READER'S DIGEST

CONDENSED BOOKS

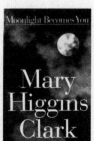

COUNTRY MORNING
by Susan Hunt-Wulkowicz

READER'S DIGEST
CONDENSED BOOKS

THE READER'S DIGEST ASSOCIATION, INC.
Montreal, Pleasantville, New York

Reader's Digest Condensed Books are published every two to three months.

The condensations in this volume have been created by The Reader's Digest Association, Inc., by special arrangement with the publishers, authors, or holders of copyrights.

With the exception of actual personages identified as such, the characters and incidents in the fictional selections in this volume are entirely the products of the authors' imaginations and have no relation to any person or event in real life.

The original editions of the books in this volume are published and copyrighted as follows:
Moonlight Becomes You, published by Simon & Schuster
distributed by Distican Inc. at $32.50
© 1996 by Mary Higgins Clark
The Outsider, published by Simon & Schuster
distributed by Distican Inc. at $25.00
© 1996 by Penelope Williamson
Harvest, published by Pocket Books, a division of Simon & Schuster
distributed by Distican Inc. at $29.50
© 1996 by Tess Gerritsen
The Falconer, published by Random House of Canada Limited at $21.00
© 1996 by Elaine Clark McCarthy

ISBN 0-88850-449-7

FIRST EDITION

ILLUSTRATORS

Kazuhiko Sano: *Moonlight Becomes You*

Joanie Schwarz: *The Outsider*, title spread; *Harvest*

Herb Tauss: *The Outsider*, interior art

Greg Harlin—Wood Ronsaville Harlin, Inc.: *The Falconer*

207-245-9703

CONTENTS

MARY
HIGGINS
CLARK

MOONLIGHT

BECOMES YOU

Sparkling autumn days in a picturesque town . . . elegant homes by the sea . . . a chance to renew old ties and make new friends. No one could blame Maggie for expecting to have a perfectly delightful time during her Newport vacation.

Guess again.

Tuesday, October 8th

Maggie tried to open her eyes, but the effort was too great. Her head hurt so much. Where was she? What had happened? She raised her hand, but it was stopped inches above her body, unable to move any farther.

Instinctively she pushed at the overhead barrier, but it did not move. What was it? It felt soft, like satin, and it was cold. She slid her fingers to the side and down; the surface changed. Now it felt ruffled. A quilt? Was she in some kind of bed?

She pushed out her other hand to the side and recoiled as that palm immediately encountered the same chill ruffles. They were on both sides of this narrow enclosure.

What was tugging at her ring when she moved her left hand? She ran her thumb over her ring finger, felt it touch string or cord. But why?

Then memory came rushing back.

Her eyes opened and stared in terror into absolute darkness.

Frantically her mind raced as she tried to piece together what had happened. She had heard him in time to whirl around just as something crashed down on her head.

She remembered him bending over her, whispering, "Maggie, think of the bell ringers." After that she remembered nothing.

Still disoriented and terrified, she struggled to understand. Then suddenly it came flooding back. The bell ringers! Victorians had been so afraid of being buried alive that it had become a tradition to tie a string to their fingers before interment. A string threaded through a hole in the casket, stretching to the surface of the burial plot. A string with a bell attached to it.

For seven days a guard would patrol the grave and listen for the sound of the bell ringing, the signal that the interred wasn't dead after all.

But Maggie knew that no guard was listening for her. She was truly alone.

She tried to scream, but no sound came. Frantically she tugged at the string, straining, hoping to hear above her a faint pealing sound. But there was only darkness and silence.

She had to keep calm. She had to focus. How had she gotten here? She couldn't let panic overwhelm her. But how? How?

Then she remembered. The funeral museum. She'd gone back there alone. Then she'd taken up the search—the search that Nuala had begun. Then he'd come, and . . .

Oh, God! She was buried alive! She pounded her fists on the lid of the casket, but even inside, the thick satin muffled the sound. Finally she screamed. Screamed until she was hoarse, until she couldn't scream anymore. And still she was alone.

The bell. She yanked on the string again and again. Surely it was sending out sounds. She couldn't hear them, but someone would. They must!

Overhead a mound of fresh, raw earth shimmered in the light of the full moon. The only movement came from the bronze bell attached to a pipe emerging from the mound. The bell moved back and forth in an arrhythmic dance of death. Round about it, all was silent. Its clapper had been removed.

CHAPTER 1

Friday, September 20th I hate cocktail parties, Maggie thought wryly. Actually, the truth is I hate cocktail parties where the only person I know is my supposed date and he abandons me the minute we come in the door.

She looked around the large room, then sighed. When Liam Moore Payne invited her to this reunion of the Moore clan, she should have guessed he would be more interested in his cousins-by-the-dozens than her. Liam, an occasional but normally thoughtful date when he was in town from Boston, was tonight displaying a boundless faith in her ability to fend for herself.

It was what Liam had told her about the Moores that had made her decide to accompany him, she remembered as she maneuvered her way through the Four Seasons restaurant on Manhattan's East Fifty-second Street. The family's founding father—or at least the founder of the family's original wealth—had been the late Squire Desmond Moore, at one time a fixture of Newport society. The occasion of tonight's reunion was to celebrate the great man's one hundred fifteenth birthday.

Going into amusing detail, Liam had explained that over one hundred descendants would be present. He had regaled her with anecdotes about the fifteen-year-old immigrant from Dingle who had considered himself to be not one of the huddled masses yearning to be free, but, rather, one of the impoverished masses yearning to be rich. Legend claimed that as his ship passed the Statue of Liberty, Squire had announced to his fellow steerage-class passengers, "In no time a-tall I'll be wealthy enough to buy the old girl." Liam had delivered his forebear's declaration in a broad Irish brogue.

The Moores certainly did come in all sizes and shapes, Maggie reflected. She watched two octogenarians in animated conversation and narrowed her eyes, mentally framing them through the lens of the camera she wished she had brought. The snow-white hair of the man, the coquettish smile on the woman's face . . . It would have made a wonderful picture.

"Having a good time?" Liam asked as he appeared suddenly beside her. Without waiting for an answer, he introduced her to yet another cousin, Earl Bateman, who studied her with interest.

She judged the newcomer to be, like Liam, in his late thirties. He was half a head shorter than his cousin, which made him just under six feet. There was a scholarly bent reflected in his lean face and thoughtful expression, although his pale blue eyes had a vaguely disconcerting cast to them. Sandy-haired with a sallow complexion, he did not have Liam's rugged good looks. Liam's eyes were more green than blue, his dark hair attractively flecked with gray.

She waited while he continued to look her over. With a raised eyebrow she asked, "Will I pass inspection?"

He looked embarrassed. "I'm sorry. I'm not good at remembering names, and I was trying to place you. You *are* one of the clan, aren't you? Your blue eyes, ivory skin, and black hair make you a Celt."

"No. I have Irish roots, but I'm no relation to this clan, I'm afraid. It doesn't look as though you need any more cousins anyhow."

"You couldn't be more right about that. Too bad, though. Most of them aren't nearly so attractive as you."

"Liam! Earl! I'm glad I came after all."

Forgetting Maggie, both men turned to enthusiastically greet the florid-faced man who came up behind them.

Maggie shrugged. So much for that, she thought.

Then she heard a voice nearby. A melodic, familiar voice—one that spurred sudden, pleasant memories. She spun around. The voice belonged to a woman who was ascending the short staircase to the restaurant's balcony area. Maggie stared, then gasped. Could it possibly be Nuala? It had been so long ago, yet she sounded just like the woman who had been her stepmother from the time she was five until she was ten. After the divorce her father had forbidden Maggie to even mention Nuala's name.

Maggie saw Liam on his way to hail another relative and grabbed his arm. "Liam, that woman on the stairs. Do you know her?"

He squinted. "Oh, that's Nuala. She was married to my uncle. I *guess* she's my aunt, but she was his second wife, so I never thought of her that way. Why?"

Maggie did not wait to answer, but began to thread her way through the clusters of Moores. By the time she reached the stairs, the woman was chatting with a group of people on the balcony level.

When Nuala had left so abruptly, Maggie prayed that she would write. She never did, though, and Maggie had found her silence especially painful. She had come to feel so close to her during the five years the marriage had lasted. Her own mother had died in an automobile accident when she was an infant. It was only after her father's death that Maggie learned from a family friend he had destroyed all the letters and gifts that Nuala had sent to her.

Maggie stared now at the tiny figure with lively blue eyes and soft honey-blond hair. She could see the fine skein of wrinkles that detracted not a bit from her lovely complexion. Childhood memories, perhaps her happiest, flooded her heart.

Nuala, who always took *her* part in arguments, protesting to Maggie's father, "Owen, she's just a child. Stop correcting her every minute." Nuala, who was always saying, "Owen, all the kids her age wear jeans." . . . "Owen, she's not just playing in mud; she's trying to make something out of the clay. For heaven's sake, recognize your daughter's creativity even if you don't like my paintings." It had been from Nuala that Maggie had learned to love art.

Typically, Nuala was dressed tonight in a pale blue satin cocktail suit and matching heels. Maggie's memories of her were always pastel-tinted. Nuala had been in her late forties when she married Dad, Maggie thought, trying to calculate her age now. She made it through five years with him. She left twenty-two years ago.

It was a shock to realize that Nuala must be in her mid-seventies. She certainly didn't look it.

Their eyes met. Nuala frowned, then looked puzzled.

Nuala had told her that her name was actually Finnuala, after the legendary Celt, Finn MacCool, who brought about the downfall of a giant. As a little girl, Maggie had delighted in trying to pronounce Finn-u-ala.

"Finn-u-ala?" she said now, her voice tentative.

A look of astonishment crossed the older woman's face. Then she emitted a whoop of delight, and Maggie found herself once again enfolded in loving arms.

"Let me look at you!" Nuala exclaimed, stepping back. Nuala's eyes searched Maggie's face. "I never thought I'd see you again. Oh, Maggie! How is that dreadful man, your father?"

"He died three years ago."

"Oh, I'm sorry, darling. But he was totally impossible to the end, I'm sure."

"Never too easy," Maggie admitted.

"Well, the poor man is dead, may he rest in peace." Aware suddenly that others were listening, Nuala slid her arm around Maggie's waist and announced, "This is my child. I didn't give birth to her, of course, but that's totally unimportant."

Maggie realized that Nuala was blinking back tears. Anxious both to talk and to escape the crowded restaurant, they slipped out together. Maggie could not find Liam to say good-bye but was fairly sure she would not be missed.

ARM in arm Maggie and Nuala walked up Park Avenue through the deepening September twilight, turned west at Fifty-sixth Street, and settled in at Il Tinello. Over Chianti and delicate strips of fried zucchini they caught up on each other's lives.

For Maggie it was simple. "Boarding school—I was shipped there after you left. Then Carnegie-Mellon and a master's in visual arts from N.Y.U. I'm making a good living now as a photographer."

"That's wonderful. I always thought it would be either that or sculpting."

Maggie smiled. "You've got a good memory. I love to sculpt, but only as a hobby. Being a photographer is more practical, and I've got some excellent clients. Now, what about you, Nuala?"

"No. Let's finish with you," the older woman interrupted. "You've got a job you like in New York. You're thirty-two and just as pretty as I knew you'd be. What about a love interest?"

Maggie felt the familiar wrench. "I was married for three years.

His name was Paul, and he graduated from the Air Force Academy. He had just been selected for the NASA program when he was killed on a training flight five years ago. It's still hard to talk about him."

"Oh, Maggie." There was a world of understanding in Nuala's voice. Maggie remembered that her stepmother had been a widow when she married her father.

Over dinner they caught up on twenty-two years. After the divorce from Maggie's father Nuala had moved to New York, then visited Newport, where she met Timothy Moore—someone she actually had dated when she was a teenager—and married him. "My third and last husband," she said. "Tim died last year, and do I ever miss him. He wasn't one of the wealthy Moores, but I have a sweet house in Newport and an adequate income, and I'm still dabbling at painting. So I'm all right."

But Maggie saw a flicker of uncertainty cross Nuala's face. "*Really* all right, Nuala?" she asked quietly.

"Oh, yes, I'm fine. It's just . . . well, I turned seventy-five last month. I've lost a number of good friends lately, and it's getting to be a bit lonely in Newport. But there's a wonderful residence—I hate the word nursing home—and I'm thinking of going to live there. The kind of apartment I want has just become available."

Then, as the waiter poured espresso, she said urgently, "Maggie, come visit me, please. It's only a three-hour drive from New York."

"I'd love to," Maggie responded. "Now that I've found you, I'm not going to let you get away again. Besides, I understand Newport is a photographer's paradise. As a matter of fact—"

She was about to say that she had cleared her calendar to take a much needed vacation when she heard someone say, "I thought I'd find you here." Startled, Maggie looked up. Standing over them were Liam and his cousin Earl Bateman. "You ran out on me," Liam said reprovingly.

Earl bent down to kiss Nuala. "You're in hot water for spiriting away his date. How do you two know each other?"

"It's a long story." Nuala smiled. "Earl lives in Newport, too," she explained to Maggie. "He teaches anthropology at Hutchinson College in Providence."

Liam pulled a chair from a nearby table and sat down. "You've got to let us have an after-dinner drink with you." He smiled at Earl. "And don't worry about Earl. He's strange, but he's harmless. His branch of the family has been in the funeral business for more than a hundred years. He even makes money talking about it."

Maggie raised her eyebrows as the others laughed.

"I lecture on funeral customs through the ages," Earl Bateman explained with a smile. "Some may find it macabre, but I love it."

CHAPTER 2

Friday, September 27th He strode briskly along the Cliff Walk, his hair blown by the stiff ocean breeze. The sun had been wonderfully warm at the height of the day, but now its slanting rays were ineffectual. It seemed to him that the shift in the air reflected the changing quality of his mood.

Till now he had been successful in his plan, but with Nuala's dinner party only two hours away a premonition was coming over him. Nuala had become suspicious and would confide in her stepdaughter. Everything could start to unravel.

Deep in thought, he paused as he came to The Breakers, that marvelously ostentatious jewel, that American palace built in the early 1890s for Cornelius Vanderbilt II and his wife, Alice.

But now he had to act quickly, and he picked up his pace. Five minutes later he came upon Latham Manor, the magnificent white marble edifice that had been a more tasteful competitor to the vulgarity of The Breakers. Originally the property of the eccentric Latham family, it had fallen into disrepair in the lifetime of the last Latham. Rescued from ruin and restored to reflect its earlier grandeur, it was now the residence of wealthy retirees.

He stopped and reached into his windbreaker pocket and pulled out a cellular phone. He dialed quickly, then smiled slightly as the voice answered.

He said two words: "Not tonight."

"Then, when?" a calm voice asked after a slight pause.

"I'm not sure yet. I have to take care of something else." Breaking the connection, he turned and began to walk swiftly.

It was time to get ready for Nuala's dinner party.

NUALA Moore hummed as she sliced tomatoes in her cheerfully untidy kitchen. The late afternoon sun was about to set, and she could feel a slight chill seeping through the poorly insulated back wall.

Even so, her kitchen was inviting with its red-and-white colonial paper, worn red brick linoleum, and pine cabinets. When she finished slicing the tomatoes, she reached for the onions. A tomato-and-onion salad marinated in oil and vinegar was a perfect accompaniment to a roast leg of lamb. Her fingers were crossed that Maggie still loved lamb. When she was little, it had been one of her favorites.

The potatoes were already bouncing in the big pot, a tray of biscuits was ready to pop in the oven, and the green beans were all prepared.

Nuala peered into the dining room, double-checking the table. Maggie would sit opposite her; cohostesses this evening, like mother and daughter. She leaned against the doorframe for a moment, reflecting. It would be wonderful to at last share this terrible worry. She would wait a day or two; then she would say, "Maggie, I have to talk with you about something important. Maybe I'm just an old, suspicious fool, but . . ."

By now Maggie should be around Bridgeport, Nuala thought. She'll probably get caught in some commuter traffic, but at least she's on her way. Maggie's on her way to me.

Nuala was about to leave the kitchen to watch the early evening news when there was a rap at the back door. Before she could look through the window to see who it was, the handle turned. She was startled, but as her visitor stepped in, she smiled warmly.

"Hello there," Nuala said. "You're not due for a couple of hours, so you can't stay long."

"I don't plan to stay long," her visitor said quietly.

AFTER HIS MOTHER MOVED TO Florida, selling the house that had been old Squire's wedding present to Liam's grandmother, Liam Moore Payne had bought a spacious condominium on Willow Street, overlooking Narrangansett Bay. Frequently he would come down from Boston on weekends to escape the hectic world of international finance.

On Friday evening, following a bracing shower, Liam stood at the bar in his study, carefully pouring Finlandia vodka into a chilled ice-filled silver goblet and stirring. Then, straining the drink into a delicate stemmed glass, he drizzled a drop of olive juice over the surface and took the first sip. "Amen," he said aloud.

It was ten of eight. He was due at Nuala's in ten minutes, but he wasn't worried about being precisely on time. Anyone who knew Nuala was aware that her cocktail hour would last at least until nine.

Liam sank onto the handsome couch covered in dark brown Moroccan leather and closed his eyes. Maggie's face floated into his mind. It was a remarkable coincidence that she happened to have a very strong tie to Newport. He had been astonished when he learned of her connection to Nuala. He remembered how angry at himself he had been for neglecting Maggie at the Four Seasons.

Maggie. He pictured her for a moment—her beautiful blue eyes and black hair, the intelligence and energy that she radiated.

Liam sipped the last of the martini and, with a sigh, hoisted himself out of his comfortable spot. Time to go, he thought. He checked his appearance at the foyer mirror, noting that the red-and-blue Hermès tie his mother had sent for his birthday went well with his navy blazer. He picked up his key ring and, locking the door behind him, set off for Nuala's party.

EARL Bateman was stretched out on his couch, a glass of wine in his hand. He knew it was time to change for Nuala's party, but he was enjoying a sense of leisure.

Earl lived in the guest wing of the Newport family home, Squire Hall, the house Squire Moore had built for his youngest daughter on the occasion of her marriage to Gordon Bateman—the Ghoul,

as Squire called him, because the Batemans had been funeral direc-
tors for four generations. Gordon Bateman's reaction had been to
convince his wife to name their home Squire Hall, a mocking tribute to his father-in-law.

After Earl finally convinced his father that he had no intention
of becoming the next Bateman funeral director, his parents sold the
mortuary to a private corporation, which retained the family name
and hired a manager to run it.

His parents now spent nine months of the year in South Carolina
and had urged Earl to take over the entire house during those
months—an offer he declined. The wing was arranged to his liking,
with his books and artifacts locked away in glass-fronted cabinets,
against the possibility of careless dusting. He also had a sweeping
view of the Atlantic; Earl found the sea calming.

At the noisy New York reunion of Squire Moore's descendants
he had stayed on the sidelines. Earl knew how gleefully some of his
cousins seized on his father's background as a funeral director.

A pox on the lot of them, he thought now as he sat up. It was ten
of eight, time to get a move on. Maggie Holloway would be at Nuala's dinner party. She was extremely attractive. Yes, her presence
would ensure that the evening would not be dull.

DR. WILLIAM Lane, director of the Latham Manor Residence,
looked at his watch for the third time in five minutes. He and his
wife were due at Nuala Moore's place at eight o'clock; it was ten of
eight now. A large, balding man in his fifties, Dr. Lane had a soothing bedside manner with his patients—an attitude of forbearance
that did not extend to his thirty-nine-year-old wife.

"Odile," he called, "for heaven's sake, get a move on."

"Right with you." Her voice, breathy and musical, floated down
the stairs of their home, a structure that once had been the carriage
house of Latham Manor. A moment later Odile rushed into the living
room. "How do I look?" She walked to the mirror over the carved
marble fireplace and smiled at her wide-eyed blond reflection.

"You look lovely. You always do," Lane said shortly. "What do
you know about Nuala's stepdaughter?"

"Her name is Maggie, and Nuala was married to her father years ago. She's going to stay for two weeks. Nuala seems very happy about it. Don't you think that's sweet?"

Without answering, Dr. Lane opened the front door, then stood aside. Odile walked past him and down the steps to the car. For a moment she paused and looked at Latham Manor, its marble façade glistening in the moonlight. Hesitantly she suggested, "When I looked in on Mrs. Hammond, she was a bit out of breath and rather pale. I wonder if you should check her before we go."

"We're late already," Dr. Lane replied impatiently. "If I'm needed, I can be back in ten minutes, but I can assure you that Mrs. Hammond will be all right tonight."

MALCOLM Norton was not looking forward to the evening. A silver-haired man with a military posture, he made an imposing appearance. It was an appearance, however, that concealed a troubled mind. Nuala's call three days ago asking him to come to dinner and meet her stepdaughter had been a shock—not the invitation itself, but the unexpected news that Nuala had a stepdaughter.

A lawyer with a general practice, working alone, Norton had seen his client list reduced drastically the past few years, partly through attrition—he had become expert at handling estates of the deceased—but also due to the arrival of several young, aggressive lawyers in the area. Nuala Moore was one of his few remaining clients.

For some time Malcolm Norton had been quietly urging Nuala to sell her home and live at Latham Manor. Until recently she had shown signs of agreeing. She admitted that since her husband, Tim, had died, the house was lonely and it cost more and more in repairs. "It needs a new roof and heating system," she had told him. "Do you think I could get two hundred thousand for it?"

He had reacted carefully. "Nuala, the real estate market here falls apart after Labor Day. Maybe next summer we'd get that much. But if you're ready to move to Latham now, I'll take the house off your hands for that price and do some basic fixing up. With Tim's insurance money and the house sale you could have the best accommodation at Latham."

"I'd like that. I'll put in my application," Nuala had said; then she had kissed his cheek. "You've been a good friend, Malcolm."

What Malcolm had not told Nuala was something a friend in Washington had passed along. A proposed change in environmental protection legislation was sure to go through, which meant that some property now protected by the Wetlands Preservation Act would be freed from development restrictions. The entire right end of Nuala's property would be included in that change. Drain the pond, cut down a few trees, and the view of the ocean would be spectacular, Malcolm reasoned. By his calculations the property alone would be worth a million dollars.

With the profit he would make, he would have enough cash to settle with his wife, Janice, retire, and move to Florida with Barbara.

Seven years younger than he, Barbara was a very pretty widow of fifty-six. Her children were grown, so she had taken the secretarial job in his office just to keep busy. It wasn't long, however, before the mutual attraction between them was palpable. She had all the warmth Janice never offered him. But she wasn't the kind who would get involved in an office affair; he would have to come to her as a single man. And all it would take to make that happen was money, he told himself.

"Well, are you ready?" His wife of thirty-five years was standing before him, arms folded.

"If *you* are," he said. He had been late getting home. This was the first time he had seen Janice since this morning. "What kind of day did you have?" he asked.

"What kind of day do I always have," she snapped, "keeping books in a nursing home? But at least one of us is bringing home a regular paycheck."

At SEVEN fifty p.m. Neil Stephens, managing director of Carson & Parker Investment Corporation, stood up and stretched. He was the only one left in the office at 2 World Trade Center in Manhattan, except for the cleaning crew. The market had been extremely volatile the last few days, and too many smaller investors became anxious to sell. It was up to him and his staff to convince them to be patient.

Well, enough for today, Neil thought. He looked around for his jacket and spotted it on one of the chairs. Neil was a big man who, at thirty-eight, managed to keep his body muscle from sliding into fat by a program of disciplined exercise, including racquetball sessions two nights a week. The results of his efforts were apparent, and he was compellingly attractive, with brown eyes that bespoke intelligence and an easy smile that inspired confidence.

Neil grimaced as he realized that he had forgotten to call Maggie to get her phone number in Newport. Just this morning he had decided to go to Portsmouth next weekend for his mother's birthday; that would put him just minutes away from Newport. Maggie had told him she would be staying there for a couple of weeks with her stepmother. He had thought they would get together there.

He and Maggie had been dating since early spring, when they met in a bagel shop on Second Avenue, around the corner from their East Fifty-sixth Street apartment buildings. They had begun chatting there whenever their paths crossed; they then bumped into each other one evening at the movies. They sat together and later walked over to Neary's Pub for dinner.

Initially Neil liked the fact that Maggie apparently took the dates as casually as he did. However, after six months, the fact that Maggie continued to act uninterested in him as anything other than a pleasant film and dinner companion was beginning to annoy Neil. He found himself becoming more and more intent on seeing her. He knew that she had been widowed five years ago, something that she mentioned matter-of-factly. But now he started wondering whether she had a serious boyfriend.

Glumly he walked over to the window. Manhattan stretched before him, ablaze with lights. When he had told Maggie his office was on the forty-second floor of the World Trade Center, she told him about the first time she had gone for a cocktail at Windows on the World, atop the center. "It was just becoming dusk. The lights of the bridges went on, and then all the building and streetlights started glowing. It was like watching a highborn Victorian lady put on her jewelry—necklace, bracelets, rings, even a tiara." The vivid image had stayed with Neil.

He had another image of Maggie, but this one troubled him. Three weeks ago he had gone to Cinema I to see the French classic *A Man and a Woman*. Halfway through the film he noticed Maggie sitting alone a few rows ahead of him. He was about to join her when he realized that she was crying. She held her hand to her mouth to prevent sobs as she watched the story of a young widow who could not accept her husband's death.

He hurried out while the credits rolled, not wanting her to see him, thinking that she would be embarrassed to be caught so emotionally vulnerable. Later that evening he was in Neary's having dinner with friends when she came in. There was nothing in her face to indicate that earlier she had been identifying with a heartbroken young widow.

Damn, Neil thought. She's gone for at least two weeks, and I have no way to reach her. I don't even have the faintest idea of her stepmother's name.

IT HAD been a good week, Maggie reflected as she turned off Route 138 in Newport. Both photo shoots had turned out exceptionally well, especially the one for *Vogue*.

But after the meticulous attention she had to give to capturing every fold of the astronomically priced gowns she was photographing, it was a joy to put on jeans and a plaid shirt. In fact, with the exception of a blue silk print blouse and long skirt she planned to wear tonight for Nuala's dinner party, everything she brought on this vacation was quite casual.

We're going to have such fun, she thought. Two uninterrupted weeks in Newport. Nuala and I really will have a chance to catch up with each other.

It had been a surprise when Liam called to say that he would be at Nuala's tonight as well, although she should have realized he spent a fair amount of time in Newport. "It's an easy drive from Boston," he had pointed out. "I go there fairly regularly for weekends."

Maggie smiled. Liam is fun, she thought, even though he does take himself too seriously. Stopping at a red light, she rechecked her directions. Nuala lived just off the fabled Ocean Drive, on Garrison Avenue. "I even have a view of the ocean from the third floor," Nuala had explained. "Wait till you see it and my studio."

She had called three times this week to be sure there were no changes of plan. "You *are* coming, Maggie?"

"Of course," she had assured her. Still, Maggie had wondered if there was an uneasiness in Nuala's voice, an uneasiness she had detected in Manhattan. She had rationalized that Nuala's husband had died only last year and she was starting to lose her friends as well. A sense of mortality has to be setting in, she reasoned.

Checking her watch, Maggie saw it was ten of eight. She would barely have time to change before the other guests arrived. At least she had phoned Nuala to let her know she was getting off to a late start. She had told her she should be arriving just about now. She turned onto Garrison Avenue and saw the ocean in front of her. She stopped the car in front of a charming clapboard house with a wraparound porch. This had to be Nuala's home, she thought, but it seemed so dark. There were no outside lights turned on, and only a faint light came from the front windows.

She pulled into the driveway, got out, and ran up the steps. Expectantly she rang the bell. From inside she could hear the faint sound of chimes. As she waited, she thought she detected a burning smell. She pressed the doorbell again.

There was still no answer. Something has to be wrong, she thought anxiously. Maggie walked over to the nearest window and crouched down, straining to see into the darkness inside.

Then her mouth went dry. The shadowy room was in wild disorder. The contents of a drawer were strewn on the carpet, and the drawer itself was leaning haphazardly against the ottoman. The fireplace was opposite the windows and flanked by cabinets. All of them were open.

What faint light there was came from a pair of sconces over the mantel. What was that? She squinted and leaned forward. As her eyes adjusted, Maggie realized she was seeing a small stockinged foot extending from behind a love seat. She lunged back to the door and twisted the handle, but it was locked.

Blindly she rushed to the car, grabbed the car phone, and punched in 911. When the call was answered, she managed to say, "I'm at One Garrison Avenue in Newport. I can't get in. I can see someone lying on the floor. I think it's Nuala."

I'm babbling, she told herself. Stop it. But as the calm questions came from the dispatcher, Maggie's mind was shouting three words: *Nuala is dead.*

NEWPORT chief of police Chet Brower stood aside as the police photographer snapped pictures of the crime scene. Aside from the savage murder—Nuala Moore had suffered multiple blows to her head—there was something about the entire picture that bothered him. There had been no reported incidents of housebreaking in this area for several months. That kind of thing started when many houses were closed for the winter and so became targets for looters.

The chief had been in the first squad car to answer the 911 call. Before forcing the front door, he and Detective Jim Haggerty had gone to the back of the house. Careful to avoid smudging existing fingerprints, he had found the door unlocked, and they had gone in.

A flame was still flickering under a pot, now burned black. The acrid smell of charred potatoes overwhelmed the other, more pleasant scent—roasting lamb. He had turned off the stove before going through the dining room into the living room.

He hadn't realized that the stepdaughter had followed them, until they reached the body and he heard her moan, "Oh, Finn-u-ala."

Then the front doorbell had chimed, and he remembered noticing that the table in the dining room was set for company. Approaching sirens announced the other squad cars, and in the next few minutes the officers had managed to get the stepdaughter and arriving guests into a neighbor's house. Everyone was told not to leave until the chief had a chance to talk to them.

"Chief."

Brower looked up. Eddie Sousa, a rookie cop, was beside him. "Some of the folks waiting to talk to you are getting restless."

"Tell them I'll be over in ten minutes," Brower said testily.

Before leaving, he walked through the house once more. The place was a mess. Even the third-floor studio had been ransacked. Not too many intruders who had just committed murder would have taken the time for so thorough a search, he reasoned.

The three second-floor bedrooms had been subjected to the same search. The contents of the largest bedroom were scattered everywhere. A pink leather jewelry chest was open. What was obviously costume jewelry was scattered on the surface of the maple lowboy. He spent a long moment studying the bedroom of the deceased in its disarray. Whoever did this wasn't a common thief or a drug-addicted burglar, he decided. He had been looking for something.

And there was something else. Moore had obviously been preparing dinner, which suggested she was in the kitchen when the intruder arrived. She had tried to escape her attacker by running through the dining room, which meant the intruder must have been blocking the kitchen door. He or she probably came in that way, and since there was no sign of forced entry, the door must have been unlocked. Unless Mrs. Moore had let the intruder in herself.

Now he was ready to talk to the dinner guests. He left Detective Haggerty to wait for the coroner.

"NO, THANK you," Maggie said as she pressed her index fingers to her temples. She vaguely realized that she hadn't eaten since noon, ten hours ago, but the thought of food made her throat close.

"Not even a cup of tea, Maggie?"

She looked up. The kind face of Irma Woods, Nuala's next-door neighbor, hovered over her. It was easier to nod assent than to continue to refuse the offer. To her surprise the mug warmed her chilled fingers and the near-scalding tea felt good going down.

They were in the Woodses' family room. Pictures were on table-tops and on the mantel—children and grandchildren, she supposed. The Woodses appeared to be contemporaries of Nuala's.

Despite all the stress and confusion, Maggie thought she had the others straight—the ones who were to have been the dinner guests. There was Dr. William Lane, the director of Latham Manor, which she gathered was a senior citizens residence. He had tried to give her a mild sedative, but Maggie refused.

Maggie observed that whenever Dr. Lane's very pretty wife, Odile, said anything, her hands began to move. "Nuala came to visit her friend Greta Shipley at the home almost every day," she had explained, her fingers gesturing in a come-hither movement as though inviting someone to come closer. Then she clasped her fingers together as though in prayer. "Greta will be heartbroken. Heartbroken," she repeated decisively. "And everyone in her art class will miss her so much."

That would be like Nuala, Maggie thought, to share her talent with others.

Malcolm Norton, who had introduced himself to Maggie as Nuala's lawyer, was standing at the fireplace. He was a handsome man, but it seemed to her that he was striking a pose. There was something superficial—almost artificial—about him, she thought.

Norton's wife, Janice, spent most of the time talking quietly to the doctor. An athletic type, she might have been attractive except for the downward lines at the corners of her mouth, which gave her a harsh, even bitter, expression.

Liam and his cousin Earl sat near each other in matching fireside chairs. When Liam came in, he had put his arm around Maggie and said, "How horrible for you," but he seemed to understand that she needed physical and mental space to absorb this by herself, and he did not take the place next to her on the love seat.

Love seat, Maggie thought. It was behind a love seat that they had found Nuala's body.

Earl Bateman leaned forward, his hands clasped in front of him, as though in deep thought. Maggie had met him only on the night of the Moore reunion, but she remembered that he was an anthropologist who lectured on funeral customs.

The sound of the doorbell made everyone look up. The police chief came in. "I'm sorry to have detained you," he said. "Several of my men will take your individual statements, so we will have you out of here soon. First, though, I have some questions I want to ask you as a group. Mr. and Mrs. Woods, I wish you'd stay, too."

The chief's questions were general, things like, "Was Mrs. Moore in the habit of leaving her back door unlocked?"

The Woodses told him that she always left it unlocked, that she even joked about forever mislaying the key to the front door, but she knew she could always sneak in the back.

He asked if she had seemed troubled recently. Unanimously they reported that Nuala had been happy and excited and looking forward to Maggie's visit.

Maggie felt tears sting the back of her eyes. And then the realization came: But she *was* troubled.

It was only when Chief Brower said, "Now, if you'll just bear with us a few minutes more while my men ask you each a few questions," that Irma Woods timidly interrupted.

"There is just one thing that maybe we ought to explain. Yesterday Nuala came over. She had handwritten a new will and wanted us to witness her signature. She also had us call Mr. Martin, a notary public, so that he could make it official. She seemed a bit upset, because she said that she knew Mr. Norton might be disappointed that she was canceling the sale of her house to him."

Irma Woods looked at Maggie. "Nuala's will asks that you visit or phone her friend Greta Shipley at Latham Manor as often as you can possibly manage it. Except for a few charitable bequests, she left her house and everything else she owned to you."

CHAPTER 3

Monday, September 30th It was obvious that Maggie Holloway was not satisfied with the theory that an intruder had murdered Nuala. At the Requiem Mass he watched when she shook her head in disbelief as the priest spoke about the random violence that claims so many innocent lives. Maggie was much too smart. She could easily become a threat.

But as they filed out of St. Mary's Church, he comforted himself with the thought that undoubtedly she would now go back to New

York and put Nuala's house up for sale. And we know who's going to step in there with an offer, he thought.

He was glad to note that Greta Shipley had been accompanied by a nurse when she arrived at the Mass and had to leave almost immediately afterward.

He didn't really want to go to the cemetery now, although he knew there was no way out of it. Later. He would go there later. . . . And alone. As with the others, his special gift would be a private memorial to her.

When the graveside service ended, Irma Woods invited everyone back to her house for refreshments. It would be a good time to learn exactly when Maggie Holloway planned to leave. Go away, Maggie, he thought. You'll only get in trouble here.

AN HOUR later, as the guests mingled, drinks and sandwiches in their hands, he was stunned to hear Irma Woods tell Maggie that the cleaning service had completed straightening the house. "So the house is ready for you, Maggie," Mrs. Woods told her. "But are you sure you won't be nervous there?"

Trying to seem casual, he moved closer, straining to hear. His back was turned toward them as Maggie said, "No, I won't be nervous. I'd intended to stay two weeks, and I shall. I'll sort out everything and visit Greta Shipley at Latham Manor, as Nuala requested."

He stiffened as she added, "Mrs. Woods, you've been so kind. I can't thank you enough. There's just one thing. When Nuala came to see you with that handwritten will, weren't you surprised that she was so anxious to have it witnessed and notarized at once?"

Mrs. Woods measured her response. "Well, yes, I did wonder. At first I just thought it was impulsive. But since her death, I've been thinking that there was more to it. It was almost as if Nuala knew something terrible might happen to her."

He drifted toward the fireplace, his mind racing. Maggie would be visiting Greta Shipley. How much did Greta know? Something had to be done. It could not be risked.

Greta. Everyone had seen her helped out of church today. Everyone would believe that the shock of her friend's death had contributed to a fatal heart attack. Unexpected, but not really a surprise. Sorry, Greta, he thought.

WHEN she was still a relatively young age sixty-eight, Greta Shipley had been invited to a reception at the newly renovated Latham Manor Residence. The new home for retirees was open and was accepting applications.

She liked everything she saw there. The house's magnificent first floor included the grand salon and marble-and-crystal dining room she remembered from her youth. The handsome library, with its deep leather chairs and cheerful fireplace, was inviting, and the smaller salon would serve as a television room.

The admission fee was steep, of course. It began at two hundred thousand dollars for a large private room and bath and climbed to five hundred thousand for a two-bedroom suite. And while the resident got exclusive use of the apartment during his or her lifetime, at the time of death, ownership reverted to the residence, which would make the rooms available for sale to the next applicant. Guests would also pay a maintenance fee of two thousand dollars a month.

Recently widowed and nervous about living alone, Greta had gladly sold her home and moved to Latham Manor. As one of the first occupants, she had a large select studio with a living-area alcove. Best of all was the secure sense of not being alone in the night. There always was a guard on the premises, a nurse on duty, and a bell to summon help if necessary.

Greta enjoyed the companionship of most of the other residents. She also kept up her long friendship with Nuala Moore. And at Greta's request Nuala agreed to give art classes twice a week at the residence.

After Timothy Moore died, Greta had begun a campaign to get Nuala to move to Latham Manor. When Nuala demurred, Greta urged her to at least put in her application so that when one of the suites became available, she would be in a position to change her mind. Nuala had finally agreed, admitting that her lawyer was encouraging her to do the same thing.

But now that would never happen, Greta thought sadly as she sat in her easy chair, the untouched dinner tray in front of her. She was still upset that she had experienced that weak spell at Nuala's funeral. She had been feeling perfectly fine until this morning.

It was reassuring to know that Nuala's stepdaughter, Maggie Holloway, would be visiting her. At the funeral parlor yesterday Maggie had introduced herself and said, "Mrs. Shipley, I know you were Nuala's closest friend. I want to make you my friend, too."

There was a tap at the door. Greta liked the fact that the staff was instructed to enter a resident's room only when invited. Nurse Markey, however, didn't seem to understand. *Just because the door isn't locked doesn't mean that she is free to barge in at any time.*

Predictably, before Greta could respond, Nurse Markey strode in, a professional smile wreathing her strong features. "How are we doing tonight, Mrs. Shipley?" she asked loudly.

"*I'm* quite fine, thank you, Miss Markey. I hope you are." Suddenly she realized that her heartbeat was beginning to accelerate.

"I hear we had a weak spell in church."

Greta put her hand on her chest.

"Mrs. Shipley, what's the matter? Are you all right?"

Greta felt her wrist being seized. As suddenly as it had begun, the pounding slackened. She managed to say, "Just give me a moment. I felt a little breathless, that's all."

"I want you to lean back and close your eyes. I'll call Dr. Lane."

Ten minutes later, propped up in bed, Greta tried to reassure the doctor that the spell was completely past. But as she drifted off to sleep with the help of a mild sedative, she could not escape the chilling memory of how two weeks ago Constance Rhinelander had died of heart failure so unexpectedly. *First Constance,* she thought, *then Nuala. Please don't let me be the third.*

No, IT had not been a nightmare; it really had happened. The full reality of the past few days settled in Maggie's mind as she stood in Nuala's kitchen in the house that now was hers.

At three o'clock Liam had helped carry her bags here from the Woodses' guest room. "Maggie, you look ready to collapse. Are you sure you want to stay here? I don't think it's such a hot idea."

"Yes," she had replied after a pause, "I do want to stay."

Instead of objecting further, he had said, "Then I'll leave you alone. But I do hope you'll rest. Don't start sorting out Nuala's things."

At the door he had put an arm around her and given her a friendly hug. Then he was gone.

Feeling suddenly exhausted, Maggie had locked the doors, then climbed the stairs. The bedroom Nuala had meant her to have was simply furnished—a maple double bed, a dresser with mirror, a night table, and a rocking chair. After dragging her bags into that room, Maggie had peeled off her skirt and sweater, slipped into her favorite robe, and climbed under the covers.

Now, after a three-hour nap, she was finally beginning to feel clearheaded. She even sensed that she was over the shock of Nuala's death. The sadness, though, that won't go away, she thought.

For the first time in four days she was hungry. The refrigerator had been stocked: eggs, milk, juice, a small roasted chicken, a loaf of bread, and homemade chicken soup. Obviously, Mrs. Woods.

She had settled on making herself a chicken sandwich when she was startled by a rap at the back door. She spun around as the handle turned.

She gasped with relief as Earl Bateman's face appeared in the oval window of the door. Chief Brower theorized that Nuala had been surprised by an intruder who had come in the back door. That thought ran through her mind as she let him in.

"Maggie, forgive me," Bateman said. "I'm heading back to Providence, and it occurred to me that you might not have locked this door. I know that Nuala was in the habit of leaving it unlocked. I didn't mean to intrude; I thought I'd just drive by and check."

"You could have phoned."

"I'm one of those holdouts who doesn't have a car phone. Sorry. I'm distressing you, and that's the last thing I want to do. I'd like to be your friend." He opened the door to leave. "I'll be back Friday afternoon. Double-lock the door, please."

He was gone. Maggie snapped the lock and sank into a chair, trembling. Then she rose, and with quick, silent steps she ran into the dark front room and knelt at the window to look out under the shade. She saw Bateman walking to the street.

At his car he stood for a long moment staring back at the house. As she watched, Bateman gave a broad wave of his hand, clearly directed at her. He can't see me, she thought, but he knows I'm here.

CHAPTER 4

Tuesday, October 1st   When the phone rang at eight a.m., Robert Stephens reached with his left hand to answer it, while his right maintained a firm hold on his coffee cup. His "Good morning" was curt, his wife of forty-three years noted with amusement. Dolores Stephens knew that her husband did not appreciate early phone calls.

Usually these calls were from one of the senior-citizen clients whose taxes he handled. He and Dolores had come to Portsmouth three years ago to retire, but Robert decided to take on a few selected clients. Within six months he had all he could handle.

The annoyance disappeared from his voice as he said, "Neil, how are you? . . . You can get up Thursday? . . . Wonderful. Your mother will be delighted. I'll call the club for a two-o'clock tee-off."

Dolores got on the line and heard the amused voice of her only child. "Tell Dad his 'Good morning' sounded more like 'Go to hell.' He hasn't finished that first cup of coffee, huh?" he said.

"You got it, dear. You will stay till Sunday, won't you, Neil?"

"You bet. I'm looking forward to it. Okay, gotta run."

Her husband refilled his cup. "Did Neil say I sounded grouchy?"

"Something like that."

Robert Stephens smiled reluctantly. "I was afraid the call was from Laura Arlington. She's all upset. Keeps calling me. She made some serious investments that haven't worked out, and she thinks now that she's getting a big runaround."

"Is she right?"

"I think she is. The broker persuaded her to invest in a small tech company that was supposed to be bought out by Microsoft. She bought one hundred thousand shares of stock at five dollars a share. As of yesterday, if you could sell it, you'd get eighty cents a share."

"Isn't she thinking of going into the Latham Manor Residence?"

"Yes. And that was the money that was going to pay for it."

"Was what this broker did illegal?"

"I don't think so, unfortunately. Unethical, perhaps, but probably not illegal. Anyway, I'm going to talk it over with Neil."

Robert Stephens walked to the large window that overlooked Narragansett Bay. A broad, athletic-looking man at sixty-eight, his once sandy hair was now white.

The water in the bay was still. "Beautiful, peaceful," he said, shaking his head. "Hard to believe that six miles from here a woman was murdered in her own home."

He looked at his wife, effortlessly pretty, her silver hair knotted at the top of her head, her features still delicate and soft. "Dolores," he said, his tone stern, "when I'm out, I want you to keep the alarm system on at all times."

"Fine," she agreed amiably. In fact, the murder of Mrs. Moore had shaken her deeply.

Dr. WILLIAM Lane was not especially pleased by Maggie Holloway's request for an appointment. Already behind in completing the load of forms the government required of him as director of Latham Manor, he found the thought of another lost half hour galling. He couldn't imagine what she needed to talk to him about. Nuala Moore had never signed the final papers committing her to move to the residence; she had decided to keep her house instead.

An uneasy thought would not go away: Was there any reason Nuala had backed out of the arrangement? And if there was, had she confided it to her stepdaughter?

He looked up as Odile wandered into his office without knocking, a habit that drove him crazy. Odile ignored his annoyance. "William, I don't think Mrs. Shipley is well. She had a little episode after the funeral yesterday and a dizzy spell last evening. Shouldn't she go into the nursing section for a few days of observation?"

"I intend to keep a close eye on Mrs. Shipley," Dr. Lane said brusquely. "Remember, my dear, I'm the one with the medical degree. You never even managed to finish nursing school." He knew it was a stupid thing to say, and he regretted it immediately, knowing what was coming next.

"I must say I've been able to put my training to good use. I've saved you a couple of times when you've made mistakes. And you might remember how close you came to losing your license to practice medicine eight years ago. You're lucky Prestige Residence Corporation even considered you for this job."

They stared at each other. Then, as usual, Odile became contrite. "Oh, William, that was unkind of me. It's just that I worry that another episode could ruin you." She reached for his hand.

Lane sighed. She was a lightweight, but she *was* pretty. Plus, she did care about him, and he knew her frequent visits to the residents delighted most of them. Odile was an asset to him.

With virtually no show of the resignation he felt, Lane stood up, put his arms around his wife, and murmured, "What would I do without you?"

It was a relief when his secretary buzzed him on the intercom. "Miss Holloway is here," she announced.

"You'd better go, Odile," Lane whispered. For once she didn't argue, but slipped out the unmarked door of his suite.

THE night before, blaming the three-hour nap she had taken earlier, Maggie had still been wide-awake at midnight. Giving up on sleep, she had gone downstairs again and in the small study found books, several of them illustrated, on the "cottages" of Newport.

She had read for two hours. As a result, when she was admitted to Latham Manor on Tuesday morning by a uniformed maid, she was able to take in her surroundings with some degree of knowledge.

The doors on the left of the entrance hall were closed, but Maggie knew the dining room would be there. To the right, what originally must have been the music room looked most inviting, with comfortable chairs and matching hassocks all richly upholstered in moss green and floral patterns. The ornately carved space above the fireplace stretched to the ceiling, filled with Grecian figures and tiny angels, except for the smooth center, where a Rembrandt-school oil painting had been hung. It really is beautiful, she thought.

Maggie realized suddenly that the maid had spoken to her. "Oh, I'm sorry," she apologized. "I was just trying to take it all in."

The maid was an attractive woman with dark eyes and olive skin. "It is lovely, isn't it?" she said. "I'll take you to Dr. Lane now."

His office was the largest in a suite of offices along the back of the house. As Maggie followed the maid down the carpeted corridor, she glanced through an open office door and noticed a familiar face—Janice Norton, the wife of Nuala's lawyer, sat behind a desk.

Maggie could not help feeling uncomfortable. She had not missed the bitter disappointment on Malcolm Norton's face when Mrs. Woods revealed that Nuala had canceled the sale of her house.

She paused to greet Mrs. Norton, then followed the maid down the corridor to the corner office. The maid knocked and, at the invitation to enter, opened the door.

Dr. Lane came around his desk to greet her, his smile cordial. "Ms. Holloway—or Maggie, if I may—I'm glad to see you. Yesterday was a very difficult day for you, I know."

"I'm sure it was difficult for everyone who loved Nuala," Maggie said quietly. "But I'm really concerned about Mrs. Shipley. How is she this morning?"

"She had another weak spell last evening, but I looked in on her just a while ago, and she seems quite fit. She's looking forward to your visit."

"When I spoke to her this morning, she asked if I would drive her out to the cemetery. Do you think that's a good idea?"

"I wish she'd wait a few days, but when Mrs. Shipley makes up her mind to do something . . . well, nothing changes it. I do think that both of her little spells yesterday were caused by her deep emotion over Nuala's death. The two of them were really very close. I told them they were like a pair of schoolgirls."

Maggie hesitated, then decided to plunge in. "Doctor, did Nuala ever confide to you that something was troubling her? Did she have a physical problem?"

He shook his head. "No, not physical. I think Nuala was having difficulty with what she perceived to be giving up her independence. I really think that she eventually would have come here."

"Then you believe that canceling the sale of her house and the hasty will she left were simply a last-minute panic attack of sorts?"

"Yes, I do." He stood up. "I'll ask Angela, the maid, to bring you up to Mrs. Shipley. And if you do go to the cemetery, please return immediately if she seems in any way distraught. After all, the families of our guests have entrusted their lives to our care."

MALCOLM Norton sat in his office on Thames Street staring glumly at his calendar for the remainder of the day. It was now entirely empty, thanks to the cancellation of his two-o'clock appointment. It wouldn't have been much of a case—just a young housewife suing her neighbor over a nasty dog bite. But the woman had phoned to say the insurance company had settled to her satisfaction.

He still could not get over the sickening realization that Nuala Moore had secretly canceled the sale of her house to him. Now he was stuck with the two-hundred-thousand-dollar mortgage he had raised on his own house. It had been hell getting Janice to agree to co-sign for the mortgage. Finally he had told her about the impending change in the Wetlands Act and about the profits he hoped to reap in reselling Nuala's property.

He could still hear Janice's furious words after they got home Friday night. "So now we have a two-hundred-thousand-dollar mortgage and the expense we went through to get it. You march down to the bank and pay it off. I don't intend to lose my home."

"You're not going to lose it," he had said. "I told Maggie Holloway that I wanted to see her about the house. Do you think she'll want to stay where her stepmother was murdered? Ms. Holloway will get out of Newport as fast as possible. By next week she'll have agreed to sell the house." She *had* to. It was his only way out of this mess.

The intercom buzzed. He picked it up. "Yes, Barbara," he said, his voice formal. He never let an intimate quality intrude into their exchanges when she was in the outer office.

"Malcolm, may I talk to you for a few minutes?" was all she said, but he sensed that something was wrong.

A moment later she was sitting opposite him, her lovely hazel eyes averted. "Malcolm, I don't know how to say this, so I'd better just plunge in. I can't stay here." She hesitated, then added, "Even loving you as much as I do, I can't get away from the fact that you're married."

"You've seen me with Janice. You know our relationship."

"But she's still your wife. It's better this way, believe me. I'm going to visit my daughter in Vail for a couple of months. Then, when I come back, I'll find a different job."

"Barbara, you can't just walk out like this," he pleaded.

She smiled sadly. "I'm giving you a week's notice."

"By that time Janice and I will be separated, I promise you. Please stay! I can't let you go." Not after all I've done to keep you, he thought desperately.

AFTER Maggie picked up Greta Shipley, they made a stop to buy flowers. As they were driving to the cemetery, Greta reminisced to Maggie about Nuala.

"Her parents rented a cottage here when we both were about sixteen. She was such a pretty girl, and so much fun. She and I were inseparable then, and she had many admirers. Tim Moore was always hanging around her. Then her father was transferred to London, and she moved there. Eventually we just lost track of each other."

Maggie steered the car through the quiet streets that led to St. Mary's cemetery in Middletown. "How did you happen to get together again?" she asked.

"Twenty-one years ago my phone just rang one day. Someone asked to speak to Greta Carlyle. The voice was familiar, but I couldn't place it. I responded that *I* was Greta Carlyle Shipley, and Nuala whooped, 'Good for you, Gret. You landed Carter Shipley!' "

Despite the warmth in the car, Maggie shivered. Thoughts of Nuala always came back to the same question: Was the kitchen door unlocked, or did Nuala unlock the door herself to let someone she knew enter her home? Chief Brower had said that he thought whoever had killed Nuala had been looking for something and, from the look of things, might not have found it.

". . . And so we picked up where we left off, went right back to being best friends," Greta continued. "Nuala told me she'd been widowed young and then the second marriage had been a terrible mistake, except for you. She was so soured on marriage that she said hell would freeze over before she'd try it again, but by then Tim was a widower, and they started going out. One morning she phoned and said, 'Gret, want to go ice-skating? Hell just froze over.' She and Tim were engaged. I never saw her happier."

They arrived at the gate of the cemetery. A carved limestone angel with outstretched arms greeted them. They parked at the top of a hill, and with Maggie's hand tucked firmly under Greta Shipley's arm they walked along the path that led to Nuala's grave. Already the ground had been resodded. The thick green grass gave the plot an air of soothing timelessness. The only sound was the rustle of the wind through the fall-colored leaves of a nearby maple.

Mrs. Shipley placed flowers on the grave. "Nuala loved that big tree. She said when her time came, she wanted plenty of shade so that her complexion wouldn't be ruined by too much sun."

As they turned to go, Greta hesitated. "Would I be imposing terribly if I asked you to stop for just a moment at the graves of some of my other friends? I saved a few flowers for them, too."

It didn't take long to make the five other stops. The headstone on the last grave was inscribed CONSTANCE VAN SICKLE RHINELANDER. The date of death was only two weeks ago.

"Was she a close friend?" Maggie asked.

"Not nearly as close as Nuala, but she lived in Latham Manor and I had gotten to know her very well." She paused. "It's all so sudden," she said, then turned to Maggie and smiled. "I'd better get back. I'm a bit tired." Maggie put her arm around the older woman and realized just how frail she seemed.

On the twenty-minute drive back to the residence Greta Shipley dozed off. When they reached Latham Manor, she opened her eyes and said apologetically, "I used to have so much energy."

As Maggie escorted her inside, Greta said hesitantly, "Maggie, I hope you'll come to see me again before you leave. When are you going back to New York?"

Maggie surprised herself by answering firmly, "I was planning to stay two weeks, and that's what I'm going to do. I'll call you, and we'll make a date."

It was not until she got back to Nuala's house and put the kettle on that she realized something was troubling her. Something wasn't right. But what *was* it?

SINCE opening his own investment firm, Liam Moore Payne had been overwhelmingly busy. The prestigious clients he had brought with him received his meticulous personal attention, earning him their complete confidence.

He had not wanted to phone Maggie too early, but when he did call, at eleven a.m., he was disappointed not to reach her. He had his secretary try her every hour, but it was nearly four o'clock when he finally heard that Ms. Holloway was on the phone.

"Maggie, at last," he began. "I was afraid you might have made up your mind to go home. I wouldn't blame you."

"I'm careful about locking up," Maggie told him. "Liam, I'm glad you called. I've got to ask you something. Did you have a discussion with Earl about me?"

"As a matter of fact, I didn't. What makes you think I did?"

She told him about Earl's sudden appearance at the kitchen door.

"You mean he was just going to check the lock without even letting you know? You're kidding."

"No, I'm not. I was shaky enough about being alone here, and then to have him just show up that way . . . It was weird."

Liam paused, then sighed. "Maggie, Earl is my cousin and I'm fond of him, but he *is* somewhat odd, and there's no question that he's obsessed with death. Do you want me to speak to him?"

"No. But I'm going to have a locksmith put dead bolts on the doors."

"I hope that means you'll be staying in Newport for a while."

"At least the two weeks I had initially planned."

"I'll be down on Friday. Will you have dinner with me?"

"I'd like that."

"All right. I'll call you tomorrow."

Liam replaced the receiver slowly. How much should he tell Maggie about Earl? he wondered. He didn't want to frighten her, but still . . . It was something he would have to think over.

AT QUARTER of five Janice Norton locked the desk in her office at the Latham Manor Residence. It was a safeguard that William Lane would have been wise to adopt. She smiled to herself, reflecting that as bookkeeper, her unquestioned access to Lane's office had been extremely useful over the years, but she sensed that now was not the right time to take advantage of her position of trust. Call it a premonition. A few times in the past Janice had refused the telephone demand, flatly saying that it wasn't safe.

Her eyes narrowed with satisfaction as she thought of the shock on her husband's face when Irma Woods had told them about Nuala Moore's will. What pleasure she had had, berating him about repaying the mortgage on their own house.

She knew, of course, that he wouldn't do any such thing. Malcolm was destined to wander forever through a field of broken dreams. Handsome, debonair, courtly, so-well-bred Malcolm. At her wedding she had been the envy of her girlfriends. Even then, on what was supposed to be the happiest day of her life, Janice had realized she had married the frog. And then she spent thirty-plus years trying to give reality the lie. What a waste!

And then the ultimate insult. Despite the way she had stuck by him all these years, Janice had realized that he was mooning over his secretary and planning to get rid of *her!*

If only he'd been the man I thought I married, Janice mused as she pushed back the chair and stood, flexing her stiff shoulders. She smoothed the sides of her skirt, taking pleasure from her slim waistline and narrow hips. In the early days Malcolm had compared her to a beautiful thoroughbred: slender, with long neck, lean legs, and shapely ankles. She *had* been beautiful when she was young. Well, look what that had gotten her, she thought ruefully.

She had spent her adult life working hard—first as a real estate agent, then as bookkeeper in this place. As a real estate agent, she used to salivate over properties that went for a song because people needed ready cash. How many times she had thought, If only I had the money . . .

Well, now she had it. And Malcolm didn't have a clue.

The phone rang. "Janice Norton," she said, holding the receiver close to her mouth.

It was the call she had hoped to receive. He didn't bother with a greeting. "Well, for once dear Malcolm got something straight," he said. "That Wetlands Act amendment absolutely will go through. That property will be worth a fortune."

She laughed. "Then isn't it time to make a counteroffer to Maggie Holloway?"

AFTER Liam's call Maggie sat at the kitchen table, sipping tea and nibbling on some cookies she had found in the cupboard. It's funny, Maggie thought, but in an odd way, being in Nuala's house is giving her back to me.

Earlier she had found a photograph album filled with pictures of herself taken during the five years Nuala had been part of her life. The unmounted picture at the very end was of Nuala and her father and herself on their wedding day. She had been beaming with joy to have a mother. The expression on Nuala's face had been just as happy. The smile on her father's lips, however, was reserved. He wouldn't let Nuala inside his heart, Maggie thought. He was the big loser when she finally left because she couldn't stand his carping. And I was the loser, too, Maggie reflected.

It was four thirty. The window over the sink framed the handsome oak tree that stood to the side of the house. It should be trimmed, Maggie thought. But why worry about that? She wasn't going to stay here. She would sort out clothes and furniture for charity. She supposed that after the will was probated, she would sell the house as is, but she preferred that it be as empty as possible; she didn't want strangers going through Nuala's home.

She began in Nuala's studio. Three hours later, grimy from the dust of cabinets cluttered with stiffened paintbrushes and dried-up tubes of oils, Maggie had a number of trash bags lined up in a corner.

Just that much clearing up changed the appearance of the room for the better. The floor-to-ceiling windows must let in wonderful northern light, Maggie thought. Nuala had urged her to bring her sculpting materials with her, so Maggie had brought along a fifty-pound tub of wet clay, several armatures—the frameworks on which the figures would be constructed—and her modeling tools.

Maggie paused for a minute. She could make a portrait head of Nuala. Except for visiting Greta and clearing out the house, she had no real plans. It would be nice to have a project, she told herself, and what better subject than Nuala?

The visit to Latham Manor and the time she had spent with Greta Shipley had convinced her that the uneasiness she had perceived in Nuala was simply the result of her concern over changing her life by moving to the residence.

Maggie sighed. I guess there's no way I can be sure. But if it *was* a random break-in, wasn't it risky to kill Nuala, then take time to search the house? Whoever was here could smell the food cooking and see that the table was set for company. Unless that someone already knew dinner was scheduled for eight o'clock and that I wouldn't be arriving until nearly that time.

"Nuala wasn't killed by a random thief," Maggie said aloud. Mentally she reviewed the people who had been expected at the dinner. Liam was the only one she really knew. It was only because of him that she had run into Nuala again, and for that she always would be grateful.

She wanted to ask Liam about Malcolm and Janice Norton. Even in that quick moment this morning when she had greeted Janice at Latham Manor, she could detect anger in the woman's expression. Because of the canceled sale? Maggie wondered. But surely there were plenty of other houses like this one available in Newport.

Something had been bothering Maggie today—something she had noticed subconsciously. She retraced her day from the time she got up to the drive with Greta Shipley to the cemetery.

The cemetery. That was it! That last grave they went to, of the Rhinelander woman, who died two weeks ago—I noticed something. But what?

In the morning I'll go back to the cemetery and look around, she decided. I'll take my camera, and if I don't see exactly what it is, I'll take pictures. Maybe whatever it is that's nagging at me will show up when I develop them.

It had been a long day. She decided to bathe, scramble an egg, then go to bed. On the way downstairs she noticed that the closet door in Nuala's bedroom was open. When she went to shut it, she saw the blue cocktail suit Nuala had worn to the reunion party at the Four Seasons. It was haphazardly draped over a hanger, as though carelessly put away.

In the course of straightening the fabric, Maggie thought she heard a soft thud, as though something had dropped. She looked down into the cluttered array of shoes in the closet and decided that if something had fallen, it would just have to wait.

She headed for her bath. The solitude she enjoyed in her New York apartment was not appealing in this house with flimsy locks and dark corners . . . in this house where a murder had been committed, perhaps by someone whom Nuala had counted as a friend.

CHAPTER 5

Wednesday, October 2nd Neil Stephens was normally able to give his undivided attention to the stock market. His clients, both corporate and private, swore by the accuracy of his predictions. But in the five days that he had been unable to reach Maggie, he had found himself distracted.

The frustration from a nagging sense that something was wrong made him uncharacteristically impatient with two of his longtime clients, Lawrence and Frances Van Hilleary, who visited his office that morning. Wearing a Chanel suit, Frances sat elegantly straight on the edge of a leather club chair and told him of a hot tip on an oil-well stock they had received at a dinner party.

Neil leaned back, trying to give the appearance of listening with attention while first Frances and then Lawrence talked excitedly of oil gushers waiting to be tapped and of fortunes to be made.

Neil took the glossy prospectus and found the contents to be exactly what he had expected. And only those with at least half a million dollars would be allowed to participate.

He cleared his throat. "Frances and Lawrence, you are two of the most generous people I've ever dealt with. You've already given away a tremendous amount of money. I firmly believe that what you have left for yourselves should not be wasted on this kind of pie-in-the-sky investment. It's much too high-risk."

There was a moment of silence. Lawrence Van Hilleary shook his head, then sighed. "Thanks, Neil. There's no fool like an old fool."

After discussing their investment portfolio, the subject changed to a decision the Van Hillearys were pondering. "We're both seventy-eight," Lawrence said, glancing fondly at his wife. "I know we look pretty good, but we can't do things we used to do. None of the kids live in the area, and the house is expensive to maintain. We're looking for a retirement community somewhere in New England."

"Where in New England?" Neil asked.

"Perhaps the Cape. Or maybe Newport. We'd like to stay near the water."

"In that case, I might be able to do some scouting for you over the weekend." Briefly he told them how several of the women whose income taxes his father handled had moved to the Latham Manor Residence in Newport and were very happy there.

When they got up to go, Frances Van Hilleary kissed Neil's cheek. "Let us know what you find out about the place in Newport."

"Of course." Tomorrow, Neil thought, I'll be in Newport, and maybe I'll bump into Maggie. Fat chance, said a niggling voice in the back of his mind.

Then the brainstorm hit him. One night when they had dinner at Neary's Pub, Jimmy Neary and Maggie talked about her pending visit to Newport. She told Jimmy her stepmother's name, and he said something about it being one of the grandest of old Celtic names. Jimmy would remember, he told himself. Tonight he would have dinner at Neary's.

AT EIGHT O'CLOCK THAT evening, as Neil was contentedly finishing sautéed scallops, Jimmy Neary joined him. Mentally keeping his fingers crossed, Neil asked whether Jimmy could remember the name of Maggie's stepmother.

"Let's see." Jimmy's cherubic face puckered in concentration. "Siobhan . . . Maeve . . . no, none of those. It's—it's— I've got it! Finnuala. And Maggie said the old girl's known as Nuala."

"At least that's a start. I could kiss you," Neil said fervently.

A look of alarm crossed Jimmy's face. "Don't you dare," he said.

MAGGIE had not expected to sleep well, but wrapped as she was in the soft eiderdown quilt, she did not wake up until the phone rang at nine thirty on Wednesday morning.

It was Greta Shipley calling. "Maggie, I wanted to thank you for yesterday. It meant so much to me. We're allowed to invite a guest for dinner on a rotating basis, and I thought that if you don't have any plans, you might consider joining me this evening."

"I'd enjoy it very much," Maggie said sincerely. Then a mental picture flashed through her mind. The cemetery. Mrs. Rhinelander's grave. Something had caught her attention there yesterday. She'd have to go back.

"Mrs. Shipley," she said, "while I'm up here, I'm going to be taking some pictures around Newport for a project I'm working on. St. Mary's has such a tranquil, old-world feeling about it, it's perfect for my purposes. I know that some of the graves we left flowers on yesterday had beautiful sea vistas behind them. I'd like to go back. Can you tell me which ones we visited?"

Greta Shipley did not seem to find Maggie's request peculiar. "Oh, they are beautifully situated, aren't they?" she agreed. "Have you got a pen and paper handy?"

"Right here." Maggie jotted down the names and directions to each plot. Now if she only knew what it was she hoped to find.

After hanging up, she got out of bed and decided on a quick shower. Wrapped in a chenille robe, her still damp hair in a towel turban, Maggie went downstairs and fixed herself a light breakfast.

Ruefully she realized that the casual clothes she had packed would not get her through her two-week stay. This afternoon she would have to get herself an extra skirt and a couple of blouses or sweaters. Dress at Latham Manor was on the formal side, plus she had agreed to have dinner with Liam on Friday night, and that probably meant dressing up.

When she was dressed for the day, in a white T-shirt, jeans, a blue sweater, and sneakers, Maggie stood in front of the mirror studying herself. Her eyes no longer held traces of the tears she had wept for Nuala. They were clear again. Sapphire blue. That's how Paul had described her eyes the night they met. It seemed a lifetime ago. She had been a bridesmaid at a wedding; he had been a groomsman.

He had sat next to her at the rehearsal dinner. We talked to each other all night, Maggie thought. Then, after the wedding, we danced practically every dance. When he put his arms around me, I felt as though I had suddenly come home.

They were both twenty-three. He was attending the Air Force Academy, she just finishing the master's program at N.Y.U. Everyone said what a handsome couple we were, Maggie reminisced. Paul was so fair, with straight blond hair and ice-blue eyes he had inherited from his Finnish grandmother. Me, the dark-haired Celt.

Why am I thinking about all this now? Maggie asked herself. It was as though she were telling Nuala, she realized. These were all the things she wanted to talk about with her. Nuala had been widowed young. She would have understood.

Back downstairs three minutes later Maggie double-locked the door and got her camera equipment into the car. Then she was on her way to the cemetery.

MRS. Eleanor Robinson Chandler arrived at Latham Manor promptly at ten thirty for her meeting with Dr. William Lane.

Lane received his aristocratic guest with charm and courtesy. He knew Mrs. Chandler's history. Mrs. Chandler's grandmother had been one of Newport's grandes dames during the city's social zenith in the 1890s. She would make an excellent addition to the residence and possibly attract future guests from among her friends.

Her financial records were a shade disappointing; she had given away a great deal of her money to her large family. However, it was clear that she was used to the best. She might well be persuaded to take the top apartment that had been intended for Nuala Moore.

Mrs. Chandler was dressed in a beige knit suit. A single strand of matched pearls, small pearl earrings, a gold wedding band, and a gold watch were her only jewelry, but each item was superb. Her classic features were framed by pure white hair.

"You do understand that this is only a preliminary meeting," Mrs. Chandler was saying. "I am not at all sure that I'm prepared to enter any residence, however attractive." Mrs. Chandler's tone was noncommittal. "I understand you have several units available."

"As a matter of fact, one of our most desirable units just became available."

"Who most recently occupied it?"

"Mrs. Constance Van Sickle Rhinelander."

"Oh, of course. Connie had been quite ill, I understand."

"I'm afraid so." Lane did not mention Nuala Moore.

They went up in the elevator to the third floor. For long minutes Mrs. Chandler stood on the terrace overlooking the ocean. "This is lovely," she conceded. "However, I believe this unit is five hundred thousand dollars."

"That's correct."

"Well, I don't intend to spend that much. I would like to see your other available units."

They were on the second floor when they passed Greta Shipley's studio apartment. A maid had just finished cleaning it, and the door was open. Mrs. Chandler glanced in. "Oh, this is lovely."

"Step in," Dr. Lane urged. "I know Mrs. Shipley won't mind. She's at the hairdresser's."

"Just this far. I feel like an intruder." Mrs. Chandler took in the large alcove seating area, the bedroom section, and the magnificent ocean views on three sides. "How much is a unit like this?"

"Three hundred and fifty thousand dollars."

"Now *that* I would pay. Is there another like it available? For that price, of course."

"Not at the moment," he said, then added, "But why don't you fill out an application?" He smiled at her. "We'd very much like to have you as a guest someday."

DOUGLAS Hansen smiled ingratiatingly across the table at Cora Gebhart, a peppery septuagenarian who was clearly enjoying the scallops over braised endive she had ordered for lunch.

She was a talker, he thought. Not like some of the others that he'd had to shower with attention before he could elicit any information from them. Mrs. Gebhart was opening up to him like a sunflower to the sun.

"Everyone's favorite nephew," one of these women had called him, and it was just the way he wanted to be perceived: the solicitous thirty-year-old who extended all the little courtesies they hadn't enjoyed for years. Intimate, gossipy luncheons at upscale restaurants like this one, followed up with a box of candy for the ones who ordered sweet desserts; flowers for those who confided stories of their long-ago courtships.

Hansen had great respect for the fact that these women were intelligent. The stock offerings he touted were the kind that even a moderate investor would admit had possibilities. In fact, one of them had actually worked out, which in a way had been disastrous for him but in the end turned out to be a plus. Because now Mrs. Alberta Downing in Providence could confirm Hansen's expertise.

"Mrs. Downing invested one hundred thousand dollars and made a three-hundred-thousand-dollar profit in one week," he was able to tell prospective clients. It was an honest claim. The fact that the stock had been artificially inflated at the last minute and that Mrs. Downing had ordered him to sell, going against his own advice, had seemed like a disaster at the time. They had had to raise the money to pay her her profits, but now at least they had a genuine reference.

Cora Gebhart daintily finished the last of her meal. "Excellent," she announced as she sipped at the chardonnay in her glass. Hansen had wanted to order a full bottle, but she had informed him adamantly that one glass at luncheon was her limit. Douglas laid his knife and fork on the plate, prongs turned down, European-style.

Cora Gebhart sighed. "That's the way my husband always left the silver on his plate. Were you educated in Europe as well?"

"I spent my junior year at the Sorbonne," Hansen responded.

"How delightful!" Mrs. Gebhart exclaimed, and slipped into flawless French, which Douglas desperately tried to follow.

After a few moments he held up his hand, smiling. "I'm afraid I'm a bit rusty."

They laughed together, but Hansen's antenna went up. Had Mrs. Gebhart been testing him? he wondered. Could she sense that he wasn't a graduate of Williams and the Wharton School of Business, as he claimed? He knew that his lean, blond, aristocratic appearance had gotten him entry-level jobs with both Merrill Lynch and Salomon Brothers, but he hadn't lasted six months at either place.

Mrs. Gebhart's next words reassured him, however. "I think I've been too conservative," she complained. "I've tied up too much of my money in trusts, so I don't have a lot left for myself. I've thought about moving into Latham Manor, but I would have to move into one of the smaller units, and I'm used to more space." She looked Hansen squarely in the face. "I'm thinking about putting three hundred thousand dollars in the stock you recommended."

He tried not to let his emotions register on his face. The amount she mentioned was considerably more than he had hoped for.

"My accountant is opposed to it, but I'm beginning to think he's a fuddy-duddy. Do you know him? His name is Robert Stephens."

Hansen did know the name. Robert Stephens took care of the taxes for Mrs. Arlington, and she had lost a bundle investing in a high-tech company he had recommended.

"But I pay him to do my taxes, not to run my life," Mrs. Gebhart continued, "so I'm going to cash in my bonds and let you make me a killing. Now that the decision is made, maybe I *will* have a second glass of wine." As the midafternoon sun bathed the restaurant in golden warmth, they toasted each other.

MAGGIE spent almost two hours at St. Mary's cemetery. The beautiful warm day ran counter to her chilling quest, but she per-

severed, revisiting all the graves she had been to with Greta Shipley and taking pictures from every angle.

Her initial hunch had been that she had detected something odd
at Mrs. Rhinelander's grave, which had been the last they had visited. For that reason she had started with the Rhinelander plot and
ended at Nuala's grave. What *am* I looking for? she asked herself.

Then Maggie drove into the center of Newport and dropped off
her film at a drugstore. She also found a boutique on Thames Street
where she was able to find two cowl-necked sweaters and two long
skirts. These additions to her wardrobe would take care of anything
that might come up for the next ten days.

Newport is special, she thought as she drove along Ocean Drive
back to Nuala's house. *My* house, she amended, still surprised at
the realization. Do I want to sell it? she asked herself. At this moment, with that glorious ocean and this lovely quaint town, I'm
not so sure.

AT FOUR thirty Nurse Zelda Markey reported as directed to the
office of Dr. William Lane. She knew Greta Shipley had complained
about her. Well, Nurse Markey was ready for Dr. Lane.

Look at him, she thought contemptuously as he frowned across
the desk at her. I bet he can't tell the difference between measles
and chicken pox. Or palpitations and congestive heart failure. She
decided that the best defense was always a good offense.

"Doctor," she began, "I know Mrs. Shipley has complained that
I walk in on her without knocking. The fact is, Mrs. Shipley is doing a great deal of sleeping—much more than she did even a few
weeks ago—and I've been concerned. I open that door without invitation only when there is no response to repeated knocking."

She saw the flicker of uncertainty in Lane's eyes. "Then I would
suggest that if Mrs. Shipley does not respond, you open the door
slightly and call in to her. She's becoming quite agitated about this,
and I want to head it off before it becomes a real problem."

"But Dr. Lane, if I had not been in her room two nights ago
when she had that spell, something terrible might have happened."

"The spell passed quickly, and it turned out to be nothing. I do appreciate your concern, but I can't have these complaints. Do we understand each other, Miss Markey?"

"Of course, Doctor."

"Is Mrs. Shipley planning to be at dinner this evening?"

"Oh, yes, and she's having a guest, Miss Holloway, the step-daughter of Mrs. Moore. Mrs. Lane was told about that."

"I see. Thank you, Miss Markey."

As soon as she left, Lane picked up the phone to call his wife at home. "Why didn't you tell me Maggie Holloway would be having dinner here tonight?" he snapped.

"What difference could that possibly make?" Odile asked in a puzzled tone.

"The difference is—" Lane took a deep breath. Certain things were better left unsaid. "I want to know about any guests who are at dinner," he said. "I want to be there to greet them."

"I know that, dear. I arranged for us to dine in the residence tonight. You'll be able to chat with Maggie Holloway then."

"All right." He paused. "I'll be home in ten minutes."

EARL Bateman kept a tiny apartment on the Hutchinson campus. He found the small liberal arts college, situated in a quiet section of Providence, an ideal spot from which to do research for his lectures.

Earl's class in anthropology was considered a major attraction. "Anthropology: The science that deals with the origins, physical and cultural development, and social customs and beliefs of mankind." Earl began any new term by having his students memorize those words. And as he was fond of repeating, he felt true knowledge of any people or culture began with the study of their rituals of death.

It was a subject that never failed to fascinate him. Or his listeners, as demonstrated by the fact that he was increasingly in demand as a speaker. Earl's fee for such engagements was now three thousand dollars, and there were more offers than he could accept.

On Wednesday one offer intrigued him to the point that he could not get it off his mind. A cable station had written to ask whether he had sufficient material to do a series of half-hour television programs on the cultural aspects of death. Of course I have sufficient material, Earl thought. Death masks, for example. The Egyptians and Romans had them. The Florentines began to make them in the late fourteenth century.

He kept his collection in a museum on the grounds of the Bateman Funeral Home. Originally a caretaker's cottage, the narrow Victorian house had been separated from the main house and property ten years earlier. The museum could be visited only by written request, and Earl personally escorted the few visitors through it. Over the years, he had gathered an impressive array of materials, all having to do with death: slides and films; recorded funeral dirges; paintings and prints; Indian funeral pyres; present-day caskets; statues; and examples of mourning attire throughout the ages.

Earl knew he had enough material for any number of programs. He was about to become famous, he mused. He, Earl, the family joke, would show those raucous cousins.

He felt his heart begin to pound. Don't think about them, he warned himself. Concentrate on developing subjects for the cable program. But first he would have a drink. Just one, he promised himself as he prepared a very dry martini. As he took the first sip, he reflected on the fact that often before death someone close to the soon-to-be-deceased experienced a premonition of what was to come.

Someone close . . . "Like me," he said aloud. "I'm not really that close to Maggie Holloway, but I'm the one who has been given the premonition. I know that Maggie is going to die very soon, just as I was sure last week that Nuala had only hours to live." Maggie's face filled his mind—that dark hair surrounding the small, exquisite features dominated by those beautiful, pain-filled blue eyes.

At least, he consoled himself, she won't experience any more pain.

ANGELA, the soft-spoken maid who had admitted her yesterday, showed Maggie in. "Mrs. Shipley is waiting for you," the maid told her. "I'll take you to her."

"Thank you."

Angela hesitated. "When Mrs. Moore had her classes here, everyone had such a good time. Just a couple of weeks ago she began by asking everyone to remember a slogan from World War Two—the kind that were on posters hanging everywhere." She smiled reminiscently. "It was the last class Mrs. Moore taught. We all miss her. Well, I'd better take you up to Mrs. Shipley," she said.

Greta Shipley's warm smile did not disguise the fact that there was a grayish pallor under her eyes. Maggie noticed, too, that when she stood up, she had to rest her hand on the chair for support. She seemed tired and distinctly weaker than she had just yesterday.

"Maggie, how lovely you look. And how kind of you to come on such short notice," Mrs. Shipley said as Angela left the room.

"Angela was telling me about one of Nuala's classes that she sat in on, the one where you all drew posters," Maggie told her.

Greta Shipley smiled. "Nuala was positively wicked! When she and I came up here after the class, she took my drawing and added her own touches to it. You must see it. It's in that second drawer," she said, pointing to the table next to the sofa.

Looking at the heavy sheet of sketching paper, Maggie felt a sudden chill. Mrs. Shipley's original sketch vaguely resembled one defense worker talking to another on a bus. Behind them a figure in a black cape and hat was obviously eavesdropping.

Nuala had drawn what was clearly her face and Greta Shipley's over those of the defense workers. The image of a nurse with narrowed eyes and an outsize ear floated above the spy.

"Does this represent anyone here?" Maggie asked.

Mrs. Shipley laughed. "Oh, yes. That dreadful sneak Nurse Markey. That day I thought it was just a joke, all her snooping around. But now I'm not so sure."

"Why is that?" Maggie asked quickly.

"I don't know," she said. "Maybe I'm just getting to be a bit fanciful. Old ladies do that sometimes, you know. Now I think we really should go downstairs."

Maggie found the grand salon to be wonderfully attractive, rich in both design and furnishings. Handsome senior citizens were seated about the room. From what Maggie could see, they ranged in age from late sixties to late eighties, although Greta whispered that an attractive woman in a black velvet suit, with a ramrod straight back, had just turned ninety-four.

"That's Letitia Bainbridge," she whispered. "People told her she was crazy to pay four hundred thousand dollars for an apartment when she came here six years ago, but she said that with the genes in her family the money would be well spent. And time has proved her right. She'll be at our table, and you'll enjoy her, I promise."

Glancing around, Maggie noticed that Dr. Lane and his wife were approaching. Odile Lane was wearing an aqua silk shirt and matching long skirt. Maggie realized that Odile was actually a beautiful woman. Dr. Lane was attractive as well. His demeanor was both welcoming and courtly.

"What a great pleasure," he said with sincerity.

Odile waved her hand, indicating the elegant room. "Maggie, what do you think of all this?"

"I think it's heaven."

"When we learned you were coming, we so hoped to have you sit at our table," Odile Lane said, "but Mrs. Shipley wasn't having any of it. She said she wanted you with *her* friends." She wagged her finger at Greta Shipley. "Naughty, naughty," she trilled.

Maggie saw Mrs. Shipley's lips tighten. "Maggie," she said abruptly, "I want you to meet some of my other friends."

A few minutes later soft chimes announced dinner.

There were ten tables in the dining room, each with place settings for eight. "Oh, tonight they're using the Limoges china and the white linen," Mrs. Shipley said with satisfaction. Maggie was seated at Greta Shipley's right. Next to her was Letitia Bainbridge, who opened the conversation by saying, "You're so pretty. I understand from Greta that you're not married. Is there anyone special in your life?"

"No," Maggie said with a smile.

"Excellent," Mrs. Bainbridge said. "I have a grandson I'd like to introduce to you. He's president of his own company."

"I've met the grandson. Forget it," Greta Shipley whispered to Maggie, then in a normal tone introduced her to the others—three women and two men. "I managed to snare the Buckleys and the Crenshaws for our table," she said. "These places become a pavilion of women, so getting any male conversation becomes a struggle."

It proved to be a lively group, and Maggie kept asking herself

why Nuala had changed her mind so abruptly about living here. Letitia Bainbridge was particularly amusing as she told stories of Newport when she was young. "All the mothers were anxious to marry their daughters off to English nobility. And there was that dreadful Squire Moore. Everyone knew he came from nothing, but he did have a bit of charm and at least the pretense of a title, so of course he married well. Squire's god was money, and he'd do anything to accumulate it. Unfortunately, that characteristic has shown up in a number of his descendants."

It was over dessert that Anna Pritchard, who was recovering from a hip operation, joked, "Greta, guess who I saw? Eleanor Chandler. She was with Dr. Lane, and she was admiring your apartment. The maid had just cleaned it, and the door was open."

"Eleanor Chandler," Letitia Bainbridge mused. "A rather forceful person. Is she thinking of coming here?"

"I don't know," Mrs. Pritchard said. "But Greta, you'd better change your locks. If Eleanor wants your apartment, she'd think nothing of having you dispossessed."

"Let her try," Greta Shipley said with a hearty laugh.

When Maggie left, Greta insisted on walking her to the door.

"I wish you wouldn't," Maggie urged. "I know you're tired."

"Never mind. Tomorrow I'll give myself a lazy day."

"Then I'm going to call you tomorrow, and I'd better find you doing just that." Maggie kissed the soft cheek of the older woman. "Till tomorrow," she said.

CHAPTER 6

Thursday, October 3rd In the six days since Nuala Moore had been murdered, Chief of Police Chet Brower's initial instinct had become a certainty, at least in his own mind: No random thief had committed that crime. It had to be someone who knew Mrs. Moore, probably someone she trusted. But who? And what was the motive?

On Thursday morning he called his deputy, Jim Haggerty, into his office to review the situation. "Mrs. Moore may have left her door unlocked, and anyone could have walked in. On the other hand, she might have opened it for someone she knew. Either way, there was no sign of forced entry."

Jim Haggerty had worked with Brower for fifteen years. Jim's mild, bespectacled appearance was not exactly a Hollywood casting director's image of supercop, but that disparity sometimes worked to his advantage. His benign demeanor tended to make people comfortable, so they relaxed and talked freely.

"Let's proceed on the premise that it *was* someone she knew," Brower continued, his brow creased with thought. "That opens the suspect list to nearly everyone in Newport. Mrs. Moore was well liked and active in the community.

"But whoever killed Mrs. Moore could hardly help seeing the preparations she'd been making for a dinner party," Brower mused. "So that means that whoever was in the house wasn't worried that somebody might arrive any minute. Which means that it is a good chance the killer will turn out to be one of the dinner guests. It's time to take a serious look at all of them." He leaned back. "What do you think, Jim?"

Haggerty proceeded carefully. "Chief, I had a hunch you might be thinking along those lines, so I did a little looking in that direction already."

Brower eyed him speculatively. "Go on."

"Well, I'm sure you saw the expression on the face of that pompous windbag Malcolm Norton when Mrs. Woods told us about the will change and the canceled sale."

"I saw it. What I'd call shock, heavily tinged with anger."

"It's common knowledge that Norton's law practice is down to dog bites and divorces. So it interested me to find out where he'd get the money to buy Mrs. Moore's house. I also unearthed a little gossip about him and his secretary, a woman named Barbara Hoffman."

"Interesting. So where did he get the money?" Brower asked.

"By mortgaging his own house, which is maybe his only asset. Even talked his wife into co-signing."

"Does she know he has a girlfriend?"

"From what I gather, that woman misses nothing."

"Then why would she jeopardize their biggest mutual asset?"

"That's what *I'd* like to know. I talked to Hopkins Realtors, and frankly, they were surprised that Norton was willing to pay two hundred thousand for the Moore place. According to them, the house needs a total overhaul."

"Then why did Norton want it? Is there oil on the property?"

"If there is, he can't touch it. The section of the property on the water side is designated wetland. The buildable part of the lot is small, and you don't have a view."

"I think I'd better have a talk with Norton," Brower said.

"I'd suggest having a talk with his wife, too, Chief. Everything I learned indicates she's too shrewd to be talked into mortgaging her house without a very good reason."

"Okay, it's as good a place as any to start." Brower stood up. "By the way, it appears Maggie Holloway's clean. Her father apparently left her a little money, and she seems to be a very successful photographer, so there's no money motive on her part. And she's telling the truth about what time she left New York. Her doorman verified it."

"I'd like to have a chat with her," Haggerty offered. "Mrs. Moore's phone bill shows that she talked to Maggie Holloway a half-dozen times the week before the murder. Maybe something Moore told her about the people she was inviting to the dinner might give us a lead."

He paused, then added, "But Chief, the thing that's driving me nuts is not having any idea what Nuala Moore's murderer was looking for when he or she ransacked that house. I'll bet my bottom dollar that's the key to this crime."

MAGGIE awoke early but waited until eleven before she phoned Greta Shipley. She had been deeply concerned about how frail Greta had seemed last evening, and hoped that she had gotten a good night's sleep. There was no answer in the room.

The telephone rang fifteen minutes later. It was Dr. Lane. "Maggie, I have very sad news," he said. "Sometime last night Mrs. Shipley died peacefully in her sleep."

Maggie sat for a long time after the phone call, numb with sadness but also angry at herself for not being more insistent that Mrs. Shipley get a medical opinion—an *outside* medical opinion—to determine what was wrong. Dr. Lane said that all indicators pointed to heart failure. Clearly she had not felt well all evening.

First Nuala, now Greta Shipley. Was there some connection? Best friends both dead in one week, Maggie thought. She had been so happy to have Nuala back in her life. And now this. . . .

Maggie thought of the time when she was six and Nuala had first given her a jar of wet clay. She had propped up a picture of Maggie's miniature poodle, Porgie, in front of her. "Try to copy him," Nuala had instructed. That had been the beginning. Ever since, Maggie had lived a kind of love affair with sculpting.

Now with the news of Greta Shipley's death, Maggie had to get her hands into wet clay. It would be therapeutic, she thought as she climbed the stairs to the third floor. It would also give her a chance to think.

She began work on a bust of Nuala but soon realized that it was Greta Shipley's face that now filled her mind. She had looked so pale last night, Maggie remembered.

It was no use trying to work now. She felt no inspiration. Another funeral! Funeral. The word jogged her memory. She thought of the pictures she had taken at the cemetery. She should pick them up and study them. But study them for what? She didn't have the answer yet, but she was sure there was one.

THE thick packet of prints was waiting for her at the drugstore. She resisted the urge to open the packet immediately. When she got home, she would study the photos carefully.

When she arrived at the house, however, she found a late-model BMW parked on the street. The driver, a man who appeared to be about thirty, hastily got out of his car and was already walking up the driveway as Maggie opened her car door.

He was well dressed, good-looking in an upscale sort of way. Still, his aggressive presence bothered her. "Miss Holloway," he said, "I'm Douglas Hansen. I wanted to reach you, but your phone number isn't listed. So since I had an appointment in Newport today, I thought I'd swing by and leave you a note. It's on the door."

He reached in his pocket and handed her his card: DOUGLAS HANSEN, INVESTMENT ADVISER. The address was in Providence.

"One of my clients told me about Mrs. Moore's passing. I wanted to tell you how sorry I was, but also to ask if you're planning to sell this house."

"Thank you, Mr. Hansen, but I haven't made any decision," Maggie said quietly.

"Before you list the place with a real estate agent, if indeed you do decide to sell, I have a client who would be interested in acquiring it through me. Her daughter is planning a divorce and wants to have a place to move to when she breaks the news to her husband. Her name is one you would recognize."

"Probably not. I don't know many Newport people," Maggie said.

"Then let's say that many people would recognize the name."

"How do you know that the house is mine to sell?" Maggie asked.

Hansen smiled. "Miss Holloway, Newport is a small town."

I'm not going to discuss this, Maggie thought. She said noncommittally, "As I told you, I have made no decision. But thank you for your interest. I'll keep your card." She started toward the house.

"My client is willing to pay two hundred and fifty thousand dollars. I believe that that amount is significantly higher than the offer Mrs. Moore was prepared to accept."

"You seem to know a great deal, Mr. Hansen," Maggie said. "Newport must be a *very* small town. I will call if I decide to sell." Again she turned toward the house.

"Just one more thing, Miss Holloway. I have to ask you not to mention this offer to anyone. Too many people would guess the identity of my client, and it could become a significant problem for her daughter. That's why they have asked me to act as intermediary."

"You needn't worry. I'm not in the habit of discussing my business with anyone. Good-bye, Mr. Hansen." She moved briskly up the walk.

The note Hansen had mentioned had been wedged in next to the door handle. Maggie took it without reading it, then slipped the key into the lock. When she looked out the living-room window, she saw Hansen driving away. Suddenly she felt terribly foolish.

Am I starting to jump at my own shadow? she asked herself. And I certainly can't ignore his offer. That's fifty thousand dollars more than Malcolm Norton offered Nuala. No wonder he looked so upset when Mrs. Woods told us about the will—he knew he was getting a bargain.

Maggie went upstairs and opened the envelope containing the photographs. The first one her eye fell on was of Nuala's grave and the fading flowers lying at the base of the tombstone.

As NEIL Stephens turned his car into his parents' driveway, he took in the trees that lined the property, their leaves ablaze with gold and amber. Before Neil could get out of the car, his mother rushed out of the house. As he stepped down, she hugged him, then reached up to smooth his hair.

"Oh, Neil, it's *so* good to see you!" she exclaimed.

His father appeared behind her. "You're running late, pal. We tee up in half an hour. We've got to be there by two, and we're having dinner at the yacht club." He clasped Neil's shoulder. "Glad you're here, son."

It was not until they were on the back nine of the golf course that his father opened the subject he'd had on his mind. "One of the old girls whose income tax I handle is on the verge of a nervous breakdown," he said. "Some young fellow talked her into investing in some fly-by-night stock, and now she's lost the money that was supposed to take care of her. She had hoped to move into that fancy retirement residence I told you about."

They talked as they walked to the next hole. "Dad, what you just told me is something I hear all the time," Neil said.

"In this instance I think there was some kind of extraordinary pressure applied. Anyhow, I wish you'd talk to her. Her name is Laura Arlington. Maybe you can go over the rest of her portfolio."

"I'd be glad to, Dad. I just hope it's not too late."

At six thirty, dressed for dinner, the three Stephenses sat on the back porch sipping cocktails and looking out at Narragansett Bay.

"You look great, Mom," Neil said with affection.

"Your mother's always been a pretty woman, and all the tender loving care she's received from me over the last forty-three years has only enhanced her beauty," his father said. Noticing their bemused expressions, he added, "What are you two smiling at?"

"You know full well I've waited on you hand and foot, dear," Dolores Stephens replied.

"Neil, are you still seeing that girl you brought here in August?" his father asked.

"Who was that?" Neil wondered momentarily. "Oh, Gina. No, as a matter of fact, I'm not. There is someone I've been seeing who's visiting her stepmother in Newport for a couple of weeks. Her name is Maggie Holloway. Unfortunately, she got away before I got her phone number here."

"What's the stepmother's name?" his mother asked.

"I don't know her last name, but her first name is unusual. Finnuala. It's Celtic."

"That sounds familiar," Dolores Stephens mused.

The phone rang. Dolores got up to answer it.

The call was for Robert Stephens. "It's Laura Arlington," Dolores said as she handed the phone to her husband. "She sounds terribly upset."

Robert Stephens listened for a minute before speaking. "Laura, you're going to get yourself sick over this. My son, Neil, is in town. I've spoken to him about you, and he will go over everything with you in the morning. Now promise me you'll calm yourself down."

EARL Bateman's last class before the weekend had been at one o'clock Thursday afternoon. He had stayed in his campus apartment for several hours grading papers. Then, just as he was about to leave for Newport, the phone rang.

It was his cousin Liam, calling from Boston. He was surprised to hear from Liam. They had never had much in common. What's this all about? he asked himself.

He felt anger build as Liam gradually got to the point of the call, the gist of which was that if Earl was going to Newport for the weekend, he shouldn't just drop in on Maggie Holloway. His visit the other day had upset her.

"I stopped in to see her because of genuine concern that she, like Nuala, might carelessly leave the door unlocked," Earl said stiffly.

Liam's voice became soothing. "Earl, Maggie isn't fey, the way poor old Nuala was. It isn't necessary to warn her, especially when it comes out more like a threat."

So he's interested in Maggie Holloway after all, Earl thought as he hung up the phone. One would never have guessed it from the way he left her by herself at the Four Seasons party. But that was typical of Liam the glad-hander.

Once again a strange feeling came over him, a premonition that something was about to go wrong, that Maggie Holloway was in danger.

The first time Earl had had such a premonition was when he was sixteen. He had been in the hospital recovering from an appendix operation. His best friend, Ted, stopped in to see him on his way to an afternoon of sailing. Something had made Earl want to ask Ted not to go out on the boat, but that would have sounded stupid.

They found Ted's boat two days later, adrift. Earl never talked about the incident. And Earl didn't let himself think about the other times the presentiment had come.

As THEY followed the maître d' into the yacht-club dining room, Robert Stephens turned to his wife. "Look, Dolores, there's Cora Gebhart. Let's go by her table and say hello. Last time we talked, I was a little harsh with her. She was going on about cashing in some bonds for one of those crazy venture schemes, and I got so irritated I didn't even ask her what it was, just told her to forget it."

Neil dutifully trailed in his parents' footsteps as they crossed the restaurant.

"Cora, I owe you an apology," Robert Stephens began expansively. "But first, I don't think you've ever met my son, Neil."

"Hello, Robert, Dolores." Cora Gebhart looked up at Neil. "Your father brags about you all the time. It's a pleasure to meet you."

"Thank you. It's nice to meet you, too. I'm glad to hear my father brags about me. Most of my life he's been second-guessing me."

"I can understand that. He's always second-guessing me, too. But Robert, you don't owe me an apology. I asked for your opinion."

"Well, that's fine. I'd hate to hear that another one of my clients lost her shirt investing in high-risk flings."

"Don't worry about this one," Cora Gebhart responded.

"Robert, the maître d' is waiting with the menus at our table," Neil's mother urged.

As they threaded their way through the room, Neil wondered whether his father had missed the tone Mrs. Gebhart used when she said not to worry. Dollars to donuts she didn't take his advice.

They had finished their meal and were lingering over coffee when their friends the Scotts stopped by their table to say hello.

"Neil, you owe Harry a word of thanks," Robert Stephens said by way of introduction. "He switched tee-off times with us today."

"Didn't matter," Harry Scott responded. "Lynn was in Boston for the day, so we planned on a late dinner."

His wife, stocky and pleasant-faced, asked, "Dolores, do you remember meeting Greta Shipley at a luncheon here for the preservation society? She sat at our table."

"Yes. I liked her very much. Why?"

"She died last night in her sleep, apparently."

"I'm so sorry."

"What upsets me," Lynn Scott continued contritely, "is that I'd heard that she had lost two close friends recently, and I'd been meaning to call her. One of the friends was that poor woman who was murdered in her home last Friday. You must have read about that. Her stepdaughter from New York discovered the body."

"Stepdaughter from New York!" Neil exclaimed.

Excitedly his mother interrupted him. "*That's* where I read that name. It was in the newspaper. *Finnuala.*"

When they got back home, Robert Stephens showed Neil the newspapers in the garage, waiting for recycling. "I'm sure Saturday's paper is in that pile," his father told him.

Two minutes later Neil was reading the account of Nuala Moore's death. As he did, his mind kept replaying the happiness in Maggie's eyes when she told him about finding her stepmother again. "She gave me the five happiest years of my childhood," she had said. Maggie, Maggie, Neil thought. Where was she now?

Nuala Moore's address was in the paper, but when he called information, he was told that the phone there was unlisted.

"Damn," he cried.

"Neil," his mother said softly, "it's quarter of eleven. Drive over there in the morning, and if you don't find her, the police will certainly know where to reach her."

"Listen to your mother, son," his father said.

"I guess so. Thanks, both of you." Neil kissed his mother, touched his father's arm, and walked dejectedly to the bedroom.

Dolores Stephens waited until her son was out of earshot, then quietly said to her husband, "I have a feeling Neil has finally met a girl he really cares about."

EVEN a painstaking examination of each photograph did not reveal to Maggie anything on those graves that should have troubled her subconscious. They all looked the same: headstones with plantings around them; grass still velvety green in this early fall season, except Nuala's, which had sod that showed some patchy spots.

Sod. For some reason that word struck a note with her. Mrs. Rhinelander's grave must have been freshly sodded as well. She had died only two weeks earlier.

Once more Maggie studied all the photographs of Constance Rhinelander's grave, using a magnifying glass to pore over every inch of them. The only thing that attracted her attention was a small hole showing in the plantings around the headstone. It looked as though a rock or something might have been removed from there.

She looked again at the best close-ups she had of the tombstone at Nuala's grave. The sod there was smooth to where the plantings began, but in one of the shots she thought she could detect something—a stone?—just behind the flowers Greta Shipley had left. There was an odd glint. . . .

Finally she laid the prints down on a corner of the refectory table and reached for an armature and the pot of wet clay. Using recent pictures of Nuala she'd found around the house, Maggie began to sculpt. For the next several hours her fingers became one with clay and knife as she began to shape Nuala's small, lovely face, the wide eyes, and to catch Nuala's spirit.

As she cleaned up, Maggie thought about the people she had dined with last evening. How distressed they must be, she thought. Maggie looked at her watch and went downstairs. Nine o'clock: Not really too late to phone Mrs. Bainbridge.

Letitia Bainbridge answered on the first ring. "Oh, Maggie, we're all heartsick. Greta hadn't been feeling well for a few weeks, but till then she was perfectly fine."

"I came to like her so much in such a short time," Maggie said sincerely. "I can imagine how all of you must feel. Do you know what the arrangements are?"

"The service is Saturday at eleven, and interment is at St. Mary's."

"I'll be there," Maggie promised.

I'M SPECIALIZING in late dinners, Maggie thought as she put on the kettle, scrambled some eggs, and dropped bread into the toaster. At least tomorrow night I can count on Liam to buy me a good meal. It would be good to see him, she reflected. He was always fun, in an outrageous kind of way.

She prepared a tray and carried it into the living room. The bookcases were overflowing with books. Large framed pictures of Tim and Nuala on vacations with friends were scattered on the walls. The deep old club chair with the hassock probably had been his, Maggie decided.

No wonder the prospect of moving to Latham Manor had proved daunting, Maggie thought. It would have been quite a wrench for Nuala to leave this happy home. But clearly she had considered moving there. That first evening, when they had dinner after they met at the Moore reunion, Nuala had mentioned that the kind of apartment she wanted in the residence home had just become available.

What apartment was it? Maggie realized suddenly that her hands were trembling. She carefully replaced the teacup on the saucer. Could the apartment that had become available to Nuala be the one that had belonged to Greta Shipley's friend Constance Rhinelander?

ALL he asked for was a little quiet, but Dr. William Lane knew he was not going to be granted that wish. Odile sat at her dressing table brushing her hair as a torrent of words poured from her.

"These days are so trying, aren't they? Everyone just loved Greta Shipley. You know, that's two of our sweetest ladies in as many weeks. Of course, Nurse Markey was concerned about that little spell Mrs. Shipley had Monday night."

"I examined Mrs. Shipley right after she had that spell," Dr. Lane said wearily. "There was no reason for alarm."

"Well, of course, you're the doctor, dear." Odile continued. "That new medical examiner is quite young and attractive. What was her name? Lara Horgan? I didn't know that Dr. Johnson had retired."

"He retired as of the first. That was Tuesday," he responded tartly. "Now, Odile, if you don't mind, I really must get some sleep."

"Oh, darling, I'm sorry. I know how upsetting this day has been." Odile put down the brush and got into bed, and at last the light went out. But now William Lane was no longer sleepy. As usual, Odile had managed to say something that would gnaw at him.

That young medical examiner *was* different from Dr. Johnson. He had always approved death certificates with a casual wave of his pen. *Be careful*, Lane warned himself.

CHAPTER 7

Friday, October 4th When Maggie awoke on Friday morning, she squinted at the clock and saw that it was seven thirty. She arose feeling groggy and headachy and decided that a brisk after-breakfast walk along Ocean Drive would help clear her head. I need that, she thought, especially since I've got to go to the cemetery again this morning. She was anxious to see what was causing the odd glint she had detected in the photograph of Nuala's grave.

The early fall day was magnificent. The sun was brilliant as it rose in the sky, though there was a cool ocean breeze. There was also the glorious sound of the crashing waves and the wonderful scent of salt and sea that filled the air. I could fall in love with this place, she thought.

After a mile Maggie turned and retraced her steps. Looking up, she realized that only a glimpse of the third floor of Nuala's house—*my* house, she thought—showed from the road. There are too many trees around it, she told herself. And I wonder why the end of the property that would afford a drop-dead view of the ocean has never been built on. Could there be restrictions against building there? I should look into that.

Back at the house, she paused long enough to have a quick cup of coffee before she left promptly at nine. She wanted to get the cemetery visit over with.

AT QUARTER past nine Neil Stephens stopped his car in front of the mailbox with the name "Moore" painted on it. He walked up to the porch and rang the bell. There was no answer.

Looking for some tangible sign that Maggie might be there, he walked to the back and peered through the window of the kitchen. He could see a coffeepot on the stove and, next to the sink, a cup and saucer. But had they been there for days or only minutes?

Finally he decided to ring a neighbor's bell and inquire whether anyone had seen Maggie. At the third house he tried, the door was answered by an attractive couple in their mid-sixties. As he quickly told them why he was there, Neil realized he had lucked out.

The couple, Irma and John Woods, told him of Nuala Moore's death and funeral and of Maggie's presence in the house. "What a sweet girl Maggie is." Irma Woods sighed. "I could tell how heartbroken she was about losing Nuala, but she isn't one to carry on. The hurt was all in her eyes."

Maggie, Neil thought, I wish I could have been here for you.

The Woodses had no idea where Maggie might have gone this

morning or how long she would be out. So Neil left a note for Maggie on the door and had her phone number tucked securely in his pocket before driving away five minutes later.

MAGGIE stopped at a florist's and bought an assortment of fall flowers to place on the graves she intended to inspect. As before, once she passed the entrance to St. Mary's, the welcoming statue of the angel and the meticulously kept plots seemed to impart a sense of peace. She drove up the winding incline that led to Nuala's grave.

As she stepped from the car, she sensed that a workman weeding the gravel path nearby was watching her. She was glad she had thought to pick up the flowers; she would rather not seem to be examining the grave. Squatting down, she selected a half-dozen flowers and laid them at the base of the tombstone.

Maggie quickly consulted the snapshot she was holding. It was fortunate she had brought the picture, she realized, because the object she was looking for could have been missed. But it was there.

She looked swiftly to the side and realized she had the workman's undivided attention. Kneeling forward, she bowed her head and crossed herself, then let her folded hands drop to the ground. Still in the posture of prayer, her fingers touching the sod, she dug around the object and freed it. When she glanced around again, the workman had his back turned to her. With one motion she yanked the object up and concealed it between her palms. As she did this, she heard a muffled ringing sound.

A bell, she thought. Why would anyone bury a bell on Nuala's grave? She walked quickly back to her car and drove slowly in the direction of the second grave she wanted to visit. She parked in a cul-de-sac, then looked around. There was no one nearby.

Opening the car window, she held the bell outside, brushing off the loose earth. It was about three inches high and surprisingly heavy, not unlike an old-fashioned miniature school bell, except for the decorative garland of flowers bordering the base. The clapper was heavy, too, she noticed. When allowed to hang freely, it no doubt could make quite a sound.

Feeling vaguely as though she were doing something amiss in tak-

ing the bell, she slid it under the seat of the car. Then she selected another half-dozen flowers and went to revisit the grave of another of Greta Shipley's friends.

Her last stop was at Mrs. Rhinelander's grave. It had been the photograph of this grave that most clearly seemed to show a gap in the sod near the base of the tombstone. As Maggie arranged flowers on the damp grass, her fingers found the indented area.

Maggie needed to think. There had to be an explanation for what she had found, Maggie reasoned. Of the six burial plots she had visited, four—including Nuala's—had bells at the base of the tombstone, each similar in weight and size. It appeared as well that one had been removed from the ground near Mrs. Rhinelander's tombstone. Only one of Greta Shipley's friends had not received this odd tribute.

A name popped into Maggie's mind: Mrs. Bainbridge. Like Greta Shipley, she had been at Latham Manor since it opened. She must have known all those women, too, Maggie realized.

Back in her car, Maggie called Letitia Bainbridge on the cellular phone.

"Come right over," she told Maggie. "I'd love to see you."

"I'm on my way," Maggie replied. She reached under the seat for the bell she had taken from Nuala's grave and put it in her shoulder bag. She shuddered involuntarily—the metal had felt cold and clammy to her touch.

IT HAD been one of the longest weeks of Malcolm Norton's life. The shock of having Nuala Moore cancel the sale of her house, followed by Barbara's announcement that she was going to visit for an extended period with her daughter in Vail, had left him numbed.

He *had* to get his hands on that house! Telling Janice about the impending change in the Wetlands Act had been a terrible mistake. He should have taken a chance and forged her name on the mortgage papers. He was that desperate.

Which was why, when Barbara put through the call from Chief Brower on this Friday morning, it took him a few moments to compose himself. "Good morning, Chief. How are you?" he said.

Chet Brower clearly was not in the mood for chitchat. "I'm fine. I'd like to drop over and talk with you for a few minutes today. When are you free?"

Norton had no intention of telling Brower exactly how free he was. "I had a closing at eleven that's been postponed till one, so I do have an opening."

"I'll see you at eleven."

Well after hearing the dismissive click, Malcolm stared nervously at the receiver. There was a gentle tap on the door, and Barbara poked her head in the office. "Malcolm, is anything wrong?"

"What could be wrong? He just wants to talk to me. I imagine it has to do with Friday night."

"Oh, of course. The murder. You and Janice did go to Mrs. Moore's for the dinner party."

She started to close the door again. "Barbara," he said, his voice pleading, "just give me a little more time. Don't leave me now." Her only answer was to close the door with a firm click.

Brower arrived promptly at eleven. He got right to the point. "Mr. Norton, you were due at Nuala Moore's home at eight o'clock the night of the murder?"

"Yes. My wife and I arrived at perhaps ten after eight. As you know, we were instructed to wait in the home of Nuala's neighbors."

"What time did you leave your office that evening?"

Norton thought for a moment. "About quarter of six. I had a closing outside the office and brought the file back here and checked on messages."

"Did you go directly home from here?"

"Not quite. Barbara . . . Mrs. Hoffman, my secretary, had been out that day with a cold. She had taken home a file I needed to study over the weekend, so I stopped at her house to pick it up."

"How long did that take?"

"About twenty minutes each way."

"So you were home around six thirty."

"Actually, it was probably closer to seven."

Janice had told him that his face could have been read like an open book when Irma Woods delivered the news about Nuala's will. So this morning Malcolm quickly had prepared answers to questions that he anticipated Brower would ask about his reaction to the canceled house sale.

In fact, the officer probed for details of the proposed sale. "Must have been a bit of a letdown," Brower mused, "but on the other hand, every real estate agent in town has a house like Nuala Moore's, just begging to be bought."

Meaning, why did I want this one? Norton thought.

"You and Mrs. Norton must have really fallen in love with it," Brower continued. "Word is you mortgaged your own house to pay for it." Now Brower was leaning back, his eyes half closed, his fingers locked together. "Anybody who wants a house that badly would hate to know that a relative of sorts was about to arrive on the scene and maybe mess things up. Only one way to prevent that. Stop the relative."

Brower stood up. "It's been a pleasure talking to you, Mr. Norton," he said. "Now, do you mind if I have a word with your secretary, Mrs. Hoffman?"

Barbara Hoffman had stayed home last Friday pleading a cold, but actually, she had wanted a quiet day to think things through. To placate her conscience, she had brought home a stack of files.

Malcolm almost never came to her house, but unexpectedly he had dropped by on Friday evening. He did not realize that her neighbor Dora Holt had stopped in. When Barbara had opened the door, he had bent to kiss her, then at her negative look had stepped back.

"Oh, Mr. Norton," she had said quickly, "I have that file on the Moore closing."

She had introduced him to Dora Holt and then made a show of going through the files. But Barbara hadn't missed the knowing smirk in the eyes of the other woman. And that was the moment when she knew the situation was intolerable.

Now, as she sat facing Chief Brower, Barbara Hoffman felt very uncomfortable.

"Then Mr. Norton only stayed a moment?"

"Yes. He took the file and left immediately."

"What file was it, Mrs. Hoffman?"

Another lie she had to tell. "I—I'm—actually, it was the file on the Moore closing." She cringed inwardly.

"Just one more thing. What time did Mr. Norton get to your house?"

"A little after six, I believe," she replied honestly.

Brower got up and nodded at the intercom on her desk. "Would you tell Mr. Norton that I'd like another moment with him please."

When Chief Brower returned to the lawyer's office, he didn't waste words. "Mr. Norton, I understand the file you picked up from Mrs. Hoffman last Friday evening was one concerning Mrs. Moore's closing. When exactly was the closing scheduled?"

"On Monday morning at eleven," Norton told him.

"You were the purchaser, but Mrs. Moore didn't have a separate lawyer representing her. Isn't that rather unusual?"

"Not really. Nuala felt it was unnecessary to involve another attorney. I was paying a fair price and was handing the money over to her in the form of a certified check."

Chief Brower stared silently at Malcolm Norton. "Just one more thing," he said. "The drive from Mrs. Hoffman's house to your home shouldn't have taken more than twenty minutes. That would have gotten you home by a few minutes past six thirty. Yet you say it was nearly seven. Did you go anywhere else?"

"No. Perhaps I was mistaken about the time I arrived home."

What does he suspect? Norton wondered.

WHEN Neil Stephens got back to Portsmouth, his mother knew from the look on his face that he had not been successful in locating the young woman from New York.

"Let me fix you breakfast," she said. "After all, I don't get much chance to fuss over you anymore."

Neil sank into a chair at the kitchen table. "I should think fussing over Dad is a full-time job. By the way, where *is* Dad?"

"In his office. Cora Gebhart, the lady whose table we stopped at last night, called and asked if she could come over and talk to him."

"I see," Neil said distractedly.

Dolores turned and looked at him. "You're worried," she said.

"I am. I should have been here to help Maggie."

Over waffles and bacon he told her all he knew about Maggie. What he didn't tell her was how angry he was at himself for not knowing more.

"She really does sound lovely," Dolores Stephens said. "I'm anxious to meet her. But listen, you've left her a note and you have the phone number. You'll surely hear from her today. Just relax."

"I know. It's just that I have this rotten feeling that there have been times when she needed me and I wasn't there for her."

"Afraid of getting involved, right?"

Neil put his fork down. "That's not fair."

"Isn't it? You know, Neil, a lot of the smart, successful young men of your generation really don't want to get involved. But some of them also never seem to grow up. I just wonder if this concern on your part doesn't reflect a sudden realization that you care a lot about Maggie Holloway, something you wouldn't admit to yourself earlier, because you didn't want to get involved."

Neil stared at his mother for a long moment. "And I thought Dad was tough."

Dolores Stephens smiled. "My grandmother had a saying: 'The husband is the head of the family; the wife is the neck.' " She paused. " 'And the neck turns the head.' "

Seeing Neil's startled expression, she laughed. "Trust me, I think of a husband and wife as equals, not game players. But sometimes what *seems* to be is not necessarily what *is*. Your father's fussing and complaining is his way of showing concern. I've known that since our first date."

"Speak of the devil," Neil said as through the window he spotted his father.

His mother glanced out. "Uh-oh, he's bringing Cora in. She looks upset."

A few minutes after his father and Cora Gebhart joined them at the kitchen table, Neil understood why she was upset. On Wednesday she had sold her bonds through the broker who had been trying to get her to invest in a venture stock he had recommended.

"I couldn't sleep last night," she said. "I had the awful feeling that I'd made a terrible mistake."

"Did you call this broker and cancel the buy?" Neil asked.

"I tried to. He said it was too late." Her lip trembled.

Neil read the prospectus and the fact sheet. It was even worse than he expected. "Yesterday you bought fifty thousand shares at nine," he told Mrs. Gebhart. "We'll find out what's happening to it today."

He phoned his office and tersely apprised a trading associate of the situation. Then he turned again to Mrs. Gebhart. "It's at seven now. I'm putting in a sell order."

She nodded her assent.

When Neil hung up, he said, "There was a rumor a few days ago that the company whose stock you purchased was being bought by Johnson and Johnson. But, unfortunately, it's just a rumor intended to inflate the value of the stock artificially. I'm terribly sorry, Mrs. Gebhart. At least we should be able to save *most* of your capital."

"What makes me furious is that this is the same broker who got Laura Arlington to invest in a fly-by-night company and caused her to lose her savings," Robert Stephens growled.

"He seemed so nice," Cora Gebhart said. "And he was so knowledgeable about my bonds."

The statement caught Neil's attention. "You must have told him about your bonds if he was so knowledgeable," he said sharply.

"But I didn't. When he phoned to ask me to lunch, he talked about the kind of clients he had—like Mrs. Downing. He told me that he made a fortune for her. Then he talked about exactly the bonds I hold."

"Who is this Mrs. Downing?" Neil asked.

"Oh, everybody knows her. She's a pillar of the Providence old guard. I did call her, and she simply raved about Douglas Hansen."

"I see. Even so, I'd like to run a check on him," Neil said.

The phone rang. Maggie, Neil thought. Let it be Maggie.

It was his associate at the investment house. Neil listened, then turned to Cora Gebhart. "He got you out at seven. Count yourself lucky."

When Mrs. Gebhart left, Robert Stephens looked at his son affectionately. "Thank goodness you were here, Neil. It would have been a shame to have Cora wiped out. As it is, this may mean that she'll have to give up the idea of moving into Latham Manor."

"Latham Manor," Neil said. "I need to ask you about that place." Neil told them about the Van Hillearys, his clients who were looking for a retirement base. "I told them I'd investigate Latham Manor for them. I'd almost forgotten."

"We're not teeing off until one," Robert Stephens said, "and Latham isn't that far from the club. Why don't you call over and see if you can make an appointment now."

"Okay, let's get it out of the way."

Dr. Lane could not have been more pleasant. "You're calling at a very good time," he said. "We have one of our best suites available—a two-bedroom unit with a terrace. Come right over."

DR. LARA Horgan, the new medical examiner for the state of Rhode Island, had not been able to figure out what was making her uneasy. The death of the woman at Latham Manor was to all appearances purely routine. Still, something about it was bothering her. The medical history of the deceased woman, Greta Shipley, had been straightforward. Mrs. Shipley had a ten-year history of hypertension and had suffered at least one silent heart attack. Dr. William Lane, the director and physician at Latham Manor, seemed competent. The staff had experience, and the facilities were first-rate.

The fact that Mrs. Shipley had had a weak spell at the funeral of her friend Nuala Moore verified the tension she must have been under. Dr. Horgan had seen a number of instances where an elderly spouse expired hours after the death of the husband or wife. Someone horrified by a dear friend's death might experience that same fatal stress.

Dr. Horgan was familiar with the circumstances surrounding the death of Nuala Moore. Multiple vicious blows to the back of Mrs. Moore's head had proved fatal. Grains of sand mixed in with blood and hair suggested that the perpetrator had found the weapon, probably a rock, somewhere on the beach and had entered the house carrying it. It also suggested that the perpetrator had known the resident of the house was small and frail. That's what's sending alarm signals to me, she told herself. The niggling feeling that Nuala Moore's death is somehow tied in with the one at Latham Manor.

Then a final thought teased her: Nurse Markey. She was the one who had found Mrs. Shipley's body. There was something about that woman she didn't like.

ON THIS Friday morning Earl Bateman was preparing a synopsis of the lectures he proposed to deliver in the potential cable-television series. When he came to the subject of tombstone rubbings, he was reminded that he had intended to look for some poignant or remarkable ones. Realizing it was a beautiful day, he decided to visit the oldest section of St. Mary's cemetery.

He was driving down the road that led there when he saw a black Volvo station wagon come out through the open gates and turn the other way. Maggie Holloway had the same car, he thought. Could she have been here visiting Nuala's grave?

Pete Brown, a cemetery worker he had come to know from his various meanderings among the old tombstones, was weeding a gravel path. Earl opened the window. "Pretty quiet around here, Pete," he offered. It was an old joke they shared.

"Sure is, Professor."

"I thought I saw Mrs. Moore's stepdaughter's car. Was she visiting the grave?" He was sure that everyone in Newport knew the details of Nuala's death.

"Nice-looking lady, skinny, dark hair, young?"

"That would be Maggie."

"Yep. And she must know half of our guests," Pete said, then laughed. "One of the fellows saw her go from one plot to another and drop off flowers. All the guys noticed her. She's a doll."

Now isn't that interesting? Earl thought. "Take care, Pete," he said, then drove slowly to the old section of St. Mary's and began wandering among the headstones. Some of the small headstones bore dates from the 1600s. He squatted by one, squinting to read the faint lettering—BETROTHED TO ROBERT SAMUELS BUT GATHERED TO THE LORD—and the dates.

Earl opened his kit to take a rubbing of the stone. He knelt down, enjoying the feel of the soft earth, which sent its cool dampness through his old trousers to his skin. As he began his careful effort to transfer the stone's poignant sentiment onto thin parchment, he found himself thinking of the young girl who lay buried beneath him.

She had just passed her sixteenth birthday, he calculated. Had she been pretty? Yes, very pretty, he decided. She had had a cloud of dark curls and sapphire-blue eyes.

Maggie Holloway's face floated before him. Clearly something was going on with her. He had to think about this.

He made one decision. Since he did not have classes on Monday, he would stay an extra day in Newport. And whether Liam liked it or not, he was going to visit Maggie Holloway.

LETITIA Bainbridge's studio apartment at Latham Manor was a large corner room with a magnificent ocean view. "Being a charter member here has its perks," she said to Maggie. "Greta and I decided to sign up right away. Trudy Nichols hemmed and hawed and ended up paying another hundred and fifty thousand for one of the largest apartments, and the poor darling only lived two years. The Crenshaws have it now. They were at our table the other night."

"I remember them. They're very nice." *Nichols,* Maggie thought. *Gertrude Nichols.* Hers was one of the graves that has the bell.

Mrs. Bainbridge sighed. "It's always hard when one of us goes, especially when it's someone from our table. And when my daughter Sarah took me to my family doctor yesterday, she told me the word is out that Eleanor Chandler is moving in here."

"Aren't you feeling well?" Maggie asked.

"Oh, I'm fine. But Sarah wanted Dr. Evans to check my blood pressure."

They sat down on slipper chairs that were placed by the windows. Mrs. Bainbridge reached over and plucked a framed snapshot from a nearby table. "My crowd," she said proudly. "Three sons, three daughters, seventeen grandchildren, four great-grandchildren. Never a week goes by that somebody in the family isn't around."

Maggie consciously stored that piece of information. Then she noticed a picture that had been taken in the grand salon there at Latham Manor. Mrs. Bainbridge was in the center of a group of eight. "Special occasion?" she asked.

"My ninetieth birthday, four years ago." Letitia Bainbridge leaned forward. "That's Constance Rhinelander on the left. She just died a couple of weeks ago, and of course you knew Greta."

"Mrs. Shipley didn't have close family, did she?" Maggie asked.

"No. Neither did Constance, but we were family for each other."

Then Maggie saw a silver bell on the fireplace mantel. She got up and crossed over to it. "Oh, isn't this lovely." She picked it up.

Letitia Bainbridge smiled. "My mother used it to summon her personal maid. My granddaughters find that a hoot, as they put it, but a lot of us old girls grew up in that milieu."

It was the opening Maggie wanted. She sat down again and reached into her purse. "Mrs. Bainbridge, I found *this* bell on Nuala's grave. I was curious as to who left it there. Is there a custom here of putting a bell on the grave of a friend?"

Letitia Bainbridge looked astonished. "I never heard of such a thing. How bizarre." She turned away.

With a sinking heart Maggie dropped the bell back in her shoulder bag. She said nothing about the other bells she had found.

There was a knock at the door, and Mrs. Bainbridge commented, "That will be the lunch tray." She raised her voice. "Come in, please."

It was Angela, the maid whom Maggie had met on her earlier visits. Maggie greeted her, then got up. "I really must run along."

Mrs. Bainbridge rose. "I'm so glad you stopped in, Maggie. Will I see you tomorrow?"

Maggie knew what she meant. "Yes, of course. I'll be at the funeral parlor and at Mrs. Shipley's Mass."

When she went downstairs, she reached into her pocketbook for her car keys and inadvertently hit the bell. A muffled ringing sound made her grab the clapper to silence it. Ask not for whom the bell tolls, Maggie thought as she walked down the steps of Latham Manor.

DR. LANE, Neil Stephens, and his father concluded their tour of Latham Manor at the entrance to the dining room. Neil took in the hum of conversation, the animated faces of the well-dressed seniors, the overall ambience of the beautiful room. White-gloved waiters were serving. "Very impressive," Neil said, nodding appreciatively.

"Do you feel that you might recommend the available suite to your clients?" Dr. Lane said gently. "Without meaning to pressure them, I can tell you that it won't last long."

"The place is most impressive," Neil said. "I'll certainly recommend that they come up and look over everything for themselves."

"Wonderful," Dr. Lane said heartily. "We like having couples here. Many of the guests are widows, but that doesn't mean they don't enjoy having men around."

Robert Stephens fell into step with them. "All right, Neil, let's be on our way. We tee up in thirty minutes."

Neil called Maggie from the car phone, but he got no answer.

Even though it was a beautiful day and he played excellent golf, Neil found the afternoon unconscionably long. He could not shake the ominous feeling that something was wrong.

ON HER way home Maggie decided to pick up groceries. She drove to a small market near the wharf. There she gathered the makings of green salad, pasta pomodoro, and some freshly prepared New England clam chowder. I've had my fill of scrambled eggs, she thought.

Pulling into the driveway at Nuala's house, she carried the groceries around to the kitchen door and let herself in. Dropping the packages on the table, she quickly locked the door. I meant to call in a locksmith, she thought. Liam would ask about that tonight.

Maggie found the phone book in a kitchen drawer and smiled at the sight of the clutter beneath it: recipes, half-burned candles, rusty scissors, paper clips, small change. I'd hate to try to find anything in this house, Maggie thought. Then she felt her throat close. Whoever ransacked this house was looking for something, and chances are he didn't find it, an interior voice whispered to her.

After she left a message on the machine of the first locksmith she called, she finished putting away the groceries and fixed herself a cup of the clam chowder. Then she went up to the studio. Restlessly her fingers reached into the pot of wet clay. Now it was Greta Shipley whose face demanded to be captured.

Maggie stayed at the worktable for an hour until the clay had taken on an approach to the likeness of the woman she had known so briefly. Finally the surging disquietude had passed and she could wash her hands and start the task of sorting out Nuala's paintings.

At three o'clock she started going through the works that had not yet been framed. In the storage closet off the studio she found dozens of Nuala's sketches, watercolors, and oils. Some of the watercolors were extraordinary. Like Nuala, she thought, they were warm and joyous and filled with unexpected depths. She especially loved a winter scene in which a tree, its branches laden and bent with snow, was sheltering an incongruous ring of flowering plants, including snapdragons and roses, violets and lilies.

Maggie became so engrossed in the task that it was after five thirty when she hurried downstairs, just in time to catch the phone that she had thought she heard ringing.

It was Liam. "Hey, this is my third attempt to get you. I was afraid I was being stood up," he said, relief in his voice.

"I'm sorry. I didn't hear the phone. I was in the studio."

"Pick you up in about an hour?"

"Fine." That should give me enough time for a soak in the tub, Maggie thought as she hung up. The house felt drafty, and in an odd way it seemed to her she could still feel the chill of the damp earth she had touched at the graves.

Feeling more relaxed after her bath, she dressed carefully in the new white sweater and long black skirt she had purchased earlier in the week, then decided that a little care with her makeup was in order. It's fun to dress up for Liam, she thought. He makes me feel good about myself.

At quarter of seven the bell rang. Liam stood on the doorstep, a dozen long-stemmed red roses in one hand, a folded sheet of paper in the other.

"You look spectacular," he told her. "Obviously, McDonald's won't do."

Maggie laughed. She quickly read the note he had brought in. "Where was this?" she asked.

"On your front door, madame."

"Oh, of course. I came in through the kitchen earlier." She refolded the piece of paper. So Neil is in Portsmouth and wants to get together. Isn't that nice. She hated to admit how disappointed she had been when he hadn't called last week before she left. She had chalked it up as another indication of his indifference toward her.

"Anything important?" Liam asked casually.

"No. Someone who's up for the weekend wants me to call."

She went back upstairs for her handbag, and as she picked it up, she felt the extra weight of the bell. Should she show it to Liam? she wondered. No, not tonight, she decided. I don't want to talk about death and graves. Not now. She took the bell out of her purse and put it on the closet shelf, pushing it back until it was completely out of sight.

Liam had made a reservation at The Black Pearl, a tony restaurant with a sweeping view of Narragansett Bay. "My condo isn't far from here," he explained, "but I miss the big house I was raised in. One of these days I'm going to bite the bullet and buy one of the old places and renovate it." His voice became serious.

"Maggie," he went on quietly, "ever since last week you haven't been out of my mind for a minute. All I've been able to think about is that if you had walked in on whatever hophead attacked Nuala, the same thing could have happened to you. I'm a big, strong guy, and I want to take care of you. I know that such sentiments are out of fashion, but it's how I feel." He paused. "And now that's entirely enough of that. Is the wine okay?"

Maggie smiled, glad that he had not asked for a response from her. "It's fine. But Liam, I have to ask you something. Do you *really* think a stranger on drugs attacked Nuala?"

Liam appeared astonished at her question. "If not, who else?"

"But whoever did it must have seen that guests were expected and yet still took time to ransack the house."

"Whoever did it was probably desperate to get a fix and searched the place for money or jewelry. The newspaper said Nuala's wedding ring was taken, so robbery *must* have been the motive."

"Yes, the ring was taken," Maggie acknowledged.

Liam smiled, breaking the dark mood that had settled over them. "Tell me about your week. I hope Newport is beginning to get under your skin. Better yet, let me continue to give you my life history."

He told her how as a child he had counted the weeks in boarding school until it was time to go to Newport for the summer, about his decision to become a stockbroker like his father, about leaving his position at Randolph and Marshall and starting his own investment firm. "It's pretty flattering that some gilt-edged clients elected to come with me," he said. "Their vote of trust led me to believe I'd made the right decision."

By the time the crème brûlée had arrived, Maggie was fully relaxed. "I've learned more about you tonight than I knew from a dozen other dinners," she told him.

"Maybe I'm a little different on my home territory," he said. "And maybe I just want you to see what a terrific guy I am. Okay, your turn. Now tell me about your week."

Maggie was reluctant to really go into things. She did not want to destroy the almost festive mood of the evening. It was impossible to talk about the week and not speak of Greta Shipley, but she put the emphasis on how much she had enjoyed her, and then she told him about her blossoming friendship with Letitia Bainbridge.

"I knew Mrs. Shipley, and she was a very special lady," Liam said. "And as for Mrs. Bainbridge . . . well, she's great," he enthused. "A real legend around here."

"What's nice is that Mrs. Bainbridge has so many protective family members nearby," Maggie said. "Just yesterday, after she heard that Mrs. Shipley died, her daughter came over to take her to the doctor because she knew she'd be upset."

"That daughter would be Sarah," Liam said. Then he smiled.

"Did Mrs. Bainbridge happen to tell you about the stunt my idiot cousin Earl pulled that sent Sarah into orbit?"

"No."

"It's priceless. Earl lectures about funeral customs. When everybody else is off playing golf or sailing, his idea of a good time is taking tombstone rubbings. But that's only a small part of it. What I'm getting to is the time he lectured on funeral practices to a group at Latham Manor, of all places. Mrs. Bainbridge wasn't feeling well, but Sarah had been visiting her and attended the lecture.

"Earl included a story about the Victorian bell ringers. Wealthy Victorians were so afraid of being buried alive that they had a hole built into the top of their caskets, with an air vent reaching up to the surface of the ground. A string was tied to the finger of the presumed deceased, run through the air vent, and attached to a bell on top of the grave. Someone was paid to keep watch for a week in case the person in the casket regained consciousness and tried ringing the bell."

"Dear God," Maggie gasped.

"Here's the best part. Believe it or not, Earl has a sort of museum up here near the funeral home that's filled with all kinds of funeral paraphernalia, and he got the brainstorm to have a dozen replicas of a Victorian cemetery bell cast to illustrate the lecture. Without telling them what they were, the jerk passed them out to twelve of these ladies and tied them onto their ring fingers. Then he told them to wiggle their fingers and pretend they were in a casket and trying to communicate with the grave watcher."

"How appalling!" Maggie said.

"One of the old girls actually fainted. Mrs. Bainbridge's daughter was so irate she practically threw him and his bells off the premises." Liam paused, then added in a somber voice, "The worrisome part is that I think Earl relishes telling that story himself."

NEIL had tried to phone Maggie several times—first from the club, and again as soon as he got home. Either she's been out all day, or she's not answering the phone, he thought. If she was in and out, she surely would have seen his note.

Neil accompanied his parents to a neighbor's home for cocktails and dinner, where he tried Maggie again at seven. It might be possible to stop by her house for a nightcap later, he thought. He was wildly restless. When everyone finally stood up to go at ten thirty, Neil justified his decision to drive by Maggie's house by telling himself that he simply wanted to be sure she was still in Newport.

His initial excitement at seeing that her car was there was tempered when he realized that a Jaguar with Massachusetts plates was parked in front of her place. Neil drove by at a snail's pace and was rewarded by seeing the front door open. He caught a glimpse of a tall man standing next to Maggie. Feeling like a voyeur, Neil accelerated and turned the corner at Ocean Drive, heading back to Portsmouth, his stomach churning with jealousy.

CHAPTER 8

Saturday, October 5th   The service for Greta Shipley was brief. All the people who had been invited to Nuala's dinner party were in attendance. Dr. Lane and his wife, Odile; and Malcolm Norton and his wife, Janice, were there. Malcolm stopped to say he would like to meet with Maggie after the funeral.

Earl Bateman had come over to speak to her before the service began. "After all this, when you think about Newport, I'm afraid that your memories of the place will be of funerals and cemeteries," he said, his eyes owlish behind lightly tinted sunglasses. He hadn't waited for an answer, but had walked past her to take a place in the first pew.

Liam arrived halfway through the service and sat down next to her. "Sorry," he murmured. "Alarm didn't go off." He took her hand, but after an instant she withdrew it. She did not want to have rumors swirling about her and Liam. But, she admitted, her sense of isolation was relieved when his shoulder brushed against hers.

The thought had crossed her mind that Greta Shipley and Nuala and all their other good friends were probably having a joyous reunion. That thought had brought with it the nagging question of the Victorian bells.

I've got to find out when and how each of those women whose graves I visited died and how many of them had close relatives, Maggie thought.

As she and Liam walked away from Greta Shipley's grave after the interment, Maggie felt a hand on her arm. A handsome woman with silver hair and remarkably straight carriage stopped her. "Ms. Holloway," she said, "I'm Sarah Bainbridge Cushing. I want to thank you for visiting Mother yesterday. She so appreciated it."

Sarah. This was the daughter who had tangled with Earl about his lecture on Victorian bells, Maggie reflected. She wanted to talk privately to her.

Sarah Cushing provided the opportunity. "Tomorrow morning I'm taking Mother out for brunch, and I'd be delighted if you could join us."

Maggie agreed readily.

"I'll pick you up at eleven o'clock, if that's all right." With a nod Sarah Cushing turned and dropped back to rejoin the group she had been with.

"Let's have a quiet lunch or dinner tonight," Liam suggested.

Maggie shook her head. "Thanks, but no. I'm going to stay at the sort-and-pack job till I drop."

Liam left Maggie at her car. She was turning the key in the ignition when a rap at the window startled her. It was Malcolm Norton.

Maggie decided to bite the bullet. "Mr. Norton, if this is about buying Nuala's house, I have absolutely no plans of selling it at this time, and I'm afraid that, absolutely unsolicited, I have already received a substantially higher offer than yours." She found it almost painful to see the poor man's horrified expression.

NEIL Stephens and his father teed up at seven o'clock Saturday morning and were back in the clubhouse by noon. This time when Neil dialed Maggie's number, he heard the phone being picked up after the second ring. When he recognized Maggie's voice, he let out a sigh of relief.

He told her how he had phoned her after she left on Friday, how he had gone to Jimmy Neary to try to get Nuala's name so he could contact her here, how he had learned of Nuala's death and was so terribly sorry. . . . "Maggie, I have to see you today," he finished.

She told him she had to stay in and finish clearing out her stepmother's personal effects.

"You still have to eat dinner," he pleaded. "Maggie, if you won't let me take you out, I'm going to arrive on your doorstep with meals-on-wheels." Then he thought about the Jaguar. "Unless somebody else is already doing that," he added. At her response a smile broke out on his face. "Seven o'clock? Terrific. I found a great place for lobster."

When Neil hung up, Robert Stephens said dryly, "I gather you reached this Maggie of yours."

"Yes, I did. We're going out to dinner tonight."

"Well, we'll be happy for you to bring her along. You know we're having your mother's birthday dinner at the club tonight."

Neil silently shook his head. Robert Stephens smiled. "A lot of people consider your mother and me good company."

"You are good company," Neil protested feebly. "Of course we'll be there. And I'm sure Maggie will enjoy being with you."

"Of course she will. Now let's get home. My client Laura Arlington is coming over at two. I want you to go over her portfolio. Thanks to that sleazy broker, she's really in bad shape."

Two hours later Neil sat in his father's office with Mrs. Arlington. She *is* in bad shape, he thought. Ten days ago Mrs. Arlington had been persuaded to buy one hundred thousand shares of some piece of trash at five dollars a share. Now it was valued below a dollar.

So five hundred thousand dollars in stock is reduced to about eighty thousand, assuming there's a buyer, Neil thought, glancing with pity at the ashen-faced woman. She's only Mother's age, he thought—sixty-six—yet right now she looks twenty years older.

"It's pretty awful, isn't it? That was the money I was going to use when one of the larger apartments in Latham Manor became available," Mrs. Arlington said. "But I have three children, and when Douglas Hansen was so persuasive, I thought, well, if I double that money, I'll have an inheritance for the children as well as being able to live in Latham Manor."

She tried to blink back tears. "Then not only did I lose my money last week but the very next day I got a call that one of the big apartments was available—the one that Nuala Moore had been scheduled to take. And seeing the confirmation of the stock purchase in writing this morning just about did me in."

Neil said, "I'm sorry this happened, Mrs. Arlington."

When she left, Neil went back to the house. His parents were in the sunroom. "Laura's a classy lady," Neil said heatedly. "I'd like to throttle that skunk Douglas Hansen. First thing Monday morning I'm going to dig up every last bit of dirt I can pin on him, and if there's any way I can file a complaint with the SEC, I'll do it."

"Good," Robert Stephens said enthusiastically.

"You sound more like your father every day," Dolores Stephens said dryly.

Later, as Neil watched the Yankees–Red Sox game, he found himself annoyed by the feeling that he had missed something in Laura Arlington's portfolio. There was something wrong there other than a misguided investment. But what?

DETECTIVE Jim Haggerty had known and liked Greta Shipley nearly all his life. From the time he was a little boy delivering newspapers to her door, he could never remember a time when she hadn't been gracious and friendly to him.

Earlier that morning, when he had attended her funeral service, he was sure that many in the congregation shared the thought that he couldn't get out of his mind: Greta Shipley's death had been hastened by the shocking murder of her friend Nuala Moore.

He had been surprised to see Maggie Holloway sitting with Liam Payne at the church. Liam always had an eye for pretty women, Haggerty mused, and Lord knows enough of them had had an eye for him over the years.

He had also spotted Earl Bateman in church. Now *there* is a guy who may be educated but who still isn't playing with a full deck of cards, Haggerty had thought. That museum of his—like something out of *The Addams Family*—gave Haggerty the shivers.

Haggerty had slipped away before the recessional, but not before he deduced that Maggie Holloway must have gotten close to Mrs. Shipley to have taken the time to come to her funeral. Maybe if she had visited Mrs. Shipley at Latham Manor, she might have learned something from her that could be helpful in understanding why Nuala Moore had canceled the sale of her house to Malcolm Norton. And it was that thinking that brought him unannounced to 1 Garrison Avenue at three o'clock that afternoon.

MAGGIE was in Nuala's bedroom, where she was separating folded clothing into piles: usable clothing for Goodwill; older, well-worn outfits for the ragbag; dressy outfits for the hospital thrift shop.

As she sorted, Maggie's mind worked on an explanation for the bells at the graves. It *had* to be Earl who had placed them there. Was it his idea of a sly joke on women from the residence, because of the uproar that had followed his lecture there? It was an explanation that made sense. He probably knew all of these women.

One of the graves did not have a bell, though. Why? she wondered. Tomorrow I'm going to go back to the cemetery and copy the dates the women died from their tombstones. There must have been obituaries in the newspaper. I want to see what those say.

The sound of the doorbell was an unwelcome interruption. It took a moment to realize that the man at the door was one of the Newport police officers who had responded to her 911 call the night of Nuala's murder. He introduced himself as Detective Jim Haggerty. Once inside the house, he settled in the club chair with the air of a man who had nothing to do except exchange pleasantries.

He began by answering a question she had not asked. "I'm afraid we're still in the dark as far as having a real suspect in mind. But this crime isn't going to go unpunished," he said.

Maggie waited.

"Ms. Holloway, I saw you in church today at the funeral for Mrs. Shipley. I guess you got friendly with her."

"Yes, I did. Actually, it was a request Nuala made in her will, but it was something I did with pleasure."

"Wonderful woman, Mrs. Shipley. Knew her all my life. Was she happy at Latham Manor?"

"Yes. I had dinner there with her the night she died, and she clearly enjoyed her friends."

"Did she tell you why her best friend, your stepmother, changed her mind at the last minute about moving there?"

"I don't think anyone knows that," Maggie said. "Dr. Lane was confident that Nuala would change it yet again and decide to take the apartment. No one can be sure of her state of mind."

"I guess I was hoping that Mrs. Moore might have explained to Mrs. Shipley her reason for canceling her reservation."

Maggie thought of the caricature Nuala had sketched on the poster, showing Nurse Markey eavesdropping. Was that still in Greta Shipley's apartment? she wondered.

"I don't know if this had any bearing," she said carefully, "but I believe that both Nuala and Mrs. Shipley were very careful of what they said when one of the nurses was around. She had a way of barging in without notice."

"Which nurse?" Haggerty asked, his tone a shade quicker.

"Nurse Markey."

Haggerty got up to go. "Any decisions made about the house, Ms. Holloway?"

"The will still has to be probated, but I'm not putting it on the market at this time. I may very well never put it up for sale. Newport would make a nice retreat from Manhattan."

"Does Malcolm Norton know that?"

"As of this morning, he does. In fact, I told him not only do I not want to sell but I have received a substantially better offer."

Haggerty got up to go. Maggie impulsively asked, "Do you know if it's possible to look up information at the newspaper office this afternoon, or is it closed on Saturday?"

"I think you'll have to wait till Monday. I happen to know that because we always have visitors wanting to look through the old society pages and read about the fancy parties."

Maggie smiled without comment.

As Haggerty drove away, he made a mental note to chat with the clerk in the newspaper office on Monday and find out exactly what information Ms. Holloway was searching for.

Maggie went back up to Nuala's room.

At six o'clock she was going through the final item of clothing in the larger closet, a pale gold raincoat that had fallen to the floor. She remembered that when she had rehung Nuala's blue cocktail suit the other day, the raincoat had been hanging precariously behind it. She ran her hand into the pockets to be sure nothing was in them.

The left-side pocket of the raincoat was empty. But when her fingertips explored the right pocket, a wad of dry dirt crumbled beneath her fingers. Surely Nuala didn't put dirt in her pocket, Maggie thought. Uncertainly she laid the coat across the bed.

There was just one task left. The shoes and boots that covered the floor of the larger closet had to be sorted through. No more for tonight, though, she decided.

It was time for the hot soak she had come to look forward to at this time of the day. And then she would get dressed for her dinner with Neil, something she now realized she was looking forward to.

JANICE and Malcolm Norton had driven together to the funeral service and interment of Greta Shipley. When Janice looked around the congregation during the eulogy, she was bitterly aware of the financial gap that existed between her and so many of the people there.

Later, at the gravesite, she felt an emotion akin to loathing as she watched Malcolm rush ahead to catch up with Maggie Holloway. My handsome husband, she thought bitterly. He had seemed to have it all: the good looks, the impeccable background, the excellent schools—Roxbury Latin, Williams, Columbia Law. But none of it had mattered; for all his credentials, Malcolm Norton was a loser.

To top it all, she thought, he was planning to leave me, and he had no intention of sharing any of the killing he expected to make off the sale of the house. Was Malcolm desperate enough to kill Nuala just to get his hands on that house? she asked herself, wondering suddenly if her husband had still more secrets he was trying to keep from her.

At the end of the walkway good-byes were exchanged. Ahead of her Janice saw Malcolm walking slowly to their car. As she neared him, she saw the anguish on his face and knew Maggie Holloway must have told him she would not sell him the house.

They did not speak as they got in the car. Malcolm stared ahead for a few moments; then he turned toward her. "I'll pay off the mortgage on our house," he said quietly. "Holloway won't sell now, and she says she has a substantially higher offer anyway."

If he ever found out that she had had a hand in the counteroffer that was made on Nuala's house, he might well be angry enough to kill *her,* Janice thought. Her nephew Doug had made the offer, but if Malcolm found that out, he would surely know that she had put him up to it. Had Maggie Holloway implicated her?

As though reading her mind, her husband turned toward her. "Surely you haven't talked to anyone, have you, Janice?" he asked.

When they reached home, he went upstairs to his room. "A bit of a headache," he said. It had been years since they had shared a bedroom.

He did not come downstairs again until nearly seven o'clock. Janice looked up as he stopped at the door of the family room. "I'm going out," he said. "Good night, Janice."

He's up to something, she thought. She allowed him plenty of time to leave, then collected her purse and car keys. She had told Malcolm earlier that she was going out to dinner. They had grown so distant that he hadn't bothered to ask her whom she was meeting.

Not that she would have told him if he had asked, Janice thought as she headed for Providence. There, at a small out-of-the-way restaurant, her nephew would be waiting. Over steaks and Scotch he would pass her an envelope containing cash, her share for supplying him with a detailed account of Cora Gebhart's financial situation.

MAGGIE thought about Neil as she dressed for their date. Over these past months she had found herself more and more looking forward to his calls and too disappointed when they didn't come.

But it was very obvious that to Neil she was an occasional date and nothing more. She really had expected him to call before she left for Newport, and now she was determined to place no special significance on this evening.

And then there was Liam, Maggie thought briefly. She didn't quite know what to make of his sudden show of interest. "Oh, well." She shrugged as she made up her lips in a soft coral shade.

She picked the outfit she had intended to wear to Nuala's dinner party—a vivid blue silk print blouse and matching skirt. A gold chain and earrings were her only jewelry, except for the oval-shaped sapphire ring that had belonged to her mother.

When she passed Nuala's bedroom on the way downstairs, Maggie entered for a moment. As she looked around, she decided definitely to make this her room. She would move into it tomorrow. I can shove the furniture around by myself, she decided.

Walking through the living room, she rearranged little things, straightening the ottoman in front of the club chair; removing some of the small framed pictures on the mantel, leaving only a few of the most flattering ones of Nuala and her husband; plumping the pillows on the couch.

In a few minutes the room took on a more tranquil, less busy feeling. I'm nesting, she told herself, more than I've ever done anyplace since that silly little apartment Paul and I had in Texas. She was at once surprised and pleased with herself.

The front doorbell rang at ten of seven. Neil was early. When she opened the door, she was careful to keep her voice and smile friendly but impersonal.

"Neil, how nice to see you."

He did not answer, but stood looking at her, his eyes troubled.

Maggie opened the door wider. "As my father used to ask, 'Cat got your tongue?' Come in, for heaven's sake."

He stepped inside and followed her into the living room.

"You look lovely, Maggie," he said finally as they stood facing each other.

She raised her eyebrows. "Surprised?"

"No, of course not. But I was sick when I heard what happened to your stepmother. I know how much you were looking forward to being with her."

"I was," Maggie agreed. "Now, where are we going for dinner?"

Fumbling with his words, he asked if she'd mind having dinner with his parents to celebrate his mother's birthday.

"Why don't we try doing this some other time?" Maggie asked curtly. "I'm sure your folks don't need a perfect stranger horning in on a family party."

"They're looking forward to meeting you, Maggie. Don't back out," Neil pleaded.

Maggie sighed. "I guess I have to eat."

She had intended to continue treating Neil with distinct reserve throughout the evening, but the warmth of his parents' greeting and their obviously sincere distress over what had happened to Nuala made it impossible not to loosen up.

"My dear, you didn't know a soul up here," Dolores Stephens said. "How awful for you to go through all that alone."

"Actually, I do know one person fairly well—the man who took me to the party where I met Nuala again." Maggie looked over at Neil. "Maybe you know him, Neil. Liam Payne. He has his own investment firm in Boston but comes to New York regularly."

"Liam Payne," Neil said thoughtfully. "Yes, I do know him slightly. He's a good investment guy."

Maggie could not resist a feeling of satisfaction at seeing the frown on Neil's face. Let him wonder if Liam is important to me, she thought. He's made it plain how unimportant I am to him.

Over a relaxing meal that included lobster and chardonnay she found herself thoroughly enjoying Neil's parents and was flattered that Dolores Stephens was familiar with her fashion photography.

"When Neil spoke about Maggie, I didn't connect you with your work," Mrs. Stephens said. "Then this afternoon, when I was reading *Vogue,* I saw your name under the Armani spread. Before I was married, I worked in a small advertising agency and we had the Givenchy account. I used to have to go to all the shoots."

"Then you know all about . . ." Maggie began, and was soon telling war stories about temperamental designers and models.

As she opened up more, Maggie told them about her inclination to keep the house. "It's too soon to be sure, I guess. But in a way, living in the house this week makes me understand why Nuala was so reluctant to give it up."

At Neil's inquiry she told them about Nuala's canceling her reservation at Latham Manor. "It was even for the large unit she had particularly wanted," she explained.

"Neil and I were over there today," Robert Stephens said. "He's scouting it for one of his clients."

"It sounds as though the apartment your stepmother didn't take is the one that's being offered right now," Neil commented.

"And it's the same one that Laura Arlington wanted," his father noted. "There's a real scramble for those places."

"Someone else wanted it?" Maggie asked quickly. "Did she change her mind?"

"No. She got talked into investing her money in a fly-by-night stock and lost it all," Neil said.

While Neil and his father got into a discussion about the bad investment Mrs. Arlington had made, Maggie found herself telling Dolores Stephens that her mother had died in an accident when she was an infant and how happy she had been the five years Nuala and she had lived together. Finally, realizing that tears were close, she said, "No more nostalgia and no more wine. I'm getting mushy."

When Neil drove Maggie home, he walked her to the door and took the key from her hand. "I'll only stay a minute," he said, opening the door. "I just want to see something. Which way is the kitchen?"

"Back through the dining room." Bewildered, Maggie followed.

He went immediately to the door and examined the lock. "That lock is so loose anyone could open it with a credit card."

"I have a call in to a locksmith," Maggie said.

"Not good enough. My dad is a wunderkind around the house, and I grew up as his unwilling little helper. I, or maybe both of us, will be back tomorrow to install a dead bolt and check the windows."

No "if you'd like" or "is that okay?" Maggie thought, feeling a surge of irritation. "I'm going out to brunch," she told him.

"Brunch is usually over by two," Neil said. "Let's figure on that time, or if you want, you can tell me where you'll hide a key."

"No. I'll be here."

Neil picked up one of the kitchen chairs and wedged it under the doorknob. "At least this will make noise if anyone tries to get in," he said. "Maggie, I don't want to alarm you, but the consensus of opinion is that whoever murdered your stepmother was looking for something, and no one knows what it was or if he got it."

"You're right," Maggie said. "That's exactly what the police think."

"I don't like you being alone," he said as they walked to the front door.

"I'm honestly not nervous, Neil. I've been taking care of myself for a long time."

"And if you were nervous, you'd never admit it to me. Right?"

She looked at him, taking in his grave face. "That's right."

He sighed as he opened the door. "I enjoyed tonight very much, Maggie. See you tomorrow."

Later, as Maggie tossed about in bed, she found she could take no satisfaction in having wounded Neil, and it was obvious she had. Game playing in relationships was not one of her favorite pastimes.

Her last thoughts as she finally began to doze off were seemingly irrelevant. Nuala had applied for an apartment at Latham Manor, then died shortly after withdrawing the application. The Stephenses' friend, Laura Arlington, had applied, then lost all her money.

Was that apartment jinxed and, if so, why?

CHAPTER 9

Sunday, October 6th   At his wife's urging, Dr. William Lane had begun the practice of joining the residents and their guests at Sunday brunch. As Odile had pointed out, visitors invited to partake of the brunch were potential future residents who might thus come to view Latham in a very favorable light. And since they had started attending the brunches, the number of people filling out forms indicating possible future interest had increased sharply.

But when he and Odile entered the grand salon that Sunday morning, Dr. Lane was anything but pleased to see Maggie Holloway with Sarah Cushing. Odile had spotted them as well. "Maggie Holloway does seem to make friends quickly," she murmured to him. Together they made their way across the room.

Maggie had not seen them approaching. When they spoke to her, she smiled and said, "Mrs. Cushing asked me to join her and Mrs. Bainbridge for brunch, but Mrs. Bainbridge was feeling a little tired this morning, so she thought it best if we didn't go out."

"You are always welcome," Dr. Lane said gallantly, and then turned to Sarah. "Should I look in on your mother?"

"No," Sarah said decisively. "She'll be along in a moment. Doctor, has Eleanor Chandler decided to become a resident here?"

"As a matter of fact, yes," he said. "When she heard of Mrs. Shipley's demise, she phoned to request that apartment."

Sarah Cushing went on. "The reason I asked about Mrs. Chandler is that I want to make it clear that she is not to be put at my mother's table. She is an *impossible* woman."

Dr. Lane smiled nervously. "I will make a special note of the seating arrangements, Mrs. Cushing," he said. "An inquiry was made yesterday about the large two-bedroom apartment on behalf of the Van Hillearys from Connecticut. Perhaps if it works out, your mother would consider having them at the table."

Sarah raised an eyebrow. "Mother does enjoy having men around."

"Mother certainly does," Mrs. Bainbridge said dryly. They all turned as she joined them. "Sorry to be late, Maggie. Do I understand that Greta Shipley's apartment is already sold?"

"Yes, it is," Dr. Lane said smoothly. "Mrs. Shipley's relatives will be here this afternoon to remove her personal effects. Now, if you'll excuse us, Odile and I should visit with some of the other guests."

Sarah Cushing was the right person for this group. Like her mother, she was a good storyteller. As Maggie nibbled eggs Benedict and sipped her coffee, she listened appreciatively to Sarah Cushing's skillful management of the conversation, directing it so that everyone was involved and cheerful.

During the second round of coffee, however, the talk turned to Greta Shipley. Rachel Crenshaw, who with her husband was sitting opposite Maggie, said, "I still can't get used to it. Greta and Constance— It was just so sudden!"

"And last year Alice and Jeanette went the same way," Mrs. Bainbridge said.

Alice and Jeanette, Maggie thought. Those names were on two of the graves I visited with Mrs. Shipley. They both had bells embedded next to the tombstones. The woman whose grave didn't have a bell was named Winifred Pierson. Trying to sound casual, Maggie said, "Mrs. Shipley had a friend, Winifred Pierson. Was she a guest here as well?"

"No. Winifred lived in her own home," Mrs. Crenshaw said.

Maggie felt her mouth go dry. She knew immediately what she had to do. She had to visit Greta Shipley's grave and see if a bell had been placed there.

When good-byes were said, Sarah Cushing stayed to visit with her mother, and Maggie headed for the front door. Then, on impulse, she turned and went up the stairs to Greta Shipley's apartment.

The door was open, and she saw the familiar signs of packing and sorting, which was being done by the relatives she had seen at the funeral. She offered brief condolences and plunged in to tell them what she wanted. "When I was visiting Mrs. Shipley, she showed me a sketch my stepmother and she had made. It's in that drawer." Maggie pointed to the table by the couch. "It was one of the last things Nuala did, and if you're thinking of discarding it, it would mean a lot to me to have it."

"Go right ahead. Take it," they chorused amiably.

Maggie opened the drawer expectantly. The sketch was gone. "It isn't here," she said.

"Then perhaps Greta either moved it or disposed of it," said a cousin who bore a striking resemblance to Mrs. Shipley. "Dr. Lane told us that after anyone passes away, the apartment is immediately locked until the family comes in and removes personal items. But do tell us what the sketch looks like in case we come across it."

Maggie described it, gave them her phone number, thanked them, and left. Somebody took that sketch, she thought.

Stepping into the hall, she almost ran into Nurse Markey.

"Oh, excuse me," the nurse said. "I just want to see if I can give Mrs. Shipley's relatives a hand. Have a nice day, Miss Holloway."

MAGGIE walked quickly away from Greta Shipley's grave, her eyes not seeing the path she was following. In every fiber of her being she felt chilled and shaken. She had found it, buried so deeply that had she not run her hand over every inch of the area at the base of the tombstone, she might have missed it.

A bell! *Exactly* like the one she had taken from Nuala's grave. Who had come back since the funeral and put that object on Mrs. Shipley's grave? she wondered. And *why?*

Liam had told her that his cousin Earl had had twelve of these bells cast to use to illustrate his lectures. He had also indicated that Earl apparently relished the fact that he had frightened the women at Latham Manor by handing the bells out during his talk. Was this Earl's idea of a bizarre joke?

It's possible, she decided as she reached her car. Revenge was a logical, if appalling, explanation.

As she drove down her street, she noticed that Neil and his father were sitting on the porch steps, a tool kit between them.

Mr. Stephens waved aside her apologies. "You're not late. It's only one minute of two. Unless my son is mistaken, he said we'd be here at two."

"Apparently, I make a lot of mistakes," Neil said, looking directly at Maggie.

She ignored the remark. "It's awfully nice of both of you to come," she said sincerely.

Robert Stephens examined the front door as he closed it. "Needs weather stripping," he observed. "Now I'd like to start at that back door Neil told me about, and then we'll check all the window locks and see which ones need replacing."

Neil stood beside Maggie, his shoulder brushing hers. She stepped away as he said, "Humor him, Maggie."

She said hastily, "I'm very grateful you're here."

Looking at Neil, dressed in a tan shirt, chinos, and sneakers, Maggie realized there was an aspect to Neil she had never seen in the city. He doesn't have that don't-invade-my-territory air about him today, she thought. He looks as though he actually might care about my feelings.

His forehead was creased with a look of worried concern, and his dark brown eyes had the same questioning look Maggie had seen there last night. As his father began working at the old door lock, Neil said in a low voice, "Maggie, I can tell something is bothering you. I wish you'd let me in on it."

"Neil, give me the big screwdriver," his father ordered.

Maggie settled in an old bentwood chair. "I'll watch. Maybe I can learn something."

For nearly an hour father and son worked, tightening some locks, noting others for replacement. In the studio, upstairs, Robert Stephens asked to examine the clay sculptures of Greta and Nuala on the refectory table.

"Is this Nuala?" Neil asked, pointing to one bust.

"There's a lot of work to do on it, but yes, that was Nuala."

On the way downstairs Robert Stephens pointed to Nuala's room. "I hope you're planning to move in there," he said. "It's twice the size of the guest rooms."

"As a matter of fact, I am," Maggie admitted.

Mr. Stephens stood at the door. "That bed should be opposite the windows, not where it is now."

Maggie felt helpless. "I'm planning to put it there."

"Come on, Neil, we'll start with the bed. Where do you want the dresser moved, Maggie?"

Neil paused long enough to say, "Don't take it personally. He's like this with everyone."

"Everyone I *care* about," his father corrected.

In ten minutes the furniture had been rearranged. The old wallpaper needed replacing, she decided. And then the floor would have to be refinished. Nesting again, she thought.

"Okay, that's it," Robert Stephens announced. Maggie and Neil followed him the rest of the way down the stairs as he said, "I'm on my way. Neil, you'll be up next weekend?"

"Absolutely," Neil said. "I'm taking Friday off again."

"Maggie, I'll be back with the other locks, but I'll call you first," Robert Stephens said as he headed out the door before Maggie could even thank him.

"He's wonderful," she said as she watched his car disappear.

"I think so, too," Neil said, smiling. He paused for a moment. "Were you at your stepmother's grave this morning?"

"No, I wasn't. What makes you think that?"

"Because the knees of your slacks are stained with dirt."

Maggie realized that with Neil and his father here, she had shaken off the uneasiness caused by finding the bell on Greta Shipley's grave.

Seeing the change in her face, Neil confronted her. "Maggie, what's the matter?" he asked, his voice intense. "You're mad at me and I don't know why, except that I didn't phone you before you left. I'll kick myself for that for the rest of my life. If I had known what had happened, I'd have been here for you."

"Would you?" Maggie shook her head, looking away. "Neil, I'm trying to work a lot of things through. Can we leave it at that?"

"I assume I have no choice," Neil said. "Look, I've got to be on my way. I have to get ready for a board meeting in the morning. But I'll call you tomorrow and I'll be here Thursday afternoon. You're staying until next Sunday?"

"Yes," Maggie replied. Unbidden, the Latham Manor Residence jumped into her mind. "Neil, last night you said that you and your father were at Latham Manor yesterday. You were looking at a two-bedroom suite for your clients, weren't you?"

"Yes. Why?"

"Nuala almost took that suite. And didn't you say that another woman would have taken it but couldn't, because she lost her money in a bad investment?"

"That's right. And he stung another client of Dad's who was on Latham's waiting list. I'm going to investigate the skunk who roped both of them into making those investments, and if I can find anything at all to hang on Doug Hansen, I'll turn him in to the SEC."

"Doug Hansen!" Maggie exclaimed.

"Yes. Why? Do you know him?"

"Not really, but let me know what you find out about him," she said, remembering that she had told Hansen she would not discuss his offer.

"Okay, I've got to go." Neil bent down and kissed her cheek. "Lock the door behind me."

She watched him drive away. The late afternoon shadows were already filtering through the trees. The house felt suddenly empty. I'll go up to the studio for a while, she decided. There were so many questions Maggie wished she could ask Nuala. Refining her features in the clay would be a way of communicating with her. She could ask questions that needed to be answered, like, Nuala, was there some reason you were *afraid* to live in Latham Manor?

CHAPTER 10

Monday, October 7th   Malcolm Norton opened his office on Monday morning at the usual time: nine thirty. He passed through the reception area, where Barbara Hoffman's desk faced the door. The desk was now cleared of all Barbara's personal belongings.

Norton shivered slightly. No clients. No appointments. The day loomed long and quiet before him. The thought occurred to him that he had two hundred thousand dollars in the bank. Why not just withdraw it and disappear?

If Barbara would join him, he would do just that. Let Janice have the mortgaged house. In a good market it was worth twice the amount of the mortgage. Equitable distribution, he thought, remembering the bank statement he had found in his wife's briefcase.

But Barbara was gone. She had not called him. She just left.

How much did Chief Brower know? Norton wondered. Everything had been so well planned. If the buy agreement with Nuala had gone into effect, he would have given her the twenty thousand he had gotten by cashing in his retirement money. They wouldn't have closed on the sale for ninety days, which would have given him time to sign a settlement with Janice, then float a demand loan to cover the purchase.

If only Maggie Holloway hadn't come into the picture, he thought bitterly. If only Nuala hadn't made a new will. If only he hadn't let Janice in on the change in the wetlands preservation laws.

Malcolm Norton sat in his dark, still office, contemplating his next move. He knew what he was going to do. The only question was when to do it.

On Monday morning Lara Horgan asked an assistant in the coroner's office to run a check on Zelda Markey, the Latham Manor nurse who had found Mrs. Greta Shipley's body.

The initial report was in by late morning and showed Markey had a good work record. During her twenty years of practice she had worked at three hospitals and four nursing homes, all within the state. She had been at Latham Manor since it opened.

"Follow up with the personnel people at the places where she's worked," Dr. Horgan instructed the assistant. "There's something about that lady that bothers me."

She then phoned the Newport police and asked Chief Brower about the Nuala Moore murder. As they were speaking, Detective Jim Haggerty stuck his head in the chief's office.

"Hold on, Lara," Brower said. "Haggerty has an expression that tells me he's onto something."

"Maybe," Haggerty said. "Maybe not." He took out his note-book. "At ten forty-five this morning Maggie Holloway went into the morgue at the Newport *Sentinel* and requested to see the obit-uaries of six women, all longtime Newport residents. Ms. Hol-loway took the computer printouts and left. I have a copy of them here."

Brower repeated Haggerty's report to Lara Horgan, then added, "We'll study those obits to see if we can figure out what made them so interesting to Ms. Holloway. I'll get back to you."

JANICE NORTON OBSERVED with cynicism that life in Latham Manor did manage to survive the momentary upheaval caused by a recent death. Spurred on by her nephew's lavish praise for the assistance she had provided in relieving Cora Gebhart of her financial assets, Janice was anxious to dip once more into Dr. Lane's applicant file. To avoid being found out, she scheduled her furtive visits when she was sure he was out of the residence.

Late Monday afternoon was one of those times. The Lanes were driving to Boston for some sort of medical affair—a cocktail party and dinner. Janice knew that the rest of the office staff would be scurrying out at five o'clock on the dot.

Lane popped his head into her office at three thirty to announce he was leaving. "Well, I hope you and Odile enjoy the evening, Doctor," Janice said as she turned briskly back to the computer.

The rest of the afternoon crawled by. It wasn't just the anticipation of getting at the files that made the day drag. It was also the nagging suspicion that someone had gone through her briefcase.

Ridiculous, she told herself. Who could have done it? Malcolm doesn't come near my room. I'm getting paranoid because that's exactly what I'm doing to Dr. Lane, she reasoned. Besides, Malcolm doesn't have enough brains to spy on me.

On the other hand, she did have a hunch he was up to something. She resolved to keep her personal bank statements and her copies of the files away from any place where he would have a chance to happen on them.

NEIL'S two meetings on Monday morning kept him out of his office until eleven. When he finally arrived there, he immediately called Maggie, but got no answer.

He called the Van Hillearys and briefly gave them his impression of Latham Manor. He then called the private investigator who worked on confidential assignments for Carson & Parker, requesting a dossier on Douglas Hansen. "Dig deep," he instructed. "This guy is a world-class sleaze."

He called Maggie again and was relieved when she picked up. She sounded breathless. "I just got in," she told him. Neil could hear anxiety and agitation in her voice. "Is anything wrong?" he asked.

"No, not at all."

Neil realized she was not going to let him in on what was bothering her. He wanted to bombard her with questions but knew better.

Instead, he said simply, "Maggie, just remember that I'm here if you want to talk."

"I'll remember."

And you'll do nothing about it, he thought. "Okay, I'll call you tomorrow."

He replaced the receiver and sat for long minutes before punching in the number of his parents' home. His father answered. "Dad, have you got those locks for Maggie's windows?"

"Just picked them up."

"Good. Do me a favor and phone over there and tell her you want to put them in this afternoon. I think something has come up that is making her nervous."

"I'll take care of it."

It was a mixed comfort, Neil thought wryly, that Maggie might be more willing to confide in his father than in himself. But at least his father would be on the alert for any hint of problems.

Neil's secretary came into his office the moment he was off the phone. As she placed a stack of messages on his desk, she pointed to the one on top. "I see your new client asked you to sell stock she doesn't own," she said severely.

"What are you talking about?" Neil demanded.

"The clearinghouse has notified us that they have no record of Cora Gebhart owning the fifty thousand shares of stock you sold for her on Friday."

MAGGIE hung up at the end of her call from Neil and filled the kettle. She wanted the feeling of hot tea warming her.

She did a quick mental review of what she had learned so far.

When she had taken Greta Shipley to the cemetery, they left flowers at Nuala's grave and the graves of five other women.

Someone had placed a bell on three of those graves, as well as on Nuala's. She had found them there herself.

There was an impression in the earth near Mrs. Rhinelander's tombstone, but for some reason that bell was missing.

Greta Shipley had died in her sleep two days later, and barely twenty-four hours after she was buried, a bell had been placed on her grave as well.

Maggie quickly read the obituaries through again. They confirmed what had occurred to her yesterday: Winifred Pierson, the woman whose grave showed no evidence of a bell, had a large, caring family. She had died with her personal physician in attendance.

With the exception of Nuala, the other women had died in their sleep. They had all been under the ongoing care of Dr. William Lane.

Dr. Lane. Sarah Cushing had rushed her mother to an outside doctor. Was it because she knew, or suspected, that Dr. Lane was not a skillful practitioner? Or perhaps *too* skillful?

No matter how one looked at it, Maggie thought, Latham Manor had been a jinx for a lot of people. What had made Nuala change her mind about going to live there? And what made Douglas Hansen, who had sold stocks to the women who lost their money, show up here wanting to buy this house? There has to be a connection, Maggie told herself.

The kettle was whistling. As she got up to make the tea, the phone rang. It was Neil's father. He said, "Maggie, I've got those locks. I'm on my way over."

Twenty minutes later he was at the door.

While he changed the locks, Maggie used the time to think. Putting together all the pieces of the puzzle she had so far, she came to a decision: She had absolutely no right to voice any suspicions about Dr. Lane as yet, but there was no reason not to talk about Douglas Hansen.

Robert Stephens came back to the kitchen. "Okay, you're all set. No charge, but can you spare a cup of coffee?" He settled in a chair, and Maggie knew he was studying her. Neil sent him, she thought. He could tell I was upset.

"Mr. Stephens," she began, "you don't know much about Douglas Hansen, do you?"

"Enough to know that he's wrecked the lives of some very nice women, Maggie. But have I ever met him? No. Why do you ask?"

"Because both the ladies you know who lost their money had been planning to go into Latham Manor. My stepmother also had planned to live there, but she changed her mind at the last minute. Last week Hansen showed up here and offered me fifty thousand dollars more for this house than Nuala almost sold it for—much more than it's worth. There's got to be more than just coincidence at play here."

EARL Bateman drove past Maggie's house twice. On the third trip he saw that the car with the Rhode Island plates was gone; Maggie's Volvo station wagon, however, was still in the driveway. He slowed to a halt and reached for the framed picture he had brought.

He rang the doorbell twice before she opened the door. It was obvious that she was surprised to see him. He quickly held up the package. "A present," he said enthusiastically. "A picture of Nuala that was taken at the Four Seasons party. I framed it for you."

"How nice of you," Maggie said, trying to smile, a look of uncertainty on her face. She reached out her hand.

Earl pulled the package back. "Aren't you going to ask me in?" he asked, his tone light and joking.

"Of course."

She stood aside and let him pass, but to his annoyance she swung the door wide open and left it that way.

"I'd close that if I were you," he said. "There's a stiff breeze." He again saw her uncertainty and smiled grimly. "And no matter what my cousin has told you, I don't bite," he said.

He walked into the living room and sat in the big club chair. He looked around. "I can see you're already putting your stamp on this place," he said. "I approve. There's a much calmer feeling. Does that love seat spook you?"

"I'll do some refurnishing," Maggie said, her tone still wary.

As she opened the package, Bateman congratulated himself on thinking of the photograph. The way her face lit up confirmed how smart he had been to think of it.

"Oh, it's a *wonderful* picture of Nuala," Maggie said enthusiastically. "She looked so pretty that evening. Thank you." Her smile was now genuine.

"You're most welcome," he said as he leaned farther back into the deep chair.

He's not going to go, Maggie thought in dismay. Bateman's eyes, too large behind the round-framed glasses, were fixed on her with an unwavering stare. His scrutiny made her uncomfortable. He's like a wire stretched too far, ready to snap, she thought.

She jumped involuntarily when the telephone rang. It was Police Chief Brower. "Ms. Holloway, I was wondering if I could stop in and see you late this afternoon," he said.

"Of course. Has something come up? I mean, about Nuala?"

"Oh, nothing special. I just wanted to talk with you. Is that all right? I'll phone before I come."

"Of course," she said. "I'm just visiting with Earl Bateman. I'll see you in a while."

With a smile she said, "That was Chief Brower. He's coming over this afternoon."

Bateman's nod was solemn. "A good police chief. Respects people. Not like security police in some cultures. You know what happens when a king dies? During the mourning period the police seize control of the government. Sometimes they murder the king's family."

Maggie sat down, oddly fascinated by the man. Earl Bateman's expression had become one of almost religious absorption.

"Did you know I lecture on funeral customs?" he asked.

"Oh, yes," she said quickly. "Remember? You told me that the first night we met."

"I'd really like to talk to you about it," Bateman said earnestly. "You see, a cable company is very interested in having me do a television series. I'd like to include some visuals."

Maggie waited.

Earl clasped his hands. Now his voice became coaxing. "You're a very successful photographer. Visuals are what you understand. It would be such a favor if you'd let me take you to see my museum today. It's downtown, right next to the funeral parlor my family used to own. Would you just spend an hour with me? I'll show you the exhibits, and maybe you could help me decide which ones to suggest to the producers. Please, Maggie."

He knows Chief Brower is coming here, Maggie thought. Liam had told her about Earl's twelve Victorian bell replicas. Suppose they're on exhibit, she thought. And suppose there are only six of them now. If so, then it would be reasonable to believe that he put them on the graves.

"I'd be glad to go," she said after a moment. "Just in case Chief Brower gets here early, I'll leave a note on the door saying that I'm with you at the museum and that I'll be back by four."

Earl smiled. "That's very wise, Maggie. That should give us plenty of time."

At two o'clock Chief Chet Brower summoned Detective Jim Haggerty to his office. When Haggerty came in, he was carrying papers identical to the ones Brower had been hunched over at his desk—copies of the obituaries Maggie Holloway had looked up at the Newport *Sentinel*.

"What did you see, Jim?" Brower demanded.

Haggerty slumped into a seat. "Probably the same thing you did, Chief. Five of the six deceased women lived at that fancy retirement home."

"Right."

"None of those five had close relatives. They all died in their sleep."

"Uh-huh."

"And Dr. William Lane was in attendance in each instance. Meaning he signed the death certificates."

Brower smiled approvingly. "You catch on real fast."

"Also," Haggerty continued, "what the articles don't say is that when you die at Latham Manor, your apartment reverts to the management, which means it can be sold again, pronto."

"I didn't think of that angle," Brower admitted. "I just spoke to the coroner. Lara's running a check on Dr. Lane. She already was investigating the background of a nurse there, Zelda Markey."

Haggerty looked pensive. "I knew Mrs. Shipley, the woman who died at Latham last week. Her next of kin are staying at the Harborside Inn, so I popped over there and talked to them. Turned out that yesterday who should be at Latham Manor but Maggie Holloway."

"Why was she there?" Brower snapped.

"She was a guest at brunch of old Mrs. Bainbridge and her daughter. But afterward she did go up and speak to Mrs. Shipley's relatives when they were packing up her effects." He sighed. "Ms. Holloway had an odd request. She said her stepmother, Nuala Moore, who taught an art class at Latham, had helped Mrs. Shipley make a sketch, and she asked if they minded if she took it. Funny thing, though, it wasn't there. But one of the residents had seen it. It was supposed to be a World War Two poster that showed a spy eavesdropping on two defense workers."

"Why would Ms. Holloway want that?"

"Because Nuala Moore had put her own face and Greta Shipley's face over those of the defense workers, and in place of the spy, guess who she'd sketched?"

Brower looked at Haggerty, his eyes narrowed.

"Nurse Markey," the detective said with satisfaction. "And one more thing, Chief. The rule at Latham Manor is that when a death occurs, the apartment is locked until the family has had a chance to take possession of valuables. In other words, nobody had any business being in there and taking that sketch." He paused. "Kind of makes you wonder, doesn't it?"

NEIL canceled a lunch date he had made and instead had a sandwich and coffee at his desk. He worked feverishly to clear his calendar for the next few days.

At three o'clock he phoned his father. "Dad, I'm coming up tonight," he said. "I've been trying to get that Hansen guy on the phone, but they keep telling me he's out. So I'm going to track him down myself. There's more going on with that guy than just giving lousy advice to old women."

"That's what Maggie said, and I'm sure she's onto something."

"Maggie?"

"She seems to think there's some kind of connection between Hansen and the women who put in applications to Latham Manor. I've been talking to Laura Arlington and Cora Gebhart. It turns out Hansen called them out of the blue."

"Why didn't they just hang up on him?"

"Apparently, using Alberta Downing's name gave him credibility. He urged them to call her for a reference. But then—and this is where it gets interesting—he talked about investments that are losing buying power because of inflation, and he just *happened* to give as examples the very stocks and bonds that Mrs. Gebhart and Laura Arlington owned."

"I need to talk to this Mrs. Downing," Neil said. "Something's definitely not right. And by the way, thanks for going over to see Maggie."

"I happen to like that young lady very much. One more thing. Hansen dropped in on Maggie last week and made an offer on her house. Maggie speculated that his offer was too high, and she's right. So while you're at it, figure out what game he's playing with her."

Neil remembered Maggie's startled reaction when he mentioned Hansen's name and how, when he had asked if she knew him, her answer had been evasive.

But I was right about one thing, he thought. She did open up to Dad. When I get to Newport, I'm going straight to her house and I'm not leaving until she tells me just what it is I've done wrong.

"I'M VERY proud of my museum," Earl explained as he held the door for Maggie to get out of her car. She had declined his offer to drive with him and was aware that he had been annoyed.

She had followed his gray Oldsmobile past the Bateman Funeral Home. The museum fronted on a side street and had its own parking, empty now except for a shiny black hearse. Maggie studied the three-story Victorian house with its wide porch and gingerbread trim. Like the Bateman Funeral Home, it was painted glistening white with black shutters. Black crepe streamers, draped around the front door, fluttered in the breeze.

"The house was built in 1850 by my great-great-grandfather," Earl explained. "It was our first funeral parlor, and back then the family lived on the top floor. When we sold the business ten years ago, we separated the house and an acre of the property. I opened the museum shortly after that." Earl put his hand on Maggie's elbow. "You're in for a treat."

Several planters filled with violets and mountain pinks were located on the broad porch railing. Bateman lifted the edge of the nearest planter and withdrew a key. "See how I trust you, Maggie? I'm showing you my secret hiding place."

Pausing at the door, he pointed to the crepe. "In our society it used to be the custom to drape the door like this to signify that this was a house of mourning."

How he enjoys this! Maggie thought, shivering. The key turned with a grating sound, and Earl pushed the door open and then stood back. "Now, what do you think of that?" he asked proudly.

A life-size figure of a man in black livery stood at attention in the foyer. "In Emily Post's first etiquette book, she wrote that when a death occurred, the butler in his day clothes should be on duty at the door until a footman in black livery could replace him."

Earl pushed aside a heavy curtain. "In this room I've staged Emily Post's version of a very small funeral. See?"

Maggie looked in. The figure of a young woman dressed in a pale green silk robe was laid out on a brocaded sofa. Long auburn ringlets spilled around a narrow satin pillow. Her hands were folded over silk replicas of lilies of the valley.

"Isn't that charming? Doesn't she look just like she's sleeping?" Earl whispered.

He took Maggie's arm. "I know you don't have a lot of time, but please come on upstairs with me to my burial section," he said enthusiastically as they ascended the stairs. "Have I mentioned a custom of the Sudan people? The principle was that the leader embodied the vitality of the nation and must never die, or the nation would die with him. So when the leader was clearly losing his power, he was secretly put to death, then walled up in a mud hut. The custom then was to believe that he had not died, but, rather, had vanished." He laughed.

They were on the second floor. "In this first room, I've created a replica of a mud hut. I've already gotten started on an outdoor museum, where the burial area can be even more realistic. It's about ten miles from here. So far I've had some basic excavation done. When it's completed, it really will be quite wonderful."

He's *crazy,* Maggie thought, a leaden sense of unease settling over her as he propelled her from room to room.

They were almost at the end of the hallway, and Maggie realized that she had not seen anything resembling bells. "What do you have on the third floor?" she asked.

"I use it for storage," he replied absently.

Then he stopped abruptly and turned to her, his eyes intense. They were in front of a heavy door. "Oh, Maggie, this is one of my best exhibits!"

Earl turned the handle and, with a dramatic flourish, threw open the door. "This depicts an aristocrat's funeral in ancient Rome." He pulled her inside. "First they built a bier; then they put the couch on it. On top of that were placed two mattresses. Maybe this would make a good opening shot for the series. The old man who made this bier for me was a real craftsman. Feel the flowers he carved into the wood." He stopped and frowned. "I do get carried away, Maggie. Forgive me."

"No, I'm fascinated," she said, trying to sound calm.

"Oh, good. Well, there's just one more room—my coffin room." He opened the last door.

Maggie stood back. She did not want to go in that room. Only ten days ago she had had to choose a casket for Nuala. "Actually, Earl, I should be heading back," she said.

"Oh. I'd like to have explained these. Maybe you'll come back. By the end of the week I'll have the newest one in. It's shaped like a loaf of bread. It was designed for a baker. I included that story in one of the lectures I gave to a Newport women's club."

Maggie realized that he might have given her the opening that she had been seeking. "Do you lecture in Newport very often?"

"Not anymore." Earl closed the door of the coffin room. "You've heard it said that a prophet is without honor in his own country, no doubt. First they expect to get you without even an honorarium; then they insult you."

She could see that his face was turning crimson. "Surely, no one insulted you?" she asked, her voice caring.

"Once," he said darkly. "It upset me terribly."

She didn't dare tell him that Liam had been the one to tell her about the incident with the bells. "Oh, wait a minute," she said slowly. "When I visited Mrs. Shipley at Latham Manor, didn't I hear that something unpleasant had happened to you when you were kind enough to speak there? Something involving Mrs. Cushing?"

"That's exactly what I mean," Earl replied sharply. "She upset me so much that I stopped giving one of my most effective lectures." As they walked down the stairs to the first floor, Bateman described handing out the replicas of the Victorian bells.

"I had them cast specially," he said with anger. "Twelve of them. Maybe it wasn't smart to let those people hold them, but that was no reason for treating me the way that woman did. Zelda was furious."

"Zelda?" Maggie asked.

"Nurse Markey. She knows my research and had heard me speak a number of times. She had told the activities chairperson at Latham how well I lecture." His eyes narrowed, became cautious. "I don't like to talk about this. It upsets me."

"But I would think that would be a fascinating lecture," Maggie persisted. "And maybe those bells would be a good visual for an opening or closing shot."

"No. Forget it. They're in a box up in the storeroom, and that's where they'll stay."

He replaced the key under the planter. "If you'd like to come back and take some pictures of the exhibits, that would be fine. You know where to find the key."

He walked Maggie to her car. "I have to get back to Providence," he said. "Will you think about the visuals and see if you can come up with some suggestions?"

"Of course," she replied as, with relief, she slid into the driver's seat. "And thank you." She had absolutely no intention of ever coming back to this place if she could help it. She turned the key in the ignition. "Good-bye, Earl. It was very interesting."

"My cemetery exhibit will be interesting, too. Oh, that reminds me. I better put the hearse back in the garage."

As Maggie drove out onto the street, she could see in the rearview mirror that Earl was sitting in the hearse, holding a phone. His head was turned in her direction. She could feel his eyes watching her intently until she was beyond his range of vision.

SHORTLY before five Monday evening Dr. William Lane arrived at the Ritz-Carlton Hotel in Boston, where a cocktail party and dinner for a retiring surgeon were being held. Odile had driven up earlier to keep an appointment with her favorite hairdresser. She had taken a room for the afternoon at the hotel.

As he drove through Providence, Lane's earlier good mood gradually dissipated; there resounded in his mind a warning.

The mental alarm had started just as he was leaving the residence, when Sarah Bainbridge Cushing called to inform him that Letitia Bainbridge had phoned shortly after lunch to say that she wasn't feeling well. She had become terribly nervous because Nurse Markey was darting in and out of her room without knocking.

He had warned the Markey woman about that very thing. What was she up to? Dr. Lane fumed. By the time he arrived at the Ritz, Lane was thoroughly on edge. When he got up to his wife's room, the sight of Odile in a frilly robe, just beginning to put on her makeup, annoyed him intensely.

"Hi, darling," she said with a smile. "How do you like my hair?" She shook her head playfully. Odile had beautiful frosted blond hair.

"It looks all right," he said.

"Only all right?" she asked, her eyelids fluttering.

"Look, Odile, I have a headache. I've had a rough few weeks at the residence."

"I know you have, dear. Why don't you lie down for a while?"

Lane glanced at his watch. "Odile, that party starts in ten minutes. Don't you think you'd better get a move on?"

"William, why are you so cross with me? I know you're terribly worried about something, but please share it with me. I've helped you before, haven't I?" She looked to be on the verge of tears.

"Of course you have," Dr. Lane said, his voice softer. Then he paid her the compliment he knew would appease her: "You're a beautiful woman, Odile."

Then, as she began to smile, he added, "But you're right. I *am* worried. Mrs. Bainbridge wasn't feeling well this afternoon, and I'd be a lot more comfortable if I were around, just in case there were to be an emergency. So . . ."

"Oh." She sighed, knowing what was coming. "But how disappointing. I was looking forward to seeing everybody here tonight and spending time with them."

It was the reaction he had hoped to receive. "I'm not going to let you be disappointed," he said firmly. "You stay and enjoy yourself. Keep the room overnight and come home tomorrow. I don't want you driving back at night unless I'm following you."

"If you're sure."

"I'm sure. I'll just make an appearance at the party now and head back. You can say hello for me to anyone who asks." The warning beep in his head had become a keening siren. He wanted to bolt, but he paused to kiss her good-bye.

She took his face between her hands. "Oh, darling, I hope nothing happens to Mrs. Bainbridge. If you suspect anything is seriously wrong, please call her own doctor in immediately. I wouldn't want you to have to sign another death certificate. Remember all the trouble at the last residence."

He took her hands from his face and held them. He wanted to strangle her.

WHEN Maggie got back to the house, she stood on the porch inhaling the salt scent of the ocean. It seemed that after the museum visit, the smell of death was in her nostrils. She took the note she had left for Chief Brower off the door. Once inside, the first thing she saw was the framed picture Earl had brought her. She would take it upstairs now, she decided.

In the studio she took the photograph out of the frame and carefully tacked it to the bulletin board by the refectory table. The photographer must have told them to smile, she thought. Smiling had come naturally to Nuala. Earl Bateman looked ill at ease, his smile forced. Still, there was nothing about him that suggested the frightening obsessiveness she had witnessed this afternoon. She remembered Liam saying once that a crazy streak ran in the family. She had taken his remark as a joke at the time, but now she wasn't so sure. Liam probably never took a bad photograph in his life, she thought as she continued to study the picture.

She went into the bedroom and opened the closet door. This would be a good time to clean out the rest of Nuala's things. The only two items that remained hanging there were the blue cocktail suit Nuala had worn that night at the Four Seasons and the pale gold raincoat that she had rehung in the closet when Neil and his father moved the bed. Every inch of the closet floor, however, was covered with shoes and slippers and boots, mostly in disarray.

Maggie sat on the floor and began sorting them out. Some of the shoes were quite new. True, Nuala wasn't a neatnik, but she never would have tossed new shoes around like that. Then Maggie caught her breath. She knew the bureau drawers had been ransacked by Nuala's killer, but had he even rummaged through her *shoes?*

The telephone rang, and she jumped. Chief Brower, she thought, and realized she would not be at all sorry to see him. Instead of Brower, however, it was Detective Jim Haggerty, calling to say that the chief would like to postpone the meeting until first thing in the morning. "He's out on an emergency right now."

"That's all right," Maggie said. "I'll be here in the morning." Then she decided to ask him about Earl Bateman.

"Detective Haggerty," she said, "this afternoon Earl Bateman invited me to see his museum." She chose her words carefully. "It's such an unusual hobby."

"I've been there," Haggerty said. "Quite a place. I guess it's not

really an unusual hobby for Earl, though, when you consider he's from a fourth-generation funeral family."

"I guess so." Again Maggie spoke slowly. "I know his lectures are successful, but I gather that there was one unfortunate incident at Latham Manor. Do you know about that?"

"Can't say as I do, but if I were the age of those folks, I wouldn't want to hear about funerals, would you?" Haggerty lowered his voice. "Earl's got serious money from his father's side. The Moore clan call him Cousin Weirdo, but I say they're jealous."

Maggie thought of Earl, frenetically charged as he dragged her from exhibit to exhibit; sitting in the hearse, staring intently after her. "Or maybe they know him too well," she said. "Thanks for calling, Detective Haggerty."

Maggie went back to the job of sorting out the shoes. This time she decided that the simplest thing to do was to bundle most of them in garbage bags. The fur-lined boots, however, were worth saving. She picked up one and put it beside her, then reached for the other.

As Maggie lifted it, she heard a single muffled clang. "Oh, no!"

Even before she put her hand down into the furry interior, she knew what she would find. As she withdrew the object, she was certain that she had found the thing Nuala's killer had been seeking—the missing bell.

Nuala took this from Mrs. Rhinelander's grave, she thought. It was the exact twin of the bell she had taken from Nuala's grave. Streaks of dry dirt clung to the rim. Other tiny particles of soft earth crumbled loose on her fingers.

Maggie remembered that there had been dirt in the pocket of the gold raincoat, and when she rehung the cocktail suit the other day, she had had the impression of something falling. Nuala was wearing her raincoat when she took this bell off Mrs. Rhinelander's grave, she thought.

Maggie knew that Earl had gone back to Providence and that the key to the museum was under the planter on the porch. The police would have no legal right to go into the museum and look for the twelve bells Earl said were there.

Earl *did* invite me to let myself into the museum at any time to try to come up with visuals for his cable programs, Maggie thought. I'll take my camera with me. That will give me an excuse for being there. I'll wait until dark; then I'll drive over. I'll look in the store-room for the box with the bells. And if I find six, I'll know he's a liar. I'll take pictures so I can compare them with the bells on the graves and the two I have. Then tomorrow, when Chief Brower comes, I'll tell him that I think Earl Bateman has found a way to take revenge on the residents of Latham Manor. And he's doing it with the help of Nurse Zelda Markey.

Revenge? Maggie froze with the realization of what she was considering. Would this form of revenge have been enough for Earl? Or could he possibly have been involved with their deaths as well? And Zelda Markey—clearly she was tied to Earl somehow. Could she be his accomplice?

ALTHOUGH it was well past his normal dinnertime, Chief Brower was still at the station. It had been a hectic afternoon.

"Where've you been?" Brower asked Haggerty sourly. "What time can Maggie Holloway see us tomorrow?"

"She told me she'll be home all morning," Haggerty said. "But I want to tell you first about a little visit I paid to Sarah Cushing. Her mother, Mrs. Bainbridge, lives at Latham Manor. Nice, smart lady."

"What made you go see her?" the chief asked.

"Something Maggie Holloway said when I phoned her for you. She mentioned Earl Bateman, and I got the distinct impression that Ms. Holloway is very nervous about Bateman."

"Of Bateman? He's harmless," Brower snapped.

"Now that's what I thought, but maybe Maggie Holloway has a sharp eye when it comes to detecting what makes people tick. Anyhow, she mentioned a little problem that Bateman had at Latham Manor not long ago. I called one of my friends whose cousin is a maid there, and she told me about a lecture Bateman gave that even caused one of the old girls to pass out. She also told me how Sarah Cushing happened to be there and that she gave Bateman what-for."

Haggerty saw the chief's mouth tighten. "So that's why I went to see Mrs. Cushing, and she told me that she hustled Bateman out for upsetting the guests with his lecture about people worrying about being buried alive, and then for handing out replicas of the bells they used to put on graves in Victorian times. Seems there would be a string or wire attached to the bell, and the other end was then tied to the finger of the deceased. That way, if you woke up in the coffin, you could wiggle your finger, the bell would ring on top of the grave, and the guy who was paid to listen for it would start digging.

"Bateman told the ladies to slip their ring finger into the loop at the end of the string, to pretend they'd been buried alive, and then to start ringing the bells."

"You're kidding!"

"No, I'm not, Chief. All hell broke loose, apparently. Mrs. Cushing said she made it her business to find out who had suggested he lecture there. That person was Nurse Zelda Markey. Sarah Cushing heard through the grapevine that Markey took care of Bateman's aunt in a nursing home years ago and got real close to the family. She heard also that the Batemans were mighty generous in rewarding her."

He shook his head. "Mrs. Cushing thinks all those ladies who died recently might have been at that lecture."

Before Haggerty even finished, Brower was on the phone to coroner Lara Horgan. At the conclusion of his conversation with her he turned to the detective. "Lara is going to initiate proceedings to have the bodies of both Mrs. Shipley and Mrs. Rhinelander, the two people who died most recently at Latham Manor, exhumed. And that's just for starters."

NEIL checked his watch at eight o'clock. Another hour and he would be in Newport. He was angry he hadn't gotten away earlier.

It hadn't been all wasted time, though. He had finally had an opportunity to think through what had nagged at him about his conversation with Mrs. Arlington, his father's client who had lost her money investing with Hansen. Finally it had registered when he remembered that Laura Arlington said she had *just* received the confirmation of her stock purchase. Those documents are mailed out right after the transaction, so she should have received it days earlier.

Then this morning he had learned that there was no record that Mrs. Gebhart had owned the stock Hansen claimed he bought for her at nine bucks a share. Today that stock was down to two dollars. Was Hansen's game to let people think they had bought a stock at one price—a stock he happened to know was on the skids—and then to wait to put the transaction through once it had reached a very low point? That way Hansen could pocket the difference. Accomplishing that would involve faking a confirmation of the order from the clearinghouse. It wasn't simple, but it wasn't impossible.

But what made that crook bid on Maggie's house? There must be something else in play there. Be home when I get there, Maggie, Neil implored silently. You're setting too much in motion, and I won't let you do it alone any longer.

AT EIGHT thirty Maggie drove to Earl Bateman's funeral museum. Before leaving home, she took the bell she found in Nuala's closet and compared it with the bell she had dug out of Nuala's grave. Both were now placed side by side on the refectory table in the studio, an overhead spotlight shining on them. Then, with her camera-equipment bag in hand, she headed out.

Fifteen minutes later she turned onto the quiet street where the funeral museum was located and drove into the parking lot.

As she approached the old house, she was surprised to see faint light emerging from behind a curtained ground-floor window. It's probably on a timer, she thought, but at least it will help me get my bearings. She had brought a flashlight to use when inside.

The key was under the planter where Earl had left it. It made a loud grating sound when she turned it in the old-fashioned lock. I really don't want to be here, Maggie thought as she darted for the stairs. She switched on the flashlight at the top of the first staircase. Keeping the beam pointed down, she continued up the next flight.

Trying not to be nervous, Maggie opened the first door on the third floor. In the low beam of the flashlight she could see that this was an exhibit in the making—a wooden hutlike structure set atop two poles. The next two rooms both contained partially completed death-ritual scenes.

The last door proved to be the one she was seeking. It opened into a large storage room, its walls covered with shelves crammed with boxes. Two racks of clothing were blocking the windows.

Where can I begin? Maggie thought, a sense of helplessness overtaking her. With a deep sigh she fought back the urge to bolt. Reluctantly she closed the door of the storeroom, hoping to prevent any spill of light out into the hall. All that clothing should be enough to make sure that nothing would show through the windows. Still, every nerve in her body urged her to get out of this place.

There was a stepladder to her left. She decided to start her search in the shelves right behind the ladder and work her way around the room. The cartons seemed to be arranged in no particular order. Some that were labeled DEATH MASKS filled a whole section of shelves; others were marked MOURNING RAIMENT, HOUSEHOLD LIVERY, DRUMS, but no bells.

It's hopeless, Maggie thought after she had been there more than half an hour. She moved the ladder, hating the screech it made on the floor. She started to climb, but as she put her foot on the third rung, her glance fell on a cardboard box wedged between two others. It was labeled BELLS/BURIED ALIVE.

She grasped the box and tugged, finally wrestling it loose. She got down from the ladder and placed the carton on the floor. With frantic haste she squatted beside it and yanked off the lid.

Brushing aside the loose popcorn packing, she uncovered the first of the metal bells, wrapped and sealed in plastic. Eagerly her fingers fished through the popcorn until she was sure that she had found everything in the box.

Everything was six bells, identical to the others she had found. The packing slip was still inside the box: "12 Victorian bells, cast to the order of Mr. Earl Bateman," it read.

I'll take shots of them and the packing slip, and then I can get out of here, Maggie thought.

She wasn't sure what first made her realize that she was no longer alone. Had she actually heard the door opening, or was it the narrow beam of light from another flashlight that had alerted her?

She spun around as he raised the flashlight, heard him speaking as it crashed down on her head. And then there was nothing but impressions of voices and movement, and finally dreamless oblivion, until she awoke to the terrible, silent darkness of the grave.

NEIL arrived at Maggie's house well after nine o'clock, much later than he had wished. Intensely disappointed to see that her station wagon wasn't in the driveway, he had a moment of hope when he noticed that one of the bright studio lights was on. But when there was no answer to the doorbell, he went back to his car to wait. At midnight he finally gave up and drove to his parents' house in Portsmouth.

Neil found his mother in the kitchen, making hot cocoa. "For some reason I couldn't sleep," she said. Neil knew that she had expected him to arrive hours earlier, and he felt guilty. "I should have called," he said. "But why didn't you try me on the car phone?"

Dolores Stephens smiled. "It occurred to me that you probably had stopped at Maggie's, so I really wasn't that worried."

Neil shook his head glumly. "I did stop. She wasn't home. I waited around till now."

"She may have had a date," Dolores said, her tone thoughtful.

"She was in her *own* car. It's *Monday* night," Neil said, then paused. "Mom, I'm worried about her. I'm going to phone every half hour until I know she's home."

His mother sat with him as he tried Maggie's number at one o'clock, at one thirty, then at two, at two thirty, and again at three. At three thirty his father joined them. "What's going on?" he asked, his eyes heavy with sleep. When he was told, he snapped, "Call the police and ask if any accidents have been reported."

The officer who answered assured Neil that it had been quiet. "No accidents, sir."

"Give him Maggie's description. Tell him what kind of car she drives. Leave your name and this phone number," Robert Stephens ordered. "Dolores, you get some sleep. I'll stay with Neil."

When his wife was out of earshot, he said, "Your mother isn't as strong as she'd like you to believe. Neither is Maggie, for that matter." He looked at his son. "I know that you haven't been seeing Maggie for that long, but why does she seem indifferent to you—sometimes even downright chilly?"

"I don't know. She's always held back, and I guess I have, too, but I'm positive there's something special going on between us. I thought about it a lot, and I've come up with one thing."

He told his father about the time he saw Maggie weeping in the theater. "I didn't think I should intrude," Neil said. "But now I wonder if maybe she knew I was there and perhaps resented the fact I didn't at least say something. What would you have done?"

"I'll tell you what I'd have done," his father said. "If I'd seen your mother in that situation, I'd have been right beside her and I'd have put my arm around her. Maybe I wouldn't have said anything, but I'd have let her know I was there."

He looked at Neil severely. "I'd have done *that* whether or not I was in love with her. On the other hand, if I was afraid of getting involved, then maybe I'd have run away."

"Come on, Dad," Neil muttered.

"And if I were Maggie and sensed you were there, I'd have written you off if you walked out on me," Robert Stephens concluded.

The telephone rang. Neil beat his father to grabbing the receiver.

It was a police officer. "We found the vehicle you described, parked on Marley Road. It's an isolated area, so we don't have any witnesses as to when it was left there, or by whom."

CHAPTER 11

Tuesday, October 8th   At eight o'clock on Tuesday morning Malcolm Norton walked downstairs and looked into the kitchen. Janice was seated at the table drinking coffee.

She made the unprecedented offer to pour him a cup, then asked, "Toast?"

He hesitated, then said, "Why not?" and sat opposite her.

"You're leaving pretty early, aren't you?" she asked.

He could see she was nervous. No doubt she knew he was up to something. "You must have had a late dinner last night," she continued as she placed a steaming cup in front of him.

"Ummmm," he responded, enjoying her unease. He had known she was awake when he came in at midnight. He took a few sips of the coffee, then pushed his chair back. "On second thought, I'll skip the toast. Good-bye, Janice."

When he reached the office, Malcolm Norton sat for a few minutes at Barbara's desk. He wished he could write a few lines to her, something to remind her of what she had meant to him, but he didn't want to drag her name into this.

He went into his own office and looked again at the copies he had made of the papers he had found in Janice's briefcase, as well as the copy of her bank statement. He had guessed what she must have been up to the other night when he saw that crooked nephew of hers hand her an envelope in the restaurant he had followed her to. Seeing her financial records only confirmed what he had suspected.

She was giving Doug Hansen privileged financial information about applicants to Latham Manor so that he could try to cheat rich old women. And Hansen was the one who made a higher offer to Maggie Holloway. He was sure of it. Janice had tipped him off about the upcoming change in the law.

If only Maggie Holloway hadn't spoiled it all, he thought bitterly. Knowing he could make a killing on the house, he would have found a way to keep Barbara.

Of course, none of that mattered anymore. He would never buy the house. He would never have Barbara in his life. He *had* no more life. But at least he had gotten even. They would know that he wasn't the empty suit Janice had sneered at for years.

He moved the envelope addressed to Chief Brower to the far corner of the desk. He didn't want it to get stained. He reached for the pistol he kept in the bottom drawer. Then he punched in the number of the police station and asked for Chief Brower.

"It's Malcolm Norton," he said pleasantly as he picked up the gun in his right hand and held it to his head. "I think you'd better get over here. I'm about to kill myself."

As he pulled the trigger, he heard the final, single word: *"Don't!"*

MAGGIE could feel the blood that matted the hair on the side of her head, which was sensitive to the touch and still ached. "I've got to be calm," she kept whispering to herself.

Where am I buried? she wondered. Probably in some isolated spot in the woods where no one can possibly find me. When she tugged the string on her ring finger, she could feel a heavy pressure on the other end. He must have attached the string to one of the Victorian bells. She ran her index finger up inside the metal tube that the string was threaded through. She should be able to get enough air through it for breathing, unless it became clogged.

Plan, Maggie told herself. She would keep tugging the string until her strength gave out. She was sure there was no clapper in the bell, but there was always the hope that the moving bell might attract attention. She also would try to shout for help at what she calculated to be ten-minute intervals. She mustn't wear out her voice too soon, though.

Of course, it might all be for naught.

AT TEN Tuesday morning Neil and his father sat tensely in Chief Brower's office as he soberly revealed the contents of Malcolm Norton's suicide note. "According to what he's written, because of a change in environmental laws, Ms. Holloway's property is going to be worth a lot of money," he said. "When Norton made the offer to Nuala Moore to buy her house, he obviously was prepared to cheat her, so it's very possible that he got wind that she was changing her mind about making the sale to him and killed her."

He paused to reread a paragraph. "It's obvious that he blamed Maggie Holloway for everything going wrong, and although he doesn't say it, he may have taken revenge on her. He's certainly managed to get his wife in serious trouble."

This can't be happening, Neil thought. Maggie isn't dead. She *couldn't* be dead.

"I've talked to Mrs. Norton," Brower continued. "Her husband came home at the usual time yesterday, then left and didn't return until midnight."

"How well did Maggie know this guy Norton?" Robert Stephens asked. "Do you think he might have forced her into her own car, then driven to where you found it? But then, what did he do with Maggie, and since he left her car there, how did he get home?"

Brower was shaking his head. "It's an unlikely scenario, but it's an angle we have to pursue. We're bringing in dogs to try to follow Ms. Holloway's scent, so if she is in that area, we'll find her. But it's a long way from Norton's home. He'd have to have acted in tandem with someone else, or he'd need to have gotten a ride home from a passerby, and both of those options seem unlikely." The intercom rang, and Brower picked up his phone. "Put him on," he said.

Brower's conversation lasted only a minute. When he got off, he said, "Malcolm Norton had dinner last night at the Log Cabin, a small restaurant near where his secretary Barbara Hoffman lived. Apparently, she and Norton ate there together frequently. The owner tells us that Norton was there until well after eleven, so he must have gone directly home."

Which means, Neil thought, he had nothing to do with Maggie's disappearance.

Brower's intercom sounded again. After listening without comment, he hung up his phone and stood. "I don't know what kind of game Earl Bateman is up to, but he just phoned to report that last night a coffin was stolen from his funeral museum."

DR. WILLIAM Lane realized that there was very little he could say to his wife this Tuesday morning. If only she hadn't come home last night and found him like that, he thought. He hadn't had a drink in ages, not since the incident at the last place he worked. Lane knew that he owed this job to Odile. She had met the owners of Prestige Residence Corporation at a cocktail party and had touted him for the director's job at Latham. Remarkably, he got the job.

He knew that the slipup last night was a sign the pressure was getting to him. The orders to keep those apartments filled; don't let them pass a month unsold. Always the implied threat of being let go if he didn't perform. Let go, he thought. Go where?

Why hadn't Odile stayed in Boston last night? he thought.

Because she suspected that he was panicking, he reasoned. He had been in a state of terror ever since he learned that Maggie Holloway had been looking for a sketch Nuala Moore had made that showed Nurse Markey eavesdropping.

He should have gotten rid of that woman long ago.

Lane found his wife drinking coffee in the breakfast room. Uncharacteristically she hadn't bothered to put on makeup this morning. She looked drawn and tired.

"Zelda Markey just phoned," she told him, a sadistic glint in her eye. "The police have asked her to be available for questioning. She doesn't know why."

"For questioning?" Lane felt the tension run through his body. It's all over, he thought.

"She also told me that Sarah Cushing gave strict orders that neither she nor you was to enter her mother's room. It seems that Mrs. Bainbridge isn't well, and Mrs. Cushing is making arrangements to transfer her to the hospital." Odile looked at him accusingly. "You were supposed to be rushing home to see Mrs. Bainbridge last night, but I hear you didn't show up at the residence till nearly eleven. What were you doing until then?"

NEIL and his father drove to the remote road where Maggie's station wagon was still parked. Now it was surrounded with police tape, and as they got out of their car, they could hear the yapping of search dogs in the nearby woods.

It was good to have the understanding presence of his father, Neil thought. Through the woods he could make out the figures of at least a dozen police. In despair he realized that they were expecting to find Maggie's body.

He bowed his head. "She can't be dead," he said.

"Neil, let's go," his father said quietly. "I don't even know why we came out here. Standing around here isn't helping Maggie."

"What do you suggest I do?" Neil asked, frustration in his voice.

"From what Chief Brower said, the police haven't spoken to this guy Hansen yet. He's expected at his office in Providence later this morning. It wouldn't hurt for us to be at Hansen's office when he comes in."

"Dad, you can't expect me to worry about stock deals now," Neil said angrily.

"No. But you did authorize the sale of fifty thousand shares of stock that Cora Gebhart didn't own. And you had to replace them with your company's money." He looked into his son's face. "Don't you see what I'm driving at? Something made Maggie uneasy about Hansen. I don't think it's coincidence that he's the guy who fronted an offer on her house. You can get him on the defensive about the stocks. But the real reason I want to see him is to find out if he knows anything about Maggie's disappearance."

When Neil continued to shake his head, Robert Stephens pointed to the woods. "If you believe Maggie's body is lying out there somewhere, then go join the search. I happen to believe that she's still alive, and if she is, I bet her abductor didn't leave her in the vicinity of the car." He turned to leave. "I'm going to Providence to see Hansen."

He got into the car and slammed the door. As he was turning the ignition key, Neil jumped in. "You're right," he admitted. "I don't know where we'll find her, but it won't be here."

EARL Bateman was waiting for Chief Brower and Detective Haggerty on the porch of his funeral museum. "The casket was here yesterday afternoon," Bateman said heatedly. "Halloween is coming," he continued. "I'm positive a bunch of kids pulled this stunt. And I can tell you right now that I *will* press charges."

"Professor Bateman, why don't we go inside and talk about it?" Brower said.

"Of course. Actually, I may have a picture of the casket in my office. I've been planning to make it the focal point of a new exhibit when I expand the museum. Come this way."

The two policemen followed him through the foyer, past the life-size figure dressed in black, to what obviously had been the kitchen—a sink, refrigerator, and stove still lined the far wall. An old-fashioned desk stood in the center of the room, its surface covered with blueprints. "I'm planning an outdoor exhibit," Bateman told them. "I have some property nearby that will make a wonderful site. Go ahead, sit down. I'll try to find that picture."

He's awfully worked up, Jim Haggerty thought. Maybe he isn't the harmless weirdo I pegged him for.

"Why don't we just ask you a few questions before you look for the picture," Brower suggested. "Was anything else taken?"

"No, nothing else seems to have been disturbed. This could have been done by someone working alone, because the catafalque is missing, too, and it would have been easy to wheel the casket out."

The telephone rang. "Oh, excuse me. That will probably be my cousin Liam. He was in a meeting when I called to tell him what happened. I thought he'd be interested."

Bateman picked up the receiver. "Hello," he said, nodding to indicate that it was the call he had been expecting. Brower and Haggerty listened to the one-sided conversation.

"A very valuable antique," he said excitedly. "A Victorian coffin. This one has the original breathing tube and was—" He stopped suddenly. Then, in a shocked voice, he cried, "What do you mean Maggie Holloway is missing?"

When he hung up, he seemed dazed. "This is terrible! Oh, I knew she wasn't safe. I had a premonition. Liam is very upset. They are very close, you know. He just heard about Maggie on the news, and he's on his way down from Boston." Then Bateman frowned. "You knew Maggie was missing?" he asked Brower accusingly.

"Yes," Brower said. "And we know she was here with you yesterday afternoon."

"Well, yes. Because she's such a successful photographer, I asked her to help me by suggesting visuals for the television series I'm going to do about funeral customs. That's why she came to see the exhibits," he explained earnestly. "I was disappointed that she hadn't brought her camera, so I told her to come back on her own at any time. I showed her where I hide the key."

"Did she come back here last night?" Brower said.

"I don't think so." He looked upset. "I hope nothing bad has happened to Maggie. She's a nice woman, and I've been quite drawn to her."

"I'd like to talk to you about a little problem you had when you gave a lecture at Latham Manor," Brower said. "I heard something about Victorian cemetery bells and your being asked to leave."

Bateman slammed his fist on the desk. "I don't want to talk about that! Only yesterday I had to tell Maggie the same thing. Those bells are locked in my storeroom, and there they'll stay." His face was white with anger.

THE morning sun had given way to clouds, and by eleven the sky was bleak and gray. Neil and his father sat on the two upright wooden chairs that, along with a secretary's desk and chair, were the sole furnishings in the reception area of Douglas Hansen's office.

The one employee was a laconic young woman who disinterestedly informed them that Mr. Hansen had been gone since Thursday afternoon and that he had said he would be in by ten today.

The door leading to the sparsely furnished inside office was open. "Doesn't exactly look like a thriving brokerage firm," Robert Stephens said.

Neil found it agonizing to simply sit there. Where is Maggie? he kept asking himself. He tried to concentrate on what his father was saying, then replied, "I doubt he shows this place to his potential clients."

"He doesn't," Robert Stephens answered. "He takes them to fancy lunches and dinners. From what Cora Gebhart and Laura Arlington told me, he can put on the charm, although they both said he sounded very knowledgeable about investments."

Both men spun their heads sharply as the outer door opened. They were just in time to catch the startled expression on Douglas Hansen's face when he saw them.

He thinks we're cops, Neil realized. He must already have heard about his uncle's suicide.

They stood up. Robert Stephens spoke first. "I represent Mrs. Cora Gebhart and Mrs. Laura Arlington," he said formally. "As their accountant, I'm here to discuss the recent investments you purport to have made for them."

"And I'm here to represent Maggie Holloway," Neil said angrily. "Where were you last night, and what do you know about her disappearance?"

MAGGIE began to shiver uncontrollably. How long had she been here? Had she drifted off to sleep? Her head hurt so much. Her mouth was dry with thirst.

How long was it since she last called for help? Was anyone looking for her? Did anyone even know that she was missing?

Neil. He said he would call tonight. No, *last* night, she thought, trying to make sense of time. I know I've been here for hours. Is it morning now, or even later than that?

Neil would call her. Or would he? She had rejected his expressions of concern. She *had* been cold to him. Maybe he had washed his hands of her.

"Find me, Neil. *Please* find me," she whispered, then blinked back tears. If only she had told him about the bells. If only she had asked him to go with her to the museum.

The museum. Mentally she replayed the attack. She saw the look on his face before he crashed the flashlight down on her head. Evil. Murderous. As he must have looked when he murdered Nuala.

Wheels. She had felt herself being wheeled. She had heard a familiar woman's voice talking to him. Maggie moaned as she remembered whose voice it was.

I've got to get out of here, she thought. I can't die; knowing this, I mustn't die. She'll do it again for him. I know she will.

"Help," she shrieked. "Help me."

Over and over she called until she finally was able to force herself to stop. Don't panic, she warned herself. I'll count to five hundred slowly and then call out three times. I'll keep doing that.

She heard a steady muffled sound from above, then felt a cold trickle on her hand. It was raining, she realized, and the rain was dripping down through the air vent.

AT ELEVEN THIRTY CHIEF Brower and Detective Haggerty entered Latham Manor. The residents knew that something was wrong. The officers were aware of the curious gazes that followed them when the maid led them to the office wing.

Dr. Lane greeted them courteously. "Come right in."

He looks like hell, Haggerty thought, taking in the bloodshot eyes, the gray lines around the doctor's mouth.

"Dr. Lane, at this point we're simply asking some questions," Brower began. "Before you took this position, you'd been unemployed for several years. Why was that?"

Lane was silent for a moment, then said quietly, "I suspect you already know the answer."

"We'd prefer to hear your version," Haggerty told him.

"We'd had an outbreak of flu in the Colony Nursing Home, where I was in charge. Four of the women had to be transferred to the hospital. Therefore, when others came down with flulike symptoms, I assumed that they'd caught the same virus."

"But they hadn't," Brower said. "In fact, in their section of the nursing home there was a faulty heater. They were suffering the effects of carbon monoxide poisoning. Three of them died. Isn't that true?"

Lane kept his eyes averted and did not answer.

"And isn't it true that the son of one of those women had told you that his mother's disorientation did not seem consistent with flu symptoms and even asked you to check for the possible presence of carbon monoxide?" Brower asked.

Again Lane did not answer.

"Your license was suspended for gross negligence and yet you were able to secure this position. How did that happen?"

Lane's mouth became a straight line. "The people at Prestige Residence Corporation were fair enough to recognize that I had been the director of an overly crowded low-budget facility, that I was working fifteen hours a day, that a number of the guests were suffering from flu and the misdiagnosis therefore was understandable, and that the man who complained was constantly finding fault with everything from the hot-water temperature to drafty windows."

He stood up. "I find these questions insulting. I suggest that you leave immediately. As it is, you have thoroughly upset our guests. Someone apparently felt the need to inform everyone that you were coming."

"That would be Nurse Markey," Brower said. "Please tell me where I can find her."

ZELDA Markey was openly defiant as she sat across from Brower and Haggerty in the small second-floor room that served as her office. "My patients need me," she said tartly. "They're aware that Janice Norton's husband committed suicide, and they've heard a rumor that she's been doing something illegal here. They're even more distressed to learn that Miss Holloway is missing."

"Ms. Markey, you're a friend of Earl Bateman's, aren't you?" Brower asked.

"To me friendship implies familiarity. I know and admire Professor Bateman. His aunt, Alicia Bateman, was a guest at the Seaside Nursing Home, where I was formerly employed."

"In fact, the Batemans were quite generous to you, weren't they?"

"They felt I was taking excellent care of Alicia and were kind enough to reward me."

"I see. I'd like to know why you thought a lecture on death might be of interest to the residents of Latham Manor. Don't you think they'll all be facing it soon enough?"

"Chief Brower, I am aware that this society has a horror of death. But the older generation has a much greater sense of reality." She hesitated. "However, I will say that it was my understanding that Professor Bateman was planning to give his talk on royal funerals through the ages. If he had stuck to that . . ." She paused for a moment, then continued, "And I will admit also that the use of the bells upset some people, but the way Mrs. Sarah Cushing treated Professor Bateman was unpardonable."

"Do you think he was very angry?" Brower asked mildly.

"I think he was humiliated, *then* perhaps angry, yes. He's actually very shy."

Haggerty looked up from his notes. An unmistakable softness had come into the nurse's tone and expression. Interesting, he thought.

"Nurse Markey, what do you know about a sketch that Mrs. Nuala Moore made with Mrs. Greta Shipley?" Haggerty asked.

"Absolutely nothing," she snapped.

"It was in Mrs. Shipley's apartment. It seems to have vanished after her death."

"That is absolutely impossible. After a resident dies, the room or apartment is locked immediately. Everyone knows that."

"Uh-huh." Brower's tone became confidential. "Nurse Markey, just between us, what do you think about Dr. Lane?"

She looked at him sharply. "I wouldn't let Dr. Lane treat my cat." She stood up. "I cannot understand how the Prestige people chose Dr. Lane to run this establishment. And before you ask, *that* is the reason I check so frequently on residents. I don't think he is capable of giving them the care they need. I'm aware that sometimes they may resent it, but I am only doing it for their own good."

NEIL and Robert Stephens drove directly to Newport police headquarters. "Damn good thing you got that restraining order in yesterday," Robert said to his son. "That guy was ready to skip. At least this way, with his bank account tied up, we stand a chance at getting some of Cora's money back."

"But he doesn't know what happened to Maggie."

"No, I guess he doesn't. You can't be an usher at a wedding in New York, offer dozens of names to vouch for you, and be up here at the same time."

"Dad, that guy has nothing in that office to indicate that he's dealing in securities," Neil said. "Those transactions are coming out of another place. And one that's probably pulling this same sort of swindle."

They arrived at the police station to find that Chief Brower was out, but Detective Haggerty saw them. "No one remembers seeing that Volvo station wagon in town last night," he said. "When Ms. Holloway's neighbors passed her house on the way to dinner at seven, her car was in her driveway. It was gone when they returned at nine thirty."

"That's all you can tell us?" Neil asked, his tone incredulous.

"We know that she went over to that funeral museum Monday afternoon. We spoke to her before she left and after she returned."

"Funeral museum?" Neil said. "What was she doing there?"

"According to Professor Bateman, she was helping him select visuals for some television series he'll be doing," Haggerty responded.

"You said, 'according to Professor Bateman,'" Robert Stephens said sharply.

"We have no reason to doubt the professor. He may be a bit eccentric, but he's got no record of any trouble." Haggerty hesitated. "I'll be totally honest with you. Ms. Holloway seemed to indicate that there was something about him that bothered her. We did learn that he was responsible for a stir one evening among a number of the residents at the Latham Manor retirement home."

Latham Manor again, Neil thought.

"Bateman also volunteered that Maggie knew where the key to the museum was hidden and that he had invited her to come back with her camera at any time."

"Do you think she went there last night? *Alone?*" Neil asked.

"I wouldn't think so. No, the fact is, there seems to have been a robbery at the museum last night. If you can believe it, a coffin is missing. We think some teenage kids are probably responsible. They may also be able to give us some information about Ms. Holloway. If she had gone into the museum and they saw her car parked there, they would have made sure she was gone before they went in."

Neil stood to leave. He had to get out of there; he had to be doing something. He could go back to Latham Manor. His excuse would be that he wanted to talk about the Van Hillearys' possible application.

"I'll check in with you later," he told Haggerty. "I'm going over to Latham Manor. Dad, what's your car-phone number?"

Robert Stephens scribbled the number on a business card. "Here."

Neil handed the card to Haggerty. "If there are any developments, try us at this number."

"Ms. Holloway's a close friend, isn't she?"

"She's more than that," Robert Stephens said brusquely. "Consider us her family."

"I *do* understand," Haggerty said simply.

The look of genuine sympathy on Haggerty's face brought Neil to an acute awareness of just how close he might be to losing someone who, surprisingly, he now couldn't imagine living without. He swallowed over the lump in his throat. Not trusting himself to speak, he nodded and left.

In the car, he said, "Dad, why do I feel that Latham Manor is at the center of all this?"

"MAGGIE, you're not calling for help, are you? That isn't wise."

Oh, God, no. He was back! His voice, hollow and echoing, was barely discernible through the rain beating on the earth above her.

"You must be getting wet down there," he called. "I'm glad. I want you to be cold and wet and scared. I'll bet you're hungry, too. Or maybe just thirsty?"

Don't answer, she told herself. Don't plead with him. It's what he wants.

"You ruined everything for me, Maggie—you and Nuala. She had begun to suspect something, so she had to die. Latham Manor— I own it, you know. Only, the outfit that manages it doesn't know who I am. I have a holding company. And you were right about the bells. Those women weren't buried alive—maybe just a little bit sooner than God intended. That's why I put the bells on the graves. It's my little joke.

"When they exhume those women, they'll blame Dr. Lane for their deaths. They'll think it was his fault that the medicines got mixed. He's a lousy doctor with a terrible record. And a drinking problem. That's why I had them hire him. Do you know how much profit there is in turning over those rooms? Lots. *Lots.*"

Maggie struggled to blot out his face from her mind.

"I guess you figured out that the bell attached to your finger has no clapper. Now figure this out: How long will you last when the air vent is clogged?"

She felt a rush of dirt on her hand. Frantically she tried to poke open the vent with her finger. More dirt tumbled down.

"Oh, one more thing, Maggie," he said. "I took the bells from the other graves. I thought that was a good idea. Sweet dreams."

She heard the thump of something hitting the air vent; then she heard nothing. He was gone. The vent was packed. She flexed and unflexed her left hand so that the string on her ring finger would keep the mud from hardening around it. Please God, she prayed, let someone see that the bell is moving.

How long would it be before she used up all the oxygen? Hours? A day? "Neil, help me," she whispered. "I need you. I love you. *I don't want to die.*"

LETITIA Bainbridge had absolutely refused to go to the hospital. "You can ride in that ambulance yourself," she tartly informed her daughter, "but I'm not going anywhere."

"But Mother, you're not well," Sarah Cushing protested.

"Who's well at ninety-four?" Mrs. Bainbridge asked. "Sarah, I appreciate your concern, but there's a lot going on around here and I don't intend to miss it."

Sarah Cushing gave up reluctantly.

"Find out why the police were talking to Nurse Markey," Mrs. Bainbridge snapped. Then, in a quieter tone, she added, "I'm so worried about that wonderful Maggie Holloway. We're all praying that she'll be found."

"I know, and so am I," Sarah Cushing agreed.

"All right, go downstairs and find out the latest. Start with Angela. She doesn't miss a thing."

NEIL had called on the car phone to tell Dr. Lane he would like to stop by to discuss the Van Hillearys' interest in residing at Latham Manor. He found Lane's voice curiously indifferent.

Neil and his father were admitted to Latham Manor by Angela, the same maid they had seen before. When they arrived, she was talking to a handsome woman in her mid-sixties. "I'll let Dr. Lane know you're here," Angela said softly.

The older woman came over to them. "I don't want to seem inquisitive, but are you from the police?" she asked.

"No, we're not," Robert Stephens said quickly. "Why?"

"Let me explain. I am Sarah Cushing. My mother, Letitia Bainbridge, is a resident here. She has become very fond of a young woman named Maggie Holloway, who seems to have gone missing, and she is anxious for any news."

"We're very fond of Maggie, too," Neil said, once again experiencing the lump in his throat. "Would it be possible to speak to your mother after we see Dr. Lane? We're groping at straws to see if Maggie may have said anything to anyone that might help us to find her." He bit his lip, unable to go on.

Sarah Cushing studied him, sensing his distress. Her frosty blue eyes softened. "Absolutely. You can see Mother," she said briskly. "I'll wait in the library for you."

The maid returned. "Dr. Lane is ready," she said.

Both men were shocked when they reached Dr. Lane's office. The man seated at the desk was radically changed. Lane looked ill and defeated. Listlessly he invited them to sit down, then said, "I'll be happy to answer your questions. However, a new director will be meeting your clients when they come up."

He's been fired, Neil thought. Why? "Look, I'm not asking you to explain the reasons behind your departure." He paused. "But I am aware that your bookkeeper had been giving out privileged financial information. That was one of my concerns."

"Yes, that has just been brought to our attention. I'm very sure it won't happen again in this establishment," Lane said.

"I can sympathize," Neil continued. "In the investment business we unfortunately face the problem of insider trading." His father was looking at him curiously, but he had to try to learn if that was the reason Lane was being fired. Secretly he suspected that it had something to do with the sudden deaths of some of the residents.

"I'm aware of the problem," Lane said. "My wife worked in a securities firm in Boston—Randolph and Marshall—before I took this position. It would seem that dishonest people crop up everywhere. Ah, well, let me try to answer whatever questions you have. Latham Manor is a wonderful residence, and our guests are very happy here."

When they left fifteen minutes later, Robert Stephens said, "Neil, that guy is scared stiff."

"I know. And it's not just because of his job." I'm wasting time, Neil thought. He had brought up Maggie's name, and Lane's only response was an expression of polite concern for her welfare.

"Dad, maybe we should skip meeting with anyone here," he said as they reached the entrance hall. "I'm going to break into Maggie's house to search it. Maybe there's something there that will give us some idea of where she was going last night."

Sarah Cushing was waiting for them, however. "Mother wants very much to meet you."

Neil was about to protest but saw his father's warning glance. Robert Stephens said, "Neil, why don't you visit for a few minutes? I'll make some calls from the car. I happened to keep an extra key to the new lock on Maggie's door in case she ever forgot hers. I told her about it. I'll call your mother and have her meet us there with it."

Neil nodded. "I'd like to meet your mother, Mrs. Cushing."

Mrs. Letitia Bainbridge was seated in a wing chair. She waved Neil in and pointed to the chair nearest her. "From what Sarah tells me, you seem to be Maggie's young man. You must be so worried. How can we help?"

Having deduced that Sarah Cushing had to be nearly seventy, Neil realized that this bright-eyed woman had to be ninety or more. She looked as if she missed nothing.

"Mrs. Bainbridge, I hope I won't upset you by being absolutely frank. Maggie had begun to be very suspicious about the recent deaths in this residence. Yesterday morning she looked up the obituaries of six different women, five of whom had resided here and who died recently. Those five women died in their sleep unattended, and none had close relatives."

Letitia Bainbridge did not flinch. "Are you talking about neglect or murder?"

"I don't know," Neil said. "I just know that Maggie started an investigation that's already leading to an order for the exhumation of at least two of the dead women and now she's disappeared. And I've just learned that Dr. Lane has been fired."

"I just found out that, too, Mother," Sarah Cushing said. "But everyone thinks it's because of the bookkeeper."

"What about Nurse Markey?" Mrs. Bainbridge asked her daughter. "Is that why the police questioned her? Because of the deaths?"

"Nobody is sure, but she's mighty upset. And, of course, so is Mrs. Lane."

This isn't getting me anywhere, Neil thought. "Mrs. Bainbridge," he said, "I can only stay a minute longer. There's one other thing I'd like to ask you. Were you at the lecture Professor Bateman gave here? The one that caused such an uproar?"

"No." Mrs. Bainbridge shot a look at her daughter. "That was another day when Sarah insisted I rest, so I missed all the excitement. But Sarah was there."

"I can assure you, Mother, that you wouldn't have enjoyed being told to pretend you were buried alive," Sarah Cushing said spiritedly. "Let me tell you exactly what happened, Mr. Stephens."

Bateman has to be crazy, Neil thought as he listened to her version of events. Had anyone checked to confirm Bateman's story that he had gone directly to Providence after he left the museum yesterday afternoon?

"I was so upset, I gave that man a real tongue-lashing," Sarah Cushing continued. "A look came over his face that almost frightened me. I think he must have a fearful temper. And Nurse Markey had the gall to defend him!"

"I'm still sorry I wasn't there," Mrs. Bainbridge said. "And as far as Nurse Markey goes," she continued reflectively, "in perfect fairness many of the residents here consider her an excellent nurse. I just find her to be nosy and intrusive." She paused, then said, "Mr. Stephens, this may sound ridiculous, but I think that whatever his shortcomings, Dr. Lane is a very kind man, and I'm a pretty good judge of character."

A HALF HOUR LATER NEIL AND his father drove to Maggie's house. Dolores Stephens was already there. She took her son's face between her hands. "We're going to find her," she said firmly.

Unable to speak, Neil nodded.

"Where's the key, Dolores?" Robert Stephens demanded.

"Right here."

The kitchen was neat. There were no dishes in the sink. The dining room and living room both were orderly. Upstairs the smallest bedroom contained the evidence of Maggie's packing up her stepmother's personal effects: Neatly tagged bags of clothing, purses, and shoes were piled there.

Neil went next to the studio. The light that he had noticed last night when he parked outside waiting for Maggie to come home was still on, pointed toward a picture tacked to the bulletin board.

He started across the room, then stopped. A chill ran through his body. On the refectory table, in the glare of the spotlight, he saw two metal bells.

As surely as he knew that night followed day, he knew that these were two of the bells that Earl Bateman had used in his infamous lecture at Latham Manor—the bells that had been whisked away, never to be seen again.

HER hand ached and was covered with dirt. She had continued to move the string back and forth, hoping to keep the tube open, but now no more dirt seemed to be falling through the air vent. The water had stopped trickling down, too.

She couldn't hear the beating of the rain anymore either. Was it getting colder, or was it just that the dampness inside the coffin was so chilling? she wondered.

But she was actually starting to feel warm—too warm. She was so light-headed. The vent is sealed, she thought. There can't be much oxygen left.

"One . . . two . . . three . . . four . . ." Now she was whispering the numbers aloud, trying to force herself to stay awake, to start calling out again when she reached five hundred.

"Make a fist," she said aloud. "All right, relax." That's what the nurses had told her to do when she was little and they were taking a blood sample.

"One hundred fifty . . . one hundred fifty-one . . ."

She had known Neil was sitting behind her that day in the theater. He had coughed a couple of times, a peculiar little dry cough that she had recognized. He had to have seen her unhappiness.

I made it a test, she thought. If you love me, you will understand that I need you—that was the thought she had willed him to hear. But when the film ended, he was gone.

"I'll give you a second chance, Neil," she said aloud now. "If you love me, you'll know that I need you and you'll find me."

"Four hundred ninety-nine, five hundred."

She began to cry out for help again. This time she screamed until her throat was raw. There was no use trying to save her voice. Time was running out.

Still, resolutely she began to count again. "One . . . two . . . three . . ."

Her hand moved with the count: flex . . . unflex . . .

With every fiber of her being she fought the urge to sleep. She knew that if she slept, she would not wake up again.

WHILE his father started downstairs to phone police headquarters, Neil hesitated for a moment, studying the picture he had found pinned to the bulletin board. The inscription on the back read, "Squire Moore Birthday Anniversary. September 20th. Earl Moore Bateman—Nuala Moore—Liam Moore Payne."

Neil studied Bateman's face. The last man to see Maggie alive. Aghast at what his subconscious was telling him, he dropped the picture next to the bells and hurried to join his father.

"I have Chief Brower on the phone," Robert Stephens said. "He wants to talk to you. I told him about the bells."

Brower came immediately to the point. "If these are two of the same bells Bateman claims are locked in the storeroom of his museum, our best bet is to confront him and hope that he'll say something to give himself away."

"I intend to be there when you confront him," Neil said.

"I have a squad car watching the museum from the funeral parlor parking lot. If Bateman leaves the premises, he'll be followed."

"We're on our way," Neil said, then added, "Wait a minute, Chief. I know you've been questioning some teenagers. Did you find out anything from them?"

He heard the hesitation in Chief Brower's voice before he answered. "One of the kids admitted that they were across the street from the museum last night. At about ten o'clock that kid claims he saw two vehicles—a hearse, followed by a station wagon—drive out of the museum's parking lot."

"What kind of station wagon?" Neil asked urgently.

"The kid isn't sure of the make, but he swears it was black."

"TAKE it easy, Earl," Liam Moore Payne said for the tenth time.

"No, I won't take it easy."

They were sitting in the office of the museum. It was nearly five o'clock, and the old-fashioned globed chandelier spread a murky glow over the room.

"Look," Liam said, "you need a drink."

"You mean *you* need a drink."

Liam got out the Scotch bottle, glasses, ice, and a lemon. "Double Scotch with a twist coming up for both of us."

Mollified, Earl waited until the drink was set in front of him, then said, "I'm glad you stopped by, Liam."

"When you called, I could tell how upset you were. And, of course, I'm more than upset about Maggie's disappearance." He paused. "Earl, I've dated her casually over the last year or so. But that night at the Four Seasons, when she'd left without saying a word to me, I realized what a jerk I'd been. But besides making me realize how important Maggie has become to me, that night gives me hope that maybe she's okay."

"What's that supposed to mean?"

"The fact that she walked out without saying a word when she was upset. She's had plenty of reason to be upset since she arrived in Newport. Maybe she just needed to get away."

"You seem to have forgotten that her car was found abandoned."

"For all we know, she got on a plane or train and left her car parked somewhere and someone stole it."

The doorbell startled both men. "I'm not expecting anyone. Maybe it's the police telling me they found the casket," Earl said.

Neil and his father joined Chief Brower in the funeral museum parking lot, and the chief cautioned Neil to leave the questioning to the police. The bells from Maggie's house had been placed in a shoe box, which Detective Haggerty now carried under his arm.

When Earl took them to the museum office, Neil was startled to see Liam Payne sitting there.

Bateman and Payne went to get chairs for the men, taking them from the funeral scene in the front room. Irritation was on Bateman's face as he snapped at his cousin. "Liam, your shoes are muddy, and that's a very expensive carpet out there." Then, in an abrupt shift, he turned to the detectives. "Have you any news about the casket?" he asked.

"No, we don't, Professor Bateman," Brower said, "but we do have news about some other artifacts we think you own."

"That's ridiculous. Nothing else is missing except the catafalque."

"Earl, take it easy," Liam Payne said soothingly. He turned to Brower. "Chief, is there any new information about Maggie Holloway?"

"No, unfortunately there isn't," Brower told him.

"Have you considered that Maggie simply wanted to escape the terrible pressures of the last week and a half?"

Neil looked at Liam scornfully. "You don't know Maggie at all," he said. "She doesn't try to escape. She faces problems head-on."

Brower ignored both men and spoke to Bateman. "Professor, we're trying to clarify a few matters. From what we understand, the bells that you had cast for your lecture on Victorians who feared being buried alive are all packed away. Is that true?"

The anger was clear on Earl Bateman's face. "I simply will not go into that Latham Manor incident again," he said sharply.

"I understand. But will you answer the question, please?"

"Yes, I packed the bells away. Yes."

Brower nodded to Haggerty, who opened the shoe box. "Professor, Mr. Stephens found these bells in Maggie Holloway's home. Are they similar to the ones you have?"

Bateman paled. He examined one of the bells. "That woman is a thief!" he exploded. "She must have stolen these last night."

He jumped up and ran up the stairs, the others following him. On the third floor he threw open the door of the storeroom and hurried to a shelf on the right-hand wall. Reaching up, he yanked at a box and pulled it out.

"It's too light. I can tell already," he muttered. He rifled through the protective plastic popcorn. Turning to the five men standing behind him, his eyes blazing, he said, "There are only five of them here. Seven are missing! Maggie must have stolen them. No wonder she kept harping on them yesterday."

Neil shook his head in dismay.

"Professor Bateman, I must ask you to accompany me to police headquarters," Brower said, his tone formal. "I have to inform you that you are now a suspect in the disappearance of Maggie Holloway. You have a right to remain silent—"

"You can forget your Miranda warning," Earl shouted. "Maggie Holloway sneaked back in here, stole my bells and maybe even my casket, and you blame *me?* Ridiculous!"

Neil grabbed the lapels of Bateman's coat. "You know Maggie never took that stuff. And you answer me something. Some kids saw a hearse and Maggie's station wagon leave here around ten o'clock last night. Which one were you driving?"

"Shut up, Neil," Brower ordered angrily.

"You mean *my* hearse?" Bateman asked. "That's impossible. It's in the garage." Bateman rushed out to the garage. He yanked up the door and ran inside, closely followed by the others.

"Someone *did* use it!" he exclaimed, peering through the vehicle's window. "Look at it. There's dirt on the carpet."

Neil wanted to throttle the man, to beat the truth from him. How had he gotten Maggie to follow him in that hearse? Or was someone else driving her car?

Liam Payne took his cousin's arm. "Earl, it's going to be all right. I'll call a lawyer."

NEIL AND HIS FATHER SAT in a waiting area at the police station. From time to time Detective Haggerty joined them. "The guy has refused a lawyer; he's answering everything. He insists that he was in Providence last night and can prove it with phone calls he made from his apartment. At this point we can't hold him."

"But he's done something to Maggie," Neil protested.

Haggerty shook his head. "He's more worried about his casket and the dirt in that old hearse than he is about Ms. Holloway. His scenario is that she brought someone with her to steal the casket and bells, someone who drove the casket away in the hearse."

"You *can't* let him go," Neil protested.

"We can't *not* let him go." The detective hesitated, then said, "This will come out anyhow, and it's something you'd be interested in knowing. We also are looking into accusations of improprieties at Latham Manor, thanks to the suicide note of that lawyer. The chief made it top priority to find out who owns Latham Manor. Guess who does? Bateman's cousin Mr. Liam Moore Payne."

Haggerty looked around as though afraid Payne would appear behind him. "I guess he's still inside. He insisted on staying with his cousin during the questioning. We asked him about owning Latham. Readily admitted it, but he doesn't want it known. Says that if people knew, he'd have the residents calling him with complaints or requests for favors. That kind of makes sense, doesn't it?"

IT WAS nearly eight o'clock when Robert Stephens turned to his son. "Come on, Neil, we'd better get home," he urged. Their car was parked across the street from police headquarters. As soon as Stephens turned the ignition key, the car phone rang.

It was Dolores Stephens. She had gone home when they left Maggie's house for the museum. "Neil, I just received a phone call from a Mrs. Sarah Cushing. She said that her mother, Mrs. Bainbridge, is a resident at Latham Manor and that you were talking to her today."

"That's right." Neil felt his interest quicken.

"Mrs. Cushing's mother remembered something that she thought might be important. Mrs. Bainbridge said that Maggie mentioned something about a bell she had found on her stepmother's grave. She asked if placing a bell like that was some sort of custom. Mrs. Bainbridge said it just occurred to her that Maggie might have been talking about one of Professor Bateman's Victorian bells. I'm not sure what any of this means, but I wanted you to know right away," she said. "I'll see you in a while."

Neil gave his father the details of the message. "What do you make of it?" Robert Stephens asked his son as he started to put the car into drive.

"Hold it a minute," Neil said urgently. "The bells we found in Maggie's studio must have been taken from her stepmother's grave and from someone else's—probably one of the women from the residence. If she *did* go back to the museum last night, it was to see if any of the bells Bateman claimed were in that box were missing."

"Here they come," Robert Stephens murmured as Bateman and Payne emerged from the police station. They watched as the men got into Payne's Jaguar and, for a few minutes, sat in the car talking animatedly. The rain had ended, and a full moon brightened the already well-lighted area around the station.

"Payne must have taken dirt roads when he came down from Boston today," Robert Stephens observed. "Look at those tires. His shoes were pretty messy, too. There's something about that guy I don't like. Was Maggie dating him seriously?"

"I don't think so," Neil said tonelessly. "I don't like him either, but he obviously is successful. That Latham Manor cost a fortune. He has his own firm now, and he was smart enough to take with him some of Randolph and Marshall's best clients."

"Randolph and Marshall," his father repeated. "Isn't that where Dr. Lane said his wife used to work?"

"That's what's been bugging me!" Neil exclaimed. "Don't you see? Liam Payne is connected to everything. He owns the residence. He must have had the final say in hiring Dr. Lane. Doug Hansen also worked for Randolph and Marshall for a brief time. He has an arrangement now whereby his transactions go through their clearinghouse. I said today that Hansen had to be operating out of another office, and I also said that he's clearly too stupid to have worked out that scheme for defrauding those women. He was just the front man. Someone had to be programming him. Well, maybe that someone was Liam Moore Payne."

"But it doesn't all quite fit together," Robert Stephens protested. "If Payne owns the residence, he could have gotten the financial information he needed without involving either Hansen or his aunt Janice Norton."

"But it's much safer to stay a step removed," Neil pointed out. "That way Hansen becomes the scapegoat if anything goes wrong. Don't you see, Dad? Laura Arlington and Cora Gebhart had applications pending. He wasn't just turning over the apartments of residents, he was cheating applicants when there were no apartments."

"What are you saying?"

"I'm saying that this Payne guy is the key to all this. He secretly owns Latham Manor. Women there are dying under what seem to be unexceptional circumstances, yet when you consider how many have died recently—all of them pretty much alone, no close family to check on them—it all starts to look suspicious. And who stands to gain from their deaths? Latham Manor does, through reselling those now empty apartments."

"Do you mean to say that Liam Payne killed all those women?" Robert Stephens asked, his tone incredulous.

"I don't know that yet," his son replied. "The police suspect that Dr. Lane and/or Nurse Markey may have had a hand in the deaths. No, I don't know who killed those women, but I think Maggie must have been getting too close for comfort for the actual killer."

"But where do the bells come in? And Bateman?" Robert Stephens protested.

"The bells? Who knows? Maybe it's the killer's way of keeping score. Chances are that if Maggie found those bells on graves and looked up those women's obituaries, she had started to figure out what really happened." Neil paused. "As for Bateman, he seems almost too weird to be able to take part in anything as calculating as this. No, I think Mr. Liam Moore Payne is our connection here."

Noting that Payne had started his car, Robert Stephens turned to his son. "I take it we're following him," he said.

"Absolutely," Neil said, then added his own silent prayer: *Please let him lead me to Maggie.*

DR. WILLIAM Lane dined at Latham Manor with some of the charter members of the residence. He explained Odile's absence by saying she was devastated to be leaving her dear friends. As for himself, while he regretted having to give up so pleasant an experience, it was his firm belief that, as the axiom goes, "The buck stops here."

"I want to reassure everyone that this sort of outrageous indiscretion will never happen again," he promised, referring to Janice Norton's violation of privileged information.

Letitia Bainbridge had accepted the invitation to dine at the doctor's table. "Do I understand that Nurse Markey is filing an ethics complaint against you stating that, in effect, you stand by and let people die?" she asked.

"So I gather. It isn't true, of course."

His farewell was gracious and to the point. "Sometimes it is appropriate to let other hands take the reins. I've always tried to do my best. If I am guilty of anything, it is of trusting a thief."

On the short walk between the residence and the carriage house that was now the director's home, Dr. Lane thought, Whatever job I get will be on my own. Whatever happened, he wasn't going to spend another day with Odile.

When he went upstairs to the second floor, Odile was on the phone, apparently screaming at an answering machine. "You can't just drop me like this. Call me. You've got to take care of me. You promised!" She hung up with a crash.

"And to whom were you speaking, my dear?" Lane asked from the bedroom doorway. "Perhaps the mysterious benefactor who hired me for this position? Don't trouble whoever it is any longer on my account. Whatever I do, I won't be needing *your* assistance."

Odile raised tear-swollen eyes to him. "William, you can't mean that."

"Oh, but I *do*." He studied her face. "You really *are* frightened. I wonder why. I've always suspected that under that empty-headed veneer, something else was going on.

"Not that I'm interested," he continued as he opened his closet and reached for a suitcase. "Just a bit curious. After my little relapse last night, I got to thinking and made a few calls of my own."

He turned to look at his wife. "You didn't stay for the dinner in Boston, Odile. And wherever you went, those shoes of yours got terribly muddy, didn't they?"

MAGGIE couldn't keep track of the numbers anymore. It was no use. It would be so easy just to close her eyes and retreat from what was happening to her.

She should have guessed that there was something dishonest about Liam's sudden attentiveness. He had been more in character when he abandoned her at the cocktail party.

She thought back to last night, to the voice. Odile Lane had been arguing with Liam. She had heard them. "I can't do it anymore," Odile had wailed. "You're insane. You promised you'd sell the place and we'd go away."

She could barely flex her hand now. It was time to scream for help again, but her voice was only a whisper. No one would hear.

Her mind kept coming back to the first childhood prayer she had ever learned: *Now I lay me down to sleep . . .*

"YOU could have told me that you owned Latham Manor," Earl Bateman said accusingly to his cousin. "Why are you so secretive?"

"It's just an investment, Earl," Liam said. "Nothing more. I am completely removed from the day-to-day operation of the residence." He drove into the parking lot of the funeral museum, stopping next to Earl's car. "Go home and get a good night's sleep."

"Where are you going?"

"Back to Boston. Why?"

"Did you come rushing down today just to see me?" Earl asked, still annoyed.

"I came because you were upset and because I was concerned about Maggie Holloway. Now, as I've explained, I'm not as concerned about her. My guess is that she'll show up soon."

Earl started to get out of the car, then paused. "Liam, you knew where I kept the key to the museum, and the ignition key to the hearse, didn't you?" he asked.

"What are you driving at?"

"Nothing, except to ask if you told anyone about where I keep them."

"No, I didn't. Come on, Earl. You're tired. Go on home."

Earl got out and slammed the door.

Liam Moore Payne drove to the end of the side street. He didn't notice a car pull out from the curb and follow at a discreet distance when he turned right. It was all unraveling, he thought glumly. They knew he owned the residence. Earl had started to suspect that he had been in the museum last night. The bodies were going to be exhumed, and they'd find that the women had been given improper medications. If he was lucky, Dr. Lane would take the fall, but Odile was ready to crack. They would get a confession out of her in no time. And Hansen? He would do *anything* to save his own skin.

All that work for nothing. The dream of being the second Squire Moore, powerful and rich, was gone. After all the risks he had taken—borrowing from his clients' securities, buying the residence and pouring money into it, figuring out Squire-like ways to get other people's money—he was just another failed Moore.

And Earl, that obsessed fool, was rich—really rich.

But fool though he was, Earl wasn't stupid. Soon he would start to put two and two together, and then he would know where to look for his casket.

Well, even if he figured it all out, he wouldn't find Maggie Holloway alive. *Her* time had run out, of that Liam was certain.

CHIEF Brower and Detective Haggerty were about to leave for the day when the call came in from Earl Bateman. "They all hate me," he began. "They're all jealous because we're rich."

"Could you get to the point, Professor?" Brower asked.

"I want you to meet me at the site of my planned outdoor exhibit. I have a feeling that my cousin Liam and Maggie Holloway have played a practical joke on me. I'll bet anything they took my casket to one of the open graves at the exhibit and dumped it there."

The chief grabbed a pen. "Where exactly *is* your exhibit site?"

When he hung up, Brower said to Haggerty, "I think we may be about to find Maggie Holloway's body."

"NEIL, look at that!"

They were driving along a narrow dirt road, following the Jaguar. When they left the main road, Neil had turned off the headlights, hoping that Liam Payne wouldn't realize they were there. Now the Jaguar was turning left, its headlights briefly illuminating a sign Robert Stephens strained to make out.

"Future site of the Bateman Outdoor Museum," he read. "That must have been what Bateman was talking about when he said the stolen casket was going to be part of an important exhibit. Do you think it's here?"

Neil did not answer. A terrible fear was exploding within him. Casket. Hearse. Cemetery.

Suppose Liam Payne had been in the museum last night and found Maggie there. He and someone else, Neil thought. It must have taken two of them to drive Maggie's car and the hearse. Had they killed her and taken her out in that coffin?

Oh, God, no, no, please!

"Neil, he may have spotted us. He's turning around."

"Dad, you follow him. Call the police. I'm staying here." Before his father could protest, Neil jumped out of the car.

The Jaguar raced past them. "Go," Neil shouted. "Go!"

Robert Stephens executed a precarious U-turn and pressed down on the accelerator.

Neil began to run. Moonlight illuminated the muddy bulldozed acreage. He could see that trees had been felled, undergrowth cleared, paths staked out. And graves dug. Scattered, the holes yawned all around the area. Was Maggie here somewhere? Had Payne been insane enough to dump the casket with her inside it in one of those open graves and then cover it with earth?

Neil began to crisscross the huge site, shouting, "Maggie . . . Maggie . . . Maggie . . ."

WAS SHE DREAMING? MAGGIE forced her eyes open. She was so tired. She just wanted to sleep. She couldn't move her hand anymore. It was so stiff and swollen. She couldn't scream anymore, but that didn't matter. There was no one to hear her.

"Maggie . . . Maggie . . . Maggie . . ."

She thought she heard her name. It sounded like Neil's voice. She tried to call out, but no sound came from her throat. With painful effort she grasped her left hand with the fingers of her right hand and forced it up and down, up and down . . .

Vaguely she sensed that the bell must be moving.

"Maggie . . . Maggie . . . Maggie . . ."

Again she thought she heard her name, only it seemed fainter and so very far away.

SHE was here. Neil was sure of it. He could feel her presence. But where? He had gone over almost all of the bulldozed area. She might be buried under any one of those mounds of dirt. He was running out of time. And so was she. "Maggie . . . Maggie . . ."

He looked around despairingly. Suddenly he noticed something.

The night was still. There wasn't even enough breeze to stir a leaf. But over in the far corner of the lot something was glistening in the moonlight. And it was moving.

A bell. Moving back and forth. Maggie! Running, stumbling around open pits, Neil reached the bell and saw that it was attached to a pipe, its opening almost packed with mud. With his hands he began to claw at the dirt around it—claw and dig and sob.

As he watched, the bell stopped moving.

CHIEF Brower and Detective Haggerty were in the police car when the call from Robert Stephens was relayed to them. "Two of our guys have picked up the chase on the Jaguar," the dispatcher said. "But Stephens thinks that the missing woman may have been buried on that outdoor museum site."

"We're almost there," Brower said. "Dispatch an ambulance and emergency equipment out here now." He leaned forward. "Turn on the siren," he ordered.

When they arrived, they found Neil clawing at the wet clay. An instant later Brower and Haggerty were beside him, their powerful hands joining in the effort, digging, digging, digging.

Under the surface the soil became looser. Finally they reached the satiny wood. Neil jumped down into the hole, scraping dirt off the surface of the casket and hurling it away. He yanked out the clogged air vent and brushed the entry site clear.

Sliding to the side of the wide grave, he got his fingers under the casket lid and with a superhuman effort yanked it partially open. He held it with his left shoulder as he reached in, grabbed Maggie's limp body, and lifted it up to the hands reaching down from above.

As her face brushed his, he saw that her lips were moving and then heard her faint whisper, "Neil . . . Neil . . ."

"I'm here, love," he said, "and I'll never let you go."

CHAPTER 12

Sunday, October 13th   Five days later Maggie and Neil went to Latham Manor to say good-bye to Mrs. Bainbridge.

"We'll be up for Thanksgiving weekend with Neil's parents," Maggie said, "but I couldn't leave without seeing you now."

Letitia Bainbridge's eyes were sparkling. "Oh, Maggie, you don't know how we prayed that you'd be all right."

"I think I do," Maggie assured her. "And your caring enough to let Neil know about the bell I'd found on Nuala's grave may have saved my life."

"That was the clincher," Neil agreed.

He and Maggie were sitting side by side in Mrs. Bainbridge's apartment. He put his hand over Maggie's, unwilling yet to have her beyond his reach.

"Has everybody pretty well settled down here?" Maggie asked.

"Oh, I think so. We're more resilient than you'd think. I understand the Prestige people have arranged to buy the residence."

"Liam Payne will need all the money he can lay his hands on to pay for lawyers, and I hope they don't do him any good," Neil said forcefully. "His girlfriend, too. I understand that Odile has confessed to deliberately switching medicines on orders from Liam."

Maggie thought of Nuala and Greta Shipley and all of the women whose lives Liam and Odile had cut short. At least I helped to stop them from killing again, she consoled herself.

"Were Janice Norton and her nephew Douglas involved in these deaths?" Mrs. Bainbridge asked.

"No," Neil said. "Chief Brower told us that he believes that Hansen and Mrs. Norton were just involved with Liam's scheme to swindle applicants to the residence. Even Odile didn't know what they were up to. They're up on fraud charges, not murder."

"According to Chief Brower," Maggie said soberly, "Odile and Liam became involved when she worked in his former brokerage firm, just when he was buying this place. When Liam proposed this scheme to her, she jumped at it. Odile dropped out of nursing school, but it wasn't because she failed her courses. She knew exactly what drugs to combine to cause heart failure. Odile claims she begged Liam not to make her tamper with Mrs. Rhinelander's medication, but he was too greedy. By then Nuala had decided to go into the manor, provided she could have a two-bedroom unit."

"Was it Connie Rhinelander's death that made Nuala suspicious?" Mrs. Bainbridge asked sadly.

"Yes, and then, when she found that bell on Mrs. Rhinelander's grave, she apparently began to be sure that something terrible was going on at the residence. She must have asked some very pointed questions of Nurse Markey, who innocently reported them to Odile."

"And Odile warned Liam," Maggie said. Oh, Finnuala.

Mrs. Bainbridge's lips tightened. "Squire Moore's god was money. I remember my father saying Moore actually bragged that it was more interesting to cheat someone out of it than make it honestly. Obviously, Liam Payne is cut from the same evil cloth."

"One last thing," Maggie said. "Odile took that sketch Nuala and

Mrs. Shipley had made. Odile knew it could get people thinking."

It was time to leave. They would drive in tandem to New York.

"We'll visit you when we get back up here in November," Maggie promised as she bent to kiss Letitia Bainbridge's cheek.

"I'm already looking forward to it," Mrs. Bainbridge said briskly, then sighed. "You are so pretty, Maggie, and so nice and so smart." She looked at Neil. "You take good care of her."

"He did save my life." Maggie smiled.

Fifteen minutes later they were ready to leave for New York. Her station wagon was already packed in her driveway. The house was locked up. For a moment Maggie stood looking at it, remembering that night only two weeks ago, when she had arrived.

"It'll be fun to come up here on vacations and weekends, won't it?" she said.

Neil put his arm around her. "You're sure it won't hold too many bad memories?"

"No." She inhaled deeply. "Not as long as you're around to dig me up when I need help." Then she laughed. "Don't look so shocked. Gallows humor has gotten me through some pretty bad times."

"From now on that will be my job," Neil said as he opened the door of the station wagon for her. "Now remember, don't speed," he cautioned. "I'll be right behind you."

"You sound like your father," Maggie said. Then she added, "And I like that just fine."

MARY HIGGINS CLARK

Ideas for novels often come from unexpected sources. Years ago Mary Higgins Clark's mother-in-law told her about a recurring nightmare she had: She dreamed of opening her eyes to find herself in a closed casket. "She grew up in England," the author explains, "and probably heard stories from her mother about people being buried alive in Victorian times, when the dead were buried quickly as a precaution against the spread of disease."

Clark never forgot her mother-in-law's frightening vision, but not until she began to write *Moonlight Becomes You* did she find a way to use it in a story. Her next step was to find the perfect background for her suspenseful tale. "The setting is always a character in my books," she says. Newport, Rhode Island, an elegant seaside resort with a tradition of charm and wealth, was just the kind of place she needed to bring her story to life. Given Clark's track record—over a dozen of her books have been best sellers—it's a safe bet that both the story and the setting of her latest book will ring a bell with readers.

THE
OUTSIDER

PENELOPE WILLIAMSON

Their worlds were as different as could be.

She, a pious young woman, followed the Plain ways, the gentle ways.

He, a man apart, knew all too well the darkness in men's souls—and in his own.

Who could have imagined that these two, brought together on a snow-drifted prairie, were destined to change each other's lives forever?

CHAPTER ONE

HE CAME into their lives during the last ragged days of a Montana winter.

It was the time of year when the country got to looking bleak and tired from the cold. The snow lay in yellowed clumps, like old candle wax; the cottonwoods cracked and popped in the raw air; and spring was still more a memory than a promise.

That Sunday morning, the day he came, Rachel Yoder hadn't wanted to get out of bed. She lay beneath the heavy quilt, her gaze on the window that framed a gray sky. She listened to the creak of the wind-battered walls and felt bruised with a weariness that had settled and gone bone-deep.

She listened to Benjo's stoking up the fire in the kitchen: the clatter of a stove lid, the rattle of kindling in the woodbox, the scrape of the ash shovel. Then the house fell quiet, and she knew he was staring at her closed door, wondering why she wasn't up yet.

She swung her legs onto the floor, shuddering at the cold blast of air that billowed up from the bare pine boards. She dressed without lighting the lamp. As she did every morning, she put on a plain dark brown bodice and skirts and a plain black apron. Over her shoulders she draped a black triangular shawl, whose two long ends crossed over her breasts and pinned around her waist. Her fingers were clumsy with the cold, and she had a hard time pushing the thick blanket pins through the stiff wool. Yet it was the Plain-and-narrow way to use no hooks and eyes or buttons. The women of the Plain People had always fastened their clothes with pins and always would.

She did her hair last. It was thick and long, curling down to her hips, and it had the color of polished mahogany. Or so the only man who'd ever seen it let down had once told her. A soft smile touched her lips at the memory. Polished mahogany, he had said. And this from the mouth of a man who'd been born into the Plain life and known no other, and surely never looked upon mahogany, polished or dull, in all of his days. *Oh, Ben.*

He'd always loved her hair, and so she had to be careful not to let it be her vanity. Pulling it back, she twisted it into a knot, then covered it completely with her *Kapp,* a starched white cambric prayer cap. She had to feel with her fingers for the cap's stiff middle pleat to be sure it was centered on her head. They'd never had any mirrors, not in this house or the house she'd grown up in.

The warmth of the kitchen beckoned, yet she paused in the cold and murky light of the dawn to stare out the curtainless window. A stand of jack pines along the hill in back of the river had died during the winter and was now the color of old rust. Clouds draped over the shoulders of the buttes, leaden with the threat of more snow. "Come on, spring," she whispered. "Please hurry."

She lowered her head against the cold glass pane. Here she was wishing for spring, but with spring came the lambing time and a month's worry and toil. This spring she'd have to live it on her own.

"Oh, Ben," she said again, this time aloud.

She pressed her lips together against her weakness. Her husband knew a better life now, the eternal life, warm and safe in God's bosom. It was selfish of her to miss him. For the sake of their son she had to find the courage to surrender to God's will.

She made herself smile as she pulled open her bedroom door and stepped into the warmth and yellow light of the kitchen.

Benjo stood at the table pouring coffee beans into the mill. At the click of the latch his eyes fastened hard on her face.

"Mem? Why are you up suh—suh—so late? Are you fuh—fuh—fuh—" He clenched his teeth as his throat worked to expel the word that was stuck somewhere between his head and his tongue.

She ached to watch her boy stutter like this. She shook her head. "I'm only feeling a little lazy is all." Gently she brushed the hair out of his eyes. She hardly had to reach down to do so anymore, he was getting that big. He would be ten years old come summer.

The days, how they could flow one into the other without your noticing. Somehow winter, no matter what, turned into spring, and the lambs came and the hay was cut and the wool was sheared. You got up in the morning and put on the clothes of your grandmother, you went to the preaching and sang the hymns your grandfather sang, and your faith was their faith and would be the faith of your children. It was this—the way the days flowed like a river into the ocean of years—that she'd always loved about the Plain life. The sweet sameness of it, the steady sureness of time passing.

"I expect we got ourselves a bunch of hungry woollies out there," she said. "You'd best get started with hitching up the hay sled while I see to our own empty bellies." She ruffled his hair again. "And I'm feeling fine, our Benjo. Truly, I am."

She watched the relief ease his face. His step was light as he went to the door, snatching up his coat and hat from off the wall spike. His father had been a big, strapping man with black eyes and hair. Benjo took after her: small-boned and gray-eyed. Mahogany hair.

He had left the door open behind him, and winter came into the kitchen on a gust of stale wind. From the porch he leaped into the yard, and his shrill whistle cut through the air. MacDuff, their brown-and-white herding collie, burst out of the willow brakes that lined the creek. The dog made a beeline for Benjo, jumping onto his chest and nearly knocking him down. Rachel shut the door on the sound of the boy's shrieking laughter and MacDuff's barking.

The burp of the coffeepot sent her flying to the stove. Judas, she'd have to hurry with breakfast if they were going to make it to the preaching without being unforgivably late. They met for worship every other Sunday, all the Plain People who homesteaded this high mountain valley. Short of mortal sickness, no one ever missed a preaching.

The hot lard sputtered as she laid a thick slab of cornmeal mush into the frying pan. She cracked the window open a bit to fan out the smoke. The mush sizzled; the wind moaned along the sill. She glanced outside. Benjo's head was slightly tilted, his gaze focused on the distance. That was when she saw him too, the stranger walking across their hay meadow. An outsider, wearing a long black duster and a black hat. Headed toward them.

HE WALKED in a lolling, floppy kind of way, like a whiskified man. No one ever walked in these parts. It was too empty a place for a body to go anywhere without a buggy or a horse.

Rachel left the warmth of the house and met Benjo in the yard. They both watched the stranger come, making his slow, staggering way right at them. MacDuff, guarding the sheep beneath the cottonwoods, stood stiff-legged, a growl rumbling deep in his throat.

The snow in the meadow had been blown into waves by the wind and frozen over. Although the wind was blowing shrill now, she could hear his boots crunch as they broke through the ice crust.

He stumbled onto one knee. The wind caught his black duster, making it billow, so that he looked like a crow, wings spread for flight. He lurched to his feet again and left a streak of bright, wet red on the old snow.

"He's huh—huh—huh—" Benjo cried, but Rachel had already lifted her skirts and was running.

The stranger's foot caught in a crest of ice and he went sprawling, and this time he didn't get back up. Rachel fell to her knees beside him so abruptly that Benjo, following close, almost ran into her.

She laid a hand on the stranger's shoulder. The man recoiled at her touch, rearing onto his knees and flinging up his head. She saw utter terror well in his eyes before they fluttered closed and he slid again to the ground in a heap of black cloth and red blood.

"Benjo," she said, "you must ride into town and fetch Dr. Henry."

He swung his head back and forth hard. "Nuh—nuh—nuh—"

She gave him a little shake. "You must. He knows you, so you won't need to talk. You can write it down for him."

Benjo's wide gray eyes stared back at her. It was always an ordeal for a boy, with his Plain dress and his Plain ways, to go into town, to go among the outsiders. Most often they merely stared, but sometimes they were cruel. To a skinny Plain boy who choked on his words, they were almost always cruel.

"Benjo, the man is dying. Go on, now. Go!"

The man *was* dying. She couldn't imagine why he wasn't already dead, with the blood he had lost, was still losing. She needed to get him into the house. She tried to lift him and couldn't.

Benjo came out of the barn, riding their old draft horse bareback. He stared at her a moment, then nudged the mare's sides with his heels. The horse broke into a trot, heading up the road to town.

Rachel scooped up a handful of snow and rubbed it in the stranger's still, white face. "Wake up, you. Wake up!"

He woke up partly. Enough to push himself half onto his knees again. She saw that his right arm was broken and bound up roughly in a sling made from a man's black silk neckcloth.

She laid his other arm over her shoulder and grasped him around the waist and somehow got him onto his feet. "We're going to walk to the house now," she said, though she doubted he heard her. The wind blew hard. His breath came in ragged gasps.

They crunched through the crusty snow, wrapped up arm in arm, so close the butt of the rifle he carried in a saddle scabbard over his shoulder kept banging her on the head. A revolver was holstered at his hip.

SHE managed to jerk the quilt off her bed before they fell into it, still locked together in their strange embrace. She bucked and heaved against him and flung him onto his back. A bright red stain had already begun to spread on her muslin sheets.

She had to struggle against his weight to pull the rifle scabbard out from beneath him. She spread open his duster. His clothes, once dandy fine, were now so blood-soaked she had to spend precious seconds trying to discover where he was hurt. She ripped open his vest and shirt.

He had a bullet hole in his left side. The hole was small and black and pulsed blood with his breathing. She made a thick pad out of a huck towel and pressed it to the wound, leaning against it hard with the heels of her hands. When she lifted the pad, she saw that while the bleeding might have slowed some, it hadn't stopped.

She ran from the room, banged out the door and into the yard. The wind whipped her skirts, frightening the chickens that scratched in the straw by the barn, scattering them. She pulled open the barn door and was struck in the face with the pungent smells of cow and chicken and sheep, sheep, sheep.

She gathered up all the cobwebs she could find, then brought them back to the house cradled in her apron.

She poured turpentine into the bullet hole. He jerked at the sting of it, but he didn't waken. She laid the webs over the wound and packed it with a clean compress. Then, backing away from the bed, she sat down in her rocking chair and for the first time really looked at the face of the outsider who lay on her bed.

He was young, no older than twenty-five, surely. His hair was the brown-black of fresh-plowed earth, his skin milk pale. He had arresting looks: high, sculptured cheekbones; long, narrow nose; wide-spaced eyes with thick, long lashes.

It was *Mutter* Anna Mary who had the healing touch. From her father's grandmother, Rachel had learned the healing lore, but the touch—that was a gift from God, and so far He had not seen fit to give it to her. Her great-grandmother said the healing touch came simply of faith. Of opening one's soul to the power of faith the way a sunflower unfurls its petals to the warmth and the light.

Rachel stood slowly and went to the bed. She laid her hands on him. Closing her eyes, she imagined her soul opening like a flower, petals unfolding one by one. His chest moved beneath her hands, a ragged rise and fall. She thought she could hear the rush and suck of his heart beating. She tried to imagine the life passing from her fingers, like a river pouring into the ocean, until she became part of the rush and suck of his heart.

But when she opened her eyes and looked down at his face, she saw the blue lips and pinched skin of coming death.

"Come along there, you. Open up."
Rachel pushed the rubber nipple between the outsider's lips and

tilted the kidney-shaped nursing bottle so that the milk would flow more easily into his mouth. "That's it, that's it," she crooned. "Suckle now, suckle it all down like a good little *Bobbli.*"

She looked over her shoulder. Judas, what was she thinking of to speak such outlandish words and to an outsider, no less? She couldn't imagine what had prompted her to do such a thing anyway, to try to feed him from a pap bottle. Only it seemed she would have to do something to replace all the blood he'd lost, or he would surely die. And she'd saved many an orphaned lamb in just this way, by feeding it a mixture of milk, water, and molasses from a nursing bottle.

SHE was out in the yard when Benjo came back with the doctor.

The phaeton lurched over the frozen ruts in the road, swaying on its high wheels. It pulled abreast of her, and she caught her image in the shiny black lacquer. She was startled to see her prayer cap askew and straggles of loose hair flying about in the wind.

"Whoa, now!" Dr. Lucas Henry called out, pulling on the reins. He gripped the crown of his beaver bowler, and the drooping curve of his tawny mustache curled around a lopsided smile. As usual, the whiskey shine was bright on his face.

"How there, Mrs. Yoder." He slurred the words, but then, she'd always thought he enjoyed for mischief's sake putting on a show of wicked drunkenness, especially for someone who was Plain.

Benjo rode up alongside the buggy. His eyes shone more with excitement now than with fear. She smiled at him, so he would know how pleased she was with him, though she said only, "Those poor woollies still haven't been fed yet."

The boy's wide-eyed gaze jerked to the house, then back to her. When she said nothing more, he headed for the barn.

The doctor swept his hat off his head. "And a pleasure it is to exchange a howdy with you too, Mrs. Yoder."

His words and actions flustered her. It wasn't the Plain way to speak empty phrases on coming and going, and she never knew quite what to do when an outsider chose to practice such manners on her. She settled for nodding her head at him.

The doctor stared down at her from the buggy a moment longer, then heaved a deep sigh. He wrapped the reins around the brake handle, picked up his black bag, and swung down onto the ground. She started for the house, leaving him to follow.

"Your boy," he said, falling into step beside her, "managed to communicate to me in his unique way that you've had trouble come a-calling in the form of a devil, a demon . . . an incubus, perhaps?" He wiggled his brows. "Dressed all in black and leaving bloody footprints in the snow."

"He's not a devil. He's one of you outsiders, and he's been gunshot," she said. "He'll die of it, I should think. I bathed the wound with turpentine and packed it with cobwebs. And I fed him from a pap bottle to make up for all the blood he's lost."

She held the door open for the doctor. He paused next to her on the threshold, his eyes full of mockery. "What a wonder you are, Plain Rachel. The very soul of ingenuity and efficiency."

She spoke the truth that was in her heart, because that was the only way she knew how to be. "I did try to heal him," she said. "I laid my hands on him. But my faith wasn't strong enough."

His voice was serious for once. "No? But whose faith ever is?"

As they stepped into the kitchen, the hot air from the cookstove and the smells of fried mush and blood hit them in the face. She waited while the doctor shrugged out of his plaid greatcoat and then his frock coat and hung them both on the spike by the cookstove, along with his hat. She was relieved to see that he wasn't as inebriated with the devil's brew as he had seemed.

He unfastened the pearl-and-gold links from his cuffs, slipped them into the pocket of his maroon brocade vest, and began to roll up his shirtsleeves. As always, he was flashy as a strutting gamecock.

He washed his hands at the slopstone and then went without asking into her bedroom. He knew where to go because he had been there once before, on the day he had brought home Ben's lifeless body. There hadn't been anything he could do on that day, though, for a man the outsiders had hanged.

"I DON'T know how he still lives," Rachel said.

The doctor had removed the compress and was studying the

wound. The hole in the stranger's side continued to seep blood. "During the Sioux wars I saw men punctured with more holes than a pie safe," he said. "Yet they clung to life. One wonders why." He'd taken an instrument from his bag and was probing the wound. "The bullet's bounced off a rib and lodged in his spleen. I'll need hot water and more light."

She hurried to fetch the water from the cookstove reservoir. She came back to find Doc Henry standing at the dying man's bedside with his head thrown back, a silver flask to his lips.

She set the water pail and an enamel basin on the floor with a loud clatter and a splash, then left. When she came back with the peg lamp, the doctor dropped the stranger's leather cartridge belt and holster into her arms. "Better put this up where—"

The weight of the belt surprised her. She juggled it in her hands, and the revolver slid out of its greasy holster and hit the floor. Something smacked into the wall, spitting splinters. The air itself seemed to explode with smoke and flame, and Rachel screamed.

Cursing under his breath, Doc Henry stooped over and picked up the gun. She watched, stiff with fear, her ears still ringing, while he emptied it of its remaining cartridges and took the gun belt back from her. He looked around the room, his gaze falling on the rough pine wardrobe Ben had built for her the year they were married.

"An oiled holster and a doctored trigger," the doctor was saying, as he turned the revolver over in his hands. "What a dangerous hombre you've brought into your saintly home, Mrs. Yoder." He gestured at the wardrobe as if to say, "May I?" She nodded.

She pointed to the corner where she had set the stranger's rifle scabbard. "There's another," she said.

He put both firearms into the wardrobe. But when he went back to the bed, she saw that there was still another, a small one tucked into a shoulder holster beneath the stranger's left armpit. Further exploration showed the man had a bowie knife tucked into a sheath in his boot. "Yup, this bum lamb of yours is sure enough a real desperado," Doc Henry drawled, putting the weapons with the others. "He's packing enough hardware to outfit Custer's army."

They undressed him then, together. The man was built lean and strong, with long shanks, a deep, muscled chest, and a taut, flat belly.

She glanced up to catch the doctor's eyes watching her, laughing at her. And though it wasn't like her at all, she blushed.

One of the doctor's pale eyebrows lifted, and his mouth curled slightly. "There's nothing wrong in admiring God's handiwork, Plain Rachel." He looked down at the wounded man. "Getting that bullet out is going to be trickier than braiding a mule's tail. Pity I haven't chloroform along with me. But then, he's already so far under, just the shock of cutting into him is liable to kill him."

The doctor's hand shook only a little as he picked up a scalpel and pressed the blade of it against the stranger's pale skin. Blood welled and the flesh gaped, and Rachel had to look away.

The stranger groaned. "Feel that, do you, dear heart?" the doctor crooned. "That's good, that's good. As long as you're suffering, you're still living." The gunshot man groaned again and jerked violently. "Don't stand there like a fence post, woman. Hold him down."

Rachel leaned over the bed and gripped the stranger's shoulders. The doctor probed and dug at the bloody wound, then straightened and held the bullet, pinched between a pair of long silver tweezers, up to the light. "A forty-four-forty," he said. "See where it's slightly flattened at one end? That's where it struck the rib."

He dropped the bullet into the basin of water. "You're looking peckish there, Plain Rachel. Don't you go fainting on me."

He had her help him sew up the hole in the man's flesh—made by a bullet and enlarged by his doctor's knife. "Suturing," he called it, which he did with a curved silver needle.

Doc Henry dressed the wound and then looked at the man's broken arm. He made a clucking noise with his tongue. "An oblique compound fracture of the radius, and it looks as if the blamed fool tried to set it himself. He sure fancies himself a tough one."

Rachel thought that surely it would take a lot of courage to set your own arm. She wondered if it had happened before or after he'd been shot and who had shot him and why, and what had been behind that wild terror she'd seen in his eyes. But then, she had so many wonderings about him, this outsider who had come staggering across her hay meadow, leaving his bloody footprints in the snow.

RACHEL SAT IN HER SPINDLE-BACKED rocker, her hands folded in her lap and her gaze on the young man in her white iron bed. They had bound up his broken arm in a sheet of surgeon's plaster, cleaned him, and dressed him in one of Ben's old nightshirts. She thought his eyes no longer looked so sunken into the bones of his face. He lay in utter stillness, but she could see the throb of the pulse in his throat.

A sound at the door made her look up. Doc Henry, clean now after using the yard pump, leaned against the jamb. A cigarette drooped from one corner of his mouth. "Well, aren't you just a-sitting there looking as pleased with yourself as a pig in pokeweed."

She beamed a smile back at him. "He's going to live," she said.

"For today." He drew deeply on the cigarette, squinting at her through the smoke. "Wild boys like him don't make old bones."

He didn't sound as if he cared much. He was a strange man, was Dr. Lucas Henry. She supposed she knew him better than she'd ever known an outsider, and yet she knew him not at all. One afternoon last spring she had sat in this very chair, beside this bed, holding the hand of her dead husband, and Doc Henry had stayed with her for a time, talking to her because he'd sensed she could not bear being alone.

Most of what he'd said that day had been merely words to fill the empty corners of the room, but some of it she'd heard and remembered. He'd been born the same year and month and very day as she, which made him thirty-four. His home had been in Virginia. She could often hear the echoes of that place in his speech. For a time he'd done his doctoring in the U.S. cavalry.

Those things he had told her about himself, and one other thing she'd only felt. He was a man apart from the world, a bleak and lonely soul.

She watched him now as he pulled the silver flask from his pocket and drank deeply. "Strictly for medicinal purposes," he said, mocking himself this time. He gestured at the bed with the flask. "The very thing that must be done with our desperado here. The nursing bottle was a fine idea. See if you can get him to take it again."

She nodded, and then the full sense of what he'd said struck her. "But I thought you would be taking him back into town with you?"

"Not unless you want to undo all our good work."

She crossed her arms, gripping her elbows. "But—"

"Change the dressing often, and for mercy's sake, don't clean the wound with turpentine again. I'll give you carbolic acid instead. And make him stay quiet. He can't afford to start bleeding again."

The doctor pushed himself off the doorjamb. He went to the bed and picked up the stranger's wrist to feel his pulse. The stranger's hand, Rachel saw, was long and fine-boned, with slender fingers.

But then the doctor's own long fingers slid down to grip the man's hand, and he turned it over almost roughly. "Have a good look at that, Plain Rachel. All pretty and smooth on the outside and a pure mess on the inside. Somebody's worked this boy brutally hard for a time in his life. And look at this finger. It takes hours of shooting practice to put a callus like that on your trigger finger."

He laid the hand on the bed, gentle now. "He's got shackle scars on his ankles, and someone's taken a whip to his back. Those are the sort of marks a spell in prison leaves on a man."

He smoothed the dark hair off the stranger's pale forehead. "So will he thank you for saving him, I wonder? And I wonder why you even bothered, for he's already caught fast in the devil's clutches. Isn't that what you believe?" His gaze lifted to hers. "You people who are so sure that only you are saved, for you alone are the chosen of God?"

She shook her head at him. "No one can be sure of salvation. We can only yield to God's eternal will and hope things turn out for the best."

He moved abruptly away from the bed and began to pack up his instruments. Except to tell her that he would be back in a day or two to check on his patient, he said nothing more. Rachel too was silent.

She went with Doc Henry out into the yard. The wind was raw and cold. She was surprised to see Benjo still on the hay sled, feeding the ewes, for it seemed that hours surely must have passed.

At his buggy Doc Henry turned and looked back to the house. Lampshine spilled from her bedroom window in a soft yellow pool.

"That boy in there . . ." he said. "He might be handsome as a

July morning, but he's also probably mean enough to whip his weight in wildcats when he's not half dead." He brushed his fingers against her cheek, touching her gently. "Have a care, Plain Rachel. The powers of darkness *do* sometimes prevail."

CHAPTER TWO

THERE was nothing quite so eye watering as the sour stink of sheep. Even with the wind blowing, Rachel Yoder could still smell the woolly monsters. They crowded around the sled, bleating, while she stood on the deck of the sled and heaved pitchforkfuls of hay out beyond them.

She braced her legs apart as Benjo drove the draft horse, pulling the sled over the frozen ruts in the pasture. When he hauled on the reins and the sled squeaked to a stop, Rachel thrust the pitchfork into a loose bale and jumped to the ground.

"Muh—Mem?" Benjo stood with one hand wrapped around a hame on the harness collar. "Mem, thuh—thuh—that outsider, is he an outlaw?"

She came up to him. "I don't know," she said gently. "Perhaps."

"Will he shuh—shuh—shuh—" The muscles of his throat clenched around the word that wouldn't come.

She put her hands on his shoulders. "Sh, now, and listen to me. The outsider has no reason to shoot us. We mean him no harm."

He stared up at her, his eyes as leaden as the clouds overhead. She saw the question in those eyes and the unspoken truth. The outsiders had had no reason to hang his father, but Benjamin Yoder had died nonetheless, choking at the end of a rope.

The boy's mouth spasmed once, and then the words burst out of him fierce and whole. "I won't let him hurt you, Mem!"

Rachel pulled him against her. She knew she ought to tell him that he mustn't resist whatever happened, for it would be the will of God. But this time her own throat closed up tight around the words and kept them from coming.

THE EWE BUTTED HER BLACK face against Rachel's thigh, making a *buuuuhh* sound deep in her throat. "It's the hay you're supposed to be eating, you silly old thing. Not me," Rachel said, laughing.

This ewe was an old one, and her mouth was so broken she could barely chew even the softest grass. She should have been culled from the band last mating season, but she'd always been such a sweet, gentle mother, producing strong and healthy babies year after year. Rachel hadn't the heart to ship her off for slaughter.

A horse's whinny floated to her on the wind, followed by the rattle of wheels over the log bridge that spanned the creek. To the outsiders all the Plain People looked alike, with their austere conveyances and their drab old-fashioned clothes. But as soon as the light spring wagon with its faded brown canvas top turned into the yard, Rachel knew who it was. Although her neighbors and family would all have been worried when they didn't see her at the preaching this morning, she had known Noah Weaver would be the one to come.

As Noah got down, Benjo came flying out of the barn to meet him. She could tell from the way her son was waving his arms and pointing to the house that Noah was now getting an earful about the outsider.

It had started to sleet. The boy led Noah's horse, still hitched to the wagon, into the big barn. Rachel snapped her fingers at Mac-Duff, and they left the paddock together. MacDuff took off after the boy in a mud-splattering gallop, barking joyfully.

Rachel walked through the slushy snow and mud in the yard with her head lowered against the stinging ice pellets. Noah waited for her with his hands on his hips, the wind tugging at his long beard. She stopped before him, and he looked down at her with brown eyes that were warm and concerned. His craggy face, with its bumpy nose and thick ginger beard that lay on his chest like a forkful of hay, was so dearly familiar to her that she wanted to laugh and throw her arms around him.

Instead she stood before him, her hands linked behind her.

White air puffed from his mouth. "*Vell,* our Rachel?"

"I've fried mush left over from breakfast, should you want it."

He smiled at her, openly, and so she let her own smile come out.

They turned together toward the house, and the wind drove the sleet at them. Noah barely snatched his hat before it went sailing.

He must have hurried over right after he'd finished his evening chores. At least as much as he was capable of hurrying. Noah Weaver was slow in thought, word, and deed. He took his own good time arriving at a place within himself, but once he got there, not even a barrel of gunpowder could budge him loose.

He plodded into her kitchen, cumbersome and big-footed as a bear. He gazed from the slopstone to the cookstove to the bathing screen. "So where is he, then—this *Englischer?*" he said, his lip curling around the word as if it tasted foul.

They were speaking *Deitsch,* the old peasant German of their roots, for the Plain didn't use the *Englische* talk except around outsiders. And only then when they chose to be friendly.

She led the way in silence to the bedroom. The outsider slept in utter stillness. As it did every time she gazed at him, her breath caught at the arresting quality of his face.

She felt Noah stiffen beside her and knew that he, at least, saw only an outsider who had come unwanted into their lives. He said nothing, though, until they were back in the kitchen.

His head jerked up and around as if he was pointing with his beard. "In your bed, Rachel?"

"He was gunshot and bleeding to death. What else was I to do? Dump him in the corner like a bundle of old gunnysacks?"

Noah shrugged out of his sack coat and hooked it on the wall spike. He took off his hat and reached to hang it there as well, but he paused, as if he had to carefully choose his words. When he turned back to her, he was very much the church deacon, with his eyes all solemn, his mouth stern. As Deacon Weaver, it was his duty to be sure everyone followed the straight-and-narrow way and conformed to the understanding of what it was to be Plain.

"That *Englischer* in there, he's tainted. He reeks of the world and the evil that's in it."

"You don't know him."

"And what do you know of him?"

Rachel had nothing to say to that. What little she did know of the outsider—the callus on his finger, the shackle scars, the whip marks, the bullet hole—was all wickedness. It spoke of the hurt he had done unto others, as much as the hurt done upon him.

She turned away and went to the stove. She forked a slab of the cold fried mush onto a plate and poured sorghum syrup over it, then brought it and a tin mug to the table. She stopped there, her hand that held the plate suspended in air. She felt a bittersweet ache in her chest at what she was about to do. Yet she did it anyway: She set the plate down in Ben's place at the head of the table.

She felt Noah move, and she looked up to catch his gaze on her. She quickly averted her face and went to the stove for the coffeepot.

When she came back to him, he was seated, his head bent in silent prayer. She thought of the many times she had stood like this beside the table, looking down at Ben's black head.

They had all been the best of friends when they were children, she and Ben and Noah. It seemed strange only now, looking back on it, that a couple of rowdy boys would welcome a shy, skinny girl three years younger into their games. Even as boys, they'd been very different: Noah, slow and steady and a little stiff in his ways; Ben, so quick to laugh and quick to anger, reckless and a little wild.

She poured coffee into Noah's cup from the battered, blue, speckled pot. He ate in silence, as was the Plain way, his gaze on the painted clay plates that lined the shelf along the far wall. Rachel had painted them herself, copying the wildflowers that burst upon the valley in the spring. She had meant to do a dozen, but she'd stopped at five when Noah showed her how she was taking too much sinful pride and worldly pleasure in what she was creating.

Now Noah lifted his empty plate and captured her gaze. "You set the food that was meant for me at Ben's place. I got to believe that—"

"I did it without thought," she said quickly, before he could go on. Her words were an outright lie, may God forgive her. By inviting him to take her husband's place at her table, she'd all but told Noah Weaver she was willing to make a place for him in her heart and bed as well. Oh, yes, she had thought of it, and then she had acted on that thought, and now she wanted it all undone.

Noah set the plate down and reached for her hand. "It's no disloyalty to him, what you did. He's nearly a whole year gone now. And the boy needs the firmness of a father's hand to guide him."

And the church frowned on a woman who went her own way, without a husband to guide her. Those were all good reasons why she should become Noah Weaver's wife.

It had seemed when they were young, she and Noah and Ben, that the three of them would always be together. But then had come the day that Noah Weaver had first kissed her, and Rachel had realized they wouldn't always be able to share everything.

On that day Noah had been up in the mow of his papa's barn, forking hay into a wagon bed. She'd tried to sneak up on him and give him a shove from behind, only he'd caught her at the last instant. Caught at her apron strings too, so that she'd gone flying with him down into the bed of hay. One moment she'd been lying in the hay, laughing, straw tickling her nose. And then his head was blocking out the sky, and his lips were pressing down on hers.

She could still remember the way that kiss had made her feel—all trembly inside, filled with strange wantings to have him kiss her again. And a wanting for Ben to do it to her as well.

So she'd gone looking for Ben later and found him at their fishing hole, stealing a nap when he should have been at his chores. He lay flat on his belly on the grassy bank, his head cradled in his arms. It was a hot day, and his sweat-damp shirt clung to his back. She could see the bulge of muscle in his shoulders and the way the curve of his ribs met his spine. She couldn't remember ever noticing these things before.

She sat down next to him and touched his black hair.

He opened his eyes and smiled at her.

"Noah kissed me on the mouth," she blurted.

He sat up in one quick, graceful movement. He studied her, his head cocked slightly. "I'll allow that," he finally said. "As long as you don't forget I'm the one you're going to marry."

She made a face at him. "Hunh. Don't you think I might have something to say to that, Benjamin Yoder?"

He leaned into her until it seemed their faces were but a breath apart. That if she did so much as breathe, their lips would touch.

She felt the heat of his breath as he spoke. "*Ja, Meedel,* I reckon so. On the grand day I do my asking, you'll be saying yes."

His hands were on her arms, and he was pulling her closer. But he abruptly let her go without kissing her at all.

She watched him gather up his pole and wicker creel and saunter away, knowing already that he was the one she loved best.

And Noah, dear Noah, had always known it too. She looked at Noah Weaver now, so many years and memories later, and his dark brown eyes stared back at her. She had seen those eyes looking back at her often over the years. Seen them bleak with hopeless yearning on the day she had taken another man as her husband. Seen them hollow with anguish the night his own wife had died in childbirth. Seen them countless times shining with the rapture of prayer.

And now because of this simple, foolish thing that she had done, she saw those eyes glowing bright as Christmas candles with hope.

Oh, she could imagine herself making a life with him, imagine him sitting at her table like this of an evening while they talked over the day and planned the morrow. But when she tried to imagine going into the bedroom with him and undressing for him . . . She pulled her hand from his and reached for his empty plate, but he caught at her wrist.

"Rachel—"

"Noah, don't say anything more, please. I'm just not ready."

He let her go, stretching to his feet. His face was flat and empty as he put on his hat and coat. But he paused at the door.

"I know," he said, "how you'll say that if the *Englischer* showed up here as he did, gunshot and bleeding, then it could never have been God's will for you to leave him to die. And you're right in that. But it's not for nothing that we Plain People have kept ourselves separate from those things that can corrupt the soul. I know it was Ben's belief that we shouldn't always turn our back on the world, but he was wrong, and now he's got you thinking you can—"

She swung around on him so fast her cap strings flared. "You stop blaming me on Ben!"

She surprised him so, his face flushed red above his beard. He looked at her now as if he'd never seen her before, as if she wasn't the Rachel he had known all his life.

She reached up and felt that a swatch of hair had slid loose from beneath her prayer cap. She thrust it back up under the starched white cambric. The gesture, one she had made a thousand times over the years, brought a reluctant smile to Noah's mouth.

"Aw, Rachel." He gave a ragged laugh. "You never change. Not even Ben could really change you, for good or for ill."

He half turned to the door, then swung back. "I saw when I drove up that you're getting low on wood. I'll send my boy, Mose, on over in a day or two with his axe."

Her smile came a little shakily. "That would be kind."

He turned and left. She watched him lead his horse and wagon from the barn and climb aboard, but he didn't drive off right away. He sat there, his shoulders hunched against the weather, one hand clutching at his hat.

She wanted to go to him and take the hurt away, to go to him and say, "I will marry you, my Noah. If I can't have Ben, I can at least have a husband who is dear to me, a friend."

She wanted to run out and say all those things. But she stayed where she was until his wagon disappeared over the rise.

SLEET still pecked at the window and pattered on the tin roof that night as Rachel took off her black shawl and apron, storing their pins in the apron belt. She removed the top pin from her bodice as well and untied the strings of her prayer cap. She took off the cap and put it in its place on the shelf beneath the window. When she looked up, she caught her reflection in the night-blackened glass. The woman who stared back at her was a stranger, with a wild tangle of hair falling over her shoulders.

She sat in her spindle-backed rocker, its rush seat squeaking softly as it took her weight. The outsider lay in her bed, a silent collection of lumps and hollows beneath the quilt. In a moment she would join Benjo, although she'd probably have to shoo off that bed hog of a dog to make room for herself. In a moment. The breath eased out of her in a soft sigh. Her head fell back.

And she let the music come.

The drumbeat of the rain on the tin roof joined in syncopation with the beat of her heart. The wind whistled like a pipe, blowing shrill. The log walls moaned with their deep bass sound.

The music became wilder. Jagged clarions of trumpets joined with bright cymbals crashing through her blood. She shook with the force of the thundering chords, shocked at their violence. Never had the music been so awesome, so wild. So forbidden.

No music was allowed in the Plain life, of course, save for the chanting of the hymnsongs on worship Sunday. Yet it seemed that all her life the music had been with her, as elemental as breathing.

She had no notion of why it came, only from where. It came from nature's songs—from the violin scrape of a cricket's wing, the clap of a thundercloud, the pop of the cottonwoods freezing.

No one knew about her music; not even Ben had known. If the church ever came to hear of it, she was sure she'd have to confess it as a sin and promise never to allow it to happen again.

But the music was her way of praying. She couldn't use mere words to speak of what was truly in her soul. The music—it did more than speak. It worshipped. When the music came, the Lord was somehow there as well.

In those first months after Ben's death, she had lost the music. There had been only emptiness then, as hard as a cold stone inside her. She'd moved through the days staggered with grief and loneliness, able to summon only a pale shadow of the faith that had always steadied and comforted her. For how could a loving God allow a woman's husband to be so unjustly hanged at the end of a rope?

Yet the music found a way to be heard, just as God always found a way. It came back to her at first in sweet bits and snatches, like the whispered perfume of apple blossoms on a spring day. Then one night she had shut her eyes and opened her heart to the wind howling through the cottonwoods. And the wind became a chariot of wondrous, booming chords, carrying her back to her faith.

And so when the music came to her on this night, Rachel opened her heart. It wasn't sweet or gentle. It was as sudden and shattering as the sound of a bullet slamming into a wall.

As always the music ended abruptly, falling into a hollow, echoing silence. Slowly she opened her eyes.

The room wavered before her, hazy from the lamp smoke. The outsider still lay in utter quiet on her bed. Lampshine reflected off the sheen of his eyes. He was awake.

Her breath caught in surprise, then in fear. She rose and went to him. In the gloomy light his eyes glittered up at her, fierce and wild.

His hand grabbed her arm. "Where's my gun?"

She sucked in a breath. "We put it up. In the wardrobe."

"Get it." His fingers, so long and slender, whitened with his grip.

"You'll shoot me."

"I'll shoot you if you don't get it."

His eyes locked with hers, and she believed him capable of anything. "I will, then. As soon as you let go of me."

She pulled away, and he let go.

The door to the wardrobe groaned as she opened it. She knelt and retrieved the leather cartridge belt from the back corner where Doc Henry had put it. Even though she'd watched the doctor empty the gun of its bullets, she was still afraid of it. Its wooden grip had the smooth worn feel of an old axe handle.

She thought the stranger had fallen back into sleep, for he lay still again, eyes closed. Yet as she held the revolver out to him, his fingers wrapped around it with an unnatural strength. She felt the breath leave him then on a sigh of relief.

"Where am I?"

"You're safe," she said softly.

His mouth pulled up at one corner, but it wasn't a smile. His gaze went to the black, empty window. "There's no such place."

"Hush now and sleep," she said. "There's nothing out there."

As she bent down to lower the wick in the lamp, her loose hair brushed over his chest and face. She felt a tug on her hair, and she saw that he had tangled his fingers in it. But then his heavy eyelids closed as if against his will. He slid into sleep again, letting go of her hair and wrapping his hand once more around his gun.

She turned off the lamp and left him to the dark and the night. His eyes, she now knew, were blue.

CHAPTER THREE

IT WAS barely noon, and Rachel was already a day's worth behind in her chores. She had cream—souring in a bucket—that needed churning, an apple duff that needed boiling, the bed linens yet to soak. But first the outsider's wound needed tending.

Rachel stuffed a wad of fresh bandages under her arm. She filled an enamel basin with vinegar water and headed for her bedroom.

Doc Henry had ordered him seen to three times a day. She was to cleanse the bullet hole with carbolic acid and sponge him down all over with the vinegar water. He'd been in a terrible feverish state since that first night. He didn't toss about and rave, though, as one might expect. Most of the time he just lay there and sweated. Except for twice, when he'd been startled awake all wild-eyed and pointing his six-shooter at some unseen menace.

Since she'd put it in his hand, he hadn't once let go of his precious gun. But Doc Henry said that because the wicked thing appeared to bring him comfort, she wasn't to take it away.

Skirts swishing, Rachel entered her bedroom just as, out in the yard, MacDuff barked. The man in the bed exploded into a blur of motion, and Rachel was staring down the black muzzle of his Colt.

She screamed and flung the basin up in front of her face, dousing herself with the vinegar water. She squeezed her eyes shut behind her puny shield. The air grew thick and still, except for the drip-drip of the water.

She lowered the basin slowly, peering over its chipped rim.

He still held the six-shooter trained right on the bridge of her nose. She tried to assure herself that she'd seen Doc Henry take out the bullets, but she didn't completely trust any outsider.

MacDuff barked again, and the outsider's whole body drew taut.

"That dog—" His voice was savage. "What's it barking at?"

She was holding her head so stiffly it seemed to creak as she turned to look out the window. MacDuff was loping in and out of the willow brakes and cottonwoods that lined the creek, a dirty gray fluff of tail flashing ahead of him.

"It's only our herding collie, chasing a jackrabbit."

The barrel of the gun jerked upward. His thumb flashed, and there was a loud metallic click, and Rachel nearly jumped out of her skin again. He sagged down into the pillows. Sweat gleamed on his face.

His gaze suddenly snapped back to the window, focusing on the running figure of her son outside. MacDuff's barking must have drawn Benjo away from his chores in the barn. The boy was going after the rabbit with his sling, whirling the rawhide cords over his head like a lasso.

"Who's that?" said the man in the bed.

"M-my son. Don't"—her throat constricted—"don't hurt him."

Out by the wild plum thickets Benjo released one of the sling's rawhide cords, and the rabbit dropped like a stone.

The man turned his eyes back to her and stared with a concentration that was frightening and tangible. Unexpectedly he smiled. "Looks like you'll be having rabbit stew for supper."

His smile disconcerted her. His eyes remained terrifying.

Her gaze dropped to the floor, where the vinegar water had made a dark wet stain, almost like blood. *Lieber Gott, lieber Gott.* If it had been Benjo to come through the door instead of her . . .

"What kind of crazy person are you?" she shouted, advancing on the bed. "Waving that wicked thing around like a fool, pointing it at innocent folk. Why, I've a good mind to . . ." She trailed off.

"You're gonna do what, lady? Take a switch to my sorry rear end?"

Flustered, she jerked her gaze away from his. "Hunh. I ought to."

She slammed the basin down on the floor. She had dropped the roll of bandages back by the door. She went and got it and slapped it on the nightstand next to her black calfskin Bible. She jerked the bedclothes down to his waist and tugged up Ben's nightshirt.

"What the—" He reached for the sheet, but she batted him away.

"Whatever you've got, mister, I've already seen plenty of it."

Blood had seeped through the white linen bandage. She leaned over him, reaching for the knot where the bandage ends wrapped and fastened around his middle. His chest heaved beneath her arm as he drew a ragged breath. She glanced up. He was studying her—her prayer cap and her brown Plain clothing.

"What are you?" he said. "Some sort of nun?"

"What a notion. I'm a daughter of the Plain People."

He flashed a bright smile that showed off his even white teeth. "You sure don't look plain to me. A bit starchy maybe, and undoubtedly a holy-howler. But definitely not plain."

"I don't know what you mean by holy-howler," she said. "We follow the straight-and-narrow way, working and praying together and trusting in the mercy of the good Lord to take care of us."

"And does He? Does your good Lord take care of you?"

It was a question only an outsider would ask. A Plain man was born knowing the answer. She felt no need to reply.

Silence fell between them, and his gaze went back to the window. She busied herself with the bandages while he seemed to be analyzing and cataloguing her bedroom, the way he'd done with her.

Her house was like most other Plain farms in the valley, a simple structure made of cottonwood logs and a tin roof. Three simply furnished rooms: a *Kuch,* or kitchen, and two bedrooms. No curtains on the windows, no rugs on the floors, no pictures on the walls. Just a Plain house. Doubtless it seemed some strange to him.

She had no idea how to be with him. She knew she could never manage a smile, but she thought she could try a bit of friendliness herself. He was, after all, a guest in her house.

She held her hand out to him. "It seems a bit late for a proper meeting, but I'm Rachel Yoder. Mrs. Yoder."

He lay there looking up at her with eyes so cold they burned. His thumb caressed the gun butt. And then he let go of his gun and took her hand. "You have my gratitude, ma'am. And my apology."

They remained that way for a moment, touching palm to palm; she was the one to pull away. "Your gratitude and apology are both accepted," she said. "While you're at it, do you have a name you'd care to give me? If only so's Benjo and I have a handle to put on you."

"You can call me Cain," he said finally.

She nearly gasped aloud. *And now art thou cursed from the earth, which hath opened her mouth to receive thy brother's blood from thy hand.* Surely no one could be born with such a name. He must have taken it on as some sort of cruel and bitter joke.

Cain. The name he killed under.

She knew her thoughts showed on her face. "If you don't like it," he said, "pick something else. I'll answer to most anything that ain't an insult." His mouth twisted. "Is this Benjo your husband?"

"My—" Her voice cracked, and she had to start over. "My son. My husband died last year."

He said nothing. His gaze had wandered to the window again; he seemed to have forgotten her.

"You haven't told me where you call home," she said.

"I don't call any place home."

He seemed about to say more, but he was interrupted by the rattle of wagon wheels over the log bridge. He swung his gun up.

Her heart was pounding as she stepped up to the window to see more of the road. The Weavers' spring wagon rolled into the yard with Noah's son at the reins.

She turned back to the outsider. He could barely hold up his six-shooter, it was trembling so hard in his outstretched hand. His chest jerked with his rough breathing, and fever sweat sheened his face.

She walked to him and put her hand against his chest, pressing him down into the bed. "It's only Mose," she said, "my neighbor's boy—come to chop up some wood for me."

His harsh breathing made his words come out as a gasp. "This neighbor and his boy, do they know about me?"

"The whole valley can't help but know about you by now."

"What are they saying?"

Through the window she watched Mose set the brake, tie the reins around its handle, and jump down. At seventeen he showed the promise of someday being as big and sturdy as his father.

"If they're Plain, they're saying you're a fool *Englischer* who went and got himself shot almost dead, and it's only by God's bountiful grace that you're not—dead, that is. As for what the outsiders are saying, you could probably imagine that better than I could. Now if you think you can be still, I'll tend to your hurt."

She used a pair of scissors to cut through his soiled bandage, since the knots were hopeless. Fresh blood seeped around the wound from all the jerking and jumping he'd been doing. It was solely by God's grace, surely, that this man still lived.

And then it occurred to her, with a sudden horror that almost made her heart stop, that she and Benjo weren't safe. That on taking him in, his enemies had become their enemies.

"The one who did this to you," she said, "is he going to be coming after you here?"

Nothing stirred behind his eyes. Nothing.

And then she realized the truth: He'd killed him. He had killed the man who had shot him; she had no doubt of it.

A terrible feeling came over her, a feeling she struggled to disown, for it was not the Plain way to seek redress against one's enemies. But the feeling was there, nonetheless. She felt *relief.* Relief that she and Benjo would be safe because this man had killed.

MOSES Weaver scuffed his feet along the rough boards of the Yoder front porch, scraping the sheep manure off his tooled leather high-heeled boots. He lifted his derby to slick back his pomaded hair, gave his checked trousers a hitch, and raised his arm to knock.

The door opened before his fist could fall. Mrs. Yoder gave him a slow look-over, pressing her fingers to her lips and making her eyes go round as shoe buttons. "Why, if it isn't our Mose. And don't you look flashy in those clothes."

His fist fell to his side, and his cheeks caught fire. "Uh, I've come to chop up that wood for you, ma'am."

"It sure is good of you. Especially when I know how your da has got you working over at your place."

He craned his head to see around her into the kitchen, but she shifted her weight to lean against the jamb. "So did you get those fancy new clothes of yours out of a mail-order wish book?"

"Yes, ma'am, with last summer's wool money." He stretched out his neck to see over her. He got a glimpse of a milk bucket and strainer sitting in the middle of the floor, a flour tin and a string of dried apples waiting on the table. With all the talk he'd been hearing, he almost expected to see the outsider lurking in there, wearing a black duster and armed with a pair of pearl-handled six-shooters.

Mrs. Yoder stepped across the threshold onto the porch, pulling the door half shut behind her.

Mose sure wished he could've gotten a look at those six-shooters. It was just the sort of wild tale to give the shivers to his girl, Gracie Zook. Sometimes, if he got Gracie worked up enough, she'd let him put his arms around her and hold her close.

He backed up. "I'll just be at that wood, then."

He got halfway to the chopping block before Mrs. Yoder called after him. "Mose? Why don't you knock on the door after you're done, and I'll give you some dried apple duff to take home with you."

Mose spun around, grinning broadly, and touched the curled brim of his new black derby in a cocky salute. She hadn't actually invited him inside, but maybe he could get a gander at the desperado after all. Wouldn't Gracie be impressed, although his father would likely have a conniption. Old Deacon Noah was of the mind that all a Plain boy had to do was get within hailing distance of the world outside, and he would be damned.

Mose looked back at the house, but Mrs. Yoder had gone inside. There'd been a lot of talk lately about his father and her marrying. Mose wished it would happen. He liked Mrs. Yoder a lot. She had a nice way of smiling and was always giving him food and asking him whether his coat was warm enough. He'd often imagined that if his own mother had lived, she'd be like Mrs. Yoder. His mother had died having another baby when he was only a year old. His aunt Fannie had moved in after that to keep house for him and Da, and if she'd ever spared so much as a smile for them, he sure couldn't remember it.

Mose shrugged out of his four-button cutaway. He didn't want to sweat stains into his new coat before Gracie got a look at it. She probably wouldn't recognize him in it, she was so used to seeing him in that ugly brown sack coat all the Plain boys wore.

It wasn't really against the rules for Mose to dress worldly, because he hadn't been baptized into the church yet. Once he took his vows, once he promised to walk the straight-and-narrow way—well, then he'd have to dress Plain, to grow a beard but not a mustache, and to quit parting his hair. But there was no sense in doing all that beforetime.

Mose carefully hung his new coat on the low branch of a nearby yellow pine, then laid a thick piece of cedar trunk on the chopping block. He raised the axe above his head and brought it down. The axe split the wood with a solid *whunk!* and a ring of its steel blade.

He winced as the sudden movement pulled at the bruises and welts on his back. He was still sore from the thrashing his father had given him for what he'd done in Miawa City last Saturday. He thought he was getting too big to be whipped, but the trouble was, he wasn't so big yet that he could stop his father from doing it.

Ach, vell, he did know of one way. He could renounce the evil world, marry Gracie, and settle down into the Plain life forever. If he did that, he would make things right between him and his father.

Mose felt his body settle into the rhythm of the swinging axe. Chips flew. Chopping firewood was hard work, but Mose liked it. It helped to calm some of the wild and edgy feelings that had been churning in his guts all winter.

Mose tossed a piece of the fresh-cut wood onto the stack and was reaching for another when a stone whizzed past his head.

"Hey!" he shouted, and whirled, a scowl pulling at his face.

Benjo Yoder trotted up, his herding collie loping at his heels. A braided rawhide sling dangled from the boy's left hand.

Mose pointed to the sling with his chin. "I 'spect you fancy yourself David the giant killer with that thing."

"I kuh—kuh—killed me a m-muskrat." Benjo held the animal up by its webbed hind feet, its long tail curled around its glossy fur.

"Phew!" Mose said, rearing back a step as the muskrat's powerful stink slapped him in the face. He looked the trophy over, then punched the boy lightly on the arm. "You gonna serve up that ol' muskrat for supper, Benjo Yoder?"

Benjo snorted a laugh. He hauled back and flung the wet carcass into a wild plum thicket. MacDuff barked and took off after it.

Mose hefted another piece of the cedar onto the chopping block. He wiped the wood dust off his axe blade and looked up in time to catch Benjo casting a worried glance back at the house.

"What's he like?"

The boy lifted his shoulders in an exaggerated shrug. There'd been no need for Mose to specify who *he* was. "Mem says I'm to stuh—stay away from him," Benjo said. "He's juh—juh—jumpy."

"Yeah?" Mose cocked a grin. "No more than you are, I reckon."

Benjo jutted out his chin. "I'm not scuh—scared of him."

It was on the tip of Mose's tongue to ask the boy if he intended to take on the desperado's six-shooters with his puny sling, but he held back. He didn't want to hurt him.

He bent over the chopping block again, rubbed his hands across the seat of his trousers, and wrapped them around the axe helve.

"Muh—Mose?" Benjo pursed his lips and bulged his cheeks, and the stubborn words shot out on a spray of spittle. "D-did you really go into the G-gilded Cage last Suh—Suh—Saturday and buy yourself a g-glass of the devil's b-brew?"

Mose straightened with a snap, bringing the axe with him. He flushed, glancing around guiltily. "So what if I did?"

"So d-did you drink it? The devil's brew?"

"I said I drank it, didn't I?"

Mose wedged the axe back into the chopping block.

Benjo was looking up at him in wide-eyed wonder, and Mose felt a bright glow. "How'd you know about the Gilded Cage?"

"I . . . I h-heard your da talking to Mem about it. He said you're buh—buh—breaking his heart."

Breaking his heart. Put like that, it suddenly didn't seem enough that Mose'd paid for his grand adventure with the lick of the old man's razor strop across his back.

"Wh-what does it t-taste like?" Benjo asked.

"What? The whiskey? It's like swallowing fire."

"Wh-what does it smell like?"

"Criminy!" Mose snatched up his axe. "If you don't quit pestering me, it'll be the Fourth of July before I'm done chopping this wood."

Benjo released a tiny sigh, turned, and shuffled away. Mose waited until the boy was at the house before he looked up.

He'd been so busy answering Benjo's questions that he'd let slip by the opportunity to ask a few of his own. Benjo probably knew all sorts of interesting things about the outsider, like what he was wanted for and how much lead he was packing and how many people he'd killed. Above all, Mose wanted to know exactly what sort of flashy duds the desperado had been wearing when he was shot.

CHAPTER FOUR

THAT night the outsider's fever settled into his chest. He breathed as if he were drowning. And Rachel found herself waiting to see if each strangled gasp would be his last.

She refused to let him go easily. In the early hours, while he could still swallow, she dosed him with onion syrup. She bathed his burning flesh with vinegar water. And she prayed for him.

Once, deep in the night, she thought he came awake. He struggled to sit up, and she leaned close in to him and laid her arm across his chest to calm him. His breathing was coming in such hard shocks now that she wondered how his ribs didn't crack. He'd ruptured his sutures again; the bandage shone wet-black with blood in the flickering lantern light.

She wasn't sure how long it was before she realized that his fevered body was now racked with chills. She covered him up with the sheet and quilt, and still he shuddered. Finally she crawled into the bed with him, fully clothed from her shawl to her prayer cap, to warm him with her body.

She had held only one naked man in her arms before this, and that was her husband. The memory of Ben, of holding Ben like this, tore at her, sharp and raw and nearly unbearable.

A man such as this one hanged my husband, she thought, and laughed while he was doing it. My Ben, to have died in such a way, and all because of outsiders like this man.

No, no. Those were the devil's whisperings. This outsider had done her no evil. She couldn't blame him for what had happened to Ben.

Later, during the gray hour that harbingered the dawn, while she held his chill-racked body tight to her breast, his bruised and weighted eyelids lifted a little. "Don't leave me," he rasped. And all the world's sorrow, all the world's loss, was in those blue eyes.

HE DIDN'T die that night or the night after that. Sometime during the third night Rachel fell asleep on her knees beside the bed where she had been praying. When she awoke after dawn, she was lying half across the bed, and she was holding his hand. Disoriented, she knew only that something was different. Then she realized what it was. The room was quiet. The outsider's choking gasps had subsided to the slow, even breathing of a deep sleep.

She pushed herself to her feet, aching, feeling battered. She looked down at his face. It seemed strange that a face could be so familiar to her eyes and yet not be dear to her heart.

She felt an odd affinity for this man. Not one of friendship and caring, for he was an outsider. Not even one of liking, for she didn't know him. Yet she wondered . . . No, it was more than that. It was almost a conviction: He had been sent to her for a purpose.

SHE was out on the sled feeding the sheep later that morning when she heard Benjo's scream.

Her son banged out the door of the house with MacDuff at his heels. The boy was running so hard he lost his hat, and his brogans kicked up big splatters of mud. Rachel stabbed the pitchfork into a hay bale, jumped off the sled, and took off after him.

They were nearly to the creek before she caught up with him. He looked frightened but also guilty.

"Benjo—" She had to stop and take a deep breath. "Benjo, what happened? Did the outsider hurt you? If he—"

"Nuh!" Benjo shook his head hard. "He d-didn't!"

He twisted out of her grasp and ran off, MacDuff barking at his heels, thinking it a game of chase. He'd been frightened but not hurt, and she wasn't likely to get any more out of him.

She came back and entered the house. It seemed she crossed that kitchen floor in three strides, such was her anger with the outsider. She entered the bedroom and brought herself right up to the bed. "What did you do to frighten my son?" she demanded.

"If anyone ought to be frightened, it's me. I woke up, and there he was, staring down at me, nose to nose, hacking and spouting like a geyser at me. All I did was point my finger at him." His mouth curled up slow at the edges. "Well, I might've said 'bang.' "

Rachel gripped her elbows, hugging herself to stifle a sudden chill. That had been mean, what he'd done.

His gaze held her quiet and still and frightened. "I don't like surprises, Mrs. Yoder. I thought your boy should know that."

"The trouble is, Mr. Cain, that you seem to be dealing frights out to us here quicker than we can duck."

"I want your boy to be careful of me," he said slowly, "but not scared. And I don't want you scared either."

She watched, mesmerized, as he laid his palm on her Bible.

"I swear to you, Mrs. Yoder, on this Book, that—"

"No, you mustn't do that!" She reacted without thought, covering his mouth with her fingers to stop his words. "You mustn't swear to me on the Bible like that. Oaths are serious things to be made only to God, and they are binding for life."

She had taken her fingers off his lips the instant she had touched him, but she had gotten a strange feeling inside, like a tickle. He stared at her a moment in that intense way of his, with his hand still on her Bible. Then he brought his hand back to his lap. "How about a simple promise, then?" he said. "If I tell you I'll not harm you or your boy, will you take my word on it?"

She stared at him, trying to understand. He seemed unable to imagine anyone trusting in him, because he trusted no one himself.

"If *you* believe you won't harm us," she said, "then we believe you."

RACHEL supposed, with such a day as she was having, it was inevitable that she would get a visit from Jakob Fischer.

She'd had a goodly number of visitors over the last three days, neighbors who had come calling with pots of mulligan stew or offers to do chores for her—like young Mose. And all of them, of course, harboring a hope of glimpsing her notorious houseguest.

But Jakob Fischer was the worst snoop among their people. Indeed, he'd been sticking his nose into others' affairs for so long that the Plain had started calling him Big Nose Jakob to his face.

She was putting a schnitz pie in the oven when the door cracked open and Jakob Fischer's nose came right on in, along with the rest of him. "I'm here to see this outsider you've got," he said, and without waiting to be announced he headed straight for her bedroom.

No sooner did he poke his nose around the jamb than he let out a thunderbuster bellow that shook the air. He flew out of the house, screaming at the top of his lungs, something about the devil having fangs on him that were as big and shiny as carving knives.

Rachel was still standing by the stove. She sighed, wiped her hands, and went in to see what the outsider had done now.

The man called Cain lay propped against the pillows, holding a long, flat metal tube up to his mouth. She could see where Big Nose Jakob might think he was seeing a devil with fangs, especially with the setting sun pouring fiery red light in through the window.

The whole thing suddenly struck Rachel as funny. She covered her mouth with her hand, but the laughter came out anyway.

The outsider took the metal tube out of his mouth. He gave her one of those wide-eyed looks her son got whenever she caught him smack in the middle of some mischief. "What did I do?" he said.

She looked away from him so that she would quit laughing. "I expect Jakob Fischer came here thinking to see horns on you, and he saw fangs instead. He thinks he's somebody, does Jakob."

"He isn't somebody?"

That nearly set her laughing again. "A person who's proud, shows off, and is pushy, we Plain say he 'thinks he's somebody.' "

He was studying her as if he didn't quite know what to make of her, but he seemed to be looking at her in a friendly way this time.

"Where is that from?" she asked, indicating the metal tube.

"My duster pocket."

She'd hung his duster on the opposite wall, and he could never have reached it from the bed. His strength of will was frightening.

"You shouldn't have gotten up like that," she said. Her gaze went to his gun—his *loaded* gun, she had no doubt—which lay now on the table by the bed.

He smiled at her scolding, turning the tube over in his hand.

"What is it, anyway?" she asked, curious in spite of herself.

"You've never seen a harmonica? I won it in a monte game."

She had no idea what a harmonica was. Or a monte game, for that matter, although that she could at least guess.

"I thought one wagered money at games of chance," she said.

"The fellow I was playing with ran out of money."

"It was that poor man's last possession, and you took it?"

"It would've been an insult to him not to."

She was trying to puzzle out this quirk of outsider logic when he put the tube thing in his mouth and blew on it. Out of it came a wonderful wailing noise. It raised the hair on her arms.

"Oh! It makes music!"

He lifted his shoulders in a little shrug. "It's supposed to. I only know the one tune—'Oh Susanna!'—and I ain't much good at it."

"Will you play it for me?" She was so excited, she forgot herself and smiled at him. "I should like to hear it just the once." She sat in her rocking chair, with her shoulders rolled forward and her hands tucked between her knees, full of anticipation, like a child.

"Here goes." He brought the metal tube back up to his mouth and blew on it, and that wonderful wailing filled the room.

Rachel closed her eyes and let the sound fill her. It was like the music the wind made. It shrieked to the heavens with joy. And when it ended, it trailed off with an eerie veil of sad moaning.

She breathed out a sigh. "Oh, that was such a wonderment."

She opened her eyes to find him staring at her. "I only know that one tune," he said, the words strangled and rough. "But I could teach you to play it if you'd like."

"No, you mustn't. Music played on worldly instruments, it isn't allowed in the Plain-and-narrow life. It was very wicked of me to ask you to play it in the first place, and now I must ask you never to do so again. Not in my house. It's against the rules we live by."

He considered her words a moment; then he smiled his naughty-boy smile. "And I don't suppose you'd want that fellow who goes around thinking he's somebody to catch you breaking the rules."

She shook her head, although she had to struggle hard to keep her face set serious.

He was looking down at the harmonica in his hand. He seemed to be searching for something to say to her. "What's that delicious baking smell?"

"A schnitz pie. It's made of dried apples and spices."

"It's a wonder to me where you found the time to bake a pie. Just lying in here and listening to you work through this day, going from one chore to another like you do, has got me plumb exhausted."

"Hunh. Obviously you've never been married, Mr. Cain. Otherwise you'd know that every woman's day is as busy as mine."

She'd never seen a person's face change so fast. She thought she caught a flash of something in his eyes, the echoes of a bleak sadness long ago put away; then there was nothing.

Now she was the one struggling to fill the silence. "Besides," she said, "idleness is the cause for all sorts of wickedness in this world."

The bleakness had left his face; he seemed amused with her again. "Do you never sin, Mrs. Yoder?"

She felt herself flush. "Well, I don't go out of my way to."

"I do."

"You do?" she asked, astonished.

"Uh-huh. I go far, far out of my way to sin. So far I can practically smell the hellfires burning."

He was teasing, surely. He was like Ben in that. He—

Thin wisps of black smoke trailed like ribbons through the air.

"Judas Iscariot! My pie!" she shouted, pushing so hard to her feet that the back of the rocker smacked against the wall.

As she ran from the room, she heard him laughing.

CHAPTER FIVE

THE outsider stood on Rachel Yoder's porch with one leg bent, the sole of his boot propped on the wall, and one thumb hooked in the leather cartridge belt that hung heavily from his hips. His hat cast his face in shadow, and his whole body looked relaxed and lazy.

At the sight of him on her porch Rachel's steps faltered. She was

already out of breath from chasing the ewes from the feeding paddock back into the pasture. Now, suddenly seeing him standing
there dressed and wearing his gun, she felt her heart give a hitch. She
crossed the yard toward him. At the bottom of the steps she stopped
and looked up at him. "You shouldn't be out of bed, Mr. Cain,"
Rachel said.

"Another day spent lyin' on my back countin' the knotholes in
the rafters, and I'll end up crazier than the bedbugs."

"There are no bugs in my bed!"

His eyes crinkled at the corners. "No, ma'am, that bed in there is
sure enough clean, and it's soft too. But it's lonesome, real lonesome."

She had to tangle her hands up in her apron to keep from pressing
them to her hot cheeks. *Lonesome.* It was indecent, what he'd said.

He pushed himself upright. He was taller than she'd thought.
Taller and with a look of elegance, with his fine gabardine trousers
tucked into glossy black leather boots, his black Stetson hat and
bottle-green vest and . . . Ben's shirt. He was wearing Ben's shirt.

He noticed what she was looking at. "I helped myself to one of
your husband's shirts. If it hurts you to see me in it . . ."

She shook her head. "No, no. As if such a thing would matter. It
was stained and torn beyond salvation—your own shirt, I mean."
His shirt had little tucks and pearled buttons set in the bosom, and
a choker collar. The shirt he had on now was collarless and button-
less and tuckless. "I'm afraid you'll have to dress partly Plain for the
time being, Mr. Cain."

"I'm not sure as how my reputation can stand that," he said.

She felt a smile pull at her mouth and fought it back.

He turned, a bit unsteady. "Would it inconvenience you if I
brought a chair out here? I thought to take a little sun, but I don't
reckon after all that I can do it on my feet."

Earlier this morning, when she'd changed the dressing, his wound
had still looked angry and sore. And after all, he'd been two weeks
in bed, consumed with fever a good part of the time. She wasn't surprised he was feeling unsteady.

"You shouldn't be up at all," she said. Yet even as she was
protesting, she was passing through the open door into her kitchen,

fetching one of her spindle chairs for him. She thought if he was going to be inflicting his disturbing presence on the world, she'd rather have him doing it out here than in her house.

As she came back out onto the porch, he took the chair from her hands and put it flush up against the wall. He lurched again when he went to sit in it, so that she had to help him, and for a moment they were side by side, her arm around his waist. But then he was in the chair, and she had taken a step back from him. He looked so worldly sitting there, so different from what she was used to.

RACHEL'S skirts swayed as she whipped the lather brush around the shaving mug, working up a thick foam. From his position in the chair the outsider was casting a concerned look up at the whirling white bristles. "Are you riled at me, Mrs. Yoder?"

Rachel whipped the lather brush even harder. "Ought I to be?"

"Heck, I don't know. A man never knows. And now that I've thought some more on your kind offer to give me a shave . . ." He stretched out his neck and rubbed his hand over his scruffy beard. "Well, the regrettable fact is, ma'am, that in my experience it ain't wise to allow a riled woman to get paired up with anything sharp."

Rachel wrung out a huck towel she'd had soaking in a basin of steaming water. "But the more regrettable fact—regrettable to you, of course—is that riled or not, I am already paired"—she unrolled the towel with a snap of her wrists—"up with a warranted Perfection razor that is sharp enough to split the hair on a frog."

With that, she slapped the hot cloth down over his face, smothering his startled yelp.

This morning she'd noticed how the outsider kept scratching at the sprouting hair on his face. The next thing she knew she'd been offering to scrape it off for him. She'd figured that even if she loaned him her husband's shaving things, with his right arm bound up the way it was, he'd never manage them on his own.

His gaze was riveted to her as she removed the towel and began to brush the lather over his thick dark beard. The soap smelled of spring laurel, and steam floated through the air, warm and moist. She waited until his eyes had drifted closed before she said, "I reckon when I see the blood start to spurt a geyser, I'll know I've scraped off too much."

His eyes flew open wide, and Rachel laughed. Once started, she couldn't stop. It felt so good. She hadn't laughed like this since Ben died.

When her laughter quieted, she looked at him. He was trying to act insulted, but his mouth gave him away. "Done making a fool of me?"

She nodded solemnly.

"Hold that razor, then. I want to know if your hand shakes."

She picked up the razor, deliberately jiggling her hand so that the blade flashed in the sun. It made her laugh again, and him as well. But the quiet that followed brought an uneasiness with it, as if they both were wary of the intimacy their laughter had stirred.

The razor made a soft snicking sound as it cut through his beard. She enjoyed watching the lean ridges and smooth skin of his face become bared by the blade. She had forgotten how young she'd first thought him. But there were hard edges to him, a toughness, that made him seem older, as if he'd been through more of life than his face could ever show.

She leaned closer to him to get at the whiskers along the far line of his jaw, and her belly pressed against his shoulder. She jerked back, her startled gaze on his face. But his eyes were focused not on her, but on something beyond. Or perhaps something within.

He fascinated her. There were so many things she wondered about him—the loneliness and the restlessness and the sin.

She washed off his face with a clean hot towel. "There you are, Mr. Cain," she said. "No, wait." She leaned over him, using a corner of the towel to wipe a last bit of foamy soap off his earlobe.

He reached up and gave one of her prayer cap strings a little tug. "Why do you wear this thing all the time?"

"We've always done so. It's part of the *Attnung,* the rules of living. The Bible says, 'For if the woman be not covered, let her also be shorn.' So we wear our prayer caps during the day."

"You ever seen a prairie fire?" the outsider asked. "The way the flames light up the clouds from underneath, turning them all scarlet and wine red? I opened my eyes that first night I was here, lying

in your bed, and I thought I was looking at a firelit cloud. I thought it was a dream, but it was you. Only, your hair was down. Why should God or any man breathing want to hide something so pretty?"

She felt a little flutter of pleasure in her chest from what he'd said. "Listen to you talk," she said. "I suspect the devil used such blather on Eve to persuade her to taste of the forbidden fruit."

"Yeah, I 'spect he did." His mouth curved into an unholy smile. "But I also reckon she liked the taste so much, the ol' devil didn't have to do any persuading at all to get her to take a second bite."

RACHEL sat on the porch steps, her arms wrapped around her bent legs, her head tilted back. The sun was a pulsing red ball behind her closed eyelids. The wind had the barest thread of warmth to it. It smelled of the thawing earth, of spring.

She stretched her legs out flat, leaned back on her elbows, and turned to look at the outsider. The man sat with his long legs sprawled over the warped boards of her porch. He sat so still she thought about getting up and going over to him to see if he was breathing.

She ought to get up in any case. She had bread to bake, clothes to wash. It was slothful just to be sitting there.

Benjo would be done with school soon too, and she wasn't sure she wanted the outsider on the porch when her son came home. Ever since he'd been scared off with the "bang," Benjo had stayed clear of the man. Rachel felt easier inside herself because of it, although she wasn't quite sure why anymore. She wanted to believe the outsider's promise that he would bring them no harm.

"A day like this is so *good,* don't you find it so, Mr. Cain? It makes you want to thank God for giving you the life to enjoy it."

Her words fell into an empty silence. She turned and saw his eyes lift quickly to the mountains, as if he didn't want to be caught looking at her. Something cold seemed to shiver across his face. She had a notion he'd just seen something or thought something that hurt him terribly. She wanted to go to him and touch him, lay her hand against his cheek. Instead she gripped her knees tighter.

"What made y'all settle away out here anyway?" he said, a strange roughness in his voice.

"The Lord." She drew out the words slowly. "We began as a larger community of Plain People that farmed the Sugarcreek Valley in Ohio. But there was a division of thought among the members. Some of us felt that the others were becoming tainted by the world—taking up modern things and doing prideful things, like posing for photographs and wearing buttons and suspenders. Why, some men even took to wearing neckcloths!"

He made a snorting sound. "Heaven forfend. I've known many a man to be led down the merry path of sin by his neckcloth."

"You ought not to laugh at things you don't understand."

His face sobered, but she sensed he was still laughing inside.

"Well," she went on, a bit tentatively, "what happened was, my *Vater,* my father, had a powerful awakening. Da saw this very valley in a dream, and he led us here to Montana. Those of us who were determined to follow the straight-and-narrow way. And during our first worship service, when the lottery chose my *Vater* to be our bishop, we knew it was a sign from God that his awakening had guided us true. But then the land turned out to be too dry for farming."

"This country's too high to grow much of anything but hay."

His comment surprised her. "Are you a farmer, Mr. Cain?"

"Oh, no. Never again as long as I draw breath."

She tried to imagine him standing spread-legged on a sled, forking hay over the wriggling backs of a bunch of hungry ewes. But the image that came to her mind was of Ben.

"It was Ben's, my husband's, idea to try sheep. Even though the Bible speaks often of shepherding and of Adam's son Abel being a keeper of sheep—still, it took my *Vater,* as bishop and leader of our church, many days of prayer to come around to the idea. To put up the plow and raise sheep instead wasn't a thing to be done lightly."

"It don't sound like he bends much, your old man."

"It isn't our way to bend. There is one Plain way of doing things and no other. Ben, though, he had a way of looking at things from the other side."

A sadness welled up inside her. She swallowed and drew in a

breath, and in the next instant scalding tears pushed against her eyes.

"You miss him." He said the words simply, his voice low and flat. But then he said in a gentle voice, "How did he die?"

Her hands made a fist. She'd never spoken aloud of the hanging; not with her *Vater* or Mem, not with any of her brothers. Not even with Noah.

"The outsiders hanged my husband for a cattle thief."

She looked at him, daring him to say he was sorry. Instead he said, "Was he?"

"Ben would sooner cut off his hands than allow them to take up a thing that wasn't his!"

Her words had come out harsh, but it was an old and festering anger that she felt. "The outsiders in this valley, most of them don't like us much, because our ways are different and we keep ourselves apart. Mostly they never do us any real hurt. Except there's this cattleman, a Scotsman by the name of Fergus Hunter. He owns a big spread on the other side of those hills over yonder."

She looked hard at the rock- and pine-studded buttes, as if she could see through them to the big white house with its gables and spool-railed galleries, to the acres of corrals and miles of fences, to the thousands of cattle that needed so much land to roam in.

"At one time this whole valley was all open range, and Mr. Hunter got used to grazing his herds wherever he pleased. He got to be what the newspapers call a cattle baron. He got so puffed up he even allowed some folk to call him that, to call him Baron. And he sure didn't like us Plain People coming here to homestead on what he'd come to think of as his land. He liked it even less when we started raising sheep. A year or so ago he went and made up this boundary to go down the middle of the valley, like some sort of line on a map. He called it a deadline and said to us, 'If you cross it, bring your coffin along.'"

The outsider made a small sighing sound, as if he'd heard this story before. "But you didn't believe him."

"Oh, we believed him. But we were not leaving here, no matter how many lines Mr. Hunter drew. We can't always avoid suffering for our faith in a hostile, sinful world."

" 'Yea, for thy sake are we killed all the day long; we are counted as sheep for the slaughter.' "

"Why, you know the Bible, Mr. Cain!" she exclaimed.

The outsider was gazing on the far mountains again, and his face had taken on his flat look. "A man can come to know the smell of a sweet-grass meadow," he said. "He can know the feel of a prime horse between his legs and the taste of a beautiful woman. He can come to know them without ever once understanding them."

She felt deflated. There was surely no knowing or understanding *him*. She thought that he probably really didn't care much at all about how a Plain sheep farmer came to die. But she wasn't going to betray Ben by leaving his story unfinished.

"About the time Mr. Hunter marked off those deadlines, he hired on this man he said was a stock inspector. He said his calves were disappearing quicker than he could slap a brand on them, and this inspector, he was to put a stop to it." She tried for a scornful laugh, but what came out was a strangled sound. "Maybe that inspector should've had a talk with those Hunter cows, because they were always wandering uninvited onto our hay meadows. One morning last spring Ben rounded them up to drive them back home."

It was her last memory of him, sitting astride their old draft horse, yipping and waving a lariat at the milling cattle that were churning up the mud in their yard.

"He was always quick to anger, was Ben, and just as quick to get over it. I suppose he did leave here that morning with the intention of giving Mr. Hunter a piece of his mind." She looked at the ragged pine-studded buttes that shielded the Hunter ranch. "They hanged him for rustling those silly strays."

"And may God be with him," the outsider said, so softly she wondered if it was more his thought than his voice she'd heard.

She nodded. "You know what Mr. Hunter said? That he was sorry. *Sorry.* He came with the sheriff out to the farm. First the sheriff explained how the mistake had happened, how a man's got a right to try and protect his cows if he thinks they're being rustled. Then Mr. Hunter said it was a terrible tragedy and how sorry he was for it."

"You don't sound like you believe much of his apology."

"Death is a hurtful thing," she said to the outsider and to herself, "but only to those left behind. The Bible says that the Lord giveth and the Lord taketh, and in our sorrow it's so easy to dwell only on the taking part. But He does give us so much. He gives a day like this one that is so pretty and full of the promise of spring. He gave me the years I had with Ben, and He gave me our son."

"I'll kill them for you if you want."

"What?" She turned sharply to look at him.

His voice was as cold as winter earth. "I'll kill this Mr. Hunter and his so-called stock inspector who hanged your husband."

She lurched to her feet, almost falling over the steps, so that she had to grab at the railing. "Don't you say these terrible things! Killing is never justified. Vengeance belongs only to the Lord."

He followed her with his empty blue gaze. "It was just an offer, because I figure I owe you for taking me in and tending to me like you've done. If you change your mind—"

"I won't." Just then the wind kicked up hard, with no hint of spring at all. She wrapped her arms around herself, shuddering. "I won't," she said again.

CHAPTER SIX

THE iron hissed as it glided over the dampened cambric cap, leaving behind a knife-sharp pleat and the smell of hot starch.

Rachel returned the iron to the hob on the cookstove. She carefully lifted the freshly pressed cap off the ironing board and carried it to the kitchen table, where three others exactly like it sat in a row, like roosting white hens.

She glanced through the open door. The morning breeze brought the mulchy smell of wet earth into the kitchen to mix with the smells of starch and hot metal. From where she stood Rachel could just see one of the outsider's glossy black boots. He'd been sitting out on the porch all day, his back to the wall. She knew that beneath his hat those restless eyes watched the road, as though waiting for someone fool enough to ride down it, so he could shoot the poor fellow dead.

I'll kill them for you if you want.

When you wanted to chase away the darkness of night, she thought, you lit a lantern. Jesus had instructed Paul "to open their eyes, and to turn them from darkness to light, and from the power of Satan unto God." She would show the outsider the light.

She smoothed down her apron and went out onto the porch. "What we spoke of earlier today, Mr. Cain . . ."

He pushed his hat back and looked up at her. "I remember having the conversation, Mrs. Yoder. Though I suspect you're now hell-bent on making me live to regret it."

"But it's about living and being hell-bent that I wish to speak more. Living, and then dying in God's own time and being held to account for our sins. What Mr. Hunter did he must answer for, but he will do his answering only to God. As will we all."

"Yeah, well, I don't figure it's Him who's going to be doing the calling and settling up the accounts when my time comes around."

"But there's where you are all wrong in your thinking. It's by living a Christian life that a soul can be cleansed and saved. And part of living a Christian life is understanding that we must love those that hate us and not take revenge on our enemies."

The outsider sighed. Loudly. "In the first instance, the enemy we're speaking of here ain't my enemy. He's yours. In the second instance, I told you I'd be the one doing the taking."

"You would take the life of a man you don't even know?"

"I do it all the time."

His words shocked her. "You're not to do it to Mr. Hunter."

He shrugged. "I offered, and you said no, thank you. So long as the man don't take a notion to come after me, I'm easy."

She turned her back on him and went into the kitchen.

RACHEL slammed the rolling pin onto the ball of dough. She pushed hard, and the dough flattened. She pulled and pushed the wooden pin with such vigor that flour floated around in a white cloud. She stopped pushing, stood in stillness a moment, then dusted her hands off on her apron and marched out onto the porch.

"The Bible teaches us, Mr. Cain, that 'whosoever shall smite thee on thy right cheek, turn to him the other also.'"

The face he turned up to her wore a polite expression, but his eyes were hooded. "I heard them Scriptures you keep throwing up at me read plenty when I was a boy. Seems like I remember Jesus Christ himself doing a lot of talking about loving your enemies. But on a day when *his* enemies were feeling particularly mean, He wound up getting crowned with thorns and hung up to die on a cross. That, lady, is what comes of turning the other cheek."

She flinched. "Jesus died so that we might be saved."

"Yeah? So what did your man die for?"

She spun around, but his hand shot out, grabbing her arm. "Don't run off again. I'll quit doing it. I promise."

"I'm not running off; I've biscuits baking— Quit doing what?"

"What I been doing to you. Like using a spur on a bronco, trying to make it buck so's you can break it."

"You've been . . . and here I thought I was . . ." Laughter burst out of her, surprising her before she could stop it and surprising him, so that he dropped her arm. They'd been hurling words back and forth at each other, she thought, like children. But they were too wide apart in their beliefs to ever really hit each other.

She saw now that it wasn't the outsider she'd been trying to lead out of the darkness; it was herself. Because that burning emptiness inside her had allowed a terrible thought to take root, the devil's weed of vengeance. But she had sought the light and found it, and the weed had shriveled and died before its awesome power.

She laughed again, feeling light-headed and lighthearted. "You will never be able to break my faith, Mr. Cain," she said. "Certainly not with something as insignificant as a pair of spurs."

NOAH Weaver heard her laughing.

He was slogging through the cluster of yellow pines and tamaracks that separated his farm from hers. He walked slowly, deliberately, through the soggy pine straw and melting snow. The sound of her laughter startled him so that he jerked to a stop.

She was leaning back against the porch railing. Her skirts slatted in the wind; her cap strings danced. She was talking with the outsider. Laughing with him. But Noah barely spared a glance for the man. His gaze stayed on Rachel.

So many times over the years Noah had watched Rachel like this—from afar. Coming to the Yoders' for a word with Ben about the shearing or the haying, when it was really her he'd come to see.

Watching the way her lower lip would puff out when she blew a sigh up her face if she was tired. The way her back would bow, supple as a willow tree, when she bent to pour him more coffee.

He approached her slowly now, prolonging the moment when it would seem that she was his alone. The outsider must have seen him, made some telltale movement, for she suddenly jerked upright and whirled.

"Noah!" she exclaimed. Her face was bright with happiness as he came up to her. "How nice of you to come calling. Mr. Cain, this is my good neighbor and my particular friend, Noah Weaver."

Noah allowed his gaze to settle on the outsider. The man looked up at him through half-closed eyes that were a pale, cold blue, then lifted his hand and laid it on his thigh. Noah realized that he'd had that hand resting on the handle of the devil's tool he wore strapped around his waist. Had probably had it there from the moment Noah walked out from behind the barn.

"Good afternoon to you, sir," the outsider said. "And how d' you do." He had a slight drawl, from Texas maybe, Noah thought.

"Myself, I'm doing fine, Mr. Outsider. As for yourself, I'd say you were fortunate in where you chose to get yourself shot."

The outsider's mouth curled into an easy smile. "Ah, but fortune is a two-faced wench." He cast a look over at Rachel, and his smile changed. "All because Mrs. Yoder went and saved my life, now I gotta be polite and let her take a crack at my black soul."

And in that moment Noah sensed something flash between the two of them, between the outsider and his Rachel.

"Whereas if it'd been your farm I'd've stumbled across, why, I suspect you'd have just let me go straight on to hell."

Noah could hear the edge in the man's voice.

He tried to clear the gritty feeling out of his throat. "None of us knows if he is saved till he gets over yonder, so we don't worry ourselves about the salvation of others, Mr. Outsider. We leave that to God. And we don't accept converts into our church."

Rachel made a funny little jerking movement. "Oh, honestly, Noah—as if he should even want to. Mr. Cain is only joking."

Noah didn't like this conversation. He felt left out of it, horrified by it. His gaze roamed over the yard, the barn, the hayfields as he struggled for something to say. "Your ewes will be dropping soon."

Rachel looked over to the paddock where her sheep munched on scattered hay. "No. Not for a while yet, I should think," she said.

Noah felt a flash of irritation with her. He knew she was right, but a woman shouldn't contradict her man in front of another.

Rachel had turned back to the outsider and tucked in her chin to hide a smile in that way she had when she was teasing. "But if they do start dropping while you're still here, Mr. Cain, we'll see if we can't make a lamb licker out of you."

"Lady, I sure do hope that ain't what it sounds like."

"Oh, it's much worse." To Noah's utter shock she laughed again.

He wondered where she'd come from, this Rachel he didn't know. How often had he preached about how a boisterous laugh and a quick retort betrayed a cocky spirit, the kind that God despised? He wondered now if Rachel had ever really listened.

He cast a glowering look at the outsider. "Now that he's up and about, I reckon he'll be moving on directly."

"Mr. Cain is hardly cured enough to straddle a horse yet."

"He can walk. That's how he came; that's how he can go."

Stormy eyes flashed at him. "Noah!"

That same easy smile pulled at the outsider's mouth. "I fear, ma'am, that your good neighbor and particular friend don't have much use for a disreputable rogue like me."

Rachel almost laughed again.

Noah looked from her back to the outsider, and hatred roiled like a storm in his belly. He was astonished by it and ashamed. He backed up, shaking his head. "I've a buckboard wheel at home that needs hooping," he said.

"Noah?" Rachel called after him, but he pretended not to hear.

MOSES WEAVER STOOD NAKED on a shelf of rock. He looked six feet down into the still water. The wind was warm on his bare skin, but he knew Blackie's Pond would be freezing, and he shivered.

He took a deep breath and dove. The cold seemed to suck the air right out of his lungs as the water closed over him. He thrust his legs hard and shot back to the surface.

Judas, it was cold. He forced himself to swim two turns around the pond, and then pulled himself out.

Shivering, he lay down on a bed of marsh grass, stretching flat out on his belly. He breathed in the loamy smell of damp earth. It was a luscious feeling just to lie there and do nothing, although he knew he'd pay for it later, once his father got a look at how that busted paddock gate he was supposed to have been fixing this afternoon was still busted.

Mose closed his eyes and felt himself drift along.

The willow brakes crackled behind him. Mose looked up, and his heart did a flip-flop in his chest. A girl stood among the rocks and willows and wild plum trees. She was dressed all in frothy white and wore a big plaited straw hat, with a white satin ribbon tied in a bow beneath her chin. Over one shoulder she carried a white lace parasol that seemed to be twirling like a carriage wheel in the wind.

Mose scrambled frantically for his clothes. He found his shirt and held it in a crumpled ball in front of his privates.

The girl was laughing at him. "You want I should turn my back?"

"Huh?"

"I'll turn my back so's you can put your trousers on. Then maybe you'll quit flushin' all the colors of berries in summer."

She did as promised, swinging around with a rustle of silky skirts. He stared at her, mesmerized. Her dress cascaded over her hips, like a lacy waterfall. And she had the tiniest waist he'd ever seen. He could have spanned it with his hands.

"I've never known anyone to get dressed so quiet. Did you fall asleep or somethin'?"

Mose came to himself with a start. He didn't bother with his longhandles but went right for his trousers. While he was pulling his shirt on, the yoke caught on his ear, and he nearly poked out his eye getting it loose. His suspenders had gotten twisted, so he left them to dangle at his hips. He stabbed his arms into his coat.

The parasol dipped, and a straw hat brim peeked around the lacy scallops. "You decent now?"

Mose swallowed hard. "Uh, *ja*. Yes, miss. Sorry, miss."

She turned with another rustle of silk and walked up to him.

She flashed a bright smile. "I wouldn't mind restin' here a spell with you," she said, "but I don't want to get stains on my dress. Do you think I could trouble you, sir, for the use of your coat?"

He almost ripped his coat in his haste to get it off. He spread his precious new four-button cutaway out on the wet grass for her. She settled onto it with a sigh and a waft of honeysuckle toilet water, tossing a thick ringlet of hair back over her shoulder. It was pale yellow, her hair, the color of wheat ripening.

"This is a nice spot, this pond," she said. "I come here in the summer sometimes for picnics. But mostly I just come to be alone when I'm feelin' blue. Sometimes I go for walks out over the prairie too. I enjoy them." She tilted her head back to look up at him, and she smiled again. "Do you ever go for prairie walks?"

"Yes, miss." He supposed herding a bunch of woolly monsters from one pasture to another might constitute a prairie walk.

Her bosom rose and fell with another sigh. "It sure is warm as summer out here today, though, ain't it?"

"Yes, miss."

Mose felt foolish, standing there bobbing his head like a windup toy and doing nothing. As he squatted down next to her, his knee joints popped like firecrackers. He flushed.

She smiled at him again. "So what do they call you, boy?"

"Uh, Mose. Moses Weaver."

She held her hand out. "I'm Marilee. That's my real name. I'm not like them other girls, puttin' on airs with their made-up names."

He wiped his sweating hand on his pant leg and took her fingers. "Pleased to be making your acquaintance, Miss Marilee."

He thought she was the prettiest thing he'd ever seen. She had high, wide cheekbones and a dainty pointed chin that gave her face a sweet heart shape. Her lips were very red. He wondered if she painted them. Fast girls, he'd heard, always painted their lips. Her skin was like freshly skimmed cream. He could see a lot of her skin.

"D-do you work at the, uh, Gilded Cage?" he asked.

"Lord, I should hope to never sink so low!" she exclaimed. She tossed her head. "I'm an upstairs boarder at the Red House."

Mose knew about the Red House. It sat on the very edge of Miawa City, between the creek and the cemetery. The house wasn't really red, of course. It was only called the Red House because of the red locomotive lantern that hung outside the front door most nights.

Mose had engaged in a lot of speculation with the other Plain boys about what went on behind that door.

She was giving him a careful look-over. "You're a Plain boy, aren't you? Your hair's been barbered, and you got on real clothes, but you're one of them Plain boys, sure enough."

Mose could feel another flush burning his cheeks. He felt shame for being Plain and an awful guilt over that feeling. "I've not joined the church yet," he mumbled. "Maybe I'll choose not to."

The girl lifted her shoulders in a little shrug that caused the big sausage curls of her hair to slide over her shoulder. "At least you got a choice. Most of us don't ever get many choices." She stood and shook out her skirts. "Lordy, it's gettin' late," she said. "I'd better be makin' tracks for home." She bent over and retrieved her parasol, unfurling it with a snap of lace and fringe.

Mose stumbled to his feet as she turned to him with another of those smiles. "Thank you, Mr. Moses Weaver, for the use of your coat." She gave him a pat on the cheek. "You're a sweet one."

Her skirts rustled and whispered as she walked back through the rocks and willow brakes, back where she had come from.

"Hey, wait!" Mose cried out. He followed after her.

He caught up with her at the road, which was really nothing more than wagon ruts cut through the prairie grass. She'd driven a smart little black shay out to the pond. It had green wheels and fringed cushions and was hitched up to a saucy-looking bay.

She had paused to look down the unfolding ribbon of wheel tracks toward the west. "It'll be turning cool again before I make it back," she said. "Would you help me to put the bonnet up?"

"Sure thing!" he exclaimed, then winced at his loud voice.

As he unfolded and fastened down the bonnet, he tried out in his head what he wanted to say to her, but everything he came up with sounded stupid. His mouth had suddenly gone dry.

"Might I pay a call on you, Miss Marilee?" he finally blurted.

He'd turned as he spoke, not realizing she was right on top of him, and they bumped into each other. He grasped her shoulders to steady her. She was looking up at him, her face serious.

"You got nice eyes," she said. "They're such a dark, deep brown. Like coffee beans. They're nice. Nice and sweet-looking."

"You got pretty eyes too." He tried to think of a way to describe them. Blue as the sky, blue as a bluebell, blue as . . .

But she was already slipping away and climbing into the shay.

She gathered up the reins and looked down at him. "You can pay a call on me if you want, Mr. Moses Weaver," she said. "But if you do, you take a bath first, you hear? I ain't puttin' up with the stink of sheep."

He watched the back of the shay sway and dip along the ruts until it was swallowed up by the rolling grassland.

He brought the skirt of his flashy four-button cutaway coat up to his nose and sniffed. He smelled of sheep, all right.

CHAPTER SEVEN

BENJO swiped a smear of apple butter off his mouth with his shirt cuff and stretched his hand across the table for another hoecake. But his mother got to the tin first, snatching it out of his reach.

"You clean your plate of those pickled beets first, Joseph Benjamin Yoder," she said. "Then you ask, politely, for someone to pass you more hoecakes. And use your napkin, not your sleeve."

"Yes'm," Benjo mumbled to his plate, which had a little bit of sowbelly beans on it and a lot of pickled beets.

The kitchen fell back into silence, but for the occasional clink of a tin fork on a tin plate and the tick of the tin-cased clock.

Another two days had passed since the outsider first tested his constitution by getting out of bed and taking the sun on Rachel's porch. But this was the first time the three of them had sat down at the table to take a meal together.

Meals were usually times of prayer and quiet contemplation in the Plain life, which seemed to suit the outsider just fine. Thus far Benjo, too, had kept quiet. But he'd been watching the outsider with such wide eyes that Rachel could practically see behind them to the questions working their way from his head to his tongue.

Just then Benjo drew in a deep, noisy breath, and Rachel held hers. A question from Benjo could know no bounds. Still, she nearly gasped aloud when it finally stuttered out.

"H-how many people have you shuh—shot dead, mister?"

The outsider slowly turned his head and looked at the boy as if he wondered where he'd sprung from. He laid his fork down gently. "Enough to make trouble for myself in this life," he said.

"Is th-that what they luh—locked you up in jail for?" Benjo asked, and Rachel dropped the hoecake she was eating into her lap.

He had stolen only that one look at the outsider all the time the man had been lying in her bed, so she couldn't imagine how her son could know Mr. Cain bore the marks of prison. Maybe the rumor of it had just gotten carried along through the valley on the wind.

The outsider was staring at Benjo from beneath heavy-lidded eyes. He pulled at his lower lip. "Let's see, I think maybe it was 'cause I didn't eat all my pickled beets like my ma told me to."

Benjo shot a wary look at his mother, then stabbed his fork into a beet. He shoved the beet into his mouth, chewed, swallowed.

"I th-think it was 'cause you kuh—killed a man. Wh-what did he do to m-make you kuh—kill him?"

"I reckon he might've asked me one question too many."

Benjo's jaw sagged open, and his face flooded red. His gaze dropped to his plate. He stabbed at another beet.

Rachel hid a smile. The man sure did like to tease.

"You done your evening chores yet, Joseph Benjamin?" she said.

"No'm. B-but—"

"But get to it."

He heaved a loud sigh, then scraped back his chair, grabbed his hat and coat, and banged through the door, chin hanging low.

No sooner was he gone than Rachel wanted him back. Maybe, with all his pesky questions, Benjo could have pried some answers out of the outsider. His broken life fascinated her. She had been watching him closely, collecting thoughts and observations like quilt pieces, but she hadn't been able to make a pattern with them as yet.

This much she thought she knew about him: His life had left a taint on him, wounds and scars that went beyond the ones on his flesh. Yet there was laughter in him and unexpected wells of gentleness. He had no home, no family, and this more than anything struck her heart with pity for him. Family, friends, a home—those were what gave life meaning and joy.

Ach, the way he was sitting there now, with his back to the wall and his eyes flitting every so often to the door, waiting, watchful, careful. She wondered how he could live with such intensity.

Rachel's chair made a loud grating noise in the quiet room as she pushed away from the table. She picked up her plate and Benjo's. On the way to the slopstone she paused opposite the outsider's place. There were, she saw, a goodly number of pickled beets still left on his own plate.

"I reckon, Mr. Cain," she said, "that you'd better finish off those beets of yours. Otherwise I just might have to send for the sheriff."

He looked down at his plate. "But, ma'am, what I really had my heart set on was some more of your deeelicious hoecakes."

She set down the plates and snatched up the tin of hoecakes, dancing just out of his reach. "Oh, no, you don't. You can't sweet-talk me into breaking the rules just for—"

He exploded out of his seat, startling her so that she skidded backward. She pressed her fist to her pounding chest and stared at him wide-eyed. He had his gun in his hand. "What—" she began, and then from the yard she heard a horse's whinny.

"See who it is." He said it calmly, but his eyes were feral.

Rachel quaked as she went to the window.

She stared through the glass. A burly man in a mud-splattered duster and a sweat-stained brown Stetson was swinging out of the saddle and making to tie an apron-faced roan to the paddock gate.

"You know him." His words were an accusation.

"It's Sheriff Getts," she admitted. She jerked around to face him, suddenly afraid of what he would think. "I didn't send for him. Truly I did not!"

He shifted his weight, and his thumb cocked the hammer of his gun. The noise seemed obscenely loud in the quiet of her kitchen.

"Don't kill him," she said. "Promise me you won't kill him here, before me and my son."

He snapped his head around to impale her with his cold, cold eyes. And then he touched her face, tracing the curve of her jaw and brushing his fingertips over her mouth. "I won't kill him here, lady, and not at all if I can help it."

She backed away from him. "I'll go see what he . . . what the sheriff wants, then," she said. And she ran for the door.

Crossing the yard, she wanted to run and keep on running over the prairie and beyond the jagged mountains to the very ends of the earth. And even then, she knew, she wouldn't be safe from what she had already allowed this man to do to her.

She kept feeling the brush of his fingers on her lips. She wanted to rub her mouth with her hand, to make the feeling go away.

The sheriff touched the curled brim of his hat, all politeness even now, as she came up alongside him. "Evenin', ma'am," he said.

He was a man long past the prime of his life, with tired blue eyes and seamed, weather-glazed skin. His gray mustache hung down over the corners of his mouth, and his belly hung over the waistband of his black britches. "Did he tell you who he is?"

Rachel tried to calm her face, to make it look innocent, before she met the lawman's eyes. "He said his name is Cain. Isn't it?"

He nodded slowly, sucking on one end of his tobacco-stained mustache. "Johnny Cain. He's a shootist by occupation, a man-killer. His purpose—some might even say his joy—is in killin'."

His joy is in killing. This was the piece of the outsider she'd known about all along and hadn't wanted to see, couldn't bear to see. It wouldn't fit into the pattern she wanted to make of him.

"Have you come to take him back to prison?"

"Nope. He ain't wanted anywheres at the moment. I checked. I do need to have a li'l chat with him, though."

He started across the yard toward the house, his boots squelching in the mud. Rachel had to hurry to catch up with him.

Inside, the outsider sat within the kitchen's shadows, his back to the wall. His Colt lay on the table in front of him, his left hand resting lightly on the grip.

"You promised to put away your gun," Rachel said.

"Now I doubt Johnny Cain ever made such a promise. He's only bein' cautious, ain't you, boy? He knows a tin badge ain't no guarantee I won't build up my own rep by takin' on his."

The sheriff had kept the bulk of his body shielded by the door. He stepped fully inside now, though he held his hands spread out at his sides. "Now what I'm fixin' to do," he said, "is hang up my gun belt on that there wall hook, along with my hat, and then I'm gonna pull a chair up to Mrs. Yoder's table here."

Rachel glanced at the outsider. His eyes rested solely on the sheriff, and his face wore a puzzled look, as if an innocent such as himself couldn't imagine what a lawman could have to say to him.

The sheriff scraped a chair up to the table and collapsed into it with a heavy sigh. "There's three dead bodies I need to account for up on Tobacco Reef. I figure you can help me do that."

"I'm always willing to oblige the law," said Johnny Cain with a smile that held no warmth.

The sheriff grinned. "That's fine, real fine." With slow, deliberate movements he fetched a briar pipe and a buckskin bag of loose tobacco out of the pocket of his muddy duster. He said nothing more until he had the pipe smoking.

He settled his thick shoulders into the chair, puffed, and studied the man across the table from him, staring intently as though assessing the broken arm and the careful way he sat to accommodate the bullet hole in his side. "Now this is what I figure happened up on that butte. It has its genesis, so to speak, with these three brothers name of Calder who ranched with their pappy up east of here. Them boys was down in Rainbow Springs a week or so back, where they spotted you in that high-stakes monte game. They got took with the stupid notion that their braggin' rights would sure be enhanced considerable if they could be the death of Johnny Cain."

Rachel shot a startled look at the outsider, but he only watched the lawman with his flat eyes.

She had taken herself as far away from the two men as she could, perching on the woodbox next to the cookstove, cradling a bowl of beans in her lap to be picked over before soaking. But though her fingers sifted through the beans, her whole awareness was held by what was being spoken of at the table.

The sheriff inflated his cheeks and blew the air out in a gusty sigh. "Now I ain't gonna speculate on how they knew just where you was headed and when you'd be passin' on through. Suffice it to say them three boys waited for you up in the rocks of Tobacco Reef. Maybe you saw the sun flashin' off of a rifle barrel, or maybe you just *knew* they was there, like your kind always knows."

Johnny Cain sat silent and motionless except for his hand, which stroked the grip of his gun once and then went still.

"However it was," the lawman went on, "you'd already turned and was firin' by the time they got off their shots. Which accounts for Rafe Calder windin' up dead in the rocks."

Johnny Cain didn't so much as flicker an eyelash.

"Now, you might not know this," the sheriff said, "but them Calder boys had a rep for being crack shots. So if they had long enough to take aim at you, they was bound to hit you. Which they did, huh?" He looked the outsider over again slowly. "One got you and another got your horse. Your horse went down, prob'ly rolled on you, which is prob'ly how your arm got busted."

He leaned back, and his fingers began to toy with his tarnished watch fob. But Rachel noticed that the outsider never once looked at the man's hands or anywhere other than into his washed-out eyes.

The lawman's spiky gray eyebrows drew together. "This is where it starts to get tricky, but this is how I'm picturin' it. You lose your six-shooter when your horse rolls and your arm gets broke. You can't reach your rifle what's still in the saddle scabbard, and them two livin' Calder boys is coming out of the rocks, their guns trained on you. So you make like an Injun and play dead."

The sheriff smiled slowly and nodded his head at the outsider. "Yup, them Calder boys keep you covered the whole while. Maybe one of 'em kicks you to see if you groan. Might be he even takes a lick at your busted arm, in which case you're one tough son of a gun. Because you just lay there playin' possum, waitin' for them to get closer. And you know they'll be gettin' closer if they're gonna take your scalp or maybe your nose or an ear—"

Rachel lurched off the woodbox, dumping the bowl from her lap, sending the beans scattering over the bare pine boards.

"Yes, ma'am," Sheriff Getts said, not taking his eyes off the outsider. "Them boys was gonna need a trophy to prove they kilt Johnny Cain." He rubbed the bit of his pipe over his lips as if in thought. "Otherwise there woulda been no point to any of it."

Rachel looked at Cain, wondering how he'd endured it. She thought of the utter terror she had seen in his eyes that day in the hay meadow when she'd first touched him.

"So you wait," the sheriff was saying. "You wait until Jed Calder puts up his gun and takes out his toad-sticker and bends over you, and then you shoot him with that boob gun you carry in a holster under your armpit. And all the whilst you're killing Jed, you're grabbin' the knife out of his hand and cuttin' the guts out of his baby brother, Stu, and I reckon by then you musta been either real sore or real scared because that boy looked like he'd been stabbed with a shovel."

Rachel shut her eyes and saw blood, smelled it. All that blood soaked and splattered on his clothes—it hadn't all been his.

For the first time Johnny Cain stirred. He flashed one of his charming, easy smiles. "You sure do tell a fine story, Sheriff."

"Uh-huh. I suppose you're gonna say you shot yourself whilst cleaning your gun, then broke your arm fallin' outta the chair."

"There ain't no law against being clumsy that I know of."

"There ought to be a law, though," the lawman growled, "against treatin' a man like a fool when he ain't one. I've known them Calder boys to be dumb as fence posts and mean as polecats their whole lives, and so their deaths sure ain't no loss to civilization. They came after you, and you only gave 'em what they asked for."

He leaned forward and tapped his finger on the silver star he wore. "But I'd be derelict in my duty if I didn't suggest that you mosey on along, soon as you're able. Before this nice little valley is overrun with fools who want to be known as the one who shot Johnny Cain."

Johnny Cain said nothing.

The lawman pushed the chair back from the table. Lumbering to his feet, he pulled the watch from his vest, then glanced at the window, glazed gold now by the setting sun. He turned to leave.

And still Johnny Cain said nothing. Not even good-bye.

Rachel went with the sheriff out into the yard. The salmon-pink light had seeped out of the clouds, leaving them a smoky gray. It would be full dark soon; a cold wind had sprung up.

The sheriff knocked the bowl of his pipe against the fence, the wind catching the sparks and embers. Leather squeaked as he put his weight in the stirrup and swung up into the saddle. Though Rachel knew his eyes were on her, she couldn't look at him.

"That Johnny Cain," he began, "don't start to feelin' tender for him. A man like him is trouble, and trouble don't like bein' lonesome. Time and luck'll run out on him someday."

She stared at him. "But what is a man to do if there are people out there waiting to shoot him in the back, to cut off his ears?"

"Which is my point exactly, ma'am. When his destiny finds Johnny Cain, you don't want to be standing anywheres near him."

CHAPTER EIGHT

JOHNNY Cain still sat at her table, his hand on his gun. Slowly he lifted his head. His eyes gleamed in the murky light, but there was no warmth there. "I've been telling you I'm the devil," he said, "and you've been trying to argue me out of it. Now you're looking at me like you expect me to sprout horns."

"I know you are not the devil, Mr. Cain."

He gave a hard, short laugh. He stood up slowly and pushed his revolver back into its holster. "But you're still going to ask me to leave. Soon as you can think of a gentle way to do it."

He brushed past her, making for the door as if he had it in his mind to leave that very moment. She went after him, although she didn't really know if she meant to stop him or see him on his way.

She nearly stumbled up the back of his boots when he halted, his hand on the jamb. "But what if there are others out there," she said, "waiting up in the buttes, waiting for you down the road?"

He kept his back to her. "They're out there, all right. And I'll kill them for it, just like I did the Calders."

"You could put your gun away. Refuse to fight."

"Turn the other cheek."

"Yes."

He spun around abruptly. "There's only the quick and the dead. Ever heard that said? Well, now you know what it means."

He grabbed the latch and jerked the door open. "I think I'll go on down to the paddock and take a look at the sheep."

She watched him walk slowly across her yard, and she thought that he moved like what he was—a man sorely hurt. She hadn't asked him to leave. He hadn't said he would stay.

THE next morning she was rattling a fresh stick of wood into the cookstove when the door to the yard opened. She turned to see that he carried a zinc bucket brimming with foamy milk.

"Why, you've done the milking," she said. She was surprised he even knew how to do such a thing as milk a cow. "And you managed it one-handed."

"Yeah, well, it sure wasn't easy. That brown bossy kept trying to kick the holy . . . dickens outta me."

She took the bucket from his hand and set it on the slopstone. He smelled of hay and of the crisp morning air.

"That brown bossy's Annabell," Rachel said. "She has real sensitive teats. You need to use gentle hands on her."

"I'll have to remember that," he said, "if I'm going to be doing the milking while I'm here."

She felt herself smile. "I'll make you into a lamb licker yet."

"Now as to that, I'm taking a wait-and-see attitude. Wait until I figure out what the heck that is, then see if I can stomach it."

She laughed as she put a pan on the fire and began to stir up the batter for flapjacks.

He went to look out the window. "I was thinking maybe if you had a sugan," he said, "or some such thing handy, I could roll it out come nighttime and bed down in the barn."

"There's a herder's wagon parked out back of the lambing sheds. You could sleep there. My husband used it when it was his turn at the summer pasturing. It's all fixed up with a bunk, even a cookstove."

He grunted, which she took to mean he would be pleased.

LATER that morning Benjo Yoder walked through the jack pines and tamaracks that draped the lower slopes of Tobacco Reef. He was thinking that maybe he was almost as good at reading trail sign as any Indian scout ever was.

He squatted on his haunches to study the fresh black droppings that lay scattered like lumps of coal over the pine straw. A bear had crossed over this deer trail not too long back, he thought.

He looked up, squinting against the sunlight that splashed through the pine boughs. It was just this time of year that bears first stuck their noses out of their winter beds to get a whiff of spring.

The brush crackled behind him.

Benjo whirled, his fingers scrabbling for his sling. Ears straining, he stared hard at the tangled thicket of kinnikinnick bushes.

A breeze came up, stirring the leaves . . . rustling, crackling.

He let out a shaky breath. It was only the wind.

He sure hadn't wanted to meet up with any bear. He had no illusions that he could take down a grizzly or even a black bear with his sling, no matter what David was supposed to have done to Goliath. Just like he knew he really wasn't any Indian scout.

Benjo ambled on down the trail, looking for more signs of the bear. Leaving the trail, he broke out of the pinewoods and descended into a coulee, his feet nearly skidding out from beneath him as he scrambled down the steep slope. He didn't see the two men on horseback until he'd nearly run right into them.

The horse that was in the lead, a sorrel gelding, shied in fright. Benjo saw that the sorrel's rider was a young man with a hawklike face, thin-boned and high-nosed. Just then the other rider nudged his horse forward a couple of steps. He pushed his hat back to reveal a long face with droopy eyes and a beard like a billy goat's. His mouth was puckered around a thick wad of chewing tobacco.

Benjo's throat locked around a scream. He was Mr. Hunter's stock inspector. The man who had hanged his father.

Benjo watched now, his eyes wide and dry, his breath whining through his throat, as the man unhooked a coiled, braided rawhide rope from off his saddle. "Well now," the man said. "I'll be damned if we didn't just catch ourselves a cattle rustler."

QUINTEN Hunter grabbed the man's arm, his fingers digging into fringed buckskin that was slick with old sweat and grease. "Put it up, Wharton." He narrowed his eyes and made his voice smooth and slick as coal oil. "Put up the rope."

For a moment longer the arm beneath Quinten's fingers stayed rigid, and a wildness flared deep in the man's pale eyes. Then Woodrow Wharton blinked and hooked the rope back on his saddle.

Quinten wondered if the boy was alone. He was certainly terrified. Quinten could hear his breath scraping in his throat. The kid stood so rigid he looked as if he would break in a stiff wind.

"You there, boy. What're you doing straying so far from home?"

"Let's go ahead and string him up, Quin."

The boy's jaw muscles were working hard, like bellows.

"Muh!" he shouted with force. "Muh—m-my friend . . . huh—huh—he'll sh-shoot you all s-stone-d-d-dead!" He whirled and broke into an all-out run, scrambling back up the slope of the coulee toward the stand of jack pines.

Quinten thrust his sorrel gelding into the path of Wharton's horse and leaned over, grabbing the shank of the bit to keep him from bolting after the boy.

Wharton stared at him, wearing a wild smile. "Scare him, Quin. I was only going to scare him."

"You scared him. Half out of what little wits he seems to have."

Wharton wiped the wet tobacco flakes off the ends of his goatee. "I always knew Injun blood made a man's hide go red. I didn't know it also turned his guts yellow."

He dug his spurs cruelly into his horse, jerking its head around hard and sending it back down the coulee in a spray of mud.

Quinten stared after him, frowning. He wondered what had motivated his father, the Baron, to take on a man like Woodrow Wharton at the Circle H. No real hand would ever dude himself up in Wild West clothes, like chaps with silver conchas and fifty-dollar boots so skintight the man's feet were starting to curl like a ram's horns. No real ranch hand packed a pair of pearl-handled Colts.

Quinten felt his jaw tighten. During the months he'd been gone his father had hired on a cowboy who seemed to know nothing about cows. A hand more handy with a gun than a branding iron.

"Maggot-brained fool," Quinten swore aloud, then shook his head at himself. He hadn't been home a day, and already he was letting his father rub him raw.

Quinten rode up the coulee through the jack pines. He had to duck under low swags of pine branches.

He stopped when he got to the shoulder of the high bluff. This was wild, tangled country. Up here the wind was blowing strong, and he had to anchor down his hat with the bonnet strings. He straightened his legs to stand up in the stirrups, stretching out his body, stretching out his mind. It felt so *good* to be home.

For almost two years he'd tried to please his father by attending college back in Chicago. He'd been shut up indoors all day, hunched over books in the winter, slaving in the heat and stink of the stockyards during the summer. But at least he'd discovered one thing of importance during his time of exile. Only nineteen years old, he already knew what he wanted for the rest of his life.

He wanted that life to be here, on the Circle H. He wanted to wake up every morning and look out to see the mountains propping up the big sky. He wanted to ride the miles of prairie and not see another living thing, except maybe for his own shadow moving ahead of him. He wanted to raise cattle and horses and a family on this land, where you could ride and breathe and feel alive.

QUINTEN HUNTER PULLED HIS galloping horse up hard beneath the ranch gate. So maybe it wasn't the prettiest place on earth, he thought. The grass was gray, and the windmill was missing a sail. But the sight of the big white house, with its gables and dormer windows and stately spool-railed galleries, still made him smile.

He rubbed his lathered horse dry with a gunnysack and gave him an extra ration of oats. Once inside the house, he paused in front of a hall stand made of stag antlers to hook his hat on one of the points. From the winter parlor he could hear his father shouting in a voice roughened by thousands of cigars, and the cool, murmuring response of his father's wife.

"I built up this spread when there was damn all out here but Indians and coyotes. You're daft if you think I'll brook the death of it."

Ailsa Hunter, his father's wife, said something then, too low for Quinten to hear.

His father roared back in his gruff Scottish brogue, "We made a bargain, you and I, and for fourteen miserable years I've kept to my end of it. So you just go on keeping to yours, or I'll—"

His father must have cut himself off, for Quinten heard nothing more. Yet he held his breath, waiting. He knew the bargain his father spoke of had something to do with him, to do with that time he had been brought to the ranch from the reservation after his mother died when he was a boy of five. For a lady born and bred as Ailsa Hunter was, to agree to take in the breed son of her husband's squaw meant one heck of a bargain struck. A devil's bargain.

Quinten started when his father appeared suddenly in the parlor doorway. He stood spread-legged, with his thumbs in his breast pockets, anger sharpening the prominent bones of his face.

The Baron had a face that was all blades: a bowie knife of a nose, a mouth that curved sharp and down like a sickle. The skin of his face and hands had been leathered by the Montana wind and the grindstone life of ranching. His hair grew thick off his broad, flat forehead, white and flowing.

The Baron looked his son over with eyes that were hard and black. "Where've you been?"

"Out riding."

"I was led to believe that you were going to start in on taming those wild broncs for the spring roundup. Now you tell me you spent the time 'out riding,' " he said with a mocking lilt on the last words. "You're a lazy scalawag, boy."

Quinten had to jerk his head back as his father's stiff finger stabbed at his face. "If you think, just because I'm letting you get away with quitting on college, that I'll tolerate you going back to the blanket, living up there on the res with your mother's people, to squat outside a bloody tepee, like some no-good breed—"

"Not *like* some breed, Baron. I am a breed."

"What you are is my son. And, by damn, you'll stay here on the ranch, and you'll work for your keep."

"Yes, sir," Quinten said to his father's disappearing back.

THAT night at dinner his father said, "It appears to me you spent precious little of your time back there book learning and most of it girling about."

The Baron sat at the head of the table, wearing pearl-gray California trousers, a black frock coat, and a gray silk four-in-hand tie fastened with a ruby stickpin. At the other end of the table sat Ailsa Hunter, in a black taffeta gown that glittered in the light cast by a matching pair of crystal candelabra. She wore pearl drops in her ears and a pearl choker collar around her neck. Her hair was the blue-black of a crow's plumage, her skin a pale translucent white. She had violet eyes. Not dark blue, but the pure deep purple of hothouse violets. Elegant and beautiful and cold.

She had been born Ailsa MacTier, the tenth daughter of a Scottish Lowland squire. It was a mystery to Quinten what had ever drawn her to this wild, crude place to marry a coal miner's son.

They could have been a Chicago society couple, man and wife enjoying a quiet evening together in one of those fine mansions gracing the lakeshore—except for the man's red-skinned son and Wild West Wharton, hired gun, who were also in attendance.

His father's tobacco-fed voice cut into Quinten's thoughts. "Well, now that you are home, Quin, you can help me to rid the valley of those holy-howling, Bible-banging mutton punchers. They think they can come here and reap the reward of those who came before. It took grit and brawn to make the Miawa what it is today."

"Well, it seems to me, Pa," Quinten said, "that any poor fool who tries to raise sheep suffers enough persecutions without you adding to them. Coyotes and bears, death camas and stomach bloat. Sheep go out looking for ways to die."

"Aye, and I hope they find every bloody one of them."

Quinten opened his mouth, then shut it. His father behaved as if there was something privileged about raising cattle. As if a cow was somehow a higher class of animal than a sheep. But Quinten suspected that what probably galled the Baron most about his "holy-howling mutton punchers" was that wool now sold at a premium, whereas the glutted beef market had crashed. The Circle H would need to put even larger cattle herds on just that many more acres of grassland for there to be a hope of a profit in the coming years.

For the first time all night Wild West Wharton unhooked his small clasp of a mouth for something besides chewing. "Something tells me that come spring it won't be a good time to be a woolly."

Quinten stared into the man's pale eyes, but he was frowning more over the memory of that skinny Plain boy. "Woodrow and I nearly rode down one of their young uns this morning. *He* at least appears to have a friend who is willing to shoot us all stone-dead."

Wharton scratched his head. "He was probably talking about that stranger who got himself shot up while passing through here a while back," he said. "One of them Plain women is supposed to've taken him in. The widow of that Plain rustler we hung last spring."

Quinten's head snapped around to his father. "You hanged a Plain man? For what? For being a cow thief? What Plain man even knows how to build a loop, let alone swing a wide one? Or was it for having the audacity to make a go of a few measly acres—"

"We caught him with a bunch of slick-eared calves, so what else were we to think?" The Baron's hand trembled slightly. "It isn't anything for you to get all wild-eyed about. It was a mistake. I told his woman—I've told everyone—it was an honest mistake."

"You remember what he was jawing about right before we hung him, boss?" Wharton's lips pulled back from his long teeth in a smile. "He said we were all gonna be done in by a rider on a pale horse—"

" 'I looked, and behold a pale horse: and his name that sat on him was Death, and Hell followed with him.' "

The quiet voice, as silky and cold as dry snow, froze them all.

Quinten looked at his father's wife. Her violet gaze was on the window that framed a fiery sunset. Streaks of copper and orange were suddenly reflected in the silver and china and crystal on the table, in the mirror of the mahogany sideboard, until it seemed the whole of heaven and earth had caught fire.

The faintest of smiles touched her lips. "His name was Death."

CHAPTER NINE

RACHEL held the lantern high as she slogged through the icy mud. It was after midnight, but she still was dressed properly in her apron and shawl. She wasn't wearing either a prayer cap or a night-cap, though, and her hair fell thick and heavy over her shoulders and down her back. The wind tugged and stirred the ends.

The first full moon of spring, round and creamy, shed a soft light over the hay meadows and over the sheepherder's wagon, where the outsider now spent his nights. Rachel climbed the steps of the wagon's small stoop and knocked.

A moment later the top half of the Dutch door swung open, and she found herself staring at his naked chest. She took a startled step backward. "They are coming, Mr. Cain," she said.

She could almost feel his gaze moving over her hair, like the touch of the wind, before it shifted to the corral next to the lambing sheds, where the ewes milled and bleated in the cold night.

"Let me just finish getting dressed, then," he said.

She waited for him at the bottom of the stoop. When he joined her, she saw that to him, getting dressed included strapping on his cartridge belt.

Their feet crunched through the half-frozen mud; the oil sloshed in the lantern she carried. Beyond, in the dark infinity of the prairie, a coyote began singing to the moon.

Benjo, with MacDuff at his side, appeared at the door to the sheds in the lantern light. He had one gloved hand wrapped tight around a pole nearly half again his length and with a hook at the end of it. "You can go fetch some water from the creek," she said to him, "if you please. And by then I should have need of that hook."

The boy leaned the sheephook against the sheds and snatched up a few empty creamery cans. He ran off, his dog at his heels.

Earlier, in preparation for this moment, Rachel had hung several lanterns on the poles of the corral. She went around lighting them now, and yellow puddles spilled onto the muddy straw and the shifting gray woolly backs.

"Mr. Cain, if you would start separating out the ones who are about to drop. That flighty one is going to be first." She pointed to a young ewe that was digging frantically in the straw to make a nest. "It's her first spring as a mother. She could have trouble."

Rachel could always spot the ones that were going to lamb in the next hour or so. It was the music. She imagined she could hear a sweet trilling, like birdsong, emanating from the ewes about to give birth. And if a ewe was headed for trouble, the birdsong became the discordant caw of the crow.

The outsider was now walking among the ewes. "It appears," he said, "like there's gonna be a lot of 'em coming all at once."

"Indeed, Mr. Cain. It's going to be a busy night. Now if you could just come over here, please, and give this new little mother your sturdy leg to push against."

A thin white sac was showing now under the ewe's tail. She flung her head back, her whole body straining, her eyes bulging. The opening widened, and Rachel could see the emerging lamb's front hooves and, between them, a tiny black nose.

The ewe was laboring hard, her upper lip peeling back with each push. The outsider had given her his leg to brace against, and now he squatted down in the straw next to her rolling head. He threaded his fingers through the puff of wool between her ears, stroking her, over and over.

Benjo trotted up just as the ewe gave a mighty strain, her rear end jerking sharply. The lamb seemed to dive out of the womb, feet and nose first, landing in the muddy straw—a glistening, steaming, nubby yellow sack of bones.

Rachel peeled the membrane away from the lamb's nose and mouth, laughing as she heard the squeaky *maa* that came with the little one's first breath. Benjo handed his mother some gunnysacking so that she could dry off the lamb's ears and keep them from freezing.

The ewe just stood there, baaing frantically and shaking her hind end. Rachel began to fear she'd turn out to be one of those mothers who refused to accept her baby. But then the ewe turned, stretching her nose out toward her lamb, and began to lick the yellow slime off its rump, making loud noises that almost drowned out the bleats and baas of the other expectant mothers.

"And here all this time I've been worried you were going to make *me* do that," the outsider said.

"The night is young yet, Mr. Cain."

He laughed; then his gaze fell back down to the ewe, who was now trying to nudge her lamb to its feet by pushing up on its little rump. A gentleness she had never seen before came over his harsh face. He looked very young, she thought, and . . . *happy.*

"M-mem?"

She turned, swallowing the lump that clogged her throat. She took the sheephook that Benjo handed her. She slid it under the lamb's belly, lifting the nubby yellow bundle of bones until it was dangling from the end of the pole, nose to the ground.

She offered the baby in this fashion to its mother, letting her see and smell it. The ewe stretched out her neck, sniffing hard to be sure the baby was hers. Slowly Rachel backed up, the lamb dangling on the pole. And the ewe followed them warily into the sheds.

The sheds, long and low, had a mixture of straw and sawdust on the floor and were divided into a honeycomb of pens, called jugs, that were just large enough to hold a ewe and her lamb. Once snug in its new home, the newborn pushed itself up onto its wobbly legs. Using gentle nudges, Rachel guided it to its mother's teat for its first meal. She couldn't linger to watch, though, for Benjo was hollering.

They hit a flurry of birthings after that, so she and the outsider had to work separately. She watched him, though, whenever she got the chance. Johnny Cain, man-killer, settled easily into the sheep midwifery business. His low and lazy drawl soothed the ewes like a lullaby, and the touch of his hands was gentle and sure.

Only once did Rachel have to pick up a small, wet yellow bundle and carry it outside the corral fence to the place that one particularly bad spring her husband, Ben, had taken to calling the bone pile. For it was inevitable that even in the good years, some lambs died, and they always lost a few of the ewes as well.

Still, as Rachel carried the dead lamb to the bone pile, she turned away so that her son and Johnny Cain wouldn't see her tears.

RACHEL suddenly realized that MacDuff was whining at her. Benjo gripped her arm, and she turned. The boy was looking up at her with wide eyes. "Muh—Mem! Y-you know that old gappy-mouthed ewe? Huh—huh—her baby's c-coming out all wrong!"

The ewe lay on the ground, quiet except for her contracting belly. Rachel could see only one tiny black hoof thrusting from her rear. Her water had broken some time ago. As Rachel knelt in the straw, the ewe looked up at her with those serene eyes that had always made her seem such a gentle, wise old thing.

"You poor old dear. Your baby's trying to come out all backward, isn't he?" She massaged the ewe's clenching belly. "I'm going to need to pull her," she said to the outsider, who had squatted down alongside Rachel. "Benjo, fetch me a bucket of water and some lye soap. And a piece of baling twine."

As they waited in silence for the boy to come back, kneeling side by side, Rachel was so very aware of Cain. Of the way his black suspenders cut his shirt into white diamonds lit by the moon, and the way his sharp cheekbone cast a deep shadow onto his beard-roughened cheek. Of the way his hand, like her own, rubbed and pulled through the wool of the sheep's shuddering belly.

Benjo came running up so fast he nearly dumped the bucket of water in her lap. "M-Mem! Is she g-g-going to d-die?"

"I don't know," Rachel said, rolling up her sleeves. She plunged her arms in the water, scrubbing hard with the soap. "I'll try to save her and her baby both. But the Lord always knows what's best."

She pushed her hand up inside the ewe's hot womb. The lamb's head was turned backward, and its other hind leg seemed to be bent up around it. The ewe stretched her neck forward and rolled her head as a fierce contraction shook her body. The squeezing muscles bore down hard, crushing Rachel's hand between the lamb's skull and the ewe's pubic bone. Tears started in her eyes. She knew now that the ewe and her lamb would both surely die.

"The lamb's head is twisted around all funny, and my hand's too big. I can't get it up in there far enough."

"Let the boy try," the outsider said.

Benjo reared back. "Nuh—nuh—nuh—"

Rachel cupped her son's face so that she could look into his eyes. "You don't have to do it. I'll not make you. But this poor old gappy-mouthed ewe, you are her only hope."

Benjo pulled his head out of her hands and nodded solemnly.

"All right, then." Rachel's breath eased out in a sigh. "The trick is to get your fingers around the lamb's nose and jaw and ease its head around until it's pointed right." She gripped his hand, his small boy's hand that she was asking to do a man's job. She could feel him trembling. "Benjo, the ewe's belly is going to try to squeeze out her baby, and when that happens, she'll squeeze your hand too."

"Wuh—will it h-hurt?"

"Yes."

"He can do it." The outsider clasped her boy's shoulder, giving it a rough shake—the kind of touch a man gave his son.

Benjo had to lie flat on his belly to push his hand and arm up inside the ewe. With every contraction he screamed aloud. Tears ran down his cheeks, but he never once let go. Each time the ewe labored, the lamb came down an inch or two. Finally she gave a mighty heave, and the lamb slid out.

The outsider was right there to cradle it. His fingers tore away the membrane from the tiny black nose. "Breathe, breathe." He chanted the words like a prayer. "Breathe, breathe, breathe."

The lamb wasn't breathing.

Rachel grabbed the yellow bag of bones from him by the rear hocks. She stood up and swung it hard in a full circle through the air. Once. Twice. The lamb let out a loud, indignant baa.

Laughing, Rachel collapsed into the straw, cuddling the bawling lamb in her lap.

Through it all, Benjo had been choking over hysterical words, while the outsider had been staring at her, wearing a look of pure wonderment. Now he let his own laughter go.

"I thought you were going to . . ." he sputtered. "Lordy, I don't know what I thought. The way you swung that poor lamb—"

"It's supposed to help them start breathing," Rachel said.

"Helps to scare the breath right out of them, I would've thought."

Her boy had been laughing as well. But now he gripped her arm. "M-mem? Wuh—wuh—wuh—"

She touched his tear-streaked face. "He'll live, our Benjo. He'll live." She laid the lamb gently back into the straw, then pushed a burlap sack into the outsider's hands. "Here, rub him down with this, Mr. Cain. Or you can go on ahead and use your tongue, if you like. Then you can lay full claim to the title of lamb licker."

A bright and dazzling smile blazed across his face. "Lady, you sure don't cut a man any slack, do you? I've a mind to . . ."

She was so caught up in his smile that it took her a moment to realize his voice had trailed off. In the next instant she saw what he had just noticed: that the ewe was lying too quietly.

Rachel pressed her hand to the ewe's brisket. It rose once and then subsided, softly, gently. She looked down into those quiet, all-knowing eyes in time to see the life fade out of them.

The outsider came up onto his haunches, shifting his weight so that the ewe was shielded from Benjo's sight. His gaze met hers, and then, together, they looked at the boy. Benjo had taken up the burlap sack himself, and he was absorbed with wiping the lamb clean.

"Hey there, partner," the outsider said. "Come along and help me carry this youngster of yours into the sheds and out of the cold."

Rachel watched them go. She couldn't bear for Benjo to be told of the ewe's death just yet.

When he was out of sight inside the sheds, she turned back to the ewe. Such a sweet, gentle mother. Rachel threaded her fingers through the tight curly wool between the ewe's ears. She leaned over and kissed her bony nose. "Good-bye, old dear."

CHAPTER TEN

RACHEL pulled her black bonnet over her prayer cap, tilting her head back to stare up into the soft and hazy sky of a Montana spring. She loved this time of year, when the earth seemed to be warming from within, erupting into a rainbow glory of color. The willow trees were swelling with brilliant red buds. Phlox blossoms pillowed the ground, pink and sweet. And high on the slopes the sage was turning from the steel gray of winter to a feathery green.

A horse's loud, nose-clearing snort cut the air, and Rachel turned, smiling wide. The outsider had led their old draft mare from the barn and stood now in the yard, his hand wrapped around the harness reins, looking at her.

"Isn't this the most glorious day?" she said as she came up to him, a breeze blowing soft and sweet against her face.

He began backing the horse between the shafts of her small buckboard. "What's put you in such a fine mood?" he said.

"I'm pleased you're coming to the preaching with us."

"Yeah, well, I'm thinking you ought to hold off on being pleased until we see how it goes."

It had been two months since he had come into their lives and nearly a month since that first night of the lambing season.

At the end of the first week of lambing Rachel had said to him, "I'll hear no more talk about you earning your keep. I'll pay you proper wages, and I'll hire you on through the end of summer and mating season." Just so he'd know that she understood there would be an end to it. Just so he wouldn't think she was some lonely Plain widow who'd fallen into a wild crush for a handsome outsider.

He had said, "Just through the end of summer, Mrs. Yoder." And she had known that, of course, there really would be an end to it someday. As there should be. Because anything else was forbidden.

During those last months, as was their way, the Plain people had all gathered every other Sunday to worship the Lord. But not the outsider.

Then last night, while the two of them were feeding the newest bum lambs in front of the stove, she had said to him, "Come with us to the preaching tomorrow."

And he had said, not surprised, indeed almost smiling, "Why?"

"So that you can come to know us, to see how we are . . . and this Sunday the preaching is at my father's farm."

A silence came between them then, as it often did, and then he said, "I'll come."

And it was her turn to ask, "Why?"

"Because," he had said, "you asked."

Now, this morning, his cheeks shone from a fresh shave, and his hair was still damp from washing. He had polished his boots and brushed his coat and put on a clean shirt of Ben's.

THE buggies and buckboards and spring wagons were lined up in Bishop Isaiah Miller's pasture like pigs at a feeding trough. As the outsider squeezed their buckboard into a shady spot, a gangly boy came running up to them. He was supposed to unhitch the horses, but when he caught sight of Johnny Cain at the reins, he skidded to a dead stop, his eyes wide.

"The way that mouth of yours is gaping open, Levi Miller," Rachel called down to her youngest brother, "it'll be a pure wonder if you don't catch yourself a fly."

This was hardly the first time Levi Miller had set those big eyes on the notorious desperado. Indeed, even though it was the busiest time of year, nearly every Plain man and boy in the valley, and a good many of the women too, had found a spare moment to come and take a gander at Johnny Cain.

The outsider had shown remarkable forbearance. Still, he'd always slipped that six-shooter of his from its holster every time he heard hooves or wagon wheels turning into the yard. He wasn't wearing that gun of his this morning, though, and all because of her, to please her. He was even pretending not to notice how her brother was gawping at him. Laughing, she climbed out of the buckboard.

Rachel nudged the boy's bony shoulder. "Are you putting down roots? Go show Mr. Cain where to pasture the horse."

She gave the bow of her bonnet a straightening tug. She didn't need to look around to see that the knots of people who'd all been standing outside the front doors of the barn were suddenly staring stock-still and openmouthed at the Yoder buckboard.

Benjo ran off to join the other youngsters at a pond in back of the lambing sheds. Rachel waited while Levi and the outsider led the mare through a gate in the nearby fence.

Meadows surrounded her father's house, which was two stories high and made not of rough cottonwood logs but of milled lumber. Snuggled up next to the big house on either side, like step blocks, were two smaller houses. In one lived her eldest brother, Sol, a bachelor. The other, called the *Daudy Haus,* was where her great-grandmother, *Mutter* Anna Mary, lived. It was tradition for the old folks to live in houses separate but not apart from the younger generations. A white spool-railed porch wrapped around all three houses, linking them like a daisy chain.

Bishop Isaiah Miller had the biggest and finest sheep farm in all the valley. He spent a good part of his days praying, studying the Scriptures, and shepherding his human flock, while Sol tended to the sheep.

The outsider came back through the gate alone, and he and Rachel walked together toward the front of the barn, where the preaching would take place. As they drew closer to the silent crowd, Rachel felt a nervous quiver. There would be consequences to face over what she had chosen to do. It was one thing to take in an outsider who'd been found gunshot and bleeding to death in your hay meadow. It was quite another to make him your hired man. And another thing entirely to bring him along to the preaching.

Rachel looked for her father. Of all those here today, he would have the most influence over whether the outsider would be allowed to stay among them for a time. But he was already in the barn, meeting with the community's other two ministers, Noah Weaver and Amos Zook, as he did before every worship service.

Her four brothers certainly appeared to have made up their collective Miller minds. In their freshly brushed Sunday sack coats and wide-brimmed felt hats, they stood in a row, glowering at the outsider.

Or rather, Abram and Samuel glowered. Levi gawped and blushed. Sol, whose big and gentle heart was incapable of glowering, looked only at her, with concern shadowing his face.

It was Samuel who broke away from the group to stride toward her and the outsider, with the others trailing after him. He stopped in front of her, hands on his hips, long black beard jutting.

"What the die-hinker do you think you're doing, bringing *him* here?"

Rachel thrust her own chin into the air. "Mr. Cain has come to witness the preaching. It's not a forbidden thing."

"He'll not understand a word," Samuel said. "He'll be bored."

"He'll be bored stiff as a corpse," Abram echoed.

Since they were already speaking *Deitsch,* presumably the outsider couldn't understand a word now. But Rachel thought the man could probably guess at the sentiment behind the words.

"I've told him he can leave whenever he wishes, and we won't be offended," she said in English. "You would deny him an opportunity to worship God in fellowship with us?"

"She's right," Sol said softly, "about the preaching, at least. It's not forbidden if he wants to come and witness."

"Aaugh . . ." Samuel waved his hand as if brushing away a pesky fly. "He'll grow tired of it all soon enough anyway."

Just then, as if they'd been given some invisible signal, the Plain women began to file into the barn. The children came running up from the pond—the girls going with the women, the boys joining the groups of men.

"I must go," Rachel said to the outsider. "We women always sit separate from the men."

His mouth broke into one of those reckless smiles with a touch of wildness in it. "Don't you worry none about me, Mrs. Yoder."

She left him, crossing over to the side of the yard where the women walked. Her steps faltered when she saw her mother. Sadie Miller's mouth and eyes were etched with shame, her shoulders bowed. In a world where a woman was judged by the daughters she raised, Rachel was her mother's singular failure.

Standing close to her mother were her twin daughters-in-law, Velma and Alta. The two younger women each held a baby resting on a hip. Together they raised their free hands to pat Sadie on the arm. Together they lowered their heads as if in silent prayer.

Rachel wanted to go to them so badly her chest ached with it, but she couldn't face her mem's shame. So instead she went alone to the fence and took off her bonnet, looping it over the top rail with the others. The black bonnets all hung upside down off the fence rail in a row, looking like coal scuttles. Rachel stood there by herself a moment, feeling lonesome, then went to join the *Meed,* the girls and young unmarried women.

THE silence lay heavy and warm over the barn.

It was a time of waiting, of moments rich with the promise of what was to come. She breathed in the barn smells of horse and cow and hay, the Sunday smells of starch and soap and shoe blacking. Her gaze moved lovingly over those in front of her. This was her life.

In this time of waiting, of silence, with her family and friends close around her, Rachel Yoder felt safe. She felt loved. For her just being here was an act of worship.

Her gaze roamed over the men's benches. The outsider sat pressed between two of her brothers, Sol and Samuel. Her son also sat with the men, his head respectfully lowered.

The silence spun out and out, until the men reached up, as if in one motion, and took off their felt hats, putting them under the benches. And Ezra Fischer, the *Vorsinger,* who led the hymnsongs during worship, shuffled slowly to his feet.

He opened his mouth, and his voice took flight. A trilling tenor so pure and sharp, it pierced the soul. His head thrown back, Ezra Fischer drew out the first note of the hymn as if it were so precious he couldn't bear to let it go. Then the rest of the men joined in.

The men's voices, deep and dark and rich, rolled in slow waves up to the rafters. The women's voices, high and sweet, melded into the low, tolling tones of the men to become one pure song rising up. It was an old hymn, mournful and yet beautiful, about exiles wandering through the land. For three hundred years the Plain People had sung this hymn in just this way, and so it would always be. Slow and unchanging, always together. One mind, one spirit.

Rachel's head fell back as the hymn thrummed through her blood, creating a tempest of joy within her. The slow chanting washed over her, purifying her and making her feel one with God.

And then they stopped abruptly, cutting off the last word, the last note. Silence descended once more.

Rachel slowly opened her eyes. She was so filled with joy and the glory of the Lord, she could have burst with it.

Breathless, she looked over to the men's side of the barn. Her gaze locked with the outsider's, who was staring at her, his face fierce and intent. She jerked her head away. And time, which had seemed suspended, as if floating in the rays of sunlight that poured through the cracks in the rafters, rippled suddenly . . . and broke.

RACHEL'S father rose to his feet. Bishop Isaiah Miller stood strong and tall in the middle of the floor. His beard was black and fleecy, but his hair had a white streak going down the very center of it, like the stripe on a skunk's back. He had awakened with that stripe the morning after he'd had the vision-dream that had led them to leave their homes in Ohio and settle in this wild and empty land. It had been taken by all as a sign of divine benediction.

He talked of days long ago, of a time in the old country when the Plain People suffered terrible torments for their faith: burnings and stonings and whippings. In the dusk of the barn his gray eyes flashed with the passion of his words.

He spoke of the will of God, of how salvation came through submission, through acceptance. Through all their sufferings, the Plain People followed the example set by Jesus Christ, who had yielded so completely to his Father's will that He suffered and died on the cross. "They spat upon Him and scourged Him with reeds. And then they led Him away and crucified Him. They passed by Him, hanging up there on his cross, and they wagged their heads and mocked Him, saying, 'If you are truly the Son of God, then why don't you come down from that cross and save yourself?' "

Rachel's eyes had drifted closed. She saw a man, bleeding, tortured, dying. Saw him throw back his head and scream in his despair. And she knew suddenly what had been behind the terror in Johnny Cain's eyes.

My God, my God, why hast thou forsaken me?

CHAPTER ELEVEN

RACHEL walked out of the dark coolness of the barn after the worship service and blinked against the sudden wash of sunlight. She fetched her bonnet and leaned against the fence, bracing her forearms on the whitewashed rail. Clouds hung over the mountains, but here in the valley it was spring—periwinkle skies, a warm whisper of breeze.

She turned and saw the outsider coming toward her, his stride fluid and elegant. He should have been stiff, she thought, after three hours of sitting on a hard, backless bench, listening to preaching and prayers that to him must surely have seemed like babble.

"You appear none the worse for wear," she said as he stood next to her, "after such a long and close brush with salvation."

"It was a near thing, though. Y'all got me so worked up, I was almost shoutin' hallelujahs."

She looked away. She had astonished herself, making a joke out of such a serious thing as a soul's salvation. He had a way of making her say things, do things, that were not herself.

"There's someone here I want you to know," she said, "and I want her to come to know you." She pushed away from the fence and started across the yard, leaving him to come with her or not.

The Plain People had gathered together again, talking in groups in the yard. A hush fell over everyone as they watched Rachel and the outsider walk side by side toward Bishop Miller's big house.

"I'm taking you to meet *Mutter* Anna Mary," she said to him. "She's what we call a *Braucher,* which means she can heal the sick with her touch alone. It's a wondrous gift of God. She's actually my father's grandmother, but all of us call her *Mutter,* mother, for she's connected to so many of us here. She is our roots."

MUTTER Anna Mary sat in a willow rocker on the gallery of her *Daudy Haus.* She'd never been a big woman, but the years had worn her down until she was little more than parched skin and frail bones. As Rachel climbed the porch steps, the old woman lifted her head. Her marbled skin pulled taut over her bones, and her eyes were like two smooth milky-white pebbles. She had been stone-blind for over fifty years.

"Rachel, my wild child," she said, although Rachel had yet to make a sound but for the rustle of her skirts. "What have you done?"

"I've brought Johnny Cain."

The outsider settled down on his haunches before the old woman. *Mutter* Anna Mary reached out her hand, and he took it.

"You have slain your brother." She said the words flat out, brutally.

He didn't answer, but neither did he pull his hand from hers.

The old woman's chest rose and fell with her breath. "And will you give to your God only silence when He says to you, 'What hast thou done? the voice of thy brother's blood crieth unto me from the ground'? Are you so full of pride, Johnny Cain?"

"I make no excuses for what I've done," he said, "and I'm not looking to change what I am."

The old woman turned her wrinkled face toward the tenuous warmth of the spring sun. She pulled her hand from his. "I would have thought you tough enough for anything. Even repentance."

"Well, ma'am, the way I see it, repenting ain't so hard. It's giving up the sinning that can get to be a challenge."

Rachel jerked back. "The men have started setting up the trestle tables and benches for the fellowship meal," she said. "Perhaps you ought to go help them, Mr. Cain."

The outsider stretched slowly to his feet. "It was a pleasure to make your acquaintance, ma'am," he said. His eyes met Rachel's for one enigmatic moment, and then he turned away. He walked the length of the gallery and down the steps.

"You sent him away," *Mutter* Anna Mary said.

Rachel knelt beside the willow rocking chair. She laid her cheek on her great-grandmother's knee. After a moment she felt the old woman's fingers stroking the crisp black cotton of her bonnet.

"He is broken," *Mutter* Anna Mary said. "You brought him to me because you hoped I would see a goodness inside him, a soul worth nurturing. And then you became frightened that I would see too much, and you sent him away. He has a soul, Rachel. Even that most wicked of Cains, who slew his brother Abel, had a soul. But for what he did, God made him a fugitive and a vagabond."

Rachel raised her head. "But *Mutter*, why can't God forgive him? If you could have seen his eyes on the day he came to me."

"Whom do you want to save this outsider for, my wild child—God or yourself?"

Rachel could feel the truth searing her face. "I want to come to know him. I want to understand how he can be as he is," she said.

"But what you know and understand, you might come to love."

Rachel was quiet. To love an outsider was a thing so wrong, so impossible, it was beyond words.

"If the weather keeps up like this, it's going to be hot as this soup come shearing time," Samuel Miller said as his sister, Rachel, set a clay bowl filled to the brim with bubbling bean soup in front of him. He wasn't speaking to her, though, but to the other men sitting with him.

The fellowship meal was the only time the Plain didn't eat in silence. The women always ate separately from the men, and they served the men first. Rarely did they join in their talk.

"Aw, our Sam's only worried about his sweat fouling the wool," Abram said. He stuffed a crusty chunk of bread in his mouth and winked at his brother while the others laughed at his joke.

Rachel smiled. She tried to catch the outsider's eye, but he and her son, who were sitting side by side, seemed to be sharing a joke of their own as a platter of pickled cucumbers and beets passed beneath their noses. Deacon Noah Weaver, on the other side of Benjo, saw what they were doing and frowned.

The men had made a place for the outsider at the trestle table and then ignored him. They spoke in *Deitsch* and let their eyes slide over him as if he were a ghost they couldn't see.

Rachel waited until the talk turned serious again. "If you men are going to speak of such things as haying and shearing and the plans for the summer pasturing, then you best do it in *Englisch*. For I've hired Mr. Cain on to work my farm through the breeding time."

Silence fell over the table. The men's heads all swiveled to look first at her, then at Bishop Miller.

But Rachel's father said nothing for the moment. He brought a spoonful of steaming soup up to his mouth and blew on it. In the tense quiet the huff of his breath sounded as loud as a gust of wind.

Rachel held her head high. It wasn't against tradition for an outsider to be hired on to work a Plain farm. Many sitting at these tables had paid Basque herders to watch over their sheep in the summer.

"I thought it would help," she said, "to hire on Mr. Cain. He can be taking Ben's turns with the haying and herding."

Noah Weaver forced a laugh. "And will he be taking Ben's turn at the shearing too? Such a worldly man as that one, why, I expect he probably figures that to shear a hundred-pound woolly monster has got to be as easy as spitting out a straw."

Since they were speaking in English now, the outsider had no trouble understanding the Plain man's words. Or the insult.

"Well," he drawled, "up till now sheep shearing hasn't much figured in my line of work." His eyes hardened. "I've had me plenty of practice, though, at recognizing a challenge when I'm given one."

Abram cocked a thumb at the outsider. "The rest of us will be clipping our tenth woolly before he's done with his first."

"You can't have a shearing contest with a man who's never done it before," Rachel protested. "It wouldn't be fair."

"Who said anything about a contest?" Noah said. "I'm saying he'll not last out the first hour of shearing, let alone the day."

"And I reckon your God gives out a prize, does He, to the man among you who shears the most sheep?"

Noah's eyes winced shut, and Rachel knew he felt shame to have been caught out in a vanity. Especially by an *Englischer.*

But her hotheaded brother Samuel leaned across the table to point at the outsider. "Might be we'll allow you to take a crack at summer herding the woolly monsters, then. Might be all those guns of yours will come in handy when the coyotes come to pay a call."

Johnny Cain's gaze went to Rachel's father.

"I reckon," the outsider said, "that your bishop would say 'the good shepherd giveth his life for the sheep.' "

Slowly Isaiah nodded. "It was the Lord Jesus Christ who said as much."

There was a moment of stunned silence; then Samuel scoffed, "How fortunate we are, then, to have this brave outsider among us, my brothers in Christ, to take on the coyotes."

Noah had folded his hands on the table, pressing them together so hard they trembled. Rachel saw that his face was flushed.

Benjo, who sat between the two men, had turned a pasty white. He held a cider jug, which he clutched tightly to his chest.

"You ever watch a coyote kill a lamb, outsider?" Noah said. "He goes for the throat, so he does, and the last thing that poor lamb sees is his life's blood spilling down the front of him as he dies."

Noah laughed.

And Benjo upturned the jug of cider into his lap.

Noah's laugh turned into a bellow. He reared to his feet, his belly and thighs knocking into the table so hard it rocked. He pulled back his hand. Benjo squawked and flung his arms over his head.

"Noah!" Rachel cried.

The outsider's arm shot up and caught Noah's wrist before the flat of his big palm could slam into the side of Benjo's head. The two men stared at each other, breathing heavily. Noah tried to wrench free, but the outsider held him fast. Benjo cringed between them, his shoulders jerking as he choked over his words.

"Nuh—nuh—nuh—"

"Noah, don't!" Rachel had started around the table toward her son, but her father grabbed her arm, stopping her. "He didn't mean to do it. I'm sure," she said. It was that talk of coyotes and blood

spilling down a lamb's front—it must have frightened the boy, for the pitcher had just seemed to slip from his hands.

Benjo took off running, and the outsider let go of Noah's wrist. Noah's hand clenched into a fist as he sucked in a sharp breath.

Rachel's father had tightened his grip on her arm to keep her from going after her son. He cast a stern look down the table. "Brother Noah."

Noah's chest shook as his breath rushed in and out of his throat. "The Proverbs admonish us not to spare the rod."

"My daughter coddles that boy too much, 'tis true. But you ought not to have given way so to the sins of anger and pride."

Noah closed his eyes, and his lips moved in desperate prayer.

His whole body shuddered hard, as if he were trying to throw off the sins that had gripped him. Then he swung around and pointed a finger at the outsider. "You see! You see what corrupting influence this man has on us all. He has brought the evil world among us!"

Noah turned and walked off, his head bowed.

The others pretended a sudden fascination with what was left in their soup bowls. Rachel stood next to her father, rubbing her arm where he had held her. Johnny Cain looked up, and their gazes met, but she could see nothing in his eyes. Throughout all that had just happened, he had shown not a shred of anger, yet he had stopped Noah from striking her son. He had cared at least that much.

Still, she thought that when the fellowship meal was done her father would tell her the outsider must go.

THE women spread quilts to sit beneath the shade of the cotton-woods that grew along the east side of the big house. Rachel found a place next to her mother and the twins. She wanted so badly to talk with her mem. But sitting there with her arms wrapped around her drawn-up legs, she could think of nothing to say.

Alta's baby started fussing. Rachel watched the other woman as she unpinned her shawl and bodice and put the baby to her breast.

"Yours suckles so much better than mine," her sister, Velma, said.

Smiling, Alta kissed the downy crown of her son's head. "But look at yours. He'll be crawling long before mine."

Rachel almost didn't feel the touch of a hand on her shoulder. She turned her head and looked into her mother's face.

"When you were a little girl," Sadie Miller said, "you used to say you were going to have thirteen babies. A baker's dozen."

Tears blurred Rachel's eyes and filled her throat. "Did I?"

Her mother nodded, so serious, so solemn. "Thirteen children and a hundred and sixty-nine grandchildren."

A startled laugh burst from Rachel's tight chest.

"Oh, yes," her mother went on. "For each of your babies was going to have thirteen babies of its own. You were only three at the time you made this declaration, but you had your brother Sol work out the mathematics of it." A crease appeared between her eyebrows. "But we always thought, your father and I, that Deacon Noah would be the one you would choose to marry."

"You never said so at the time."

"It was your life to live, Rachel."

My life to live as long as I kept to the straight-and-narrow path, she thought. And of course, she had. She always would.

Rachel glanced at her mother. They'd never talked this way before, and she was afraid of saying the wrong thing.

"Mem, have I changed so much from that girl you remember?"

Sadie turned her head away, and Rachel nearly gave up. But then Sadie gripped her sleeve. "It's not too late for you to have more babies." Sadie's hand fell to her lap. "He's always wanted you, has Noah Weaver. That man has always wanted you worse than a mud hen on a tin roof wants rain."

A smile flickered in her eyes, and Rachel felt herself smile in return. Her smile widened to include the twins, then all the women, spread out over their hand-pieced quilts. Her gaze went beyond—to the men at the trestle tables lingering over their empty soup bowls, to the children who had gathered around the pond again.

A thousand times her eyes and heart must have taken in such a scene. It was all the same, and so was she.

This is what it means to be Plain, she thought, this certainty of changelessness, of always belonging. This is what she'd really brought the outsider here to see. These people defined not the means to her life, but life itself, and she wouldn't know who she was without them. They would always be a part of her in ways she could never be to others. To any outsider, even him.

THOSE who died Plain were buried in a cemetery on a hill behind the Miller big house. It was a pretty spot, shaded by cottonwoods and carpeted with buffalo grass. A snake fence had been built around the graves, but one grave lay outside the fence, separate. No stone or wooden cross marked it, though everyone knew it was there.

Rachel's steps faltered as she passed by that grave on her way to the gate, but she didn't look at it. Couldn't bear to look at it.

Ben's grave was with the others, safe inside the fence. She had picked wildflowers, and now she knelt and put them in an empty can and wedged it into the earth beneath a rough-hewn granite marker.

She arranged the flowers so that they made a pleasing picture. "Here you are, Ben. A little something just for pretty." That's what he'd always said to her. *A little something just for pretty.* It was one of the rituals of spring, like watching the newborns take their first steps—Ben picking her flowers. Now she did it for him. "We had us a nice crop of fat lambs this year, including six sets of twins."

The rawhide hinges of the gate squeaked as it opened. Rachel scooted around on her knees. It was Noah.

"I was just telling Ben what a sweet crop of lambs we have."

"And did you tell him how you've been letting an *Englischer* work his evil wiles on you?"

Rachel said nothing, only got stiffly to her feet. She pushed past him, but he grabbed her arm, swinging her back around.

His lips tightened and twisted down at the corners, making him look mean. "That outsider, he sure does think he's somebody, he does. And now he's got you thinking you're somebody too."

She tried to pull free of him, but his grip tightened, twisting her head around toward the gate and the solitary grave that lay beyond it. "That's what comes of pride, of thinking you're somebody. Is that how you want to wind up, shunned in life and then in death?"

She squeezed her eyes shut. She wouldn't look.

"Do I need to tell you what to think, Rachel? How to be? 'Be ye not unequally yoked together with unbelievers; for what fellowship hath righteousness with unrighteousness? And what communion hath light with darkness?' "

She wrenched loose of him with such force she stumbled. Lurching upright, she backed away from him. "I've done nothing wrong. Do you think I could face Ben if—"

"Ben is dead!" He closed the space between them. "Listen to me, Rachel. Send the outsider away before it's too late. Light cannot be found in darkness. Or truth among lies."

She shook her head. "Oh, Noah. Surely you know nothing can seduce the truth from my heart."

He stared at her with eyes that were wet with anguish. "Once. Once I thought I knew you. But no longer."

This time she was the one to take a step toward him. She thought at first her legs weren't working right, the way the grass trembled and the ground shuddered beneath her feet. A heavy rumbling was pounding her ears, like thunder rolling across the sky.

She saw Noah's face change, contort with horror as his eyes focused beyond her onto the farmyard below. She spun around.

A herd of cattle about a hundred strong stampeded down the lane that led to the farmhouse, their sharp hooves churning up the grass.

The sheep in the meadow waddled in panicked retreat. In the farmyard men shouted, women and children screamed, running, knocking over trestle tables and benches, scattering quilts, running for the shelter of the barn and the houses, and still the cattle came. The pretty white pasture fences acted as a funnel for the crazed beasts.

And standing alone in their path was Benjo.

CHAPTER TWELVE

THE herd of cattle bore down on Rachel's son with hooves that could trample bones to dust. She screamed his name, although she knew he couldn't hear her over the churning roar. She lunged for the cemetery gate and plunged down the hill, all the while knowing she'd never get to her son in time. She could see his head jerking.

"Benjo!"

The shout hadn't come from her, although her mouth was open and she was screaming.

"Benjo!" the outsider shouted again, and he was there, running down the lane, running fast. And still he was too far away.

The earth shook. The thunder of the pounding hooves reverberated against Rachel's ears. The outsider launched himself the last few feet, knocking the boy to the ground, covering him with his own body as the panicked cattle swarmed and crashed over them. Rachel could see nothing but motley red hides and slashing hooves and black bawling mouths in white faces and, once only, the flash of something pale that might have been his shirt or his hand.

For just a moment the bellowing, trampling herd parted around the man and the boy. They seemed nothing but a pile of clothing in the mud of the road, but then the man stirred. He pushed himself up on his elbows and in his one good hand he had a small pistol. He fired point-blank into the crush of wild cattle that was once again bearing down on them.

The rumble and roar of the thudding hooves drowned out the shots. Rachel saw one of the steers slew sideways and stumble.

The rest turned then, bolting in rolling-eyed terror. They crashed into the whitewashed fence, smashing it to splinters, and exploded into the pasture, trampling the frenzied sheep in their path.

Rachel ran to her son and threw herself onto her knees beside him in the mud. She ran her hands over him, over and over every inch of his body.

"He's all right."

The words broke through the sounds of bellowing cattle, bleating sheep, men shouting, someone praying. A woman's sobs.

She looked at Johnny Cain. He had a gash below his eye, and his clothes were in tatters, exposing bruised and bleeding flesh. A deep cut in his hand—the hand that still held the fancy pearl-handled pistol—dripped blood into the hoof-churned mud.

Rachel took that hand and lifted it to her mouth. But he pulled away as his gaze narrowed on a single sweat-foamed horse coming toward them. Rachel realized that she had seen men on horseback with the cattle all along. Men who might have been trying to turn the cattle if they had not been driving them to this destruction. Fergus Hunter's men, who hated the Plain People and wanted them gone.

The outsider got slowly to his feet. Rachel stood as well, bringing Benjo with her. She looked across the ruined pasture. Sheep carcasses lay on the ripped and flattened grass. The thick stand of jack pines at the edge of the horseshoe-shaped meadow had finally blunted the cattle's wild stampede. Men on horseback, Hunter men, had the herd bunched beneath the trees now.

The sheep that weren't dead bleated wildly. The cattle too were nervous, humping their tail ends, shaking their heads, lowing. One of the men had left the herd and was trotting toward them.

"Take your boy," Cain told Rachel, "and run back to the house."

Rachel grabbed Benjo's arm, dragging him down the road.

Her father and her brothers and Noah all stood unmoving at the front of the yard, with the rest of the community behind them. They would come no farther; they would shout no warnings or challenges or curses, for it was the Plain way to meet threats from the outside world with silence and with acceptance.

The rider reined his horse up in front of Cain in a slurry of wet mud. A man with a short pointed beard and a long-barreled buffalo gun in his hand, he spewed tobacco spittle out the corner of his mouth. "My name's Woodrow Wharton. You ever hear of me?"

"I can't say that I have," the outsider said in his easy drawl.

The man nestled the gun's butt into his shoulder and sighted down the barrel. "They say you're the genuine article, a dead shot."

Rachel waited for the outsider to raise his own gun and kill him with it, kill this man who had hanged her husband and sent stampeding cattle to trample her son.

Woodrow Wharton's lips lifted off his teeth like a snarling dog's. "But then, a man," he said, "can't be a dead shot with nothing but an empty boob gun to hand. Can he, Johnny Cain?"

One of the other cowboys had left the cattle and was riding hard toward them now, shouting something. It distracted the stock inspector for a moment; then his eyes burned brighter. "It's a pure shame, it truly is, for me to have to put a hole in a man of your rep."

Johnny Cain smiled. "Are you going to do it, sir, or is it your intention to bore me to death talking about it?"

The light faded from Woodrow Wharton's eyes, and the hand that cradled the gun tightened its grip.

A harsh, strangled sound erupted from Benjo's throat. He started to run toward the outsider. Rachel made a wild grab for Benjo, and then she was running herself, running past him now. She tried to scream but felt as if her chest were being crushed. Something flew past her eyes, like the blurred beat of a hummingbird's wings.

The stock inspector's horse leaped as if bee-stung, shrieking and rearing, just as the buffalo gun fired. The roar of it smacked against Rachel's ears and stopped her heart. White smoke hazed the air. Then she saw the outsider and he was still alive, his gaze riveted on Woodrow Wharton, who now knelt in the mud. Wharton no longer had his buffalo gun, but he was reaching for the revolver at his hip.

A bullet whipcracked through the air. Wharton's spooked horse reared again, jerking loose the reins, and cantered off. Wharton fell back, his hands flailing at the air as he choked on his tobacco chaw.

At first Rachel thought the outsider had somehow managed to fire his empty pistol after all. But Wharton's angry eyes were on the other Hunter man, the one who'd come riding at them hard, shouting. Smoke wisped from the gun in the cowboy's hand.

"You forget which side you're on, breed," Wharton said.

"We've done enough," the cowboy said softly.

Turning his back on Wharton, he walked his horse through the shredding smoke. He drew abreast of the outsider, and the two men exchanged a long look, and then he turned his gaze on Rachel.

She had drawn Benjo up against her. The young man stared down at them.

"I'm Quinten Hunter, the Baron's son. I'm sorry we spoiled your frolic." He twisted sideways in the saddle to look at the pasture where his cattle milled and bunched and tore at the tender spring grass. "They're wild this time of year," he said, "after the winter and all. We were doing some cutting out for branding when a sage hen flew up from her nest, cackling, and set them off."

Rachel said nothing. She didn't believe him. There was a bitterness in her mouth, like the taste of ashes after a prairie fire.

"That's it, Quin. Why don't you just coddle them some more before the slaughtering." Wharton had gotten to his feet. He jerked around and limped off down the road to chase after his horse.

The other Hunter men had started to haze the cattle, quieted now, out of the Miller pasture and back down the lane. Quinten Hunter tipped his hat and rode off to join them.

He left behind a breath-held quiet, as if the very heart of the earth had suddenly stopped beating. The Plain People walked slowly down the road, praying as they came. Sol stopped before the shattered fence. He seemed unable to look beyond it to the blood-smeared pasture. Levi bent over a dead ewe.

Rachel knelt and gripped her son's face between her hands, pressing her lips hard to his forehead.

"M-Mem!" Benjo twisted away from her, and then the outsider was there before them, holding out his hand to Rachel's son.

"I'd be honored to shake your hand, Benjo Yoder."

Surprise stilled the boy; then he reached up, and the outsider's hand closed around his. "You got a quick eye with that sling of yours. A man can be mighty grateful to have a partner with a quick eye."

Benjo's chest swelled, and his face came alight with the outsider's praise, and Rachel's eyes stung with fresh tears. "You did a remarkable thing, and I am so proud of you," she said. "But it is only for the three of us to know. You mustn't speak of it to the others."

Benjo nodded, his mouth set serious now.

Rachel faced the outsider. She searched for words, spirit-lifting words like those he had given as a gift to her son. Words that she could give to him in turn to thank him for what he'd done.

"Rachel. Rachel, my child."

The sound of her father's voice, full of comfort and love, was nearly her undoing. She pressed her lips together and closed her eyes. And when she opened them again, it was to look into her father's dear face. For a moment she thought he would throw his arms around her and pull her close, but it was not the Plain way.

"I'm all right, Da." She draped her arms over Benjo's shoulders, linking her hands together over his heart. "We're both all right."

"Rachel. The Lord has indeed been merciful."

This time it was Noah who spoke, and she tried to smile at him and at her brother Samuel who stood with him.

Isaiah Miller turned to the outsider. "Outsiders sought to take my grandson from me," he said in his careful English, "but you, an outsider, gave him back to me."

Cain's gaze flickered over to Rachel. "Yeah, well, y'all ought to do what the men want: Sell out and move on."

Isaiah nodded slowly. "It's all in the Bible. I say, what if God is only testing our resolution? 'They that trust in the Lord shall be as mount Zion, which cannot be removed.'"

"Hunter and his hired guns sure enough seem resolved to remove you folk. And if they can't remove you, it's not too big a stretch before they resolve to bury you."

Samuel stepped up to thrust his finger in the outsider's face. "You speak of death, and you smile your devil's smile. But you'd be dead now if God hadn't caused that horse to spook when it did."

Benjo paled, and his left hand slid up to cover the sling that was tucked into the waist of his broadfalls.

The outsider gently pushed Samuel's finger aside. He flashed the most devilish of smiles. "Well, it must've been a miracle."

THAT evening Rachel listened to the hymns from the porch of her father's house. It was tradition for the young people to gather at the end of a worship Sunday to have a sing. It was a time of courtship, with the girls sitting on one side of the long trestle table and the boys on the other.

"You're to come in now."

Rachel turned. It was her brother Sol. He reached out with his big clumsy fingers and pushed a loose strand of her hair back under her cap.

Their father sat at the long kitchen table, the rest of her brothers and Noah on their feet behind him. They waited for Isaiah to be the first to speak. Yet he sat in silence, with the big family Bible open before him, combing his thick beard with his fingers.

"We have been thinking," her brother Samuel said, though it was not his place to do so, "that you don't need to hire some outsider to work your farm. We will give you the help you need."

She knelt beside her father at his chair, folded her hands in her lap, and bowed her head. "Is this what you think, Da?"

Isaiah pressed his hands flat on the table. "I will tell you what I know. I know that he's not one of us. That he can never be."

"He's not like other outsiders," Rachel said. "He doesn't drink the devil's brew. He's careful not to blaspheme. He—"

"He brought a gun with him to the preaching," Noah said flatly. "A gun that saved our Benjo's life."

Rachel felt her father's hand settle on her head. "But still," he said, "for all the good the outsider has done, he is not one of us."

"I only sought to hire help for the farm until I marry again."

"That's easily solved," Samuel said. "Marry tomorrow."

Rachel raised her head. She looked at her father so that he might know the truth of what she said. "Ben is still in my heart."

Samuel spat out a short laugh, with something sharp in it. "I say that if the *Englischer* stays through the summer, then, mind you, come mating season he'll be gone and you will be ready to marry."

At any other time she would have laughed, for it was such a preposterous thing. To tell her, a grown woman and with a child of her own, whom she must marry and when. But she couldn't laugh, not looking into her brother Samuel's face, flushed as it was with anger.

Her gaze went to Noah. "If he stays," she said, "then I promise that come mating season, I will marry again."

She waited for her father to speak, but he gave her only silence. She thought she should leave before she started to cry or said too much. She'd already said too much.

THE croaking of the bullfrogs by the pond rumbled in the blue dusk. Rachel waded through the thick grass looking for wildflowers. She felt unstrung. She knew the outsider would find her, wanted him to find her. Yet when he came, she turned her back on him.

"What did they do to you?" he said.

"Nothing." She caught at her lower lip, tears blurring her eyes.

He thrust his hands in his coat pockets and turned away from her. "They want me to leave," he said.

"I promised Noah I would marry him after the breeding season."

To that he said nothing. But then, he didn't understand the cost of her promise, or perhaps he didn't care.

She cut through the grass with long strides, heading for the hill behind the big house. When he didn't come along, she stopped and waited for him. After a moment he caught up to her.

At the cemetery she didn't go through the gate. She knelt beside the grave that lay outside it. "My brother Rome is buried here," she said. "Do you know why he's apart from the others?"

He studied the grave. "He was an outsider," he finally said.

"No. Not in the way that you are." She took in a deep breath. "Rome went to one of those revival meetings one day, on a lark, and a saddlebag preacher laid his hands on him, and the next thing Rome is saying he'd been born again in Jesus; he'd been saved."

She brushed her hand across her face, breathed again. "How this happened, we don't know. He wouldn't confess to being wrong, and so he was placed under the *Bann* by the church for having a *fremder Glaube,* a strange belief. He was shunned. Shunned by us all."

"Why didn't he just leave, then?"

She looked up at him, her eyes wide. "This was his home. How could he leave his home? Only to us it was as if he had died. He moved among us, but he was dead. And then one day he did die."

The outsider knelt beside her and took her in his arms. She clung to his coat, and he held her, stroking her back.

"I want you to stay," she said.

CHAPTER THIRTEEN

IT GOT hot early that spring of '86, the spring the outsider was hired on to work Rachel Yoder's sheep farm. A haze built up in the mountains, and overhead the sky blazed so blue it hurt to look at it and stayed empty but for a few feathers of cloud.

Folk said a drought was in the making, and everyone prayed for rain. But no rain came. And on the morning the outsider was to pay his first visit to town, the sun came up smoking and the wind died early, so that by midday the whole valley lay sweltering beneath a blanket of gummy, heavy air.

"Isn't this a fine summer's day we're having in spring?" Rachel said to him as he loaded the wagon with crocks of her clotted cheese. "The grasshoppers started singing even before the sun came up."

Cain growled something about how now they wouldn't shut up. She laughed back at him, not caring that the heat made him grumpy.

The wagon made a song as it creaked and clattered its way to town over the ruts in the road. The harness chains jingled, and the old mare's plodding hooves beat a sleepy tattoo on the baked dirt.

Rachel often dreaded going into town—the outsiders all stared so and could be so mean. But today a feeling of excitement gripped her, as if they were off on some grand adventure. She knew a part of her happiness came from sitting with him here in her spring wagon, with Benjo between them. He almost looked as if he belonged with her now. His flashy clothes, all but the black duster, had been ruined in the cattle stampede, so Ben's broadfalls, sack coat, and felt hat had been added to the Plain shirt. He still wore his own fancy stitched boots and black suspenders. And, always, his revolver.

Like the road they traveled on, the Miawa Valley itself had the undulating shape of ripples on a washboard, with Miawa City tucked into the lowest dip of the rolling buttes and hills. The first thing a body saw when topping the rise before town was a meandering creek lined with diamond willows and aspens. Otherwise the town was a sparse collection of ramshackle buildings made of logs weathered to the color of old buffalo bones.

They passed the cemetery first. Then came a two-story gray clapboard house that was encircled by a double gallery and had a red locomotive lantern hanging from a hook next to the front door. Three women in silk wrappers and hair papers sat perched on the upper balcony rail like a flock of bright-colored finches.

"Th-that's the house where all the Jezebels live," Benjo declared.

Rachel hauled her son's pointing finger back into the wagon. "If you're going to flap at something, make it these flies on my cheese."

Benjo twisted around to pick up a bundle of willow branches. He waved the makeshift fan over the crocks of clotted cheese that his mother hoped to trade to defray the cost of their monthly supplies.

As for Rachel, she kept her eyes carefully on the road ahead and off that house of sin.

"You going to roost up there all day?"

Rachel looked at the outsider's raised hand. He stood in the road waiting to help her climb out of the wagon.

Her face burned as he took a step closer and clasped her around the waist, swinging her down and onto the warped boardwalk. She gasped aloud and clung to his shoulders like a child.

It had been a polite thing to do, nothing more. Yet she had been so aware of the hard strength of his hand and arm pressing into her back. Of how, just for an instant, their faces had been close enough for his lips to have touched hers.

She looked around her, feeling disoriented, as if she'd never seen Tulle's Mercantile, Wang's Chop House, the Slick-as-a-Whistle Barber and Bath, or the town's four honky-tonks and dance halls.

"We better get those crocks out of the hot sun," Cain told Benjo. "After Doc Henry cuts this plaster off my arm this morning," he added, "I'm going to go buy me a horse. Want to help me pick it out?" Cain set a couple of the crocks by Tulle's Mercantile.

Benjo looked like he'd just been given the moon.

"A horse?" Rachel said.

He grunted as Benjo slapped another crock of clotted cheese into his hands. "Lady, if I ever do got to make a quick getaway, it sure ain't gonna be on that slug mare of yours."

"Oh." Of course he would need a horse. After all, he wasn't going to stay forever. When he left, he would certainly need a horse.

He took off his hat to cuff the sweat from his forehead. His hair was getting as long as any Plain man's.

He dropped the hat back on his head and gave its brim a rakish slant. "I'll try not to do any misbehaving today, Mrs. Yoder, but I ain't promising." His arm settled over Benjo's thin shoulders. "Come along, partner."

Rachel watched them walk off down the boardwalk, feeling strangely left out. He was taking her son along with him to buy a horse that he would then use to leave them.

MARILEE shifted her hips on the black leather cushion and focused her eyes on the ceiling. It was so hot she could practically hear the heat, as if the very air were panting and sweating. Dr. Lucas Henry straightened up, going to a white porcelain basin to wash his hands. "Marilee, my sweet Marilee," he said, his voice slurring. His mustache quirked up at one corner, surprising her into a smile. "You are, by the bye, in an interesting condition."

Her smile perished into a wail. "Aw, shoot!"

She sat up, folding her hands over her middle, swaying dizzily.

He had taken a couple of steps back to lean against a glass-fronted cabinet filled with thick tomes, medicine bottles, and gruesome-looking instruments. His arms were folded across his chest.

"This is all your fault, Lucas Henry, curse your miserable hide."

"*My* fault? What quirk of womanly logic has led you to—"

"That female preventive you been givin' us girls up at the Red House didn't prevent nothin'. First Gwendolene and now me. Lord, Mother Jugs is gonna throw a pure hissy fit when I tell her."

"Every occupation has its hazards." The doctor unfolded his arms. "While you put your lovely gown back on, I'll put together an herbal infusion for your morning sickness."

She twirled a finger in the air. "Whoopee. If it works as well as your preventive did, it'll have me pukin' clean into next year."

He laughed. "Marilee, Marilee. Shame on you for your blasphemy. Don't you know we doctors are God?"

As she slid off the examining couch, she could feel herself smiling. She did so love the way he said her name: *Marilee, Marilee.*

She jerked on her petticoat and knotted the tapes. She sucked in her belly until it felt pressed against her backbone, so she could fasten the sateen buttons on the front of her corset without having to loosen the back laces. She tied on her crinoline bustle, giving her bottom a little wriggle so that it settled properly.

She was already feeling fat, and she wasn't even showing yet. In a few months she'd be wide as the back end of a cow and twice as ugly.

Fear cramped in Marilee's belly, making her queasy again. She didn't want to lose her looks; they were all she had. Marilee had figured out early where all her blessings—and all her miseries—would come from in this life. She had a face sweet and pretty enough to break a man's heart, and she had beguiling ways. And she practiced them too. Even the other girls up at the Red House, who were all jealous of each other, thought she was sweet as sugar. But then, her daddy, who himself was as mean as they came, always used to say that when his little Marilee called the tune, even the gators had to dance.

And everybody danced, except for Doc Henry. She'd tried everything she could think of to beguile him. She'd even tried being herself, and that was risky, what with him being an educated Virginia gentleman and her being ignorant trash from the Florida swamp.

But then, it didn't take a lot of fancy words and genteel manners to do what she did. When Lucas Henry came to the Red House, he always picked her. He came to satisfy his carnal urgings, nothing more. She was the fool who'd fallen in love.

Marilee pulled her pink foulard dress over her head. Her fingers trembled as she put on her straw bonnet, anchoring it to her pouf of curls with a faux pearl pin. She fastened her chatelaine pocket to the hook at her waist. She tiptoed to the door, slowly eased it open, and poked her head out into the parlor. It was empty.

She straightened her back and glided into the room with her head held high, pretending that she lived here and was entertaining company for tea. It was a small house, with only four rooms: this parlor, the room he did his doctoring in, his bedroom, and a kitchen.

A brown tweed frock coat hung from the arm of a bentwood coat tree. She lifted one of the sleeves and rubbed it against her cheek. It smelled fresh, with just a hint of sandalwood. It was one of the things she liked most about him, his clean smell.

A beautiful hide trunk stood against one wall, and above it hung an army officer's sword. He'd once done his doctoring in the cavalry. That was one of the few things she knew about him.

She heard a footstep behind her and swung around. He stood at the threshold to the kitchen, holding a small wicker tray of dried flowers. "I was fetching the chamomile for your infusion," he said.

She could smell the sharp tang of the dried flowers even from across the room, and she couldn't help smiling at him. "You're like someone's old granny, you know that? What with the way you're always growin' herbs and roots to make potions with, 'stead of dosing people proper with patent medicines like other docs."

"Dulling one's pain with alcohol is certainly an option. But a bottle of Rose Bud whiskey is cheaper and far more effective."

Her smile faded slightly, for she hadn't understood him; she never understood half of what he said.

Sighing, she watched while he made up the potion for her morning sickness at his big rolltop oak desk. He wrapped it up in an old scrap of newspaper and told her how to brew it into a tea to drink every morning before she got out of bed. She put the small parcel in her chatelaine pocket and took a dollar out of it to pay him for his doctoring. He accepted the dollar, just like she took the three dollars from his hand every other Saturday night. Gentleman to the end, he saw her to the door.

She cocked her head at him. "See you tomorrow, then?"

"Of course, my sweet Marilee. After all, too much virtue can lead to too little vice."

She laughed and tossed her head, and she swiveled her hips as she walked away from him, bouncing her bustle.

She waited until she heard his door close behind her before slowing her steps. She could feel her face sagging, feel a band of misery tightening around her throat, feel the tears welling up.

She stumbled along the boardwalk and into the small alley that cut between Tulle's Mercantile and a saloon that was still only half built. The tang of new-cut wood pinched her nose.

She collapsed onto an upturned nail keg, and she breathed through her mouth to keep from crying, but from deep within her the sobs came, exploding in a downpour of tears, tears that weren't only for this moment but for all the hurting of her life.

DR. LUCAS Henry sat in his brown leather wing chair, his bleary gaze focused on the surface of his rolltop desk. A single celluloid hairpin lay on the green felt blotter. He'd found the hairpin on his examining couch a few moments ago. It must have fallen from Marilee's hair. Poor, sweet Marilee.

He'd brought the hairpin back with him into the parlor, along with a fresh bottle of Rose Bud. He had also fetched a clean glass from the kitchen, but then he hadn't bothered with it, choosing instead to drink straight from the bottle.

He picked up the hairpin and flipped it over and over between his fingers until he dropped it. When he picked it up, he tossed it into the empty fire grate, just as there was a knock on the door.

He took another swig from the bottle. He felt the black depression settle over him. Some days—most days—it felt as if he lived in the bottom of a well with no hope of crawling out.

The knock came again, louder.

" 'Physician, heal thyself,' " he quoted aloud.

He stood up, swaying as his booze-sodden legs sought a safe purchase on the Turkey carpet. He took his spectacles from his pocket and hooked them with exaggerated care over his ears. He made his way to the door and flung it open, blinking against the sunlight.

"Please, do come in," he said, slurring the words.

Johnny Cain walked through the door.

"I suppose you're here to get that plaster sawed off," Lucas said.

Cain took off the Plain hat he was wearing and hooked it on the bentwood coat tree. "So long as you don't saw off my arm along with it."

It was a simple matter to remove the surgeon's plaster and splints. Lucas cut through the gypsum with a saw. When he was done, Cain stretched out the healed arm, flexing his fingers.

"Your killing hand, is it?" Lucas said.

"Killing and other deeds, both wondrous and wicked."

The doctor nodded at the desperado's hand. "That one might not serve you so well for deeds of any sort in the future. It was a bad break. Your arm may seem much as before, but the bone's been weakened. I wouldn't trust it with my life."

"I never figured on dying in bed anyway." Johnny Cain looked up at him, smiling, but Lucas saw that his eyes were empty.

"How about a drink?" Lucas said.

"No, thank you. I'll take some water, though."

"The kitchen's in there, back through the parlor."

He followed behind Cain. "There's a *Harper's Monthly* been making the rounds," Lucas went on, "with a story that has you killing your first man when you were but a tender fourteen. Or was it twelve? In any event, twenty-seven more are said to have followed that poor unfortunate into the grave in the intervening years, dispatched by your lightning-quick draw. Have I got the tale right?"

Cain worked the pump, then bent over the sink to drink, his shirt pulling taut across his back. "I haven't stopped to do a tally recently."

Laughing, Lucas waved a hand. "You probably noticed, by the proliferation of stray dogs scavenging in what passes for a street around here, that our fair town doesn't have an excess of law enforcement. Hence, you may slaughter the citizenry with relative impunity. Although, as I'm both physician and undertaker, you might want to spare a thought for the trouble you'd be putting me to."

The kitchen was small, barely large enough for an old sawbuck table and a potbellied stove. Cain stood at his ease in front of the big stone sink, his quick and dangerous hands hanging at his sides.

"Tell you what," he said. "I'll shoot them stone-dead so's you don't have to do any doctoring, and I'll do it where it don't show so's you'll have little work in making them pretty for the burying."

Lucas laughed again. And then the laughter faded as he stared into Johnny Cain's eyes and realized that if the man had ever had a soul, the devil had long ago claimed it.

"Why do you do it?" he said to Cain.

"Do what?"

"Live the way you do. Hasn't it occurred to you that it's a flamboyant, self-indulgent, rather prolonged form of suicide?"

"So's drowning yourself in a bottle."

The doctor tried to swallow through the tightness in his throat. "What of our dear Plain Rachel?" he went on. "Have you spared a thought for what you're doing to her? She who is not plain at all, with her dark red hair and those big solemn gray eyes. She who is so innocent, so pathetically innocent. You could destroy her utterly."

Cain's voice expressed only mild inquiry. "Why do you care?"

"I like her. And when I'm not wallowing too deep in my drunkenness, I admire her, bound as she is by her faith that is gentle and yet so severe. In this world, but not of it."

Cain started to pass through the door. Then he stopped and turned. His stare was an insult, filled as it was with that cold indifference. "You're right, Doc. I do have it in my mind to seduce Rachel Yoder. But not for all the obvious reasons."

CHAPTER FOURTEEN

THE livery was the only building in town to wear any paint, and the paint it sported was the bright red of a spit-polished apple. Benjo Yoder had waited for Cain in the gray twilight shade cast by the building. Even on hot days, passing through the livery's sliding double doors was like dipping your toe into a pool of springwater. Cool moist air enveloped Cain and Benjo, redolent of hay and manure. From the yard came the pang-ping-pang of hammer on steel.

They found the hostler, Trueblue Stone, at the smithy out back, fastening a new handle onto a battered black-bottomed boiling pot. Trueblue wore only a pair of tattered trousers and a big leather apron that fell all the way to the domed toes of his hobnailed boots. The bare skin of his arms and back was shiny and black. He spoke to his horses with words that came from a place called Africa.

The men fell into a conversation about horses, and when Trueblue was finished with the pot, they went to the corral. There were five horses for sale, four geldings and a young mare. "Which one do you fancy?" Cain asked.

It took Benjo a moment to realize the question had been directed at him, and his chest stretched with surprise and pleasure. But with Trueblue standing there, Benjo knew he had no hope of getting any of his words out from around his twisted-up tongue. He pointed to the mare, a chestnut with a blaze on her face and white stockings.

"She is the prime one of the lot, all right: nice sleek coat, bright eyes, a long arch to her neck, and a clear-footed gait. You've a good eye, partner." Cain made the boy's chest swell even more.

Cain dickered with Trueblue for a long time over the price, and then they dickered some more over a saddle and bridle. Benjo loved watching Johnny Cain, and he loved listening to him talk in that cool, slow way of his. He even pretended to be him sometimes, tilting his hat over one eye and moving in an easy, loose-jointed way.

Afterward, out again on the hot and dusty street, Cain wiped the sweat off the back of his neck and said, "You know, Benjo, I sure have got me a touch of dry throat, what with all the argufying I had to do with Trueblue Stone over the cost of that mare you talked me into. How about if I was to buy us a couple of sarsaparillas?"

Grinning, Benjo nodded. "Puh—puh—puh—" *Please.*

They walked side by side down the boardwalk, and Benjo relished the looks and the whispers they were attracting. And when they stopped in front of the Gilded Cage saloon, he thought he would explode from nervous excitement, although the moment lost some of its shine when Cain said, "Maybe you better wait out here."

Benjo waited until the saloon's batwing doors had stopped swinging behind Cain's back before he knelt down and peered beneath them. He saw a tobacco-stained puncheon floor sprinkled with sawdust. A whiskified man sat slumped over a table, snoring. Two more men stood at a brown felt-covered table, knocking ivory balls around with long, skinny sticks.

Benjo heard the ring of jingle-bobs and the scrape of spurs behind him. He backed up on his hands and knees, out of the way of the door. His gaze went up winged, silver-studded black leather chaps to a fringed white buckskin shirt and a cowhide vest, settling finally on a billy-goat beard, a bulging cheek, and pale, wet eyes.

A strange light appeared in those eyes when they fell on Benjo.

"You sure do keep turning up where you don't belong, don't you, boy?" Woodrow Wharton said.

Wharton's lips peeled back from his pointed teeth, and he sent a stream of tobacco juice whizzing close to Benjo's face. Laughing, he slammed his hand on the swinging door and disappeared into the murky shadows of the Gilded Cage.

WHENEVER RACHEL'S FATHER preached of the Plain being strangers in a strange land, it put her in mind of Tulle's Mercantile. Today, with shafts of bright sunlight streaming through the bay window to haze the air with dancing dust motes, it especially seemed a mythical place, full as it was of so many tempting things.

Like that bolt of yellow sateened muslin, so shimmery it looked shot with sunbeams. She stroked the cloth. What did one make out of such a bright material? She wished she could think of a purpose for it that wasn't worldly. A Plain woman wasn't supposed to covet such a thing, but she did.

"How there, Miz Mutton Puncher. What can I do for you today?"

Rachel jerked her hand back and whirled, color flooding her cheeks. Mr. Tulle had a nose like a crow's beak and a whittled brown face, and his black button eyes were scowling at her as if he suspected her of soiling things with her sheep-grubby hands.

Like most outsiders, he'd always made her uncomfortable, and she stumbled through her list of purchases: flour, salt pork, soda crackers, hominy, brown sugar, a five-gallon tin of coal oil, a bag of Arbuckle coffee beans. A couple of yards of that yellow muslin.

He packed her purchases into hardtack cases, but he didn't offer to help her carry them out to the wagon. She had to make several trips and was just coming out of the mercantile for the third time when she saw Benjo running down the boardwalk toward her.

Suddenly she realized that Benjo wasn't the only one running. People were spilling out of the shops, shouting and excited.

Benjo slammed into her, spitting and sputtering. She let him drag her after him, fear burning a hot path up her chest.

It was the outsider; she knew it. He'd killed someone, was going to kill someone. Someone had killed him.

Benjo wormed his way through the knot of men at the slatted wooden doors of the honky-tonk, pulling her with him. She stopped on the threshold, blinking against the sting of tobacco smoke and the sudden darkness after the bright sunlight.

"Hard-boiled eggs tend to be yellow inside," she heard a man say. Shadows suddenly moved, flattening against the wall.

Two men stood before the long, wooden bar. One, Johnny Cain, faced the mirror behind the bar, his hand wrapped around a bottle of sarsaparilla. The other man was Woodrow Wharton, and he had a gun in his hand.

He spit tobacco juice. "I believe I spoke to you, sir," he said.

Slowly Johnny Cain turned his head, tilting it slightly so his eyes could clear his hat brim. "Pardon me," he said, and he smiled.

His shoulder dipped as he backhanded the bottle against the bar. The bottle burst into a spray of sarsaparilla and shattering glass. The jagged shard in Cain's hand slashed across Wharton's mouth.

The man screamed. One hand, the hand without the gun, flew up to his mouth.

"No!" Rachel cried, and took a step toward them.

Johnny Cain's head whipped around, his eyes flaring.

Wharton's gun came up, pointing, but Cain was already snatching his own gun from its holster as he whirled back, so fast that all Rachel saw was a flash and a puff of smoke. An explosion ripped the air.

Wharton was slammed backward with the force of a mule kick. His back hit the bar, and he hung there for a heartbeat, staring slack-jawed, as if in surprise. Johnny Cain fired three more shots. Slowly Wharton's legs folded, and he slid to the floor.

Powder smoke drifted past Rachel's eyes. A smell like brimstone pinched her nose. As she stared, hard fingers dug into her arm, and she was spun around abruptly. Johnny Cain slapped the batwing doors open, dragging her behind him, and people were suddenly scurrying out of their way.

She looked around and saw Benjo trotting along the boardwalk after them, and she breathed her first breath in an eternity.

When they got to the wagon, the outsider turned her to face him. It hurt to look into his eyes. But all he said was, "You and the boy better stay here."

As he walked off, she could feel her heart beating, and each breath needed a deliberate effort. After a time she and Benjo climbed into the wagon. Her mouth was dry, her belly sour.

"I told everyone he doesn't drink the devil's brew."

She hadn't realized she'd voiced the thought until Benjo jumped. The words burst out of him, whole and complete as they rarely did. "We got thirsty buying the horse. He only went in there to get us some sarsaparillas."

Rachel shocked and horrified herself by laughing.

"That man," Benjo went on, "he's the one who hung Da. I'm glad he's duh—duh—duh—"

"Dead," Rachel said.

She shivered. She wondered what the outsider was doing now. Maybe he was seeing about burying the man. The street was as empty now as a ghost town. But then, there was no marshal in Miawa City for anyone to summon, and Sheriff Getts might be anywhere in the territory. Cain had no law to answer to. Except God's law.

He came out of the livery then, leading a tacked-up chestnut mare. His face was as smooth and cold as pond ice.

He knotted the horse's reins around the wagon's tailboard. The wagon dipped and rocked as he climbed aboard. He had, Rachel suddenly saw, Woodrow Wharton's blood splattered on his shirt.

By THE time the wagon pulled into the yard, a storm had moved in. Sheets of lightning backlighted the clouds, followed by great claps of thunder that seemed to rip the heavens apart.

The skirling wind tore at Rachel's skirts as she and Benjo and MacDuff herded the ewes and lambs to the lee of a gently sloping hill, away from the danger of flooding coulees and lightning-struck cottonwoods. She didn't see what the outsider did or where he went. They hadn't spoken once on the drive home. She despised him for what he had done, and she despaired of him. But a dark, ugly corner of her soul was in awe. And gratified. Oh, yes, gratified. Woodrow Wharton was dead, and she was glad.

They stayed with the sheep to keep them bunched. Although the storm was bright and noisy for a time, it gave up no rain. Only after the storm had passed did she go to see if the outsider had put his new horse in the barn or if he had used it to ride away.

The barn was cool. Her old gray draft horse was in one of the stalls, crunching on oats. In another his flashy chestnut mare was drawing up great mouthfuls of water from the trough.

Cain hadn't moved or made a sound, but she knew somehow

where to find him. He sat at the far end of the barn on the dirt floor, with his shoulders pressed to the wall, his arms hanging over his bent knees. He lifted his head as she walked up to him. For a moment she saw through the cold, glittering windows of his eyes into his shrouded, tangled soul, but then his eyelids came down like shutters.

"Don't touch me," he said, surging to his feet.

She took a step toward him, and he flinched. But she kept coming until she was close enough to wrap her arms around his waist and press her face against his chest. She could feel him trying to hold himself very still, as if he feared to draw even so much as a single breath.

"Please don't touch me, Rachel. I'm filthy," he said, and she knew he wasn't talking about dust and sweat. But he let her hold him anyway, until he stopped shuddering.

DOWN in the valley at the big house, a piano waltz floated sweet and lilting out the parlor's open windows.

Quinten Hunter stood outside in the shadows of the gallery and watched his father's wife. Her back swayed gently as her hands stroked the black and ivory keys in the candlelight.

The waltz she played was one of his favorites. He was starting to tap his boot in time with the music when the front door to the house opened. A match hissed and flared in the night, lighting the sharp bones of his father's face.

"That you out here in the dark, Quin?" the Baron said. "I thought you were catting in town with the rest of the boys."

"Woody's being buried in the morning," Quinten said. "I didn't go to the Red House with the others, because I don't believe in going to funerals with a boozed-up head. It's disrespectful."

The Baron blew out a puff of cigar smoke. "Who made up that rule of etiquette? Besides, Woodrow Wharton was a bloody-minded fool to let things get personal between himself and a shootist of Johnny Cain's rep, then try to best the man in a quick-draw contest. We ought to be able to drive those mutton punchers on out of here without having to come up against Cain's gun."

"He's living with them," Quinten said. "Maybe he figures that gives him a stake in the issue."

"So he should be getting a real education, then, on how perilous is the life of a sheep farmer. What with droughts and coyotes and these hot dry days we've been having." The Baron drew deeply on his cigar. "You can never tell, for instance, when a stray spark is going to set those woolly farms to blazing like pitch torches."

Quinten leaned his head back. "Pa, don't . . ."

"Don't what?"

He turned his head, trying to see the Baron's face in the night. "Why are you so hell-bent on pushing things with those Plain folk?"

His father's words seemed to come ripping out of his big chest with a dark desperation. "I'm in deep as a tar baby to the stockyard banks, Quin. And stuck fast. Which means I got to run more cows this year to make even half of what I made last year—"

"But we're already overstocked and overgrazed as it is."

"You're making my point for me, boy. Those cows, they got to eat. Throw in this killing drought, and the simple fact is, I need what those Plain folk got. I need their grass."

"But they don't want to sell out to us. To you, I mean," Quinten amended, flushing. "You can't just make them give it up."

His father laughed and said, "Aye, that I can, lad o' mine. Ride on up to the reservation and take a good look at what's left of your ma's people; then tell me if the world's not divided into those that take and those that are made to give it up."

Quinten swallowed hard and looked away, toward unseen grassland that went on for mile after mile and would never be enough.

CHAPTER FIFTEEN

Rachel loaded a water butt onto a small dumpcart and dragged it out to where the men were making hay. Windrows of the freshly mowed timothy grass ribbed the meadow. The hot wind blew thick with the smell of it, sweet and rich. Two days ago the hay had been mowed and raked and left to dry; today they were stacking it. Mose Weaver and the outsider did the forking. Noah did the layering and rolling because that required the most skill. It surprised her, but the outsider seemed to like making hay. He called it "sweet and sweaty work."

It was the Plain way for neighbor to help neighbor, even though Noah sure enough resented Johnny Cain's participation in the task. "That outsider, he doesn't know beans about hay," he'd grumped to her after the first day.

The men finished off the windrow they were loading before they came for water. The hay crackled as it was forked and stacked. Prickling dust swirled into the hot air, coating their faces and hair so white their heads looked dipped in cornstarch.

Benjo and the outsider were the first ones to the water butt. She gave them each a dipperful, and they slurped it down.

"Is it hot enough for you, Mr. Cain?" she asked him.

"Heck, no," he said, drawling out the words teasing and lazy. "Back where I come from, we call this middlin' weather. We don't say it's hot enough till the water in the creek gets to boilin'."

"Wuh—we don't say it's hot enough," Benjo chimed in, "till the r-rocks start to melt."

Laughing, Rachel looked from the man to the boy and back to the man again. They looked like big-lipped clowns, their mouths and chins washed clean while the rest of their faces were still chalky white with hay dust. "If you two aren't a pair of a kind," she said.

Noah Weaver tossed the dipper back into the water butt with a splash. "Hard work is good for a man's soul," he said.

"Noah has always built the best haystacks in the valley, haven't you, Noah?" Rachel said. "High and tall and straight."

Noah stared at her, a tightness around his eyes. "The righteous man doesn't swell up with pride in his work; he just does it." He turned on his heel, saying over his shoulder, "There's still plenty hay that needs stacking sometime before next winter." And the tone of his voice made the boys jump and trot after him.

The outsider lingered behind, though, his gaze following the Plain man's stiff back.

"I'm sorry," Rachel said. "He doesn't mean to always be scolding. He's just . . . being Deacon Noah."

Cain said, "Aw, I've been ridden with sharper spurs."

The hot wind plucked at her loose cap strings, making them dance. She tossed them out of the way over her shoulders. She could feel his eyes on her, hotter than the summer wind.

"We're having rivels and puddins for dinner," she said. "It's a haymaking tradition. And peppermint tea is cooling in the creek."

"I ain't asking what rivels are in case I don't want to know."

She spun around, laughing at him. "Hunh. Once you're done building me a haystack to the moon, Mr. Cain, I expect you'll be hungry enough to eat anything."

She took off for the house at a run, her skirts tossing gaily.

TO RACHEL the clang of the bell on the leading wether—a neutered male sheep—was a joyous song marking the end to a good day.

She drove the herd of ewes and their lambs onto the rough stubble of the newly shorn hay meadow and saw the woollies settled and munching happily. Although she had dishes to wash and a kitchen to scrub down, she stayed in the pasture. She stood in the hay stubble and let the hot wind blow wild through her.

Slowly she tipped her head back and let herself be drawn up, up, up into the deep blue of the evening sky, the endless and empty sky.

"A body could get lost up there if she isn't careful."

The outsider stood leaning against the trunk of a jack pine, his hat dangling from his fingers. She stared at his reckless face with its flaring cheekbones, his fierce mouth, his eyes. . . . Those eyes weren't cold, not cold at all.

She stared up into his face, a face that had somehow become beloved to her, and a wild yearning swelled open inside her.

Just then one of lambs took a notion to buck, spooking the whole flock into a run, so that they flowed around Rachel and Cain and down the sloping meadow.

They laughed, and their laughter—his mellow and deep, hers light and airy—became a carol of bells. The woollies bleated and baaed, bass and tenor notes. Grasshoppers rasped in the tall grass along the creek. A killdeer trilled sweetly, and a chickadee burbled.

"Oh, do you hear it, Johnny! Do you hear the music?"

She whirled to face him in her excitement. "I hear them, you see—all the sounds the earth makes. I hear the wind and the creek and all the noises the animals make—the sheep and birds and frogs. I hear them all in my head, and it comes together into music. I don't know how. I can't explain it, except that I know it's wicked."

He lowered his head slightly. "What's wicked about taking the songs of life and making a symphony out of them?"

She turned away from him, suddenly shy. She began to walk toward the house, and he fell into step beside her. She felt lightheaded and light-footed.

"Have you ever done any dancing?" she asked him.

"I have been to a few fandangos in my time."

Somehow they had stopped walking and were facing each other. He surprised her by starting to sing a lilting song about a girl named Annie Laurie. He was fitting his palm to hers, entwining their fingers, while his other hand was lifting her arm by the wrist and draping it over his shoulder, and then he was sliding his arm around her waist.

And they were dancing.

He twirled her around and around in dipping, sweeping circles, and she clung to him as he turned her faster. Her head fell back, and she opened her eyes to the wide blue sky spinning crazily above her while the earth tilted and swayed beneath her floating feet.

And then suddenly their bodies slowed and drew closer, and his mouth came down over hers, pressing her lips. She dug her fingers into the hard muscles of his back to hold on. And they might have been dancing still, for the way the sky spun and the earth tilted.

It lasted forever and ended too soon. His mouth let go of hers.

"I want you, Rachel," he said. "I want to lie with you."

She put her fingers on his mouth. Her heart was fierce with panic. "No. We can never," she said. "Not only is it a terrible sin, but what you would take from me is so much less than what I would end up giving. And there's nothing you can give me," she said, pulling away. "Not even if you somehow came to love me, because you are an outsider."

She turned and walked away from him. She kept her back stiff and her head up, because she didn't want him to know how hard this was when she needed him and loved him so much. It was a need so elemental, so consuming, that it was like needing air to breathe.

"You ask too much, Rachel," he shouted after her.

THAT night the wind blew hot and smelled sweet of fresh-cut hay and sunbaked earth.

The men on horseback pulled up on the north bank of the creek, where they were shielded by the thick willow brakes and cottonwoods. The small log farmhouse, the slope-roofed barn, the squat lambing sheds all looked quiet.

"You sure you got the grit for this, lad o' mine?"

"I'm less worried about my grit than about your good sense," Quinten Hunter said. "The whole valley's like a tinderbox."

His father laughed. "But in the end, you'll do what I tell you, where I tell you. Won't you?"

"Yes, sir." Quinten gave a hard smile, but the branding iron he carried was heavy in his sweating hand. The Circle H mark glowed fire red in the dark, like a giant eye.

"Let's get it done, then," the Baron said, and sent his horse splashing across the creek and toward the stacks of fresh-mown hay.

Quinten spurred his own horse on. Three Hunter cowhands crossed the creek on their heels. These others had joined up with Quinten and his father shortly after they had left the campfire they'd built to heat the iron, and Quinten had paid them little mind. The Baron had made it plain that tonight at least he was putting the Circle H brand and all that it stood for into the hand of his breed son.

They rode through a flock of sheep, scattering the bleating animals. Inside the farmhouse a dog barked. One of the cowhands fired two shots from his six-shooter, and a door slammed shut.

Quinten put the burning brand to a haystack. White smoke curled up from the iron, and the hay melted into tongues of flame.

From out of the night a gun fired. The cowhand next to Quinten slumped over in his saddle with a soft cry.

"Cain!" the Baron shouted. He pointed his gun toward a sheepherder's wagon that was parked next to the barn and fired off three shots. The two other Circle H men opened fire as well.

The gun fired again from the sheepherder's wagon, and Quinten heard a bullet kiss the air over his head.

Just then the haystack went up in a sheet of flames, silhouetting them against the horizon like wooden ducks at a shooting gallery.

"Let's get out of here," his father bellowed, but Quinten had already dug the heels of his boots hard into his horse's sides.

They all rode low on their horses' necks back across the creek and through the cottonwoods, firing off random shots. When they were sure they weren't being pursued, they pulled up their mounts and looked back at the sheep farm. They could see figures with water buckets running to and fro.

"THE devil should be well pleased with his work on this night."

Rachel pulled her gaze away from the blackened, smoldering stack of hay that Noah had built so high and tall for her. She looked at him, her good neighbor and friend. He had seen the fire from his farm and ridden over to help put it out. Now his face was streaked with soot, his eyes red-rimmed from the smoke.

She lifted the Circle H branding iron that she held awkwardly in her hand. "It wasn't the devil," she said.

He shook his head, his mouth set stubborn. "This happened because the outsider killed that stock inspector."

She threw the branding iron into some willow brakes. The outsider, along with her son and Noah's boy, Mose, were laying wet gunnysacks over the smoldering mound of hay.

"Perhaps you're right," she said. "Perhaps if Mr. Cain hadn't provoked them, they would've set fire to your haystacks instead."

Noah's gaze searched her face. Then he turned and strode away.

The outsider had left the boys and was coming toward her. He was barefoot and wore his Plain man's broadfalls with no shirt. But his gun was strapped around his hips.

She couldn't help wondering if those Hunter men would have managed to put their burning brand to all of her haystacks instead of just the one if Johnny Cain hadn't been here to shoot his gun.

He stopped in front of her. His chest was streaked with soot and sweat and marked with red blisters from flying sparks and embers.

"This time I'm killing them for you," he said.

She closed her eyes; she was so tired. And she felt that terrible burning emptiness in her belly, the need to make them pay for what they had done. She thought of how all she had to do was keep quiet and let Johnny Cain, man-killer, do what he wanted.

She exhaled a breath. "You gave me your promise you wouldn't. It was understood between us when you said you'd stay."

"And I've told you before: You ask too much."

She pressed her hands flat against her belly, but the burning emptiness didn't go away. "What you are thinking, what you're wanting, would destroy my soul. And you say I ask too much."

CHAPTER SIXTEEN

IT WAS evening, and Moses Weaver stood among the wooden markers of the Miawa City cemetery, trying to screw up the courage to go visit his first woman. The cemetery was as close as he'd been able to bring himself yet to the Red House. Mose figured he might as well get used to the cemetery anyway, since this was likely where he would be ending up real soon. His father would kill him for what he was about to do. And it would all be worth it, he thought, if he could have but a few moments of heaven on earth with Miss Marilee.

But first he had to get himself through the front door. The ground had saved up most of the day's blistering heat and was now releasing it back into the night air. He was sweating rivers beneath his flashy mail-order clothes.

He climbed the steps of the Red House's broad veranda. The famous locomotive lantern swayed in the wind, and its red light flickered in the half-moon window above the door.

He gave the door a timid rap and was surprised when it opened almost immediately. He found himself staring down into the slit-eyed face of a man as shriveled as a seed husk. Mose had never seen an Oriental before. He slapped off his hat. "I'm here to see Miss Marilee."

The man bowed and said something in a scratchy voice that Mose couldn't understand. He hoped it was the Chinese for "come right on in," because that was what he did.

From the hallway the Oriental waved at a curtain of blue glass beads and squawked more Chinese. A string of brass bells suddenly appeared in the little man's clawlike hands. He rang them with vigor, then shuffled off on silk slippers into the shadows.

Mose passed through the beads, clicking and clacking, and entered a room stuffed from floor to fanlight with things: plaster busts and glass vases, brass spittoons and lacquered boxes. Even the furniture was all doodadded up, with tidies on the chairs and sofas and Arab scarves draping every conceivable flat surface.

Mose settled onto a plush purple sofa, the cushions closing around him. He rested his hat on his knee and tried not to fidget.

The beaded curtain was slapped open as a woman came into the room. She was so skinny she would've had to walk twice to make a shadow. She wore a simple black skirt and bodice, with long cuffed sleeves and a high neck—not too different from what Plain women wore. She went over to a hurdy-gurdy and began to crank the handle, banging out a tune so loud it made Mose's ears jangle.

Mose heard a knock at the door, footsteps, and a voice rough as a whetstone bellowing a greeting. The Oriental's brass bells rang, the bead curtain clicked and clacked open, and Mose's heart, which had been lying quiet in his belly, suddenly thrust up into his throat and nearly choked him. Fergus Hunter strolled into the room.

The cattleman's gaze flickered immediately over Mose and dismissed him. He exchanged howdies with the skinny woman, who left the hurdy-gurdy to pour him a glass of whiskey from a decanter. Fergus Hunter was dressed fine in a dark suit, white brocade vest, and gray silk tie with a pearl stickpin. The gaslight glinted off his thick gold watch chain, which was hung with a crystal fob.

The beads clicked and clacked again, and a young man entered the parlor. Mose recognized him as the Baron's son.

"I decided to let my boy loose on the town tonight," the cattleman boomed to the skinny woman. "Isn't that right, Quin?"

Two red spots the size of dollars appeared beneath the boy's thin, sharp cheekbones. He seemed embarrassed by his father, and Mose could sympathize with that.

Mose saw that the Baron had now returned his attention to him and was giving him a slow once-over. Mose swallowed.

"Why, I didn't think you pious Plain boys ever succumbed to the calico fever," the Baron said, shaking his head in mock surprise. But then a genuine smile stretched his wide mouth as the beads clacked open again. "Well, if it isn't Miss Marilee."

Mose snatched his hat off his knee and pumped his arms, propelling himself out of the sofa and onto his feet. Marilee entered the parlor on a waft of honeysuckle toilet water and wearing a wispy scarlet silk wrapper.

The Baron grinned around the cigar in his mouth and tried to slide his arm around Marilee's waist. "Come here, m'girl. Let's you and me take a walk upstairs."

She gave his cheek a pat as she drifted by. "You can just wait your turn, Fergus Hunter." She turned a smile that was as bright as new paint onto Mose. "I see I got me a special caller tonight."

The Baron's face colored, but he smiled amicably enough. "Sure, then, Marilee. You go and take care of the woolly puncher."

Marilee slipped her arm through Mose's and pulled him out into the hallway toward a spooled-banister staircase. The bead curtain swayed and clicked behind them.

Marilee mounted the stairs slowly, her hips rocking from side to side. Mose felt his heart quake as he followed her up the stairs, her silky scarlet wrapper shifting and whispering before him.

She startled him by suddenly whipping around and snapping her fingers beneath his nose. "Thunderation, where's my head tonight? I nearly forgot to collect your three dollars."

He fumbled for the coins in his vest pocket. "I brought it. I just didn't know when was the proper time to give it to you."

Her fingers curled around the dollars, making a fist, but she flashed that bright, crooked-toothed smile at him. "You did take a bath, didn't you, Moses? 'Cause you know I can't abide the smell of sheep." With that, she pulled him into the room.

AFTER A LONG WHILE THE ceiling of the room came into view.

Marilee had rolled away from him to sit up on the bed. A sweet smile softened her face. "You're real nice, Moses. A poor, innocent babe who's so lost in the woods even the trees don't know what to do with him. But nice."

Mose lay on the bed and watched her, feeling a stirring again in that part of him he wasn't supposed to think about but which seemed lately to have been occupying all his waking moments. He had released his soul to a dark desire, sure enough. The terror of the sin and its certain wages of hellfire haunted him already.

"Your time's about all used up," she said to him over her shoulder, "and I got Mr. Hunter a-waitin' downstairs for me."

Mose sat up. "Why can't he go with one of the other girls?"

"'Cause it's me he always asks for in particular."

He cleared a lump that felt the size of a crab apple from his throat. "I don't want you to be with him."

She whirled and bent over to thrust a stiff finger under his nose. "Now, you listen to me, boy. Don't you go gettin' your head all twisted around backward. I'm a workin' girl, see."

"Will you . . ." He cleared his throat again. "I would sure consider it an honor, Miss Marilee, if you would go on a picnic with me."

She slapped her hands on her hips, blowing out a big sigh. "Oh, Lord. Now he wants to go on a picnic—"

"Tomorrow?"

She sighed again. "Surely I got to wonder what's made me go all soft in the head." She sucked in her lower lip. "Not tomorrow," she said. "We'll go on a picnic real soon, though. Now you gotta git."

CHAPTER SEVENTEEN

SHE rubbed her fingertips along the skin of his forearm, right below his rolled-up shirtsleeve. "You ain't exactly no flannelmouth."

Mose stared at Marilee, enjoying the pink and pretty picture she made. She was dressed in some fluffy thing the color of primroses.

Pinpricks of sunlight pierced her flat-brimmed straw bonnet, freckling her ear and jaw.

"What's a flannelmouth?" he said.

She grinned at him. "Someone whose gums're always flappin'."

Mose squinted against the brassy sun as he looked out over the rolling miles of prairie. The hot, dry days that had followed one after the other with no respite had already burned the grass a golden brown, although it was only June. The sky was a gray-yellow color.

His first thought had been to have their picnic at Blackie's Pond, where they'd met. But there wasn't enough shade, so they'd moved up the hill a ways to this stand of cottonwoods and box elders.

They sat as deep into the shade as they could get, on one of his aunt Fannie's quilts, which he'd spread over the ground. When Marilee had promised to go on this picnic with him, he hadn't known whether to believe her. But here she was, and she had a delighted, almost childlike glow about her.

When he had driven up to the Red House earlier in a borrowed shay, she had come tripping out the door looking as fresh and promising as a sunrise, carrying a cloth-covered basket. "I ain't never yet been on a picnic with a man who didn't forget to bring along the victuals," she told him. "So I decided to provide them for myself." She had laughed then, a bright, quick laugh that made his belly tingle and his chest feel all soft and warm, and Mose had thought he must surely love her.

Now she lifted the cloth off the top of the basket, smiling at him. "It's only common doin's—fried chicken and candied-yam pie."

She held out a chicken leg to him, wrapped up in a cloth napkin. It smelled delicious. He was about to take it from her when he heard the sound of hooves drumming the ground. Three men were riding toward them. Hunter men.

"Run," she said.

His head whipped around to her. "I'm not leaving you—"

She pushed him hard in the back. "Go on, you fool. Git!"

He stood up because he wanted to meet whatever was coming on his feet. Fear clawed at his innards, though.

The man on the lead horse, a stranger to him, began uncoiling a rawhide lariat. The roiling fear in Mose's belly made his knees buckle. They were going to do to him what they'd done to Ben Yoder.

He ran then, sprinting out across the prairie. He could hear hooves pounding the sunbaked ground behind him. He ran harder.

He cast a look over his shoulder. The Hunter hired hand was thundering down on him, swinging the lariat in a wide, floating loop over his head. Mose stretched out his legs, straining every muscle in one desperate forward lunge.

The lariat sailed and settled over him. He hit the ground hard. He heard laughter, and then the rope jerked, and he was hauled brutally back to the cottonwoods and Marilee and the ruins of their picnic.

The rope went slack, and he slid to a stop. He lay there, gasping for breath, trying not to show his fear, while the three Hunter men dismounted and stood around him.

"Get up onto your knees," said the one who'd roped him.

Swaying and lurching, fighting down dizziness and nausea, Mose got to his feet. He tossed the dusty hair out of his eyes and looked up into the face of his murderer.

The man was short and slender, with a heavy upper lip, side-whiskers, and a small gray beard elegantly trimmed to a point. He was dressed fine, with a whiskey-colored velvet vest, a tall black hat, and a white silk tie. He looked like a cultured man, but he had a hog's eyes, small and dark and darting. He was smiling.

Mose's gaze shifted to the other two. One was Fergus Hunter's son, and he looked almost as ill as Mose felt. The other seemed to be just an ordinary cowboy, dressed in chaps and a gray Stetson. He had Marilee in front of him, her arms gripped fast in his big hands.

"What are you going to do to him?" she asked, trembling.

"You should be worrying about what we're going to do with *you*, Miss Marilee of the Red House," said the man with the rope, who, Mose decided, was another stock inspector—a hired gun.

He met Mose's eyes, smiling still. "I said onto your knees, woolly puncher." And he backhanded Mose hard across the face, driving him down where he wanted him.

Mose's head swam.

"I don't reckon you've ever been on a cattle drive, have you, boy?"

the man said. "Well, there's a lesson we give out on the trail to wet-behind-the-ears youngsters like you who don't know how to behave." He shot a look over at Marilee. "What we do is, we whup his bare hide with a pair of chaps until he's too sore to ride a horse . . . or a woman."

His hand snaked out, gripping Mose by the hair, and he began to drag him deeper into the cottonwoods. Mose fought back, but there were three of them. Two of them tied him facedown over a log, with his trousers pulled down to his knees.

He heard the first blow coming before he felt it—a whoosh through the air—and he nearly screamed aloud at the fiery slash of pain. The leather chaps blistered his flesh. The whipping went on and on until the pain became a constant, screaming agony and the blows blended one into the other.

When it was over, he lay there, tied down, his flesh on fire. Through the pain he heard the hired gun say, "Take her over to that quilt."

Marilee screamed. Mose jerked against the ropes that bound him and nearly screamed himself as a fierce new wave of pain crested over him. "Leave her alone!" he cried. The hired gun laughed.

Mose could hear the scuffling, her gasping cries—then silence.

The Hunter son spoke now. "Why do you have to do this?"

The hired gun's legs came around into Mose's view. He had a knife. "You heard your pa say how she had to be taught a lesson."

The hired gun caught Mose's agonized expression, and his grin widened. He walked around the log, tossing the knife from hand to hand. Marilee screamed once, a desperate wail, and then she began to cry and plead. "Oh, God, don't do that to me, please, please."

Mose yelled, pulling against the ropes. Tears filled his eyes.

Marilee screamed and went on screaming, and Mose was screaming as well, begging them to stop whatever it was they were doing to her, which he couldn't see, only hear.

After a time the hired gun came back around the log. Mose stared up at him through blurred eyes. Marilee wasn't screaming anymore.

"I understand," the hired gun said, "that there's a man who lives with you Plain People, name of Johnny Cain."

Mose nodded, swallowing, trying to keep from sobbing out loud.

The man's hard smile grew even harder. "You tell him Jarvis Kennedy works for the Circle H now and that Johnny Cain is a dead man. All he's got to do is pick his moment."

He walked off in a jangle of spurs, and Mose heard the squeak of leather as they mounted up and then the thud of hooves, fading into stillness.

He called to Marilee. He could hear her whimpering now, but she wouldn't answer him. It took a long while to work his hands free of the ropes. His buttocks were fiery raw.

He crawled to her on his hands and knees. She was curled into a tight ball among something that looked like sheaves of wheat, something he didn't quite understand until she uncurled enough to look up at him.

"My hair, Mose. They cut off all my hair."

Her hair, her pretty hair, looked like the stubble left in the field after the hay was cut. It had been sheared off close to her scalp.

"Aw, Marilee. I'm so sorry."

She whimpered and straightened her legs. There was a lot of blood on her skirt.

Suddenly her whole body jackknifed. Marilee clutched at her belly and screamed over and over again.

WHAT was left of the haystacks they'd built such a short while ago stood baking and tanning in the heat. Mose walked slowly toward them, each step an effort and an agony. He kept shivering even though he was sweating.

A briny taste soured his mouth. *Lieber Gott,* had Marilee screamed! He had driven the shay wildly across the prairie back to town, with fear and rage punching his heart. He'd gone running with her in his arms, still screaming, into Doc Henry's house. That was when the doc had told him she was losing her baby, a baby Mose hadn't even known she was going to *have.*

The hired gun had promised Mose he would be too sore to ride a horse, but the rage in Mose's heart had made it possible for him to get on his mount and ride back across the valley to the Weaver farm and beyond. The rage made it possible now for him to be walking across the Yoder south pastures in search of Johnny Cain.

MOSE looked now at the quick-draw rig the outsider always wore on his hip, even in such a place of peace as a pasture full of sheep. But it wasn't easy getting it out—his own trouble and what he meant to do about it and the help that he would need from Johnny Cain.

They stood side by side among the grazing sheep, he and Cain, and it was as if he were two Mose Weavers. One, a Plain boy and a sheep farmer, and the other, this Mose, who was far far different.

He cleared his throat. "Before you came to be with us, did you do stuff for money? I mean, how much did someone have to pay you?"

Cain took off his hat. "Pay me to do what?"

"Kill a man."

The outsider turned his head and gave Mose a long, steady stare. "Who is he?"

"He said his name's Jarvis Kennedy. He's the new Hunter stock inspector, and he said to tell you Johnny Cain is a dead man and that all you have to do is choose your moment."

The outsider's mouth pulled into a hard, tight smile.

"Also, well, maybe you don't care, but he raped a woman—Miss Marilee from the Red House—who's a friend of mine."

He was beginning to feel foolish. He had expected the outsider to be outraged when he heard the story of what happened, but he wasn't. The outsider said nothing, and so Mose had to go on.

"Since I want him dead, I'm willing to pay you."

"You can't afford me."

Mose nodded, swallowed. He had figured such would be the case. "Will you teach me how to quick draw, then? He raped my friend, and with or without your help I'm going to kill him for it."

The outsider moved so fast Mose didn't see him coming until his hand was gripping his neck, pushing his head up, and Mose was staring into eyes that were as lifeless and hard as blue glass.

"First," Johnny Cain said, "you are talking too stupid to live, boy. Second, I don't care about you or your whore and her trouble. But Mrs. Yoder seems fond of you, and so for her sake I'm gonna give you one lesson with my Colt. One lesson, and what you choose to learn from it will be your own business."

Cain let him go, stepping back. "Are you ready?"

Mose nodded, stretching out his neck. His legs felt weak.

The outsider slipped his revolver from the holster and held it out to Mose butt first. Mose reached to take the gun, when it suddenly spun around in the outsider's hand. Mose heard a loud click, and he was suddenly looking at the black bore of the Colt's muzzle.

And Johnny Cain was smiling that smile, the smile of a man-killer. "What are your favorite flowers, boy?"

Mose squeezed his eyes shut and waited, waited. Then the sense of the man's words finally penetrated his fear, and he understood that Cain wasn't going to kill him, had never had any intention to.

He jumped, though, when Cain released the hammer. He opened his eyes in time to watch the revolver slide back into its holster. Cain had already turned his back on him and was walking away.

But after a few steps he stopped, stood still, then turned back around. "I guess I am a little sorry about your friend," he said.

MARILEE opened her eyes onto the familiar sight of a paper trellis of ribbons and roses. Doc Henry was standing over her, looking worried. This pleased her, for it meant he must care for her at least a little.

Her throat hurt, and she swallowed. "The baby's gone, isn't it?"

"I'm sorry."

She pressed her head back into the pillow, squeezing her eyes shut. A sob exploded out of her. "It hurts, Luc. It hurts so bad," she cried, trying to push herself up.

"I know, I know." He held her tight for a moment, then eased her back down onto the bed. "I'll give you one of my herbal infusions in a moment. And maybe some patent medicine too, just to be safe. You'll be some time in healing, Marilee."

It was a long time before she was able to find the courage to ask him if she would be able to have another baby. And it was a longer time still before he spoke, and before he did, she saw the answer come first into his eyes. That was when she began to cry again.

CHAPTER EIGHTEEN

I T WAS hot. Blistering, sweat-cooking, drought-making hot. Hot winds shriveled the grass and dried up the water holes. Not a drop of rain fell. And it was still only the second week of June.

It was hot, and it was shearing time.

Noah Weaver watched the sheep come waddling one by one out of the bathing pool, water-laden and staggering with it. It had been hard work this year, damming up the low-running creek and scooping out a puddle big enough to make a woolly bath. But a clean crop fetched higher prices, and at least in this hot weather the sheep would be dry enough to shear in no time.

Samuel Miller, who had the enviable job of standing in the pool and making sure none of the sheep rolled over and drowned, tossed a smile at his brothers. He pretended to wring the sweat out of his beard. "Judas. It's hot enough to make the devil feel t'home, *ja?*"

Abram laughed, but then his face sobered quick enough. "It's a drought we're in the making of. You tell me if we're not."

Sol nodded, his mouth so tight it disappeared into his beard.

Noah clamped his own lips together, reminding himself to think of these days as a trial sent by the Lord to be endured with meekness and humility. God was testing him, saddling him with scorching days, a drought, and Johnny Cain all in one summer.

He had been looking forward to this day, though. The day they sheared Rachel's sheep. He had made the outsider a promise—*ach, vell,* you could call it a challenge, wicked though that might be— that the man wouldn't be able to last through a day of shearing.

Noah looked over to where his son, Mose, was wrangling the drying sheep into the shearing corral. For a moment their gazes met. Then his son's face took on that sour, flat-chinned look, and he turned around, giving Noah the stiff back, the cold shoulder.

Noah had told his boy that once his backside healed, he would take up the strap and give him a fresh set of welts. But when the day came, he hadn't done it; he hadn't had the heart for it. Besides, he sensed that the boy wasn't going to be taking any more whippings from anybody, ever again. He'd been changed sure enough by what had happened with the cattlemen and that strumpet from the Red House, changed in ways that Noah didn't understand. It frightened him, for his son seemed more lost than ever—lost to God and the church.

Lost to him.

THE men had gathered inside the shearing shed.

The good thing about shearing time, Noah thought, was that it brought families and friends together. Everyone had something important to do. Fannie Weaver and the Miller wives were already in the kitchen, preparing huge quantities of food, for shearing built up a prodigious appetite. Mose would soon be funneling the bleating, frightened woollies into the cutting chute. Rachel would stand on top of the chute fence to open the gate, sending the sheep into the catch pen. Five at a time, one for each of the shearers.

Even the children worked. Levi would tie up the fleeces and toss them up to Benjo, who would pack them into burlap sacks, the woolbags.

Noah himself, along with Sol, Abram, and Samuel, would do the fleecing. The outsider would take Ben's place with them on the shearing floor of the shed, and not an hour would he last. And then they would all see what Rachel had to say to that.

Noah handed a pair of gleaming shears to the outsider. Cain gripped the looped handle and squeezed the hafts.

"Give me a sheep!" Noah hollered to Rachel, who had already taken her place at the cutting chute.

A fat old ewe came waddling through the woolbag curtains that had been hung up between the catch pen and the shearing floor. Noah hooked her under her front legs. She kept running, right up onto her hind legs, and Noah dumped her onto her rump easily. He gripped her tight to his body with his knees to keep her from wriggling free. The ewe let out a loud bleat.

Noah worked quickly, and the soft and greasy wool began to unfold smoothly in a spiraling ivory circle.

The ewe emerged from the pile of her wool big-eyed and naked. She shook herself hard, no doubt feeling strange, and then trotted off.

Noah looked up from his stooped position and showed his teeth in a hard smile. "Now, let's see how you do, outsider."

Noah asked for a big yearling wether. Rachel came into the shed along with the sheep to watch.

The outsider had trouble from the start. It wasn't as easy as it looked to cut the wool off a living, panting, squirming sheep. The outsider's big mistake was not gripping the wether's body tightly enough with his knees. Cain had it only half shorn when the wether slithered free, gathered its legs underneath it, and ran off, trailing fleece. The outsider had to chase after it, and Rachel laughed so hard she had to sit down on a stack of woolbags and hold her belly.

They all were laughing by then. Even Noah.

When the poor sheep was finally shorn entirely of its wool, it staggered off, blood-spotted and sporting ratty patches where Cain's shears had either missed completely or nicked the hide.

"I've cut him to pieces," the outsider said, looking miserable.

"Actually, you've a deft hand," Noah told him grudgingly. "You'll pick up the rhythm of it in no time."

"I think, Mrs. Yoder, that you'd better just give me the old ones with tough hides," the outsider said. As Noah watched, feeling like an outsider himself, their laughter blended in a music all their own.

THERE were sounds, Noah thought, that belonged just to the shearing time. The snick and click of the blades, as the shears were clasped and released, clasped and released, over and over.

A shearer calling, "Give me a sheep!" And Rachel coaxing one through the chute, *poorrrr-poorrrr-pooorrr,* sounding sometimes like a kitten and sometimes like a mourning dove. Noah loved the sound of Rachel singing to her sheep.

Ja, and the sound of his own panting breaths, of his sweat drip-drip-dripping like a rainspout onto the shearing floor.

And a new sound this year. Johnny Cain crooning softly to his sheep as he sheared them. The outsider seemed to have a genuine fondness for the woollies, which both astonished and bothered

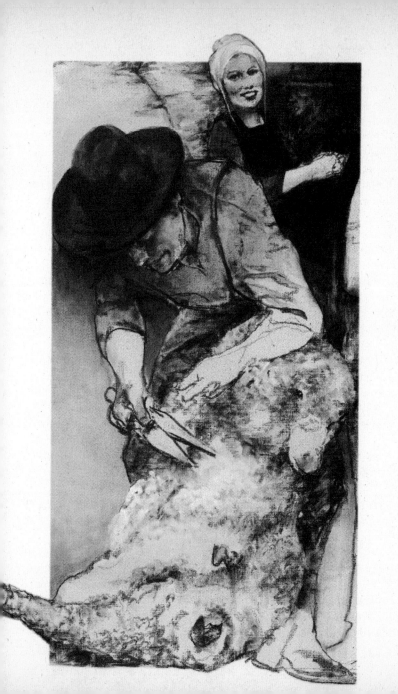

Noah. He found himself liking the outsider, and he didn't want to.

Noah finished with a ewe and looked up to see that Benjo was standing on top of a full woolbag. "Time to rest a spell," he called out to the others. Time to catch their breaths, stretch their backs.

Noah went to the water butt, stumbling a little. He brought a dipperful of water over to the outsider, and the two men stood staring at each other, sweat pouring in streams down their drawn faces.

Rachel sailed in, a teasing light in her eyes. "What is this I see? You lazy men taking a rest already, and the morning not yet half gone."

Noah watched her with helpless yearning as she went to the water butt. When she finished drinking, she walked on past him to Benjo and helped finish sewing shut the woolbag. And then she went to *him.* To the outsider.

They stood close together, and Rachel's eyes shone like morning dew. Her whole body seemed to be leaning, straining to span the distance between them, as if all of her was saying to the outsider, *Touch me, touch me, touch me.*

IT WAS still blistering hot a week later, when Quinten Hunter and his father made the long trip to the stockyards at Deer Lodge to buy more beefs for their overstocked and overgrazed range.

This morning the pens and corrals that usually teemed with livestock were mostly empty. Only the middle pens held a couple of hundred ragged cows, which stood listlessly around the feeding and watering troughs, their heads hanging low in the heat.

"Where is everybody?" the Baron said.

"Busted."

A tall, thin man walked over to them from beneath the shade of a water tank. He was coated in red prairie dust from the crown of his black Stetson to the fringe on his worn chaps.

He pointed to the cows in the middle pens. "You're looking at all I got left of a ranch over in east Oregon. I been trying to hang on, but with the market glut and beef prices falling, there ain't no way."

The Baron surveyed the herd. "They're a pretty ragged bunch."

"They're trail weary, is all. Otherwise they're prime stock. All they need is a season or two of fattening up."

After some negotiations the transaction was completed on a word and a handshake. His father had gotten a good deal, but Quinten didn't know where the money was going to come from. He didn't want to know. He told himself he ought to be concentrating instead on the logistics of how they would trail their newly acquired cows up to the Miawa.

The cattleman started to walk off, but then he turned around, pointing down the road to a pair of wagons filled with huge jute sacks stuffed with wool and piled high as haystacks.

"Now, there, sir, is the business you and I should be in. Sheep. Why, I bet them mutton punchers could buy us out twice over." The cattleman spit in the dirt, then walked off.

Quinten came up to stand alongside his father as they watched the heavily loaded wagons trundle toward them.

The man at the reins of the lead wagon had a thick ginger-colored beard. The wide brim of his hat flapped in the wind. The driver of the second wagon was a beardless youth, and Quinten knew him. Remembering how he knew him stirred a shame that Quinten felt as a queasiness deep in his belly.

JUST as the Miller, Yoder, and Weaver farms all shared in the labor of their shearing, so too did they share in the selling of their fleeces. It was tradition. In good years the woolbags would be many and stuffed full, and it would take two big hay wagons, each pulled by a six-mule team, to carry them to market.

As the deacon, and thus less susceptible to temptation, Noah Weaver was always given the task of going out into the dangerous and corrupting world to find a buyer for their wool. Always before, he had chosen one of the Miller brothers to drive the second wagon, but on a morning three days ago he had said to his son, "You're a man grown enough, I should think, to come along with me to Deer Lodge this season and deal with the wool broker."

So it was a changed Mose who had gone along with his father from farm to farm, loading the woolbags into the wagons. A Mose whose thoughts were dwelling on the traditions of the Plain life and his part in them. We are a good people, he thought. Strict and narrow in our ways, but our backs are wide and our hearts are giving.

But then the morning after the woolbags were all loaded, when the mule teams were hitched up and they were ready to set off, Mose had come out of the house wearing his flashy mail-order clothes. His father said nothing, only looked at him with disappointment showing in his face. Mose set his jaw at a stubborn tilt, climbed onto the seat of the hay wagon, and picked up the reins.

LATER, near the town stockyards, Mose was thinking of Gracie Zook and smiling, when he saw Fergus Hunter step into the path of his father's wagon. They pulled up hard on their teams, and their heavily laden wagons jolted to a stop, creaking and groaning. Mose's leader mules shied and bucked in the traces, and Mose had his hands full getting them back under control.

When he looked up again, he saw that Fergus Hunter's son had come to stand by the man's side. Their gazes, Mose's and the other boy's, met and then jerked apart. Shame burned hot in Mose's cheeks as he remembered how that boy had last seen him—bent over a cottonwood log, getting whipped by the Hunters' hired gun.

The cattleman's black eyes were studying Noah now from beneath the brim of his hat. "I believe," he said, "that you are one of the preacher gentlemen I talked to last year. About you and your people selling your rangeland to the Circle H."

The wind came up, bringing with it the smell of cattle and sun-baked dust. And fear. Mose could smell the fear on himself.

But if his father was afraid, he didn't show it. Noah sat in silence long enough for the cattleman to think he wouldn't be getting a response; then he said, "*Ja*. And our minds, they have not changed."

Fergus Hunter's mouth thinned into a tight smile. "Now that is peculiar, it is. Because I understand that you folk've been having a run of bad luck lately. Stampedes and hay fires and such."

Noah sat in his wagon, immovable and silent as a boulder.

The cattleman heaved an elaborate sigh. "And what with the way trouble always seems to run in bunches . . ." He shook his head, taking a cigar out of his vest pocket. "Well, I have to admit to you, sir, that I don't know a whole lot about the business of sheep. Cattle being more in my line, you understand." He put the cigar in his mouth and struck a long stove match on the wheel rim of Noah's wagon. "But a man picks up stray bits of facts here and there," he went on, holding the burning match up to the end of the cigar. "Like I been told, for instance, that nothing catches alight quicker than a bunch of oily fleeces."

The flame wavered and then brightened, and Mose's heart jolted. That match tossed into a wagon bed full of woolbags, and they could all turn into one enormous pillar of fire.

"We will not sell to you, outsider," Noah said. "And you can never defeat us. The Lord said to Abram, 'I am thy shield, and thy exceeding great reward.'"

The cattleman shook his hand, and the flame went out. He turned on his heel and strode off, back toward the stockyards.

"He wouldn't have done it," Fergus Hunter's son said. "He was only— He wouldn't have done it."

Noah said nothing to the boy, nor did he look at him. He gathered the reins, sitting up taller, although to Mose's eyes his father's broad back and shoulders already seemed to fill the world.

"Hie!" Noah shouted to his mules, and his wagon lurched ahead.

"Hie!" Mose shouted, feeling a fierce pride in his father.

CHAPTER NINETEEN

THE rocking of the wagon wheels over the rough ground was a cradlesong. The music left Rachel smiling as the wagon lurched over the sheep path cut through the pine-studded mountain slopes.

Each June the Yoder, Miller, and Weaver farms combined their sheep into a common herd—earmarking the animals to tell them apart—then drove them up onto the summer pastures in the mountains. The men from each farm took turns at the sheepherding.

Rachel couldn't be a summer shepherd. It wasn't woman's work. But when it came the Yoder turn for the herding, she did the camp tending. In her wagon bed now were white sacks of salt for the sheep and rawhide-covered boxes packed with coffee and beans and bacon for the shepherd. And on this day she was bringing these supplies to Johnny Cain.

The spring wagon lurched over a boulder, and the provision boxes banged and rattled. "Are you holding on back there?" she called to Benjo, who was perched, legs swinging, on the open tailboard, with a fresh-baked shoofly pie under his tender loving care.

She got a muffled umph in response.

"You get your sticky fingers out of that pie," she said. She hadn't needed to turn around; she knew her boy.

They plunged out of the mellowed and muted shadows of the tree-shaded path and into the harsh sunlight of a clearing.

From across the meadow the dented tin stovepipe of the sheep wagon flashed a welcome. A few sheep were scattered over the sun-lit grass, but most were shaded down among the trees. MacDuff was there, tongue lolling, tail thumping. She didn't see the outsider.

Rachel and Benjo unharnessed and watered the horse, and teth-ered her loosely so she could graze. They unloaded the provisions, then took a walk among the herd. The sheep were much prettier now that their wool was coming in again. The new growth had a soft, knotty feel to Rachel when she rubbed a ewe's head.

"What have you done with your shepherd?" she asked the ewe, who looked back at her with eyes that were sweet but empty.

Benjo headed deeper into the pines, his eyes searching. Rachel came along with him. They heard a panicked baa first, followed by loud sucking noises and a man's low, melodious cursing.

"You perfidious daughter of a— Any woolly as muttonheaded as you deserves to drown."

"Don't listen," Rachel said to Benjo. But she had to suck on her cheeks to keep from laughing at the sight that greeted her eyes.

A fat, bawling ewe stood mired shank-deep in a bog. Too mud-logged to climb out, she stood shivering and complaining to the outsider, who was pushing on her rump, trying to shove her out.

Rachel didn't think he knew they were there, but then he said, "You going to stand there and cling to your high ground, Mrs. Yo-der? Or get down here in the mud with the rest of us sinners."

"I believe I will cling, Mr. Cain."

Benjo, with a boy's love for anything wet and dirty, happily slogged into the mire to help. He took the right loin, Cain took the left, and together they heaved. The ewe exploded out of the bog like a cork out of a bottle. She huffed and bleated and shook her head, and then trotted off to join the rest of the flock as if nothing had happened.

The man and the boy slogged out after her, bringing a good part of the bog with them. Cain swiped the grit out of his mouth with his shirt cuff, and Rachel came to him. Using the hem of her apron, she wiped the mud splatters off his face, and all the while she was doing it, she was looking into his eyes and smiling.

They walked back to the clearing together, the three of them, like a family. Rachel slanted a glance up at him. He was looking so fine. The days spent beneath the summer sun had tanned his pale skin to the golden color of apple cider. Their gazes met.

"So, Mr. Cain," she said, "how have you survived your first days of summer herding?"

"Well, I started talkin' to the woollies last Tuesday, and by Friday they were answerin' back, but I didn't really start to worry till this morning, when what they said started makin' sense."

Laughing, she put a little skip into her step. She would have slipped her arm through his and drawn herself closer to him while they walked—if he were her man. But he wasn't her man.

WHEN the outsider and Benjo went to fish the creek for their supper, Rachel decided that she would do a bit of housekeeping in the sheep wagon. The top half of the Dutch door was open to let in air. She climbed the narrow steps and pushed in the latch to the bottom half, wincing at the squeal of unoiled hinges.

It was cleaner inside than she had expected, although there was a coffeepot sitting on the stove that had sure seen better days. She popped the lid and wrinkled her nose at the tarry sludge stirring in the bottom. But she didn't set about brewing up a fresh pot right away. Instead she unpacked the last of the provision boxes she and Benjo had carted up from the farm. At the bottom of the box, wrapped in butcher paper, was a gift she had made for Johnny Cain.

The yellow sateened muslin caught the light, shimmering, as she slid it from the brown paper.

She had done a wicked thing, buying the cloth that terrible day in Miawa City. Then once she had it in her possession, she had done another wicked thing: She had sewn a set of ruffled curtains.

The sheep wagon had a single window, on the side where the table was. But it was a fair size, big enough to let in the light and big enough for curtains made of yellow sateened muslin.

Kneeling on the table, she strung the curtains across the window with a piece of rope. She'd just folded the hinged table back up when she heard the scrape of boots on the steps. She spun around, putting space between herself and the window, trying to look busy with the coffeepot. She was floating with sweet anticipation.

She wiped her hands on her apron, tucked a loose bit of hair beneath her prayer cap. "So did you two catch any fish?"

"A whole mess of sockeye." The outsider's gaze was drifting around the wagon, alighting everywhere but on her. "I thought you and Benjo could take the bunk tonight," he said. "I've been bedding down outside most nights anyway."

"I've a surprise," she blurted, smiling, floating, loving him so much. "These I made up special just for you." She swung around, showing him the curtains. "A little something just for pretty."

She turned back to him, smiling, even as she began to see that all the color had left his face, and his eyes had gone stark and hard.

He turned on his heel and left the wagon, left her, without a word.

SHE made a campfire out in the meadow and cooked the salmon he and Benjo had caught for supper, but he never came to eat it. Later that evening, lying snug up against her son in the bunk in the herder's wagon, saying her prayers, her gaze went to the window. The curtains were gone.

THE wail of a cougar woke her.

She sat up. Benjo stirred in his sleep, but dreamed on. She used a struck match to find her half boots and her shawl to pull around her night rail, but she waited until she was through the door of the sheep wagon before she lit the wick in the coal oil lantern.

MacDuff stood at the bottom of the steps, legs braced and growling. Some of the sheep were bleating and milling in alarm. Her lantern cast long shadows over the grass as she walked among the sheep, murmuring, soothing them. She prayed the cougar had passed them by.

Johnny Cain, her shield and comfort, seemed to have deserted her.

The woollies settled down again, went back to their dreams of green meadow grass. But Rachel didn't go back to the bunk and her own troubled dreams. She extinguished the lantern and let herself be swallowed up by the deep blue night.

Then she sensed a movement at the far edge of the clearing. The outsider was wearing his black duster, so she could barely tell where he left off and the night began. They stared at each other, and the air around them trembled.

He came toward her suddenly, his duster flaring darkly, throwing shadows over her. He held a ripped and wadded-up ball of the yellow muslin in his hands.

She took a step back, and he stopped. He drew in a deep breath and then another. "I won't hurt you."

"I know, Johnny," she said, sparing him with a lie. For he could hurt her in so many ways.

The yellow cloth fell from his fists, fluttering to the ground. "Don't leave me, then," he said.

She took a step toward him. Then he reached out, pulling her closer, and she came. He sat at the base of a rock, bringing her down with him, turning her and settling her between his thighs. She leaned her back against his chest and wrapped her arms around her drawn-up legs.

His breath stirred warm against her neck. "I always thought of sheep as being white, but they're gray," he said. "They're the color of the gravy we had every Sunday for supper over soda biscuits."

"Your folks, they were poor, then?"

His arms, which had been wrapped loosely around her, tightened. "There's this orphanage in east Texas, only they call it something more fanciful—the Blessed Are the Merciful Foundling Home for Boys. It has this big iron fence and a gate in front of it. They told me that was where they found me, like an abandoned dog."

She picked up his hand, his scarred and beautiful hand, and wrapped her own hands around it as if she cradled a wounded bird.

"Every spring they'd have this day in church where they'd put us up for adoption, as they called it." His laugh caught on a tearing sound. "Aw, Rachel, we were so pathetic. The way we'd scrub our faces and slick back our hair and put on begging little smiles, each of us hoping he'd be the one to be picked out from the others. But we were always brought back come winter, because there was never meant to be any adoption. The home was only renting us out to the local farmers for their planting and the harvest."

Rachel bit her lip.

"The summer I was ten I was rented out to a Mr. Silas Cowper, who was a hog farmer. He claimed to have owned slaves before the war, and he sure enough thought he owned me. I don't know if there was any slave ever worked as hard as he worked me.

"I ran away first chance I got, but he caught me easy enough, with dogs that he bred for bullfighting. He dragged me back to his place, and he put shackles on my legs and arms and chained me to a post in the barn, next to this big carcass hook."

He was talking in a raw, hoarse voice now. She could feel a hard trembling going on deep inside him.

"Cowper took this hog and hooked it through the neck, then gutted it. He dropped it into a barrel of boiling hot water to make it easy, he said, to scrape the hair off its hide. He was talking to me, see, all the while he was doing it, telling me how he owned me and that if I ever ran off again, he'd do to me exactly what he'd done to that hog. And I believed him."

He breathed heavily. "From then on he kept me chained to that post in the barn when he wasn't working me, except for the nights when he hung me from that carcass hook and laid my back open with a hog whip. It took me a whole year to weaken a link in that chain enough to bust it."

The darkness and the silence of the night lapped around them.

His voice was flat and cold now. "I figured that if I wasn't going to wind up like a butchered hog, then I had to make sure Cowper couldn't come after me. So before I ran away that second time, I took up a pitchfork and stabbed him in the gut with it. I did it three times to make sure he was good and dead."

Rachel brought his hand up to her mouth, pushing her pursed lips hard on his knuckles. Just a boy. He'd been just a boy, just like Benjo, when those terrible things were done to him. When he had done that terrible thing.

He turned her around to face him. "Don't," he said. "Don't cry for me."

She looked down. More tears fell. "I love you."

She heard his breath catch. "Don't do that either," he said.

"It's too late."

He picked up the ruined yellow muslin from the ground and held it out to her, as if offering it as a gift. "I killed a woman once," he said, and his voice was flat and hard and cold again.

"She was a dance hall girl in a town whose name I don't remember, and I don't remember hers either, because I never knew it."

She watched as his hand that held the yellow muslin curled into a fist, and her heart was aching for him, aching for herself. "Don't tell me any more, Johnny. I don't want to know any more."

He went on anyway. "I was coming out of the livery when I heard a man hollering my name. I didn't know the fellow. He was just another quick gun looking to take on my rep. We started shooting, and there was all this dust and smoke. And through it I saw her come running out of that saloon where she worked. I saw her. I know I saw her, but I couldn't stop firing, because it's something you learn, you see—not to stop until your gun is empty.

"And she took one of my bullets high in the chest. She was wearing a dress made out of shiny yellow stuff like this."

He opened his fist and let the muslin flutter back to the ground.

"I went over and looked down at her, and then I got on my horse and rode away. I kept thinking I ought to be feeling something. I *tried* to feel bad for her, for what I had done, but there was nothing inside of me but this emptiness. I felt real tired, that's all. . . ."

He put a hand on her jaw, silencing her lips with his thumb, even though she hadn't yet spoken. "I had some hard luck, Rachel, but a better man than me would've faced up to life differently."

Her lips moved against his fingers. "If you come to the Lord with true repentance in your heart, you will be forgiven all your sins."

"I'm a man-killer, Rachel—a creature that kills because it's in his nature to kill." His mouth curved into a terrible smile. "I don't believe your God has that much forgiveness in Him."

She cupped his face with her hands, gripping him tightly, almost shaking him. "Then let me be your faith."

But in his eyes she saw the desolation of a man who believed there was no way off the dark path he had chosen to follow.

She couldn't bear it. She pulled his head to her breast, and she smoothed his hair as a mother would. But only for a moment. He lifted his head, and she thought he would kiss her, but he said, "Will you do something? Will you take down your hair?"

She reached up and took off her nightcap. One by one she took the pins from her hair, and it fell over her shoulders in a thick, slinky mantle.

He stared at her a long time. With trembling hands he cupped her hair and lifted it to his face, as if he would drink of it.

"You'd better leave me now," he said.

"I love you," she said. "Soon I'll show you how much I love you."

SHE did not go up on the mountain again. Young Mose Weaver took over the camp-tending chores, and one day in July, Mose went up the mountain to stay for his turn at the herding, and Rachel knew the outsider would be coming home to her. Hoped he was.

She sent Benjo to her father's farm to help Sol whitewash the new fence they had built. She dragged out her galvanized tin tub and heated gallons of bathwater on the stove. She washed her hair.

By late afternoon, when her whole body was humming with sweet anticipation, Johnny Cain appeared at her side. After waiting for him half a day, she hadn't heard him come.

"You came home," she said. "I wasn't sure you would."

"Is this my home, Rachel?"

"For as long as you want it to be."

He gave her a soft, slow smile. Rachel looked into his eyes and fell in love all over again.

He swung her up into his arms and carried her into the bedroom. The sun filtering through the cottonwoods outside the window cast a tea-green light over her plain white iron bed and star-patterned quilt.

He set her back onto her feet. Stepping back, she took off her prayer cap and laid it in its place on the shelf beneath the window. Then she let down her hair.

He watched her—and then she watched him as he unbuckled his gun belt. Giving up its embrace, he hooked it around the bedpost.

She came to him. "Feel my heart," she said. "Feel it beating."

They fell onto the bed, onto a quilt of blue and white stars.

FANNIE Weaver walked quickly along the path that led through the woods separating their farm from the Yoder place. The pines and tamaracks spread their thick-needled branches overhead, blocking out the sun. Fannie hated the woods. They were too dark and smothering.

It had been her brother Noah's idea that she bring the bucket of blackberries to Rachel. They grew in wild abandon on their side of the creek, way more than they could ever eat or preserve. It was only right, Noah had said, that they share God's abundance with others.

Fannie emerged from the woods in back of the Yoder barn. Crossing the yard to the house, she went up the porch steps. The door creaked a little beneath Fannie's hand as she opened it. The Plain never knocked on each other's doors during the daylight hours, for no one ever did anything that was better left unwitnessed.

At the moment, though, the kitchen was empty, and Fannie was pleased to find it so. If Rachel was here, she would have been tempted to linger, and the next thing Fannie knew, she'd have been running home through the shadowy woods after sunset. With Rachel off doing farm chores somewhere, Fannie could put the blackberries on the table and leave.

She did pause long enough on the threshold of the kitchen to glance around and inspect Rachel's housekeeping. She took a step toward the table, and the house moaned.

She thought it was the wind, until she heard it again. Deeper this time. Then another moan, coming from the bedroom.

With quiet steps she crossed the kitchen and walked right up to the door, for it was partway open.

Fannie gasped at what she saw. She whirled away. Staggering, she banged the bucket against the wall. It fell from her hand, clattering, spilling berries as she ran from the house.

CHAPTER TWENTY

RACHEL was making a slipped-custard pie.

It was a foolish thing to be doing so late at night, but she needed something to occupy her head and hands, because when her hands were idle, they started to shake, and she was too full of feelings to think.

She ran a spatula around the edge of the custard, separating it from the plate. *Da will be the one to come. No—it is the deacon's place to confront a Plain one who has been caught out in a sin. Noah, I can face. It will be hard, but I would sooner face Noah than Da.* She shook the plate gently, loosening the custard. *I'll have to face them all eventually, though—Da and my brothers, Mem, oh, poor Mem. I'll have to confess my shame before them all and say I'm sorry. But what if I'm not sorry? I love him. I would do it again. I will do it again. . . . Rachel, Rachel, what are you saying? You are damning your soul. I don't care. Yes, I do care. I don't want to care, but I do.*

She held the plate of custard above the flaky piecrust shell. Slowly, slowly she tilted the plate, and the custard began to slip. Her Benjo and Johnny Cain were out in the barn, getting a late start with the evening milking, for it was barely an hour before midnight.

So when she heard the barn door bang, her hand only jerked the littlest bit. The custard began slipping too fast, though. When she heard a stuttering shout that was unmistakably Benjo in a panic, the custard slid slickly off the plate to land with a plop on the floor.

Rachel hurried to the window, looking out into the night-blackened yard. Lantern light spilled out the open barn doors, and she could see twisting, whirling shadows. Shadows of men fighting.

She flung herself out the door and ran toward the barn. They were all there—Noah Weaver and three of her brothers, Sol and Samuel and Abram—men with clenched fists and rage in their hearts, there to hurt the man she loved more than any other in this world.

She came hurtling through the door in time to see Sol throw his full weight into a violent punch that snapped Johnny Cain's head back and sent him slamming into a stall door.

Rachel gasped to see her lover's face. Blood oozed from his mouth and from a cut on his cheekbone. Yet he wasn't fighting back. Even with Samuel and Abram now taking turns to pummel him, he just stood there with his arms hanging loose at his sides.

"You stop it this instant!" Rachel shouted in *Deitsch.*

Sol didn't stop. He smashed his fist into Cain's face again, then followed with a savage blow to his belly. Cain grunted, doubled over, staggered, tripped on a sawhorse, and fell to his knees. Noah pulled back his brogan and kicked him in the kidneys.

Rachel seized a hay rake off a wall hook and ran at them with it, shrieking, "You stop, stop it, stop it!"

But it was the outsider who stopped it by shouting her name.

The quiet that followed was immediate and complete. Benjo had his back pressed against a stall door. His eyes were staring wild.

"Get off my farm." She waved the hay rake at them, jabbing the air with it. "Get away from me and mine."

Cain had pushed himself up. He brushed his forearm across his nose, staining his sleeve with blood. Rachel leaned toward him, yearning to go to him, to comfort him and ease his hurt.

The lantern flared as Noah took a step, holding out a clumsy hand toward her, his voice shaking. "Rachel, please—"

"Don't say my name! Don't you dare to say my name!"

Samuel pointed a finger at Cain, who still knelt in the straw.

"There's nothing left to your name, now that *he's* had you for his whore."

"You take back your filthy words, Samuel Miller—"

"No. I'll not!"

He brushed past her and through the barn doors as if he couldn't get out fast enough. Abram followed, pausing only long enough to say to her, " 'She that liveth in pleasure is dead while she liveth.' "

"And what of your deeds this night?" she shouted after them. "You too will be answering for them on Judgment Day!"

She turned to her brother Sol, who stood as if his body felt too weighted to move. The knuckles on his right hand were scraped.

"Sol," she said, nearly choking over his name, crying. "I know what you are. How could you have had a part in this?"

Sol faced her squarely. "If we wish to destroy a weed, we must pull it up by the roots," he said, and left the barn.

Of those Plain men who claimed to love her, only Noah remained. It was too hurtful to look at him, so she focused her gaze on his hanging lantern. "You will take yourself away from here, Noah Weaver, and you will never set foot in my house again."

"He wanted you, and so he took you," Noah said, his voice bleak. "He took you, and you let him."

"And that justifies what you've done? To beat on a man with fists, with vengeance in your hearts—that has never been the Plain way."

He lifted his hands, palms out, and took a single stumbling step toward her. She saw the silver glint of tears on his cheeks, in his beard. "You remember that night, Rachel, the night of my Gertie's death? You said I was dear to you. Those were your words, Rachel. You said, 'You are so dear to me, my Noah.' You led me to believe that if it wasn't for Ben, you would have been mine. And now—"

"And now you have just torn my heart out at the roots. I never want to look into your face again."

His arms fell to his sides, and something seemed to collapse inside of him. He turned away. But he stopped at the door, and bracing his hand hard against the frame, he turned to face her.

"And him, Rachel? An outsider and a man-killer? What can he give you besides misery and eternal damnation?"

HE WAS SITTING IN A CHAIR IN her kitchen, not saying anything, while she doctored his hurts. Crowfoot salve for his cuts. An elder-flower infusion for his swollen eye. She chanted *Mutter* Anna Mary's *Brauche* prayers, though she understood now that her faith would never be strong enough.

With tender care she eased his ripped and blood-splattered shirt over his head. A raw, purpling bruise spread over his belly.

"Benjo," she said, slowly and carefully.

The boy had been hovering over by the cookstove. He hadn't once taken his eyes off Johnny Cain. He jumped when she said his name.

"Benjo, go rake out the barn." She pointed to the door. "Go!"

Choking over words of protest, her son ran from the house.

Rachel knelt before the outsider. She slid her arms around him and pressed her open mouth to his bruised flesh.

His hand closed over her head, crinkling her prayer cap. "Aw, Rachel, Rachel. Don't, darlin'. I've taken worse beatings—"

"I know you, Johnny Cain," she said, the words vibrating against his stomach. "I know you, and so I love you."

His hand tightened on her cap. "Rachel, what happened to your brother Rome?"

She raised her head. He was looking down at her with empty eyes, but she could see the pulse beating in his neck, fast and hard. "Your particular friend, Deacon Noah, he said I was to ask you."

"I told you what happened. He was banned from the church, shunned by his family, and he died."

"How did he die?"

She sat back on her heels. Her throat felt as if a hand were wrapped around it, choking her.

"How did he die, Rachel?" Cain asked, relentless.

"He hanged himself in our father's barn."

He didn't move or make a sound, but she could feel something change in him. She looked up into his eyes.

"What?" she cried. "What is it?"

He bent over and took her face in his hands. "Before your broth-ers started walloping me, I told them I would marry you."

"Oh," she said. She hadn't imagined he would do such a thing. She thought the caring had all been on her side. Tears welled in her eyes. She covered his hand with hers, holding it, so that she could turn her head and press her lips into his palm.

"Be my wife, Rachel."

She shook her head, and the tears splattered. "I love you, Johnny Cain. I will always love you. But a Plain woman must marry Plain, or she will be lost, shunned forever by her friends and family."

He leaned close and brushed his mouth across hers. She reached up and wrapped her arms around his neck, holding him, and laid her head on his shoulder.

She didn't know how long they stayed that way, but eventually she slipped gently out of his grasp. She didn't want him to feel how cold she was. "To lie unwed with a man is a grave sin," she said, all calm and matter-of-fact, "but it can be forgiven."

"What are you going to have to do in order to be forgiven?"

"I will go before the church and confess my sin with you. I will beg to be absolved and will vow never to sin in that way again."

"And?"

The cold, crushing sensation sharpened in her chest. "And you will leave here, never to return."

He sat there, saying nothing, his eyes and face a black void, like the darkness beyond the lantern light. There wasn't anything about him to tell her he was hurting. But she knew him now. She wanted to hold him, hold him tight against the pain, but she didn't dare.

She went to him the next Sunday morning.

He was in the barn, scraping caked dirt and dung out of his little mare's left rear hoof with a hoof pick. He straightened up as soon as he saw her.

He was no longer dressed Plain. He had on a white shirt with a crisp linen collar and a vest the color of rhubarb wine, decorated with shiny jet buttons. His trousers were black with a thin gray stripe running through it. He looked fine, not at all like a sheep farmer.

She petted the mare's velvet nose. Her throat was tight, full of the things she wanted to say. "It's happening this morning at the preaching," she said. "My confession and repentance. Will you take me there, and will you promise not to leave until it's over?"

He muttered an oath. "What do you think I'm made of, Rachel?"

All that is fine and frightening, all that is sinful and beautiful, she thought. She tried to smile, but it came out all wrong.

"Please, Johnny. I need you with me." She backed up a step and then another. She turned and walked toward the open barn doors.

"Do you think it a sin, Rachel, the love we made?"

She didn't answer, because she didn't know what the answer was.

THE sun was a molten copper ball in a hard blue sky. The wind rippled the tawny grass. It luffed the brim of Rachel's bonnet.

It was only herself and the outsider in the buckboard this time. Her brother Sol had come over with his wagon to bring her to the preaching, but she had sent him on his way with Benjo instead. It had seemed a terrible enough thing that her son would have to witness her shame as she confessed her sins. She couldn't bear having him endure with her what would come before: that long walk past the silent rows of benches, through that sea of black and white prayer caps and black hats. Those long, slow moments on her knees, of waiting, of time passing. Not sweet this time, but bitter and hard.

The old horse shook her harness and plodded along. Johnny Cain's horse, saddled and groomed and tied to the back of the buckboard, was following along behind.

I must do this, I must. For my son and family. I must do this, or there will be no place for me at the table.

She looked at him, but he kept his eyes on the road.

I can't become separate like you, Johnny. I can't live on the outside. She had always been joined—like a limb to a tree—to the church and to her family and to God. If she broke off, she would die.

She thought this moment must have always been in her future, like a prophecy. Beginning with that day he had come staggering across her hay meadow and ending with this—when she must choose between her family and God, and her love for Johnny Cain.

I must do this. I must.

THIS SUNDAY THE PREACHING was in Noah Weaver's barn. The doors were open, and everyone was already inside, waiting for her.

The outsider pulled the buckboard to a stop.

"When you hear the hymnsong," Rachel said, feeling feverish, "then you'll know it's been done. Then you will go."

She watched his fist clench around the reins. "Rachel, I— If this is what your God demands of you, then I don't want to know Him."

"Oh, no, no. You mustn't say that; you mustn't think it. Don't turn away from God because of me. Please."

He wrapped the reins around the brake handle and swung out of the buckboard. She started to climb down, but he was suddenly there to steady her, an excuse to touch one last time.

"Rachel."

It was her father who spoke her name. At the sound of it she turned and walked away from the outsider and back into her Plain life.

Bishop Isaiah Miller stood before her in his freshly brushed Sunday coat. He wore the pain she'd given him in his eyes.

"You will make yourself right with the church, *ja,* our Rachel? You will make it right."

She managed a nod, and it seemed to satisfy him.

They started to walk together toward the barn. Rachel wanted to turn around, to look back at Johnny Cain, but she was afraid that if she did, then she wouldn't be able to take one more step toward a life without him.

"Da," she said, "this is too hard, I don't think I can bear it."

He wrapped his arm around her shoulders, clumsy and yet tender. "You'll feel better once you can walk again in righteousness."

He stood there, holding her. She wanted it to last forever.

BISHOP Isaiah Miller stood with tears running into his beard. He read in a quavering voice from the Bible about the prodigal son and about the faithful shepherd and his lost sheep.

Rachel Yoder knelt on the straw-strewn floor, facing the church, facing her family, her friends, her Plain life. She tried to make herself listen to the holy words, to endure this as she must, with humility, with a yielding joy and hope in her heart. But her mind kept wandering, and her heart echoed with hollowness.

"Rachel Yoder, if you believe you can face the All-Highest God with a penitent heart, then confess to your sins now in the name of God, and you shall be forgiven them."

The straw prickled her knees. The silence was heavy and solemn.

"I confess that I failed to keep myself separate. That I made the outsider Johnny Cain part of my family, allowing myself and my son to be touched by his worldly ways and corrupting influences."

He'd been a hard worker around the farm, and so good with Benjo. And he wasn't as tough as he liked to pretend.

"I confess to the sin of fornication with the outsider."

His mouth had always looked so hard. It had been such a sweet surprise to feel how soft and warm his lips were.

"I confess to the sin of pride, of thinking I could bring salvation to the soul of the outsider, when only God can grant it."

He had killed in the coldest blood. If she went back to her Plain life, he would go back to his old life. And eventually he would die bleeding on a saloon floor.

"I confess . . . I confess . . ."

The sunlight pouring through the open doors was blinding. Her vision blurred and whitened at the edges. She heard weeping and a rustling of feet, and then all she heard was her own heartbeat.

I must do this.

"I confess," she said, her voice rising, "to having fallen into love with the outsider Johnny Cain. You say he is separate and so I cannot love him, but tell that to my heart. The love I bear for him, it just comes over me and it doesn't stop, it goes on and on."

She tried to draw in a breath, but it caught in her throat. "He is separate, you say. He is an outsider. But I think to myself, If God loves all of his creatures, even the unbelievers, why then would He demand of me that I deny the love I bear for this one man?"

Behind her, her father said something, a hard, desperate whisper. Sol had his head buried in his hands. Noah had his fist pressed hard to his mouth. Tears washed over her mem's face.

"I know what I must do," she said, rising, lifting her gaze to that dazzling, white sunlight beyond the doors. "I looked for the sorrow in my heart, for the shame I must feel for what I've done, but it isn't there. Mem, Da, my brothers and sisters in Christ, I am so sorry. But my heart is too full of my love for him."

The first step was the hardest; then she was running.

SHE didn't see him at first, and she feared that he might already have left her. But he sat beneath a box elder tree at the top of the lane, with his back pressed against its furrowed trunk. When he saw her, he stood up.

She cried out, a shout of joy, and ran to him. And then she was in his arms.

His hands took hold of her face gently, made her eyes look up into his. "Come be my wife," he said.

From the open doors of the barn, low and slow, came the funeral-bell toll of the first hymnsong.

"Mem!"

Benjo burst into the sunlight, running hard, his hand holding down his hat. "Mem! Wuh—wait!"

He threw himself against her, and she held him tight.

She looked up at Johnny Cain. "I want to go home, please. Take us home."

THE circuit preacher wasn't due in Miawa City for another month, so they went up to the Blackfoot Indian reservation to be married by the missionary there. In a small log church Rachel and Johnny Cain spoke the vows that made them man and wife.

She hadn't been able to stop herself from thinking how different this was from her wedding to Ben, when her father had pronounced his blessing over their clasped hands.

She was given no such blessing now.

The vows were the same, though, then and now. And both times, then and now, there was love.

NOAH stood on the porch, looking at the door. He drew in a deep breath. He had his duty as deacon to perform. He would speak to her one last time. Then her name would never again pass his lips.

He had to knock twice, and when she pulled open the door, the sight of her tore a gasp from his throat. She had on her Plain dress, but wore no apron, no modest shawl. Her dress was unpinned at the neck. Her hair fell over her shoulders and arms in a dark red silken quilt, caressing her hips. He swallowed, hard.

"Noah." His name was a whisper on her lips, dark with sorrow.

He straightened his back. "Rachel Yoder, you have been placed under the *Bann* by all members of the church of God. You will be shunned and avoided by us until the time of your repentance. Never will we speak your name, from this moment forth, until such time as you repent, or if you do not repent, then to us you are dead."

Her eyes misted. But she looked at him with resolution. "You have done your duty, Deacon Weaver, and I have taken your words to my heart. But I'll not be repenting, ever."

Cloaked by dim shadows within the kitchen, the outsider had moved up behind Rachel. Noah saw that for once the man wasn't smiling that devil's smile.

"I don't know why you have done this," Noah said. "To seduce a Plain woman from her family, her life, her God—why? If she matters to you at all, why did you choose to become her damnation?"

The outsider stirred. He laid a hand on Rachel's shoulder.

"She isn't damned," the outsider said. "No God worth worshipping, no heaven worth striving for, would ever turn her away."

Noah shook his head. There was only one path to salvation—the straight-and-narrow way.

"Noah?" She was crying now, a few tears that she wasn't able to help. "Will you tell Da, tell my family, that I still love them all so very much and that I'm sorry, so sorry."

Noah opened his mouth to speak, but his throat locked. He should have reminded her that he could no longer speak her name. It was his duty as deacon to do that, but he still loved her too much.

So he only swallowed, nodded, and dragged the weight of his feet and legs off the porch and toward the barn and the woods that separated her place from his.

CHAPTER TWENTY-ONE

FOR Rachel time passed both sweet and hard that summer.

It was like nothing she could ever have imagined, her life with him. She would look at him sitting at the man's place at her table, and her heart would catch anew with awe and excitement to think he was hers.

Or she would suddenly be swept up into his arms in the middle of the yard, and he would be humming a tune and whirling her around and around in a dance, and she would think of the Bible words: *For ye have not passed this way heretofore.*

By marrying an outsider, she supposed she had gone *Englische,* but she didn't feel that way. She no longer wore her prayer cap, though. Not because he'd asked it of her, but because to her the cap was a symbol of what she once was and could never be again.

Otherwise she dressed as she always had, for much of what she was inside of herself was still Plain. Yet she felt something vital was missing. She was less than herself, as if a limb had been cut off.

And then there were those times she would look at Benjo, and the fear would burn hot in her breast. For although she was shunned, Benjo was not. His kin and his church were still there for him to have, and she would be sure he had them. She would raise him Plain and send him to the preaching and fellowship every other Sunday. He would go often to the farms of his relatives; he would eat at their tables. And then one day he would kneel in a Plain barn, and he would say the traditional words, "It is my desire to be at peace with God and the church," and he would have to shun her then, his mother. He would be lost to her. But if he didn't choose the Plain church, if he joined her in the world instead, then he would be lost to God. As she was lost to God.

IT WAS the first worship Sunday after she was banned. That night, after it had grown dark, and supper had been cooked and eaten, and the dishes washed, and her son pried out of the kitchen and sent off to bed, Rachel went by herself out to the paddock fence. She stood there listening to the saw of the crickets, to the gentle purl of the creek, to the soughing of the summer wind, opening her heart to the music—only the music wouldn't come. And suddenly she was doubled over the fence rail, burying her face in her arms and sobbing.

She didn't even know he had come until he'd already gathered her up in his arms and was walking back to the house, with her face buried in his chest and her sobs quieting now.

He laid her on the bed, and then he lay down next to her.

"Hold me, Johnny," she said. "Hold me tight."

LATER, in the middle of the night, she was sitting in her spindle-backed rocker, staring into the darkness. He got up and went to her. He knelt at her feet and took up her hands, which she had clenched in her lap.

"The music is gone," she said to him.

"It'll come back."

"No, it can't come back. The music was God."

SHE was sitting on the porch one afternoon, with the butter churn between her knees, cranking on the handle, when she saw a Plain woman walking down the road.

Rachel's arm slowed its cranking. And long before the woman turned into the yard, Rachel knew it was her mother.

She couldn't imagine what terrible thing had happened in the lives of her family that would send her mem here. A death, surely—it could be nothing less for Sadie Miller to break the *Bann*.

Sadie Miller stopped at the bottom of the steps. Her prayer cap, starched and bleached, blazed white under the sun.

"Mem, what are you doing here? You shouldn't have come. If anyone's seen you, if they find out . . ."

Rachel's mother lifted her head. "I won't come again," she said. "Only this once. I had to see with my own eyes how you are."

Rachel's heart ached. "It's hard for me some days, but I'm happy," she said to her mother, and the truth felt good to say, good to acknowledge. "I love him so very much, Mem. He is everything to me."

Her mother said, "It's a wonderful and hurtful love you must have for him. Hurtful because you've given up everything to possess him. And wonderful because you believe him to be worth it all."

Her mother looked at her in a way she'd often done when Rachel was a girl, with a mixture of exasperation and confusion and surprise. "I don't know if God's always so smart," she said, "in the way He matches us all up, the one to the other. Sure enough, I wasn't the right mother for you."

Something caught at Rachel's chest. "Oh, Mem—"

"There you see, always you don't let me finish. I used to look at you growing up—*ja,* and even after you married and had a boy of your own—I used to look at you and think to myself, This is my daughter? And I'd feel such a wonderment, that you had come from me. For sure I could never see how that could be. You've always been so strong, so complete inside yourself. Like a hymnsong always sung in the same sure way, you always knew right where you wanted to go, how you wanted to be."

"I don't feel so much that way now," Rachel said.

"You will again. You are so strong, my daughter."

My daughter. Rachel hadn't known how badly she'd needed to hear those words, and they were doubly sweet and painful because she knew she would never hear them again after this.

Tears filled her eyes. As she walked down the steps and into her mother's arms, she moved as if blinded. It was an awkward embrace, and it left them both feeling a little shy and foolish, so that when they pulled apart, neither could look at the other.

Rachel's mother dabbed at her eyes with the corner of her apron. "I never said it to Rome. And I've had to swallow back many a bitter regret since. So I'll not leave here without saying it to you."

She dropped her apron and stared up into her daughter's face, as if she were etching it into memory. "You aren't dead to us, our Rachel. Not to your da or to your brothers or to me, no matter how we must behave to you. You are with us always, in our hearts."

Rachel watched her mother turn and walk away from her.

QUINTEN HUNTER STOOD ON the gallery of the big house. What he saw on this afternoon hurt. The prairie grass was so brown, the sage foothills gray with dust. Tag ends of clouds clung to the mountains, but they were empty of rain.

He went into the house in search of his father. As he walked down the hall toward the Baron's study, he could hear that tobacco-fed voice growling to someone about "this bloody drought."

Quinten knocked and went through the door in one motion.

The Baron was sitting in his leather swivel chair behind his massive black walnut desk. He had put his dusty boots on the desktop because he knew how it would irritate his purebred wife.

Ailsa, elegant in brown silk, was sitting in a Boston rocker that was stenciled in gilt and that caught the sunlight pouring through the lace panels on the windows. She didn't look irritated, only untouchable.

"Ah, there you are, m'boy," his father said, waving his cigar expansively. "I was just telling your mother that we've been having buzzard's luck lately, eh? Can't kill anything and won't nothing die."

The Baron referring to his wife as his bastard's mother—Quinten thought she probably hated that above all things, although you would never know it to look at that cool, remote face.

"If cattle prices don't start coming back up, it won't pay us to ship them to market this year," his father was saying. "Yet did you hear what those holy-howler mutton punchers got for their wool? The range is getting sheeped out, and they're getting rich off it."

"What does it matter?"

The words, spoken in Ailsa's snowbank voice, silenced the room. Quinten could hear the tick of the oak hanging clock.

"It matters!" The Baron swung his boots off the desk. "Listen. We had the range once, and we'll have it again." He held a match to the end of his cigar, sucking and puffing to get it going. Then he pointed with the smoking end of it at a pile of gunnysacks on one corner of his desk. It was the first Quinten had noticed of them.

"Tonight," his father said, "we're going to booger those mutton punchers so bad they'll be run out of this valley for good."

Quinten felt weary and scared. "Getting rid of the Plain folk won't drive cattle prices back up or put rain in the clouds," he said.

His father picked up one of the sacks and shook it before Quinten's face. "Life isn't owed to you, boy. You got to earn it. If you want this ranch, it's time you learned how to fight for it."

"Johnny Cain married that Plain widow he was working for. That sheep farm of hers now belongs to him, and there's a man who's always lived by the gun. He won't run."

"Johnny Cain might be more feared in these parts than the Almighty, but he's only one man. And one man just gets trampled in the dust until there's nothing left of him or his gun."

"I want no part of this," Quinten said.

"You'll have a part of it. Or you'll have none of it."

Quinten nodded, hearing his father's threat, accepting it. Tasting the certainty, not only that what they were about to do was wrong but that the consequences were going to be bad.

CHAPTER TWENTY-TWO

A COYOTE howled a last sad lament to the deepening night.

Benjo Yoder shivered and then looked to see if the other boy had noticed. But Mose was busy turning the grouse that was sizzling on a stick over the campfire while trying to wave the billowing smoke away with his hat. The wind was blowing wild tonight, swirling and gusting, and they kept having to shift around the fire.

The sheep were bunching—the ewes calling to their lambs, and the young ones answering. The woollies liked to huddle during the night, protecting themselves from the darkness, Benjo supposed.

He felt proud that he'd been sent up alone to do the camp tending for Mose this week. This wasn't the first summer he'd been given the responsibility. He'd done it once or twice before, and he thought he was probably getting big enough to handle a few weeks of shepherding too. But his mem would have none of that yet.

Benjo watched while Mose opened a couple of cans of deviled ham with a knife and emptied them into a pair of battered metal dishes for their dogs. MacDuff dug right in, but Mose's dog, being female, approached her food with a bit more daintiness, even sniffing it at first. She was getting real old, was Lady.

The grouse had turned a nice golden color, dripping fat that flared in the flames and made a delicious sizzling. Benjo punched at the fire with a stick, sending red sparks spiraling into the night.

He thought at first it was the sparks that set the sheep off.

Until the men with no heads came riding at them from out of the black night.

MacDuff let out a bark, but it was Lady who charged, growling, at the galloping phantoms. There was a shot; then Lady went down in a spray of blood and fur. Mose reached for his Winchester, but it was Benjo who screamed as the other boy's arm spurted blood and bony splinters.

The men on horseback spread out over the clearing, going after the frenzied sheep. Mose lay on the ground, writhing in pain. The most Benjo was able to do was stand up. All of him, his muscles and bones, had locked up with fear.

He understood why he'd thought the men were headless. They had gunnysacks pulled over their heads, with holes cut in them for their eyes. But their horses' Circle H brands were plain in the firelight.

And they had clubs in their hands. They rode among the bleating, milling sheep, smashing their woolly skulls. MacDuff, snarling, went after a blaze-faced sorrel, leaping up at the rider's leg with his teeth.

The man on the sorrel twisted in the saddle and swung his club, catching MacDuff with a terrible thwack. The dog went flying backward, yelping and smacking hard into the ground. He lay whimpering, with his hind leg twisted crooked.

Benjo cursed inside his head. He pulled out his loaded sling. He gripped the two ends of the rawhide cords in his left hand and whipped the sling hard above his head. He let go of one cord sharply, and the rock whizzed through the night air.

He'd aimed for the red glint of reflected firelight in the slit of the mask—the man's eye—and the rock struck true. The man shrieked, grabbing for his face, blood spilling from between his fingers.

Eye for eye! Eye for eye! Benjo screamed in his head.

Another man came galloping up to the campfire. He had a torch in his hand, which he set alight. He held the torch high as he spurred his horse, jerking its head around by the reins.

"No, Pa! Don't!" cried the man on the blaze-faced sorrel. Where the eye slit in the gunnysack mask had been, there was only blood.

The man with the torch was laughing. He leaned over and set the blazing wood to the back of a fat ewe. The ewe turned into a bawling torch and ran, frenzied, into the middle of the flock, touching off the entire herd in one blazing lanolin-fed fireball.

The masked men rode around the clearing, clubbing all the woolly heads they could find, sending others off into the pines with their fleece in flames. And then they seemed suddenly to ride back into the black night from where they had come.

Only one man had stayed behind. He hadn't been doing any sheep killing. He'd just sat there on his horse and watched, his cocked shotgun in his hand.

Now he sent his horse in a slow walk toward the campfire. Benjo, the sling hanging empty from his hand, watched the man come.

The burning sheep had set the pines and the buffalo grass on fire. The fire lit up the whole clearing with an eerie red glow. And the world was full of terrible noises: the crackle of flames, Mose's cries, MacDuff's whimpers, the screaming bleats of the sheep.

The man brought his horse right up to Benjo. He leaned over, and the mask made him seem as if he were looking at Benjo with a blinkless stare. "You know a Johnny Cain, boy?"

"H-he's my father," Benjo said.

He couldn't see the man's smile, but he could feel it, like a cold draft from behind the gunnysack. "You tell him that Jarvis Kennedy is plumb wore out waiting for him to rediscover his guts. He can find me in the Gilded Cage anytime tomorrow."

He turned his horse's head around and started off, but then he came back. "If he don't show, then I'll be coming to wherever he's at." The man laughed. "You tell him I am his Armageddon."

MOSE'S blood seemed to be everywhere, lying in puddles on the grass, smeared over the pine straw, splattered over his clothes.

Benjo knelt beside him, and Mose looked up, wild-eyed with pain and fear. "Benjo . . . I need to get to a doctor, bad."

Benjo nodded his head extra hard so that Mose would be sure to see. There was no way he was ever getting any more words out of his throat, which felt as if it had a noose around it. A hangman's noose.

He didn't realize he was crying until he brushed the hair out of his face and his hand came away wet. He took off his coat and wrapped Mose's arm up with it.

Somehow he got both Mose and MacDuff into the wagon bed, although he couldn't have explained afterward where he found the strength. The sky rained cinders, blistering their skin. The whole mountain was going up in flames. Thick roiling clouds of black smoke rolled overhead, burning their throats raw. Benjo drove the wagon, lurching, over the trail. He looked back once. It was as if heaven had gone up in flames.

RACHEL stood in the yard watching as her son drove up and turned into the yard, hours before she expected him.

Behind her, she heard the door bang shut, heard her *Englische* husband come out of the house. She didn't have to turn around and look to know he was already wearing his gun.

She was running alongside the wagon before Benjo could pull it to a complete stop. She saw that Mose Weaver was lying in the wagon bed, his arm wrapped up in Benjo's coat. MacDuff was back there, too. She thought he was dead until his head moved.

Her boy's face looked bloodless beneath a covering of soot and ash. For an instant Rachel's gaze lifted to the mountain where their sheep summered. The mountain was on fire.

Benjo's lips pulled back from his teeth, his throat worked hard, but the words weren't coming. Mose Weaver, though, was conscious enough to tell them most of what had happened.

This time Rachel's husband didn't offer to kill Hunter's men for her. He didn't even bother to tell her he *was* going to kill them. He just went about the business of getting himself ready to do it.

Their old draft mare's head was dragging the ground, and her legs were splayed with exhaustion. He unhitched her from the harness and brought out his own horse. There was no thought, no feeling, nothing showing on his face. Nothing.

"I'm going with you," Rachel said.

He gave her a curt nod. "I want you and Benjo both with me, where I can keep you safe. But you do what I tell you once we get into town, Rachel. You stay put where I tell you to stay put."

"Johnny." She touched his arm. "Think about Jesus. About how although his person was always yielding, his heart was never weak."

Cain's hard blue gaze met hers. "You remember what I told you about killing that hog farmer? I told you how I killed him, but I never said how I felt about it. After I'd done it, when I looked down on him, I knew he'd broken me, because I was still scared of him. Even with him dead, I was scared of him. And I hated him worse than ever then, because I knew I was never going to be free. I was always going to be his slave. But not ever again, Rachel. I'll not be a slave to another man ever again. I won't yield, I won't run, I won't turn the other cheek."

"I will pray for you, Johnny Cain," she said.

"I HAD to take the Weaver boy's arm off," Doc Henry said.

He spoke to the woman who sat on his black horsehair sofa. Rachel had one arm wrapped around her son, and she was holding him close. At Lucas Henry's words she bowed her head to pray.

Johnny Cain stood at the window looking out at the deserted street, drawn into a taut alertness deep inside himself.

Lucas was worried about the boy. "I set your dog's leg," he said, his voice gentle, yet firm. "What was his name again?"

The boy's head jerked, his throat clenching. "Muh—"

"MacDuff, isn't it?" Lucas asked. "Well, he's going to be just fine. Though he might not run as fast as he used to."

The boy's left hand hovered near his sling. A couple of hours ago Lucas had cleaned out and sewn up the right orbit of young Quinten Hunter, who had lost an eye to a rock hurled from that sling.

But then, young Quinten and his father had set fire to a whole herd of sheep and had shot off a boy's arm. So who was he to say Quinten didn't get what he deserved, Lucas thought.

The door banged open without a knock. Noah Weaver stood at the threshold, his eyes searching.

Lucas started toward him, but the big man pushed him aside and headed for the back room. "I had to amputate his arm," Lucas said. "He's had a severe shock to his nervous system, and he's lost a lot of blood. He shouldn't be moved."

The doctor might as well have been talking to a stone wall. The Plain man's broad back disappeared into the back room. He came out with the boy in his arms, carrying him like a babe, his cheeks, his beard, gleaming wetly with tears. The boy groaned, his eyelids fluttering, but he didn't awaken.

"He is my son," Noah Weaver said. "I am taking him home."

Rachel stood up, holding out her hand to him. "Noah . . ."

The Plain man looked at her, then through her. He walked straight and sure out the open door, his son in his arms.

They all stood unmoving, and Lucas could hear no sound but his own breathing. Then Johnny Cain left the window and walked to the door, just walked to the door and went through it.

His wife watched him go.

JOHNNY Cain walked out into the middle of the sunbaked street. He walked slowly. His hat was pulled low, shading his eyes, so he could see better. He flexed his fingers, unconsciously limbering the muscles for the draw.

He felt a single, quick pulse of fear, and then nothing.

He stopped across the street from the Gilded Cage saloon, directly in line with the swinging summer doors. He leaned against the post of a hitching rail, next to a horse trough, and waited.

Jarvis Kennedy burst out of the doors, firing, a Colt in each hand. But Cain had seen the toe of his boot coming a full second before the rest of him. His revolver was in his hand in a motion so quick and smooth and natural that it was like the act of breathing.

His first bullet ripped Jarvis Kennedy's throat open. Blood spilled down the front of his white vest and shirt. The second bullet got Jarvis in the back as he was spun around. He fell through the saloon's doors. He was dead before he hit the floor.

Cain was already swinging the barrel of his Colt to the right, aiming, firing at the man who was coming at him from an alley.

Shotgun pellets splintered the trough behind Cain, but he ignored them. The first of his bullets went through the man's coattails; the second went where it was supposed to—right where a gold watch chain stretched across his belly. The man screamed, doubling over, his arm clutching at his middle. He started to crawl, bleeding, back toward the mouth of the alley, and Cain fired again. The man jerked and went still.

The sound of the last shot fell, echoing, into a breath-held silence. Skeins of gun smoke drifted past on the wind. Cain opened his Colt, ejected the empty cartridges, and reloaded, his fingers moving sure and fast. He could taste the bitterness of gunpowder.

He knew there was someone else in the alley, but whoever it was had apparently quit on the notion of dying today. Cain kept his gun cocked, his finger a hairbreadth from squeezing the trigger.

A young man with long dark hair and a bandage wrapped around his head to cover one eye inched out of the shadows into the light, his hands raised high in the air. "I threw down my gun!" he called out, his voice breaking. "That's my father, please . . ."

Cain didn't move. The young man fell to his knees and crawled through the dust to the man who lay in a spreading pool of blood.

Cain waited. He waited a long while, gun in hand, because you could never be too careful.

Something banged behind him. He whirled. . . .

When he saw Rachel come running out Doc Henry's front door, crying his name, he had already fired.

"Johnny!" she shouted, and felt something slam into her chest, knocking the breath out of her, and she fell.

She saw the face of her *Englische* husband. His sweaty face was streaked with dust, his eyes were glittering brightly, and she tried to smile at him, to say his name. But there was a terrible pain inside her chest, and she thought her eyes must be filling up with blood, because the world was turning red.

Johnny.

CHAPTER TWENTY-THREE

JOHNNY Cain sat in the dust with his wife's head in his lap, and he watched her die.

The bullet hole in her chest bubbled blood. Her eyes widened, focusing on his, then slowly drifted closed. Her lips formed his name.

"No, please," he tried to say. He curled his body over her and pressed his face hard into her chest. He felt hands pulling him off her; he heard Doc Henry saying they ought to get her inside.

The boy was there too. He couldn't look at the boy.

He stood up and backed out of the way, letting them have her, because it didn't matter; nothing mattered.

He looked down at his hand. His gun was still there.

SHE was breathing still, but barely, and it was a sucking chest wound. Lucas Henry had never seen anyone live with a sucking chest wound.

He had laid her on the couch in the examining room. There was nothing he could do but drink and watch her die.

Her boy sat on the floor in the corner, with his knees drawn up beneath his chin. Every so often his head would jerk and his mouth would open, but no words would come out.

Lucas heard footsteps crossing the parlor. He turned, unsteady on his feet. "Cain?" he said.

But it wasn't Johnny Cain. It was Miss Marilee of the Red House. She had herself all decked out in black taffeta, her idea of the respectable matron out to do a good deed, he supposed.

"I've come to help you lay her out," she said, her mouth solemn.

"She isn't dead yet," he said.

She stared at him, her eyes wide, her forehead wrinkling a little. "Then why aren't you doing something to help her?" she asked.

He sighed. "Because she has a .44-caliber bullet lodged next to her left pulmonary artery, the bullet having first ruptured the lung, which has brought about pneumothorax, or air in the pleural cavity. Does that answer your question, Miss Marilee?"

He brought the bottle of Rose Bud up to his mouth with one hand while the other lowered the sheet, exposing the wound. It pulsed blood and air with her weakening heartbeat. "Or maybe you'll understand this better: She's dying, and I haven't the skill or the knowledge to prevent it from happening."

Marilee leaned over for a look, her black taffeta skirts rustling. "Can't you get the bullet out?"

"It would take a miracle. And she'd likely die anyway."

Her eyes met his, and a hard, calculating look came over her face. "I think you're scared to try, Lucas Henry. You're scared because you know you'd have to put down that bottle to do it."

"Ah, sweet Marilee." He curled his lip and tried to put a cutting edge on his tongue, but he could hear the quaver in his voice. "I'm beginning to think your sweetness is more like spun sugar—all air."

Her chin went up. "I can be real nice when I want to be and mean when I have to be. But one thing I ain't ever been is a coward."

He stared at her. He knew he couldn't do it. He thought maybe if he hadn't pickled his brain and palsied his hands with the booze for so many years, he could have done it. But now it was too late.

A man couldn't really be redeemed for all that he had done by a single act, could he?

"All right, damn you," he said. He looked around the room, terrified to begin. He had never set out to perform a miracle before. Miracles were for fools who believed.

His gaze fell on Rachel's son. "Get him out of here," he snapped.

Marilee coaxed the boy to his feet and gently led him to the door. Lucas stopped her with a hand on her arm. "Take this with you too," he said, and held out what was left of the Rose Bud.

The sweat was running cold on his trembling flesh. "Maybe we should pray for that miracle," he said. "Well, Miss Marilee, do you think God'll listen to the prayers of a drunk and a chippy?"

She gave him the sweetest smile he'd ever seen. "I always figured God listens to the prayers of sinners first, Luc. We're the ones who need his help the most."

GREAT COLUMNS OF BLACK smoke rolled over the burning prairie grass. Flames leaped along the buttes and ridges, flinging cinders, sparks, and ashes up against the bruised sky. The wind was blowing from the south. It had driven the fire down the mountain and across the cattle rangelands of the Circle H.

The big house was a pile of black, smoldering ruins when Quinten Hunter rode up to it. Strangely, the long line of stately cottonwoods still stood.

It was beneath the cottonwoods that he found his father's wife.

She must have saved the horses; at least she had saved one for herself. Quinten got off his own horse and went to stand beside her. She didn't look at him. She looked at the ruins of the house where she had lived for sixteen years, and she said nothing.

Quinten's eye, where his eye used to be, throbbed with fierce pain. "He's dead," Quinten said to her, to his father's wife. "Johnny Cain killed him."

She faced him and stood still for a very long time, and then he saw tears well in her eyes and spill over onto her cheeks. She turned abruptly away from him and mounted her horse. Her skirt rode up around her knees, revealing black lisle stockings and button shoes. He looked up into her face, so beautiful, so cold, and shining wet with an incomprehensible grief. "Where are you going?" he said.

He didn't think she would answer, but she did. "I don't know."

Quinten watched her ride away, watched until she disappeared. And a body could see a long way in Montana, even a one-eyed body.

RACHEL'S son walked through Miawa City, searching for Johnny Cain. A sooty black cloud had swallowed up the sun. The street was deserted, and it made Benjo feel scared, scared of being alone forever. He found Johnny Cain beside the livery barn, sitting in the dirt with his back pressed up hard against the wall.

He made a lot of noise, walking, because Cain had his Colt in his hand and he was jumpy. But Cain didn't seem to hear or see him.

As Benjo watched, he brought the gun up to his mouth.

Benjo opened his own mouth, but nothing would come out. He took the last few stumbling steps at a hard run and threw himself at Cain's arm, his fingers wrapping tight around the wrist of the man's gun hand. The blow jarred the gun away.

The man's eyes stared back at Benjo.

"I killed her, partner," Cain said. "I killed her."

Benjo shook his head hard, and tears splattered from his eyes. "Fuuuuhhh!" he shouted. "Fuh—fuh—fuh—father!"

He let go of Cain's wrist and grabbed for the gun, knocking the barrel up into the air. The gun fired, and the crack of the shot echoed in the hot, thick air.

Benjo wrenched the gun free from Cain's hand, and he flung it away from them with the same hard, violent motion he used to hurl his sling. They watched together as the gun flew, end over end, far, impossibly far, to land with a splash in Miawa Creek.

And Johnny Cain screamed.

He stopped the ragged noise of it with his hands, pressing his hands against his face, his breath coming in tearing sobs.

Benjo wrapped his arms around the man's shuddering back. "D-Doc Henry— He's g-going to muh—muh—make a muh—muh—muh—" *Miracle.*

Dr. Lucas Henry walked into his parlor, wiping his hands on a towel, and looked up to find Johnny Cain standing at his open door with Rachel's son at his side. The man's and the boy's hands were gripped together in a single fist. It was hard to tell who was holding on to whom.

Cain said, "The boy told me she's not dead yet. That you were trying to save her."

Lucas shrugged. "I've managed to remove the bullet and to repair some of the damage. But I can't lay claim to saving her yet. She has to survive the surgery. And the risk of pneumonia is considerable."

Lucas knew his words were callous, but he was too tired to care. When he lifted the bullet out of Rachel's lung and saw the faint tremor of a pulse in her neck, he had felt more powerful than God. Now, though, all he wanted was another slug of whiskey.

"I've put her in my own bed for now," Lucas said. "You can go on in to her."

It was the boy, though, who moved, pulling the man after him.

They walked hand in hand up to the bed. Cain stood looking down on her. "Rachel," he said, her name a torn whisper.

He dropped abruptly onto his knees beside the bed. He wrapped one arm around the waist of Rachel's son. The other hand stretched out and gripped the sheet that lay across her breast. His back bowed and his head came down, pressing into her dark red hair that lay like a spill of wine over the pillow.

LUCAS leaned against his open front door, a half-empty bottle of Rose Bud dangling from his hand. He heard the rustle of black taffeta, smelled honeysuckle toilet water. Miss Marilee of the Red House came to stand beside him.

"That Johnny Cain, he sure does love his woman," she said. "It's gonna go real hard on him if she dies, after what he done."

" 'Two loves I have of comfort and despair,' " Lucas drawled. He slanted a look at her. "That's Shakespeare, Miss Marilee."

"I don't know about that, Luc. But I know there's all sorts of love. Deep and shallow, pure and naughty. Blessed and cursed. But the best love is the kind that comes back at you from the person you give it to, bright and blindin' like the sun bouncin' off a mirror."

"I had a love like that once, and I wound up killing her for it." The words shocked him, coming out as they did without thought or premeditation. He turned full around to face her so that she could know him for what he was. "And I do mean that literally, my dear. I am as much a wife-killer as Johnny Cain in there."

He lifted the bottle of Rose Bud. "Now I don't want you to get things all backward, Miss Marilee. I didn't become a drunk because I killed my wife. I killed my wife because I'm a drunk."

He turned away from her. "She begged me to quit, and I told her I would, but I never really meant it. One night I came home—inebriated, of course—and found her packing her clothes in a trunk, leaving me just like she promised. We argued, and I hit her, and she fell down a flight of stairs and broke her neck. She wanted to save me, and I knew it, and so I destroyed her before she could. Don't you think that must have been the way of it, sweet Marilee?"

She shook her head. "It don't change things, me knowin' what you did. I love you, Luc Henry, and it won't ever change things either if you can never find it in you to love me back."

Lucas closed his eyes, swallowing back a sigh. "You think you know what you're saying, but you don't. You think you'll be able to change me, but you can't. I will still end up hurting you."

"Oh, don't you understand, Luc? *Life* is going to end up hurtin' me, so why not you?"

He stared at her. Her eyes, wet and wide, could shame the blue right out of heaven. She was sweet and pretty, and he thought she probably really did love him, in spite of everything.

She looked away. "I thought I'd go on up to the Red House and have myself a bath," she said after the silence had stretched out too long. "But I'll come back later if you want a little company."

"It's not Saturday."

She gave him a punch on the arm. "Oh, you! I never said nothin' about sportin'. There's always conversation. You ever done that with a woman—engage in a little conversation?"

He laughed and felt his heart warm.

She gave the place on his arm where she had just hit him a little rub. "I'll come back. I ain't nothin' if not persistent."

Lucas watched her until she turned down the road toward the Red House. Then his attention was caught by the churning dust of a Plain man's wagon. The man pulled the wagon up and climbed out. He walked slowly toward Lucas. He didn't come all the way up to the house, but he stood in the middle of the road, his long black beard lifting and falling with the hot, gusting wind.

"If you're here for Rachel, I can tell you she lives for the moment, although I can't promise anything more, and you're not taking her anywhere without first going over my own dead body. But you can come in and see her if you want."

Lucas didn't think he would get a response from the man. There was no expression on that bearded face or in the pale gray eyes.

But then the man said, "No. My daughter is dead to me, but you come tell me if she dies, *ja?*"

"Yes, I'll tell you," Lucas said, not understanding. And yet he had the feeling that just by being here this big, gruff Plain man had been forced to surrender some of his rare and precious innocence.

THE night lay silent over Miawa City, but inside Doc Henry's house a lamp was lit at the bedside of the sleeping woman. A man sat nearby in a winged leather chair, his head nodding.

It was the music of the wind that woke her: whining in the kitchen stovepipe, whistling under the tin roof, clanging the signboard of the saloon next door.

Rachel breathed, pleased that it didn't hurt quite so much anymore. She felt fuzzy-headed, as if her senses were wrapped up in wool. Wisps and veils of strange memories clung to her mind.

The man in the chair stirred and leaned over her. His face was dark with a days-old growth of beard. His eyes were haggard and red-rimmed, but even in the murky light of the coal oil lamp she could see that they were happy.

"I'm not gonna outlive this love, lady," said Johnny Cain. "So I'd take it kindly if you wouldn't die on me."

She smiled at him, for she knew now she wasn't going to die and because he had said in his roundabout way that he loved her.

"Johnny, I dreamed. And in the dream I heard the most beautiful music. I wanted to stay there with the music, but I couldn't. I had to come back to you and our Benjo."

"You've had pneumonia. You almost died so many times we all lost count, and Doc Henry said he was going to write you up as scientific evidence that miracles do happen."

"Do you think it was a miracle?"

His gaze broke from hers and fell to the hands he had clasped between his knees. When he raised his head again, she saw the old wariness in his eyes, but a fragile hope was there as well. He *needed* to believe, and maybe that was all faith really was, she thought. Simply a need to believe.

"I love you, my *Englische* husband," she said.

A stain of color spread across his sharp cheekbones. "Yeah. Me too," he said. "I mean, I feel the same as you do. For you."

She laughed, even though it hurt to do so. She had thought they were forever parted, and now they had it all again—their lives, their love. Her gaze traveled lovingly over him and stopped at his hips.

No gun belt. No gun.

"It's somewhere at the bottom of Miawa Creek," he said, although she hadn't spoken.

"And is it there to stay, Johnny? Or will you only buy another?"

His eyes met hers, and they were no longer empty, no longer cold. "I love you, Rachel. So much it scares me, and I have a hard time even saying the word. But I can't become Plain for you. And I can't change what I've done or the man I've been."

"I know what you are," she said. "I've always known. But the past is done, and God with his miracle has given us a future."

She had to touch him. She lifted her hand at the same time that he reached for it. He kissed her palm. "Rachel, I want . . ."

"What is it you want, Johnny Cain?"

They shared a smile, as deep and intimate as a kiss. "Only to go home and raise sheep and watch our Benjo grow into a man, and spend the rest of my life loving you. Just that."

"You ask for a lot, outsider."

He laid the back of her hand against his cheek. His smile was so tender and fragile. "What I've learned of love, I've learned from you. I don't believe in anything, but I believe in you."

He brought her hand to his lips. "There was a song," he said, "a hymn we sang in church when I was a boy." And he said the words in a voice that was deep and roughened with all the feelings he was showing her, offering to her as a gift with his love.

" 'Amazing grace, how sweet the sound. . . .' And more I don't remember, except for this. 'I once was lost but now am found.' "

PENELOPE WILLIAMSON

Not many Marine Corps veterans go on to become successful romance writers. In fact, the list of those who have may begin and end with Penelope Williamson. Before becoming an award-winning author, she marched to the tune of "The Halls of Montezuma" for six years, rising to the rank of captain in what she calls "one of the most macho societies in the world." Following her stint in the military, she worked for a few years in the high-tech world of computers before devoting herself full-time to writing novels. Her favorite subject? "I'm fascinated by women trying to break out of what the world wants them to be"—women like *The Outsider*'s Rachel Yoder.

The theme of independence runs through all of Williamson's novels, including *Keeper of the Dream* and *A Wild Yearning,* both of which won the Romance Writers RITA Award. It's also a theme that runs strongly through the author's own life. She credits her father—an air force officer—with encouraging her to believe she could do anything she set her mind to. Thanks to him, she says, "I didn't realize that women weren't allowed to do certain things."

Currently living in California, Williamson is already at work on her next book. It will follow the life of a woman raised in the strict society of upper-class Rhode Island during the late nineteenth century. Will her heroine break out of the role set for her by society? Stay tuned.

VEST

Tess Gerritsen

Heart transplant surgery.
Emergencies at all hours.
The chance to save lives.
For aspiring young heart
surgeon Abby DiMatteo,
it's the most exhilarating,
exhausting work there is—
the kind of job you have to
be willing to give up your
life for.

As Abby is about to
find out.

ONE

HE WAS small for his age, smaller than the other boys who panhandled in the underpass at Arbatskaya, but at eleven years old, he had already done it all. He had been smoking cigarettes for four years, stealing for three and a half, and turning tricks for two. This last vocation Yakov did not much care for, but it was something Uncle Misha insisted upon. How else were they to buy bread and cigarettes? Yakov, being the smallest and blondest of Uncle Misha's boys, bore the brunt of the trade. The customers always favored the young ones, the fair ones. They did not seem to care about Yakov's missing left hand; indeed, most did not even notice his withered stump. They were too enchanted by his smallness, his blondness, his unflinching blue eyes.

Yakov longed to grow out of the trade, to earn his keep by picking pockets, like the bigger boys. Every morning when he woke up in Misha's flat, he would reach up with his one good hand and grasp the head bar of his cot. He'd stretch and stretch, hoping to add another fraction to his height. A useless exercise, Uncle Misha advised him. Yakov was small because he came from stunted stock. The woman who'd abandoned him in Moscow eight years earlier had been stunted, too. Yakov could scarcely remember her, nor could he remember much of anything else from his life before the city. He knew only what Uncle Misha told him, and he believed only half of it. At the tender age of eleven, Yakov was both diminutive and wise.

So it was with his natural skepticism that he now regarded the man and woman talking with Uncle Misha over the dining table. They had come to the flat in a large black car with dark windows. The man, Gregor, wore a suit and tie, and shoes of real leather. The woman, Nadiya, was a blonde, dressed in a skirt and jacket of fine wool, and she carried a hard-shelled valise. She was not Russian— that much was evident to all four boys in the flat. She was American or English and spoke in fluent but accented Russian.

While the two men conducted business over vodka, the woman's gaze wandered about the tiny flat, taking in the old army cots, the piles of dirty bedclothes, and the four boys huddled together in anxious silence. She had light gray eyes, pretty eyes, and she studied each of the boys in turn. First she looked at Pyotr, the oldest at fifteen. Then she looked at Stepan, thirteen, and Aleksei, ten. And finally, she looked at Yakov.

She said to Misha, "You are doing the right thing, Mikhail Isayevich. These children have no future here. We offer them such a chance!" She smiled at the boys. Stepan, the dullard, grinned back.

"They will need time to learn the language," said Uncle Misha.

"Our agency is quite familiar with transitional needs. They will stay for a while in a special school to give them time to adjust."

"And if they cannot?"

Nadiya paused. "Every so often, there are exceptions. The ones with emotional difficulties." Her gaze swept the four boys. "Is there one in particular who concerns you?"

Yakov knew that he was the one with the difficulties of which they spoke, the one who seldom laughed and never cried, the one Uncle Misha called his "little stone boy." Yakov did not know why he never cried. The other boys, when hurt, would shed fat and sloppy tears. Yakov would simply turn his mind blank, the way the television screen turned blank at night after the stations shut off.

Uncle Misha said, "They are all good boys. Excellent boys."

Yakov looked at the other three boys. Pyotr had a jutting brow and shoulders hunched forward like a gorilla's. Stepan had small wrinkled ears, between which floated a walnut for a brain. Aleksei was sucking his thumb. And I, thought Yakov, looking down at his stump, I have only one hand. Why say we are excellent?

"That one there looks undernourished." Gregor pointed to Yakov. "And what happened to his hand?"

"He was born without it."

"It should pose no problem," said Nadiya. She rose from the chair. "We must leave. It's time."

"But so quickly? We have no time to say good-bye?"

A ripple of irritation passed through the woman's eyes. "A moment. We don't want to miss our connections."

Uncle Misha hugged the boys in turn. When he came to Yakov, he held on a little longer, a little tighter. "Remember your uncle," Misha whispered. "When you are rich in America. Remember how I watched over you."

"I don't want to go to America," said Yakov.

"It's for the best. You have to go."

Yakov looked at the other boys grinning at each other. They are happy about this, he thought. Why am I the only one with doubts?

The woman took Yakov by the hand. "I'll bring them to the car. Gregor can finish up here with the papers."

"Uncle?" called Yakov.

But Misha had already turned away to stare out the window.

Nadiya shepherded the four boys into the hallway and down the stairs. They were already on the ground floor when Aleksei suddenly halted. "Wait! I forgot Shu-Shu," he cried, and went tearing back up the stairs.

"Come back here," called Nadiya. "You can't go up there!"

"I can't leave him," yelled Aleksei, thudding up the steps.

"Come back here now!" The woman was about to chase after him when Pyotr said, "He won't leave without Shu-Shu."

"Who the devil is Shu-Shu?" she snapped.

"His stuffed dog. He's had it forever."

She glanced up toward the fourth floor, and in that instant Yakov saw in her eyes something he did not understand—apprehension.

She stood as though poised between pursuit and abandonment. When the boy came running back downstairs clutching the tattered

Shu-Shu, the woman seemed to melt in relief against the banister.

"Got him," crowed Aleksei, embracing the stuffed animal.

"Now we go," the woman said, ushering them outside.

The four boys piled into the back seat of the car. It was cramped, and Yakov had to sit halfway on Pyotr's lap. Pyotr shoved him. He shoved back.

"Stop it," ordered the woman from the front seat. "Behave yourselves." She glanced up at the building, toward Misha's flat.

"Why are we waiting?" asked Aleksei.

"Gregor. He's signing the papers."

"How long will it take?"

The woman sat back and stared straight ahead. "Not long."

A CLOSE call, thought Gregor as the boy Aleksei left the flat for the second time. Had the little brat popped in a moment later, there would be hell to pay.

Gregor turned to the pimp. Misha was standing at the window staring down at the street, at the car where his four boys sat. When he turned to face Gregor, his eyes were actually misted with tears. But his first words were about the money. "Is it in the valise?"

"Yes," said Gregor. "Twenty thousand American dollars. Five thousand per child. You did agree to the price."

"Yes." Misha sighed and ran a hand over his furrowed face. "They will be adopted by proper families?"

"Nadiya will see to it. She loves children, you know. It's why she chose this work." Gregor had to get him away from the window. He pointed to the valise, which was resting on an end table. "Go ahead. Check it if you wish."

Misha went to the valise and unsnapped the catch. Inside were stacks of American bills. He stood staring at the money, not with a look of triumph, but a look of disgust. He closed the valise and stood with head bowed, hands resting on the hard black plastic.

Gregor stepped up behind Misha's balding head, raised the barrel of a silenced automatic, and fired two bullets into the man's brain. Misha collapsed facedown, toppling the end table as he fell. The valise thudded onto the rug beside him.

Gregor snatched up the valise before the pooling blood could reach it. He glanced around the room to assure himself that his work here was done. Then he left the flat and went downstairs.

Nadiya and her charges were waiting in the car. She looked at him as he slid behind the wheel, the question plain in her eyes. "You have the papers all signed?" she asked.

"Yes. All of them."

Nadiya sat back with a sigh of relief.

There were sounds of scuffling in the back seat. Gregor glanced in the rearview mirror and saw that the boys were shoving each other. All except the smallest one, Yakov, who was staring straight ahead. In the mirror their gazes met, and Gregor had the eerie sensation that the eyes of an adult were staring out of that child's face.

Then the boy turned and punched his neighbor in the shoulder. That made Gregor smile. No reason to worry, he thought. They were, after all, merely children.

IT WAS midnight, and Karen Terrio was fighting to keep her eyes open. Fighting to stay on the road.

She had been driving for the better part of two days now, had left right after Aunt Georgina's funeral, and she hadn't stopped except to pull over for a quick nap or a hamburger and coffee. Lots of coffee. She knew she should try to catch another quick nap before pressing onward, but she was so close, only fifty miles from Boston.

A Burger King sign beckoned from the darkness ahead. She pulled off the highway. Inside, she ordered coffee and a muffin, and sat down at a table. At this hour, there were only a few patrons in the dining room, all of them wearing pasty masks of exhaustion.

At the next table sat a depressed-looking woman with two small children, both of them quietly chewing on cookies. Those children, so well behaved, so blond, made Karen think of her own daughters, asleep in their beds. When you wake up, she thought, I'll be home.

She refilled her coffee cup, snapped on a plastic cover, and walked out to her car. Her head felt clear now. She could make it.

She started the engine and pulled out of the parking lot, back onto Route 90.

Dr. Abby DiMatteo was tired, more tired than she'd ever been in her life. She had been awake for thirty straight hours, and she knew her exhaustion showed. While washing her hands in the sink of the surgical intensive care unit, she had glimpsed herself in the mirror and had been dismayed by the smudges of fatigue under her dark eyes, by the disarray of her hair, which now hung in a tangled black mane. It was already ten a.m., and she would be lucky to get out of the hospital by five. Just to sink into a chair right now would be luxury.

But one did not sit during Monday morning attending rounds. Certainly not when the attending physician was Dr. Colin Wettig, chairman of Bayside Hospital's surgical residency program. A retired army general, Dr. Wettig had a reputation for crisp and merciless questions. Abby was terrified of him. So were all the other residents.

Eleven surgical residents now stood beside bed 11 in the SICU, forming a semicircle of white coats and green scrub suits around the residency chairman. The group had already discussed treatment plans and prognoses of four post-op patients. It was Abby's turn to present this case.

Though she held a clipboard in her arms, she did not refer to her notes. She presented the case from memory, her gaze on the General. "The patient is a thirty-four-year-old Caucasian female, admitted at one this morning after a head-on collision on Route 90. She was intubated and stabilized in the field, then airlifted here. On arrival to the ER she had evidence of multiple trauma. She was unresponsive to all stimuli, with the exception of some questionable extensor posturing—"

"Questionable?" asked Dr. Wettig. "What does that mean? Did she or did she not have extensor posturing?"

Abby felt her heart hammering. She swallowed and explained. "Sometimes the patient's limbs would extend on painful stimuli, sometimes they wouldn't."

"How do you interpret that, using the Glasgow coma scale for motor response?"

"Well, since a nil response is rated a one and extensor posturing is a two, I suppose the patient could be a . . . one and a half."

There was a ripple of uneasy laughter among the residents.

"There is no such score as a one and a half," said Dr. Wettig.

"I know that," said Abby. "But she doesn't fit neatly into—"

"Just continue with your exam," he cut in.

Abby took a breath and continued. "Vital signs were blood pressure of ninety over sixty and pulse of a hundred. She had no spontaneous respirations. Her rate was fully supported by mechanical ventilation. Head exam revealed both depressed and compound skull fractures. Severe swelling and lacerations made it difficult to evaluate facial fractures. Her pupils were mid-position and unreactive."

She described the physical findings. The normal breath sounds. The unremarkable heart. The benign abdomen. Dr. Wettig did not interrupt. By the time she'd finished describing the neurologic findings, she was feeling more self-assured.

"So what was your impression," asked Dr. Wettig, "before you saw any X-ray results?"

"Based on the mid-position and unreactive pupils," said Abby, "I felt there was probable midbrain compression, most likely from an acute subdural or epidural hematoma." She paused, and added with a quiet note of confidence, "The CT scan confirmed it. Neurosurgery performed an emergency evacuation of the clot."

"Let's take a look at how things are this morning," said Dr. Wettig, moving to the bedside. He shone a penlight into the patient's eyes. "Pupils unresponsive." He pressed a knuckle, hard, against the breastbone. She remained unmoving. "No response to pain."

All the other residents had edged forward, but Abby remained at the foot of the bed. While Wettig continued his exam, she felt her attention drift away on a tide of fatigue. She stared at the woman's head, recently shorn of hair. The hair had been a thick brown, she remembered, clotted with blood and glass. There had been glass ground into the clothes as well. In the ER, Abby had helped cut the blouse. It was a blue-and-white silk with a Donna Karan label. Abby thought of how sometime, somewhere this woman must once have stood in a shop flipping through blouses, listening to the hangers squeak as they slid across the rack.

Dr. Wettig straightened and turned to Abby. "You diagnosed a subdural hematoma. It's been evacuated. So why are her pupils still mid-position and unreactive?"

Abby hesitated. "The . . . pupillary changes, the extensor posturing of the limbs—they were high midbrain signs. Last night I assumed it was because of the subdural hematoma, pressing downward on the midbrain. But since the patient hasn't improved, I guess that indicates a midbrain hemorrhage. It could be due to shearing forces. Or residual damage from the subdural hematoma."

Dr. Wettig turned to the other residents. "A midbrain hemorrhage is a reasonable assumption. With a combined Glasgow coma scale of three"—he glanced at Abby—"and a *half*," he amended, "the prognosis is nil. The patient has no spontaneous respirations, no spontaneous movements, and she appears to have lost all brain-stem reflexes. At the moment I have no suggestions other than life support. And consideration of organ harvest." He gave Abby a curt nod. Then he moved on to the next patient.

One of the other residents gave Abby's arm a squeeze. "Hey, Di-Matteo," he whispered. "Flying colors."

Wearily Abby nodded. "Thanks."

CHIEF surgical resident Dr. Vivian Chao was a legend at Bayside. As the story went, two days into her first rotation as an intern, her fellow intern suffered a psychotic break and had to be carted off. Vivian was forced to pick up the slack. She moved her belongings into the on-call room, and for twenty-nine days she did not step out of the hospital. On the thirtieth day her rotation ended, and she walked out to her car, only to discover that it had been towed away. The parking-lot attendant had assumed it had been abandoned.

Four days into the next rotation Vivian's fellow intern was struck by a bus and hospitalized with a broken pelvis. Again someone had to take up the slack. Vivian moved back into the hospital on-call room.

When Abby first heard the Vivian Chao stories, she'd had a hard time reconciling the legend with what she saw: a laconic Chinese woman who was so petite she had to stand on a footstool to operate. Though Vivian seldom spoke during attending rounds, she could always be found standing fearlessly at the very front of the group, wearing an expression of cool dispassion.

That afternoon Vivian approached Abby in the SICU. By then Abby was moving through a sea of exhaustion. She didn't even notice that Vivian was standing beside her until the other woman said, "I hear you admitted an AB-positive head trauma."

Abby looked up from the chart where she'd been recording patient progress notes. "Yes. Last night. Bed eleven. Why?"

"I've been following a medical patient on the teaching service. End-stage congestive failure. Blood type AB positive. He's been waiting a year for a new heart." Vivian went over to the chart rack, pulled Karen Terrio's chart out, and flipped open the metal cover. Her face showed no emotion as she scanned the pages.

"She's only ten hours post-op," said Abby, glancing toward bed 11's cubicle. "It seems a little early to be talking harvest."

"Maybe. Maybe not." Vivian slid the chart back on the rack. "This is the best match that's come up for my patient."

"I think this is premature. No one's even talked to the husband."

"Someone's going to have to."

"She has kids. They'll need time for this to sink in."

"The organs don't have time," said Vivian, and walked out.

An SICU nurse appeared. "Karen Terrio's husband's back with the kids. Can I send them in?"

Abby stepped into Karen Terrio's cubicle and looked at her. "Wait," she said. "Not yet." She quickly smoothed out the blankets. She wet a paper towel and wiped away the flecks of dried mucus from the woman's cheek. Then, stepping back, she took one last look at her. And she realized that nothing she could do would lessen the pain of what was to come for those children.

She sighed and nodded to the nurse. "They can come in now."

BY FOUR thirty Abby's afternoon rounds were completed. It was, at last, time to go home. But as she closed the last chart, she found herself drawn once again to bed 11. She stepped into the cubicle and stood gazing numbly at Karen Terrio.

She didn't hear the footsteps approaching from behind. Only when a voice said "Hello, gorgeous" did Abby turn and see brown-haired, blue-eyed Dr. Mark Hodell smiling at her. It was a smile meant only for her. On most days Abby and Mark managed to share a quick lunch together or, at the very least, exchange a wave in passing. Today, though, they had missed seeing each other entirely, and the sight of him now gave her a quiet rush of joy. He bent to kiss her. Then, stepping back, he eyed her uncombed hair and wrinkled scrub suit. "Must've been a bad night," he murmured sympathetically. "How much sleep did you get?"

"I don't know. Half an hour."

"I heard you batted a thousand with the General this morning."

She shrugged. "Let's just say he didn't use me to wipe the floor."

"That qualifies as a triumph."

She smiled. Then her gaze shifted back to bed 11, and her smile faded. "I admitted that patient last night," said Abby. "Thirty-four years old. A husband and two kids. They were here just a little while ago. They stood looking. Just looking at her. But they wouldn't touch her. I kept thinking, You have to. You have to touch her now, because it could be your last chance." Quickly she ran her hand across her eyes. "I hear the other guy was driving the wrong way, drunk. You know what really gets me, Mark? He'll survive. Right now he's sitting upstairs in the orthopedic ward whining about a few broken bones." Abby took a deep breath, and with the sigh that followed, all her anger seemed to dissipate. "I'm supposed to save lives, and here I am wishing that guy was smeared all over the highway." She turned from the bed. "It must be time to go home."

Mark ran his hand down her back, a gesture of both comfort and possession. "Come on," he said. "I'll walk you out."

They left the SICU and stepped into the elevator. As the doors slid shut, Abby felt herself wobble and melt against him. At once Mark took her into the warm, familiar circle of his arms, where she felt safe.

A year before, Mark Hodell had seemed a far from reassuring presence. Abby had been an intern. Mark had been a thoracic-surgery attending physician, a key surgeon on the Bayside cardiac transplant team. They'd met in the OR over a trauma case. Mark had already been scrubbed and gowned when Abby entered the OR. She'd been nervous, intimidated by the thought of assisting the distinguished Dr. Hodell. She'd stepped up to the table. Shyly she'd glanced at the man standing across from her. What she saw above his mask was a broad, intelligent forehead and a pair of beautiful blue eyes. Very direct. Very inquisitive.

Together they operated. The patient survived.

A month later Mark asked Abby for a date.

She turned him down. Not because she didn't *want* to go out with him, but because she didn't think she *should.*

A month went by. He asked her out again. This time temptation won out. She accepted. Four months later Abby had moved into his Cambridge home. It hadn't been easy at first, learning to live with a forty-one-year-old bachelor. But now, as she felt Mark holding her, supporting her, she could not imagine living with, or loving, anyone else.

"Poor baby," he murmured, his breath warm in her hair.

"I'm not cut out for this."

"Abby, you're going through the worst of it now. You've got two more days on trauma. You just have to survive two more days."

"Big deal. Then I start thoracic—"

"A piece of cake in comparison. Trauma's always been the killer."

She burrowed deeper into his arms. "If I switched to psychiatry, would you lose all respect for me?"

"All respect. No doubt about it."

"You're such a jerk."

Laughing, he kissed the top of her head. "Many people think it, but you're the only one allowed to say it."

They stepped off on the first floor and walked out of the hospital. It was autumn already, but Boston was sweltering in the sixth day of a late September heat wave. As they crossed the parking lot, she could feel her last reserves of strength wilting away. By the time they reached her car, she was scarcely able to drag her feet.

"I'll be home in an hour. Shall I pick up a pizza?" he asked.

"None for me. All I want tonight"—she sighed—"is a bed."

TWO

IN THE night it came to her like the gentlest of whispers: *I am dying.* That realization did not frighten Nina Voss. For weeks, through the changing shifts of three private-duty nurses, through the daily visits of Dr. Morissey, Nina had maintained her serenity. And why should she not be serene? Her life had been rich with blessings. She had known love and joy and wonder. And she had known the peace of mind that comes only with the acceptance of one's place in God's universe. She was left with only two regrets. One was that she had never had a child. The other was that Victor would be alone.

All night her husband had maintained his vigil at her bedside, had held her hand through the long hours of labored breaths and coughing. Sometime near dawn, through the haze of her dreams, she heard him say, "She is so young. Only forty-six. Can't something else, anything else, be done?"

Something! Anything! That was Victor. He did not believe in the inevitable. But Nina did.

She opened her eyes and saw that night had finally passed and that sunlight was shining through her bedroom window, beyond which was a sweeping view of her beloved Rhode Island Sound.

So many dawns I have known. I thank you, Lord, for every one.

"Good morning, darling," whispered Victor.

Nina focused on her husband's face, smiling down at her. Some who looked at Victor Voss saw the face of authority. Some saw genius or ruthlessness. But this morning, as Nina gazed at her husband, she saw only the love. And the weariness.

She reached out for his hand. "You must get some sleep, Victor."

"I'm not tired." He kissed her hand, his lips warm against her chilled skin. They looked at each other for a moment. Oxygen hissed softly through the tubes in her nostrils, and she saw a tear trickle down his cheek. Oh, but Victor did not cry! She had never seen him cry, not once in their twenty-five years together. She had always thought of Victor as the strong one, the brave one. Now, as she looked at his face, she realized how very wrong she had been.

"Victor," she said, and clasped his hand, "you mustn't be afraid."

Quickly, almost angrily he mopped his hand across his face. "I won't let this happen. I won't lose you."

"You never will."

"No. That's not enough! I want you here on this earth. With me."

"Victor, if there's one thing . . . one thing I know"—she took a deep breath, a gasp for air—"it's that this time . . . we have here . . . is a very small part . . . of our existence."

She felt him stiffen with impatience and withdraw. He rose from the chair and paced to the window, where he stood gazing out.

"I'll take care of this, Nina," he said.

"But Victor . . ."

He turned and looked at her. His shoulders, framed by the window, seemed to blot out the light of dawn. "It will all be taken care of, darling," he said. "Don't you worry about a thing."

IT WAS one of those warm and perfect evenings, the sun just setting, ice cubes clinking in glasses. It seemed to Abby, standing in the walled garden of Dr. Bill Archer, that the air itself was magical as clematis and roses arched across a latticed pergola. The garden was the pride and joy of Marilee Archer, whose loud contralto could be heard booming out botanical names as she shepherded the other doctors' wives from flower bed to flower bed across the lawn.

Bill Archer laughed. "Marilee knows more Latin than I do."

They were gathered next to the brick barbecue: Bill Archer, Mark, the General, and two surgical residents. Abby was the only woman in that circle. It was something she'd never grown accustomed to—being the lone female in a group.

It was Mark who anchored her in this circle of men. He and Bill Archer, also a thoracic surgeon, were close colleagues. Archer, chief of the cardiac transplant team, had been one of the doctors who'd recruited Mark to Bayside seven years before. It wasn't surprising that the two men got along so well. Both of them were hard driving, athletic, and fiercely competitive. Their friendly rivalry extended from the ski slopes of Vermont to the waters of Massachusetts Bay. Both men moored their J-35 sailboats at Marblehead Marina, and so far this season the racing score stood at 6–5 in favor of Archer.

As the conversation veered toward hull maintenance and keel design, Abby's attention drifted. That's when she noticed two late arrivals: Dr. Aaron Levi and his wife, Elaine. Aaron, the transplant-team cardiologist, was a painfully shy man. Already he had retreated with his drink to a far corner of the lawn. Elaine was glancing around in search of a conversational beachhead. This was Abby's chance to flee the boat talk. She went to join the Levis.

"Mrs. Levi? It's so nice to see you again."

Elaine returned a smile of recognition. "It's . . . Abby, isn't it?"

"Yes, Abby DiMatteo. I think we met at the residents' picnic."

"Oh, yes, that's right. Which rotation are you on now?"

"I start thoracic surgery tomorrow."

"Then you'll be working with Aaron."

"If I'm lucky enough to scrub on any transplants."

"You're bound to. The team's been so busy lately. They're even getting referrals from Massachusetts General, which tickles Aaron pink." Elaine leaned toward Abby. "They turned him down for a fellowship years ago. Now they're sending *him* patients."

"The only thing Mass Gen has over Bayside is their Harvard mystique," said Abby. "You know Vivian Chao, our chief resident?"

"Of course."

"She graduated top ten at Harvard Med. But when it came time to apply for residency, Bayside was her number one choice."

Elaine turned to her husband. "Aaron, did you hear that? Really, you're already at the top here. Why would you want to leave?"

"Leave?" Abby looked at Aaron, but the cardiologist was glaring at his wife. Their sudden silence puzzled Abby.

Then Aaron cleared his throat. "It's just something I've toyed with," he said. "You know. Getting away from the city. Moving to a small town." He took a gulp of his drink. "It was just a fantasy."

In the odd silence that followed, Abby heard her name called. She turned and saw Mark waving to her.

"Excuse me," she said, and crossed the lawn to join him.

"Archer's giving the tour of his inner sanctum," said Mark. "Come on." He took her hand and led her into the house.

Archer was already waiting in a room at the end of the second-floor hall. In a grouping of leather chairs were seated Drs. Frank Zwick and Rajiv Mohandas.

Abby noticed she was standing in a museum of antique medical instruments. In display cases were exhibited a variety of tools both fascinating and frightening: scalpels and bloodletting basins, leech jars, obstetrical forceps with jaws that could crush an infant's skull.

"Isn't Aaron coming?" asked Archer.

"He's on his way up," said Mark.

"Good."

The door opened then, and Aaron came into the room. He said nothing, only nodded as he sat down in a chair.

"Can I offer you a splash of brandy, Abby?" said Archer.

Abby smiled. "All right. Thanks."

Archer poured Abby's drink and handed it to her. The room had fallen strangely quiet, as though everyone was waiting for this formality to be completed. It struck her then: She was the only resident in the room. There were six other surgical residents circulating downstairs in the garden. But here, in Archer's private retreat, there were only the five men on the transplant team. And Abby.

She sat down on the couch, next to Mark, and sipped her drink. Archer sat down across from her. "I've been hearing some good things about you, Abby, from the General."

"Dr. Wettig?" Abby couldn't help a surprised laugh.

"He thinks you're one of the best level-two residents in the program. I've worked with you, so I know he's right."

Abby shifted uneasily on the couch. Mark gave her hand a squeeze.

That gesture was not missed by Archer, who smiled. "Obviously, Mark thinks you're pretty special. And that's part of the reason we thought we should have this discussion." He reached for the brandy decanter and poured himself a scant refill. "Our transplant team's interested in only the best. We're always looking over the residents for fellowship material." He paused. "And we were wondering if you might have an interest in transplant surgery."

Abby flashed Mark a startled look. He nodded.

"It's not something you have to decide anytime soon," said Archer. "We have the next few years to get to know each other. It may turn out transplant surgery's not something you're even vaguely interested in."

"But it is." She leaned forward, her face flushing with enthusiasm. "I guess I'm just surprised. And flattered. There are so many good residents in the program. Vivian Chao, for instance."

Mohandas said, "There's no question Dr. Chao's surgical technique is outstanding. I can think of several residents with excellent technique. But you have heard the saying? 'One can teach a monkey how to operate. The trick is teaching him *when* to operate.' "

"I think what Raj is trying to say is, we're looking for good clinical judgment," said Archer. "And a sense of teamwork. We see you as someone who works well with a team. When you're sweating it out in the OR, all sorts of things can go wrong. We have to be able to pull together, come hell or high water. And we do."

"We help each other out, too," said Frank Zwick. "Both in the OR and outside it."

"Absolutely." Archer glanced at Aaron. "Wouldn't you agree?"

Aaron cleared his throat. "Yes. We help each other out. It's one of the benefits of joining this team."

"One of the many benefits," added Mohandas. "For example, when I completed my surgery residency, I had a number of student loans to pay off. So that was part of my recruitment package. Bayside helped me pay off my loans."

Abby nodded ruefully. "I'm just beginning to feel the pain from the college and medical school loans."

"Anyway, it's something for you to think about," Archer said, standing up. "One thing, though. You're the only resident we've approached. It would be wise if you didn't mention this to the rest of the house staff. We don't want to stir up any jealousy."

"Of course not," said Abby.

"Good." Archer looked around the room. "I think we're all in agreement about this. Right, gentlemen?"

There was a general nodding of heads.

"We have consensus," said Archer, smiling. "This is what I call a real team."

"So WHAT do you think?" Mark asked as they drove home.

Abby threw back her head and shouted deliriously, "I'm floating! Wow, what a night!"

"You're happy about it, huh?"

"Are you kidding? I'm terrified."

"Terrified? Of what?"

"That I'll screw up. And blow it all."

He laughed. "Hey, we've worked with all the residents. Believe me, you're our number one choice. We're all together on this."

She fell silent for a moment. "Even Aaron Levi?" she asked.

"Aaron? Why wouldn't he be?"

"I don't know. I was talking to his wife tonight. I got the feeling Aaron isn't very happy. Did you know he was thinking of leaving?"

"What?" Mark glanced at her in surprise.

"Something about moving to a small town."

For a while Mark drove without saying a word. "You must have misunderstood," he said at last.

She shrugged. "Maybe I did."

"LIGHT, please," said Abby.

A nurse reached up and adjusted the overhead lamp, focusing the beam on the patient's chest. It was a small chest, a small woman. Mary Allen, eighty-four years old and a widow, had been admitted to Bayside a week earlier complaining of weight loss and severe headaches. A routine chest X ray had turned up an alarming find: multiple nodules in both lungs. For six days she'd been probed, scanned, and x-rayed, and still the diagnosis was unclear.

Today they'd know the answer.

Dr. Wettig picked up the scalpel and stood with blade poised over the incision site. Instead of cutting, though, he looked at Abby. "How many open lung biopsies have you assisted on, DiMatteo?"

"Five, I think."

Wettig held out the scalpel. "This one's yours, Doctor."

Abby looked at him in surprise. The General seldom relinquished the blade, even to his upper-level residents. She took the scalpel, felt the weight of stainless steel settle comfortably in her grasp. With steady hands she made her incision along the fifth rib's upper edge. Another, deeper incision parted the intercostal muscles.

"Okay, retract," said Abby.

The ribs were spread apart. The ventilator pumped another burst of air, and a small segment of lung tissue ballooned out of the incision. Abby clamped it, still inflated, and focused her attention on the exposed segment of lung tissue. It took only a glance to locate one of the nodules. She ran her fingers across it. "Feels pretty solid," she said. "Not good." She began to resect the wedge of lung containing the nodule.

Wettig nodded. "This one's aggressive. Eight months ago she had a normal X ray. Now she's a cancer farm."

Abby completed the resection and sutured the cut edge of lung. Wettig offered no comment. He merely watched, his gaze as chilly as ever. The silence was compliment enough. At last, the chest closed, the drain tube in place, Abby stripped off her bloodied gloves.

"Now comes the hard part," she said as the nurses wheeled the patient out of the OR. "Telling her the bad news."

"She knows," said Wettig. "They always do."

They followed the squeak of the gurney wheels to recovery. In the curtained stall Mary Allen was just beginning to stir. She moved her foot, moaned. With her stethoscope Abby listened to the patient's lungs, then said, "Give her five milligrams of morphine, IV."

The nurse injected an IV bolus of morphine sulfate—just enough to dull the pain yet allow a gentle return to consciousness. Mary's groaning ceased.

"Post-op orders, Dr. Wettig?" the nurse asked.

Abby glanced at Wettig, who said, "Dr. DiMatteo's in charge here," and left the room. Another vote of confidence for Abby.

She took the chart to the desk and began to write: "Diagnosis: post-op open lung biopsy for multiple pulmonary nodules. Condition: stable." She wrote steadily, orders for diet, meds, activity.

"Dr. DiMatteo?" It was a voice over the intercom.

"Yes?" said Abby.

"You had a call from neurosurgery about ten minutes ago. They want you to come by. Something about a patient named Terrio."

"Did they say why?"

"They want you to talk to the husband."

"Okay, thanks." Sighing, Abby closed the chart and went to Mary Allen's gurney for one last check of the cardiac monitor, the vital signs. The patient was moving, groaning again. Still in pain.

Abby looked at the nurse. "Another two milligrams of morphine." Then she headed off to meet with Joe Terrio.

IT WAS three p.m., sixty-one hours since a drunk driver had slammed into Karen Terrio's car. She was thirty-four years old, HIV-negative, cancer free, infection free. She was also brain-dead. In short, she was a living supermarket of healthy donor organs. With one terrible harvest half a dozen different lives could be saved.

Abby pulled up a stool and sat down across from Joe. She was the only doctor who'd actually spent much time talking with him, so she was the one the nurses had called to speak to him now. To convince him to sign the papers and allow his wife to die.

"Joe," said Abby, "her heart is strong. It could keep going for some time. But not forever. The body knows that the brain is dead."

Joe looked across at her, his eyes red-rimmed with tears. "I know." He rubbed his face with his hands. "I know." Then he looked up at the monitor again, the one spot in the room he seemed to feel safe to stare at. "It all seems too soon."

"It isn't. There's only a certain amount of time before the organs go bad and can't be used. And no one is helped by that, Joe."

He looked at her. "Did you bring the papers?"

"I have them."

He scarcely looked at the forms. He merely signed his name and handed them back. A nurse and Abby witnessed the signature.

ABBY found Vivian Chao dressing in the OR locker room. Vivian had just emerged from four hours of emergency surgery, yet not a single blot of sweat stained her discarded scrub clothes.

Abby said, "We have consent for the harvest. Joe Terrio just signed the papers."

"Good. I'll order the lymphocyte cross match." Vivian snapped the padlock on her locker shut. "You have a minute? I'll introduce you to Josh, my patient on the teaching service. He's in medical ICU."

They left the locker room and headed down the hall toward the elevator. "You can't judge the success of a heart transplant until you've seen the before and the after," said Vivian. "So I'm going to show you the before. Maybe it'll make things easier for you."

"What do you mean?"

"Your woman has a heart but no brain. My boy has a brain and no heart. Once you get past the tragedy, it all makes sense."

JOSHUA O'Day was asleep in bed 4.

"He's sleeping a lot these days," whispered the nurse, a sweet-faced blonde with HANNAH LOVE, R.N. on her name tag.

"Change in meds?" asked Vivian.

"I think it's depression." Hannah sighed. "He's such a terrific kid, you know? Really nice A little goofy. But lately, all he does is sleep or stare at his trophies." She nodded at the bedside stand, where various sports and Scouting awards had been lovingly arranged.

The boy looked much younger than Abby had expected. Seventeen according to his chart. He could have passed for fourteen. A thicket of plastic tubes surrounded his bed—IVs, and arterial and Swan-Ganz lines. "How long has he been sick?" asked Abby.

"He hasn't been to school in a year," said Vivian. "Coxsackie virus B hit him two years ago. Within six months he was in congestive heart failure. He's been in the ICU for a month now, just waiting for a heart." She paused and smiled. "Right, Josh?"

The boy's eyes were open. He blinked a few times, then smiled at Vivian. "Hey, Dr. Chao."

"Josh, I brought someone along to meet you. This is Dr. Di-Matteo, one of our surgical residents."

"Hello, Josh," said Abby.

It seemed to take the boy a moment to fully refocus his gaze. He didn't say anything.

"Is it okay for Dr. DiMatteo to examine you?" asked Vivian.

"Why?"

"When you get your new heart, you'll be like that crazy Road Runner on TV. We won't be able to tie you down long enough for an exam."

Josh smiled. "You're so full of it." He pulled up his gown.

Abby lay her stethoscope against his heart and listened to it fluttering like a bird's wings against the cage of ribs, the whole time aware of the boy's gaze, wary and untrusting. When she finally straightened and slipped her stethoscope back into her pocket, she saw the look of relief in the boy's face.

"Is that all?" he said.

"That's all." Abby smoothed down his hospital gown. "So, who's your favorite team, Josh?"

"Red Sox. My dad taped all their games for me. When I get home, I'm going to watch 'em all." He took a deep breath of oxygen-infused air and looked up at the ceiling. Softly he said, "I want to go home, Dr. Chao."

"I know," said Vivian.

"I want to see my room again. I miss my room." He swallowed, but he couldn't hold back the sob. "I just want to see my room."

At once Hannah moved to his side. She gathered the boy into her arms and held him. He was fighting not to cry, his fists clenched. "It's okay," murmured Hannah. "Baby, you just go ahead and cry. I'm right here with you." Her gaze met Abby's over the boy's shoulder. The tears on the nurse's face weren't Josh's, but her own.

In silence Abby and Vivian left the room.

At the MICU nurses station, Abby watched as Vivian signed in duplicate the order for the lymphocyte cross match between Josh O'Day's and Karen Terrio's blood.

"How soon can he go to surgery?" asked Abby.

"Tomorrow morning. The sooner the better. The kid's had three episodes of V. tach in just the last day. He doesn't have much time."

"Dr. Chao?" said the ward clerk.

"Yes?"

"I just called SICU about that lymphocyte cross match. They said they're already running a match against Karen Terrio. But it isn't with Josh O'Day."

Vivian turned from Abby and looked at the clerk. "What?"

"They're running it on some private patient named Nina Voss."

"But Josh is critical! He's at the top of the list."

"All they said was the heart's going to that other patient."

In three quick steps Vivian was at the telephone, punching in a number. A moment later Abby heard her say, "This is Dr. Chao. I want to know who ordered that lymphocyte cross match on Karen Terrio." She listened. Then, frowning, she hung up.

"Who ordered it?" asked Abby.

"Mark Hodell."

THREE

ABBY and Mark had made reservations that night at a restaurant near their Cambridge house. Though it was meant to be a celebration to mark the six-month anniversary of their moving in together, the mood at their table was anything but cheerful.

"All I want to know," said Abby, "is who the hell is Nina Voss?"

"I told you, I don't know," said Mark. "Now can we drop it?"

"The boy's critical. He's been on the list for a year. An AB-positive heart finally becomes available, and you're bypassing the system? Giving the heart to some private patient who's still at home?"

"We're not *giving* it away, okay? It was a clinical decision."

"Whose decision was it?"

"Aaron Levi's. He asked me to order the screening labs on the donor. Now can we change the subject?"

She watched him sip his wine. He wasn't looking at her, wasn't meeting her gaze. "Who is this patient?" she asked. "The nurses told me she was flying in from Rhode Island."

"She and her husband live in Newport during the summer."

"Who's her husband?"

"Some guy named Victor Voss. That's all I know about him."

She paused. "How did Voss get his money?"

"Did I say anything about money?"

"A summer home in Newport? Give me a break, Mark."

He still wouldn't look at her. So many times before, she'd look across a table at him and see all the things that had first attracted her: the direct gaze, the forty-one years of laugh lines, the quick smile. But tonight he wasn't even looking at her.

She said, "I didn't realize it was so easy to buy a heart."

"You're jumping to conclusions."

"Two patients need a heart. One is a poor, uninsured kid on the teaching service. The other has a summer home in Newport. So which one gets the prize? It's pretty obvious."

Mark reached for the wine bottle and poured himself another glass. "Look," he said, "I spend all day in the hospital. The last thing I feel like doing is talking about it. So let's drop the subject."

They both fell silent. The subject of Karen Terrio's heart was like a blanket, snuffing out the sparks of any other conversation. Abby thought, Together only six months, and already the silences have started.

She said, "That boy reminds me of my brother, Pete. Pete was a Red Sox fan."

Mark said nothing, his shoulders hunched in discomfort. He'd never been at ease with the subject of Pete. But then, death was not a comfortable subject for doctors. Every day we play a game of tag with that word, she thought. We say "expired" or "could not resuscitate" or "terminal event." But we seldom say "died."

The celebration dinner was a bust. They ate with scarcely another word between them.

Back in the house, Mark retreated behind his stack of surgical journals. That was the way he always reacted to their disagreements—withdrawal. Damn it, *she* could deal with a healthy argument. It was the silence she couldn't stand.

Later they lay side by side in bed, not touching. But suddenly Abby couldn't stand the silence any longer. "I hate it when you do this," she said. "I just want you to keep talking to me."

"All right. What do you want me to say?"

"Anything! The boy's in MICU. He's only seventeen."

"It's not my decision alone. The whole transplant team is involved. Even Jeremiah Parr."

"Why the hospital president?"

"Parr wants our statistics to look good. And all the research shows that outpatients are more likely to survive a transplant."

"Without a transplant Josh O'Day's not going to survive at all."

"I know it's a tragedy. But that's life."

She lay very still, stunned by his matter-of-fact tone. "You could change their minds," she said.

"It's too late. The team's decided."

"What *is* this team anyway? God?"

Quietly Mark said, "Be careful what you say, Abby."

"You mean about the holy team?"

"The other night, at Archer's, we all meant what we said. In fact, Archer told me you're the best fellowship material he's seen in three years. But we need people who'll work with us, not against us."

"Even if I don't agree with the rest of you?"

"It's part of being on a team, Abby. We all have our points of view. But we make the decisions together. And we stick by them." He reached out to touch her hand. "Come on," he said softly. "There are residents out there who'd kill for a transplant fellowship at Bayside. Here you're practically handed one on a platter. It is what you want, isn't it?"

"Of course it's what I want. It scares me how much I want it."

"Then don't blow it, Abby. Please. For both our sakes."

"You make it sound as if *you're* the one with everything to lose."

"I'm the one who suggested your name. I told them you're the best choice they could make." He looked at her. "I still think so."

For a moment they lay without talking. Then he reached over and caressed her hip. Not a real embrace, but an attempt at one.

It was enough. She let him take her into his arms.

THE simultaneous squeal of half a dozen pocket pagers was followed by a curt announcement over the hospital speaker system: "Code blue, MICU. Code blue, MICU."

Abby joined other residents in a dash for the stairway. By the time she'd jogged into the MICU, a crowd of medical personnel was thronging the area. She pushed into the knot of white coats and scrub suits. At their center lay Joshua O'Day. Hannah Love was administering chest compressions. Abby glanced up at the cardiac-monitor screen. Ventricular fibrillation. The pattern of a dying heart.

"Seven and a half ET tube!" a voice yelled.

Abby noticed Vivian Chao crouched behind Joshua's head, the laryngoscope ready. The crash-cart nurse passed an endotracheal tube to Vivian, while the respiratory tech, holding an anesthesia mask to Josh's face, manually pumped oxygen into the boy's lungs.

"Okay," said Vivian, "let's intubate."

The tech pulled the mask away. Within seconds Vivian had the ET tube in place, the oxygen connected.

The medical resident glanced up at the monitor. "Still in V. fib. Let's have the paddles. Two hundred joules." He slapped the defibrillator paddles onto the chest. "Everyone back."

The burst of electricity shot through Joshua O'Day's body. He gave a grotesque jerk and then lay still.

"Still in V. fib," someone said. "Bretylium, two fifty."

Hannah automatically resumed chest compressions. She was flushed, sweating, her expression numb with fear.

"I can take over," Abby offered.

Nodding, Hannah stepped aside. Abby positioned her hands on Joshua's thin, brittle chest and began to pump. She concentrated: lean, release, lean, release.

"Everyone back again!" someone yelled.

Abby pulled away. Another jolt of the paddles, another spasm.

A new voice joined in the bedlam. "Let's try a bolus of calcium chloride. A hundred milligrams," said Aaron Levi. He was standing near the footboard, his gaze fixed on the monitor.

The bolus was injected into the IV line.

"Okay, try the paddles again," said Aaron. "Four hundred joules."

Another jolt. The tracing on the monitor shot straight up. As it settled back, there was a blip. Then another. And another.

"I'm getting a pulse," said a nurse. "I feel a pulse!"

"BP seventy over forty. . . . Up to ninety over fifty."

A collective sigh seemed to wash through the room. At the foot of the bed Hannah Love was crying unashamedly. Welcome back, Josh, Abby thought, her gaze blurred with tears.

Gradually the other residents filed out, but Abby felt too drained to leave. In silence she helped the nurses gather up all the used syringes and glass vials, the aftermath of every code blue.

It was Vivian who broke the silence. "He could be getting that heart right now." She was standing by the bedside stand with Joshua's trophies. She picked up a Cub Scout ribbon. "He could've gone to the OR this morning. Had the transplant by ten o'clock. But you wouldn't give me a decision. You just delayed. And delayed. If we lose him, it's your fault, Aaron." Vivian looked at Aaron Levi, whose pen had frozen in the midst of signing the code sheet.

"Dr. Chao," said Aaron quietly, "would you care to talk about this in private?"

"I don't care who's listening! The match is perfect." She took a deep breath. "I don't know what the hell you think you're doing."

"Until you calm down, I'm not going to discuss this with you," said Aaron. He turned and walked out.

Vivian stood white-faced, watching Josh's chest rise and fall with each *whoosh* of the ventilator. "I'm transferring him," she said.

"What?" Abby looked at her in disbelief. "Where?"

"Massachusetts General. Transplant service. Get Josh ready for the ambulance. I'm going to make the calls."

Hannah Love protested. "He's in no condition to be moved."

"If he stays here, we're going to lose him," said Vivian. "Are you willing to let that happen?"

Hannah looked down. "No," she said. "No. I want him to live."

"Ivan Tarasoff was my professor at Harvard Med," said Vivian. "He's head of their transplant team. If our team won't do it, then Tarasoff will."

"Even if Josh survives the transfer," said Abby, "he still needs a donor heart."

"Then we'll have to get him one." Vivian looked straight at Abby. "Karen Terrio's."

That's when Abby understood exactly what she had to do. She nodded. "I'll talk to Joe Terrio now."

"It has to be in writing. Make sure he signs it."

"What about the harvest? We can't use the Bayside team."

"Tarasoff likes to send his own man for the harvest. We'll assist. We have to do it fast, before anyone here can stop us." Vivian looked at Abby. "Okay, DiMatteo. Go get us a heart."

NINETY minutes later Abby was scrubbing in. She completed her final rinse and, elbows bent, backed through the door into OR 3.

Karen Terrio, the donor, lay on the table. Vivian, gowned and gloved, stood at one side. "Signed and sealed?" she asked.

"In triplicate. It's in the chart." Abby herself had typed up the directed-donation consent, a statement specifying that Karen Terrio's heart be given to Josh O'Day, age seventeen.

It was the boy's age that had swayed Joe Terrio. He'd been sitting at his wife's bedside, holding her hand, and had listened in silence as Abby told him about a seventeen-year-old boy who loved baseball. Without saying a word, Joe had signed the paper. And then he'd kissed his wife good-bye.

Abby was helped into a sterile gown and gloves. "Who's doing the harvest?" she asked.

"Dr. Frobisher from Tarasoff's team," said Vivian. "He's on his way now."

"Any word about Josh from Mass Gen?"

"Tarasoff called ten minutes ago. They've got his blood typed and crossed and an OR cleared. They're standing by."

Five minutes later the OR door swung open, and Dr. Frobisher pushed in. "Size nine gloves," he snapped.

At once the atmosphere in the room stretched taut. No one except Vivian had ever worked with Frobisher before, and his fierce expression did not invite any conversation. With silent efficiency the nurses helped him gown and glove.

He stepped to the table. "History on this patient?"

"Head injury. Brain-dead. Donor forms all signed. She's thirty-four, previously healthy, and her blood's been screened."

Frobisher picked up a scalpel and touched the blade to Karen Terrio's chest. In one swift slice he cut straight down the center, exposing the breastbone. "Sternal saw."

In moments he was in the chest cavity, his scalpel poised over the pericardial sac. He delicately slit open the membrane. At his first glance at the beating heart he gave a soft murmur of satisfaction. Glancing across at Vivian, he asked, "Opinion?"

"It's beautiful," she said, eyes shining. "It's just the heart for Josh."

Frobisher said to the nurse, "Iced saline! Get the Igloo ready. And someone better call an ambulance for transport."

Vivian looked at Abby. "We'll need you for the delivery."

"What about my patients?"

"I'll cover for you. Leave your beeper at the OR desk."

Already Frobisher's scalpel was moving swiftly, freeing up the heart for removal. The organ was still pumping. Now it was time to stop it, to shut down the last vestiges of life in Karen Terrio.

Frobisher injected five hundred cc's of a high-potassium solution into the aortic root. The heart beat once. Twice. And it stopped, paralyzed by the sudden infusion of potassium. Abby couldn't help glancing at the monitor. There was no EKG activity. Karen Terrio was finally, and clinically, dead.

A nurse poured iced solution into the chest cavity, quickly chilling the heart. Frobisher got to work, ligating, cutting. Then he lifted out the heart and swished it gently in a basin of cold saline. A nurse stepped forward, holding a plastic bag. Frobisher eased the rinsed organ into the bag. More iced saline was poured in. The heart was double-bagged and placed in an Igloo cooler with ice.

"It's yours, Dr. DiMatteo," said Frobisher. "You ride in the ambulance. I'll follow in my car."

Abby picked up the Igloo. She was pushing out the OR doors when she heard Vivian's voice calling after her, "Don't drop it."

AT MASS GEN, a nurse in green scrubs was waiting at the ambulance dock. Carrying the Igloo, Abby stepped out of the ambulance and followed the nurse through the ER and into an elevator.

"How's the boy doing?" asked Abby.

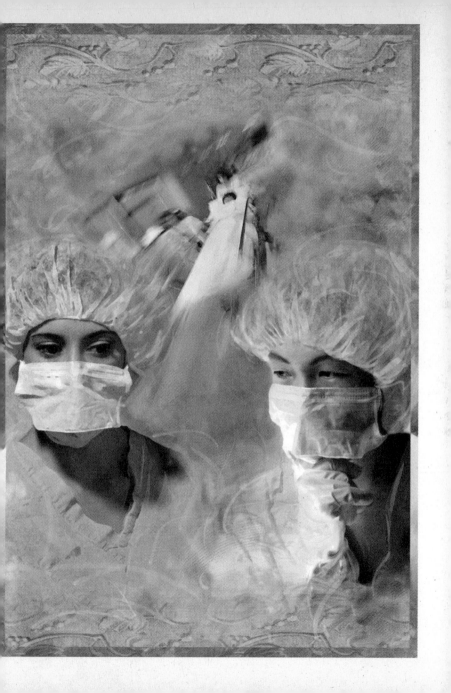

"He's on bypass. We couldn't wait."

"He coded again?"

"He doesn't *stop* coding."

They stepped off the elevator, made a quick jog through a set of automatic doors, into the surgery wing.

"Here. I'll take the heart," said the nurse, reaching for the cooler. "If you put on fresh scrubs, you can go in."

"Thanks. I think I will."

By the time Abby slipped into the OR, the surgeons had already removed Josh O'Day's diseased heart. Abby eased around to the head of the table and stood beside the anesthesiologist. Overhead, the cardiac monitor showed a flat line. There was no heart beating in Josh's chest; the bypass machine was doing all the work.

The anesthesiologist glanced at Abby. "You from Bayside?"

"I'm the courier. How's it going so far?"

"Touch and go for a while. But we're over the worst of it. Tarasoff's fast." He nodded toward the chief surgeon.

Ivan Tarasoff, with his snowy eyebrows and mild gaze, was the image of everyone's favorite grandfather. No showmanship, no high-flying ego, just a quiet technician laboring at his job.

Abby looked up again at the monitor. Still a flat line.

Josh O'Day's parents were crying in the waiting room, sobs mingled with laughter. Smiles all around. It was six p.m., and their ordeal was finally over.

"The new heart's working just fine," said Dr. Tarasoff. "It's a good strong heart. It should last Josh for a lifetime."

"We didn't expect this," said Mr. O'Day. "All we heard was that they moved him here, that there was some kind of emergency. We thought—we thought—" He turned away, not able to speak.

A nurse said gently, "Mr. and Mrs. O'Day? If you'd like to see Josh, he's starting to wake up."

A smiling Tarasoff watched as the O'Days were led toward the recovery room. Then he turned and looked at Abby, his blue eyes glistening. "That's why we do it," he said. "For moments like that."

"It was close," said Abby.

"Too close." He shook his head. "Tell Vivian to give me a little more warning next time."

"Vivian knew what she was doing. Sending the kid to you."

"Vivian Chao always knows what she's doing." He laughed. "You're in the Bayside surgery program with her?"

Abby nodded. "Second year."

"Good. Not enough women in the field. Too many macho blades. All they want to do is cut."

"That doesn't sound like a surgeon talking."

"A little blasphemy," he whispered, "is a healthy thing."

Abby glanced at her watch. "I've got to get back to Bayside. I probably shouldn't have stayed for the surgery. But I'm glad I did." She smiled at him. "Thanks, Dr. Tarasoff. For saving the boy's life."

He shook her hand. "I'm just the plumber, Dr. DiMatteo," he said. "You brought the vital part."

IT WAS after seven when the taxi delivered Abby to Bayside. As she walked into the lobby, the first thing she heard was her name being paged. She picked up the in-house phone. "This is DiMatteo."

"Doctor, we've been paging you for hours," said the operator.

"Vivian Chao was supposed to cover for me. She's carrying my beeper."

"We have your beeper here at the operator's desk. Mr. Parr's looking for you."

"It's seven o'clock. Is he still in?"

"He was five minutes ago."

Abby hung up, her stomach fluttering with alarm. Jeremiah Parr was the hospital president, not a physician. She'd spoken to him only once before. Now he was paging her at seven in the evening.

This can't be good, she thought as she rode the elevator to the second floor.

The administration wing was dimly lit by a single row of fluorescent ceiling panels. Abby walked beneath the strip of light, her footsteps noiseless on the carpet. At the far end of the hall, light was shining under a closed door. Someone was in the conference room.

She went to the door and knocked.

It swung open. Jeremiah Parr stood gazing at her. Behind him, seated at the conference table, were half a dozen men. She glimpsed Bill Archer, Mark, and Mohandas. The transplant team.

"Dr. DiMatteo," said Parr.

"I'm sorry. I didn't know you were trying to reach me," said Abby. "I was out of the hospital."

"We know where you were." Parr stepped out of the room. Mark came out right behind him and shut the door, both men confronting Abby in the dim hallway.

"Come into my office," said Parr. The instant they stepped inside, he slammed the door. "Do you understand the damage you've done? Do you have any idea?"

Abby looked at Mark, but his face told her nothing. It scared her that she could not see past the mask, to the man she loved.

"Josh O'Day's alive," she said. "The transplant saved his life. I can't consider that any kind of mistake."

"Abby," said Mark, "we're not questioning your instincts. They were good. Of course they were good."

"What's this crap about instincts, Hodell?" snapped Parr. "They stole a damn heart! They knew what they were doing."

"Following the orders of her chief resident is exactly what Abby was supposed to do. And that's all she did—obey orders."

"There have to be repercussions. Firing the chief resident isn't enough."

Fired? Vivian? Abby looked at Mark for confirmation.

"Vivian admitted everything," Mark said. "She admits that she coerced you and the nurses to go along with her."

"I hardly think Dr. DiMatteo is so easily coerced," said Parr. "There was that directed-donation form in the chart." Parr turned to Abby. "Drawn up and witnessed by you."

"Joe Terrio signed it willingly," said Abby. "He agreed the heart should go to the boy."

"Which means no one can be accused of organ theft," Mark pointed out. "It was perfectly legal, Parr. Vivian knew exactly which strings to pull, and she pulled them. Including Abby's."

Abby started to speak, to defend Vivian, but then she saw the cautionary look in Mark's eyes. *Careful. Don't dig yourself a grave.*

Parr turned to Abby, his face rigid with anger. "We have a patient who came in for a heart. And now we have no heart to give her. What the hell am I supposed to tell her husband? 'Sorry, Mr. Voss, but the heart got misplaced?' Dr. DiMatteo, you made a decision that wasn't yours to make. Victor Voss has already found out about it. Now Bayside's going to have to pay for it. Big time. As of right now, you're out of the residency program."

Abby stared at him in shock. Her throat had closed down.

"You can't do that," said Mark.

"Why not?" said Parr.

"For one thing, it's a decision for the program director. Knowing the General, I don't think he'll take to having his authority usurped. For another thing, our surgical house staff is already stretched thin. We lose Abby, that means thoracic service rotates call every other night. They'll get tired, Parr. They'll make mistakes. If you want lawyers on your doorstep, that's how to do it."

Jeremiah Parr glared at Mark. "This is temporary. Believe me, this is only temporary." He turned to Abby. "You'll hear more about this tomorrow. Now get out of here."

Too numb to think, Abby somehow managed to walk out of Parr's office. She made it down the hallway and stopped. Felt the numbness give way to tears as Mark came up beside her.

"Abby"—he turned her around to face him—"it's been a battle-field here all afternoon. What did you think you were doing today?"

"Saving a boy's life!" Her voice cracked, shattered into sobs. "It's exactly what we *should* have done." She made an angry swipe at her tears. "If Parr wants to get back at me, then let him. I'll present the facts to any ethics committee. Maybe I'll get fired. But I'll go down kicking and screaming." She turned and continued down the hall.

"There's another way. An easier way." Mark caught her arm. "Let Vivian take the fall. She accepted the blame. She did it to protect you and the nurses. Leave it at that."

"But she saved her patient's life. You don't fire someone for that!"

"She violated the number one rule here: Play with the team. This hospital can't afford loose cannons like Vivian Chao. A doctor's either with us or against us." He paused. "Where does that put you?"

"I don't know." She shook her head. "I don't know anymore."

"Consider your options. Vivian's finished her residency. She's already board-eligible. She could find a job. But all you've got is an internship. You get fired now, you'll never be a surgeon. What're you going to do? Spend your life doing insurance physicals?"

"No." She took a breath and let it out in a rush of despair. "No."

Mark nodded. "Then listen to me, Abby. I can talk to Archer and the others. If we all stick by you, Parr will have to back down."

"That's a big if."

"You can help make it happen. First let Vivian take the blame. She was chief resident. She made a bad judgment call."

"But she didn't!"

"You saw only half the picture. You didn't see the other patient."

"What other patient?"

"Nina Voss. She was admitted today. Maybe you should take a look at her. See for yourself that the choice wasn't so clear."

Abby swallowed. "Where is she?"

"Fourth floor. Medical ICU."

EVEN from the hallway Abby could hear the commotion in the MICU: the cacophony of voices, the whine of a portable X-ray machine, two telephones ringing at once.

"Dr. DiMatteo, perhaps you should come and see this," said Aaron Levi with a look of barely suppressed rage. He had just emerged from cubicle 5.

A few of the nurses were staring at her; most were pointedly looking the other way. Abby went to the window of cubicle 5. Through the glass she saw a woman lying in the bed, a fragile-looking woman with white-blond hair and a face as colorless as the sheets. An ET tube had been inserted down her throat and was hooked up to a ventilator. She was fighting the machine, her chest moving spasmodically as she tried to suck in air. The machine wasn't cooperating. Alarms buzzed as it fed her breaths at its own preset rhythm, ignoring the patient's desperate inhalations. Both of the woman's hands were restrained. A nurse was attempting to calm the patient down, but the woman, fully conscious, stared up with an expression of sheer terror. It was the look of an animal being tortured.

"That's Nina Voss," said Aaron.

Abby was silent, stunned by the horror in the woman's eyes.

"She was admitted eight hours ago. At five o'clock she coded. Ventricular tachycardia. Twenty minutes ago she coded again. She was scheduled for surgery tonight. The team was ready. The OR was ready. Then we find out the heart that should have gone to this woman has been stolen. *Stolen,* Dr. DiMatteo."

Abby was transfixed by the ordeal she was witnessing in cubicle 5. At that instant Nina Voss's eyes lifted to her. It was only a brief meeting of gazes, an appeal for mercy. The pain in those eyes left Abby shaken. "We didn't know," she whispered. "We didn't know her condition was critical."

No matter what she said, she could not justify the suffering beyond that window. She scarcely noticed a man crossing toward her from the nurses station. Only when he said "Is this Dr. DiMatteo?" did she focus on the man's face. He was in his sixties, tall and well dressed, the sort of man whose very presence demands attention.

Quietly she answered, "I'm Abby DiMatteo." But as she said it, she realized what she saw in the man's eyes. It was hatred, pure and poisonous. The man stepped toward her.

"So you're the other one," he said. "You and that Chink doctor."

"Mr. Voss, please," said Aaron.

"You think you can mess around with me?" Voss yelled at Abby. "There'll be consequences, Doctor. Damn you, I'll see that there are consequences." Hands clenched, he took another step toward Abby. "I want her out of this hospital! I don't want to see her again!"

"Mr. Voss," said Abby, "I'm so sorry. I can't tell you how sorry—"

"Just get her the hell away from me!" roared Voss.

Aaron quickly moved between them. He took Abby by the arm and pulled her away from the cubicle. "You'd better leave," he said.

Meekly she nodded. "All right," she said softly. "I'll leave."

THREE hours later Stewart Sussman pulled up at the curb on Tanner Avenue, and from his car he studied number 1451. The house was a modest cape with dark shutters and a covered front porch.

Sussman left his car and walked up the porch steps to the front door. He rang the bell, and a moment later a man opened the door, eyes red-rimmed. "Yes?" he said.

"I'm sorry to disturb you, Mr. Terrio. My name is Stewart Sussman. I'm an attorney. I've been sent here by someone who's very concerned about the circumstances surrounding your wife's death."

"Circumstances?"

"She was a patient at Bayside Medical Center, is that correct?"

"Look, I don't want any damn ambulance chaser bothering me tonight." Joe started to close the door, but Sussman put out a hand to stop it.

"Mr. Terrio," Sussman said, "I have reason to believe one of your wife's doctors made an error. It's possible Karen didn't have to die. I can't be certain of that yet. But with your permission I can look at the record. I can uncover the facts."

Slowly Joe let the door swing open again. "Who sent you?"

Sussman gazed back with a look of sympathy. "A friend."

FOUR

NEVER before had Abby dreaded going to work, but as she walked into Bayside Hospital that morning, she felt she was walking straight into the fire. Last night Parr had threatened repercussions; today she'd have to face them. But until Wettig actually stripped her of her hospital privileges, she was determined to carry on as usual. She was going to do her job and do it well. She owed it to her patients—and to Vivian. Only an hour before, they had spoken on the phone, and Vivian had said, "Someone there has to speak up for the Josh O'Days. Stay with it, DiMatteo. For both of us."

The moment Abby walked into the SICU, she heard the lowering of voices. By now everyone must know about Josh O'Day. Though no one said a word, Abby could see the nurses' uneasy looks. She went to the rack and gathered her patients' charts for rounds. She placed the charts in a cart and wheeled it out to the cubicle of the first patient on her list, Mary Allen, still under close observation following her biopsy.

She lay on the bed, her eyes closed. Abby went to the bedside and said, "Mrs. Allen?"

The woman stirred awake. "Dr. DiMatteo," she murmured.

"How are you feeling today?"

"Not so good. It still hurts, you know."

Abby saw from the chart that the nurses had been giving morphine around the clock. Obviously, it wasn't enough.

"We'll give you more medicine for the pain," said Abby. "As much as you need to keep you comfortable."

"To help me sleep, too. I can't sleep." Mary gave a sigh of profound weariness. "I just want to go to sleep, Doctor. And not wake up. You're my doctor. Couldn't you do that for me?"

"We can make the pain go away," said Abby.

"But you can't take away the cancer, can you?" Her eyes regarded Abby with a look that pleaded for honesty.

"No," said Abby. "It has spread to too many places. We can give you chemotherapy to slow it down. Gain some time for you."

"Time?" Mary gave a resigned laugh. "What for? To lie here another week, another month? I'd rather have it over with."

Abby took Mary's hand. "Let's take care of the pain first. If we do that, it could make everything else seem different."

Mary simply turned on her side, away from Abby, shutting her out. "I suppose you want to listen to my lungs," she said.

They both knew the exam was merely a formality. Abby went through the motions anyway. When she was finished, her patient still lay with her back turned.

"We'll be transferring you to a room on the ward," said Abby. "It'll be quieter there."

No answer. Just a deep breath, a long sigh.

Abby left the cubicle feeling defeated. She opened Mary's chart and wrote, "Patient expresses wish to die. Will increase morphine sulfate for pain control and change code status." She wrote the transfer orders and handed them to Cecily, Mary's nurse.

"I want her kept comfortable," said Abby. "Titrate the dose to her pain. Give her as much as she needs to sleep."

"What's our upper limit?"

Abby paused, considered the fine line between comfort and unconsciousness. She said, "No upper limit. She's dying, Cecily. She wants to die. If the morphine makes it easier, then that's what we should give her, even if it means the end comes a little sooner."

Cecily nodded, a look of unspoken agreement in her eyes.

IT WAS four p.m. Abby had been on duty since seven that morning, and she had another twenty-four hours on duty to go. But so far, no axe had yet fallen. In fact, Colin Wettig had taken her aside to tell her, in his usual gruff way, that she'd received outstanding evaluations for trauma rotation.

It will all work out, she thought as she stood in the OR watching a patient whose operation she had just assisted on wheeled out to recovery. Somehow this will all turn out just fine.

The circulating nurse poked her head in the door. "Dr. Di-Matteo? They want to see you in administration."

"Now?"

"They're waiting for you," said the nurse, and left.

Abby pushed through the OR door and headed grimly for the elevator.

With the same dread she'd felt last night, she stepped off onto the second floor and headed to Jeremiah Parr's office. She knocked on the door. "Come in," she heard Parr say.

Taking a shaky breath, she stepped inside.

Parr rose from his seat at a conference table. Also in the room were Colin Wettig and a woman whom Abby did not recognize, a fortyish brunette in a nicely tailored blue suit.

"Dr. DiMatteo," said Parr, "let me introduce you to Susan Casado, the hospital's corporate attorney."

An attorney? This is not good.

Abby took a chair next to Wettig. Then Parr said, "Dr. DiMatteo, perhaps you could tell us about your role in the care of a Mrs. Karen Terrio."

Abby frowned. This was not at all what she'd expected. "I performed the initial evaluation on Mrs. Terrio," she said. "Then I referred her to neurosurgery. They took over her case."

"So how long was she under your care?"

"Officially? About two hours, more or less."

"And during those two hours, what did you do exactly?"

"I stabilized her. Ordered the necessary labs. My admitting notes and orders would be in the medical record."

"Do you remember anything you did that might have negatively affected the patient's course?"

"No."

"I understand the patient expired."

"She'd suffered massive head trauma. A motor vehicle accident. She was declared brain-dead." Abby glanced around the table. "Could someone please tell me what's going on?"

"What's going on," said Parr, "is that our insurance carrier, Vanguard Mutual, received notification a few hours ago that you—and Bayside—are being sued for malpractice by Joseph Terrio."

The air went out of Abby's lungs. She knew they were waiting for her to respond, but all she could manage was a shocked look.

"I take it you weren't expecting this," said Susan Casado.

"I . . ." Abby swallowed. "No. No, there has to be a mistake."

"Damn right there's a mistake," said Wettig. Everyone looked at the General, who had, until then, sat in stony silence. "I've reviewed the record myself. Every page of it. There's no malpractice there. Dr. DiMatteo did everything she should have done."

"Then why's she the only doctor named in the lawsuit?" said Parr.

"I'm the only one?" Abby looked at the attorney. "What about neurosurgery? The emergency room? No one else was named?"

"Just you, Doctor," said Susan. "And your employer—Bayside."

Abby sat back, stunned. "I don't believe this."

"Neither do I," said Wettig. "This isn't the way it's done, and we all know it. Lawyers usually name every M.D. who came within a mile of the patient. Something else is going on here."

"It's Victor Voss," said Abby softly.

"Voss?" Wettig waved dismissively. "He has no stake in this."

"He's out to ruin me. That's his stake." She looked around the table. "Why do you think I'm the only doctor named? Somehow Voss has gotten to Joe Terrio. Convinced him I did something wrong. If I could just talk to Joe—"

"Absolutely not," said Susan. "It would be a sign of desperation. If there's really no malpractice here, they'll drop the suit."

"What if they insist on going to trial anyway?"

"It would make no sense. The legal expenses alone would—"

"Don't you see, *Voss* must be footing the bill. He doesn't care about winning or losing. He could pay an army of lawyers just to keep me running scared. Track down every patient I've ever cared for. Convince every single one of them to file suit against me."

"And we're her employer," said Parr. He looked ill.

Susan said, "We're still early in the game. We have months to maneuver, to plan a response. In the meantime"—she looked at Abby—"you may also consider hiring your own private counsel."

Abby swallowed. "I don't know how I'm going to afford one."

"In your particular situation, Dr. DiMatteo," said Susan, "you can't afford not to."

FOR Abby, being on call that night was a blessing in disguise. A flurry of calls and pages kept her on the run all evening. There was little time to brood over Joe Terrio's lawsuit, though every so often she would find herself hovering dangerously close to tears.

At ten o'clock she was finally free to retreat to the on-call room. Too demoralized to talk to anyone, she lay down on the bed and stared at the ceiling. Her whole body felt lifeless.

She finally moved at ten thirty, when the phone rang. She sat up and reached for the receiver. "Dr. DiMatteo."

"This is the OR. Drs. Archer and Hodell need you up here."

"I'll be there." Abby hung up with a sigh. Any other time she'd already be on her feet, raring to scrub. Tonight she could barely stand the thought of facing Mark and Archer across an operating table.

She found them on the twelfth floor, in the surgeons lounge. They were standing by the microwave, their voices lowered in private conversation. The instant they saw her, though, both of them smiled.

"There you are," said Archer. "All quiet in the trenches?"

"For the moment," said Abby. "I hear you two have a case."

"A transplant," said Mark. "But we can't get hold of Mohandas. We may need you to assist. Feel up to scrubbing in?"

"A heart transplant?" The quick shot of adrenaline was exactly what Abby needed to shake off her depression. "I'd be thrilled."

"One small problem," said Archer. "The patient is Nina Voss."

Abby stared at him. "They found her a heart so soon?"

"We got lucky. The heart's coming in from Burlington. Victor Voss would have a stroke if he knew we were using you. But we're calling the shots right now. We may need another pair of hands in that OR, and on such short notice you're the obvious choice."

"Are you still up for it?" asked Mark.

Abby didn't even hesitate. "Absolutely," she said.

At eleven thirty p.m. they got the call from the thoracic surgeon at Wilcox Memorial Hospital in Burlington, Vermont. The donor organ was being rushed to the airport. The flight, by emergency charter, was expected to take an hour and a half.

By midnight the Bayside Hospital transplant team was assembled and dressed in surgical greens. Along with Bill Archer, Mark, and anesthesiologist Frank Zwick, there was a small army of support staff—nurses, a perfusion technician for the bypass machine, cardiologist Aaron Levi, and Abby. At one thirty a.m. the call came in from Logan International: The plane had landed safely.

That was the cue for the surgeons to head to the scrub area. As Abby washed her hands, she could look through the window into OR 3, where the rest of the transplant team was already busy with preparations. On the operating table, at the center of a tangle of EKG wires and IV lines, lay Nina Voss. Dr. Zwick stood at her head, murmuring to her gently as he injected a bolus of pentobarb into her IV line. Her eyelids flickered shut. Zwick placed the mask over her mouth and nose. With the Ambu bag he pumped a few breaths of oxygen, then removed the mask, swiftly intubated her, and connected the tube to the ventilator.

The OR doors banged open as Mark, Archer, and Abby, freshly

scrubbed, walked in with hands held up. By the time everyone was fully garbed in sterile gowns and gloves, Nina Voss had been prepped and draped.

The phone rang. Everyone watched as the nurse answered it. Seconds later she announced, "The courier's on his way up."

"Okay," snapped Archer, "let's cut."

From where Abby stood, she caught only a slanted glimpse of the procedure. Archer and Mark were working in concert, making a midline sternotomy incision, exposing fascia, then bone.

The wall intercom buzzed. "Dr. Mapes from the harvest team is here. He'll be in as soon as he changes," came the message from the OR front desk. Moments later Dr. Mapes entered, wearing surgical greens. He was a small man with an almost Neanderthal brow and a nose that jutted out like a hawk's beak under the surgical mask.

"Welcome to Boston," said Archer, glancing up at the visitor. "I'm Bill Archer. This is Mark Hodell."

"Leonard Mapes. I scrubbed with Dr. Nicholls at Wilcox."

Archer said, "So what'd you bring us for Christmas, Len?"

"Nice one. I think you'll be pleased."

"Let me finish cannulating, and I'll take a look."

Cannulation of the ascending aorta was the first step to connecting the patient to the bypass machine. That machine would assume the job of the heart and lungs, collecting venous blood, replenishing its oxygen, and pumping it back into the patient's aorta.

Archer, using silk sutures, sewed two concentric "purse strings" in the wall of the ascending aorta. With a scalpel tip he made a tiny stab in the vessel. Bright blood spurted out. Swiftly he inserted the arterial cannula into the incision and tightened the purse strings. The bleeding slowed to an ooze, then stopped as he sewed the cannula tip in place. The other end of the cannula was connected to the bypass machine's arterial line. Mark, with Abby retracting, was already starting on the venous cannulation.

"Okay," said Archer, "let's unwrap our present."

A nurse unpacked the Igloo cooler and lifted out the organ, wrapped in two ordinary plastic bags. She untwisted the ties and slid the naked organ into a basin of sterile saline.

"Seems on the small side," said Abby. "How big was the donor?"

"Forty-four kilograms," said Dr. Mapes.

Abby frowned. "Adult?"

"An adolescent, previously healthy. A boy."

Abby caught the flicker of distress in Archer's eyes. She remembered then that he had two teenage sons.

"We won't let this one go to waste," he said.

Working together now, Archer and Mark snared shut the inferior and superior venae cavae, cutting off return blood to the heart. The heart was now a useless sac. Nina Voss's circulation was under the complete control of the bypass machine. Also under its control was the body temperature. By chilling the fluids, the body could be cooled down to twenty-five degrees Celsius—profound hypothermia. This would preserve the newly implanted myocardial cells and lessen the body's oxygen consumption.

Zwick turned off the ventilator. There was no need to pump air into lungs when the bypass machine was doing the work. Transplantation could now proceed.

Archer cut the aorta and pulmonary arteries. Blood gushed out into the chest, spilled onto the floor. At once a nurse threw a towel down to soak up the mess. Next Archer transected the atria and reached into the chest cavity. Nina Voss's sick heart, pale and flabby, was now lifted away and dropped into a basin. What remained was a gaping hollow. The EKG line on the monitor screen was flat.

Mark lifted the donor heart from the basin and lowered it into the chest, rotating it to match up the left atrial chambers.

"Lot of blood pooling in here," said Archer. "Suction, Abby."

The hiss of the suction machine gave way to a tense silence as the surgeons worked more quickly now. Archer soon snipped away the suture needle. "Right atrial anastomosis done."

"Perfusion catheter," said Mark.

A nurse handed him the catheter. He introduced it into the left atrium and infused four-degree-Celsius saline. The chilled liquid cooled down the ventricle and flushed out any air pockets.

"Okeydoke," said Archer, repositioning the heart to sew the aortic anastomosis. "Let's hook up these pipes."

Mark glanced up at the wall clock. "Look at that. We're ahead of schedule, folks. What a team."

The intercom buzzed. It was the OR desk nurse. "Mr. Voss wants to know how his wife is doing."

"Fine," called Archer. "No problems. Tell him to hang in there."

The intercom shut off. Archer glanced across at Mark. "Voss rubs me the wrong way. Likes to be in control. But then, I guess if I had his money, I'd call the shots, too."

"Where does his money come from?" asked a nurse.

Archer glanced up in surprise. "You don't know about Victor Voss? VMI International? Everything from chemicals to robotics." He tied off the last suture. "Aorta done. Cross clamp off."

"Perfusion catheter coming out," said Mark, and turned to Abby. "Get those two pacing wires ready for insertion."

Archer picked up a fresh suture needle and began the pulmonary anastomosis. When he tied off, Mark said, "Pacing wires on."

"Isuprel infusion going in," said Zwick. "Two micrograms."

They watched and waited for the Isuprel to take effect, for the heart to contract. "Come on," said Archer. "Don't let me down."

Slowly the heart tightened into a fist-size knot, then fell flaccid.

Zwick said, "Increasing Isuprel to three mics."

There was one more contraction. Then nothing.

"Four mics," said Zwick, dialing up the IV infusion.

The heart tightened, relaxed. Contracted, relaxed.

Zwick glanced up at the monitor. QRS spikes were now tracing across the screen. "Rate's up to fifty. Sixty-four. Seventy."

Archer said to the circulation nurse, "Get on the intercom, will you? Tell recovery we're about to close."

"Rate's one ten," said Zwick.

"Okay," said Mark, "let's take her off bypass."

Zwick flipped on the ventilator. Everyone in the room seemed to exhale a simultaneous sigh of relief. "Let's just hope she and this heart get along," said Mark.

"We know how close the HLA match is?" asked Archer. He turned around to look at Dr. Mapes.

There was no one standing behind him. Abby had been so

focused on the operation, she hadn't noticed that the man had left.

"He walked out twenty minutes ago," one of the nurses said.

"Didn't even get a chance to shake his hand," said Archer. He turned back to the patient on the table. "Okay, let's close."

FIVE

NADIYA had had enough. All the whining, all the demands of eleven boys, all the pent-up energy that regularly erupted into swearing and shoving had sucked away her strength. That, and now the seasickness. Gregor was sick as well, as were most of the boys. On the roughest days, when the ship's hull pounded like a hammer on the anvil of the North Sea, they all lay groaning in their bunks.

Yakov had never had such a good time. Unstricken by even a twinge of nausea, he roamed the ship. He would visit the engine room, that noisy hell of grinding pistons and diesel fumes, and when he got hungry, he would wander into the galley, where Lubi, the cook, would offer him tea and beet soup. Then there was the dusty cargo hold to explore and the deck with its tarp-covered lifeboats to hide in. The only place he could not wander was the far aft section. He could not find any passage to get in there.

His favorite place of all was the bridge. The navigator would greet Yakov with an indulgent smile and allow him to sit at the chart table. There he'd trace the course they had already sailed—from the port of Riga, down the Baltic Sea, through a channel and around the top of Denmark, and across the North Sea. Soon, the navigator told him, they'd be crossing an even bigger sea: the Atlantic Ocean.

"They won't live that long," Yakov predicted.

"Who won't?"

"Nadiya and the other boys."

"Of course they will," said the navigator. "Everyone gets sick in the North Sea. It has to do with the inner ear."

"I'm not sick. Is there something different about my inner ear?"

"You must be a born sailor."

Yakov looked down at the stump of his left arm and shook his head. "I don't think so."

The navigator smiled. "You have a good brain. Brains are far more important. In America if you're clever, you can become rich."

"Do you like America?" Yakov asked.

"Wouldn't know. They always order us confined to quarters as soon as we get into port. I never see a thing."

"Why does the captain order this?"

"The captain doesn't. It's those people in the aft cabin."

"What people? I've never seen them."

"No one ever does, but someone eats the food Lubi sends up."

"Why don't you just leave the ship and stay in America and get rich."

The navigator grunted. "They pay me enough. I can't complain."

"So it's a good job to be a ship's navigator?"

"No."

"But you get paid a lot."

"It's only because the Sigayev Company pays very well."

"Why?"

"I keep my mouth shut."

Yakov was quiet a moment, then asked, "Are you doing something illegal? Is that what you're not supposed to talk about?"

The navigator sighed. "My only responsibility is to guide this ship from Riga to Boston and back to Riga. I don't ask questions."

The boy watched him for a while in silence. Then he said, "Do you think anyone will adopt me?"

"Of course someone will."

"How do you know?"

"Someone paid for your passage. Arranged for your papers."

"I've never seen my papers. Have you?"

"It's none of my business." He waved Yakov aside. "Why don't you go play somewhere else?"

Reluctantly Yakov left the bridge and went out on deck. He was the only one there. He stared down at the water splintering before the bow. Suddenly he found he couldn't breathe; the image of swirling water was suffocating. Yet he didn't move. He stayed, gripping the rail with his one hand, letting panicky thoughts of cold, deep water wash through him. He had not felt fear in a very long time. He was feeling it now.

HER brother, Pete, was sitting in a chair by Abby's bed, looking at her. He wore his blue Cub Scout uniform. Where is his cap? she wondered. And then she remembered that it was lost, that she and her sisters had searched and searched the roadside but had not found it anywhere near the mangled remains of his bicycle.

He had not visited in a long time. When he did, it was always the same. He would sit looking at her, not speaking.

She said, "Where have you been, Pete?"

He just sat watching her, his eyes silent. A musical note seemed to be calling to him. He looked toward another room. He was starting to shimmer, like water that has been stirred. Another bell-like jangle led to total disintegration. There was only darkness.

And the ringing telephone in the on-call room.

Abby reached for the receiver. "DiMatteo," she said.

"This is the SICU. I think maybe you'd better come down."

"What's happening?"

"It's Mrs. Voss in bed fifteen—the transplant. She's running a fever, thirty-eight point six, and her pulse is ninety-six."

"I'll be there." Abby hung up and switched on the lamp. It was one a.m. The chair by her bed was empty. No Pete. Groaning, she climbed out of bed and stumbled to the sink, where she splashed cold water on her face. Wake up, wake up, she told herself. You have to know what the hell you're doing. She couldn't afford to make any mistakes. Not now, and certainly not with this patient.

The lights were dimmed for the night in the SICU. In the gloom of the nurses station the electrical patterns of sixteen patients' hearts traced across sixteen screens. A glance at screen 15 confirmed that Mrs. Voss's pulse was running fast—a rate of 100.

The monitor nurse picked up a ringing telephone, then said, "Dr. Levi's on the line. He wants to talk to the on-call resident."

"I'll take it," said Abby, reaching for the receiver. "Hello, Dr. Levi. This is Abby DiMatteo."

There was a silence. "You're on call tonight?" he said, and she heard a distinct note of dismay in his voice. She understood at once: Abby was the last person he wanted to lay hands on Nina Voss.

She said, "I was just about to examine Mrs. Voss. She's running a fever."

"Yes. They told me about it." Again there was a pause.

She plunged into that void, determined to keep their conversation purely professional. "I'll do the usual fever workup," she said. "I'll examine her. Order a CBC and cultures, urine, and chest X ray. As soon as I have the results, I'll call you back."

"All right," he finally said. "I'll be waiting for your call."

Abby donned an isolation gown and stepped into the cubicle. A single lamp shone dimly above the bed. Under that soft cone of light Nina Voss's hair was a silvery streak across the pillow. Her eyes were shut. Abby moved to the bed and said softly, "Mrs. Voss?"

Nina opened her eyes. "Yes?"

"I'm Dr. DiMatteo." Abby saw the flicker of recognition in the other woman's eyes. She knows my name, thought Abby.

Nina Voss said nothing, merely looked at her.

"You have a fever," explained Abby. "We need to find out why. How are you feeling, Mrs. Voss?"

"I'm . . . tired. That's all," whispered Nina. "Just tired."

"I'll have to check your incision." Abby turned up the lights and gently peeled the bandages off the chest wound. The incision looked clean—no redness, no swelling. She pulled out her stethoscope and moved on to the rest of the fever workup.

At last Abby straightened and said, "Everything seems to be fine. But there must be a reason for the fever. We'll be getting a chest X ray and collecting blood samples." She smiled apologetically. "I'm afraid you're not going to get much sleep tonight."

Nina shook her head. "I don't sleep much anyway. All the dreams. So many dreams."

"Bad dreams?"

Nina took in a breath, slowly let it out. "About the boy." Softly she touched her hand to her chest. "This was a boy's, wasn't it?"

Abby nodded. "That's what I heard in the operating room."

"You were there?"

"I assisted Dr. Hodell."

A small smile formed on Nina's lips. "Strange that you should be there, after . . ." Her voice faded.

"Mrs. Voss," said Abby, "the first heart . . ." She looked away. "There was a boy. Seventeen. Boys that age—they want cars or girl-friends. But this boy, all he wanted was to go home." She sighed. "I didn't know you, Mrs. Voss. You weren't lying in that bed. He was. And I had to make a choice." She felt tears wet her lashes.

"He lived?"

"Yes, he lived."

Nina nodded. Again she touched her own chest. She said, "This boy's alive, too. I'm so aware of his heart. Some people believe that the heart is where the soul lives. Maybe that's what his parents be-lieve. I think about them, too. And how hard it must be. I never had a child. If it was my son, I'd want to know that some part of him is still alive." She pressed her hand against the bandages. She was cry-ing now, the tears a sparkling trickle down her temple.

Abby reached for the woman's hand and was startled by the force of Nina's grasp, the skin feverish, the fingers tight with need. Above the bed a line skipped across the green glow of the oscilloscope. The heart of an unknown boy, beating a hundred times a minute, pumping fevered blood through a stranger's veins.

IT TOOK thirty-five minutes before Abby had the developed X ray in hand. She examined it for signs of pneumonia. She saw none.

It was three a.m. She called Aaron Levi's house.

Aaron's wife answered, her voice husky with sleep. "Hello?"

"Elaine, this is Abby DiMatteo. I'm sorry to bother you at this hour. May I speak with Aaron?"

"He left for the hospital."

"How long ago?"

"Uh, it was just after the second phone call. Isn't he there?"

"I haven't seen him," said Abby.

There was a silence on the other end of the line. "He left home an hour ago," said Elaine. "He should be there."

"I'll page his beeper. Don't worry about it, Elaine." Abby hung up, then dialed Aaron's beeper.

By three fifteen he still hadn't answered.

"Dr. D.?" said Sheila, Nina Voss's nurse, "The last blood culture's been drawn. Is there anything else you want to order?"

What have I missed? thought Abby. Think. A post-op fever. Where was the infection coming from?

"What about the organ?" said Sheila.

"The heart?"

"I used to work with a renal transplant service. We had this patient, a kidney recipient with post-op fevers. His infection turned out to be fungal. They tracked down the donor record and found out that the donor's blood cultures were positive, but the results didn't come back until a week after the kidney was harvested."

"Where's the donor information kept?" Abby asked.

"It would be in the transplant coordinator's office downstairs. The nursing supervisor has the key."

"Could you ask her to get the file for me?"

Abby opened Nina Voss's chart. On the New England Organ Bank donor form—the sheet that had accompanied the heart from Vermont—were the blood type, HIV status, and a long list of other lab screens for viral infections. The donor was not identified.

Fifteen minutes later the phone rang. It was the nursing supervisor, calling for Abby. "I can't find the donor file," she said. "And there's nothing here under Mrs. Voss's medical-record number. I've double-checked. Are you sure it isn't somewhere up in the SICU?"

"I'll ask them to look. Thanks." Abby hung up and sighed. Missing paperwork was the last thing she felt like dealing with. She looked at the SICU records shelf. If the missing file was buried somewhere in that, she could be searching for an hour. Or she could call the donor hospital directly.

Directory assistance gave her the number for Wilcox Memorial in Burlington. She dialed and asked for the nursing supervisor. A moment later a woman answered. "Gail DeLeon speaking."

"This is Dr. DiMatteo, calling from Bayside Hospital in Boston," said Abby. "We have a heart transplant recipient here who's running a post-op fever. We know the donor heart came from your OR. I need a little more information on the donor's medical history."

"The organ harvest was done here?"

"Yes. Three days ago. The donor was a boy. An adolescent."

"Let me check the OR log. I'll call you back."

Ten minutes later she did—not with an answer, but with a question. "Are you sure you have the right hospital, Doctor?"

Abby glanced down at Nina's chart. "It says right here 'Donor hospital, Wilcox Memorial, Burlington, Vermont.' "

"Well, that's us. But I don't see a harvest on the log."

Abby scanned the OR nurses' notes and saw the notation "0105: Dr. Leonard Mapes arrived from Wilcox Memorial." She said, "One of the surgeons who scrubbed on the harvest was Dr. Leonard Mapes. That's the same guy who delivered it."

"We don't have any Dr. Mapes on our staff. In fact, I don't know of any Dr. Mapes practicing anywhere in Burlington. I don't know where you're getting your info, Doctor, but it's obviously wrong."

"But—"

"Try another hospital."

Slowly Abby hung up. For a long time she sat staring at the phone. She thought about Victor Voss and his money, about all the things that money could buy. She thought about the amazing confluence of events that had granted Nina Voss a new heart. A matched heart.

She reached once again for the telephone.

"YOU'RE overreacting," said Mark, flipping through Nina Voss's chart. "There has to be a reasonable explanation for this."

"I'd like to know what it is," said Abby.

"It was a good excision. The heart came packed right, delivered right. And there *were* donor papers."

"Which now seem to be missing."

"The transplant coordinator will be in at nine. We can ask her about the papers then. I'm sure they're around somewhere."

"Mark, there's one more thing. I called the donor hospital. There's no surgeon named Leonard Mapes practicing there. In fact, there's no such surgeon practicing in Burlington." Abby paused. Softly she said, "Do we really know where that heart came from?"

Mark said nothing. He seemed too dazed, too tired to be thinking straight. It was four fifteen. After Abby's phone call he'd dragged himself out of bed and driven to Bayside. Post-op fevers required immediate attention, and although he trusted Abby's findings, he had wanted to see the patient for himself.

"Why all this secrecy about the donor anyway?" asked Abby.

"Standard procedure. Donor records are confidential. They're always kept separate from the recipient's chart. Otherwise you'd have families contacting each other. The donor side would expect undying gratitude. The recipient side would resent it or feel guilty. It leads to one giant emotional mess." He rubbed his eyes. "We're wasting time on this issue. It'll all be resolved in a few hours."

"All right. But if there's any question about this, New England Organ Bank wants to discuss it with you."

"How did NEOB get involved?"

"I called them. They have this twenty-four-hour line. I told them you or Archer would get back to them."

"Archer can handle it. He'll be here any moment."

"He's coming in?"

"He's worried about the fever. And we can't seem to get hold of Aaron. Have you paged him again?"

"Three times. No answer. Elaine told me he was driving in."

"Well, I know he got here. I just saw his car down in the parking lot. Maybe he got busy on the medical floor." Mark flipped through Nina Voss's chart to the order sheets. "I'm starting antibiotics. Broad spectrum. We can't take a chance she's infected somewhere."

At six a.m. the first dose of IV Azactam was dripping into Nina's vein. Two hours later a second antibiotic, piperacillin, was infused.

By then Abby was making morning SICU rounds, her wheeled cart piled with charts. It had been a bad night—just one hour of sleep before that one a.m. phone call and not a moment's rest since then. Fueled by two cups of coffee and a view of the end in sight, she pushed her cart along, thinking, Four more hours and I'm out of here.

She passed by cubicle 15 and glanced in. Nina was awake. She saw Abby and weakly managed a beckoning wave. Abby left her charts by the door, donned an isolation gown, and stepped inside.

"Good morning, Dr. DiMatteo," murmured Nina. "I'm afraid you didn't get much sleep because of me."

Abby smiled. "That's okay. I slept last week. How do you feel?"

"Like quite the center of attention." Nina glanced up at the IV antibiotics hanging over the bed. "Is that the cure?"

"We hope so. You're getting broad-spectrum antibiotics. If you have an infection, that should take care of it."

"But you don't really know what's causing this."

"No," Abby admitted. "It's more of an educated shot in the dark."

Nina nodded. "I thought you would tell the truth. Dr. Archer wouldn't, you know. He was here earlier, and he kept telling me that everything was taken care of. But the truth doesn't scare me."

"I'm sure he didn't want to worry you," said Abby as she gazed at the monitors.

She heard Nina say softly, "Victor."

Abby turned. Only then, as she faced the doorway, did she realize Victor Voss had just stepped into the cubicle.

"Get out," he said. "Get out of my wife's room." He took a step toward her and caught hold of her arm with a grip that hurt.

"Victor, don't!" said Nina.

Abby gave a cry of pain as she was wrenched forward. He thrust her out of the cubicle, shoving her backward against the wheeled cart. She felt herself falling as the cart slid away. She landed hard on the floor. The cart, still rolling, slammed against a counter. Abby, stunned by the impact, looked up to see Victor Voss standing over her. He was breathing hard, not from exertion, but from fury.

"Don't go near my wife again," he said. "Do you hear me, Doctor? *Do you hear me?*" Voss turned to the shocked personnel standing in the SICU. "I don't want this woman near my wife. I want that written in the chart and posted on the door. Now." Then he walked into his wife's cubicle and yanked the curtain across the window.

Two of the nurses hurried over to help Abby to her feet.

"I'm okay," said Abby, waving them away. "I'm fine." She went over to the cart. Her charts were on the floor, loose pages and lab slips scattered everywhere. Face burning, she gathered up all the papers. By then she was fighting tears. I can't cry, she thought. Not here. I won't cry.

Abby looked up. Everyone was watching her. She left the cart right where it was and walked out of the SICU.

Mark found her three hours later in the cafeteria. She was sitting at a corner table, hunched over a cup of tea. The tea bag had been left soaking so long that the water was as black as coffee.

Mark pulled out a chair across from her and sat down. "Voss was the one who threw the tantrum, Abby, not you."

"I'm just the one who landed on her butt in front of everyone."

"He shoved you. That was assault. You can press charges. Something you can use as leverage against any more of those nutty lawsuits."

She shook her head. "I don't want anything more to do with Victor Voss. Let's forget the whole thing." To change the subject, she said, "Did Aaron agree about starting antibiotics?"

"I haven't see Aaron all day."

She frowned. "I thought he was here."

"I beeped him, but he never answered."

"Did you call his home?"

"I got the housekeeper. Elaine left for the weekend, visiting their kid at Dartmouth." Mark shrugged. "This isn't Aaron's weekend for rounds anyway. He's probably taking a vacation from all of us."

"A vacation." Abby sighed and rubbed her face. "Yes, that's what I want. A beach and a few palm trees and a piña colada."

"Sounds good to me, too." Reaching across the table, he took her hand. "Mind if I join you?"

"You don't even like piña coladas."

"But I like beaches and palm trees. And you." He leaned across the table and kissed her.

Abby glanced at her watch. It was noon at last. Mark walked her out of the cafeteria and across the hospital lobby. As they pushed through the front doors, he said, "I almost forgot to tell you. Archer called Wilcox Memorial and spoke to some thoracic surgeon named Tim Nicholls. Turns out Nicholls assisted on the harvest. He confirmed the patient was theirs and that Dr. Mapes did the excision."

"Then why isn't Mapes listed on the Wilcox staff?"

"Because he was flown in from Houston. We knew nothing about it. Apparently, Mr. Voss didn't trust just any Yankee surgeon."

"So the harvest *was* done at Wilcox Memorial."

"Nicholls says he was there. Whatever nurse you spoke to last night must've been looking at the wrong log sheet. If you'd like me to call and confirm it again—"

"No. Just forget it. It all seems so stupid now. I don't know what I was thinking." She looked across at her car at the far end of the parking lot. "I'll see you at home," she said. "If I'm still awake."

Mark put his arms around her, tipped her head back, and kissed her. "Careful driving home," he whispered. "I love you."

She walked across the lot, dazed by fatigue and by the sound of those three words still echoing in her head: *I love you.*

Abby looked back to wave at him, but he had already vanished through the lobby doors. "I love you, too," she said, and smiled.

She turned to her car, her keys already out of her purse. Only then did she notice that the lock button was up. What an idiot. She'd left the car unlocked all night. She opened the door.

At the first foul whiff of air, she backed away, gagging on the stench. And repulsed by the sight of what lay inside. Loops of rotting intestine were coiled around the gearshift. Unidentifiable tissue was smeared across the passenger seat. And on the driver's side, propped up against the cushion, was a single bloody organ.

A heart.

SIX

"IT WAS a pig's heart. They probably left it in my car the night before, where it baked all day in the heat. I still can't get rid of the smell."

"The man is messing with your head," said Vivian Chao. "I say you should fight back."

Abby and Vivian pushed through the front doors and crossed the lobby to the elevators. It was Sunday noon at Massachusetts General, and the public elevator was crammed tight with visitors and with get-well balloons, bobbing overhead.

"We don't have any proof," murmured Abby. "We can't be sure Voss is the one doing this."

"Who else would it be? Look what he's done already—manufacturing lawsuits, shoving you in public. I'm telling you, DiMatteo, it's time to press charges. Assault. Terroristic threatening."

"The problem is, I understand why he's doing it. He's upset."

They stepped off the elevator onto the fourth floor and headed up the hall toward the cardiac surgery wing.

"He has the money to make your life hell for a very long time," said Vivian. "You've got one lawsuit against you already. There'll probably be more."

"I think there already are. Medical records told me they've had six more chart requests from Hawkes, Craig, and Sussman. That's the law firm representing Joe Terrio."

Vivian stared at her. "What? You're going to be in court for the rest of your natural life."

Abby nodded. "Sometimes I wonder if it was all worth it."

"Worth it?" Vivian stopped outside room 417. "Take a look. You tell me." She knocked on the door, then stepped into the room.

The boy was sitting up in bed, fussing with a TV remote. If not for the Red Sox cap on his head, Abby might not have recognized Josh O'Day, so transformed was his appearance by the rosy flush of health. At his first glimpse of Vivian he grinned hugely.

"Hey, Dr. Chao!" he whooped. "I wondered if you were *ever* coming to see me."

"I came by twice," said Vivian. "But you were always asleep." She shook her head in mock disgust. "Typical lazy teenager."

They both laughed, and Vivian nodded toward Abby. "You remember Dr. DiMatteo, don't you?"

Josh looked uncertainly at Abby. "I think so. I mean . . ." He shrugged. "I forgot some things, you know?"

"That's nothing to worry about," said Vivian. "When your heart stops, you don't get enough blood to your brain. You can forget a few things." She touched his shoulder. "At least you didn't forget me." And she added with a laugh, "Though you may have tried."

Josh looked down at the blanket. "Dr. Chao," he said softly, "I don't ever want to forget you."

Neither one spoke for a moment. They seemed frozen by embarrassment in that awkward pose—Vivian's hand on the boy's shoulder, the boy looking downward, his face hidden under his cap.

There was a knock on the door, and a woman called out, "Joshie?"

"Hey, Mom," said Josh.

The door swung open, and the room was invaded by O'Days, sweeping in with them a forest of helium balloons and the smell of McDonald's fries. They swarmed around the bed with exclamations of "Look at him!" "He looks so good!" "Doesn't he look good?" Josh bore it all with an expression of sheepish delight.

Vivian slipped away from his bedside to where Abby was standing. Through the crowd of O'Days, Abby caught a glimpse of Josh. He was looking their way. He gave them a helpless smile, a wave. Quietly Abby and Vivian left the room. Vivian said, "So, Abby, to the question 'Was it worth it?' that's your answer."

THIS one smelled pretty bad. Homicide detective Bernard Katzka glanced across the autopsy table and saw that the stench had gotten to Lundquist. His younger partner was turned away from the table, gloved hand over his nose and mouth, his movie-star good looks twisted into a squint of nausea. Lundquist had not developed the stomach for autopsies; most cops never did. Over the years Katzka had trained himself to focus not on the humanity of the victim, but on the purely organic nature of death—a specimen stripped, examined, and catalogued. To view a body any other way was to invite nightmares. Three years before, Bernard Katzka had watched his wife die of cancer. He had already lived his worst nightmare.

He focused impassively on the body now being autopsied. The corpse was a fifty-four-year-old white male, a cardiologist by profession—Aaron Levi. His identity had been confirmed by the widow. The experience must have been profoundly upsetting to her. Viewing the corpse of a loved one is difficult enough. When that loved one has been hanging by the neck for two days in a warm and unventilated room, the sight would be truly horrifying.

Dr. Rowbotham had completed the thoracoabdominal incision and exposed the pleural cavity. Rowbotham had served thirty-two years with the M.E.'s office, and very little seemed to surprise him. He was dictating in his usual monotone as his foot clicked on and off the recording pedal.

"Take a look, Slug," he said to Katzka. The nickname had nothing to do with Katzka's appearance, which was average in every way. Rather, it was a reflection of his unflappable nature. Among his fellow cops the running joke was that if you shot Bernard Katzka on a Monday, he might react by Friday. But only if he was really ticked.

Katzka leaned forward to peer inside the chest cavity, his expression as flat as Rowbotham's. "I don't see anything unusual."

"Exactly. It's all consistent with asphyxiation."

"So I guess we're out of here, huh?" said Lundquist. Already he was sidling away from the table, impatient to get on to other things.

Katzka did not move.

"We really need to watch the rest, Slug?" asked Lundquist. "It's a suicide." He yanked off his gown, revealing bulky shoulders.

"This one feels different to me." Katzka thought his young partner needed to learn the fallibility of first impressions.

Rowbotham removed the organs and then the brain. Lundquist, now looking a little green, sat down in a chair by the sink and dropped his head in his hands.

"Nothing unusual," Rowbotham said. "Now we get down to the nitty-gritty. The neck."

The belt ligature had already been removed. Rowbotham examined the furrow left behind on the neck. "Your classic inverted V shape," he noted. "No surprises so far." He lifted his scalpel and began the neck dissection.

As Rowbotham's blade sliced through the skin of the anterior neck, Katzka said, "You seem pretty sure it's suicide."

"The only other possibility is homicide, and homicidal hanging is almost unheard of. If someone was strangled first, you'd see a different ligature pattern. Not this inverted V. And forcing a man's head in a noose . . . Well, that would almost certainly leave other injuries. He'd fight back."

"What if he was drugged and unconscious?"

"We'll do a tox screen, Slug, just to make you happy."

Lundquist, by now recovered, cut in. "I say we just leave it as a suicide."

"I would. Except for the lights."

"What lights?" said Rowbotham, his eyes finally registering interest behind his protective goggles.

"Dr. Levi was found hanging in an unused patient room the hospital was having renovated," explained Katzka. "The workman who found the body was almost certain the lights were off."

"Go on," said Rowbotham.

"Dr. Levi died very early Saturday morning, well before sunrise. Which means he either hung himself in the dark or someone else turned off the lights."

"I CAN'T believe it," Elaine kept saying. "I just can't believe it." She was not crying, had sat dry-eyed through the burial. She now sat in a chair in her living room, a tray of finger sandwiches on her lap, and she said again, "I can't believe he's gone."

Abby took an olive sandwich and passed the tray along. It moved from hand to hand down a succession of guests. At least two dozen people were in the room, seated solemnly on couches and chairs or standing around in small groups, but no one was saying much.

The sandwich platter had made its round and now came back empty to Abby. "I'll refill it," she said to Elaine. She rose from the couch and went into the kitchen. There she found the marble countertops covered with platters of food. She was unwrapping a tray of shrimp when she looked out the kitchen window and noticed Bill Archer, Raj Mohandas, and Frank Zwick standing outside on the flagstone terrace. They were talking, shaking their heads. Leave it to the men to retreat, she thought. A bottle of Scotch sat on the umbrella table, positioned for easy refills. As Zwick reached for it, he caught sight of Abby. He nodded and gave a quick wave. Then the three men crossed the terrace and walked away, into the garden.

"So much food. I don't know what I'm going to do with it," said Elaine. Abby hadn't noticed that she had come into the kitchen. Elaine stood gazing at the countertop and shaking her head.

"I'm so sorry," said Abby. "If only there was something I could say to make it easier."

"I just wish I could understand. He never said anything. Never told me he . . ." She swallowed and looked at Abby. "You spoke to him that night. Was there anything he might have said—"

"We discussed one of our patients. Aaron wanted to make sure I was doing all the right things."

"That's all you talked about?"

"Just the patient. Aaron didn't seem any different to me. Just concerned. I never imagined he would . . ." Abby fell silent.

Elaine picked up a tray and put it in the refrigerator. "There was no warning," she said. "Oh, I know he wasn't happy in his job. He kept talking about leaving Boston. Or quitting medicine entirely."

"Why was he so unhappy?"

"He wouldn't talk about it. When he had his own practice in Natick, we'd talk about his work all the time. But after we moved here, it was as if I didn't know him anymore. He'd come home and sit down like a zombie in front of that damn computer. Sometimes late at night I'd wake up and hear those weird beeps and clicks. And it was Aaron, sitting up all alone, playing some video game."

Outside, the three men were returning from their garden walk. Abby watched them cross the terrace to the kitchen door. They entered the house and nodded to her in greeting.

"Nice little garden," said Archer. "You should go out and take a tour, Abby."

"I'd like to," she said. "Elaine, maybe you'd come out and show me . . ." She paused.

There was no one by the refrigerator. Elaine had left the room.

A WOMAN was praying by Mary Allen's bed. She had been sitting there for the last half hour, head bowed, hands clasped together as she murmured aloud to the good Lord Jesus, imploring him to purify Mary's body and her unclean soul so that she might finally accept His word in all its glory.

"Excuse me," said Abby. "I'm sorry to intrude, but I need to examine Mrs. Allen."

The woman kept praying. Abby was about to repeat the request, when the woman at last said, "Amen," and raised her head. She had unsmiling eyes and dull brown hair with the first streaks of gray. She regarded Abby with a look of irritation.

"I'm Dr. DiMatteo," said Abby. "I'm taking care of Mrs. Allen."

"So am I," the woman said, rising to her feet, cradling a Bible to her chest. "I'm Brenda Hainey, Mary's niece."

"I didn't know Mary had a niece. I'm glad you're able to visit."

"I only heard about her illness two days ago. No one bothered to call me." Her tone of voice implied this was Abby's fault.

Abby moved to the bedside and said softly, "Mrs. Allen?"

Mary opened her eyes. "I'm awake, Dr. D. Just resting."

"How are you feeling today?"

"Still nauseated."

"It could be a side effect of the morphine. We'll give you something to settle your stomach."

Brenda interjected. "She's getting morphine?"

"For the pain." Abby turned to the niece. "Mrs. Hainey, could you leave the room, please? I need to examine your aunt."

"It's Miss Hainey," said Brenda. "And I'm sure Aunt Mary would rather have me stay."

"I still have to ask you to leave."

Brenda glanced at her aunt, obviously expecting a protest. Mary Allen stared straight ahead, silent. Brenda clutched the Bible tighter. "I'll be right outside, Aunt Mary."

"Dear Lord," whispered Mary as the door shut behind Brenda, "this must be my punishment."

"Are you referring to your niece?"

Mary's tired gaze focused on Abby. "Do you think my soul needs saving?"

"I'd say that's entirely up to you and no one else."

WHEN ABBY EMERGED FROM the room, she found Brenda Hainey waiting right outside the door.

"Doctor, about that morphine. Is it really necessary?"

"I think your aunt would say so."

"It's making her drowsy. All she does is sleep."

"We're trying to keep her as pain free as possible. The cancer's everywhere. It's the worst kind of pain imaginable. The kindest thing we can do is to help her go with a minimum of discomfort."

"What do you mean 'help her go,' Doctor? I happen to know for a fact it's not legal to medically assist a suicide."

Abby felt her face flush with anger. Fighting to control it, she said as calmly as she could manage, "You misunderstand me. All we're trying to do is keep your aunt comfortable."

"There are other ways to do it."

"Such as?"

"Calling on higher sources of help."

"You're certainly welcome to pray for your aunt. But if I recall, there's nothing against morphine in the Bible."

Brenda's face went rigid. Her retort was cut off by the sound of Abby's beeper.

"Excuse me," said Abby coolly, and walked away, leaving the conversation unfinished. A good thing, too; she'd been on the verge of saying something really sarcastic. With Joe Terrio's lawsuit lurking on the horizon and Victor Voss determined to get her fired, the last thing she needed was another complaint lodged against her.

She picked up a phone in the nurses station and dialed the number on her beeper readout.

A woman's voice answered. "Information desk."

"This is Dr. DiMatteo. You paged me?"

"Yes, Doctor. There's a Bernard Katzka standing here at the desk. He's wondering if you could meet him here in the lobby."

"I don't know anyone by that name. I'm sort of busy up here. Could you ask him what his business is?"

There was a background murmur of conversation. When the woman came back on, her voice sounded oddly reticent. "He's a policeman."

THE MAN IN THE LOBBY LOOKED vaguely familiar. He was in his mid-forties, medium height, medium build, with a face that was neither handsome nor homely. His hair, a dark brown, was starting to thin at the top, a fact he made no effort to conceal. As she approached him, she had the impression he recognized her as well—his gaze had singled her out the moment she stepped off the elevator.

"Dr. DiMatteo?" he said. "Detective Bernard Katzka, homicide."

Just hearing that word startled her. They shook hands. Only then, as she met his gaze, did she remember where she'd seen him—Aaron Levi's funeral. He'd been standing slightly apart from everyone, a silent figure in a dark suit. During the service their gazes had intersected. At the time, she'd registered almost no impression of the man. Looking up at his face now, she found herself focusing on his eyes, which were a calm, unflinching gray. If not for the intelligence of those eyes, one might never notice Bernard Katzka.

She said, "I saw you at Aaron Levi's funeral. Or am I mistaken?"

"I was there."

Abby waited for an explanation, but all he said was, "Is there somewhere we can talk?"

"Can I ask what this is all about?"

"Dr. Levi's death."

She glanced at the lobby doors. The sun was shining, and she had not been outside all day. "There's a little courtyard with a few benches. Why don't we go out there?"

It was warm outside, a perfect October afternoon. They sat down on a bench in front of a small fountain. For a moment nothing was said. The silence made Abby uneasy, but it did not appear to disturb her companion. He seemed accustomed to long silences.

"Elaine Levi gave me your name," he said. "She suggested I talk to you."

"Why?"

"You spoke to Dr. Levi on the phone early Saturday morning. Do you remember what time that was?"

"Around one a.m., I guess. He called the SICU and asked to speak to the on-call resident. I happened to be it that night."

"Why was he calling?"

"A patient was running a post-op fever, and Aaron wanted to discuss a plan of action. Now, do you mind telling me what this is all about?"

"I'm trying to establish the chronology of events. So, did you talk to Dr. Levi again after that call?"

"No. I called, but he'd already left the house."

"What time was that?"

"I don't know. Maybe three o'clock, three fifteen."

"You didn't call his house any other time that morning?"

"No. I tried paging his beeper several times, but he never answered. I knew he was somewhere in the building because his car was in the parking lot."

"What time did you see it there?"

"I didn't. My boyfriend—Dr. Hodell—saw it when he drove in around four a.m. Look, why is homicide investigating this?"

He ignored her question. "Elaine Levi says there was a call around two fifteen. Her husband answered the phone. A few minutes later he got dressed and left the house. Do you know anything about that call?"

"No. It wasn't me. I spoke to Aaron only once. Now, I'd really like to know why you're asking me these questions. This can't possibly be a routine thing you do."

"No, it's not routine."

Abby's beeper went off. It was the residency office—not an emergency, but she was getting fed up with this conversation anyway. She rose to her feet. "Detective, I've got work to do. I don't have time to answer a lot of vague questions."

"My questions are quite specific. I'm trying to establish who made calls at what time that morning. And what was said."

"Why?"

"We're considering the possibility that Dr. Levi's death was something other than suicide."

She stared at him, then slowly sank back down on the bench. "Are you saying he might have been murdered?"

Katzka didn't answer. He sat motionless, revealing nothing.

"*Did* Aaron hang himself?" she asked.

"The autopsy findings were consistent with asphyxia."

"That's what you'd expect. It sounds like a suicide. Why aren't you convinced?"

He hesitated, then said, "Two days before he died, Dr. Levi brought home a brand-new computer."

"That's all? That's the basis for your questions?"

"He used it to do several things. First he made plane reservations for two to St. Lucia in the Caribbean. Also, he sent E-mail to his son at Dartmouth, discussing plans for Thanksgiving break. Two days before committing suicide, this man is making plans for the future. But at two fifteen a.m. he climbs out of his bed and drives to the hospital. Takes an elevator to a deserted floor. Ties a belt to the closet dowel, loops the other end around his neck, and simply lets his legs go limp. Consciousness wouldn't fade at once. There would be time to change his mind. He has a wife, a kid, and a beach on St. Lucia to look forward to. But he chooses to die. Alone and in the dark." Katzka's quiet gray eyes held hers. "Think about it."

Abby swallowed. "I'm not sure I want to."

"We know Dr. Levi's car was found in its usual parking spot at the hospital. We don't know why he drove here. Except for that two-fifteen call, which we've found was made from Bayside, you're the last person we know of who spoke to Dr. Levi. Did anything he said strike you as not quite right?"

She thought about it. And she remembered how dismayed Aaron had sounded when she'd first come on the line.

"Dr. DiMatteo?" His expression took on new alertness.

"I remember he didn't sound very happy that I was the resident on duty."

"Why not?"

"Because of the particular patient involved. Her husband and I— we'd had a conflict." She looked away. "I'm sure Aaron would've preferred that I stay miles away from Mrs. Voss."

"Mrs. *Victor* Voss?" Katzka said.

"Yes." Abby looked at him again. "You know the name?"

Katzka sat back, exhaling softly. "I know he founded VMI International. What surgery did his wife have?"

"A heart transplant. She's doing much better now. The fever resolved after a few days of antibiotics."

Katzka was staring at the fountain. Then he abruptly rose to his feet. "Thank you for your time, Dr. DiMatteo," he said. "I may call you again." He turned and swiftly walked away. The man had gone from absolute motionlessness to the speed of sound. Amazing.

Her beeper chirped. It was the residency office again. She returned to the lobby and picked up the house phone.

A secretary answered her call. "Residency office."

"This is Abby DiMatteo. You paged me?"

"Oh, yes. You have a certified letter up here."

"Who sent it?"

There was a sound of shuffling papers. Then, "It's from Hawkes, Craig, and Sussman, attorneys-at-law."

Abby's stomach went into free fall. "I'll be right there," she said, and hung up. The Terrio lawsuit again. Her hands were sweating as she rode the elevator to the administrative floor.

The residency-office secretary was on the telephone. Abby saw the envelope in her mail cubicle and ripped it open.

At first she didn't understand what she was reading. Then she focused on the plaintiff's name, and the meaning at last sank in. Her stomach had ended its free fall. It had crashed. This letter wasn't about Karen Terrio. It was about another patient, a Michael Freeman. An alcoholic, he had unexpectedly ruptured a swollen blood vessel in his esophagus and bled to death in his hospital room. Abby had been the intern on his case. Now Michael Freeman's wife was suing, and she had retained Hawkes, Craig, and Sussman to represent her. Abby was the only defendant named in the lawsuit.

Abby fled straight to her on-call room, locked herself in, and sat down on the bed. She stared at the letter, thinking about all the years, all the work it had taken to get to this point in her career. She thought about the nights she'd fallen asleep over her books. The weekends she'd worked double shifts as a phlebotomist, drawing blood to earn her tuition. She thought about the hundred and twenty thousand dollars in student loans she had to pay off.

And she thought about Pete, who'd been the reason for it all—

the brother she'd wanted to save and hadn't been able to. Most of all, she thought of Pete, hospitalized and comatose for months, now eternally ten years old.

Victor Voss was winning. He'd said he would destroy her, and that was exactly what he was going to do.

Fight back. It was time to fight back.

Her beeper went off. Would they never leave her alone? She picked up the phone and dialed zero. "DiMatteo," she snapped.

"Outside call for you, Doctor," said the operator. "Let me put it through."

There were a few clicks; then a woman said, "Dr. DiMatteo?"

"Speaking."

"This is Helen Lewis at New England Organ Bank. You left a message last Saturday about a heart donor. We expected someone at Bayside to call back, but no one did. So I decided to check back."

"I'm sorry. I should have called you, but things have been crazy around here. It turns out it was just a misunderstanding."

"Well, that makes it easy, since I couldn't find the information anyway. If you have any other questions, just give me a—"

"Excuse me," Abby cut in. "What did you just say?"

"The data you requested isn't in our system."

For a solid ten seconds Abby was silent. Then she asked slowly, "Are you absolutely certain it's not there?"

"I've searched our files. On the date you gave for the harvest, we have no record of a heart donor. Anywhere in Vermont."

SEVEN

"**H**ERE it is," said Colin Wettig, laying open the *Directory of Medical Specialists*. "Timothy Nicholls. M.D., Tufts. Residency, Massachusetts General. Specialty, thoracic surgery. Affiliated with Wilcox Memorial, Burlington, Vermont." He slid the book onto the conference table. "So there really is a thoracic surgeon named Tim Nicholls practicing in Burlington."

"When I spoke to Nicholls on Saturday," said Archer, "he claimed he was at the harvest and it took place at Wilcox Memorial. Unfortunately, I haven't been able to find anyone who was in the OR with him. And now his staff tells me he's taken a leave of absence. I don't know what's going on, Jeremiah, but it's starting to smell rotten."

Jeremiah Parr shifted uneasily in his chair and glanced at attorney Susan Casado. He didn't bother to look at Abby, sitting at the end of the table, next to the transplant coordinator, Donna Toth. Maybe he didn't *want* to look at her. Abby, after all, was the one who had initiated this meeting, bringing this mess to everyone's attention.

"What exactly *is* going on here?" Parr asked.

Archer said, "I think Victor Voss arranged to keep the donor out of the registry system. To shunt the heart directly to his wife."

"Explain to me how donor assignments are *supposed* to work," said Parr. "Because I don't understand how this happened."

"The system's pretty straightforward," said Donna Toth. "We have both a regional and a national waiting list of patients needing organs. The national system's the United Network for Organ Sharing, or UNOS for short. The regional one is New England Organ Bank. Both systems rank patients only in order of need. The list has nothing to do with wealth, race, or social status."

"Where was Mrs. Voss on the list?"

"Number three on the AB blood-type list," Donna answered.

"What happened to the first two names?"

"I checked with NEOB. Both names were reclassified as code eights a few days later."

"Meaning they died?" Susan Casado asked softly.

Donna nodded. "They never got their transplants."

Parr groaned. "So Mrs. Voss got a heart that should have gone to someone else."

"That seems to be what happened."

"How did *we* get notified of the donor?" asked Susan.

"A phone call," said Donna. "That's how it usually happens. The transplant coordinator at the donor hospital will check the latest NEOB waiting list and call the contact number for the first patient on the list."

"So you were called by Wilcox's transplant coordinator?"

"Yes. I've spoken to him before on the phone, about other donors. So I had no reason to question this particular donation."

Archer shook his head. "I don't know how Voss managed this. Every step of the way it looked legal and aboveboard to us. Someone at Wilcox obviously got paid off. My bet is it's their transplant coordinator. So Voss's wife gets the heart, and Bayside gets suckered into a cash-for-organs arrangement. And we don't have any of the donor paperwork to double-check this."

"It's still missing?" asked Parr.

"I haven't been able to find it," said Donna. "The donor records aren't anywhere in my office."

"So what are we going to do about this?" said Abby.

Her question was met with a momentary silence.

"I'm not sure what we should do," said Parr. He looked at the attorney. "Are we obligated to follow up on this?"

"Ethically, yes," said Susan. "However, there are consequences if we do. First, there's no way we could keep this from the press. Second, we'd be, in a sense, breaching patient confidentiality. That's not going to sit well with a certain segment of our patient population."

Wettig snorted. "Meaning the bloody rich ones."

"The ones who keep this hospital alive," corrected Parr.

"Exactly." Susan continued: "If they hear we spurred the investigation of someone like Voss, they're not going to trust us to keep *their* records private. And what if this is made to look like we were part of the conspiracy? We'd lose our credibility."

Abby glanced at Archer, who looked stunned by the possibility. This could destroy the Bayside transplant program.

"How much of this has already gotten out?" asked Parr. He looked at Abby. "What did you tell NEOB, Dr. DiMatteo?"

"When I spoke to Helen Lewis, I wasn't sure what was going on. Neither of us was. That's how we left it. Unresolved."

Parr sighed with relief. "All right. So it's just in this room."

Susan Casado shared Parr's look of relief. "We've still got a shot at damage control. Tell Helen Lewis that it was a directed donation, so it never went through NEOB. Then let's just move on."

"In other words," said Wettig, "stick our heads in the sand."

"See no evil, hear no evil. We just need to install safeguards to ensure it doesn't happen again." Parr glanced around the table. He seemed to take the lack of response as a sign of general assent.

But Abby couldn't hold her silence. "What happens to Victor Voss?" she asked. Yet she knew the answer: Nothing would happen to him. Nothing ever happened to men like Victor Voss. He could buy a heart, buy an entire hospital. And he could buy lawyers, too, enough to turn a lowly surgical resident's dreams into scorched earth. "He's out to ruin me," she reminded the others. "He's dumped offal in my car. He's initiated two lawsuits, with more on the way, I'm sure. It's hard for me to just move on."

"Dr. DiMatteo," said Parr, "this hospital's reputation is on the line. We need everyone to pull together, including you."

"What if it all comes out anyway? Bayside's going to be accused of a cover-up. And this'll blow up in all your faces."

Parr and Susan exchanged nervous glances. Susan said, "That's a risk we'll have to take."

A BBY stripped off her OR gown and pushed through the double doors. It was nearly midnight. The patient, a stabbing victim, was now in recovery. All was quiet in the trenches.

She wasn't sure she welcomed the lull. It gave her too much time to brood over what had been said at that afternoon meeting.

My one chance to fight back, she thought, *and I can't. Not if I'm going to be a team player and keep Bayside's interests at heart.*

Several times that evening, she'd been on the verge of picking up the phone and calling Helen Lewis. That's all it would take to get NEOB into the picture. One phone call to expose Victor Voss. Now, as she headed to the on-call room, she was still mulling over what she should do. She unlocked the door and stepped inside.

It was the fragrance she noticed first. She switched on the lamp and stared at the vase of roses on the desk.

A rustle of sheets drew her gaze to the bed. "Mark?" she said.

He came awake with a start. For a moment he seemed unsure of where he was. Then he saw her and smiled. "Happy birthday."

"Oh! I completely forgot." She went to the bed and sat down beside him. "It's midnight. How long have you been here?"

"Two hours." He moved aside to make room for her on the narrow mattress. She pulled off her shoes and lay down beside him. At once she felt comforted by the warmth of the bed and of the man. She thought of telling him about the meeting this afternoon, about the second lawsuit, but she didn't want to talk about any of it.

"I can't believe I forgot my own birthday. Maybe I wanted to forget it. Twenty-eight already."

Laughing, he wrapped an arm around her. "Such a decrepit old lady."

"I *feel* old. Especially tonight."

"Yeah, well then, I feel ancient." He kissed her. "And I'm not getting any younger. So maybe now's the time."

"Time for what?"

He cupped her face in his hand. "To ask you to marry me."

She stared at him, unable to say a word, but so filled with happiness she knew the answer must be plain in her eyes.

"I knew a couple of nights ago that this was what I wanted," he said. "You were on call, and when I went up to bed, I saw your things on the dresser. Your hairbrush. Jewelry box. That bra that you never seem to put away." Softly he laughed. "Anyway, that's when I knew I never want to live anywhere without your stuff lying on my dresser. I don't think I could. Not anymore."

"Oh, Mark." Through tears she saw him smile.

"So what do you think, Dr. D.?" he whispered. "Can we fit a wedding into our tight schedules?"

Her answer was half sob, half laughter. "Yes. Yes, yes, *yes!*" And rising up, she rolled on top of him, her arms thrown around his neck, her mouth finding his.

SHE had been beautiful once. Sometimes when Mary Allen looked at her own hands and saw the wrinkles and brown stains of age, she would wonder with a start, Whose hands are these? Not mine, not pretty Mary Hatcher's. Then the flash of confusion would pass, and she'd look around the hospital room and realize she'd been dreaming again. Not a true dream, but a sort of lingering mist. She was grateful for the morphine. It took away her pain, and it opened some secret gate in her mind, allowing images to flow in, images of a remembered life, almost over now.

She closed her eyes, and that secret gate swung open. A path to the sea. Hedges of beach roses, pink and sweet-smelling. Warm sand swallowing up her toes. Waves tumbling in from the bay.

She heard a door swing open. A real door. Heard soft footsteps.

Suspended in her morphine daze, she had to struggle to open her eyes. When at last she did, she found that the room was dark except for one small circle of light, hovering nearby. She made out a darker patch that had materialized by her bed. Something not quite solid, not quite real. She wondered if this, too, was a morphine dream. She felt a hand grasp her arm with a cold, rubbery touch. Her breath came out in a rush of fear. This was not a dream. This was real. The hand was there to lead her somewhere, to take her away.

A voice said softly, "It's all right, Mary. Just time for you to sleep."

Mary saw the penlight playing on her arm. Her IV. She watched as a gloved hand produced a syringe. The plastic cap was removed and a needle glittered in the dim light. She felt a fresh stirring of alarm and said, "I want to see my nurse. Please call my nurse."

"There's no need." The needle tip pierced the IV injection port. The plunger began its slow and steady descent. Mary felt a warmth flush through her vein. She realized that the syringe was very full, that the plunger was taking far longer than usual to deliver its dose of painless oblivion. Not right, she thought. Something is not right.

"I want my nurse," she said. She managed to lift her head and call out weakly, "Nurse! Please! I need—"

A gloved hand closed over her mouth and shoved her head back to the pillow. Mary reached up to pry away the hand, but it was clamped too tightly over her mouth. She thrashed, felt the IV rip loose, felt the disconnected tubing dribbling saline. By now the liquid warmth had spread from her arm to her chest and was rushing toward her brain. She tried to move her legs and found she couldn't. Found, suddenly, that she didn't care. The hand slid away.

She was running. She was a girl again, her hair long and brown and flying around her shoulders. The sand was warm under her bare feet, and the air smelled of beach roses and the sea.

The gate hung wide open before her.

THE ringing telephone pulled Abby from a place that was both warm and safe. She stirred awake and found an arm wrapped around her waist—Mark's. Somehow, despite the small bed, they'd managed to fall asleep. She reached for the phone. "DiMatteo."

"Dr. D., this is Charlotte on Four West. Mrs. Allen has expired. The interns are all busy at the moment, so we wondered if you could come down and pronounce the patient."

"Right. I'll be there." Abby hung up. Mrs. Allen. Dead. It had happened sooner than she'd expected. She felt relieved that the ordeal was finally over, and guilty that she should experience such relief at all. It was three in the morning. She pulled on her shoes. Mark was snoring softly. Smiling, she leaned over and gave him a kiss. "I do," she whispered in his ear, and left the room.

Charlotte met her at the Four West nurses station. Together they walked to Mary's room at the far end of the hall.

"We found her at two a.m. rounds. I checked her at midnight and she was sleeping, so it happened sometime after that."

"Have you called the family?"

"I called the niece, the one listed in the chart. She's on her way now. We've been cleaning things up for the visit."

"Cleaning?"

"Mary must have pulled her IV out. There was saline spilled on the floor." They entered the patient's room.

Abby's task took only moments. She placed her fingers on the carotid artery. She lifted the gown and lay her stethoscope on the chest. She shone a penlight into the eyes. Then she picked up Mary Allen's chart, recorded the results, and wrote, "Patient pronounced expired at 0305." She closed the chart and turned to leave.

Brenda Hainey was standing in the doorway.

"I'm sorry, Miss Hainey," said Abby. "Your aunt passed away in her sleep. It was sometime after midnight."

"Was anyone with her when it happened?"

"There were nurses on duty in the ward."

"But no one was here in the room?"

Abby hesitated. Decided that the truth was always the best answer. "No. She was alone. I'm sure it happened in her sleep. It was a peaceful way to go." She stepped away from the bed. "You can stay with her for a while if you want. I'll ask the nurses to give you some privacy." She started past Brenda toward the door.

"Why was nothing done to save her?"

Abby turned back to look at her. "Nothing could be done. She had terminal cancer."

"She came into the hospital only two weeks ago. I think you people made her sicker."

By now Abby's stomach was churning. "There was nothing we could do," she repeated.

"Why wasn't her heart shocked at least?"

"She was a no-code. That means we don't shock her or put her on a breathing machine. It was your aunt's wish, and we honored it. So should you, Miss Hainey." She left before Brenda could say anything else. Before *she* could say anything she regretted.

She found Mark still asleep in the on-call room. She crawled into bed, with her back to his chest, and pulled his arm over her waist. Mark sighed and nestled closer to her. She took his hand and clasped it to her heart. *I do.* She smiled in spite of the sadness of Mary Allen's death. It was the beginning of a new life, hers and Mark's. The death of an elderly patient was a sad thing, but here in the hospital was where lives passed on. And where new lives began.

IT WAS midmorning when the taxi dropped Brenda Hainey off at her house in Chelsea. She had not eaten breakfast, had not slept since that call from the hospital. She had prayed at her aunt's bedside until the nurses had come to take the body to the morgue.

Now, climbing the steps to her front porch, she looked forward to a quiet breakfast and a long nap. She unlocked the door and saw that an envelope with her name on it had been deposited through the door slot. Just her name. No return address.

She broke the seal and unfolded the enclosed slip of paper. There was one typewritten line: "Your aunt did not die a natural death." It was signed "A friend."

FRANK Zwick glanced up from the patient on the operating table and said, "I understand congratulations are in order."

Abby had just walked into the OR to find Zwick and the two nurses grinning at her.

"I never thought that one would get hooked," said the scrub nurse. "Just goes to show you, bachelorhood *is* a curable illness. When did he pop the question, Dr. D.?"

Abby slipped her arms into the sterile gown and snapped on gloves. "Two days ago."

"You kept it a secret for two whole days?"

Abby laughed. "I wanted to make sure he wasn't going to suddenly change his mind."

She finished draping the patient and looked up as Mark pushed through the doors. He donned gown and gloves, and took his place across the table from her. They grinned at each other.

The intercom buzzed. A voice over the speaker said, "Is Dr. DiMatteo in there?"

"Yes, she is," said the circulating nurse.

"Mr. Parr needs her out of the OR."

"Tell him we're in surgery!" said Mark.

"He knows that. We need Dr. DiMatteo out here," repeated the intercom. "Now."

Abby backed away from the table and nervously stripped off her gown. Something was wrong. Her heart was already racing as she pushed through the OR doors and walked to the front desk.

Jeremiah Parr was standing there. Beside him were two hospital security guards and the nursing supervisor. No one was smiling.

"Dr. DiMatteo," said Parr, "could you come with us?"

"What's this all about?" said Abby. "Where are we going?"

"Your locker." Flanked by the two guards, Abby followed Parr to the women's locker room. The nursing supervisor first cleared the area of personnel, then beckoned Parr and the others inside.

"Could you open your locker, please?" said Parr.

Abby reached for the combination padlock, then stopped and turned to Parr. "I want to know what this is all about first."

"Just *open the locker.*"

Abby glanced at the guards, then at the nursing supervisor. They were watching her with heightened suspicion. She thought, I can't win. If I refuse to open it, they'll think I'm hiding something.

She opened the lock, and Parr stepped closer. So did the guards. They were standing right beside him as she swung open the door.

Inside were her street clothes, her purse, a flowered toilet bag for on-call nights, and the long white coat she used for attending rounds. She unzipped the flowered bag and held it open for everyone to see—toothbrush and tampons and Midol. She zipped up the bag and opened her purse. No surprises in there either. She put the purse back in the locker and took the coat off the hook. The instant she did, she knew there was something different about it. It was heavier. She reached into the pocket and felt something cylindrical and smooth. A glass vial. She took it out and stared at the label: MORPHINE SULFATE. The vial was almost empty.

"Dr. DiMatteo," said Parr, "please give that to me."

Too stunned to think of an alternative action, she simply handed it to him. "I don't know how it got there," she said.

Parr turned to the guards. "Please escort Dr. DiMatteo to my office."

"THIS is bull," said Mark. "Someone set her up. We all know it. It's part of the same pattern of harassment!"

"This is entirely different, Dr. Hodell. This is a dead patient." Parr looked at Abby. "Dr. DiMatteo, why don't you just tell us the truth and make things easier for all of us?"

Abby glanced around the table at Parr and Susan Casado and the nursing supervisor. She said, "I told you, I don't know how the morphine got in my locker. I don't know how Mary Allen died."

"You pronounced her death," said Parr. "Two nights ago."

"The nurses found her. She'd already expired."

"You were on call the night Mrs. Allen expired of a morphine OD. And today we find this in your locker." He set the vial on the table. "A controlled substance. Just the fact that it's in your possession is serious enough."

Abby stared at Parr. "You just said Mrs. Allen died of a morphine OD. How do you know that?"

"A postmortem drug level. It was sky-high."

Mark said, "Why would anyone order a postmortem morphine level? She was a terminal cancer patient."

Parr looked at Susan Casado, who said, "One of Mrs. Allen's relatives asked us to look into it. She received some kind of note implying the death was suspicious. We notified Dr. Wettig, and he ordered an autopsy."

"Then what you're saying," said Mark, "is that the patient was deliberately overdosed."

There was a long silence. Parr said, "Yes."

"This is ridiculous! I was with Abby that night, in the on-call room."

"You were together the whole time?" said Parr.

Mark hesitated. He doesn't really know, thought Abby. He'd slept through all her phone calls, hadn't even stirred when she'd left to pronounce Mrs. Allen at three o'clock. He was about to lie for her, and she knew that it wouldn't work. She said, "Mark was in the on-call room with me. But he slept all night."

"What about you, Dr. DiMatteo?" said Parr. "Did you stay in the room?"

"I was called to the wards several times. But you know that already, don't you?"

Parr nodded.

"You think you know everything," said Mark. "So tell me this. Why would she do it? Why would she kill her own patient?"

"It's no secret she has sympathies with the euthanasia movement," said Susan Casado.

Abby stared at her. "What?" She couldn't breathe.

"We've spoken with the nurses. On one occasion Dr. DiMatteo was heard to say, quote"—Susan flipped through the pages of a yellow legal pad—"If the morphine makes it easier, then that's what we should give her. Even if it makes the end come sooner. Unquote."

"That had nothing to do with euthanasia! I was talking about pain control, about keeping a patient comfortable."

There was a knock, and Dr. Wettig walked in and shut the door behind him. He stood at the end of the table and looked at Abby.

"She says she knows nothing about it," said Parr.

"I'm not surprised," Wettig said. "You really don't know anything about this, do you, DiMatteo?"

Abby met the General's gaze, determined to make him see that she had nothing to hide. "I didn't kill my patient. I swear it."

"That's what I thought you'd say." Wettig reached into his lab-coat pocket and produced a combination padlock. He set it down on the table. "This is from Dr. DiMatteo's locker. I called a locksmith. He says it's a spring-loaded model, a piece of cake to open. One sharp blow is all it takes. Also, there's a code on the back. Any registered locksmith can use that code to obtain the combination."

Parr glanced at the lock, then gave a dismissive shrug. "That doesn't prove anything."

"What's wrong with you people?" said Mark. "Can't you see what's happening here? An anonymous note. Morphine conveniently planted in her locker. Someone's setting her up."

"To what purpose?" said Susan.

"To discredit her. Get her fired."

Parr snorted. "You're suggesting someone actually murdered a patient just to ruin Dr. DiMatteo's career?"

Mark started to answer, then seemed to think better of it. It was an absurd theory and they all knew it.

"You have to agree, Dr. Hodell, that a conspiracy is pretty far-fetched," said Susan.

"Not as far-fetched as what's already happened to me," said Abby. "Look at what Victor Voss has already done. He assaulted me, put bloody organs in my car. And then there are the lawsuits—two of them already. And that's just the beginning."

There was a silence. Susan glanced at Parr. "Doesn't she know?"

"Apparently not."

"Know what?" said Abby.

"We got a call from Hawkes, Craig, and Sussman just after

lunch," said Susan. "The lawsuits against you have been dropped."

Abby reeled back in her chair. "I don't understand."

"If Victor Voss *was* trying to harass you, it appears he's stopped. This has nothing to do with Voss."

"Then how else do we explain this?" said Mark.

"Look at the evidence." Susan pointed to the vial. "I think we can all draw the same conclusion."

The silence was suffocating. Abby saw that no one was looking at her, not even Mark.

At last Wettig spoke. "What do you propose to do, Parr? Call in the police?"

"Let's keep them out of this," said Mark.

"If you people want to call this murder, then the police should be involved," said Wettig. "Call in a few reporters as well. Get it all out in the open—that's the best policy." He looked directly at Parr. "*If* you're going to call this murder." It was a dare.

Parr was the one to back down. He cleared his throat and said to Susan, "We can't be absolutely certain that's what it is."

There was another pause. Then Abby spoke. She scarcely recognized her own voice; it sounded like a stranger's, calm and steady. "I'd like to return to my patients now. If I may," she said.

Wettig nodded. "Go ahead."

"Wait," said Parr. "She can't go back to her duties."

"You haven't proved anything," said Abby, rising from her chair.

"We have one charge that's indisputable," said Susan. "Illegal possession of a controlled substance." She looked at Parr. "We don't have a choice. The potential for liability is sky-high. If something goes wrong with any of her patients and people find out we knew about this morphine business, we're dead." She turned to Wettig. "So's the reputation of your residency program, General."

Susan's warning had its intended effect. Liability was something they all worried about. This time Wettig didn't argue.

Parr rose to his feet, the decision now made. "Dr. DiMatteo, until further notice you're on suspension. You're not to go on the wards or anywhere near a patient. Do you understand?"

She understood. She understood perfectly.

EIGHT

TODAY the sea was calm. Yakov was finally able to coax Aleksei from his bunk to go exploring. The first place Yakov took him was the engine room. They wandered for a while in the clanking darkness. Then they went up to the bridge, where the navigator was too busy to talk to them. Yakov could not demonstrate his special status as a regular visitor.

Next they headed to the galley, but the cook was in a cranky mood. He had a meal to prepare for the aft passengers, a demanding pair no one ever saw. He grumbled as he set two glasses and a wine bottle on a tray and slid it into the dumbwaiter. He pressed a button and sent it whirring upward, to their private quarters.

"I'm hungry," said Yakov.

"You're always hungry," said the cook. "Go cut yourself a slice of bread. The loaf is stale, but you can toast it."

The two boys rummaged in drawers for the bread knife. Holding down the loaf with the stump of his left arm, Yakov sawed off two slices. He slid the first piece into the toaster, and a furry ball of gray suddenly popped out of one slot and leaped to the floor.

"A mouse!" shrieked Aleksei. "There's a mouse!"

The gray ball scampered around Aleksei's dancing feet, then shot off, vanishing under a cabinet.

Something was burning on the stove. Cursing, the cook ran to turn off the flame. "A mouse in my kitchen! And look at this. Ruined. I'll have to start over again. Bloody mouse."

"He was in the toaster," said Yakov.

"Probably left it full of his poop," said the cook.

Yakov cautiously peered into the toaster. No more mice, but lots of mysterious brown specks. He slid the toaster toward the sink, intending to dump them out.

The cook gave a shout. "Hey, there's water in that sink! And look, the thing is still plugged in. If you put that in there and you touch the water, you're dead. Didn't anyone ever teach you that?"

"Uncle Misha never had a toaster."

"It's not just toasters. It's anything that plugs in, anything with an electric cord. You're as stupid as all the others." He waved his arms. "Go on, get out of here, both of you. You're a nuisance."

The boys left and played on deck for a while, until they grew chilled. Sheer boredom took them at last to the one place on the boat where Yakov knew they would bother no one and no one would bother them. It was his secret place. He had found it on his third day of exploring, when he had spotted the door in the engine-room corridor. He had opened that door and found it led to a stairwell shaft. Wonderland.

The shaft soared three levels. A circular staircase spiraled up and up, and leading off the second level was a flimsy steel walkway. A blue door led aft from the walkway. But it was always kept locked, and Yakov had stopped even bothering to try it.

Yakov and Aleksei climbed up to the top level, then went down the staircase, setting off lovely clatters. At the bottom Yakov showed Aleksei an empty crate, which he'd found shoved under the stairs. They crawled inside. There they lay in darkness among the crate's wood shavings and listened to the engines' rumble.

"This is my secret place," said Yakov. "You can't tell anyone about it. Swear to me you won't tell."

"Why should I? It's a disgusting place. It's cold and wet."

"If you don't like it, you can get out. You're no fun." Yakov gave him a kick through the wood shavings. Stupid Aleksei. Anyone who carried a filthy stuffed dog everywhere could not be expected to enjoy adventures.

Somewhere above them a door squealed and clanged shut. The walkway was rattling now, the sound of every footstep shattering to a thousand echoes in the stairway shaft.

Yakov crawled to the opening and peered out of the crate at the walkway above. Someone was knocking at the blue door. A moment later the door opened, and he caught a glimpse of blond hair as a woman vanished inside. The door closed behind her.

Yakov retreated back into the crate. "It's just Nadiya."

"Is she still out there?"

"No. She went in the blue door."

"What's in there?"

"I don't know. It's always locked."

For a while they rested side by side, Aleksei clutching Shu-Shu. They lay immobilized by boredom, by the sleep-inducing rumble of the engines, and by the sway of the sea.

"I don't like Nadiya," said Yakov at last.

"I do. I wish she was my mother."

"She doesn't even like children."

"Does so. The other boys like her, too."

Stupid Aleksei, thought Yakov. Stupid everyone. Nadiya had them all fooled. Eleven boys on the boat, and each and every one of them was in love with her. Yakov shared their fascination, but his was not because of adoration. He was afraid of her.

It was all because of the blood tests.

On their fourth day at sea, when the boys were still puking and moaning in their bunks, Gregor and Nadiya had come around carrying a tray of needles and tubes. "It will be only a small prick," they'd said, "a small tube of blood to confirm you are healthy. No one will adopt you if they cannot be assured you are healthy." The pair had moved from boy to boy, weaving a bit from the rough sea. At each bunk they'd asked the boy his name and fitted him with a plastic bracelet on which they'd written a number. Then Gregor tied a giant rubber band around the boy's arm and slapped the skin a few times to make the vein swell. Some of the boys cried, and Nadiya had to hold their hand while Gregor drew the blood.

Yakov was the only boy she was unable to comfort. No matter how she tried, she could not make him hold still. He did not want that needle in his arm, and he had given Gregor a kick to emphasize the point. That's when the real Nadiya took over. She pinned Yakov's one arm to the bed, holding it there with a grasp that pinched and twisted at the same time. As Gregor drew the blood, she had kept her gaze fixed on Yakov, had spoken quietly, even sweetly to him. Everyone else heard only murmured words of reassurance. But Yakov, staring into those pale eyes of hers, saw something entirely different. Afterward he gnawed off his plastic bracelet.

Aleksei still wore his. His certification of good health.

"Do you think she has children of her own?" asked Aleksei.

Yakov gave a shudder. "I hope not," he said.

IN THE night Yakov awakened and sensed at once that something was different. He realized it was the engines that had changed. That ceaseless rumble had muffled to a soft growl.

He crawled out of his bunk and went to give Aleksei a shake. "Wake up," he whispered. "We've stopped moving. I'm going up to take a look. Come with me."

"I don't care. I'm sleeping."

"Don't you want to see land? We must be near land." Yakov bent closer to Aleksei, his whispers softly enticing. "Maybe we can see the lights. America. You'll miss it unless you come with me."

Aleksei stirred a bit. "All right, all right." He sat up and put on his shoes. They tiptoed past the double bunks of sleeping boys and climbed the stairway to the deck.

Outside, a soft wind was blowing. They looked over the railing, straining for a view of city lights, but the stars met only a black and formless horizon.

"I don't see anything," said Aleksei. "I'm going back to bed."

They had just reached the stairway when they heard a series of sharp thuds. Suddenly the deck was ablaze with light. Both boys froze, blinking at the unexpected glare.

Yakov grabbed Aleksei's hand and tugged him under the bridge stairway, where they crouched, peering out between the steps. They heard voices and saw two men in white overalls walk into the circle of floodlights. Together they bent down and gave something a tug. There was a scrape of metal as some kind of cover was forced aside. It revealed a new light, this one blue. It shone at the center of the floodlit circle, like the forbidding iris of an eye. Both men straightened and looked up at the sky. Toward a distant growl of thunder.

Yakov, too, looked up. The thunder was moving closer. It deepened to a rhythmic *whup-whup.* The two men retreated from the floodlights. The sound drew right overhead, churning the night like a tornado. Aleksei and Yakov watched as a helicopter descended into the wash of light and touched down on the deck.

One of the men in overalls reappeared, running bent at the waist. He swung open the helicopter door. Yakov could not see what was inside; the stairway post was blocking his direct view. He eased out onto the deck just far enough to see around the post. He caught a glimpse of the pilot and one passenger—a man.

"Hey!" came a shout from overhead. "You! Boy!"

Yakov glanced straight up and saw the navigator peering down at him from the bridge deck.

"What are you doing down there? You come up here right now, before you get hurt. Come on!"

Yakov scurried up the stairway, with Aleksei right on his heels.

"Don't you know enough to stay off the main deck when a chopper's landing?" yelled the navigator. He pulled them inside the wheelhouse. He pointed to two chairs. "Sit. Both of you."

"We were just watching," said Yakov.

"You two are supposed to be in bed."

"I *was* in bed," whimpered Aleksei. "He made me come out."

The roar of the helicopter made them all turn to look. They watched as it lifted into the sky, then veered off, to be swallowed by the night.

"Where does it go?" asked Yakov, going to the bridge window.

"You think they tell me?" said the navigator. "They just call me when it's coming in for a pickup, and I turn the bow into the wind."

"What does it pick up?" asked Yakov.

"I don't ask. I just do what they tell me."

"Who?"

"The passengers in the aft cabin." He tugged Yakov away from the window and gave both boys a push toward the door. "Go back to your bunks. Can't you see I have work to do?"

STEPAN was not at breakfast. By then the news of his departure during the night had already spread to Yakov's cabin, so when he sat down at the table that morning and faced the boys across from him, he knew the reason for their silence. They did not understand why Stepan should be the first to be chosen. They'd all thought he'd be among the leftovers or would be consigned to some unlikely family who favored idiot children. But he was gone now. Gone to new parents who'd chosen him, Nadiya said.

The rest of them were the leftovers.

NINE

SHE was in her late forties, with the thin, dry face of a woman who had long ago lost her estrogenic glow. In Bernard Katzka's opinion, that alone did not make a woman unattractive. A woman's appeal lay not in the luster of her skin and hair, but in what was revealed by her eyes. Lundquist, his partner, was of the masculine school that believed women were not worth a second glance once they'd crossed the menopausal finish line. No wonder he had looked so relieved when Katzka agreed to interview Brenda Hainey. Katzka was the one detective in homicide who had the patience to hear out her bizarre charges. And this was precisely what he had been doing for the last fifteen minutes.

"I've spoken to the hospital about this," Brenda Hainey was saying. "I went straight to their president, Mr. Parr. He promised he'd investigate, but that was five days ago, and so far I've heard nothing. So I called your people."

Katzka almost sighed but caught himself. He knew she would take it for what it was—an expression of weariness. He said, "May I see the note?"

She pulled a paper from her purse and handed it to him. It had one typewritten line: "Your aunt did not die a natural death. A friend."

"Do you know who might have sent this?" he asked.

"I have no idea. Maybe one of the nurses. Someone who knew enough to tell me."

"Have you spoken to your aunt's doctors?"

"I'd prefer not to."

"Why not?"

"Given the situation, I'm not sure I trust them."

"I see." Katzka picked up his pen and flipped open his notebook. "Why don't you give me the names of all your aunt's doctors?"

"The physician in charge was Dr. Colin Wettig. But the one who really seemed to be making all the decisions was that resident of his. I think she's the one you should look at. Dr. DiMatteo."

Katzka glanced up in surprise. "Abigail DiMatteo?"

Brenda said cautiously, "You know her."

"I've spoken to her. On another matter."

"Well, you should take a close look at Dr. DiMatteo."

"Why her in particular?"

"She's the one who wanted my aunt dead."

IT WAS with reluctance that Katzka drove to Bayside Hospital that afternoon after Brenda Hainey's visit. Brenda's charges struck him as improbable, but still, there was the matter of that note. At the hospital's public-information office he confirmed that Mary Allen had indeed expired on the date Brenda said she had and that the diagnosis had been undifferentiated metastatic carcinoma. Dr. Wettig was unavailable, so Katzka had Abby DiMatteo paged.

A moment later she called back.

"This is Detective Katzka," he said. "We spoke last week."

"Yes. I remember."

"I have some questions on an unrelated matter. Can I meet you?"

He heard a sigh, then a reluctant "Okay. I'm in the medical library. Second floor, administrative wing."

In Katzka's experience the average person enjoyed talking to homicide cops. People were curious about murder, about police work. Dr. DiMatteo, however, had sounded genuinely unwilling to speak to him. He wondered why.

He found the hospital library tucked between data processing and the financial office. Dr. DiMatteo was standing beside the photocopier, collating papers. It surprised him to see her performing such a clerical task. He was also surprised to see her dressed in a skirt and blouse rather than scrub clothes. From the first day he'd met Abby, he'd thought her an attractive woman. Now, seeing her in a flattering skirt, with all that black hair hanging loose about her shoulders, he decided she was really quite stunning.

She looked up and gave a nod. She seemed nervous, even wary. "I'm almost finished," she said. "I have one more article to copy."

"Not on duty today?"

She placed another page on the Xerox machine and hit the COPY button. "I'm not scheduled for the OR. So I'm doing a literature search. Dr. Wettig needs these for a conference." She stared down at the copier, as though the machine required all her concentration. When the last pages rolled out, she took them to a table, where other stacks lay waiting, and sat down. He pulled out the chair across from her. She picked up a stapler. Still not looking at him, she asked, "Have there been new developments?"

"On Dr. Levi, no. This is a different matter. A patient of yours."

"Oh?" She picked up a stack of papers and slid it between the stapler teeth. "Which patient are we talking about?"

"A Mrs. Mary Allen."

Her hand paused for a second in midair. Then it came down, hard, on the stapler.

"I understand she died last week here at Bayside."

"That's right."

"Can you confirm that her diagnosis was undifferentiated metastatic carcinoma?"

"Yes."

"Then her death was expected?"

There was a hesitation. At last she looked up at him. He realized she was sitting absolutely still. Almost rigid. "Can I ask why you're pursuing this?"

"A relative of Mrs. Allen's came to us with some concerns."

"Are we talking about Brenda Hainey, the niece?"

"Yes. Brenda Hainey received an anonymous note. It claimed that Mary Allen didn't die of natural causes. Do you have any reason, any reason at all, to think there might be substance to that?"

He could have predicted several likely responses. She might have laughed and said this was all ridiculous. She might have told him that Brenda Hainey was crazy. Or she might have shown puzzlement, even anger, that she was being subjected to these questions. What he did not expect was her actual response.

She stared at him, her face suddenly white. And she said softly, "I refuse to answer any more questions, Detective Katzka."

SECONDS after he left, Abby reached for the nearest phone and paged Mark. To her relief he immediately answered her call.

"That detective was here again," she whispered. "Mark, he knows about Mary Allen. Brenda's been talking to him. And he's asking questions about how she died."

"You didn't tell him anything, did you?"

"No. I . . ." She took a deep breath. The sigh that followed was close to a sob. "I didn't know what to say. Mark, I was ready to spill my guts. If I just came out and told him everything—"

"Don't. What if he doesn't believe you? He'll take one look at that morphine in your locker and jump to the obvious conclusion."

"But Mark, what if Mary Allen *was* murdered? Then there *should* be an investigation. We should bring this to the police ourselves."

"It's your decision. But I want you to think long and hard about the consequences."

She already had. The publicity. The possibility of arrest. She'd gone back and forth, knowing what she should do, yet afraid to take action.

I'm a coward. My patient's dead, maybe murdered, and all I can worry about is saving my own skin.

The hospital librarian walked into the room, wheeling a squeaky cart of books. She sat down at her desk and began stamping the inside covers. *Whap. Whap.*

"Mark, I'll talk to you later. I've got to go now." Abby hung up and went back to the table. She stared at the stack of photocopied articles. This was the extent of her work today. She was a physician who could no longer practice, a surgeon banished from the OR.

The *whap, whap* had ceased. She realized the librarian had stopped stamping her book covers and was now eyeing Abby.

Like everyone else in this hospital, she, too, is wondering about me.

Flushing, Abby gathered up her papers and carried them to the librarian's desk.

The librarian reached for the copier log. "How many copies?"

"Two hundred. You can charge them to Dr. Wettig's office."

As Abby set the stack of papers down, the name "Aaron Levi, M.D." seemed to jump out at her from the top page. The article's title was "Comparison of Cardiac Transplant Survival Rates Between Critically Ill and Outpatient Recipients." The authors were Aaron Levi and a Lawrence Kunstler. She stared at Aaron's name, shaken by the unexpected reminder of his death.

The librarian, too, noticed Aaron's name, and she shook her head. "It's hard to believe Dr. Levi's gone."

"I know what you mean," Abby murmured.

"And to see both those names on the same article."

"Excuse me?"

"Dr. Kunstler and Dr. Levi."

"I'm afraid I don't know Dr. Kunstler."

"Oh, he was here before you came." The librarian closed the copier log. "It must have happened six years ago at least."

"What happened six years ago?"

"Dr. Kunstler jumped off the Tobin Bridge."

Abby focused again on the article, on the two names at the top of the page. "He killed himself?"

The librarian nodded. "Just like Dr. Levi."

THOUGH it was drizzling outside, Abby drove all the way home that afternoon with her window open. The stench of rotting pig organs still lingered in her car. She didn't think the smell would ever disappear. It would be a permanent reminder of Victor Voss's rage.

The Tobin Bridge was coming up—the place where Lawrence Kunstler had chosen to end his life. She slowed down. As she drove onto the bridge, she wondered if Kunstler had been conscious after he hit the water, whether he had struggled against the current. She wondered, too, about Aaron. Two doctors, two suicides. She'd have to ask Vivian about Kunstler. If he had died only six years ago, Vivian might have heard of him.

As she waited at the toll booth, Abby took one last backward look at the bridge, past a maroon van idling behind her. They knew each other, Aaron and Kunstler. They worked together. They wrote that article together.

That thought kept going around in her mind as she navigated the streets back to Cambridge. As she turned onto Brattle Street, she happened to glance in the rearview mirror. The maroon van was still behind her. It, too, drove onto Brattle.

She drove another block, past Willard Street, and looked again at the mirror. The van was still there. On impulse she turned left, onto Mercer. So did the van. She turned left again, onto Camden, then right, onto Mt. Auburn. She kept glancing in the mirror, waiting for the van to come into view. Only when she'd reached Brattle again and the van hadn't reappeared did she allow herself a sigh of relief.

What a nervous Nellie.

She drove straight home and pulled into the driveway. Mark wasn't back yet. She stepped into the house. It was gloomy inside, the afternoon light gray and watery through the windows. She was about to switch on a lamp when she heard the low growl of a car on Brewster Street. She looked out the window.

A maroon van was moving past the house. As it approached her driveway, it slowed to a crawl, as though the driver was taking a long, careful look at Abby's car.

Lock the doors. Lock the doors.

She ran to the front door, turned the dead bolt, and slid the chain into place, then ran to the back door and locked it. Back in the living room, she peeked outside. The van was gone.

She left the curtains open and the lights off. Sitting in the dark living room, she stared out the windows and wondered if she should call the police. With what complaint? She sat for close to an hour, watching the street, hoping that Mark would come home.

The van didn't appear. Neither did Mark.

She picked up the phone and dialed Vivian. The clamor of the Chao household came through the line in a lively blast of laughter and shouted Cantonese. Vivian said, "I'm having trouble hearing you. I'm going to change extensions." After what seemed like an endless wait, Vivian picked up the extension. "Okay, Grandma, you can hang up," she yelled. The chatter of Cantonese was abruptly cut off.

Abby said, "There was a doctor on the transplant team who died six years ago. Did you know him?"

"Yeah. But it wasn't that long ago. More like four years."

"Do you have any idea why he committed suicide?"

"It wasn't a suicide. It was an accident. There was some defect in his furnace, and carbon monoxide collected in the house. It killed his wife and baby girl, too."

"Wait. I'm talking about a guy named Lawrence Kunstler."

"I don't know anyone named Kunstler. That must have happened before I got to Bayside."

"Who are *you* talking about?"

"An anesthesiologist. The one before they hired Zwick. Hennessy—that's the name."

"He was on the transplant team?"

"Yeah. He wasn't here very long. I remember he was thinking about moving back west when it happened."

"Are you sure it was an accident?"

"What else would it be?"

Abby stared out the window at the empty street and said nothing.

"Abby, is something wrong?"

"Someone was following me today. A van."

"Come on."

"I keep thinking about Aaron. And Lawrence Kunstler. He jumped off the Tobin Bridge. And now you're telling me about Hennessy. That's three, Vivian."

"Two suicides and an accident."

"That's more than you'd expect in one hospital." Abby drew her legs up on the chair and hugged herself for warmth. For self-protection. "I'm getting scared. You know, a detective questioned me about Aaron's death, and he said it might not be a suicide."

"Does he have any evidence?"

"If he did, he certainly wouldn't tell me."

"He might tell Elaine."

Of course. The widow. The one who'd want to know.

After she hung up, Abby dialed Elaine. The phone rang four times. Then she heard a recording: "The number you have dialed is no longer in service. Please check your listing and dial again."

Abby redialed. The same thing happened. She hung up and stared at the phone. Why had Elaine changed her number? Who was she trying to avoid?

Outside, a car splashed through the rain. Abby ran to the window and peered out. A BMW was pulling into the driveway. She offered up a silent prayer of thanks. Mark was home.

TEN

MARK refilled his wineglass and set the bottle down on the restaurant table. He had wanted to eat out to celebrate their engagement. "Sure, I knew them both," he said. "I knew Larry Kunstler better than Hennessy. Larry was one of the guys who recruited me here, straight from my fellowship. He was an okay guy."

"Why didn't you ever tell me about them?" Abby asked.

"It never came up."

"I would think *someone* would mention them. Especially after Aaron died. The team loses three colleagues in six years, and no one says a thing. It's almost as if you're all afraid to talk about it."

"It's a pretty depressing thing to talk about. We try not to bring up the subject, especially around Marilee Archer. She knew Hennessy's wife. She even arranged her baby shower."

"The baby who died?"

Mark nodded. "It was a shock. A whole family, just like that."

"It was definitely an accident?"

"They'd bought the house a few months before. They never got the chance to replace the old furnace. Yes, it was an accident."

"But Kunstler's death wasn't."

Mark sighed. "No, Larry's was not an accident." He took a sip of wine, then another, but he seemed to have lost any enjoyment in its taste. Or in the food.

They skipped dessert and left the restaurant, both of them silent and depressed.

Mark drove through thickening fog and intermittent rain. The whisk of the windshield wipers filled in for conversation, until he said softly, "I want to show you something, Abby. I want to know what you think about it. Maybe you'll think I'm just crazy. Or maybe you'll be wild about the idea."

"What idea?"

"It's something I've been dreaming about. For a long time now."

They drove north, out of Boston, kept driving through Revere and Lynn and Swampscott. At Marblehead Marina, he parked the car and said, "She's right there, at the end of the pier."

"She" was a yacht.

Abby stood shivering and bewildered on the dock as Mark paced up and down the boat's length. His voice was animated now, more than it had been all evening. "She's a cruiser," he said. "Forty-eight feet, fully equipped. She could take us anywhere we'd want to go. You're looking at freedom, Abby. Freedom!"

She shook her head. "I don't understand."

"It's a way out. Of the city. Of the hospital. We buy this boat. Then we bail out of here and *go*."

"Where?"

"Anywhere."

"I don't want to go anywhere. I've worked so hard. I'm not going to give up now."

"What about *me?*"

She stared at him. And realized that, of course, this *was* all about him. The soon-to-be-married man, suddenly seized with the urge to run away from home.

"I want to do this, Abby," he said, his eyes glittering, feverish. "I put in an offer on this boat. That's why I got home so late. I was meeting with the broker."

"You made an offer without telling me? I'm way over my head in student loans and you're buying a *boat?*"

"It's like buying a second home. It's an investment."

"It's not what I'd invest my money in."

"I'm not spending *your* money."

She took a step back and stared at him. "You're right," she said quietly. "It's not my money at all."

"Abby." He groaned.

The rain was starting to fall again, cold and numbing against her face. She walked back to the car and climbed inside. He got into the car as well. For a moment neither one of them spoke. The only sound was the rain on the roof.

He said quietly, "You don't understand," and she heard a strange and unexpected note of desperation in his voice. He started the car.

They drove halfway home without speaking. Then Abby said, "Maybe we should rethink the engagement. Maybe getting married isn't really what you want, Mark."

"Is it what you want?"

She looked out the window and sighed. "I don't know," she murmured. "I don't know anymore."

It was the truth. She didn't.

THE one advantage of being relieved of ward duties was that Abby could skip out for the whole afternoon and no one at Bayside would care. She decided to drive to Elaine's house. As she headed west on Route 9 to Newton, she remembered the day of Aaron's funeral and how no one had mentioned the two previous deaths. Not even Elaine, who must have known about them. Not even Mark.

If he kept this from me, what else hasn't he told me?

She pulled into Elaine's driveway and sat there for a moment, trying to shake off her depression. But the pall remained. It's all falling apart for me, she thought. My job. And now I'm losing Mark. The worst part about it is, I don't have any idea why it's happening.

Over the last few days, ever since the night she'd brought up the subject of Kunstler and Hennessy, everything had changed between her and Mark. They lived in the same house and slept in the same bed, but their interactions had become purely automatic.

She got out of the car and climbed the steps to the front door. She rang the doorbell. When no one answered, she tried knocking, then rang again. And again. The front door was locked; she circled around to the back garden. The kitchen door was also locked, but just off the patio was a sliding glass door. Abby gave it a tug, and it glided open. She called, "Elaine?" and stepped inside.

The room was vacant. Furniture, rugs—everything was gone, even the pictures. Her footsteps echoed as she went through more bare rooms. The house was swept clean. She walked outside and stood in the driveway, feeling completely disoriented. Only two weeks before, she had sat in the living room and eaten finger sandwiches. Now she wondered if she'd hallucinated the whole scene.

Still in a daze, she got into her car and backed out of the driveway. She drove on automatic pilot, her mind on Elaine's bizarre disappearance. To uproot her life so abruptly after Aaron's death didn't seem rational. Rather, it seemed like something one did out of panic.

Suddenly uneasy, she glanced in the rearview mirror. She'd made it a habit to check the mirror ever since Saturday, when she'd first glimpsed the maroon van.

There was a dark green Volvo driving behind her. Hadn't it been parked outside Elaine's house? She couldn't be sure. She hadn't really been paying attention. The Volvo blinked its lights on and off.

She accelerated. The Volvo did too. She turned right, onto a major thoroughfare. Ahead stretched a suburban strip of gas stations and minimalls.

Witnesses. Lots of witnesses.

She'd had enough of being pursued, enough of being frightened. She swerved into the parking lot of a shopping mall. The Volvo followed her. She slammed on the brakes, and the Volvo screeched to a halt inches from her rear bumper.

Abby scrambled out of her car and ran back to the Volvo. Furiously she rapped at the driver's window. "Open up, damn you!"

The driver rolled down his window and looked out at her. "Dr. DiMatteo?" said Bernard Katzka. "I thought it was you."

"Why have you been following me?"

"I saw you drive away from the house."

"No, *before*. Why did you follow me before?"

"When?"

"Saturday. The van."

He shook his head. "I don't know about any van."

She backed away. "Forget it. Just quit tailing me, okay?"

"I was trying to get you to pull over. Didn't you see me flash my lights?"

"I didn't know it was you."

"I'd like to talk to you. Or are you going to refuse to answer questions again?"

"That depends on what you're going to ask me."

"It's about Dr. Levi."

She thought about it and decided that questions could go both ways. She glanced toward the mall. "I see a doughnut shop over there. Why don't we go in and have a cup of coffee?"

IN THE Dunkin' Donuts, Katzka came right to the point. "Why were you at the house?"

"I came to see Elaine. I wanted to talk to her."

"About what?"

"Personal matters."

"It was my impression that you two were just acquaintances. Is that how you'd characterize the relationship?"

"Yes. I guess so."

"So why did you come to see her?"

She took a deep breath. "Some strange things have happened to me lately. I wanted to talk to Elaine about it."

"What things?"

"Someone was following me last Saturday. A maroon van. I spotted it on the Tobin Bridge, then again at home. It scared me."

He regarded her in silence, as though trying to decide if it really was fear he was seeing in her face. "What does this have to do with Mrs. Levi?"

"You're the one who got me wondering about Aaron. About whether he really committed suicide. Then I found out two other Bayside doctors have died."

Katzka's frown told her this was news to him.

"Six years ago," she said, "there was a Dr. Lawrence Kunstler. He jumped off the Tobin Bridge."

Katzka said nothing, but he shifted forward in his chair.

"Then four years ago there was an anesthesiologist," continued Abby. "A Dr. Hennessy. He and his wife and baby died of carbon monoxide poisoning from a broken furnace."

"Unfortunately, that kind of accident happens every winter."

"And then there's Aaron. That makes three. All of them were on the transplant team."

"What are you formulating here? That someone's stalking the transplant team? Killing them off one by one?"

"I'm just pointing out a pattern. You're the policeman. You should investigate it."

Katzka sat back. "How is it you got involved in all this?"

"My boyfriend's on the team. Mark doesn't admit it, but I think he's worried, and they're wondering who's going to be next. But they never talk about it."

"So you're worried about your boyfriend's safety?"

"Yes," she said simply, leaving out the larger truth—that she was doing this because her relationship with Mark was crumbling. She wanted Mark back. All of him.

Obviously, Katzka had expected her to say more. Instead she quickly avoided his gaze. And asked a question of her own. "Why were you watching Elaine's house?" she asked. "That's what you're doing, isn't it?"

"I was talking to the next-door neighbor. When I came out, I saw you pull out of the driveway."

Her gaze lifted to his. "Why are you still investigating a suicide?"

"The widow packs up and leaves practically overnight, with no forwarding address. That's unusual."

"You're not saying Elaine's guilty of anything, are you?"

"No. I think she's scared."

"Of what?"

"Do you know, Dr. DiMatteo?"

She found she could not look away, found there was something about the quiet intensity of his gray eyes that held her transfixed. She felt a completely unexpected flicker of attraction, and she had no idea why this man, of all people, should inspire it.

"No," she said. "I have no idea what Elaine's running from."

"Maybe you can help me answer another question, then. How did Aaron Levi accumulate all his wealth?"

She shook her head. "He wasn't particularly wealthy, as far as I knew. A cardiologist earns maybe two hundred thousand, tops."

Katzka sat back, thinking. He wasn't looking at her now but was staring at his coffee cup. There was a depth of concentration to this man that intrigued her.

"Detective, how much wealth are we talking about?"

He looked up at her. "Three million dollars."

Stunned, Abby could only stare at him.

"After Mrs. Levi vanished," he said, "I thought I should take a closer look at the family finances. So I spoke to their C.P.A. He told me that shortly after Dr. Levi died, Elaine discovered her husband had a Cayman Islands bank account. She asked the C.P.A. how to access the money. And then, without warning, she skipped town." He looked at her questioningly.

"I have no idea how Aaron got that much money."

"Neither does his accountant."

They were silent a moment. Abby asked softly, "Do you know where Elaine is?"

He shook his head. "At the moment, Dr. DiMatteo," he said, "I don't think she wants to be found."

THREE million dollars. How had Aaron Levi accumulated three million dollars? All the way home she considered that question. And why had he hidden his wealth even from Elaine? The Cayman Islands was where people stashed their money when they wanted it kept out of sight of the IRS.

Abby pulled into her driveway. Found herself surveying the neighborhood for a maroon van. It was getting to be a habit—that quick glance up and down the street.

She walked in the front door and gathered up the usual pile of mail. She lugged it into the kitchen, where she sorted everything into two piles: his junk, her junk. It was four o'clock. Tonight, she decided, she'd cook a nice dinner. Why not? She was now a lady of leisure. While Bayside took its sweet time deciding her future, she could stay busy fixing things up between her and Mark.

She scooped up her half of the junk mail, carried it to the trash can, and stepped on the pedal of the pop-up lid. Just as the mail was tumbling in, she glimpsed a large brown envelope stuffed at the bottom. The word "yachts" caught her eye. She dug out the envelope. At the top left was printed:

> East Wind Yachts
> Sales and Service
> Marblehead Marina

It had been addressed to Mark but sent to a P.O. box.

She went to Mark's desk in the living room and opened the bottom drawer. Inside were his insurance papers, mortgage papers, car papers. She found a tab with "Boat" written on it. There was a folder for *Gimme Shelter,* his J-35 sailboat. There was also a second folder. It looked new. On the tab was written "H-48." She pulled out the H-48 file. Inside was a sales contract from East Wind.

She sank into a chair, feeling sick. *You bought it anyway and kept it a secret,* she thought. *It's your money, all right. I guess this makes it perfectly clear.*

Her gaze moved to the bottom of the page, to the terms of sale. Moments later she walked out of the house.

"CASH for organs. Is it possible?" asked Vivian.

In the midst of stirring cream into his coffee, Dr. Ivan Tarasoff stopped and glanced at Vivian and Abby. "Do you have any proof of this?"

"Not yet. We're just asking you if it's possible. And if so, how could it be done?"

Dr. Tarasoff sank back on the couch and sipped his coffee as he thought it over. It was four forty-five, and except for the occasional scrub-suited resident passing through, the Mass Gen surgeons lounge was quiet. Tarasoff, who'd come out of the OR only twenty minutes before, still had a surgical mask dangling around his neck. Watching him, Abby was comforted once again by the image of a grandfather—the gentle blue eyes, the silver hair, the quiet voice.

"There've been rumors, of course," said Tarasoff. "Every time a celebrity gets an organ, people wonder if money was involved."

"What rumors have you heard?"

"That one can buy a higher place on the waiting list. I myself have never seen it happen."

"I have," said Abby. "Two weeks ago. Mrs. Victor Voss. She was third on the waiting list, and she got a heart. The two people at the top of the list later died."

"UNOS wouldn't allow that. Or NEOB. They have strict guidelines."

"NEOB didn't know about it. In fact, they have no record of the donor."

"We think Voss paid to keep it out of the system so it could go to his wife," added Vivian.

"This is what we know so far," said Abby. "Hours before Mrs. Voss's transplant Bayside's transplant coordinator got a call from Wilcox Memorial in Burlington that they had a donor. The heart was harvested and delivered to our OR by a doctor named Mapes. Donor papers came with it, but somehow they got misplaced. No one's seen them since. I looked up the name 'Mapes' in the *Directory of Medical Specialists*. There's no such surgeon."

"Then who did the harvest?"

"We think it was a Tim Nicholls. His name *is* listed. He trained a few years at Mass Gen. Do you remember him?"

Tarasoff shook his head. "I'd have to check the residency records."

"We're thinking this is what happened," said Vivian. "Mrs. Voss needed a heart, and her husband had the money to pay for it. Somehow the word went out. Tim Nicholls happened to have a donor. So he funneled the heart directly to Bayside, bypassing NEOB. And various people got paid off, including some of the Bayside staff."

Tarasoff looked horrified. "I've referred patients to Bayside myself. It's one of the top transplant centers in the country. Why would they risk getting into trouble with NEOB and UNOS?"

"The answer's obvious," said Vivian. "Money."

"I'll find out what I can about Nicholls," said Tarasoff. "If there's a shadow organ procurement network out there, I want to know about it."

"So do we," said Abby. "But we have to be very careful, Dr. Tarasoff. In the last six years three Bayside doctors have died. Two suicides and an accident. All of them were on our transplant team."

Tarasoff looked shocked. "You're trying to scare me, aren't you?"

Abby nodded. "You should be scared. We all should."

OUTSIDE, in the parking lot, Abby and Vivian stood together under a gray, drizzling sky. Shivering, Abby pulled her slicker tighter and glanced around the lot. No maroon vans.

"We don't have enough," said Vivian. "We can't force an investigation yet. And if we tried, Victor Voss could just cover his tracks."

"Nina Voss wasn't the first one. I think Bayside's done this before. Aaron died with three million dollars in his account. He must have been getting payoffs for some time."

"You think he got second thoughts?"

"I know he was trying to get out of Bayside. Out of Boston. Maybe they wouldn't let him go."

"That could be what happened to Kunstler and Hennessy."

Abby sighed. "I'm afraid that's exactly what happened to them."

"We need to find out the names of other transplants and where they were on the waiting list."

Abby said, "I can do that."

"I'd help you out, but Bayside won't let me in its doors anymore. They think I'm their worst nightmare."

"You and me both."

Vivian grinned, as if it were something to be proud of. Then her gaze became direct and uncompromising. "Okay, Abby, now tell me why we're keeping this from Mark."

Abby released a deep breath. The answer spilled out in a rush of anguish. "I think he's part of it."

"Mark?"

Abby nodded and looked up at the drizzling sky. "He wants out of Bayside. He's been talking about sailing away. Escape. Just like Aaron did before he died."

"You think Mark's been taking payoffs?"

"A few days ago he bought a boat. Not just a boat. A yacht."

"He's always been crazy about boats."

"This one cost half a million," whispered Abby. "He paid in cash."

ELEVEN

IT WAS six that evening when Abby walked into the medical records department in the hospital basement. As she'd expected, the room was nearly deserted for the dinner hour. Heart pounding, she approached the clerk's desk and smiled. "I'm compiling statistics for Dr. Wettig on transplant morbidity. Could you pull up a list on your computer of the names and record numbers of all heart transplants done here in the last two years?"

"For a records search like that, we need a request form from the department."

"They've all gone home by now. Could I get that form to you some other time? I'd like to have this ready for him by the morning. You know how the General is."

The clerk laughed. Yes, she knew exactly how the General was. She sat down at her keyboard and called up the "Search" screen. Under "Diagnosis," she typed in "Cardiac Transplant," then the years to be searched. She hit the ENTER button, and one by one a list of names and record numbers began to appear. The clerk hit PRINT. Seconds later the list rolled out of the printer. She handed the page to Abby.

There were twenty-nine names. The last one was Nina Voss.

"Could I have the first ten charts?" Abby asked. "I might as well start working on this tonight."

The clerk vanished into the file room. A moment later she re-emerged, hugging a bulky armful of files. Abby lugged the charts to a desk. She opened the first folder to the patient-information sheet and copied all the details down onto a yellow legal pad. She also copied the date and time of transplant and the names of the doctors in attendance: Aaron Levi, Bill Archer, Frank Zwick, Rajiv Mohandas. And Mark. As expected, there was no donor information on the chart. That was always kept separate from recipient records. However, among the nurses' notes she found written, "0830—harvest reported complete. Donor heart now en route from Norwalk, Connecticut. Patient wheeled to OR for prep."

Abby wrote, "0830. Harvest in Norwalk, Conn."

She worked straight through the evening, didn't allow herself even a break, except to call Mark to tell him she'd be home late. At ten fifteen she arrived home to find that Mark was already in bed and the lights were out. She was relieved that she would not have to answer any questions. She undressed in the dark and climbed into bed.

At seven forty the next morning she was back in medical records. She requested five more charts, quickly took notes, gave the charts back to the clerk, and left.

She spent the day in the medical library, looking up more articles for Dr. Wettig. It wasn't until late afternoon that she returned to medical records. She requested ten more charts.

VIVIAN finished off the last slice of pizza. It was her fourth slice, and where her elfin body put it all was a mystery to Abby. Vivian wiped her hands on a napkin. "So Mark still doesn't know?"

"I haven't said a thing to him. I guess I'm afraid to."

"You're not afraid of *Mark,* are you?"

"I'm afraid he'll deny everything. And I'll have no way of knowing if he's telling the truth." Wearily Abby rubbed her face. "I've looked at twenty-five files so far. Mark's name is in every one."

"So is Archer's. And Aaron's. That doesn't tell us anything. What else have you learned?"

"All the records look pretty much the same. The donors are where things get interesting." Abby leaned toward Vivian. "Not all of the charts mention which city the donor organ comes from. But a number of them do. And there seems to be a cluster. Four of them came from Burlington, Vermont. I find it interesting that a town like Burlington ends up with so many brain-dead people."

Vivian's gaze met hers in a stunned look. "We were hypothesizing donors who are simply kept out of the registry system. But that doesn't explain a cluster of donors in one town. Unless . . ."

"Unless donors are being generated."

They fell silent.

"Can I have the dates on those four Burlington harvests?" said Vivian. "I'm going to check them against the Burlington obituaries. Maybe we can identify the names of the four donors and find out how they ended up brain-dead."

"Not all obits list the cause of death."

"Then we may have to go to the death certificates. Which means a trip to Burlington. A place I've been dying to visit." Vivian's tone of voice was almost breezy. That warrior-woman bravado act again. But she couldn't hide the note of apprehension.

"Are you sure you want to do this?" said Abby.

"If we don't, then Victor Voss wins. And the losers are going to be people like Josh O'Day." She paused, then asked quietly, "Is this what *you* want to do, Abby?"

Abby dropped her head in her hands. "I don't think I have a choice any longer."

AT SEVEN thirty the next morning Abby pulled into her parking space at Bayside. She sat in her car for a moment, eyeing the steady drizzle. Only mid-October, she thought, and already this dreary foretaste of winter. She had not slept well last night. Glancing in the rearview mirror, she scarcely recognized the haggard stranger staring back at her. A flash of maroon in the mirror caught her eye. She snapped her head around just in time to see a van retreating behind the next aisle of cars. She waited for another glimpse of it. It didn't reappear.

Quickly she stepped out and began to walk toward the hospital. The weight of her briefcase felt like an anchor. Her heart was slamming against her chest. It didn't calm down until she was inside the building. She took the stairwell to medical records. This would be her final visit; she was down to the last four names on the list.

She lay the request slip on the counter and said, "Excuse me, may I have these charts, please?"

The clerk, usually friendly, seemed to freeze. "I'm sorry, Dr. Di-Matteo. I've been told not to release any more files to you. Dr. Wettig said he never authorized any chart search. He said if you came in, we're to refer you to his office immediately."

Abby felt the blood drain from her face. It seemed to her the room had suddenly fallen silent. She turned and saw that three other doctors in the room were all watching her. She walked out.

Her first impulse was to leave the building, to avoid the inevitable confrontation with Wettig and just drive away. She wondered how long it would take to reach Florida and the beach and palm trees. She'd never been to Florida. She'd never done so many things. She could do them all now if she'd just walk out of this hospital, climb in her car, and say, "Forget it. You win." But she didn't. She stepped into the basement elevator and punched 2.

At the administrative floor she got out. The residency office was around the corner, past Jeremiah Parr's suite. As she walked past Parr's secretary, she saw the woman reach sharply for the phone.

Abby turned the corner and walked into the residency office. There were two men standing by the secretary's desk, neither of whom Abby had ever seen before. The secretary looked up at Abby and blurted, "Oh! Dr. DiMatteo—"

"I need to see Dr. Wettig," said Abby.

The two men turned to look at her. In the next instant Abby was startled by a flash of light—a camera flashbulb.

"What are you doing?" she demanded.

"Doctor, would you care to comment on the death of Mary Allen?" one of the men said.

"What?"

"She was your patient, wasn't she? Is it true you're an advocate of euthanasia?"

Abby stepped back. "Get away from me. I'm not talking to you." She turned to flee the office and almost collided with Jeremiah Parr, who'd just walked in the door.

"I want you reporters out of my hospital *now*," Parr snapped. Then he turned to Abby. "Doctor, come with me."

Abby followed Parr out of the room, down the hall, and into his office. He shut the door and turned to look at her. "The Boston *Herald* called half an hour ago," he said. "Then the *Globe*, followed by about half a dozen other newspapers. It hasn't let up since."

Abby stared at Parr. "Did Brenda Hainey tell them?"

"I don't think it was her. They seemed to know about the morphine. And the vial in your locker. Things she didn't know."

There was a sharp rap on the door, and Dr. Wettig walked in. "What the hell do I do about those reporters?" he said.

"You'll have to prepare a statement, General. Until then, no one talks to anyone."

Wettig gave a curt nod. Then his gaze focused on Abby. "May I see your briefcase, Dr. DiMatteo?"

"Why?"

"You know why. You had no authority to search those patient records. I'm ordering you to turn over all the notes you took."

Wordlessly she handed it to him. She watched him open it and remove her notes. She should have stashed them before coming up here. But she'd been too focused on what she would say, how she would explain herself to Wettig.

He handed the briefcase back to her and regarded her for a moment in silence. Then he shook his head. "You would have made a fine surgeon, DiMatteo. But I think you need help. I'm recommending you seek psychiatric evaluation. And I'm releasing you from the residency program, effective today." She heard a note of genuine regret in his voice when he added, "I'm sorry."

DETECTIVE Lundquist had interviewed Abby for two hours now, asking his questions while pacing around the cramped interview room. If it was a tactic designed to make her feel threatened, then it was working. Abby had been afraid of him from the moment he'd walked into the room. *She* was the one who'd walked into the police station of her own volition and had asked to speak to Detective Katzka. Instead they had sent in Lundquist, and he had questioned her with the aggression of an arresting officer.

The door opened, and at last Bernard Katzka walked into the room, his impassive face offering no reassurance whatsoever.

"Am I under arrest?" she asked.

"Not at the moment. This is only a preliminary investigation."

"Look, I walked in here on my own because I *wanted* to talk to you. I've willingly answered all this man's questions. If you're putting me under arrest, then I'll call an attorney. But I want to make it clear that I've done nothing wrong."

Lundquist and Katzka exchanged glances. Then Lundquist said, "She's all yours, Slug," and moved off into a corner.

Katzka sat down at the table.

"I suppose you're going to ask the same questions," said Abby.

"I've already heard most of your answers." He nodded at the mirror in the far wall. It was a viewing window, she realized. He'd been listening to the session with Lundquist. She wondered how many others were watching her behind that glass. It made her feel exposed. She shifted her chair and gazed directly at Katzka. "So what are *you* going to ask me?"

"You said you think someone is setting you up. Someone administered a morphine overdose to your patient, Mrs. Allen. Then he— or she—planted a vial of morphine in your locker. And now you're being followed around town by a maroon van. And you think these incidents were all engineered by Victor Voss?"

"That's what I thought. But maybe it's someone else."

Katzka sat back and regarded her. "Tell us about the heart transplants again, Doctor."

She sighed. She'd gone over this already with Lundquist. Judging by his disinterested response, it had been a waste of time. Now she was expected to repeat the story, and it would be a waste of more time. "There's a computerized registry that decides which patient gets a heart first. Our regional system is run by New England Organ Bank. They're absolutely democratic. You're prioritized according to your condition, not your wealth. Now, let's say you're rich and you're worried you'll die before they find you a heart. Obviously, you'll be tempted to go outside the system to get an organ."

"Can it be done?"

"It would have to involve a shadow matchmaking service. A way to keep potential donors out of the system and funnel their hearts directly to wealthy patients. Or there's even a worse possibility—they're generating new donors."

"You mean *killing* people?" It was Lundquist who spoke. "Then where are all the dead bodies? The missing persons reports?"

"I didn't say that's what's happening. I'm just telling you how it could be done." She paused. "I think Aaron Levi was part of it. That might explain his three million dollars."

Katzka's expression had scarcely changed. His impassivity was beginning to irritate Abby.

She said, "Don't you see? It makes sense why those lawsuits against me were dropped. They probably hoped I'd stop asking questions. But I didn't stop. And now they have to discredit me because I can blow the whistle on them. I could ruin everything."

"This is very creative," said Lundquist, and laughed.

Katzka lifted his hand in a terse gesture to Lundquist to shut up. "Dr. DiMatteo," he said, "I'll be honest with you. This is not coming across as a likely scenario."

"It's the only one I can think of."

"Can I offer one?" said Lundquist, his gaze on Abby. "Your patient Mary Allen was suffering. So you slipped her an extra dose of morphine. Problem is, one of the nurses saw you do it and sent an anonymous note to Mary Allen's niece. Suddenly you're in trouble, looking at charges of homicide. So you cobble together a conspiracy theory. One that can't be proved—or disproved. Doesn't that make more sense, Doctor?"

"But that's not what happened." She leaned forward, hands clenched. "I did not kill my patient."

Lundquist looked at Katzka. "She's not a very good liar, is she?" he said, and walked out of the room.

For a moment neither Abby nor Katzka spoke.

Then she asked, "Am I under arrest now?"

"No. You can leave. Dr. Hodell's been waiting for you." He rose to his feet and opened the door. "I'll be talking to you again, Doctor."

She walked down the hall and into the waiting area. Mark was standing there. "Abby?" he said softly.

She let him take her into his arms, but her body registered his touch with a strange sense of detachment. As if from a distance, she heard him say, "Let's go home."

Through the security partition Bernard Katzka watched the couple walk toward the door, observing how closely Hodell held the woman. It was not something a cop saw every day. Affection. Love. Love was something he himself had not felt in a long time. And at that moment he envied Mark Hodell.

"MORE flowers, Mrs. Voss. They were just delivered. Do you want them in here? Or shall I put them in the parlor?"

"Bring them in here, please." Sitting by the window, Nina watched the maid carry the vase into her bedroom and set it down on a night table. The fragrance of sage and phlox and late summer wildflowers wafted toward her. "Put them here, next to me."

"Of course, ma'am." The maid moved the vase to the small tea table beside Nina's chair. She had to make room for it by taking away a vase of Oriental lilies. "They're not your usual flowers, are they?" the maid said, her tone not entirely approving.

"No." Nina smiled at the unruly arrangement. She picked out a daisy and breathed in its pungent scent.

"Wouldn't you rather have the lilies next to you?" the maid asked. "They smell so lovely."

"They were giving me a headache. Who are these flowers from?"

The maid opened the tiny envelope taped to the vase. " 'To Mrs. Voss. A speedy recovery. Joy.' That's all it says."

Nina frowned. "I don't know anyone named Joy."

"Maybe it'll come to you. Would you like to go back to bed now?"

"I've had enough of lying in bed. I'd like to sit here for a while. By myself."

The maid hesitated. Then with a nod she left the room.

At last, thought Nina. At last I'm alone.

For the past week, ever since she'd left the hospital, she had been surrounded by people: private-duty nurses and doctors and maids. And Victor. Most of all, Victor, hovering at her bedside. Protecting her, insulating her. Imprisoning her in this house.

All because he loved her. Perhaps he loved her too much.

She heard his footsteps and looked up as he came into the room.

"Louisa told me you were still up," he said. "You should be taking your nap."

"I'm fine, Victor."

"You don't look strong enough yet."

She met his gaze. Firmly she said, "I'm going to sit here, Victor. I want to look out the window."

There was a silence. Then he said, "What are these?" pointing to the vase of flowers by her chair.

"They just arrived. Someone named Joy sent them."

"You can pick these kinds of flowers at the roadside." He lifted the vase and carried it to a table in a far corner. Then he brought the Oriental lilies back and set them beside her. "At least these aren't weeds," he said, and left the room.

Nina stared at the lilies. Exotic and perfect. Their cloying fragrance sickened her. She blinked away an unexpected film of tears and focused on the tiny card lying on the table—the one that had come with the wildflowers. Joy. Who was Joy?

As she took the card, she noticed that something was written on the back. "Some doctors always tell the truth," it said. And beneath that was a phone number.

ABBY was home alone when Nina Voss called at five p.m.

"Is this Dr. DiMatteo?" said a soft voice. "The one who always tells the truth?"

"Mrs. Voss? You got my flowers."

"Yes, thank you. And I got your rather odd note."

"I've tried every other way to contact you. Letters. Phone calls."

There was a pause, then a quiet "I see."

"I have to see you, Mrs. Voss. And it has to be without your husband's knowledge. Can you arrange it?"

"First tell me why."

Abby hesitated. "It's about your heart. The one you got at Bayside. No one seems to know where it came from."

The silence that followed was broken only by the sound of Nina's breathing, rapid and irregular.

"Mrs. Voss?"

"I have to go."

"Wait. When can I see you?"

"Tomorrow."

"How? Where?"

There was another pause. Just before the line went dead, Nina said, "I'll find a way."

THE rain beat a relentless tattoo on the striped awning over Abby's head. For forty minutes now she had been standing in front of Cellucci's Grocery, shivering. She flinched as a Progresso Foods truck suddenly roared away from the curb, spewing exhaust. When she looked up again, she saw that a black limousine had stopped across the street. The driver's window rolled down a few inches and a man called, "Dr. DiMatteo? Come into the car."

She hesitated, then crossed the street and opened the rear door.

In the gloom of the car Nina Voss looked pale and shrunken. Her skin was a powdery white. "Please get in, Doctor," she said.

Abby slid in beside her and shut the door. The limousine pulled away from the curb and glided noiselessly into the stream of traffic.

Nina was so completely bundled up in a black coat and scarf that her face seemed to be bodyless in the car's shadows. This was not the picture of a recovering transplant patient. Abby remembered Josh O'Day's ruddy face, his liveliness, his laughter. Nina Voss looked like a talking corpse.

"I'm sorry we're late," said Nina. "We had a problem leaving."

"Does your husband know you're meeting me?"

"No," Nina said. "Now, I need to know. What has Victor done?"

"I was hoping you could tell me."

"You said it had to do with my heart." Nina touched her hand to her chest. "What do you know about it?"

"Your heart didn't come through normal channels. Almost all transplant organs are matched to recipients through a central registry. Yours wasn't. According to the organ bank, you never got a heart."

The corpselike face stared at her in silence.

"I think your husband bought it," said Abby.

"People can't just buy hearts."

"With enough money, people can buy anything."

Nina said nothing. By her silence she admitted her acceptance of that fundamental truth: Money can buy anything.

The limousine turned onto Embankment Road and drove west along the Charles River. Its surface was stippled by falling rain.

Finally Nina asked, "How did you learn about this?"

"Lately, I seem to have a lot of free time on my hands. It's amazing what you can accomplish when you find yourself suddenly unemployed. And the more I learn, Mrs. Voss, the more scared I get."

"Why come to me about this? Why not go to the authorities?"

"Haven't you heard? I have a new nickname these days: Dr. Hemlock. They're saying I kill my patients with kindness." Wearily Abby gazed out at the river. "I have no job, no credibility, and no proof."

"What *do* you have?"

Abby looked at her. "I know the truth." And she explained how Nina Voss got her heart on the night of the transplant.

Nina retreated into silence. She seemed to be shrinking away into the woolen coat.

"You weren't the first one," said Abby.

The white face stared back numbly. "There were others?"

"At least four. We're talking about four hearts, four dead people." Abby paused. "I have no proof," she said. "I can't get through to New England Organ Bank or anyone else. They all know I'm under investigation. That's why I came to you. That night we met in the ICU, I thought, There's a woman I'd want as a friend." She paused. "I need your help, Mrs. Voss."

For a long time Nina said nothing. At last she seemed to come to a decision. She released a deep breath and said, "I'm going to drop you off now. Would this corner be all right?"

"Mrs. Voss, your husband bought that heart. If he did it, so can others. We don't know who the donors are. We don't know—"

"*Here,*" Nina said to the driver.

The limousine pulled over to the curb. Abby didn't move. She sat for a moment, not speaking. The rain tapped on the roof.

"Please get out," whispered Nina.

"I thought I could trust you. I thought . . ." Slowly Abby shook her head. "Good-bye, Mrs. Voss." She climbed out of the limousine and shut the door. As she watched the car glide into the dusk, she thought, I'll never see her again.

Then, shoulders slumped, she turned and walked away.

NINA Voss wrapped herself tighter in her cocoon of black wool and stared at the rain streaking across her window. She thought of what she would say to Victor. And what she would not, could not say. This is what has become of our love, she thought. Secrets upon secrets. And he is keeping the most terrible secret of all.

She lowered her head and began to cry—for Victor and for what had happened to their marriage. She wept for herself as well, because she knew what had to be done and she was afraid.

The rain streamed like tears down the window. And the limousine carried her home, to Victor.

TWELVE

SHU-SHU needed a bath. The older boys had been saying this for days, had even threatened to toss Shu-Shu into the sea if Aleksei did not give her a good cleaning. But Aleksei liked the way the stuffed dog smelled. She had not been washed, ever, and each scent she wore was like a different memory. The smell of his babyhood. The smell of being caressed and sung to and loved.

Hugging Shu-Shu, Aleksei burrowed deeper under his blanket. I'll never let them give you a bath, he thought.

Anyway, there weren't so many of *them* left to torment him. Five days earlier a boat had appeared through the fog and had drifted alongside them. While all the boys watched, Nadiya and Gregor had walked back and forth, calling out name after name: "Nikolai Alekseyenko!" "Pavel Prebrazhensky!" There were whoops of triumph as each name was called. *Yes! I have been chosen!*

Later the ones not chosen, the ones left behind, remained huddled at the rail, watching in silence as the launch carried the chosen boys to the other ship.

"Where do they go?" Aleksei asked.

"To families in the West," Nadiya answered. "Now come away from the rail. It's getting cold up here."

The boys didn't move. After a while Nadiya didn't seem to care if they stayed up on deck or not, and she left to go below.

"Families in the West must be stupid," said Yakov.

Aleksei turned to look at him. Yakov was staring fiercely out to sea, his chin jutting out. He clutched the rail with his one hand, his gaze directed at the other ship as it glided back into the fog. Then he walked away.

Over the next few days Aleksei scarcely saw him.

Tonight, as usual, Yakov had disappeared right after supper. He was probably in his stupid Wonderland, hiding out in that crate, Aleksei thought. He pulled the blanket over his head and fell asleep, curled up in his bunk with dirty Shu-Shu cradled against his face.

A HAND shook him. A voice called softly in the night, "Aleksei."

"Mommy," he said.

"Aleksei, it's time to wake up. I have a surprise for you."

Slowly he drifted up through layers of sleep, surfacing into darkness. He recognized Nadiya's scent.

"It's time to go," she whispered. "I'll take you to her, Aleksei. Out of all the boys, you've been chosen. You're very lucky. Now come. But be quiet."

Aleksei sat up. Nadiya reached up and helped him off the bunk.

"Shu-Shu," he said.

Nadiya put the dog in his arms. "Of course you can bring your Shu-Shu." She took his hand. She had never held his hand before. The sudden rush of happiness shook him fully awake. He was holding her hand, and they were walking together, to meet his mother. Somehow he remembered: This is how it feels to hold your mother's hand.

They left the cabin and walked down a dimly lit corridor. He was stumbling through a joyous daze, not paying attention to where they were going, because Nadiya was taking care of everything. They pushed through a door.

Into Wonderland. The steel walkway stretched before them. Beyond it stood the blue door. Aleksei stopped.

"What is it?" asked Nadiya.

"I don't want to go in there. There are people living there."

"You have to, Aleksei. Don't be difficult." Nadiya gripped his hand more firmly. "This is where you must go."

"Why?"

Suddenly she seemed to understand that a different tactic was called for. She crouched down and took him firmly by the shoulders. "Do you want to ruin everything? Your mother expects an obedient little boy, and now you are being very disagreeable."

His lips trembled. He tried hard not to cry, because he knew how much adults hated children's tears. But the tears were starting to fall anyway, and now he probably had ruined everything.

"Nothing is settled yet," said Nadiya. "She can still choose another boy. Is that what you want?"

Aleksei sobbed, "No."

Nadiya straightened. "Then come. Hurry, or we'll be late." She put her arm around him.

He began to walk, only because she was there beside him, hugging him close. The way he was hugging Shu-Shu close. As long as they held each other, the three of them, nothing bad would happen.

Nadiya knocked at the blue door. It swung open.

YAKOV heard them on the walkway above. Aleksei's whining. Nadiya's impatient coaxing. He crawled to the edge of the crate and cautiously peered up at them. They were crossing to the blue door now. A moment later they vanished through it.

Why does Aleksei get to go in there and not me?

Yakov slipped out of the crate and up the stairs to the blue door. He tried to open it, but as always, it was locked. Defeated, he went back to his hiding place. He waited for them to come back out, but it was taking a long time. What were they doing in there? After a while he became sleepy and dozed off.

Sometime later he was awakened by a rumbling sound. At first he thought it was the ship's engines. Then he realized the sound was growing louder and that it was coming from the deck above.

It was a helicopter.

GREGOR twisted the ties and set the plastic bag in the cooler. He handed the cooler to Nadiya. "Take it. It needs ice. Go on, do it."

She seemed to recoil in horror. Then, breathing deeply, she took the cooler, set it on the countertop, and began scooping ice into it. He noticed that her legs were not quite steady. The first time around was always a shock to the system. Even Gregor had had his queasy moments. Nadiya would get over it.

Gregor turned to the operating table. The anesthetist had already zipped up the shroud and was now gathering up the bloodied drapes. The surgeon was slumped against the counter. Gregor regarded him with distaste. There was something disgusting about a doctor who let himself get so grotesquely fat. The surgeon did not look well tonight. His hands had trembled through the entire procedure.

"My head hurts," the surgeon groaned.

"You've been drinking too much. Probably got yourself a hangover." Gregor grasped one end of the shroud. Together he and the anesthetist lifted their burden and slid it onto the gurney. Next Gregor picked up the pile of dirty clothes and the stuffed dog, which was lying on the floor, its ratty fur soaked with blood, and put it all on top of the shroud. They wheeled the gurney to the disposal chute, where they deposited everything. Then Gregor stripped off his gloves and went to the sink to scrub his hands.

Suddenly there was a loud crash, the clatter of falling metal instruments. Gregor turned.

The surgeon was lying on the floor, his face bright red, his limbs jerking. Nadiya and the anesthetist stood frozen in horror.

"What's wrong with him?" demanded Gregor.

"I don't know!" said the anesthetist. He knelt beside the convulsing man and made a few helpless attempts to revive him, but moments later the surgeon was dead.

"What do we do now?" said the anesthetist.

"We need another surgeon," Gregor said. "We'll have to head into port sooner than planned." He suddenly glanced upward. So did Nadiya and the anesthetist. They all heard it now: the *whup-whup* of the helicopter. Gregor looked at the cooler. "Is it ready?"

"I packed it with ice," said Nadiya.

"Go, then. Bring it up to them." Gregor looked back down at the corpse. He gave it a kick of disgust. "We'll take care of the whale."

FROM his hiding place under the bridge stairway, Yakov watched the helicopter descend from the darkness and land. Its door swung open as a figure appeared at the edge of the deck. It was Nadiya. She crossed the deck, her body bent forward. She leaned inside the helicopter door and handed something to the pilot. A box. Then she backed out and retreated to the edge of the deck again.

A moment later the helicopter lifted off. Yakov eased around the stairway to watch as the craft rose, then thundered away, vanishing into the night.

A hand grabbed Yakov's arm. He gave a cry as he was yanked backward and spun around.

"What the hell are you doing up here?" said Gregor.

"Nothing!"

"What did you see?"

Yakov only stared at him, too terrified to answer.

Nadiya had heard their voices. Now she crossed the deck toward them. "What is it?"

"The boy's been watching again. I thought you locked the cabin."

"I did. He must have slipped out earlier."

"I've had enough of this one anyway." Gregor gave Yakov's arm a jerk, pulling him toward the stairway hatch. "He can't go back with the others." He turned to open the hatch.

Yakov kicked him in the back of the knee. Gregor shrieked, releasing his grip. Yakov ran. He heard Nadiya's shouts, heard footsteps pounding after him. Too late he realized he had run straight onto the landing deck.

There was a loud clank, and the deck lights flared on. Yakov was trapped in the very center of their brilliance. Shielding his eyes, he stumbled blindly away from the sounds of pursuit. But they were moving in now, grabbing his shirt. He flailed.

Someone slapped him across the face. The blow sent Yakov sprawling. He tried to crawl away but was yanked up by the hair. Gregor shoved him forward across the deck, toward the stairwell hatch. Yakov kept stumbling. He couldn't see where they were going as they went down some steps and moved along a corridor. A door swung open, and Yakov was tossed over the threshold.

"You can rot in there for a while," said Gregor, and slammed the door shut.

Yakov heard the latch close, heard footsteps fade away. He was alone in the darkness. He drew his knees to his chest and lay hugging himself. A strange trembling seized his body. He could hear his own teeth chattering, not from the cold, but from some quaking deep in his soul. Whimpering, he put his thumb in his mouth and began to suck.

THIRTEEN

FOR Abby, mornings were the worst. She would awaken feeling that first sleepy flush of anticipation for the day ahead. Then suddenly she'd remember, I have nowhere to go. She would lie in bed, listening to Mark getting dressed, and she would feel so engulfed by depression she could not say a word to him. They'd scarcely spoken in days. This is how loves dies, thought Abby, hearing him walk out the front door. Not with angry words, but with silence.

This morning she fled the house. She walked blocks and blocks, not really caring where she went. The weather had turned cold, and by the time she finally came to a halt, on the Harvard University Common, her ears were aching. She realized it was well past lunchtime. She didn't know where to go next. Everyone else seemed to have a destination. But not her.

She and Vivian had run out of leads. Yesterday Vivian had flown to Burlington. When she'd called Abby last night, it had been with bad news: Tim Nicholls's practice had closed down, and no one knew where he was. Dead end. Also, Wilcox Memorial had no records of any harvests on those four dates. Another dead end. Finally, Vivian had checked with the local police and had found no records of missing persons or unidentified bodies. Final dead end.

She walked home, thinking, They've covered their tracks. We'll never beat them.

As soon as she stepped back in her front door, she saw a message on the answering machine. It was from Vivian, asking Abby to call back. She'd left a Burlington number. Abby dialed but got no answer. As she hung up, she glanced out the window. Parked at the far end of the street was a maroon van.

She grabbed the phone and dialed Katzka.

"Detective Katzka," he said in his usual flat, businesslike voice.

"This is Abby DiMatteo. The van that was following me—it's parked right outside my house."

There was a pause. "You live on Brewster Street, right?"

"Yes. Please send someone right away."

"Just sit tight and keep the doors locked. Got that?"

"Okay." She let out a nervous breath. "Okay."

Fifteen minutes later a familiar green Volvo pulled up across the street from the van. She hadn't expected Katzka himself to show up, but there he was, stepping out of his car. At her first glimpse of him she felt an overwhelming sense of relief. He'll know what to do, she thought. Katzka was clever enough to deal with anything.

He crossed the street and slowly approached the van.

Abby pressed closer to the window, her heart suddenly pounding. As Katzka shifted slightly toward her, she noticed that he'd drawn his gun. She hadn't even seen him reach for it.

He edged forward and glanced in the window. Apparently he saw nothing suspicious. He circled around to the rear of the van and peered through the back. Then he holstered his gun and looked up and down the street.

At a nearby house the front door suddenly swung open and a man in gray overalls stormed down the steps, yelling and waving. Katzka responded with his trademark unflappability and produced his badge. The other man took out his wallet and showed his ID.

For a while the two men stood talking. At last the man in the overalls went back inside. Katzka walked toward Abby's.

She let him in the front door. "What happened?"

"Nothing."

"Who's the driver? Why's he been following me?"

"He says he has no idea what you're talking about."

"I'm not blind! I've seen that van here before."

"The driver says he's never been here."

"Who is the driver anyway?"

Katzka pulled out his notebook. "John Doherty, Massachusetts resident. Licensed plumber. The van is registered to Back Bay Plumbing. And it's full of tools." He closed his notebook and regarded her with his usual detachment.

"I was so sure it was the same one," she murmured.

"You still insist there was a van?"

"Yes, damn it!" she snapped. "There *was* a van!"

He reacted to her outburst with a slightly raised eyebrow. She forced herself to take a deep breath. A burst of temper was the last thing this man would respond to. He was all logic, all reason. Mr. Spock with a badge.

"I'll check Doherty's information. But I really do believe he's just a plumber." Katzka glanced toward her living room. The phone was ringing. "Aren't you going to answer it?"

"Please don't leave. Not yet. I have a few things to tell you."

He had already reached for the doorknob. Now he paused, watching as Abby picked up the phone. "Hello?" she said.

A woman's voice responded softly, "Dr. DiMatteo?"

Abby's gaze shot to Katzka's. He seemed to understand just from her glance that this call was important. "Mrs. Voss?" said Abby.

"I've learned something," said Nina. "I don't know what it means. If it means anything at all."

Katzka moved to Abby's side. He bent his head toward the receiver to listen in.

"What did you find out?" said Abby.

"I made some calls. To the bank and to our accountant. On September twenty-third Victor transferred funds to a company called the Amity Corporation. In Boston."

September 23, thought Abby. One day before Nina Voss's transplant. "What do you know about Amity?" asked Abby.

"Nothing. Victor's never mentioned the name." There was a silence. Abby heard voices in the background. Then Nina's voice came back on. Tenser. Softer. "I have to get off the phone."

"How large was the transaction?"

For a moment there was no reply. Abby thought perhaps Nina had already hung up. Then she heard the whispered answer.

"Five million," said Nina. "He transferred five million dollars."

"THIS has to be the wrong place," said Abby.

She and Katzka were in Roxbury, parked on a run-down street of barred storefronts and businesses on the verge of collapse. The Amity building was a four-story brownstone. Over the entrance hung the sign AMITY MEDICAL SUPPLIES, SALES AND SERVICE.

Abby gazed across the street at the shabby display window full of crutches and canes, oxygen tanks, and bedside commodes, and said, "Why would he transfer five million dollars to *this* business?"

Katzka opened his door. "I'll see what I can find out. Look around. Ask a few questions."

"I'll go in with you."

"No. You stay in the car." He started to step out, but she pulled him back. He regarded her in that quiet way of his.

"Look," she said, "it's my life they've messed up. This could be my one chance to fight back."

"Then let's not screw it up, okay? Someone in there could recognize you. Do you want to risk that?"

She sank back. Katzka was right. She sat shaking her head, angry about her own impotence. Angry at Katzka for having pointed it out.

She watched him cross the street and walk into the shabby entrance. Five minutes passed. Then ten.

Katzka, Katzka, what are you doing in there?

Twenty minutes went by. It was after five now, and the anemic sunshine had already faded to a gloomy dusk. Rush hour. The traf-

fic was beginning to thicken even on this street. Through the flow
of cars she caught only intermittent glimpses of the front entrance.
Then suddenly there was a gap in the traffic, and she saw a man
emerge from the side door of the Amity building. Abby felt her
heart kick into a gallop. She recognized that face. The grotesquely
heavy brow. The hawklike nose. It was Dr. Mapes, the courier
who'd delivered Nina Voss's donor heart to the operating room.

Mapes began walking. Halfway up the street, he stopped at a
blue Trans Am parked at the curb. He took out a set of car keys.

Abby looked back at the Amity building, hoping, praying for
Katzka to appear. She looked back at the Trans Am. Mapes had
climbed inside now and was starting the engine. Easing slightly
away from the curb, he waited for a break in the traffic.

Abby cast a frantic glance at the ignition and saw Katzka's keys
dangling there. This could be her only chance. She scrambled into
the driver's seat and started the car. She lurched into traffic, elicit-
ing a screech of tires and an angry honk from a car behind her.

A block ahead, Mapes glided through the intersection just as the
light turned red. Abby squealed to a stop. There were four cars between her and the intersection and no way to get around them. She
sat counting the seconds. The Trans Am was barely in view now,
just a glint of blue in a river of cars. What the hell was wrong with
this light?

At last it turned green, but still no one was moving. Abby leaned
on her horn, releasing a deafening blast. The cars ahead of her finally began to move. She stepped on the accelerator, then let up on
it. Someone was pounding at the side of her car.

Glancing right, she saw Katzka running alongside the passenger
door. She braked.

He yanked open the door. "What are you doing?"

"Get in."

"No. First you pull over—"

"Get the hell in!"

He blinked in surprise. And got in.

At once she goosed the accelerator. Two blocks ahead a flash of
blue streaked rightward. The Trans Am was turning onto Cottage

Street. If she didn't stay right on his tail, she could lose him. She swerved left across a double line, raced past three cars in a row, and screeched back into her lane just in time. She heard Katzka snap on his seat belt as they turned onto Cottage.

"Are you going to tell me?" he said.

"The guy in the blue car came out of the Amity building."

"Who is he?"

"The organ courier. He said his name was Mapes."

The Trans Am looped around the traffic circle, then cut away east. "He's heading for the expressway," said Katzka.

Abby entered the circle and peeled off after the Trans Am. Her heart ramming her chest, she merged into traffic and spotted Mapes way ahead on the expressway, switching to the left lane.

She tried to make the same lane change, only to find a truck muscling in, refusing to yield. Abby signaled, nudged closer to his lane. The truck simply tightened the gap. This had turned into a dangerous game of chicken now, but Abby was too pumped up on adrenaline to be afraid. She floored the accelerator and shot left, right in front of the truck.

"What the hell!" yelled Katzka. "Are you trying to get us killed?"

"I don't care. I want this guy."

Up ahead, the Trans Am had switched lanes again. It peeled to the right, onto the turnoff for the Callahan Tunnel.

"Damn," said Abby, cutting right as well. She shot across two lanes, and they entered the cavelike gloom of the tunnel. Graffiti whipped past. Concrete walls echoed back the *whoosh-whoosh* of cars slicing the air. When they reemerged into the gray dusk, the Trans Am left the expressway. Abby followed.

They were in East Boston now, the gateway to Logan International Airport. That must be where Mapes was headed.

She was surprised when, instead, he rattled across a railroad track and worked his way west into a maze of streets. Abby slowed down, gave him some space. Now her challenge was to avoid being noticed. They were heading along the wharves of Boston's Inner Harbor. Behind a chain-link fence, rows and rows of unused ship's containers were stacked three-deep, like giant Legos. And beyond the container yard was the industrial waterfront. The Trans Am turned left and drove into the container yard.

Abby parked beside the fence and peered through. She saw the Trans Am drive to the foot of the pier and stop.

Mapes got out of his car. He strode onto the dock, where a small freighter was moored, and gave a shout. After a moment a man appeared on deck and waved him aboard. Mapes climbed the gangplank and disappeared into the vessel.

"Why did he come here?" she said. "Why a boat?"

"Are you sure it's the same man?" said Katzka.

"If it isn't, then Mapes has a double working at Amity." She paused. "What did you find out about the place anyway?"

"You mean before I noticed someone stealing my car?" He shrugged. "It looked like what it's supposed to be—a medical-supply business. I told them I needed a hospital bed for my wife, and they demonstrated some of the latest models."

"How many people in the building?"

"I saw three. One guy was in the showroom, two on the second floor, handling phone orders."

"What about the upper two floors?"

"Warehouse space, I assume. Nothing about that building worth pursuing."

"You could subpoena their financial records. Find out where Voss's five million dollars went to."

"We have no basis on which to subpoena any records."

"How much evidence do you need? I *know* that was the courier. I know what these people are doing."

"Your testimony isn't going to sway any judge." His answer was honest—brutally so. "I'm sorry, Abby. But you know as well as I do that you have a whopping credibility problem."

She felt herself closing off against him, withdrawing in anger. "You're absolutely right," she shot back. "Who'd believe me? It's just the psychotic Dr. DiMatteo babbling nonsense again."

They said nothing for a while.

"It's not that I don't believe you," Katzka said finally.

She looked at him. "No one else does. Why would you?"

"Because Dr. Levi didn't hang himself," said Katzka.

Abby frowned at him. "I thought the autopsy was confirmatory."

"We got the toxicology results back just last week. They found traces of succinylcholine in his muscle tissue."

She stared at him. *Succinylcholine.* It was used every day by anesthesiologists to induce muscle relaxation during surgery. In the OR it was a vitally useful drug. Outside the OR its administration would cause the most horrible of deaths. Complete paralysis in a fully conscious subject. Though awake and aware, one would be unable to move or breathe. Like drowning in a sea of air.

Abby swallowed. For a moment she was too horrified to speak. She didn't dare even consider what Aaron's death must have been like. She looked through the fence toward the freighter.

"I want to know what's on that boat," she said. "I want to know why he's gone there." She reached for the door.

He stopped her. "Not yet. Let's wait." He glanced at the fading sky, then at the fog thickening over the water. "It'll be dark soon."

"How long has it been?"

"Only about an hour," said Katzka.

Abby hugged herself and shivered from the cold. "Interesting you should put it that way—*only* an hour. It feels like all night."

"It's a matter of perspective. I've put in a lot of time in surveillance. Early in my career."

Katzka as a fresh-faced rookie—she couldn't picture that. "What made you become a policeman?" she asked.

He shrugged. "It suited me. What made you become a doctor?"

She wiped a streak across the fogged windshield. "I don't quite know how to answer that."

"Is it such a difficult question?"

"The answer's complicated. If I had to give a reason, I guess it would be my brother. When he was ten, he had to be hospitalized. I spent a lot of time watching his doctors, seeing how they worked."

Katzka waited for her to elaborate. When she didn't, he said softly, "Your brother didn't live?"

She shook her head. "It was a long time ago." She was glad

Katzka remained silent; she did not feel up to answering more questions, up to reviving the images of Pete lying on a gurney in the ER, the blood splashed on his new tennis shoes. And then there had been the months of watching him lie in a coma, his flesh shrinking away, his limbs contracting into a permanent self-embrace.

She told Katzka none of this, yet she sensed he understood all he needed to know. Communication by empathy. It was not a talent she'd suspected he possessed. But then, there were so many things about Katzka that she found surprising. And fascinating.

He looked out and said, "I think it's dark enough."

They stepped out of the car and walked through the open gate into the container yard. The freighter loomed in the mist. They walked onto the pier, passing a tower of empty crates.

At the ship's gangplank they paused, listening to the slap of water on the hull, to the myriad groans of steel and cable. Katzka touched her arm, his contact warm and solid. "I'm going to look around on board." He stepped onto the gangplank. He'd taken only a few paces when a pair of headlights swung through the gate. It was a van, now rolling toward them across the container yard.

The headlights' beams caught Abby, trapped at the end of the pier. The van skidded to a halt. Shielding her eyes against the glare, Abby could see almost nothing, but she heard doors slam. Heard footsteps on the gravel as the men moved in to cut off escape.

Katzka materialized right beside her. "Okay, just back off," he said to the men. "We're not here to cause any trouble."

The two men, now silhouetted by the headlights, hesitated only a second. Then they began to advance. Abby didn't see what happened next. All she knew was that Katzka suddenly dropped to a crouch, that there was a crack of gunfire and the zing of something ricocheting off the concrete pier behind her.

She and Katzka lunged at the same time for the cover of the crates. He shoved her head to the ground, then returned fire. There was a tattoo of retreating footsteps, a terse exchange of voices. Then the sound of the van being started, the engine revving.

Abby raised her head. To her horror she saw that the van was rolling toward them, bearing down on the crates like a battering ram.

Katzka took aim and fired, shattering the windshield. The car bumped crazily onto the pier, swerved right, left, then kept coming. Abby registered a blinding glimpse of headlights. Then she flung herself off the pier and hurtled into pitch darkness.

The plunge into icy water was shocking. She sputtered back to the surface, choking on brine and spilled diesel. She heard men shouting on the pier above, then a thunderous splash. Water boiled up and washed over her head. She surfaced again, coughing. At the end of the pier the water seemed to be glowing a phosphorescent green. The van was sliding under the surface, its headlights casting two watery beams of light that faded to black.

Katzka. Where was Katzka?

She whirled around in the water, scanning the blackness, salt stinging her eyes. She heard a soft splash, and a head popped out of the brine a few feet away. Treading water, Katzka glanced in her direction and saw that she was holding her own. Then he looked up. There were two men, maybe three, their footsteps thudding up and down the pier. They were yelling to each other, but their shouts seemed garbled and unintelligible.

Not English, thought Abby, but couldn't identify the language.

Overhead, a light appeared, the beam skimming the water.

Katzka dove. So did Abby. She swam toward the blackness of open water. Again and again she came up, gasped in a breath, then dove again. When she resurfaced a fifth time, she was in darkness.

There were now two lights moving on the pier, the beams scanning the mist like a pair of relentless eyes. She heard the splash of water somewhere close, and she knew Katzka had surfaced nearby.

"Lost my gun," he panted. "Keep swimming. Next pier."

The night suddenly lit up with shocking brilliance. The freighter had turned on its deck lights, illuminating every detail on the pier. There was a man on the gangplank, his rifle aimed at the water.

"*Go,*" said Katzka.

Abby dove, clawing her way through liquid blackness. Deep water scared her. She came up for another breath but could not seem to get enough air, no matter how deeply she gasped.

"Abby, keep moving!" urged Katzka. "Just get to that next pier."

Abby glanced back toward the freighter. She saw that the search-lights were tracing an ever larger circle on the water, that the beam was flitting toward them. She slipped once again underwater.

By the time she and Katzka finally clambered out onto land, Abby could barely move. She crawled up rocks slippery with oil and seaweed. Crouching in the darkness, she vomited.

Katzka took her arm, steadied her. Weakly she raised her head.

"Better?" he whispered.

"I'm freezing."

"Then let's get someplace warm." He glanced at the pier looming above them. "I think we can make it up those pilings. Come on."

They scrambled up the rocks, slipping and sliding on the seaweed. Katzka made it onto the pier first, then hauled her up after him.

The searchlight sliced through the mist, trapping them in its glare. A bullet ricocheted off the concrete right behind Abby.

"Move!" said Katzka.

They sprinted away. The searchlight pursued them, the beam zigzagging through the darkness as they ran toward the container yard. Bullets spat up gravel all around them. Ahead loomed the con-tainers, stacked in a giant maze of shadows. They ducked down the nearest row, heard bullets pinging on metal. Then the gunfire ceased. Voices drew near. They seemed to come from two directions.

Katzka grabbed Abby's hand and pulled her deeper into the maze of containers. They ran to the end of the row, turned left, and kept running. Then both of them halted.

At the far end of the row a light winked.

They're in front of us!

Katzka veered right, turned down another row. Stacked contain-ers towered on both sides of them like the walls of a chasm. They heard voices and corrected course again. By now they'd made so many turns, Abby couldn't tell if they were moving in circles.

A light danced ahead of them. They halted, spun around to retrace their steps. And saw another flashlight beam moving toward them.

In panic Abby stumbled backward. Reaching out to steady her-self, she felt a cleft between two containers. The gap was barely wide enough to fit into.

Grabbing Katzka's arm, she squeezed into the opening, pulling him after her. Deeper and deeper she wormed, until she bumped up against the wall of an adjacent container. No way forward. They were trapped here, wedged into a space narrower than a coffin.

The crunch of footsteps on gravel approached.

Katzka's hand reached out to grip hers. Her heart was slamming against her chest. She heard voices now.

A light danced past the cleft opening. Two men were standing close by, conversing in puzzled tones in an unrecognizable tongue. They had only to shine their flashlights into the gap, and they'd spot their prey.

Abby closed her eyes, too terrified to look. She didn't want to be watching when that beam of light flooded into their hiding place. Her limbs were rigid with tension, her breath coming in short, shallow gasps. She heard a scrape of shoes across the ground. Then the footsteps moved away.

Abby and Katzka remained frozen, hands clasped together. Twice they heard their pursuers pass by; both times the men moved on.

There was a distant rumble, like the growl of thunder somewhere over the horizon. Then for a long time they heard nothing.

It was hours later when they finally emerged from their hiding place. They crept down the row of containers and stopped to scan the unnervingly silent waterfront. The mist had lifted, and overhead, stars twinkled faintly in a sky washed by city lights.

The next pier was dark. They saw no men, no lights, not even the glow of a porthole. The freighter was gone.

FOURTEEN

IT WAS nearly midnight when Detective Lundquist dropped off an exhausted Abby at her front door. She saw that Mark's car was not in the driveway. He's had an emergency at the hospital, she thought. It was not unusual for him to be called to Bayside late at night to tend a gunshot wound or a stabbing.

She went to the answering machine, hoping he'd left a voice memo on the recorder. All she found were two phone messages, both from Vivian. She was still in Burlington. It was too late now to call her back. She'd try in the morning.

Upstairs, she stripped off her wet clothes and stepped into the shower. As the hot water beat down, she stood with her eyes closed, thinking. Dreading what she'd have to say to Mark. The time had come to confront him. The uncertainty had become unbearable.

After she got out of the shower, she called in a page for Mark. She was startled when the phone rang almost immediately.

"Abby?" It wasn't Mark but Katzka. "Just checking to see if you're okay. I called a little while ago, and there was no answer."

"I was in the shower. I'm fine, Katzka. I'm just waiting for Mark to get home."

A pause. "You're by yourself?"

His note of concern brought a faint smile to her lips. Scratch that armor of his, and you'd find a real man under there after all.

"I locked all the doors and windows," she said. "Just like you told me." Over the phone she could hear the squeal of a police radio, and she could picture him standing on that dock, the emergency lights flashing on his face. "What's happening over there?"

"We're waiting for the divers. The equipment's already here."

"You really think the driver's still trapped in the van?"

"I'm afraid so." He sighed, and it was a sound of such profound weariness, she gave a murmur of concern.

"You should go home, Katzka. You need a hot shower and some chicken soup. That's my prescription."

He laughed. It was a surprising sound, one she'd never heard from him before. "Now, if I could just find a pharmacy to fill it." Someone spoke to him. Katzka turned to answer. Then he came back on the line. "I have to go. You sure you're okay there? You wouldn't rather stay in a hotel?"

"I'll be fine."

"Okay." There was a brief silence. He seemed reluctant to hang up. At last he said, "I'll check back with you in the morning."

"Thanks, Katzka." She hung up.

Again she paged Mark. Then she lay down on the bed and waited for him to call back. He didn't.

As the hours passed, she tried to calm her growing fears by tallying up all the possible reasons he wasn't answering. He could be asleep in one of the hospital on-call rooms. His beeper could be broken. He could be in the OR. Or he could be dead. Like Aaron Levi. Like Kunstler and Hennessy.

At three a.m. the phone finally rang. In an instant she was wide-awake and reaching for the receiver.

"Abby, it's me." Mark's voice crackled on the wire, as though he were calling from across a long distance.

"I've been paging you for hours," she said. "Where are you?"

"I'm in the car, heading to the hospital right now." He paused. "Abby, we need to talk. Things have . . . changed."

She said softly, "Between us, you mean?"

"No. No, this has nothing to do with you. It never did. You just got sucked into it, Abby. I tried to get them to back off, but now they've taken it too far."

"Who has?"

"The team."

She was afraid to ask the next question, but she had no choice now. "All of you? You're all involved?"

"Not anymore. Mohandas and I came to a decision tonight. That's where I've been—at his house. Abby, we decided it's time to end this. We're going to blow this thing wide open." He paused, his voice suddenly breaking. "I've been a coward. I'm sorry."

She closed her eyes. "You knew. All this time you knew."

"I knew some of it, not all. I didn't *want* to know. Then you started asking all those questions. And I couldn't hide from the truth any longer." He released a deep breath. "This is going to ruin me, Abby."

She still had her eyes closed. She could see him in the darkness of his car. Could imagine the misery on his face. And the courage. "Come home, Mark. Please"

"Not yet. I'm meeting Mohandas at the hospital. We're going to get those donor records."

"Do you know where they're kept?"

"We have an idea. With just two of us it could take us a while. If you helped us, we might get through them by morning."

She sat up in bed. "Where are you meeting Mohandas?"

"Medical records. He has the key." Mark hesitated. "Are you sure you want to be in on this, Abby?"

"I want to be wherever *you* are. We'll do this together. Okay?"

"Okay," he said softly. "See you soon."

Five minutes later Abby climbed into her car. The streets of West Cambridge were deserted. It was three fifteen a.m., but she could not remember feeling so awake. So alive.

At last we're going to beat them! she thought. And we're going to do it together. The way we should have done it from the start.

She crossed the River Street bridge and headed onto the ramp for the turnpike. There were few cars traveling at that hour, and she merged easily with sparse eastbound traffic.

Three and a half miles later the turnpike came to an end. As Abby curved onto the Southeast Expressway ramp, she suddenly became aware of a pair of headlights bearing down on her from behind. She accelerated, merging onto the southbound expressway.

The headlights pulled closer, high beams glaring off her rearview mirror. Suddenly the car swooped left into the next lane. It pulled up beside her until they were almost neck and neck.

She glanced sideways. Saw the other car's window roll down. Glimpsed the silhouette of a man in the passenger seat.

In panic she floored the accelerator. Too late she spotted the car stalled ahead of her. She slammed on the brakes. Her car spun and caromed off the concrete barrier. Suddenly the world tilted sideways. Then everything was tumbling over and over. She saw darkness and light. Darkness, light.

Darkness.

LIGHT.

And pain. Short, sharp explosions of it in her head. She tried to scream, but no sound came out. She tried to turn away from that piercing light, but her neck seemed trapped in a choke hold.

"Abby. Abby, hold still!" a voice commanded. "I have to look in your eyes."

She twisted, felt restraints chafing her wrists and ankles.

"Abby, it's Dr. Wettig. Look at me. Come on, open your eyes."

She opened her eyes, forced herself to keep them open, even though the beam of his penlight felt like a blade piercing her skull.

"Follow the light. That's good, Abby. Okay, both pupils are reactive." The penlight, mercifully, shut off. "I still want that CT."

Abby could see the shadow of Dr. Wettig's head against the diffuse brightness of the overhead lights. There were other heads on the periphery of her vision, and a white privacy curtain billowing in the distance. Pain pricked her left arm; she gave a jerk.

"Easy, Abby." It was a woman's voice. "I have to draw some blood. Hold very still. I have a lot of tubes to collect."

Now a third voice. "Dr. Wettig, X ray's ready for her."

Suddenly Abby knew exactly where she was. This was the Bayside emergency room. Something terrible must have happened.

"Mark," she said, and tried to sit up. "Where's Mark?"

"Abby, listen." Wettig's voice was low and impatient. "We're trying to reach Mark. I'm sure he'll be here soon. Right now you have to cooperate, or we can't help you. Do you understand?"

She stared up at his face, and she went very still. So many times before, as a resident, she had felt intimidated by his flat blue eyes. Now, strapped down and helpless under that gaze, she felt more than intimidated. She felt truly, deeply frightened.

She heard the curtain whisk open, felt a lurch as the gurney began to move. Now the ceiling was rushing past in a flashing succession of lights, and she knew they were taking her deeper into the hospital. Into the heart of the enemy. She didn't even try to struggle; the restraints were impossible to fight.

Think. I have to think.

They turned the corner, into X ray. They moved her onto the table and buckled straps across her chest and hips. "Hold still," the CT technician commanded.

As the scanner slid over her head, Abby closed her eyes. She tried to think, to remember the accident.

She remembered getting into her car, driving onto the turnpike. Then her memory tape had a gap. The accident itself was a complete blank. But the events leading up to it were coming into focus.

By the time the scan was completed, she'd managed to piece together enough memory fragments to understand what she had to do next. If she wanted to stay alive.

She was quietly cooperative as she was transferred back onto the gurney—so cooperative, in fact, that the CT technician left off the wrist and ankle restraints and buckled on only the chest strap. Then he wheeled her into the X-ray anteroom.

"The ER's coming to get you," he said. "If you need me, just call. I'm right in the next room."

When he had left, Abby reached up and unbuckled the chest strap. As she sat up, she felt the room whirl. She pressed her hands to her temples, and everything seemed to settle back into focus.

The IV. She ripped the tape off her arm, wincing at the sting, and pulled out the catheter, concentrating on stopping the flow of blood from her vein. She climbed off the gurney, took a lab coat off the door hook, and pulled it on over her hospital gown. She was struggling to think, to see through a white haze of pain as she moved to the door. Her legs felt sluggish as she pushed into the hallway.

It was empty. At the far end was an emergency exit. She struggled toward it, thinking, If I can just reach that door, I'll be safe.

She lunged against the emergency-exit bar and pushed out, into the night. Alarm bells started ringing. At once she began to run. She stumbled off the curb into the parking lot. She had no plan of escape; she knew only that she had to get away from Bayside.

There were voices behind her. A shout. Glancing back, she saw three security guards run out of the ER. She ducked behind a car—too late. They had spotted her.

She lurched to her feet and began to run again. Her pursuers' footsteps pounded closer, moving in from two directions at once. They surrounded her. One guard grabbed her left arm, another her right. She kicked, punched. Tried to bite them.

But now there were three of them, and they were dragging her back to the emergency room. Back to Dr. Wettig.

"They're going to kill me!" she screamed. "Let me go!"

"No one's going to hurt you, lady."

"You don't understand. *You don't understand!*"

The ER doors whisked open. She was swept inside and strapped onto a gurney as she kicked and thrashed.

Dr. Wettig's face appeared, white and taut above hers. "Five milligrams Haldol IM," he snapped.

"No!" shrieked Abby. *"No!"*

A nurse materialized, syringe in hand. She uncapped the needle. Abby lurched, trying to buck free of the restraints.

"Hold her down, damn it," said Wettig.

Hands clamped over her wrists. She was twisted sideways, her right buttock bared.

"Please," she begged, looking up at the nurse, "don't let him hurt me. Don't let him."

Abby felt the icy lick of alcohol, then the prick of the needle.

"Please," she whispered. But she knew it was already too late.

"It will be all right," said the nurse. And she smiled at Abby. "Everything will be all right."

FIFTEEN

"No skid marks on the pier," said Detective Carrier. "The windshield's shattered. And the driver's got what looked to me like a bullet hole over the right eye. You know the drill, Slug. I'm sorry, but we're going to need your gun."

Katzka nodded and gazed down at the water. "Tell the diver he'll find my gun right about there. Unless the current's moved it."

Carrier gave Katzka a pat on the shoulder. "Go home. You look like hell."

Katzka walked wearily back up the pier, through the gathering of crime-lab personnel. The van had been pulled out of the water hours before, and they'd already traced its registration to Bayside Hospital, operations and facilities. The driver's body had been removed half an hour before. His license had identified him as Oleg Boravoy, age thirty-nine, a resident of Newark, New Jersey. They were still awaiting further information.

Katzka crossed the container yard to where his own car was parked, and slid inside. Groaning, he dropped his face in his hands. At two a.m. he'd gone home to shower and catch a few hours of sleep. Shortly after sunrise he'd been back on the pier. I'm too old for this, he thought. Too old by at least a decade. All this running around and shooting in the dark was for the young lions.

Someone tapped on his window. He looked up and saw it was Lundquist. Katzka rolled down the glass.

"Hey, Slug, you okay?"

"I'm going home to get some sleep."

"Yeah, well before you do, I thought you'd want to hear about the driver. They ran the name Oleg Boravoy through the computer. Bingo, he's in there. Russian immigrant, came here in '89. Three arrests, no convictions."

"What charges?"

"Kidnapping and extortion. The charges never stick, because the witnesses keep disappearing." Lundquist leaned forward. "The Newark cops say Boravoy's Russian Mafia."

Katzka frowned. "What's Boravoy's connection to Bayside?"

"We don't know."

"What about that freighter? You talk to the harbormaster?"

"The ship's registered to some New Jersey firm called the Sigayev Company. Her last known port of call was Riga."

"Where's that?"

"Latvia. I think it's some breakaway Russian republic."

The Russians again, thought Katzka. He thought of Abby Di-Matteo, and his anxiety suddenly sharpened. He hadn't spoken to her since that one a.m. phone call. Just an hour ago he'd been about to call her again. But as he was dialing her number, he realized that his pulse had quickened. And he'd recognized that sign for what it was. Anticipation. A joyful, aching, completely irrational eagerness to hear her voice. They were feelings he had not experienced in years, and he understood, only too painfully, what they meant. He had quickly disconnected. And had spent the last hour in a deepening depression.

Now he gazed off toward the pier. He said to Lundquist, "I want anything there is on the Sigayev Company. I want any links to Amity and to Bayside Hospital."

"On my list, Slug."

As Katzka started his car, Detective Carrier was crossing toward them, waving. "Hey, Slug," said Carrier, "did you get the message about Dr. DiMatteo?"

Instantly Katzka turned off the engine. But he couldn't shut off the sudden roar of his own pulse. He stared at Carrier.

"There's been an accident."

A LUNCH cart rattled down the hallway. Abby woke up with a start and found she was lying in sheets damp with sweat. She tried to turn in bed but found she couldn't; her hands were tied down, her wrists sore from chafing. With a sob of frustration she sank back against the pillow and stared at the ceiling. She heard the creak of a chair. She turned her head.

Katzka was sitting by the window. In the glare of midday his unshaven face looked older and wearier than ever before. "I asked them to take off the restraints," he said. "But they told me you'd pulled out a few too many IVs." He rose and came to her bedside. "Welcome back, Abby. You're a very lucky lady."

"I don't remember what happened."

"Your car rolled over on the Southeast Expressway."

"Was there anyone else . . ."

He shook his head. "No one else was hurt. But your car was pretty much totaled." There was a silence. She realized he was no longer looking at her. He was looking somewhere at her pillow instead.

"Katzka," she said softly, "was it my fault?"

Reluctantly he nodded. "It appears you were traveling at a high rate of speed. You must have braked to avoid a vehicle stalled in your lane. You veered into a barrier. And rolled across two lanes."

She closed her eyes. "Oh, my God."

Again there was a pause. "I'm afraid they found a shattered container of vodka in your car."

She opened her eyes and stared at him. "That's impossible."

"Abby, you can't remember what happened. Last night on the pier was a traumatic experience. Maybe you felt the need to unwind. To have a few drinks at home."

"I'd remember that! I'd remember if I'd been drinking."

"Look, what's important right now is—"

"*This* is important. Can't you see? They're setting me up again!"

He rubbed his hand over his eyes. "I'm sorry, Abby," he murmured. "Dr. Wettig just showed me your blood alcohol level. They drew it last night in the ER. It was point two one."

He wasn't facing her now but was gazing blankly out the window, as though just the act of looking at her had taken too much out of him. She closed her eyes and concentrated on channeling her rage. It was all she had left, the only weapon with which she could fight back. They had taken everything else away from her. They had taken even Katzka.

She said slowly, "I was not drinking. You have to believe me."

"Can you tell me where you were going at three in the morning?"

"I was coming here to Bayside. Mark called me, and I was coming to—" She stopped. "Has he been here? Why isn't he here?"

His silence was chilling. She turned her head to look at him but could not see his face.

"Katzka?"

"Mark Hodell hasn't been answering his pages. No one seems to know where he is."

She tried to speak, but her throat felt as if it had swollen shut, and the only sound that came out was a whispered "No." She didn't realize she was crying, didn't even feel the tears sliding down until Katzka gently wiped her cheek with a tissue.

"I'm sorry." He brushed her hair off her face, and just for a moment his hand lingered there, fingers resting protectively on her forehead. He murmured, "I'm so sorry."

"Find him for me," she whispered. "Please find him for me."

"I will."

A moment later she heard him walk out of the room. Only then did she realize he had untied the restraints. She was free to leave the bed, to walk out of the room. But she didn't. She turned her face into the pillow and wept.

At two o'clock Dr. Wettig came in. He stood by her bed, flipping through the pages of her chart. "Dr. DiMatteo?"

She didn't answer him.

"Detective Katzka tells me you deny drinking any alcohol last night," he said.

She said nothing.

Wettig sighed. "The first step toward recovery is acknowledging you have a problem. I should have been more aware. But now it's all out in the open. It's time to deal with the problem."

"What would be the point?" she said dully.

"The point is, you have some sort of future worth salvaging. There will be other careers open to you besides medicine."

Her response was silence. The loss of her career felt almost insignificant at that moment, compared to the greater grief she felt over Mark's vanishing.

"I've asked Dr. O'Connor to evaluate you," said Wettig. "He'll be in sometime this evening."

"I don't need a psychiatrist."

"I think you do, Abby. You have to get beyond these delusions of persecution. I'm not going to approve your release until O'Connor clears it. We're all very concerned about you, Abby. *I'm* concerned about you. That's why I'm ordering a psychiatric evaluation. It's for your own good, believe me."

She looked straight at him. "Go to hell, General."

To her immense satisfaction he flinched and stepped away from the bed. He slapped the chart shut. "I'll check in on you later, Dr. DiMatteo," he said, and left the room.

Only moments ago, before Wettig had walked in, she had felt too weary to fight. Now every muscle had tensed, and her stomach was in turmoil. She sat up. The dizziness lasted only a few seconds. It was time to get moving. To regain control of her life. She crossed the room and opened the door a crack.

A nurse looked up from her desk and stared directly at Abby. "Do you need something?"

"Uh, no," said Abby, and quickly retreated.

They were keeping her a prisoner.

She went to the nightstand and picked up the phone. She called her home, punched in her access code, and listened to the messages from her answering machine. There had been another call from Vivian, and by the tone of her voice the call had been urgent. She'd left a Burlington number. Abby dialed it.

This time Vivian answered. "You barely caught me. I was just about to check out of here."

"You're coming home?"

"I've got a six-o'clock flight to Logan. Listen, this trip has been a wild-goose chase. There were no harvests done in Burlington. It's just a cover. And Tim Nicholls provided the official paperwork."

"And now Nicholls has vanished."

"Or they got rid of him."

They fell silent. Then Abby said softly, "Mark's missing."

"What?"

"No one knows where he is. Detective Katzka says he doesn't answer his pager." She paused, her throat closing over.

"Oh, Abby. Abby . . ." Vivian's voice faltered.

In the brief silence Abby heard a click. Then the line went dead. She hung up and tried to call again, but there was no dial tone. She tried the operator. Still no dial tone. The hospital had disconnected her telephone.

AT FIVE thirty p.m. the vampire was back, carrying her tray of blood tubes and lab slips and needles. "I'm sorry, Dr. DiMatteo. But I need to stick you again."

Abby was standing at the window staring at the dreary view. "This hospital's sucked all the blood I have to give," she said.

Behind her came the clatter of glass tubes. "Doctor, I really do have to get this blood. Dr. Wettig ordered it." The phlebotomist added with a quiet note of desperation, "Please don't make things hard for me."

Abby turned and looked at the woman. She seemed very young. Abby was reminded of herself at some long-ago time. A time when she, too, was terrified of Wettig, of doing the wrong thing.

Sighing, Abby went to the bed and sat down. She held out her left arm and watched impassively as the rubber tourniquet was tucked into place with a snap. She made a fist. As the needle pierced her skin, Abby looked at the phlebotomist's tray, at all the neatly labeled tubes of blood.

Suddenly she focused on one specimen in particular, a purple-topped tube with the label facing toward her. She stared at the name: VOSS, NINA. SICU BED 8.

"There we go," said the vampire, withdrawing the needle. "Can you hold that gauze in place?"

Automatically Abby pressed the gauze to her arm. Nina Voss is back in the hospital, she thought. Something has gone wrong with the new heart. She remembered Nina's appearance in the gloom of the car. The pale face, the bluish tinge of her lips. Even then her transplant was already failing. Organ rejection.

The phlebotomist had left. Abby went to the closet. There she found a bulging plastic bag. It contained her shoes, her blood-stained slacks, and her purse. Her wallet was missing, but a thorough search of the purse turned up a few loose nickels and dimes at the bottom. She would need every last one.

She zipped on the slacks, tucked in her hospital-gown top, and stepped into the shoes. Then she went to the door and peeked out.

The regular nurse wasn't at the desk. However, two other nurses were in the station, one talking on the phone, another bent over paperwork. Neither was looking in Abby's direction.

Abby glanced down the hall and saw the meal cart rattling into the ward, pushed by a volunteer in pink. The cart came to a stop in front of the nurses desk. The volunteer pulled out two meal trays and carried them into a patient room. The cart blocked the nurses' view as Abby walked past their desk and headed for the stairwell.

Six flights up, she emerged on the twelfth floor. Straight ahead was the OR wing. From a linen cart in the hallway she picked up a surgical gown, a cap, and shoe covers. Completely garbed in blue, like everyone else, she just might pass unnoticed. She turned the corner and walked into the SICU.

Inside, she found chaos. The patient in bed 2 was coding, all the personnel frantically pressing into the cubicle. No one even glanced in her direction as she walked past the monitor station and pushed into cubicle 8. The door swung shut behind her.

Nina Voss was sleeping. She seemed to have shrunk since Abby had last seen her. Her body looked as small as a child's.

Abby picked up the nurses' clipboard hanging at the foot of the bed. In a glance she took in all the parameters recorded there. The rising pulmonary wedge pressure. The slowly falling cardiac output. Abby hung the clipboard back on the hook. As she straightened, she saw that Nina's eyes were open and staring at her.

"Hello, Mrs. Voss," said Abby.

Nina smiled and murmured, "It's the doctor who always tells the truth."

"How are you feeling?"

"Content." Nina closed her eyes. "Content that it's almost over."

Abby moved to her bedside and took the other woman's hand. "I never got the chance to thank you for trying to help me."

"It was Victor I was trying to help."

"I don't understand."

"He's like that man in the Greek myth—Orpheus. The one who went into Hades to bring back his wife. He wants to bring me back. He doesn't care what it takes. What it costs." She opened her eyes again. "In the end," she whispered, "it will cost him too much."

They were not speaking of money. Abby understood that at once. They were speaking of souls.

The cubicle door suddenly opened. Abby turned to see a nurse staring at her in surprise.

"Oh! Dr. DiMatteo, what are you—" She swiftly assessed all the monitors and IV lines.

Checking for signs of sabotage.

"I haven't touched anything," said Abby.

"Mrs. Voss needs her rest." The nurse swiftly ushered Abby out. "She's scheduled for surgery tonight. She can't be disturbed."

"What surgery?"

"The retransplant. They found a donor."

Abby stared at the closed door to cubicle 8. She asked, "Does Mrs. Voss know?"

"What?"

"Did she sign the consent form for surgery?"

"Her husband signed it. Now please leave immediately."

Without another word Abby turned and walked out of the unit. She kept walking until she reached the elevators. The door opened. She stepped inside and quickly turned to face the door.

They found a donor, she thought as the elevator descended. Somehow they found a donor. Tonight Nina Voss will have a new heart.

By the time the car reached the lobby, she had worked out the sequence of events. She had read the records of other Bayside transplants; she knew what was going to happen.

The elevator door opened. She stepped out, eyes focused on the floor. She walked out the front doors and into a driving wind.

Two blocks away, cold and shaking, she ducked into a phone booth. Using her precious cache of nickels and dimes, she called Katzka's number.

He wasn't at his desk. The policeman who had answered the extension offered to take a message.

"I have to talk to him now! Doesn't he have a pager?"

"Let me transfer you to the operator."

A moment later the operator came on. "I'm sorry. We're still waiting for Detective Katzka to respond. Can he reach you at your current number?"

"Yes. I mean, I don't know. I'll try him later." Abby hung up. She was out of coins. But there was one more person she could call.

Half the phone book had been torn away. With a sense of futility she flipped through the white pages anyway. She was startled to actually find the listing: I. Tarasoff.

Her hands were shaking as she dialed collect.

Please talk to me. Please take my call.

After four rings she heard Ivan Tarasoff's gentle "Hello?" Then, "Yes, I'll accept the charges."

She was so relieved, her words spilled out in a rush. "I didn't know who else to call. I can't reach Vivian. And no one else will listen to me. You have to go to the police. Make them listen!"

"Now slow down, Abby. Tell me what's happening."

She took a deep breath. "Nina Voss is getting a second transplant tonight," she said. "Dr. Tarasoff, I think I know how it works. They don't fly the hearts in from somewhere else. The harvests are done right here. In Boston!"

"Now, Abby, I understand from Mr. Parr that you've been under a great strain lately. Isn't it possible this is—"

"*Listen.* Please listen to me!" She closed her eyes, forcing herself to stay calm. To sound rational. "Vivian called me today from Burlington. She found out the organs didn't come from Vermont."

"Then where are the harvests done?"

"I'm not entirely sure. But I'm guessing they're done in a building in Roxbury. Amity Medical Supplies. The police have to get there tonight. Before the harvest can be done."

"I don't know if I can convince them."

"You have to! Dr. Tarasoff, this isn't just an organ matchmaking service. They're generating donors. They're *killing* people."

In the background Abby heard a woman call out, "Ivan, aren't you going to eat your dinner? It's getting cold."

"I'll have to skip it, dear," said Tarasoff. "There's been an emergency." His voice came back on the line, soft and urgent. "I don't think I need to tell you that this whole thing scares me, Abby."

"It scares the hell out of me, too."

"Then let's just drive straight to the police. Drop it in *their* laps. It's too dangerous for us to handle."

"Agreed. One hundred percent. Could you come and get me? I'm freezing. And I'm scared."

"Where are you?"

"I'm in a phone booth a few blocks east of Bayside."

"I'll find you."

"Dr. Tarasoff?"

"Yes?"

"Please," she whispered, "hurry."

SIXTEEN

A DARK Mercedes crawled along the road and came to a stop beside the phone booth. Abby could just make out that it was Tarasoff. She ran to the passenger door and climbed inside. "Thank God you're here. Let's get out of here."

As Tarasoff pulled away from the curb, she glanced back to see if anyone was following them. The road behind them was dark.

"Do you see any cars?" he asked.

"No. I think we're okay."

Tarasoff released a shaky breath. "I'm not very good at this. I don't even like to watch crime shows."

"You're doing fine. Just get us to the police station."

Tarasoff glanced nervously in the rearview mirror. "I think I just saw a car. I'm going to turn here. Let's see what happens."

Abby looked back but saw nothing. As they rounded the corner, she kept her gaze focused on the road behind them. She saw no headlights, no other cars at all. Only when they slowed to a stop did she turn and face forward. "What's wrong?"

"Nothing's wrong." Tarasoff cut the headlights.

"Why are you—" Abby's words froze in her throat as her door swung open. Suddenly hands reached in, and she was being dragged out into the night. She fought blindly against her captors but could not succeed in loosening their grips. Her hands were yanked behind her back and the wrists bound together. Her mouth was taped. Then she was lifted and thrust into the trunk of a nearby car. The trunk lid slammed shut, trapping her in darkness.

They were moving. She rolled onto her back and kicked upward again and again, until she could scarcely lift her legs. It was useless; no one could hear her. Exhausted, she curled up on her side and forced herself to think.

Tarasoff. How is Tarasoff involved?

Slowly, as she lay there in the cramped darkness, the puzzle came together, piece by piece. Tarasoff was chief of one of the most respected cardiac transplant teams on the East Coast. His reputation attracted desperately ill patients from around the world, patients with the money to go to any surgeon they chose. What they could not buy was what they needed to stay alive: hearts. Human hearts.

That's what the Bayside transplant team could provide. She remembered what Tarasoff had once said: "I've referred patients to Bayside myself." He was Bayside's go-between. Their matchmaker.

She felt the car brake and turn. The tires rolled across gravel, then stopped. There was a distant roar, a sound she recognized as a jet taking off. She knew exactly where they were.

The trunk lid opened. She was lifted out into a buffeting wind that smelled of diesel fuel and the sea. They half carried, half dragged her down the pier and up the gangplank. She caught only a glimpse of the shadowy freighter deck, and then she was dragged below, down steps that rattled and clanged.

A door screeched open, and she was thrust inside, into darkness. Her hands were still bound behind her back. She could not break her fall, and her chin slammed to the floor. Pain drove through her skull.

She rolled onto her back and struggled to focus. She could make out Tarasoff's silhouette, standing in the faintly lit doorway. She flinched as one of the men bent down and ripped off the tape.

"Why?" she whispered. "Is it the money?"

"Money means nothing," Tarasoff said, "if it can't buy you what you need."

"Like a heart?"

"Like the life of your own child. Or your own wife, sister, or brother. You, of all people, should understand that, Dr. DiMatteo. We know all about little Pete and his accident. Think, Doctor, what would you have given to have saved your brother's life?"

She said nothing. By her silence he knew her answer.

"Imagine what it's like," he said, "to watch your own child dying. To have all the money in the world and know she still has to wait her turn. Behind the alcoholics. The drug abusers. The welfare cheats who haven't worked a day in their lives." He paused. "Imagine."

The door swung shut. The latch squealed into place.

Abby was lying in pitch darkness. She heard the rattle of the stairway as the three men climbed back to the deck level. Then she heard only the wind and the groan of the ship straining at its lines.

Imagine. She closed her eyes and tried not to think of Pete. But there he was standing in front of her, proudly dressed in his Cub Scout uniform.

What would I have done to save you? Anything.

In the darkness something rustled. Abby froze. She heard it again, the barest whisper of movement. *Rats.* She squirmed away from the sound and struggled to her feet.

There was a soft click. The sudden flare of light flooded her retinas. She jerked backward. A bare bulb swung overhead, clinking against the dangling pull chain.

It was not a rat she had heard in the darkness. It was a boy.

They stared at each other, neither one of them saying a word. Though he stood very still, she could see the wariness in his eyes, his legs, thin and bare beneath shorts, tensed for flight. He looked about ten, very pale and very blond. She noticed a bluish smudge on his cheek and realized with a sudden start of outrage that the smudge was not dirt, but a bruise.

She took a step toward him. At once he backed away. "I won't hurt you," she said. "I just want to talk to you."

A frown flickered across his forehead. He shook his head and said something, but his answer was incomprehensible to her. Now it was her turn to frown and shake her head. They looked at each other in shared bewilderment.

Suddenly they both glanced upward. The ship's engines had just started up. Moments later Abby felt the rocking of the hull. They had left the dock and were now under way.

Even if I get out of these bonds, out of this room, there's nowhere for me to run.

In despair she looked back at the boy.

He was no longer paying any attention to the sound of the engines. Instead he had edged sideways and was staring at her bound wrists tucked close to her back. He looked down at his own arm. Only then did Abby see that his left hand was missing, that his forearm ended in a stump. He looked back at her and spoke again.

"I can't understand what you're saying," she said.

They regarded each other in mutual frustration. Then the boy lifted his chin. She realized that he had come to some sort of decision. He circled around to her back and tugged at her wrists, trying to loosen the bonds with his one hand. The cord was too tightly knotted. Now he knelt on the floor behind her. She felt the nip of his teeth, the heat of his breath against her skin as he began to gnaw, like a small but determined mouse, at her bonds.

"I'M SORRY, but visiting hours are over," said a nurse. "Wait. You can't go in there. Stop!"

Katzka and Vivian walked straight past the nurses desk and pushed into Abby's room. "Where is she?" demanded Katzka.

Dr. Colin Wettig turned to look at them. "She's missing."

"You told me she'd be watched here," said Katzka. "What's happened to her?"

"That's a question you'll have to ask Dr. DiMatteo."

It was Wettig's flat voice that angered Katzka. That and the emotionless gaze. "She was under your care, Doctor. What've you people done with her?"

"I don't like your implications."

Katzka crossed the room, grabbed the lapels of Wettig's lab coat, and shoved him against the wall. "Damn you," he said. "Where did you take her?"

Wettig's blue eyes at last betrayed a flicker of fear. "I told you, I don't know where she is! The nurses called me at six thirty to tell me she was gone. We've alerted security. They've already searched the hospital, but they can't find her."

Vivian stepped forward and tried to pull them apart. Abruptly Katzka released Wettig. The older man swayed backward against the wall. "I thought, given her delusional state, she'd be safer in the hospital," he said. "I didn't realize she might be telling the truth after all." Wettig pulled a slip of paper from his pocket and handed it to Vivian. "The nurses just gave me that."

"What is it?" said Katzka.

Vivian frowned. "This is Abby's blood alcohol level. It says zero."

"I had it redrawn this afternoon and sent to an independent lab," Wettig explained. "She kept insisting she hadn't been intoxicated. I thought that if I could confront her with undeniable evidence, I could break through her denial."

"You told me her alcohol was point two one."

"That was the one done at four a.m. in Bayside's lab."

"But now there's no alcohol in her system," said Katzka.

"Which tells me that either her liver is amazingly fast at metabolizing it," said Wettig, "or Bayside's lab made a mistake."

"Is that what you're calling it?" said Katzka. "A mistake?"

Wettig looked drained. And very old. "I didn't realize . . . didn't want to consider the possibility—"

"That Abby was telling the truth?" said Vivian.

Wettig shook his head. "My God," he murmured. "This hospital should be shut down if what she's been saying is true."

Katzka felt Vivian's gaze. He looked at her.

She said softly, "Now do you have any doubts?"

FOR hours the boy had slept in her arms, his breath warm against her neck. He lay limp, arms and legs askew, the way children do when they are deeply, trustingly asleep. He had been shivering when she'd first embraced him. She'd massaged his bare legs, and it was like rubbing cold, dry sticks. Eventually his shaking had stopped, and she'd felt that flush of warmth that children give off when they finally fall asleep. Then she, too, slept for a while.

When she woke up, the wind was blowing harder. She could hear it in the groaning of the ship. Overhead, the bare lightbulb swayed. The boy whimpered and stirred. He gave a soft moan and shuddered awake. As he looked up at her, recognition dawned in his eyes.

"Ah-bee," he whispered.

She nodded. "That's right. Abby. You remembered." Smiling, she stroked his face, her fingers tracing across the bruise. "And you're . . . Yakov."

He nodded.

They both smiled, and Abby brushed her mouth across one silky blond eyebrow. When she lifted her head, she felt the wetness on her lips. Not the boy's tears, but hers. She turned her face against her shoulder to wipe away the tears. When she looked back at him, she saw he was watching her with that strange, rapt silence of his.

"I'm right here," she murmured, smiling.

After a while his eyelids drifted shut, and his body relaxed once again into the trusting limpness of sleep.

"SO MUCH for the search warrant," said Lundquist, and kicked the door. It flew open and banged against the wall. Cautiously he edged into the room as Katzka flipped on the wall switch.

Both men blinked as light flooded their eyes. It shone down with blinding intensity from three overhead lamps. Everywhere they looked, they saw gleaming surfaces. Stainless steel cabinets. Instrument trays and IV poles. Monitors studded with knobs and switches.

In the center of the room was an operating table. Katzka approached it and stared down at the straps hanging from the sides— two for the wrists, two for the ankles, two longer straps for the waist and chest.

"This is bizarre," said Lundquist. "What kind of surgery were they doing here?"

Katzka looked at the table again. At the straps. Suddenly he thought of Abby, her wrists tied down on the bed, tears trickling down her face. The memory was so painful he gave his head a shake to dispel the image. Fear was making it hard for him to think. If he couldn't think, he couldn't help her. He couldn't save her. Abruptly he turned and walked out the door.

Back outside, on the sidewalk, he and Lundquist stood and looked up at the Amity building. When he had been inside it the day before, Katzka had seen only what he was supposed to see. He had not seen the top floor, that table with the straps. Less than an hour before, Lundquist had traced the building's ownership to the Sigayev Company—the same New Jersey company to which the freighter was registered. That Russian Mafia connection again. How deep into Bayside did it reach?

Lundquist's cellular phone chirped. He reached into the car.

Katzka remained in front of the building, his thoughts shifting back to Abby and where he should look next.

"Slug!" Katzka turned to see Lundquist waving the telephone. "It's the coast guard. They've got a chopper waiting for us."

FOOTSTEPS clanged on the stairway. Abby's head snapped up. In her arms Yakov slept on, unaware.

The door swung open. Tarasoff, flanked by two men, stood there. "It's time to go." He glanced at Yakov. "Wake him up, too."

Abby hugged Yakov closer. "Not the boy," she said.

"Especially the boy."

She shook her head. "Why?"

"He's AB positive. The only AB we happen to have in stock at the moment."

She stared at Tarasoff. Then she looked down at Yakov, his face flushed with sleep. Through his thin chest she could feel the soft beating of his heart. Nina Voss is AB positive, she thought.

One of the men grabbed her arm and hauled her up. The boy tumbled to the floor, where he lay blinking in confusion. The other man barked a command in Russian. Yakov stumbled to his feet.

Tarasoff led the way. Down a dim corridor, up a staircase, and through a hatch, to a steel walkway. Straight ahead was a blue door.

Suddenly the boy balked. He started to run. One of the men snagged him by the shirt. Yakov spun around and sank his teeth into the man's arm. Howling in pain, the man slapped Yakov across the face. The impact was so brutal it sent the boy sprawling.

"Stop it!" screamed Abby.

The man jerked Yakov to his feet and gave him another slap. Now the boy stumbled toward Abby. At once she swept him into her arms. The man moved toward her, as though to separate them.

"You stay away from him," Abby yelled.

Yakov clung to her, shaking, sobbing into her shoulder. She whispered, "Sweetheart, I'm with you. I'm right here with you."

The boy raised his head. Looking into his terrified eyes, she thought, He knows what's going to happen to us.

She and the boy were shoved forward through the blue door.

They passed into a different world. The corridor beyond was paneled in bleached wood; the floor was white linoleum. Their steps echoed in the corridor as they walked past a spiral staircase and turned a corner. At the end of the passage was a wide door.

The boy was shaking even harder now. And he was getting heavy. She set him down on his feet and cupped his face in her hand. Just for a second their gazes met, and what could not be communicated in words was now shared in that single look. Then she took Yakov's hand and gave it a squeeze. Together they walked toward the wide door. One man was in front of them, one behind them. Tarasoff was in the lead. As he unlocked the door, Abby tensed for the next move. Already she had released Yakov's hand.

Tarasoff pushed the door, and it swung open, revealing a room of stark white. Abby lunged. Her shoulder slammed into the man in front of her, shoving him against Tarasoff, who stumbled across the threshold to his knees.

The man behind Abby tried to seize her arms. She swung at his face, her fist connecting in a satisfying thud. She spied a flash of movement. It was Yakov, darting away and vanishing around the corner. Now the man she'd shoved was on his feet again, coming at her from the other direction. Together the two men trapped her between them and lifted her. She didn't stop fighting and thrashing as they carried her through the doorway into the white room.

"You've got to control her!" said Tarasoff.

"The boy—"

"Forget him. He can't go anywhere. Get her up on the table."

"She won't hold still!"

Abby heard Tarasoff fumbling in cabinets. Then he snapped, "Give me her arm. I need to get at her arm!"

Tarasoff approached, syringe in hand. Abby cried out as the needle plunged in. She twisted but couldn't break free. She twisted again, and this time her limbs barely responded. Her eyelids wouldn't stay open. She tried to scream but could not even draw the next breath.

"Get her in the next room," said Tarasoff. "We have to intubate now, or we're going to lose her."

The men carried her inside and slid her onto a table. Though fully awake, she could not move a muscle. But she could feel everything. The straps tightening around her wrists and ankles. The pressure of Tarasoff's hand tipping her head back. The cold steel blade of the laryngoscope sliding into her throat. Her shriek of horror echoed only in her head; no sound came out. She felt the plastic ET tube snaking down her throat, gagging, suffocating her. She could not turn away, could not fight for air. The tube was connected to an Ambu bag. Tarasoff squeezed the bag, and Abby's chest rose and fell in three quick, lifesaving breaths. Now he took off the Ambu bag and connected the ET tube to a ventilator. The machine took over, pumping air into her lungs at regular intervals.

"Now go get the boy," snapped Tarasoff. One of the men left. The other, the anesthetist, stepped closer to the table.

"Fasten that chest strap," said Tarasoff. "The succinylcholine will wear off in another minute or two. We can't have her thrashing around while I start the IV."

Already the drug's effect was starting to fade. Abby could feel her chest muscles begin to spasm against the insult of that tube. Tarasoff started the IV. As he straightened, he saw that Abby's eyes were open now and staring at him. He read the question in her gaze.

"A healthy liver," he said, "is not something we can take for granted. There's a gentleman in Connecticut who's been waiting over a year for a donor." Tarasoff hung a second IV bag on the pole. "He was delighted to hear we've finally found a match."

All that blood they drew from me in the ER, she thought. They used it for tissue typing.

He continued with his tasks. Connecting the second bag to the line. Drawing medications into syringes. She could only look at him mutely as the ventilator pumped air into her lungs. A clock on the wall read eleven fifteen.

Tarasoff heard the sound of the door open and shut again. He turned and said, "The boy's loose. They're still hunting him down. So we'll take the liver first."

Footsteps approached the table. Another face came into view and stared down at Abby. So many times before, she had looked across the operating table at that face. So many times before, she had seen those eyes smiling at her above a surgical mask. They were not smiling now.

No, she sobbed, but the only sound that came out was the soft rush of air through the ET tube. *No. . . .*

It was Mark.

SEVENTEEN

GREGOR knew that the only way out of the ship's aft section was through the blue door, and it was locked. The boy must have gone up the spiral staircase.

He began to climb, his arm still throbbing where the boy had bit him. That little brat had caused trouble from the start.

He reached the next level and stepped off the staircase onto thick carpet. He was now in the living quarters of the surgeon and the anesthetist. Aft were two private cabins. Forward was a well-appointed saloon. Gregor searched the cabins first, then started toward the saloon. Before he reached it, he heard a muffled whine.

He entered the saloon and turned on the lights. Where was the boy? He circled the room, then stopped.

The dumbwaiter.

He ran to it and pried open the doors. All he saw were cables. The boy had already escaped into the galley. Gregor headed back down the staircase. This was not a catastrophe. The galley was already secured. The boy was still trapped.

"I'M SORRY, Abby," said Mark. "I never thought it would go this far."

Please, she thought. Please don't do this.

"If there was any other way . . ." He shook his head. "You pushed it too hard. And then I couldn't control you."

A tear slid from her eye and trickled into her hair. Just for an instant she saw a flash of pain in his face. He turned away.

"It's time to gown up," said Tarasoff. "Will you do the honors?" He held out a syringe to Mark. "Pentobarb. We want to be humane about this after all."

Mark hesitated. Then he took the syringe and turned to the IV pole. He uncapped the needle and poked it into the injection port. Again he hesitated. He looked at Abby.

I loved you, she thought. I loved you so much.

He pushed the plunger.

The lights began to dim. She saw his face waver, then fade into a deepening pool of gray.

THE galley door was locked. Yakov tugged again and again at the knob, but the door would not budge. Frantically he glanced around the galley, considering all the possible hiding places. All of them offered only temporary concealment. Eventually they would find him.

He would have to make it difficult for them. He looked up at the lights. There were three bare bulbs shining overhead. He ran to the cupboard, plucked out a ceramic coffee cup, and threw it at the nearest light. The bulb shattered and went dark.

He was about to aim at the next bulb when his gaze suddenly fell on the cook's radio. It was set in its usual place on top of the cupboard. His gaze followed the radio's extension cord as it trailed down to the countertop, where the toaster sat.

Yakov glanced at the stove and spotted an empty soup pot. He dragged the pot off the burner and carried it to the sink. He turned on the faucet.

A RADIO was playing at full volume. Gregor pushed open the galley door. Drums and electric guitars blasted away in the darkness. He felt for the wall switch and flicked it on. No lights. He took a step forward, and his leather sole crunched on glass.

The little bastard's smashed out the lights. He's going to try to slip by me in the dark.

Gregor shut the door, locked it, and turned to the darkness. "Come on, boy," he yelled. "Nothing's going to happen to you!"

He heard only the radio blaring away. He moved toward the

sound, then paused to light a match. The radio was sitting on the countertop right in front of him. As Gregor switched off the music, he noticed the meat cleaver lying on the countertop. Beside it lay scraps of what looked like brown rubber.

So he's got his hands on the cook's knives, has he?

The match flickered out. Gregor took out his gun and called out, "Boy?" Only then did he notice that his feet were wet. He lit another match and looked down.

He was standing in a pool of water. Already it had soaked into his shoes. In the wavering light of the flame Gregor scanned the area around his feet and saw that the water had spread halfway across the floor. Then he saw the extension cord, the end sliced off, one coil glistening at the edge of the pool. In bewilderment he scanned the length of the cord as it snaked across the floor and looped upward to a chair.

Just before his match flickered out, the last image that Gregor registered was the faint gleam of blond hair and the figure of the boy, his arm stretched toward the wall socket.

The end of the cord was dangling from his hand.

TARASOFF held out the scalpel. "You make the first incision," he said, and saw the other man's look of dismay.

You have no choice, Hodell. You're the one who tried to recruit her. You're the one who made the mistake. Now you have to correct it.

Mark took the scalpel. Sweat had broken out on his forehead, and he paused, the blade poised over the exposed abdomen. They both knew this was a test—perhaps the ultimate one.

Go ahead. Archer did his part by taking care of Mary Allen. Just as Zwick did with Aaron Levi. Now it's your turn. Prove you're still part of the team. Cut open the woman you once made love to. Do it.

Mark took a breath and pressed the blade to the skin.

Do it.

Mark sliced. A long, curving incision. The skin parted, and a line of blood welled up and dribbled onto the surgical drapes.

Tarasoff relaxed. Mark was not going to be a problem after all. He had, in fact, passed the point of no return years before as a surgical fellow. A night of heavy drinking, a few snorts of cocaine. The next morning a strange bed and a pretty nursing student strangled to death on the pillow beside him. And Mark with no memory of what had really happened. It was all very persuasive.

And there had been the money to cement the recruitment.

The carrot and the stick. It worked almost every time. It had worked with Archer and Zwick and Mohandas. And with Aaron Levi, too—for a while. Theirs had been a closed society, meticulous about guarding their secrets. And their profits, enough to buy the very best doctors, the very best team—a team Tarasoff had created. The Russians merely supplied the parts and the brute force. In the OR it was the team that performed the miracles.

Tarasoff assisted Mark, positioning retractors, clamping bleeders. They were in the abdominal cavity now.

The lights flickered and almost went off altogether.

"What's going on?" said Mark.

They both looked up at the lamps. The lights brightened again to full intensity.

"Just a glitch," said Tarasoff. "I can still hear the generator."

"This is not an optimal setup. A rocking ship. The power going off—"

"It's a temporary arrangement. Until we find a replacement for the Amity building." He nodded at the surgical site. "Proceed."

Mark raised his scalpel and paused. Perhaps the reality of what he was doing was starting to sink in.

"Is there a problem?" Tarasoff asked.

"No." Mark swallowed. Once again he began to cut, but his hand was shaking. He lifted the scalpel and took a few deep breaths.

"We haven't a lot of time, Dr. Hodell. There's another donor to harvest."

"It's just . . . Isn't it hot in here?"

"I hadn't noticed. Proceed."

Mark nodded. Gripping the scalpel, he was about to make another incision when he suddenly froze.

Tarasoff heard a sound behind him—the sigh of the door as it *whished* shut. Mark, staring straight ahead, lifted his scalpel.

The explosion seemed to punch him in the face. Mark's head snapped backward; then his body slumped to the floor.

Tarasoff spun around to look at the door, and he caught a glimpse of blond hair and the boy's white face.

The gun fired a second time. The shot went wild, the bullet shattering a glass door in the supply cabinet. Shards rained onto the floor. The anesthetist ducked for cover behind the ventilator.

Tarasoff backed away, his gaze never leaving the gun. The hand clutching it was shaking too hard now to shoot straight. He's only a boy, thought Tarasoff. A frightened boy whose arm kept wavering indecisively between the anesthetist and Tarasoff.

Tarasoff glanced at the instrument tray and spotted the syringe of succinylcholine. It still contained more than enough to subdue the child. Slowly he edged sideways, stepping over Mark's body. Then the gun swung back toward him, and he froze.

The boy was crying now, his breath coming in tearful gasps.

"It's all right," soothed Tarasoff. And he smiled. "Don't be afraid. I'm only helping your friend. She's very sick."

The boy's gaze focused on the table. On the woman. He took a step forward, then another. His breath suddenly escaped in a high, keening wail. He did not hear the anesthetist flee from the room. Nor did he seem to hear the faint rumble of the helicopter.

Tarasoff took the syringe from the tray. Quietly he moved closer. The boy lifted his head, and his cry rose to a despairing shriek. Tarasoff raised the syringe.

At that instant the boy looked up at him. And it was no longer fear but rage that shone in the boy's eyes as he aimed Gregor's gun.

And fired one last time.

THE boy would not leave her bedside. From the moment the nurses had wheeled Abby out of recovery and into the SICU, he had stayed right beside her—a pale little ghost haunting her bed. Now he stood gripping the side rails, his gaze silently pleading with her to wake up. At least he was no longer hysterical, the way he'd been when Katzka had come across him on the ship. He'd found the boy leaning over Abby's butchered body, sobbing, imploring her to live. Katzka had not understood a word of what the boy was saying. But he'd understood perfectly his panic. His despair.

There was a tapping on the cubicle window. Turning, Katzka saw Vivian Chao motioning to him. He joined her outside the cubicle.

"That kid can't stay here," she said. "He's getting in the way."

"Give the boy some time with her, okay?" Katzka turned and gazed through the window at the bed. And he found himself struggling to shake off the superimposed image that would haunt him for the rest of his days: Abby lying on the table, her abdomen slit open. The boy whimpering, cradling her face. And on the floor, lying in a lake of their own blood, the two men—Hodell already dead, Tarasoff unconscious and bleeding but still alive. Like everyone else aboard that freighter, Tarasoff had been taken into custody.

Soon there would be more arrests. Even now the authorities were closing in on the Sigayev Company. Based on what the freighter's crew had told them, the scope of the operation was wider—and far more horrifying—than Katzka could have imagined.

He blinked and refocused on the here and now: Abby, lying on the other side of that window, her abdomen swathed in bandages, the monitor tracing the steady rhythm of her heart. Just for an instant he felt the same flash of panic he'd experienced on the ship, when Abby's heartbeat had started skipping wildly across the monitor. When he'd thought he was about to lose her and the chopper bringing Vivian and Wettig had still been miles away. He touched the glass and found himself blinking again. And again.

Behind him Vivian said softly, "Katzka, she'll be okay. The General and I do good work."

Katzka nodded. Without a word he slipped back into the cubicle.

The boy looked up at him, his gaze as moist as Katzka's. "Ah-bee," he whispered.

"Yeah, kid. That's her name." Katzka smiled.

They both looked at the bed. A long time seemed to pass as they stood sharing a vigil over this woman whom neither of them knew well but about whom they already cared so deeply.

At last Katzka held out his hand. "Come on. You need your sleep, son. And so does she."

The boy hesitated. For a moment he studied Katzka. Then reluctantly he took the offered hand. They walked together through the SICU. Suddenly without warning the boy slowed down.

"What is it?" said Katzka.

The boy paused outside another cubicle. Katzka, too, looked through the glass. Beyond the window a silver-haired man sat in a chair by the patient's bed. His head was bowed in his hands; his whole body was quaking with silent sobs. There are things even Victor Voss cannot buy, thought Katzka. Now he's about to lose everything. His wife. His freedom.

Katzka looked at the woman lying in the bed. Her face was white and fragile. Her eyes, half opened, had the dull sheen of impending death.

The boy pressed closer to the glass. In that instant, as he leaned forward, the woman's eyes seemed to register one last flicker of life. She focused on the boy. Slowly her lips curved into a silent smile. And then she closed her eyes.

Katzka murmured, "It's time to go."

The boy looked up. Firmly he shook his head. As Katzka watched in helpless silence, the boy turned and walked back into Abby's cubicle.

Suddenly Katzka felt weary beyond belief. He looked at Victor Voss, a ruined man who now sat with his body crumpled forward in despair. He looked at the woman in the bed, her soul slipping away even as he watched. And he thought, So little time. We have so little time on this earth with the people we love.

He sighed. Then he, too, turned and walked into Abby's cubicle.

And took his place beside the boy.

TESS
GERRITSEN

PHOTO: COURTESY OF TESS GERRITSEN

You never know where author Tess Gerritsen is going to turn up. Some readers may recognize her name from her nine romance thrillers. Internet surfers may find her while exploring such on-line forums as Women in Peril and Medical Mysteries, as well as one on gardening. "It's funny how many on-line messages I'm getting about *Harvest,*" she says. Her neighbors, meanwhile, know her as a pretty good Irish fiddler who plays in a dance band.

And some people may even remember Gerritsen's days as a doctor. She enjoyed a successful career as an internist in the early 1980s, then retired to raise her family. It was during her first maternity leave that she began writing romantic thrillers. Recently, however, Gerritsen realized that she could combine the human touch of her romances with her years of experience as a physician. *Harvest* marks her first foray into the realm of medical suspense, but it will not be her last. Her next thriller is already in the works.

Gerritsen lives in Maine with her husband and two school-age sons, who provided the inspiration for the characters Yakov and Josh in *Harvest.*

the
falconer

Elaine Clark McCarthy

India Blake's greatest love is her exotic garden of wildflowers.

Rhodri MacNeal's greatest love is flying his glorious falcons.

Alone, on separate paths, they assume they'll go on like this forever. What fate has in store for them is something else entirely.

*D*o I remember that first sight of him clearly now, after all that has been? I should have been struck speechless. I should have swooned. Instead, I walked toward him quite calmly, or I thought I was calm. Yet I do remember wondering if I had combed my hair that morning. I do remember being glad I had worn a bra and wishing it were not so plain and businesslike. And I remember thinking of one more thing to add to my "before I die" list—not the list I'd written out, of things a person can actually arrange on purpose, but the mental list of things I would most likely die without: passion. It is a measure of how dazzled I was that I completely failed to see any significance in such a thought at that particular moment.

Why? He looked fierce and remote, a little unreal in a way I couldn't fathom. It wasn't his physical self that seemed not of this world. One of my chaotic thoughts stood out quite clearly: Here is a man made of flesh. Nor was it that he behaved strangely. He smiled a proper social smile, twin to the one on my own face.

I said, "I've come to see your hawks." And he said, "They're in the truck." As if he already knew who I was, had been expecting me. His voice was strong, quiet. I remember his sleeves were rolled back, and I could see the veins in his forearms. I felt a little dizzy and wondered if it was a new symptom of my illness, but it passed.

He told me later that his mouth had been dry, that he could hear the blood pounding in his ears. I believed him when he said it, but now I wonder. Could we really have recognized each other with a single glance? Maybe it was only the beauty of the morning, our acute aloneness, that made us see each other so clearly. We must have added the rest in retrospect. His cottony mouth, my sense of falling skyward, outward, opening up.

My head is full of mental snapshots, a memory album. I never owned a camera, but if I had, how different the picture collection would have been. Instead of family groupings, I have a close-up vision of a leaf I held as a small child—brown and curling, with more curl on the left than on the right. Instead of wedding pictures between red plush covers, I see a glass of lemonade on my mother's kitchen table at the old house, half empty, with a fly on the rim. Instead of graduation, there's my mother's face as the cancer killed her, her flesh so shrunken that she looked like a small, fierce bird.

And now there's Rhodri as I walk toward him in the October sunshine, the edge of a redwood tree's shade just touching his shoulder. So clear that I could this instant count the smile lines at the corners of his eyes, the number of times the bird in the redwood above us cried out, the number of times my heart thudded as he walked toward me. Oh yes, I do remember. I remember it all.

The Betrayer ⟫

THE young doctor who told India about her cancer looked her right in the eye as he did it. He seemed to think he could brace her with his own firmness, but his gaze bounced off her inturned look as she absorbed the blow. He gave it to her all at once. Inoperable. Six months at the most. I'm sorry.

"Yes," she said, "I see."

See what? he almost asked. Her eyes looked as if she were staring into the next world already. After she left, he broke a rule and had a small nip of the medicinal brandy kept in the corner cabinet.

Emerging from his office, India stopped outside the door to slip her sweater on over her sleeveless blouse. She saw how the hazy autumn light shed its glory on the potholed street, so that the row of old pickup trucks in front of the hardware store, the dog lying on the apron of the gas station, even the raccoon-ravaged trash can on the sidewalk in front of Murphy's Feed and Seed blazed forth their beingness, and she was pierced with a strange sensation that tightened her throat. Love. She set her jaw and started up the street to where she'd left the old jeep, in front of the grocery store.

I am walking along quite normally, she thought. I am putting one foot in front of the other, and no one will notice that I'm different.

In the blacked-out window of the dentist's office she caught sight of her reflection. No change at all. She had seen that same face half an hour before, on her way down to the doctor's office, unsuspecting. An ordinary woman, not too pretty, not too plain. Khaki pants, a white shirt, a beige sweater, her straw-colored hair pulled away from her face, no makeup, just her lean and sun-scorched self. She stopped and looked more closely at this body she had lived in so comfortably, now the betrayer. There was a saying: By the time you're forty, you have the face you deserve. She was only thirty-seven; she would have to try to deserve this face a little early.

She stared for a long time, as if she needed to memorize her own features, the cocked wing of each eyebrow that gave her a perpetual look of startled attention, the way her high-bridged nose finished in a point, the embarrassingly sensuous mouth with its lack of a philtrum notch in the upper lip. Of all this, what had she created herself? The faint crease between her brows, a frown mark not from bad temper but from years of forgetting to wear sunglasses. Smile lines at the corners of her mouth that could mean either a cheerful attitude or something more sardonic. Ambiguous signs, but there was nothing else. The rest, even the leanness, had been given, brought about by forces beyond her reach. Like her whole life.

The bell of the First Baptist Church rang twelve, and doors all down Main Street sprang open. People popped out like cuckoos from a clock, hurrying off to lunch.

Across the street, Jean Jones locked up the library and waved. "Going to eat?"

India shook her head.

"Come on, you're too thin. Besides, I could use some company." Jean crossed the dusty street and took India's arm. "You look poleaxed; something wrong?"

"No, I'm all right," she lied automatically. If she told anybody, it would be Jean, but she wasn't ready yet.

"You're sure? I saw you come out of the doc's."

"Just my annual." They turned into Carly's Cosy Nook and grabbed a corner booth. The smell of frying onions made India feel a little sick.

"I thought you had that a month ago."

"Jean! Change the subject!"

"All right, all right! What are you going to have?"

India looked at the menu, encased in plastic, the leatherette edges frayed with use. Five kinds of burger, eight ways to fix eggs, club sandwich, and tuna melt. Sandwiches come with fries, potato salad, or dirty rice. It all looked the same, same, same as it had always looked. She didn't see a thing she thought she could put in her mouth. "Maybe I'll skip it."

Jean frowned and opened her mouth, then closed it, turned her eyes back to her menu, and didn't look up again until Carly came along with her order book. "Hey there, Jean. India." There was a subtle difference in the way she said their names, as if Jean was a buddy, India an unknown quantity. India had never wondered about this, though it was Carly's usual way of greeting them. Now, trying to figure out why she had been so oblivious, India missed Jean's order and the pause that should have cued her to give her own.

"Sorry, sorry! Just coffee." She forced herself into the moment, and while they waited for Jean's lunch, India babbled. She talked about the weather, warm for October. She talked about the row of sugar pines she was planting behind the house. She talked about the butcher's new truck. Anything. Jean listened and watched, and India could hear her wondering what was up.

Finally the food and coffee came. Jean tucked into her blue plate meat loaf while India watched. Sunlight through the window gleamed on the plate; if she blurred her vision a little, she could see rainbows on the gravy. "Is it an unusually beautiful day, or is it me?"

Jean gave her another narrow glance. "What kind of question is that? You're acting very odd."

"Do you ever wonder about the way things look? About what we see and what we miss? Is it the way we're looking? Or is it . . . Never mind." She could see Jean wasn't following her line of thought; she wasn't sure she was following it herself.

"What's going on, India? What is it?"

"It's like there are signals. A pattern that wants to be noticed. I know it sounds crazy." India laughed, wondering if she sounded as out of control as she felt; and everyone in the place glanced at her. "I've got to get outside." She put down a dollar for her coffee and dashed. Jean might think she was off her rocker, but it was Jean's unique talent to think that without making it a judgment.

She walked around town, fascinated by how different everything suddenly looked. How golden, how clear. The post office an epiphany, the fragrance from the bakery an almost unbearable pleasure. Only when, turning the bend where Main Street changed into the road to Arbuckle, she saw the Baptist church, did she halt in confusion. Beyond it lay the old graveyard. She quickly moved toward it. She would not shirk even this.

Earthquakes and torrential rains had tipped some of the stones to drunken angles. Her parents' stone still stood upright: LEONORA BLAKE, 1916–1979. ROLAND BLAKE, 1899–1960. Farther back lay Grandmother India Fairweather, BELOVED WIFE, and her quiet husband, Jonathan. "Father never spoke a word," India's mother had said time after time, as her mind wandered and complaint became her only mode of speech. Poor mother—India's daughter, then a different India's mother—born to be a butterfly but doomed to live as a fragile, pretty cuckoo in an eagle's nest. All turned to dust.

In the farthest corner, Hiram and Beatrice Jenkins, TOGETHER IN GOD, missionaries retired to the mountain air for the sake of Hiram's lungs. Great-grandmother had dressed in black every day of her life and managed what no other woman of her line since had ever come close to: the forming of her daughter into another edition of herself—India the First, taciturn, correct, a woman made of stone. Let them lie. The graveyard had always opened in India a wondering sympathy for her mother. It was the only thing that could.

Now she saw for the first time that there was a space beside her mother's grave where someone else might finally rest. Deliberately she sat exactly there, turning away from the stones and looking outward. The dead had the best view in town, down the valley to the west. On a fine morning you could see a hundred miles, but now the sun was shining into India's eyes; that was why they watered so.

Twilight

I CAN see my husband Dougie's head against the dying daylight square of the bedroom window. His profile. What is that vertical line right down the middle? Ah, the clear tube of the IV that drips painkiller into my arm. His craggy jaw was once his most outstanding feature; now it's his eyebrows, grown bushy already, though he's barely into his forties. They give his face the look of a startled owl. Why did I marry him? Why did I stay? Too late to think about that. I have more urgent questions now.

He hasn't spoken; there was never much to say. I know the time running through his head is counting toward the day, maybe the hour, the minute, when he can be with his girlfriend openly. Poor Dougie. It's funny, really, that this shell, this husk of me upon a bed, can tie him here like a lover: my stringy hair, sunken, blotchy cheeks, bones draped in skin. They won't let me have a mirror, but I know. Mother was my mirror, years ago. It's different when it's yourself. Not as bad in some ways. Not what I thought.

I felt for a moment as I woke today that it was Rhodri's body, not mine, lying on this bed. I grasped my own shoulder, but it was his flesh I felt under my hand, solid and warm. Was he thinking about me then? I know he was, just as he's in my mind each minute, sometimes a hairbreadth below the surface, yet always there. I don't even have to close my eyes to see him, throwing a hawk into the sky, and my body tenses with love and loss. Sometimes I can't tell which is real and which a vision: Rhodri with his wide-winged bird or my fast-dwindling remains trapped in this bed.

I had it almost figured out just as I faded into sleep last time. What it all meant. Why I found the falconer too late. Something to do with God, I think. Or gods, the old ones, who liked a good laugh. Taking their ease on Olympus, lifting their cups of foaming nectar, and meddling in our lives for sport.

It's these awful drugs. They blur my mind when I want to concentrate. So little time left, and no answer yet. There has to be a clue somewhere, encrypted in the shapes of things: the streaks of jet vapor white across the sky, the mocking dance the flames do in a fireplace at night, the way the falcons' wings turn up at the tips as they glide. A tendency toward the sky. Is that it?

The night is coming. I must think. What if I slide my punctured arm under the covers, pinch the tube, and stop the flow of drugs, hide it beneath my elbow? How soft and slack the skin; it feels a hundred years old. There. Now let the mind grow clear as night draws in. Dougie didn't notice, hasn't stirred. Was that a snore?

First Star ◑

*I*NDIA Blake was plump the whole first half of her life. All through grade school and high school. Not fat. Just an extra thirty pounds rounding her cheeks, giving her a little second chin, making a bulge above her waistband. Plump and shy. Never a date, never a pajama party. How could she invite anyone to her house? Crazy mother in her bathrobe all day, hair grown greasy on its rollers. Her mother sewed, built crazy clothes that India refused to wear. Things she'd seen on TV. Bell-bottoms with ruffles all down the legs, and Nehru jackets in gray-blue chintz with big pink flowers, to be worn with strings of cheap beads. India longed to fly from that house, up over the mountains to a land far away.

Dougie Davern was four years ahead of her in school, his jaw still firm, his eyebrows thick but not yet bushy. Captain of the football team, Golden Boy, American icon. Their eyes never met a single time the one year they were both students at White Creek High. Then he was gone. She dreamed. Perhaps she dreamed of him because he was gone. The falconer once said, "You can tell about people by their absences. By the shape of the emptiness they leave behind." The emptiness Dougie left in her fifteen-year-old heart was the shape of an anchor. She thought it would hold her steady, that it meant something firm and strong. She dreamed of finding solace and contentment in his arms.

She had always felt the world calling, drawing her away from the little Sierra-foothill town of her birth. She used to run away from home at every change of season until she was eleven, when her mother found the key to keep her locked in place: grotesque accounts of what would happen to a girl-child on her own. There were terrible men who would cage her and do dark and nameless things. For months after this, India pushed her dresser in front of her bedroom door at night and slept with the light on. Now she wonders where her mother got those nightmare visions. Somehow this question is even more frightening than the stories themselves.

Despite the horror tales, which she finally taught herself to disbelieve, her yearning to depart grew stronger, more insistent. She made plans. She would go to college in the East, find a career that would take her far away: paleontology, archaeology, the history of art. When she was grown and strong, she would wander.

Meanwhile the clutch of her mother's needs tightened like claws around her life. Why, she asked again and again, did they call it inflation when all it did was shrink the pension India's father had left? They could barely afford to eat. There was no money for the school trip, the summer camp (foolish waste, when they lived at the mountain's knees already); no money for a car or insurance for a teenage driver, let alone college. Seeing her mother's glee at having this excuse to keep her near, India smiled through her teeth; she knew that all she had to do was wait.

The long purgatory of high school finally ended. The scholarships were all arranged; she was nearly free. But as she stepped toward the brink, her mother found one final claim. Cancer, the ace of trumps.

For five years India tended her, at first working part-time at the local bakery just to get out of the house each day, in the end not even free enough for that. Five years of barring the door to keep her mother from wandering, drunk, into the street (always money for booze—India never did figure out how she managed it); of listening to tirades of despair, then silence; of cleaning the messes, holding the wasting hand—even at the end unrecognized and unnoticed.

By the time Leonora Blake died, India's dreams were in moth-balls, the scholarships long gone. But Dougie Davern was back, meeting her eyes at last. She was so tired. Even though everything else had changed from the days when she had loved him from afar, there was this one dream left.

She married him. She had thinned down, carved to bone by her service and her sacrifice. Gone was the baby fat, the second chin. She was like a marble angel with a lamp inside: high, broad cheek-bones and enormous haunting dark brown eyes that glowed. No more the timid, apologetic girl, but a woman who had laid out her dead, whose dreams lay buried in the carapace of stern necessity.

"What are you thinking?" Dougie would ask when she fell into a reverie about the past. She felt pressured, pried at. She wanted to shake the dark thoughts off, not dwell on them, not dig and exam-ine, trying to find words soft enough to tell it without howling.

"Come on, you can tell me, pet." He urged her often, seemed hungry for her confidence the more she held it back, crouching beside her chair as she stared out the window at the dusk. "Come on, it can't be that awful. Isn't that what love is—perfect trust?" His voice went all soft and squishy when he said it, setting her teeth on edge. "It wouldn't matter what you'd done," he swore, and she had to laugh at how far his imaginings were from the truth.

Once, she relented, spoke to him about her mother's final weeks, about how alone she'd felt, how at the end of a day of bedpans, spit-out food, and curses she would crawl into her own bed and lie there shaking, trying not to cry.

"You can cry now," he said. "It's safe here. Go ahead." His eyes gleamed; she saw that he wanted her to weep, that he was eager for her to be weak and in need of comfort.

Even though she did her best to protect it at the start, his passion soon wore off or burned away in her flame, like the moth-wing stuff it really was. Numbly she noted her own indifference. She stayed. She had filled her time, read every travel or history book in the library, gone on expeditions into the mountains, bringing home rare grasses and seeds and building a garden of native flowers by sheer determination. Transplanted roots they said would die; germinating seed they said would grow only in the wild. She would never again bow down to "can't." She would gather deer droppings to fertilize the meadow plants, scrape up sods of forest floor to carry back for the delight of her tamed darlings. She was a force of nature, the earth mother—not all billowing hips and flowing milk, but lean and strict and hardworking: a priestess, a warrior woman, a queen.

She became interested in the lore of the native people, their herbal knowledge, their rituals. The silent, town-bred remnant of the local tribe opened to her stillness, her edge, her cool kindliness, like the kindness of water running over stone. They gave her a name (maybe it was one of their subtle, secret jokes), calling her after the fox's vertebra she'd found in the forest and wore on a silk cord around her neck: Fox Bone Woman.

Sometimes she thought she might be as crazy as all the other women in her family: her namesake grandmother; her giddy dipso-maniac mother; even her dour great-grandam glaring in black bom-bazine from the parlor wall. But even if she was like them, a sprout of the same root, it made no difference. Still she stood alone.

Night

I CAN stand the pain. It's white, and seems to turn and turn like a dog before lying down. The nurse tiptoes in. "I'm awake," I tell her. I can see her expression of concern, and I lower my eyelids a fraction to look sleepier, am rewarded by hearing what she whispers as she hands Dougie the evening paper.

"Great tragedy." I think at first they are talking about me, that somehow my death has made the evening paper, though it hasn't happened yet. At least I think not.

"Horrible way to go," he agrees, the paper rustling. "Heroic."
Can't be me. Not heroic.

"Who?" I ask uneasily, though what could be left in the world to
make me uneasy this near eternity myself?

"One of the smoke jumpers," she says. "Rhodri MacNeal." She
mispronounces his name, saying Rod-ri instead of Rory. Most people do, unless they know. The newspaper, as usual, has got the
details wrong. He's no smoke jumper. He is—he was—a pilot.

For a moment I am tempted to release the IV line and let
nepenthe flow. But my annoyance at the story's inaccuracy gives me
time to think, collect myself, hold on. This is a different pain,
another question, and I have no time.

Then comes the second shock as news proceeds from brain to
heart. How can I bear it? I've been lying here so long, my only glad-
ness knowing that he was out there somewhere, he and the falcons,
still flying. How? A new question to add to "why?" and make the
puzzle deeper. Why such grief, when I knew I would never see him
again? Oh, heart! My love. It's too hard. I don't know how to go on.

Last Things ⟯⟯

SHE'D thought, as she wandered the town after her doctor's
appointment, about telling Dougie. The doctor had offered to
do it, but she had warned him off. She could predict with awful certainty her husband's reaction. This was just the sort of event that
kicked Dougie's sense of destiny into high gear. There would be
speeches, tears, another grand repentance no doubt; and Clarissa,
or the current girlfriend, would be banished to await the outcome.
The more India thought about it, the more impossible it seemed. It
could wait. She would be better able to bear his effusions of sincere but superficial grief once her own initial shock had passed.

When Dougie got home that night, he found India still awake,
to his embarrassment. She was making some kind of list and did not
seem to notice the pungent remainder of Clarissa's personal scent
that clung to him.

"Whew. Had to walk all the way around the old Bower place four or five times today. Some young fellow from Santa Barbara kept me up there for two hours. . . ." It was the best he could do on the spur of the moment, but luckily, she wasn't paying much attention. He dove for the bathroom and a midnight shower. Never thought to question this break in their routine. Poor Dougie lacked even the most vestigial scrap of imagination, taking for granted that his transparent lies had served their purpose well enough, for India never seemed to guess. Or else wouldn't she have made a fearful scene? Take that as given. At such moments India almost loved him for his innocence.

But this night he could have brought Clarissa herself into their bed, giggles and bitten nails and push-up bra and all. India's concentration had never been so complete. So far the tally read "see the ocean, balloon ride, river raft, find a thunder egg." She was surprised at herself. Sitting at the plain pine bedroom desk to plan what she wanted to do before she died, she had expected a flood of desires. But she was only writing down those goals that were still possible to reach. It would be pointless to write "visit Hawaii." A man who attempts to sell insurance and real estate in a community of three thousand cannot afford such luxuries, even for a wife about to die.

She omitted other things because they were beyond her power to arrange, but they made up an involuntary mental list: seeing a comet shower, the aurora borealis, the blooming of the century plant. And all those hawks endlessly hovering over every meadow; she had never seen one stoop, not once. A lean and hungry life they must lead. So much patience, so rarely rewarded.

But hadn't she heard something about falcons once, weeks ago? Jerry at the post office had mentioned "some foreign fellow living up toward Vreeland, who keeps falcons, hunts with them!" She'd been waiting in line behind Marie Hacker, had to endure her gush and reminiscences of dear Leonora, with whom she'd been in school.

Marie had evidently asked a question about the overheard matter of falcons, and Jerry was spouting off as he took a box from Godiva off the highest shelf. "I asked Mike Barstead, the game warden, you know. He says it's all aboveboard, regulated just like fishing. You have to have a license; that's the government for you. Got to have a license just to own a hawk. Fact."

His face changed when he saw India behind Marie; his manner became more formal. "I've got your package out the back. It said to keep in a cool, dry place, so I put it under the steps. Coolest place we've got." Marie had raised a fuss then, scolding Jerry for putting her chocolates near the ceiling, where the air was warmest.

India wrote it down: "fly a falcon." The first thing on the list she had felt really excited about. A perfect place to start.

It hadn't been as easy as she expected. Jerry recalled nothing. "Falcons? I never said anything about falcons! You must of heard it somewhere else."

She tried the local vet, who suggested a bird specialist down in Vinton, but a phone call netted no new information. The pet store in Deer Creek was no help either.

Normally, once she'd set her sights on something, she was as single-minded as a tree root pushing up a slab of sidewalk, but now things were different. Time mattered. She'd been about ready to forget the falcons, move on to the next item on her list. "I don't know where else to look," she was saying to Jean Jones as they waited for the butcher to tenderize Jean's Swiss steaks. "Maybe I dreamed it. There's no sign of a tame falcon from here to Route 5."

"What's this sudden interest in falcons?" Jean asked.

"Falcons?" the butcher said. "You looking for a falcon?"

"You know one, Plunk?" she asked.

"Sure. There's a guy comes in here every two-three weeks, buys a gross of frozen quail. Asked me if I could ever get any dead chicks for these hawks he keeps. He bought the old Oneida homestead, off the Vreeland Road. Name's Rhodri MacNeal." Plunk had pronounced it right. Rory.

He had no phone, of course, but she thought she could find her way, though she hadn't been up there for years. She set out the next morning, aiming toward the ridge above China Flat, and found the place within an hour, half by cloudy recollection, half by guess. No one was there. The old cabin had been newly roofed; and freshly graveled paths led from a fiberglass-covered carport to rebuilt front steps and from there to a row of new wood cages on the uphill side of the house: six separate enclosures big enough to walk into, with a screened-in passageway outside their slatted doors. The smell was sharp, slightly bitter, and clean, almost overpowered by the scent of new wood.

She sat on the front step, chilled by the morning shade, to write a note on the back of a grocery receipt, the only paper she could find in the jeep: "Dear Mr. MacNeal." Then she heard a truck grunting its way up the slope in four-wheel drive. She half rose, feeling like a trespasser, as it came into view around the last bend— a bright red pickup with a homemade camper shell. Whimsical, incongruous: a small brown-shingle house with red-shuttered windows like a Gypsy caravan, and little open skylights on the roof. All for some birds. India smiled in astonished delight as the truck stopped and he emerged. Rhodri MacNeal. The falconer.

The Falconer ———————————————————— ☽

PEOPLE often remarked that Rhodri MacNeal resembled his hawks, with his keen gold-brown eyes and his narrow, high-bridged nose. He had played with the idea in an idle moment, brushing his rusty-brown hair straight back from his forehead and observing with surprise the numerous glints of gray. With his hair thus and an imperious frown, he thought he did resemble Morgaine, his female peregrine. But as soon as he let the hair go, it flopped forward, his mouth relaxed, and all resemblance vanished. He might not have thought so if he could have seen his profile, but he rarely did. He was not a man for mirrors.

The new place was shaping well. When he'd left Idaho, his Forest Service co-workers had all wished him good luck and added the usual gloomy predictions that speed a parting friend—in this case, that prices in California would be sky-high, Rhodri would never be able to afford a house. Plus the people were weird, different, and the forest would be overrun with tourists. He had never seen the name of White Creek before he heard about the job there, so he had doubts about the tourists. Didn't expect the people to be any weirder than those in isolated small towns anywhere. As for the prices, he had a plan for that, one that fit right in with his need for solitude and space. He would buy an old cabin so far off the beaten path that the owner had given up on selling it. Get it cheap.

He'd had little chance to check his judgments about the tourists or the local citizens, but the cabin had been easy enough to find. It was even more ramshackle and remote than he'd dared to hope, though not quite as inexpensive.

The birds' accommodations had to be built first, of course. After so many moves he could fling up a row of cages in a couple of days, while the hawks stayed in the truck. Once that was done, he had tackled the cabin roof, which clearly had had no attention for decades. Everyone he met (up to now, only the Forest Service fire crew he flew for, the postmaster, and the butcher) told him that it rarely rained until winter hereabouts. He had never lived in such a place, didn't see how such weather could exist. He had visions of eating cold beans out of a can because every pot he owned was busy catching drips. He bought shingles.

In spite of his hurry, it took two full weeks to lay the new roof, because late summer was the fire season and he had to work. In August there were four major blazes, one of them lasting six days. He lost count of how many passes he flew, how many loads of fire retardant he dropped on how many burning hillsides.

He was forty-four years old, unmarried and unmissed. At Christmas each year he sent a card to his cousin in Aberdeen, and that was that. He hadn't been back to Scotland in twenty years. His family had moved from Inverness to Toronto when he was nine, and his vowels had altered there enough to confuse Canadians and Scots about the same.

He'd been a bit solitary, even as a kid—child of a writer and a '50s ecology radical. He could never picture his mother without a pen behind her ear, a blot of ink on her middle finger, hurrying through any nonwriting task that had preempted her attention. She'd mothered him casually, with a slightly absentminded love.

It was his dad who'd brought him up, tramping around the Scottish Highlands and then the woodlands of Ontario counting nature's losses. He'd learned to read by locating which boxes to check on endless tallies on his father's clipboard and by sitting in his father's lap finding the keys on the typewriter that added up to impassioned letters to editors who rarely printed them. Knew how to pitch a tent before he learned to write, how to capture and tag a wild bird before he had his first date. It was always a relief to let the birds go again, a relief and a sorrow, and those nights he often dreamed of taking wing himself—and in waking life vowed one day he would.

As he grew older, his mother's bemused affection became more personal. It was as if she could relate to him only in the modality of literature; he had to present a theme, an unexpected metaphor or hidden meaning. He remembered clearly the sharp, focused look she'd turned on him when at his eighth birthday party (a picnic in a sunny glen beside the river Carron) he'd said to her, "This is like *Wind in the Willows*."

"How?" she'd asked.

Pinned down, he'd looked for details. "Not the trees. The stream, I guess. The noise it makes, and the grass along the bank."

She'd only nodded, a faint smile. He felt he'd accomplished something, that she approved. He tried to repeat the act, but it fell flat. That taste of her attention had whetted his appetite, though, and he wouldn't give up. He tried writing stories to show her, but that didn't work. Brought home botanical specimens, stray animals, friends. He learned a lot about what she was indifferent to: news of the world, complaint, his father's work. Then one day she saw him handling a piece of quartz he'd been carrying in his pocket for weeks, a squat crystal he'd picked up on one of his father's trips. She asked what it was, and without thinking, he told her, "A thing that fits my hand," and demonstrated how his four fingers precisely encircled its girth, how his thumb fitted in the slightly concave blunt end. He saw her look impressed again.

He never found the rule for her brief bursts of interest but discovered in himself an instinct that often worked. Brought home the friend who was trying to read all of Trollope in one year, the carved peach pit picked up next to a dead fire left by unknown trespassers in the wilderness. Each time he found a new key, they talked, and more and more often he could find a key in talk itself.

"You're a peculiar bird," she said to him once. "You'll do something strange in life." At sixteen that wasn't what he wanted to hear, and he had let it drop. She'd died soon after that, an aneurysm that he pictured shattering her brain, so he never got to ask exactly what strange thing she foresaw in his future. Certainly nothing like the life he'd actually picked.

Two years later, while Rhodri was in his first year of college, his father was killed helping fight a forest fire. Suddenly it all came clear: Rhodri would make his dreams of flying real and at the same time do battle with the enemy that had taken his father's life. He left McGill and came to the States, joining the air force to earn the skills that he would need. Vietnam was no part of his master plan, but his experience there, the hardest sort of flying you could ever do, looked well on his résumé once he'd survived. He'd done it all—helicopters, parachute runs, transport, and now the chemical drops, which he liked best because he flew alone. But the airplanes had never really answered his dream. It wasn't until he found the falcons that he knew what flight was all about.

There had been women, of course. The usual hormonal madness of adolescence muted by shyness and confusion. Several calf-loves and one fairly long and wholly unrequited obsession with a prom queen two years his senior. As he matured, he was puzzled to note that the women he met seemed to fall into three types: ones who wanted to cling and be sheltered, ones who wanted to control and be master, and ones who just wanted sex. He knew there had to be other sorts than that, but he never seemed to find them. It was surprising how many of the sex-loving sort there were—pleasant companions who made no inconvenient demands. It was enough for now. His heart remained asleep.

Turning forty had troubled him. Though unconventional in their careers, his parents had been in other ways very much in tune with their times, and echoes of this '50s Calvinism still had the power to provoke thought. He didn't feel lonely, got on well with the others on the fire crew, and enjoyed the time he spent at work. But returning to his aerie was always a relief. The birds were good company: dignified in repose and glorious in flight, sometimes comical as well, when like greedy children they tried to hide their kill with outstretched wings, glaring defiance at him.

How was it possible to have a life so perfect and yet to feel an emptiness? He tried to chalk it up to the influence of early impressions, vestigial, as pointless as an appendix, but the feeling persisted without regard for his rationalizations.

The house above China Flat was exactly what he'd always wanted. Solitary, sheltered, but from the sleeping loft commanding a view that seemed to go to the earth's edge without a single sign of humanity. Best of all, this came with only a ten-minute drive down to the mile-wide meadows of China Flat, where the birds could be worked, and again, miraculously, no other house in sight.

He liked to fly them early in the day, with the sun just turning the dew to mist. There were days, like this one, when the world seemed to shift modes, reality becoming magic, and every falconer who ever lived looked through his eyes at the bird as she soared and stooped. He felt as if he might turn and find a king with his company watching from restless mounts; he could almost hear the jingle of the bridles, the crunch of horses' teeth on a stolen mouthful of meadow grass, the snuffling and muttering of dogs as they explored the fragrant earth. The birds flew perfectly; the sun was never in his eyes; he could not take a step wrong.

As he drove back up to the house, he felt his exaltation floating around him like a feather cape. All the more shock to see at first a scruffy old army jeep blocking the spot where he normally parked, and next moment a woman, apparently cloaked in white, rising from his own front step and emerging from the shadow of the house into the clear early light. As if out of the past into the present. It must have been an optical illusion, but it seemed to Rhodri that in the shadows she had been dressed in mist. In the light her clothes were plain enough: white jeans and a man's white dress shirt, some kind of bone on a cord around her neck. He stepped out of the truck and faced her across the yard.

I KEEP coming back to that first proof of magic on that chilly morning when he stepped toward me and changed my life. What was left of my life. I run the moment over and over through my head. It's better than the drugs they give me. It keeps the pain away; it never fails. Surely that means something. If I could run that moment through my head enough, let it circle until it filled me right up, I might even escape somehow, might spin out into infinity and away from the constant irritations of being cared for.

Bad line of thought. The spell is broken, and as if she heard it break, here comes that dratted nurse to keep me from building it back up. Clarissa had better look to her laurels; this nurse will edge her out of Dougie's affections. Trays with soup, newspapers, little consoling words. By the gleam of interest in his eye I can see he's getting far more pleasure out of her nursing than I am.

They whisper but do not look my way. The evening sky has faded; the awful yard light's glare obscures the night. Shall I whisper too? Tell them it hurts my eyes and ask to have it out? Even now Dougie twitches with impatience when I ask him to turn off his lovely gadget—the floodlights that come on like magic as the day recedes. He never could understand my preference for the natural night; he was as proud as any pioneer wresting a few acres of garden from the prairie grass. Mine! his wattage cries, claiming the land, the sky, and his rulership. Once he even canceled a tryst with Clarissa just because he was so furious that I would turn that light out the minute he was gone.

When I was small, I was allowed to have anything I wanted to eat on my birthday. Dessert first. Cold pie for breakfast and hot pie for lunch. Though it's not my birthday, I hum a little of the birthday song as Dougie leaves his nice hot soup to go turn out the light.

There. Suddenly the top of the window shows one bright star in a sea of inky blue-black, while below I can see the pale remnant of the day lying along the horizon, exhausted. I look for fire glow,

Rhodri's pyre, but there's nothing. It must be to the north, up toward . . . China Flat. Seized with a panic, I ask the nurse for the newspaper, demand to be propped up, telling her to hurry. But panic is more than my strength can sustain, and I end in letting her read it to me—about the fire. And as soon as I hear the first paragraph, I am hit with a wash of relief, or drugs. My struggle has released the IV tube, and once again I'm sinking as the narcotic seeps into my brain. I hear the rest through a fog. He wasn't the pilot that morning; he'd gone to assist the jumpers, and his chute had failed to open. It doesn't make much sense. Rhodri never jumped. I suppose they've got it wrong again and I will never know the truth. I can only hold fast to the knowledge that at least it didn't happen near his house; the cages are not burning. For a drugged moment I forget that without Rhodri the safety of the cages is nothing.

Six Pairs of Eyes ＿＿＿＿＿＿＿＿＿＿＿ ◎⟩

*T*HE falconer moves without haste, passing back and forth between his truck and a flat area where he lays out his equipment, seemingly oblivious to the tremors India feels each time he comes near her.

He explains as he works. "These are perches for the goshawks; they've been bow-shaped since the Middle Ages." He shows her three heavy-looking metal arches with spikes beneath the flat bases at either end, and then sets them aside on the ground.

The birds are perched on two Astroturf-covered pipes running lengthwise along the inside of the Gypsy-cottage truck bed. India wonders when he will reach in and take one on his hand, expects this each time he leans into the little cabin, is disappointed each time he emerges with no more than another inanimate object.

"They say the design began at Agincourt," he goes on about the perches, "when the archers stuck their bows into the ground to give the nobles' falcons a place to perch. Now they're made of steel, you see, with this Astroturf wrapped round the top for the birds to stand on. Not so very authentic, but it's for the good of their feet."

The slight burr of his *r*'s, the rounded vowel sounds, give his speech a rough, homely quality. It sounds cozy, should be cozy, but India can feel an answering vibration in her spine, like the slow, sleepy rasp of a cat's tongue.

The perches don't look much like bows, being too small and too acutely bent. "Wouldn't the bowstring get in the way?" she asks, summoning her logical faculties back by force. "Those longbows were what won the battle at Agincourt. If I'd been one of the archers, I wouldn't've let them spoil my weapon just to make a perch for someone's pet."

He laughs. "Perhaps you're right." Then he takes out a hawk, and India loses interest in her quibble. It's about fifteen inches from hooded head to the talons gripping Rhodri MacNeal's leather-gauntleted wrist, its breast a golden-white with dark brown speckles, its wings and tail various shades of gray, in handsome scallops.

"This one is Morgaine," he says. "She's a falcon, which is to say a female peregrine. The males are called tiercels, from the Latin *tertius,* which means 'third.' They're about a third smaller—unusual in the bird kingdom, but it works for them because they share territory during the time it takes to bring the young up. Both parents mind the nest and feed the eyases, which is what the young are called. Being different sizes, they prey on different creatures. That's how they can share the same territory without competing."

"Very sensible of them." She blushes because she can't seem to find a thing to say that doesn't sound inane. The bird sits beautifully still in its leather hood, which is prettily decorated with stamped designs of some kind of flower India doesn't recognize. The shape is sinister, like the helmets of the Third Reich.

Rhodri holds the bird easily on his left fist. There's a leather thong attached to the gauntlet, and with his right hand he passes its loose end through the metal ring joining the two ends of the jesses. India is proud that she knows this word for the leather straps attached to the hawk's ankles, but can't think of a way to use it in a sentence. "We have special knots," he says, "because we have to do everything one-handed. Right-handed. You always carry a hawk on the left, so even most left-handers do it exactly like this."

"She's beautiful," says India, longing to touch yet fearful of that great hooked beak. She notices that the falconer offers the falcon no caress. The only handling was when he pushed his wrist against the bird's legs so that she had to step onto it or fall backward.

He carries the falcon to the cage, removes the hood, sets her on her perch, and unties the jesses from his glove. "They're hooded to keep them calm while they're carried about."

India nods. "Why do they come back to you?" she asks. Chides herself for thinking the answer is obvious; they come back because he's a force of nature, irresistible.

He moves back and forth from truck to cages, one trip for each bird, explaining as he goes. "They come back because they're hungry. You have to feed them every single time, feed them on the fist, always. They're sated now. If I tried to fly one, she'd just take off, and I might never see her again. No matter how careful you are, you lose one from time to time. It's part of the sport."

India is feeling a bit chilled standing in the redwood's shade, and moves to a patch of sunlight nearer the cages, nearer the path he takes moving each bird. "Still, it must be infuriating to lose one."

"Oh, I didn't say I liked it! They're a lot of work to train."

She's angry with herself now. She came to fly a falcon, and it isn't going to happen, and instead of paying attention to the birds, rapidly disappearing into their cages, she's mesmerized by the man, can't take her eyes off him, his bare forearms, the way the ruddy gold hairs gleam in the sunlight. She should be attending to his words, finding sensible things to ask. He's explaining the arcana of the falcons' diet, their long history, the differences between the longwing and the shortwing varieties, but she can only watch the falconer himself, listening with her eyes, her mind bedazzled.

Until he says, "The books don't go into the philosophy of the sport, but I think it was more than a hunt. It's some kind of ritual allegory. All the work, and then letting it go, trusting it will come back to you. And in another sense, the struggle to master nature, to merge with it, to become one with the force of life even in its darker aspect. You throw the bird up, and she catches the air under her wings and climbs it like a ladder to heaven. And the moment she pauses, turns . . . It's like the way you're supposed to feel when you pray, but never do. At least I never did."

He's moved all the birds into cages now. He pulls off the glove and turns to look at India. She's speechless. He's grabbed her heart and thrown it into the sky. "You're a poet," she says.

He smiles at some thought this provokes. "I'm a falconer," is his reply.

Good-bye Without Leaving

H E NOTICED her wedding ring. She saw his eye flick past it and felt a distance between them increasing. She stood frozen, caught by a confusion of impulses: to take it off, to cover it with her other hand, to wish that she had removed it long ago. It has annoyed her daily for years, sliding around on her thin finger, slipping off and losing itself among the pots and pans as she does dishes. But she couldn't very well remove the ring and pocket it right before his eyes. She crossed her arms over her chest and immediately felt embarrassed. Would he think she was attempting to hide her breasts?

"How did you get into falconry?" she asked.

He had seen something on TV soon after his return from Vietnam. He'd been stationed at Wright-Patterson, training new pilots on the latest Sikorsky helicopters, feeling restless and dissatisfied. He knew he would get no more training that was useful to his long-range goal; he was simply working out his hitch. Then this PBS program came on. He was watching TV to fill an empty evening, and it changed his life. He did the research, wrote, phoned, and when he was discharged, he was ready. He took his savings and flew straight to Scotland, for two years lived and worked in the only falconry school in the English-speaking world, and found himself a soul.

"Soul?" she said. "Do you really believe that?"

"I know it. It's right here." He pointed to his solar plexus with a grin. "When I watch the birds, I can feel it, something like a heart. Bigger."

She didn't get the grin. "Are you serious?"

"Partly. It's strange, flying. You look down and you see patterns that are only visible from the air. A river wandering across the land, with all its little tributary streams, looks just like the veins in a leaf. The ocean looks like a huge piece of rough silk. Do you ever feel as if things are trying to talk to you?"

"Sometimes." She smiled a little at the irony of it—of him asking if things talked to her and of her reply, so calm, so equivocal, and all the while she struggled to hide her feeling that every atom of his physical self was calling to her: Closer, come closer. He didn't seem to be aware of it.

"You'll be thinking I'm some kind of a crackpot," he said.

"Oh no. I've seen it too. The way everything has a shape . . ." She felt foolish. Of course everything had a shape. What a stupid thing to say.

"Yes," he said.

There was nowhere to take it. They'd been standing too long, he unconsciously picking at a chalky spot on the leather glove, she in her ridiculous arm-folded pose. The sun was higher. She supposed he had work to do. She backed away a step.

"I'm sorry you didn't get to see them working. Maybe you could come back another time, earlier in the day?"

"You wouldn't mind?"

"I'd like to show you. Only I fly them just a little after dawn, about six thirty. Can you come that early?"

"Oh yes. That's not a problem. Shall I meet you here?"

He hesitated a moment, then said yes. Perhaps he was already having second thoughts. She thanked him formally and took her leave. The day seemed to dim a little as she drove away.

HE HAD thought at first she was a ghost. They'd told him when he bought the old place that there was one, but gave no details as to age or gender. He knew well that any lonely spot, unlived in for years, would attract such an idea. And what was a ghost, anyway, but another sort of person?

As she came into the sunlight, he realized she was not that other sort of person, though what sort she was he could not tell. Certainly not the usual sort. Maybe some kind of cross between a woodsy woman and a barbarian queen.

She walked toward him as if she owned the earth, her large dark eyes seeming to open his face and inquire into his mind. No hello, no apology for trespassing. Right to the point: "I've come to see your hawks." And instead of questioning her—who are you, how did you find me, and why?—he merely said, "They're in the truck."

He found it difficult to remember exactly how it had gone after that. He'd babbled, droning on and on about the hawks as he caged them, probably boring her to death. She'd made an intelligent remark about that old legend of the bowmen at Agincourt inventing the falcon perch. All these years he'd taken that tale as gospel, and in seconds she'd demolished it. Of course she was right; once you doubted the story, its weaknesses suddenly revealed themselves. What self-respecting archer would shove his weapon into the dirt for some filthy, militarily useless bird to spoil with its talons? It had come over him that she would understand anything he said; more, that she could instantly tell the true from the false, like an oracle.

Which hardly accounted for the other feelings, the warm pull of tension in his lower belly, the desire to reach out and touch that odd upper lip right where the philtrum ought to be. To pick up and examine the piece of bone that hung just between her breasts.

Seeing that she wore a wedding ring, he tried to abandon those thoughts, but they sprouted legs and ran after him, refusing to be left behind. He could see them, shaped like body parts trotting along in his wake. She had laughed until the tears came when he told her this later on. No particular body parts, just little flesh-colored potato shapes with arms and legs and tiny bowler hats, running furiously down a dirt road. "Very tasty little thoughts they are too," she said (later), and demonstrated her theory of what they represented, until everything else blurred away.

He'd schooled himself to see her as nothing more than an attractive married woman with a curiosity about the birds. He'd told her everything, and she had listened, expressed her interest, and thanked him politely, trying to appear satisfied. How was it possible for her to be satisfied when she had not seen them fly? He made the offer, half expecting her to turn it down with some excuse: Oh, I have to make breakfast for my family. I could never come that early.

Instead, her tone when she said "That's not a problem" awakened all those thoughts again. It was a tone that said, without shouting it—indeed trying to conceal it—that her husband was another sort of person too. A foolish sort, if he had made himself so negligible in her life that she could come and go without comment no matter what the hour. Rhodri felt the tension in his upper abdomen loosen and realized for the first time that he had almost been holding his breath for her answer. And then the other tension returned tenfold.

"What's your name?" he asked, following her to her jeep.

"India," she said. "After my grandmother."

"It suits you," he said. He didn't ask for the rest of it. The rest of it was entirely beside the point.

Messages in Sanskrit

So THAT was how we met. Debating the existence of meaning in the early morning sunlight of October, air clear and ripe with the scent of pine, ringing with birdcall. It reminded me of when I was a little girl, opening the screen door after breakfast and being reborn, from dim house into shining day. How each time the world seemed to pick me up and swing me high over its head, like a laughing father full of joy.

If things have meaning, that meeting surely did. It was all there: the bright promise of completion and the valedictory light of the dying year. Large things within small things, the falcon's power of flight restrained by leather straps with bells. Fourteen years of marriage in a phrase, and death itself in the claw of a half-tamed bird.

And what of me? Death was inside me too, and inside him, as it is within everyone. And yet the sun shone, and I for one was happy. All the rest is that. How happy I became. Happy. Such a childish word. A small word for a feeling so immense that the sky was barely able to cover it. I thought it was something to leave behind, for Rhodri to recall. Instead, he's dead before me, and I'm the only one left with the memory, and barely time enough to play it through again. Heaven in retrospect.

Forward   ⸬

S HE slept lightly that night, frequently rousing to check the sky. Yet when the alarm clock gave its preparatory click at five thirty, she heard it in time to hit the switch before it rang, and rose refreshed, glad to leave Dougie asleep. Not that he would wonder where she went; he was too used to her absences, too indifferent.

The first smoky light of dawn was filtering through the treetops; the birds were waking up. Her thoughts about this meeting had come in starts and stops. She caught herself planning an outfit of dark green slacks, snug and flattering, a white silk shirt, her suede jacket. She rejected that idea, deriding the impulse; she might as well show up in a miniskirt and spike heels. What would she wear if she were meeting Jean? She ended up erring on the side of utility: a pair of pale gray bush pants she often wore on her plant-hunting hikes, a pale gold flannel shirt, a charcoal-gray wool pullover. As she looked at the chosen clothing laid out on the spare-room bed, she laughed at herself. She had picked the colors of the birds.

Again in the shower, start and stop. She soaped with scented gel, then washed the smell off and later skipped perfume, though she normally wore it. No makeup, that was standard. She did blow-dry her hair, arguing that it would be cold out there. She'd catch her death (that would be ironic) with wet hair. When she was done, the shoulder-length pale gold mass shone like a halo. She fastened it back as usual, but with her best tortoiseshell clip.

And wondered why she was being so stern with herself. Certainly she had no qualms about Dougie. It had been years since he'd shown any desire to exercise his "conjugal rights." Yet she would not deliberately set out to seduce some stranger, though he warmed her thoughts to the boiling point. Better to turn to drink, like her mother, than to sink so low in her own estimation. She took off the tortoiseshell clip and used one of her cloth-covered elastic bands.

The miniskirted tart of her imagination followed her out the door and shivered in the early morning chill. India almost felt sorry for her in her skimpy rabbit coat and stockings. Then she forgot about it as the morning possessed her.

The sun was not yet over the horizon, but near enough that there was light to bring up halftones. The pines a greenish black, the scar of the driveway in between a brownish white. She stopped to listen, and heard a vibrant silence. It would be a pity to shatter that stillness by starting the jeep, but she found herself equal to it.

She had never been through town so early in the morning. No cars, no lights except in the bakery, where the owner, her part-time boss, toiled to make the town's breakfast bread. India sped past, then stopped, made an illegal U-turn, and zipped back to tap on the bakery window, begging a couple of new-baked rolls.

Off again, with the rolls under her sweater to keep them—and herself—warm, she regretted the impulse as too accommodating. Too friendly. But she couldn't regret the heat. It was time to put the top on the jeep for the winter; the wind in her face was painfully sharp.

And always there was a thought of him beneath everything else. Incoherent. Not a picture, nor a fantasy, nor a desire. He was just there, like someone hiding behind a tree or standing slightly beyond the edge of her vision.

There were plenty of attractive men in town. Some you might even say were better-looking than Rhodri MacNeal. Men with faces kind or handsome or dissolute; bodies ruggedly strong, broad, tall, muscular, or fine, and many gone to seed. Deep voices, booming laughs. Plenty who were game for a fling with a married woman. There had never been even a twitch of temptation. Why not?

As she drove up the steep and ill-paved Vreeland Road, she grew warmer. Sugar pine and Douglas fir provided shelter, and the chill lessened as she slowed, maneuvering around tight curves, gearing down for potholes the size of bathtubs. When she turned up the Oneida Road toward Rhodri's house, the pavement ran out entirely and the going became even slower. She wondered how so much impatience could fit inside her finite chest.

She was assailed by doubts as she drew closer. His hesitation after she'd accepted his invitation—he didn't really want her there, was only being polite. He'd seen her ring. Of course any worthwhile man would have important scruples about making love to a married woman. Realizing what she'd just thought, she groaned aloud, and everything she'd been trying to ignore burst plain upon her.

She stopped the jeep, switched off the engine, and sat shaking in the middle of the road. Face it, face it, face it. She didn't want to look. She didn't know why she didn't want to look. Wasn't it the stuff of legend, of song and story? Discontented wife finds solace and fulfillment with handsome stranger? She had always hated those stories, with their implication that a woman's happiness depended on a man. So tacky. Pathetic opiate for weak females of little imagination and less dignity.

But oh she wanted him. She wanted his hands to reinvent her skin. She wanted his eyes to find her behind her face and release her. She wanted her heart thrown into the sky; she wanted to fly. She wanted it before the dark closed in. So much dark, and so soon.

The only trouble was, she didn't know if he could want it too. But he might. Please, whatever God may be, he might.

RHODRI had promised himself he wouldn't wait for her. The husband might claim her after all, or some other duty, or just the lack of real desire to be there. He wasn't going to stand around like a flightless bird, hoping. The moment the sun edged over the horizon, he'd be gone. It was due at six thirty-two. Three more minutes. Of course, they might measure the time of rising where it was flat; it would take longer to climb over the top of a mountain ridge. Three more minutes and she would be late.

It was horribly like being a teenager again—the nervousness, the certainty that he would offend her somehow, misread signals, act the fool. He told himself over and over that it couldn't matter. Whatever he might have thought her tone of voice meant, she *was* married, and in these days, with marriage so easy to get out of, what could it mean but that she wanted to stay with her husband? She wasn't the sort of woman to have a meaningless fling; he felt quite sure of that. So. She was only coming up to see the falcons worked. That was all. A curiosity, a new experience for her. It was enough. Would have to be enough. After all, she was married.

He checked his watch. Six thirty-two. But the sun had not yet put its edge above the mountaintop. Rhodri went into the house and brought out a thermos of coffee, put it on the truck's seat. He checked the birds again, making sure the folding chair he'd added to his usual load wasn't going to slide around and hurt one of them. It would be all right; he had his imagination on a rein again. Morgaine shifted uneasily on her perch, and he regretted the cologne he'd put on after the sitz bath. Some kind of water heater was definitely going to have to be next on his list of home improvements.

Six thirty-five. He looked to the east, and there it was, just the tiniest sliver of gold, right at the top of the highest peak. His whole body seemed to fill with disappointment. Stupid. She was married.

Then came the sound of her jeep, whining up the last steep grade just out of sight, and his heart rose with a leap, like one of the birds taking flight.

Breaking Fast ⟶

SHE drew right up beside his truck—better than stopping at a distance and having to walk toward him while he watched. He was smiling, so that for the first time, she saw his eyes lit up, the pleasant creases of his face. When she stepped out of the jeep, she realized what a peculiar bulge the rolls made under her sweater, and she pulled them out. "Breakfast," she said.

"Great. I've got coffee." He reached into the front seat through the truck window and pulled out a large red thermos and then a pair of wide-bottomed cups.

"Aren't you freezing?" she asked. He was wearing only jeans and a yellow-and-black-plaid wool shirt, and the sleeves of that were rolled up to the elbow.

"I run hot. Why don't you pour the coffee, and I'll get you something to wear over that sweater."

She held the thermos and watched him as he walked toward his house—the way his back curved into the heavy shoulders, the way he held himself a little stiff. He knows I'm watching, she thought, and smiled, and then she turned and put the cups down on the hood of the truck and poured coffee into them.

When he came back, carrying a Pendleton jacket, a heavier version of his own shirt, she was leaning on the truck, the smile still on her face, her hands around a mug.

"You look pretty pleased with yourself," he said, handing it to her. "Put that on. It'll get warm soon, now that the sun's up."

"Thanks." She set her cup on the truck hood and slipped her arms into the jacket, too large for her even over her shirt and bulky sweater. The sleeves hung down inches beyond her fingertips, and she stood there looking at them and laughed, feeling about fifteen.

He grinned and took one sleeve and turned it back, and it scared her how much she yearned for him to just lean down and kiss her. She pulled back, turned up the other sleeve herself.

"Time to get going," he said, acting as if he hadn't noticed, but he was silent as they climbed into the truck.

"Do you have to fly them this early?" she asked quickly, knowing better than to let the silence grow pronounced.

"Doesn't matter, as long as you do it at the same time every day. I picked dawn because I'm finished in time to go to work."

"What do you do?"

"Fly for the Forest Service. Drop chemicals on forest fires. Search and rescue. Whatever they want. You?"

She shook her head. "Nobody ever asked me that before. I'll have to think about it." She handed him a roll and bit into her own, a good excuse not to talk.

He dropped into a low gear to ease them down the same impossible road she'd just come up. What do you do? Such a simple-sounding question—like "Who are you?"—with no answer that could encompass the truth. Between sips of coffee and bites of bread she did her best. She told him about the bakery, how she'd progressed from counter work to decorating cakes, but it was only occasional work in such a small town. About the garden, the illegally transplanted California poppies, the lupine and the sage, the unidentifiable plant that grew just at the snow line, with flowers so small you could hardly see them. About her friends from the tribe, the herbal baths they took for certain ills, the things the old women knew. She laughed. "I sound like some kind of crazy medicine woman, brewing potions, gathering strange stuff in the moonlight, conning secrets out of the elders of the tribe."

"You ought to write the secrets down," he told her. "People would be interested. Don't let it get lost."

"I should," she agreed, knowing there was too little time left. "So much gets lost."

When they arrived at China Flat, he showed her how to set up. Brisk and businesslike, he handed her the three bow perches and indicated the line where she should anchor them, just so far apart. He planted three others in a line parallel to hers, perches made of blocks of wood atop metal posts, also covered with Astroturf. Hooding each bird for the thirty-foot walk, he moved them from the truck to the perches, tied them, and took the hoods off. Then he got out the folding chair and placed it where she could watch, farther into the meadow and to one side, well out of the way. She stuck her hands under the front of the jacket for warmth, and sat.

The first bird leaped from the perch onto Rhodri's fist when he went to pick her up. It was the peregrine he called Morgaine, one of the three longwings. Once more he dropped the little hood over her head, tightening it by pulling two strips of leather at the back, one with his free hand and one with his teeth. He'd slipped into the lecture mode of their first meeting, telling her how the longwings were used to hunt only flying prey. The shortwings, which, unlike the longwings, were aerodynamically equipped with braking power, were used to hunt ground prey: rabbits, for preference.

"You have to weigh her first," he explained as he nudged Morgaine onto a scale. "Each bird has a flying weight. If she's too heavy even by an ounce, she might not be hungry enough to come back. She's one pound fourteen ounces today; that's all right."

He carried the bird twenty feet or so into the meadow beyond the perches, and slipping her hood off, he held her high. She seemed to rise on tiptoe, and expelled a dropping. "We call that muting; they usually do it before they take off. Makes them that much lighter." He raised his arm a bit, almost tossing her into the air. India watched the bird's rapid rise, each beat of her mighty wings thrusting her higher. She reached an altitude of perhaps forty feet and turned to glide back toward Rhodri, dipping down, then rising again in a movement like flirtation.

"She'll cruise around a little, warming up; we'll just let her do that for a few minutes." India watched. The falcon never went far, always turning and seeming to accelerate as she flew back toward him.

Rhodri was getting something out of his supply box: a string with a couple of robin-size gray wings tied together at one end.

"This is the lure. Now watch." He stepped out to where he'd released the falcon, gave a long, sharp whistle, and swung the lure around and around his head. Morgaine turned, seeming to see it even before her head came around. She bore down on it like a winged express train, at the last moment thrusting her legs forward, so that Rhodri's sudden yank was barely in time to snap the lure from between her outstretched talons.

"Did you see? They kill with their talons, not their beaks. Grab and twist. The beak's just for eating; it's the knife and fork." He swung the lure again, and again yanked it out of the falcon's grasp just as it seemed she could not fail to seize it. India was sitting forward on the chair, holding her breath. It was so beautiful.

"Now we'll see about your nerve, shall we? I'll fly her right over your head. Did you notice how she drops down below the lure and then rises to take it from below? She'll be coming right at you."

He moved behind India, and she heard the string hum as he swung the lure in the air. Morgaine saw it and swooped down nearly to the ground, no more than fifteen feet in front of India. Then the hawk rose to the bait, and India saw the glowing golden eyes coming almost straight toward her, felt the breeze of wings inches above her head, and laughed out loud in absolute delight.

IT WAS THE LAUGH THAT DID IT. All the changes of the morning vanished, and Rhodri barely jerked the lure out of Morgaine's reach in time, had to summon all his strength to walk forward into India's sight. He'd been in turn nervous, impatient, excited, wounded, soothed, interested, impressed—his emotions bobbing up and down like a cork on the ocean. No more; it was all solidified into an iron determination to have and hold this woman, married or not.

"That was great!" she was saying. "It was . . . It was . . ." Her face was radiant. He'd never seen anything so glorious in all his life.

"Want to try it?"

"Can I?" She jumped to her feet, her eagerness visible in every line of her body. She was so alive. He could feel her vitality like an electric field, was sure his hair was standing on end.

"Sure. It's not hard." He brought her the lure. She met him halfway. He had to be very careful their hands didn't touch as he passed it to her; the spark would surely short-circuit every nerve in his body. "Just swing it around your head, and when she's getting close, give it a yank." He stepped back and watched, feeling her pleasure, her concentration as she looked around first to see where the hawk was, then carefully arranged the string, checked the hawk again, and waited to start her swing until the bird was turning toward her.

"She sees it!"

"That's it. Just keep it up there . . ." Again the falcon stooped near the ground and rose to take the lure. "Now!"

His coaching was unnecessary. Just as the powerful talons were stretched forward to clutch, India jerked the lure sideways and down, laughing with delight.

"Perfect. Like you were born to it."

"Don't they get cross?"

"They're very persistent. Go ahead; have another go."

She threw the lure three or four more times while Rhodri watched. "It's like teasing death," she said, "or . . . You know those nature programs—sometimes they'll show a litter of some kind of cubs, fox or wolf or lion? When I watch those, I always wish I could be one of the cubs and play too. It's like that."

She seemed to grow sad, looped the line of the lure, and handed it back to him.

"I'll bring her in this time," he said. "You watch; then you can do it with the next bird."

He fetched a skinned quail out of the cooler, explaining, "They like quail better than what's on the lure." Concealing the food in his fist, he tossed the lure up again and swung it in its circles, and this time when Morgaine reached for it with those inch-long talons, it was there. She dropped to the ground with it, and Rhodri pulled her toward him by reeling in the lure. He made a clicking sound with tongue and teeth, showed her the meat. She abandoned the lure and jumped onto his wrist. Letting only a bit of the meat show, he quickly did his one-hand knotting trick to fasten her to the gauntlet by her jesses, then let her pull the meat up. She tore into it, and in less than a minute she'd consumed it all. "Nothing to it," he said. "Your turn now. Take Sir Kay; she's always next."

"Funny name for a female. Wasn't Sir Kay one of Arthur's knights?"

"Hawks are like boats; they're all called 'she,' no matter what the actual sex."

He put Morgaine back on her perch and handed the glove to India. She pulled it over her left hand eagerly, no flinching away from the smear of quail guts near the fist. She quietly approached the bird and pressed her wrist just above its feet. Sir Kay balked, would not get on, wings flapping wildly as she tried to keep her balance against India's push. India didn't give up, and finally, grumpily, the bird complied. "I'm not too sure about this knot," she said.

"Pull the tail out of the last loop," he instructed. "Now all you have to do is pull on it, and the rest will unravel. Be sure you've got a good grip on the jesses first."

"I get it." She threaded the jesses between the gauntlet's fingers just as she'd seen him do, untied the tether, and without further question tied the same knot to fasten Sir Kay to the glove. When she rose and turned toward him, her face shone with pride and pleasure. He wished he had a camera, but it didn't matter. He would remember that moment for the rest of his life.

I DON'T feel tired. Why would I? Lying in this bed for so long now, it's a miracle I can sleep at all. Drugs. Dougie still there in his chair. He's doing his "duty." Poor Dougie. I wonder why *he* stayed. And how appalling of me never to have questioned that before. I certainly didn't give him much to stick around for. Maybe he was afraid of what Frank, his dad, would say—an awful man who liked me. One more thing I never understood. One among many.

Frank said once, "Dougie wishes he were an Eskimo, so he could put me out on the ice." Right to Dougie's face. He meant it to wound, and I could see it did, though Dougie just laughed. Said something about holding with those who favored fire, and looked superior. He liked to show off the bits he remembered from college, especially at moments such at this. It was clear from Frank's expression that he had never heard the phrase, probably never even heard of Robert Frost, and didn't know what Dougie meant. One of those guys who sends his kid to college and then can't deal with it when he comes back better educated than his old man. He looked bewildered, just for a split second, and I felt sorry for him, though I never could keep that up for long.

So I said—I was so proud of this—I said, "I would have taken you for more of an ice man myself, Dougie," and I turned to Frank and recited the whole poem so he'd know. Emphasizing the relevant parts, especially the bit about ice being like hate. Dougie was so astonished at hearing me quote Frost in his father's knotty-pine–paneled rec room that he missed the insult, but Frank got it. He smiled at his son, and Dougie shut up, unable to figure out how he'd ended up losing that round. What a sorry little scene.

Still, I suppose living is the best revenge—whether well or not doesn't really matter. And he will live, will move Clarissa into the house as soon as he decently can, unless he decides he prefers the nurse. They'll make love in this very room. Maybe even be happy here. I hope they will. It's been empty so long, with an emptiness the shape of me. When I die, the air will come back into the room that I've filled with my absence. Why? My friends seemed present enough. Reba at the bakery with Earl—nothing but flour and sugar in their conversation all day long, but how she laughed, even when something went wrong. The time she dropped a tray of bagels onto the chocolate-frosted cake for Jimmy Davenport's eleventh birthday and invented chocolate-frosted bagels. Laughed until she was beet red.

Damn these drugs; my mind wanders. Though of course these things too are shapes. Laughter, scorn, wandering itself, even a chocolate bagel might mean something. I brought a couple to the falconer once; he didn't like them much. Didn't care for sweets, he said as he licked a drop of salty sweat out of that little hollow at the base of my throat after an afternoon in bed. We'd been laughing, and I was weak and tired and still filled with something light, like helium. It was toward the end, when the cancer's insidious foreclosure proceedings were getting too insistent to ignore. Now it owns the house, and I'm about to be evicted. A soul on the street. Or not.

One time Rhodri asked, "Do you believe in angels?" I had never given it much thought. He said, "I think we leap from our discarded bodies like a falcon off the fist, spread our new wings, and just take off." That would be nice—to have wings, to play with the falcons without having to keep them hooded, without having to tie those one-handed knots.

Claiming Freedom

"IT'S not your fault," Rhodri said as they rode up toward his house, only five birds in the back of the truck. "You did everything right. You expect to lose about thirty percent of your birds. I've lost half a dozen myself over the years."

India was too close to tears to speak. That lovely creature, leaping from her wrist and rising into the sky. It turned and swooped back overhead, then tilted right and rose and rose and rose. Behind her Rhodri had started to whistle—a loud, shrill sound that would probably carry for miles in the cold morning air, but seemed, for all the response it got, not to be reaching the departing bird at all. "Damn," he had finally said. India stood watching until the bird was lost to sight, her throat closing with disappointment.

"Come on," he urged. "Don't take it so hard. She'll probably be back tomorrow or the next day. I've been training them on that spot for weeks, ever since they finished their molt. She'll know where to come when she gets hungry."

"Do you think so?"

"Half of them do. Don't worry about it. It wasn't your fault."

She laughed a little shakily. "She probably did it just to discourage me."

"She's always been an ornery one." "Ornery" sounded strange in his muted Scots accent, a lot more *r* than most Californians would use. His exotic vowels soothed her; there was magic in being from somewhere else.

"How far do you think she'll go?"

"No telling. She has no territory of her own here, so she'll live up to her species' name and wander a bit. Some falconers attach a small radio transmitter before they fly a bird so that if it takes off, they can track it. Waste of time, in my book. Short of ruining good longbows for perches, I like to do things the old way."

"You should come and talk to Josephine Red Smoke sometime. She'd like you. She'd like the hawks. She might not think much of the cages, though."

"I don't think so much of them myself, but without them you're just a bird watcher. The cage is the price I pay to be a falconer."

She thought some about prices. "It helps to know what you're buying."

"Aye, it does that."

They seemed to arrive back in no time at all. He pulled the truck under the port and shut it off, but didn't get out. Turned to look at her. She was facing forward, but felt his eyes on her profile. "You're a bit hawklike yourself," he said. "That Roman nose, like mine. There's destiny in some shapes. You should take up the sport." She turned to look at him then; he seemed to have read her mind.

"How long would it take? To learn it, I mean. To get one of my own and train it?"

"It's the right time of year to start. You can't do anything in the summertime because of the molt, but by fall that's over, and the game season starts. You could begin now, learn a lot in the next few months. You have to serve a two-year apprenticeship before you're allowed to own one yourself."

"Too long," she said, unsure how much to tell him. A new fear occurred to her: that he might be patient. Careful. Testing the water with each step, waiting for signs, thinking there was time. If she hinted that her days were numbered, would he be put off? Or was he disinterested in the first place? And if he did have some feeling for her, even the smallest beginning of a feeling, surely she should warn him. It was all so slippery, impossible to grasp. She shivered.

"I'm keeping you out here in the cold. Come inside, and I'll make a fire." The day, begun with such a bright promise of sun, had turned cloudy, dark.

"I am a bit chilled." She argued to herself, Why all this shyness and hanging back? The image of that miniskirted, desperate floozy self leaped to her mind's eye for an answer. Horrible if he looked at her and saw that. She climbed out of the truck.

"I'll just build a fire and then put the birds away." He led the way down the gravel path, opened the door, and turned to look at her, standing back. "It isn't much," he said. "Bachelor digs. Don't be shocked." Stepping past him, she peered into the dim house, her eyes taking a moment to adjust. Then she crossed the threshold.

There was only one room—a deep armchair at the far end, a kitchen table with two straight chairs nearer by, close to the cookstove and sink. Another table against the same wall at the room's dark farther end. The bed was above that end of the space, in a loft. She looked for a light switch, then laughed at herself. There were no wires going to this place, so far from town. A kerosene lantern, two kerosene lamps, and beneath the sleeping loft a state-of-the-art, freestanding, fuel-efficient fireplace, its chimney pipe angled out the back. Pale silver light entered through windows on three sides. India could hear the ticking of a clock in the loft.

Rhodri stepped in after her and shut the door, and even with her face turned the other way, she could feel herself blushing bright enough to light the whole place. She half expected his hands on her shoulders next, but he stepped around her, went to the fireplace, and stirred a poker among the embers of an earlier fire, throwing in more wood from a pile nearby. It blazed up quickly. "Sit here." He drew the armchair nearer the warmth. "I'll be right back."

He was out the door again before she could move, leaving her to look around. But there was little to see, and she was tired from her early morning, the excitement and the sorrow. She sat in the armchair and leaned her head back. And fell asleep.

ON AUTOMATIC pilot, Rhodri put the birds away quickly. He cursed to himself as he passed Sir Kay's cage with Morgaine, last to go in. Stupid bird to go off like that just when India was enjoying herself so much. She was a difficult woman to read—one moment laughing like a child, the next sad and remote, or again suddenly impressive, like a falcon about to take wing. Hard to follow her lead. Yet she hadn't said or done anything that definitely meant no trespassing. And he had caught one look, that moment when she turned toward him after he'd said she looked like a hawk, a look that for just a moment seemed to pierce him to the bone.

He gathered more wood and returned to the house, and there she was in the armchair, curled up asleep. Lightly, it seemed, for she roused when he put down the wood, though he did it as quietly as he could. "Coffee?"

"I'd better. I don't want to nod off driving back."

"Not much chance of that in this weather. It looks like it might snow." If it did, she would be caught here. He wished for the first time that he had a phone for her to call out, so that no search party would appear if she failed to come home. Foolish thought.

"Not likely," she said, and it took Rhodri a second to remember they'd been discussing snow. "We're only at about three thousand feet, not high enough to get snow very often."

Rhodri was scooping coffee into the filter. "Can I help?" she asked.

"Nothing to do. Stay near the fire; keep warm. You'll need a good toasting before you try to go anywhere in that open jeep." He brought the kettle to the woodstove and put it on, set cups and the coffeepot and coffee in its filter on the little table nearby, then lifted one of the kitchen chairs to straddle and look at her. "You can see I don't get much company, or I'd be better equipped."

"You keep it nice and clean."

He felt a guilty grin forcing its way onto his face. "I did a bit of tidying last night. Just in case."

"Did you indeed?" She smiled back, a smile that looked like relief. "I like the way it smells. Pine needles and new shingles and"—she paused and sniffed—"earth. It smells real."

Some kind of tension had gone out of her. She lay back in the armchair relaxed, a woman in no hurry. Yet she kept her gaze on him—not a daunting stare, but moving as he moved, listening with her eyes, meeting his hungry look fearlessly and with no defense. Some Rubicon had just been crossed. "Why" was always a mystery, and never more than now. He thought of the ancient Eleusinians, who celebrated the unknown in their worship, and he understood the impulse to give thanks for things concealed from sight.

Surprise Party ————————————————

I DON'T know how we managed it, that strange transition from fear and doubt to confidence. It was more than just knowing he'd put his house in order on the chance I might come in. Maybe it was the fact that I'd slept the moment I arrived there, at the heart of his domain. I always found it difficult to sleep in strange places, difficult to sleep next to Dougie all those years. And when I opened my eyes, there he was, putting logs into a log box with the most exquisite care, as if they were made of china and might break. I felt so much at home. The firelight made his skin seem red-gold, and the warmth of the fire was creeping out into the room, so that my icy toes began to thaw, and everything was perfect as it was, the best of all possible worlds at last.

It wasn't even lunchtime, but it felt like night, the sky had grown so dark. I never gave a thought to what Dougie might think if I didn't make it home. I'd been caught by weather or night many times in the past, going to a friend's house if shelter was required, or sleeping in the down bag I carried on my treks. Never in weather this cold, but I don't think Dougie would have noted such a detail.

LOOK at that. As if he'd heard me think his name, Dougie's stirring. He'll have an awful crick in his neck. Yes, there, he rubs it, looks around, and starts guiltily to see me watching him. I suppose by some people's standards he is guilty. Yet I don't feel this myself, and not because I've been "unfaithful" too. The truth is, he's more like a brother to me. He owes me nothing. It might even be the other way around, though I always had a part-time job and the rent from Mother's house to pay my way. I kept his house, cooked his meals, and did not fret him with complaints. Can I call that a fair trade?

I think I must, as no means now remain to me to pay a debt.

But what is this? He's coming over to me, even turning the lamp so there's some light to see each other by. He looks a wreck.

"Are you okay, Dee?" he asks, using the bland nickname he invented to disguise the strangeness of "India" to his ears.

"In what sense?" I have to ask, though it's time to get past all that.

"No pain?"

"Not much. It doesn't matter."

"They can give you more—"

"No!" I say quite sharply. "No," again, trying to sound calm and rational so that he won't feel qualified to insist. I've already had some experience of how they take you over, no more a person but a Cancer Doll, a thing to which they apply strange remedies for its own good, regardless of the Me still resident.

Tit for tat. I did it to my mother; now I get it back. The words on the fluid bags have changed, but the essence remains the same. How she used to struggle, pulling the needles out until the visiting nurse was in despair. Like a wolf with its foot caught in a trap. Her mad eyes, so like the falcon's that day when it met my gaze as it swept past. Her nose, which had always been so broad and pudgy, was by then whittled down to bone. She tried to spit, but her mouth was dry, and all she could do was make a little noise—*phtt, phtt.*

"I have to tell you . . ." Dougie's voice draws me back. "Dee? We need to talk."

"I don't need to talk," I say. "I don't need anything." Not quite the truth, but I have no time to try to explain my whole life to Dougie now. And I don't want to hear his remorse. I'm surprised at him. Confession and absolution for this poor lapsed Catholic? He'd do better to see the priest.

"No. I'm going to say it, Dee."

"One last time," I tell him, "don't call me Dee. Call me my real name. Then maybe I'll listen."

"Oh." He pauses, abashed. If he had a hat in his hands, he would be holding it by the brim, rotating it round and round and round. "I never realized . . ."

"I said it once or twice."

"No, you . . ." He pauses, seeing, for once, the uselessness of that. "I guess I didn't hear you." Didn't listen, is more like it. "I'm sorry . . . India."

"You don't have to say. I know about Clarissa. It's all right."

"It isn't that."

I'm speechless. What can it mean? Does Dougie have a hidden depth—even one—that I've missed? It's all too likely, I'm afraid. I must make what amends I can. A vision of the rising falcon comes between us for a moment; I seem to hear the little bells. No, it's the spoon rattling on the tray the nurse brings in. Bad timing. "Go away," I say, surprising even myself with such rudeness. "Just for a minute?" Better. I will make a lady of myself yet. Something I never gave a damn about.

She goes. "Talk fast," I say. "Time is short." A little gallows humor to cheer us both up.

"I knew," he says, speaking slowly, seeming to choose his words, "about you and . . . that you went to bed with someone else. Not who. Just . . . you found someone."

I'm stunned again, twice in one night, and by a man whose

capacity to surprise me I'd thought exhausted by . . . Well, never mind by what. He goes on. "I don't blame you. That's what I want to say. I know I hurt you, with Clarissa and . . ." All those others, he doesn't say. I hear it anyway. "I was wrong. I'm sorry. I never loved them, really. I was faithful to you in my way. But you couldn't know that. I understand. You had your revenge. I forgive you."

Revenge! I'm so angry that I shout with laughter though it wears me out. "Oh, Dougie," I tell him, "what a lovely speech! You must have practiced all day." Where have I been keeping all this bitterness? Why can I not express it without an instant flood of remorse?

He doesn't know what to think. But never mind. There's not enough time left to make every wrong right. Besides, by the time the first sod falls on my coffin lid, he will have redesigned this whole event into a heartfelt rapprochement. He will surely tell the next woman, with tears streaming down his face, that he forgave me as I lay here almost on death's doorstep, and how we were both purified in that heartrending moment. He will move on. What else could he do? There was never any point in being cross with him.

It's this death business; it's put me off my stride. I used to be much kinder, or so I'd like to think. I didn't laugh at Mother the eighty-seven times she begged my pardon for ruining my life. I told her honestly that my life wasn't ruined at all. It never occurred to me to wonder whether that was really the comfort she wanted. It's only now, living through my own death, that I begin to see: She wanted forgiveness for her sin, not to have it denied. I should have said, "Yes, you did destroy my youth, turn my hopes to ashes, trample on my dreams. My life's an utter shambles, such was your power. But I love you anyway, and so I forgive you." If I'd said that, might she have died content? Sorry, Mother, I didn't understand.

As Dougie doesn't understand about the falconer. How Rhodri seemed to hear me in a way that made me hear myself, so that I rose, wingbeat by wingbeat, into another sort of being; how he made me fly.

And here's that nurse come back, hesitating just inside the door. "Just checking." There's a steaming cup on the tray. I wave my hand, a feeble gesture. Why won't they leave me be?

The Higher Plane ──────────────────── ⟫

*R*HODRI and I talked into the afternoon that day, laying the groundwork for our ephemeral house. Started with the particulars of our separate pasts, the ways that had led us to where we were. He spoke of his life as if it were an integrated whole, each part interlocked with every other, though he'd lived in five countries and half a dozen states. I spoke of mine as a series of accidents, though I've spent my whole life in a single town. But even as I said this, I saw that it was false, that every part of who I was and what I'd been had grown from what came before, that I had built each brand-new and separate (I thought) edifice of self from pieces I had salvaged from the one just lost.

I told him about the garden of native plants, the propagation techniques I'd figured out for myself because I couldn't find them in the books, the way I'd laid the lupine, the poppies, and the violets out in stars and swirls, ranged the creeping plants in a green rainbow, from dark, glossy evergreens to the pale chartreuse of the soft-leaved meadow plant I'd never managed to identify. As I talked about it, I saw that it had been to me as the falcons were to him, a way to slip sideways between society's demands and the savage freedom that the caged heart keeps in secret.

He told me about his struggle to find an alternative to his gas generator. He had to have a freezer to keep the quail frozen and was quickly driven to admit that there was no way to run it but electricity. He could have used the same source of power to run lights indoors, but wanted fire in his house, wanted it semi-tamed at his command, to serve his needs. And to keep him keen and clear about the thing he fought.

He talked about threads running through his life: fire, flight, mountains, and solitude.

I talked about the bakery, about the tribe's mask ceremonies that they'd never let an Anglo watch before I came, told him the tales of how I got the jeep and found the fox bone both the same day. I didn't speak of death. A silence fell. I saw I'd offered only emptiness again.

"All right," I said. I sounded exasperated, even to myself, and restless where I'd been at ease for hours. I got up on the pretense of pouring the dregs of my coffee down the sink, and said what I had to with my back to him, looking out the window at the dark, cold day. "I'm going to die. I haven't told anyone else, but I guess I've got to tell you. I'd like to pretend it isn't happening, to go on as long as I can without admitting it to anyone. But there it is. Too big to ignore. Sorry about that. Sorry."

I heard him stand up, walk across the bare board floor to me. He turned me around, put his arms around me, held me like a mother, and I put my face against his chest and for the first time wept. Bawled. Choked and sobbed and even, God help me, bellowed. He stood there and let me until I stopped. A long time, stroking my hair, rubbing my back.

Finally I seemed to be cried out. I pulled away. My head ached, and my whole face felt swollen. I poured some water on my hands from the bottle by the sink and splashed my face.

"Tell me about it," he said.

"Not much to tell. Cancer. Like my mother, only faster. That's one good thing, at least. Hers took five years, horrible years. The doctor says I won't live through the spring."

I turned and looked at him for the first time since I'd said it. He was frowning slightly. "That's fast."

"It is now." I surprised myself. "Before, I didn't think it made much difference. Six months or sixty years, it didn't matter—just more of the same. Nothing to cry about."

I thought I'd ruined everything, falling apart like that. Pity was the last thing I wanted from him or anyone else. I'd never been one to blub, hadn't done it but once since I was a kid, when my mother's heavy arm around my shoulders, her boozy breath in my face, had transformed my misery into inturned rage, never again to give her such a chance. Poor baby! Not this child. I wanted more from her than that.

Rhodri and I went for a walk. He helped me on with the jacket again, wrapped a scarf around my neck, found gloves, ridiculously large on my hands. He brought along a lap robe and a rolled-up ground pad, tucking them both under one arm and taking my hand. I had to laugh. "You'd make some child a terrific mother," I told him as we started up the old logging road behind his house.

"Too bad about that," he replied, and I felt I had touched a sore place.

"Never married?"

He shook his head. "Never even thought about it."

"That shows great strength of character." I hadn't meant to let that face show, but he just smiled. I was so distracted by the feel of his hand enclosing mine, a sensation I hadn't experienced since childhood, that I scarcely noticed the elder saplings encroaching on the old dirt road, the wild thyme, the strawberry plants. None native to this spot, just more of mankind's clumsy bootprints, as infuriating as the scar of the road itself, and more pernicious. But when we turned up the first switchback and came face to face with the apple tree, I stopped. "Just look at that! I ask you!"

"What?" he asked.

"Some idiot buried his apple core. Can't people ever just be in a place without changing it?"

"Even the bare fact of someone being there changes it. I've been looking for years for a spot in the world where no man or woman has ever stood before." He tugged my hand, urging me past the apple tree and my annoyance. "I don't mean the top of K2, or Antarctica. Just somewhere so far off the beaten track that no one's ever been there. I don't think it exists anymore. We'd have to go back in time, maybe to when the land bridge first formed, before the Asian tribes came east. I'd like to go so far back that we could stand on top of this mountain and be absolutely, utterly alone."

I'd felt that way myself, could see it plainly as he spoke. "You'd feel as empty as a jug. The wind could blow right through you."

We had to scramble up the last steep feet, and then we were on the ridge, not much more than a yard wide, the whole other side of the mountain disclosed beneath our feet. Turning back the way we'd come, I could see the new roof of his house a hundred feet below, shingles in a pattern like dancing diamonds. Several miles past that, the China Flat. Hawks circled; it was too far to tell if any of them trailed leather straps with little bells attached.

He unrolled the ground pad, and we sat and stared out. "This is as close as we're going to get to unexplored territory now," he said. He put his arm around my shoulder, and we looked awhile in silence. "Close enough." I knew he didn't mean the mountain.

"My great-grandmother used to hike," I said. I'd forgotten this, but it all came back. "You might think because we've lived in this area for four generations, there'd be a load of lore, but it wasn't like that. Whatever Grandma knew about her mother, she didn't pass it on, or if she did, Mother was too gin-saturated already to soak it up. But there was an old teacher, Miss Murphy, when I was a kid, who'd known Great-grandma after Great-grandpa died. Told me she used to hike—take a mule up into the hills and tie it by a stream and walk and walk. People thought she was peculiar."

"If she'd stood right here, she would have seen just what we're seeing, bar my cabin roof."

We'd fallen into a strange neutralness, so that his arm around my shoulders, though comforting, lit no spark. Yet I wasn't disappointed. There was no sag of spirits. Rather a mild elation, like the first whiff of laughing gas. "She was a sour old thing by all accounts. I don't know why she went into the woods; maybe she came to kneel on cold stones and mortify her flesh." I hadn't made my point. "The thing is, I don't think she would see just what we're seeing, even if she were standing right here this very minute."

"Don't you think you and I are seeing the same thing, then?"

"Probably not. Maybe the meadow where we lost the hawk. But to you it's a place where lots of other stuff has happened. Where that same hawk came back every time but the last. And the roof of your house is a thing you made yourself. For me there's different thoughts. See over there." I pointed. "That highest peak but one on the left? I sat there with a pointy rock digging into my butt for an hour one afternoon, watching a bald eagle build a nest. Didn't dare leave until she was out of sight. And on the far side of the next mountain over, I found a clump of yellow violets in bloom a year ago May, and in September I went back and dug out a bit of the rootstock, and it grew in my garden this summer. I could go on for hours; every place we can see from here has some memory attached. Sometimes I've thought of leaving Dougie and going someplace entirely different, just to see what a virgin landscape might be like."

"It doesn't work," he said. "You carry the old landscape along with you, and bits pop out and attach themselves to the new scenes. Before you know it, it's all right there again. You lay the shingles in that diamond pattern because that's the way you did it on the roof you helped your father lay when you were ten. The new meadow orients itself to lie the way the meadow in the Scottish Highlands lay the first time you ever flew a hawk. You can't get away from your own head." I could see it as he spoke—the young boy on the rooftree earnestly pounding roofing nails beside his father. Sunlight.

"Lucky to have good things in it, then." I laid my own head briefly on his shoulder, then lifted it again to look at him. "So tell me, falconer, where are you now?"

"I'm here," he said. "I'm really here. I'm here at last."

On the Mountaintop ꙮ

*R*HODRI had felt her confession of mortality like a knife through his chest. He'd heard about knife wounds: no pain at first, only a violent jolt and a sense of shock. He'd moved toward her almost involuntarily, turned her to him, held her for dear life, and as she began to cry, the pain burst up, searing, so that he almost cried out. Before their lives had truly touched, the end was in sight. Until he felt their loss, he had not recognized his own hopes.

He held himself there for her like a man of stone, liquid lava burning within, but for her a warm firmness where she could rest and pour her grief. His arms ached with the restraint of his tenderness, the desire to tighten and press her to him forever. He would have to save his own grief for another time, too soon.

Finally she seemed emptied out, flaccid for the moment, like a beast that has just given birth. He took her out of doors, for some instinct to let her touch the earth and renew her strength. Up to the top of the mountain, where the wind could scour them both.

It seemed to work. Her voice grew stronger as she told him about the meanings hidden in their view. He could see her in her sturdy boots, tramping the hillsides to search out the wildwood's treasures. As her strength flowed back, his grief ebbed, so that when she turned to face him, all that was left of its heat had pooled and concentrated just below his navel. She smiled that glorious smile that showed the origin of the lines bracketing her mouth, and he at last reached out and touched her face, the hesitant, sweet curve of her upper lip. Her mouth relaxed, but the smile stayed in her eyes. Tracing the lip line down to one corner and cupping her cheek in the palm of his hand, he bent toward her very carefully until their lips met. He could feel her trembling.

The fire below his navel flared white-hot. It was no longer grief, though a hint of sorrow did remain. Laying her back on the ground pad, peeling their bodies to the day's cool air, he made love to her.

She was amazed at how quickly her numbness gave way to red desire. A slow, delightful agony of want. Astonishing knife-keen pleasure of have. She opened her eyes a moment, saw a hawk circle around them once. Nothing had ever felt like this.

Alone at Last

*E*VEN lying here, hours from death, I still tingle when I think about it. And burn with anger and regret that we didn't meet years ago when there was still time. Back in 1978, when Mother was at her worst, Rhodri was looking for another job. He had grown tired of flying air survey on loan to the United Arab Emirates, though the money was fantastic. He'd saved enough to buy his house. Was looking for a job back in the Americas. There'd been an offer in California then, up near Mount Lassen, but he'd turned it down in favor of something in South Dakota, more suitable for hawks.

It's the closest he ever got to intersecting my orbit—not so very close. Mount Lassen's several hundred miles north. We combed our pasts, searching for ways we might have met before. I went down to L.A. once with Dougie soon after we were married, to go to Disneyland. Rhodri's never been near the place. He was at Yosemite once, to help put out a big fire there in the early '80s. I wasn't close.

Our attempts to find a way we might have met grew more and more fanciful. What if I'd taken a driving trip from White Creek to Ann Arbor, and what if at the same time he had decided to trek from Rapid City to Memphis? And what if our cars had both broken down in Kansas City, where our paths would cross, and we'd gone for repairs to the same garage on the same day? We might have had years together, if only we hadn't been so far apart.

What if I'd left Dougie in the summer of '85, when I was so close to it?

It's hard to remember how I used to feel about Dougie, how I used to be. When I told Jean Jones—the only friend I had in town after five years in that house with Mother—that Dougie had asked me to marry him, she said, "About time you had some happiness." Looking back, I notice it didn't strike me as funny at the time.

I know that's not much evidence, but it seems better than the purely negative fact that when I found out about him and Prinny Dufour, it hurt.

First of all, it hurt because Prinny didn't have one thing about her I could envy. She was and still is a plain, worn-out–looking woman, too thin, too hoarse, and wearing too much makeup. She's older than I am and has made a twenty-year career out of pulling beers at the three local bars, moving from one to the next each time she has a fight with the boss. By the time she gets back to where she started, there's usually new management.

It wasn't that she was sleeping with Dougie and the whole town knew it. All right, I did mind that, but that wasn't the worst of it. The worst was the way I found out. She staged a confrontation. In the bakery, while I was at work. "Let him go. I love him and you don't" (bring on the violins), in front of Reba and Earl. I couldn't make up my mind whether to reach for the gun Earl kept under the cash register or to go for a chocolate cream pie and hit her square in the face, so I just stood there gaping at her, to my lasting regret.

I ought to have put that on my last-chance list: throw a chocolate pie at Prinny Dufour. Strange I didn't think of it.

Dougie apologized very nicely, actually got down on his knees (in the kitchen, not a public place) and promised that it had all been "a terrible mistake"—that he had "lost his mind," it was "just physical," "it's really you I love," and it "would never happen again." And I stood there looking down at the top of his head (he was crying noisily into the hem of my skirt) and realized that I no longer loved him, I could hardly remember that I ever had, and I was flooded with relief. I wonder why on earth I was wearing a skirt.

When I told Jean about this, she asked, "What are you going to do?" and for a moment I couldn't think what she meant.

"You mean leave him?" It was like a revelation. I pictured myself in a tailored suit, gray wool maybe, with a discreet chalk stripe, striding along a city sidewalk with a briefcase and a breezy look.

Doing what? For months that question tortured me. On the one hand, I had my mother's house rented and bringing in a little income. I could sell it, but I wouldn't get much. Who's going to buy a house built in 1892, wired for electricity in 1908 and again in 1952, and plumbed in 1935 and left to rust? The floors sagged; none of the windows fit. I was lucky to get two hundred a month for it from Billy Boseman, whose mother had thrown him and his twenty cats into the street when he forgot her sixty-fifth birthday.

On the other hand, I had no work experience. Nobody carries a briefcase to a job piping roses on birthday cakes. I'd heard about those city rents—more than I made in three months in White Creek, so that even if I worked full-time, there wouldn't be enough.

Meanwhile Dougie was being extremely sweet. Flowers. Candy. Not original, but at least he was trying. Every night he came home early, undressed in the bathroom, put his own dirty clothes into the laundry hamper (instead of strewing them on the floor), and asked politely if I was in the mood. And though I never was, I sometimes said yes, because it didn't matter much and seemed to please him so. He said things like "I know you can't forgive me right away, but I'm going to show you . . ." Never exactly saying what.

"Go on, girl," Jean kept urging me. "Get out while you can." But

I held back. Prinny was giving me the evil eye every time we met, but Dougie hadn't been near her since the shoot-out at the bakery, I knew that. I looked around my house and found it good. More than good. It was my place. The kitchen cabinets I'd refaced myself with fumed oak; the garden of healthy native plants in formal beds, a cross between *Wild Kingdom* and Versailles; my mountain walks.

My mother's house. Could I part with that? Four generations, mother to daughter, each one before me dying in the front bedroom. I've thought of making them take me there to die myself, but what would become of Billy and the cats?

I still haven't reached the heart of it. Why did I stay? I'm a mystery to myself. All I can remember is that the idea of leaving gradually faded away. I spent more and more time in the garden and on walks, got interested in the medicinal uses of the plants, and forced my acquaintance on Josephine Red Smoke, the tribal matriarch who lived above the beauty parlor and always seemed to have three or four infants "staying" with her. She taught me the native names of the plants, what they were for. She let me hold the babies. She sold me the jeep and gave me my name: Fox Bone Woman. I felt new and strong, complete with or without the marriage. And when Dougie stopped apologizing and began again to stay out late, I noticed and said nothing, and my life was set.

Now it seems that if I'd left, I might have had a chance. Some accident surely would have drawn me to South Dakota to meet Rhodri there. Or if not there, a few years later I might have gone to Idaho. Fate might have washed me up anywhere, if only I'd had the sense to let go of the rock I was clinging to. If only I'd believed there was a Fate.

With This Ring ⟫

*W*E FINALLY came down off the mountain, and by then it was midafternoon. Some choices had to be made. Both of us knew that the only thing for it was to have me stay with him. In a town the size of White Creek you can't say hi to a stranger in the

street without having to explain it three thousand times before breakfast the next day. But the minute you get past that bend in Main Street, out onto the Arbuckle Road, you just about disappear.

Rhodri brewed up another round of coffee to warm me for my trip back, where I'd pick up what I needed for a stay of some sort. We weren't being too specific. We were like Wendy and John and Michael after Peter Pan has taught them to fly; we'd stopped thinking and were just doing it.

I sat in that armchair by the fire, took off my ring, and looked at it. Rhodri saw it in my hand when he brought the coffee. His eyebrows rose, but he didn't say anything. "I don't know what to do with it," I said.

"It's a problem," he agreed. I was so glad he hadn't said "Throw it out" or pretended not to understand.

"I don't even know what it is," I said. "Symbol of a promise I never should have made in the first place, and broke today without a moment of regret."

He kissed me and handed me my coffee. "What's he like?"

"Oh, Lord. Another impossible question. Where do I start?"

"I shouldn't have asked. It's not the right question."

"I guess not. All I can say is, if he found out, I don't think he'd be hurt." It wasn't much, but even at that, it was more compunction than I'd felt about Dougie for many a long year. Strange time to discover these feelings in myself.

I stuck the ring in my pants pocket and drank my coffee, and that was the end of that.

Rhodri's Argument

*H*E FIGURED people would have to know about them at some point. He could rent a hospital bed down in Vinton, but sooner or later nurses would be required, and anyway her husband would have to be told. She'd been on the mountain for ten days now without her absence from home exciting any comment, but six months or more would surely be a different story.

"What are you thinking?" she asked him.

"Just trying to figure whether I'll need a bigger generator."

"What for?"

"So you can have one of those electric hospital beds that goes up and down when you push the button."

"Uh-oh," she said, and his gut lurched.

She wasn't going to stay. Didn't want him to see her fall apart. It wasn't exactly a quarrel, but definitely was an argument. "You think I'd turn squeamish on you?"

"It isn't that."

"Nothing's going to change me. You could turn into a snail, and I'd love you just the same. We've got so little time as it is. Don't make it less."

They'd been in their favorite spot—in front of the fire, where they'd constructed a sort of nest out of their sleeping bags. She touched his face. He could never resist that look, the steady gaze that saw into his soul. "It could never be less," she said.

"You know I'll do whatever you want. It doesn't matter. Only let me be with you."

"Oh, heart, I want that too. Forever, if there is such a thing."

"How not?" he asked. "Something like this can't melt into the void. We're taking huge pieces of the power of the universe and forging them into a bond between us and a ward around us that will never come apart. Don't you feel that?"

"I feel it, but . . ."

"Don't say but. You've got to believe it; that's an essential part. My mother used to say people find what they expect after death. We used to pity all those poor Calvinists, sitting on hot coals forever because it's what they imagined."

"Where's your mother, then?"

He laughed. "She had a vision of heaven as a huge library. She's up there, still writing away."

"And you?"

"I'll fly. With you. That's all I want."

It made him fearful the way she said, "I hope." She didn't believe it yet.

Twenty-four Days, Four Hours, and Fifteen Minutes ————— ☽

*I*T'S NO wonder Dougie figured it out. I was hardly home a minute while my time with Rhodri lasted. The only reason I didn't suspect that he suspected must have been that after the ring question I slipped completely into my new life. Nothing else existed, just Rhodri, the hawks, and the mountaintop.

I did go home late that first afternoon, but didn't stay the night. Stuck the ring in the back of the drawer where I keep old sweaters and left a note saying I was off and not to worry. I didn't like writing it, but I put it as a P.S.: "I'll be back." I didn't bother to explain. Maybe I subconsciously figured that he'd think I was out exploring again. I'd done it enough times before, sometimes as long as ten days. Mostly, I didn't care. I grabbed clothes, toothbrush, whatever. I was in such a hurry to get back I could hardly concentrate. Took time for a shower, since hot water was a pump-and-stove thing at Rhodri's place, but forgot nightgowns and underwear. Forgot my slippers too, which I sorely missed.

If Rhodri hadn't had to go down to Lanark to the airfield every weekday afternoon to work, we might have died of love. I spent the time while he was gone playing house, wearing my own jeans and his big shirts and socks, washing the windows, reading his falconry books, cooking dinners for us both. What would have been deadly chores in any other place were fairy-tale tasks. I mastered the woodstove, the balky pump, the flue's persnickety demands.

I often slept, and pretended it was normal to need a four-hour nap after a good night's rest. Pretended it was because of the waking up to make love, the sleepy urge sometimes coupling us before we were fully conscious. Each time he reached for me, my flame leaped up to meet him; each time I reached for him, he rose to readiness in a rush of heartbeats, like a bird taking the air.

With those naps I managed to hide my growing weakness. On the days he was off-duty, it was harder, sometimes a real struggle to stay bright, and those nights I might have been slower to awaken to his slumberous caress. We even slept all night the last two Sunday nights. At least I never woke up.

He had only a small mirror, propped above the kitchen sink, where he shaved each morning. I saw my face and wished I had something to hide the circles that appeared beneath my eyes. I felt my ribs growing more prominent. In the firelight one night Rhodri traced them with his finger. "You're not eating enough."

"Shhh," I said. "None of that talk. I haven't changed; I'm never going to change. Don't even think it." I knew it was useless, but wanted to stave it off as long as I could. Never to let him see me fading, let alone the way Mother got. I remembered that with knife-like clarity: the bedsores and stinking breath, the anger she felt at her own incontinence and vented on me while I cleaned her up. If she'd been crazy before, she became in the last days almost a demon, forgetting who I was and screaming in my face. No, I had no plan to make him go through that.

We flew the falcons together every day—the five of them. Sir Kay never came back. Rhodri had a smaller bird, a male called Gawain, cross between a merlin and a goshawk, that he called mine. I flew all the birds at different times. The shortwings were funny, their mad, suspicious eyes and the way they'd jump off the rabbitskin lure to snatch at a much smaller piece of a dead chick. "Not very bright," Rhodri remarked. "Every falconer knows a bird in the hand is worth two in the bush. We made up that saying ourselves, but the birds never seem to figure it out."

ONE night as we lay in the dark together after our bodies' fire had been satisfied, he said, "There is one thing I haven't told you yet. Something I've never told a soul."

There was a tone in his voice I hadn't heard before. I was flooded with panic and tried to make a joke. "Don't tell me you were Jack the Ripper in a former life."

"Not quite as grim as that. I have a daughter."

A picture of Dougie's worried face and a hospital ceiling flashed in my mind as I searched for the way to answer this. "I'm jealous."

He laughed. Not a merry laugh. "It's not like that."

He hadn't even known about her birth. Visiting in Toronto after his stint in South Dakota, he'd been having lunch with some old family friends when this woman dropped by. Someone he'd slept with once, on a visit to the city five years before, between his time in the Emirates and taking up the job he'd then just left. She had her daughter with her, a girl who'd recently turned four. He couldn't take his eyes off her, she looked so much like his mother.

When the woman left, he made a clumsy excuse and went with her. Janet, her name was. He didn't know what to say. The child was right there—Gillie, her big solemn eyes watching him with what he felt as a far from casual curiosity. "We've got to talk," he said.

"There's nothing to talk about," Janet replied.

"You don't want me to say it all right now, do you?"

"I thought you were more of a gentleman than that," she said. He didn't care what she thought.

She dropped the child at a friend's house, took Rhodri to a little park nearby. "Don't get ideas," she'd said. "I've been married to Paul since she was a year old. She thinks he's her father. There's no place for you in this picture."

He'd been too furious to speak, clenched his hands to hide their trembling and lest he take this woman by the throat and change the course of both their lives. Even talking about it years later, in my arms, I could feel him struggle with the pain. His whole body seemed to vibrate with it. "It was like she'd robbed me in cold blood."

Janet had been perceptive enough to see his rage. "It wasn't on purpose, Rhodri. I'm the one that should be angry. I'm the one that got knocked up and had to deal with the consequences. You can't blame me for making a life for us."

He wanted to tell her she could have written and told him. He would have come back, married her, anything. He didn't say it, didn't know whether he would have or not. They'd hardly known each other their one night, hardly knew each other now. "Don't upset the applecart," Janet had begged. "She has a good life, two parents who love her, security, everything a child needs. Knowing about you could only mess her up."

He knew she was right. He left Toronto for the last time, dropped the friends they had in common. The new job was challenging, and there was a new sort of hawk to fly, the shortwings they were breeding in Mexico.

He couldn't stop thinking about Gillie, how when she met his eyes for a moment, it was like seeing his mother look at him from the child's face. He hired a private investigator to make sure she was all right, to send him a picture once a year. From his lonely distance he'd watched her grow more and more like the grandmother she would never know about. She was fourteen now, getting to the difficult part. He worried. "I've thought about writing her a letter— something she'd get if she looked, but not otherwise. But I don't know what I'd say." He didn't cry. I held him until his limbs relaxed. A daughter. Age fourteen.

It was a long time before I went to sleep. All the old questions were clamoring in my head. Why had I stayed? How could I have left? Was this revelation another proof that the forces of the world had meant us to be together, or was it just another damn coincidence? I saw the shape but not yet what it meant.

Night and Day

THEY seem to be running some kind of midnight Olympics around here. Every time I close my eyes, there's that nurse to take my temperature, to turn me so I don't get bedsores, to plump my pillows. I don't want my pillows plumped. I want to be left alone. Dougie is back in his armchair, snoring again. I suppose our little talk was cathartic for him. I always thought if I left him, he'd fall apart, but here I go, and I suppose he'll be all right. He'll find someone else to keep track of his glasses and his crossword puzzles and to cook him low-fat food so his little pot doesn't turn into a big pot. Clarissa, or this nurse, or someone else. It beats me how such a befuddled soul can attract so much loving assistance. He's got the sympathy of every female in town; they all know I'm half crazy and neglect him. They'll have to put me in a double-wide grave so there'll be room for all the women who want to dance on it.

If, if, if. If I'd sold my mother's house instead of renting it out all these years, I could have gone. Maybe I would have gone to Toronto, been the one he slept with that night. Round and round. Would he have loved the girl I was then? It seems to me, looking back, that I had no character at twenty-three. I was like yesterday's balloon, most of my buoyancy gone, just enough left to drift along near the ground. Couldn't see any way to go back and pick up the path I'd planned to take five years before, couldn't see any way to go forward, couldn't seem to move at all, of my own volition.

I said something like that to Jean once, and she said it was grief, posttraumatic shock, a delayed reaction. I think it was more the bewilderment of the maggot when you remove its protecting rock. Sunlight! Wait! I'm not ready to move to the next instar yet! The exposed larvae squirm about, trying blindly to nuzzle their way back to the dark. I married Dougie, lost my chance to find Rhodri while there was still time. Still, as Dougie is fond of saying (his only philosophical comment), we'll never know what would have happened if what did happen hadn't happened.

Outward Bound _____ ❧

*R*HODRI and I did all the things on my list: the balloon ride, the visit to the ocean, the river raft. We searched for a thunder egg in the desert, half a day's drive away, but we found only agate and a small piece of polished rose quartz some tourist had probably dropped. We stayed in the desert overnight, awake and looking at the zillion stars. He said the vault of heaven was like a dome of glass over one of those Christmas scenes you shake, with stars instead of snow, and we were safe inside it and would endure forever.

We found a flat place amid the scrubby madrona and dusty sage, made a circle of stones, and built a fire. There wasn't a human sound except our voices. Hardly a sound at all, just the crackling of the fire.

I can see his face. He was looking at the flames, and I was looking at him, how the firelight gilded his profile. The sparks flew up. "What do you think we would have fought about?" I asked.

He smiled at me and shook his head. "Do people always fight?"

"If they care," I said, expressing an opinion I'd never been conscious of. "Only I couldn't bear it if you were angry with me."

He poked the ground with the stick he'd been using to stir the fire. "You might get upset about how much time I have to spend with the birds. Bored, maybe, if I talked about them too much."

"Never. They're so much a part of you. But you might get tired of having me tag along. Maybe I'd get in your way or be clumsy."

"Should we have a fight now?" he asked, smiling as if he were almost daring me to say yes. I might have laughed, only I realized he'd caught me.

"I'd like to, in a way."

He nodded.

"Only I don't think I can," I said.

"Maybe we could just pretend we'd fought, skip ahead to the making up?" He threw the stick into the fire and moved closer to me, facing me. "I didn't mean it," he said. "I'm sorry." His eyes were full of sorrow too; I could hardly breathe.

"It doesn't matter," I whispered, hearing the fire crackle, hearing the stars sigh. "It's all right." I kissed him, and he picked me up and carried me to our sleeping bags. It was like a dream to feel so loved, so wanted, so complete.

It was cold; we huddled together all night, got up at dawn, and drank gallons of coffee to get warm. As we flew Morgaine in the early desert light, a wild hawk appeared, and the two of them did a kind of dance, circling each other in elaborate loops until it made me dizzy to watch. Rhodri seemed unconcerned, and sure enough, the wild hawk broke off and went its way, and Morgaine came to his whistle. The morning cold brought tears to my eyes.

That was the first expedition, when I still had some strength. Luckily, the rest were easier.

Nothing to do in a balloon but gawk as you sail above the valley's agribusiness, with its clean-ruled quilt of fields, a patchwork of food and safety and separateness.

Nothing to do in a raft but enjoy the floating ride, horizon narrowed to the river's edge, ever changing and ever the same.

And when it came to looking at the ocean, that was the least effort of all. I never even got out of the truck. There was no temptation, in November, to actually touch that water. We drove north awhile on a road that overlooked the beach. Empty. I couldn't believe the vastness. It seemed bigger than the sky. I was sorry we hadn't brought the birds. What would they have made of it?

Back home by late afternoon, I fell asleep as Rhodri lit the fire, and I woke to find him looking at me with worry written large upon his face. "All that fresh air," I lied, and was careful after that. Rested when he wasn't looking. Ate as much as I could. By the third week I was sleeping almost every minute he wasn't there. In his presence I managed to hide the growing pain, though sometimes in bed at night my legs would twitch and jerk. Then came the day—thank God it happened while he was at work—I started to trek across the room and found myself on the floor, sitting in a pool of my own urine. The spell passed, and I got it all cleaned up and out of sight before he came home, but not out of mind. Our time was nearly up.

We lay in front of the fire that night, and I traced the outline of his face, a memory exercise. He leaned on one elbow and looked down at me, and the orange glow of the flames glinted gold in his eyebrows, yellowed the silver threads in his fox-brown hair. I drew the lines on his forehead with my fingernail, traced his crow's-feet and his smile lines, the crease across his chin. He could tell something was up. He didn't ask. "I'm going tomorrow," I said.

"No," he said. "Stay here. Let me take care of you. How can I not be there? How can I not be the one who holds your hand, brings your food, sits with you?"

"There's more to it than that."

He knew what I meant. I'd spoken of my mother's death, how I didn't want him to remember me like that, wasted and witless, how I didn't want to see him seeing me like that.

"A month, a year, a lifetime, what's the difference? Love is whole. We've had it all already." I said it, but I don't know if I believed it myself. "All I have left is to be able to remember us like this. I don't want you pitying me, and you wouldn't be able to help it."

He gathered me to him, held me right up into his heart, so hard I knew he was memorizing too, and I held him with as much strength as I had. I felt his shoulders under my hands, the strong, thick blades well muscled, where wings would be attached. I felt him rise with desire, and my own flame burned up to meet him, and the fire inside us and outside us seemed all one burning light that might lift us straight to heaven on the tower of joy and anguish in our hearts.

HE HELPED me gather up my stuff. I put on the white pants and white shirt I'd been wearing the first morning I came up, but left the fox's vertebra behind, hidden under his pillow for him to find. We stood beside the jeep for a long time, silent. The birds in their mews clamored, urging me on my way. "Think of me as dead already," I said. "Don't picture the rest of it. Promise."

"I promise."

He helped me into the jeep and followed in his truck all the way down the Oneida Road, down the paved, potholed Vreeland Road, down the Arbuckle Road, just to the edge of town. Stopped by the Baptist church and watched me out of sight as I watched him—tiny in the rearview mirror that said across his chest, "Objects in mirror are closer than they look"—until the turn of Main Street broke the thread. Jean tells me she saw me and shouted from the sidewalk, asking where I'd been. I don't remember that, or answering "mountaintops," or driving past the school, up the slope of the driveway. Don't remember a thing until I walked into the kitchen, and there was Dougie, wearing an apron, and God alone knows where he got *that,* and I said, "I'm home." He dropped one of the good plates.

The End ⟫

SO WHAT does it mean? I've been over it dozens of times as my life ebbs away. Two sides to every coin: heads, we found each other in spite of everything; tails, it was too late. "Too late for what?" Rhodri asked me once. Too late for everything: for a lifetime of sharing, for quarrels and making up, for really knowing each other. Yes, that's the real ache. Three weeks of constant talk is just a start, where things are supposed to begin. Even skipping as much small talk as we could, there are vast tundras still untracked. I don't know what color his mother's eyes were, or whether he was ever stung by a wasp. I don't know whether he went to his senior prom or whether he likes daffodils. I never got to fly in an airplane with him or see him with other people. Never found out what he wanted to put into that letter to Gillie he had yet to write. Probably never did write. It seems now that it was all about me, as if we'd agreed it was no use filling my head with him when it would soon go blank. So instead he listened, and in the end I told him as much as I could fit. Is that some kind of immortality? Short-term life extension, at least. It would have been good to die and wake up in his skull, I think. His thoughts seemed as clear and sharp as snowmelt.

"Why do you love me?" I asked him once.

"I don't know," he answered immediately. "Other women have pleased me, made me laugh, engaged my interest for a week or two, but there was always some kind of distance. Emotionally, touching them was like touching a hologram. You I can feel even when you're not in sight. Feel you right down to the heart."

My thoughts are going in circles, I know. I've grown too weak to straighten them out. In a while it will be dawn, another dreary dawn. Dougie will get up, go and shave. The nurse will come and clean me up. And still no answer, not a hint. And time is running out.

Only consider how everything he touched was changed. My life in total and in many parts. A sort of laying on of hands. Perhaps I even expected that his magic would penetrate not just my female parts but my whole body, and bring about remission of the crab crawling toward my backbone. Yet in a sense he did change even that—from "death, a trifle premature" to "glorious life, cut short."

Example: As we drifted down the American River in our boat of air and rubber, I told him about Sitting on the Rock. There's a small stream that runs through White Creek, turning tame and pastoral in the little level space occupied by the town. This stream runs behind the backyard of my mother's house, and in the middle of it a flat rock rises a couple of feet above the normal water level. Which is only about ten inches.

In times of trouble I would use that spot as my secret refuge—hardly secret, as there was no place more visible for a country mile. But the stream was broad, and my mother had an aversion to wetting her feet (or any other part except her throat), and so when crisis burst upon the house, I made my escape to where she would not go. I don't know why this was so effective. She would stand on the bank, ten feet from where I perched, and tell me what she thought in words both loud and rude. The one time she did risk pneumonia and plunge into the stream to shout from closer up, she neglected to take her shoes off, and the slippery leather soles gave her no foothold on the river stones. She fell, was doused, and as I told the story to Rhodri, I remembered the rest: She laughed. All her crossness had just vanished. She sat there in the water and splashed some toward me, actually giggling. And now I recall that sometimes she could be like that. Yes. Playing with me like an overexcited child, wild and clever and out of control. Not just that day but other times as well. Times I forget as often as I remember them, and when they do come back, I'm puzzled all over again at their repeated loss. I'm filled with a kind of pleasure/pain that bewilders me. It made me glad Rhodri was there.

I told the story to him with a lot of detail: the fuzz of the cottonwood trees sticking to her wet dress, the way she'd scared the fish, the slotted spoon she'd been carrying. I laughed, thinking of how her shoes had oozed water in a gush when she stepped out onto the stream's bank.

Rhodri said, "There, you see, you do believe in something. Some kind of magic made that place safe for you." And as soon as he said it, it was as if the light had changed in my memory, as if I were looking at myself upon that rock at a different time of day or from a different spot along the bank, and I saw that it was true. I had gone there because the rock was sacred to me in some way and gave me strength. Its power had turned my mad mother into a playmate for me, the elusive key suddenly found at just the right moment, even if in the end it vanished and she was changed back.

Here's the bottom line: The shape of his desire was me; the shape of mine was him. If nature abhors a vacuum, how was it we weren't drawn together like two magnets? The only answer is, there is no Fate. No guardian angels, no benign deity who cares about our souls, not even a perfect clock set going and abandoned by the Celestial Clockmaker. Nothing but blind happenstance. Think how many poor souls that leaves without their perfect mates, their ideal jobs, even the well-suited children they might have had in an orderly universe. We're all just out there bouncing in a vacuum, using our feeble will to turn this way or that, and only a lucky few happen to bounce into the place or person that will make their lives complete.

I said that to the falconer, and he laughed at the picture of us as tiny homunculi flying through life like popcorn in a popper, but disputed my conclusion. "After all," he always ended his argument, "we did find each other at last." Too late, that was my point. But it was difficult to maintain it while his mouth burnished my skin until it felt as hot as a live coal. Passion's a kind of magic, I'll admit, but still no sort of argument.

The Long-Awaited Dawn ———————— ☽

THE birds are waking up. Dougie is not. He's snoring again, his head thrown back. He looks very uncomfortable. This is the worst time of day, the gray of dawn that ought to mean hope and life but somehow always smells of despair. Mother waking up sober, with a groan, out of cigarettes. My sheets are damp with sweat, and this is the coldest time of day. I'll catch my death. Ha ha.

It was this time of day I had awakened in the hospital and realized my hopes of a child were sunk. The five-month baby who took only a few breaths and then expired. The problem that had expelled her prematurely. All in letters of fire against the gray sky of dawn. Dougie was there, asleep. He's good at sickbeds, I have to give him that. He woke up and saw my silent tears pouring from the corners of my eyes, down over my temples, and into my ears. He got tissues and blotted most of them away, leaving little cold puddles in the hard-to-reach places. He held my hand and didn't speak. His eyes were wet too. Maybe it was that, those unshed tears at dawn, that kept me with him all these years.

That should have been Rhodri's child. Same year, three thousand miles apart. Mine was a girl, too, they said.

I try to lift my head and find I can't. It won't be long now. There's no pain, but my thoughts are extra clear, or maybe I'm so doped up I only think they're clear. I riffle through the deck of memories once again, comparing shapes. Falcon wing, angel wing, airplane wing; longbow and perch; the curve of the birds' flight and the curve of Rhodri's shoulder under my fingers. The lines on a map, on a globe; Rhodri's flights. My own dot, made of much traveling back and forth in the same small space. If I were an electron, I'd be hot.

There, the sun's coming up. Just the pinpoint gleam of it at the horizon, quickly leaping to a sliver, an arc. And someone knocking on the door, and Dougie waking up.

The nurse comes, something in her hand. "Is she awake? Oh, good. Someone brought a card." She puts it in my hand; I can barely lift it. "India," it says on the outside. Rhodri's handwriting.

"Who?" I ask. "Who brought this?"

"Dan Jones." Jean's husband, Forest Service boss. "He's been up to that fellow's house, the one who died? To see about some parakeets, but they were gone. He found this, so he brought it along as soon as he could. . . ." Before I die, she meant.

I'm so weak I can barely open the envelope. My fingers fumble and shake, not just from feebleness. Inside is a picture of Morgaine on my hand. I remember the day he took it, almost the last day, though he didn't know it. He'd bought one of those disposable cameras, took a whole roll of me and the birds. When he'd moved up close to get this shot, Morgaine had objected to his approach, his strange crouch as he leaned forward to snap it. Her wings were spread, her bright eye fearsomely intent. That's all the picture shows, the bird and the gloved hand beneath. On the back it says, "I'll be waiting."

"I didn't know you knew the pilot," Dougie says.

"Did you not?" The envelope slips off the edge of the bed, but I hold the picture to my heart. It's almost too much to grasp. I know the answer already but move toward it step by step. No birds; therefore he let them go. He put this message out where I would surely get it. Therefore he knew he was going to die. Therefore . . . he died on purpose. To make the message true, to be there, because he knew there is a "there," waiting for me. I can't take it in, though in a sense I already have. Again he's changed the whole of my life, past and present, up, down, and sideways, at a stroke. Rewritten history.

I'm stunned by the strength of his belief. It seems to grasp me in sinewy arms from the picture in my hand, shouting that there *is* a pattern, a meaning, and a truth. A place beyond this one, where we'll fly together. And how can I doubt it now, when he knew it well enough to shed his life? It would be like doubting the falcon's flight, the fire's warmth, the bond between us.

In the blaze of this new knowledge I see something else—that I, who always thought I was so strong, have been in fact a coward, weak. All my life. Afraid to trust, afraid to try, afraid to risk. Barricaded in my room for fear of fear itself. Crippled by doubt. But now it's not too late. Finally it's not too late. I *can* take up my life and walk. Could have done it anytime.

I see the picture slip out of my fingers as I rise. The nurse reaches for my wrist, looking alarmed. I really don't know why. I stretch my wings; they're wide and they tingle. I try an experimental wave to get the feel of them. Then with one powerful stroke I'm lifted to the sky, and there he is, just as he promised. See how he shines! Smiling, he reaches out to take my hand. A voice somewhere below me says, "My God, she's gone," and as I swoop into his arms, I think, They've got it wrong again. I'm really here. I'm here. I'm here at last!

ELAINE CLARK McCARTHY

Elaine Clark McCarthy's first encounter with falcons had a powerful effect on her. While doing research for a novel set in medieval England, the author decided to soak up some atmosphere by attending a falconry demonstration. She recalls, "It was just the most extraordinary sensation to see this bird coming straight at you with these mad yellow eyes. Sent a chill up my spine. I'll never forget it."

The historical novel, though, fell by the wayside when McCarthy, inspired by *The Bridges of Madison County,* decided to write a love story instead. "I thought, I've been dreaming about romance all my life; maybe I ought to give this a shot. So I did."

As the author pondered the plot for her story, she remembered that rush of pleasure she'd felt when the falcon had swooped over her head, and how it had made her laugh. Soon the unforgettable characters of the falconer, Rhodri, and his ladylove, India, were pouring onto the page.

McCarthy, whose next novel will be set in Venice, Italy, lives in California's Monterey Bay area with her husband and daughter, as well as with a menagerie of the four-legged cat and dog variety—but no winged pets.